ZODiAC ACADEMY 9

RESTLESS STARS

CAROLINE PECKHAM
SUSANNE VALENTI

BOOKS BY CAROLINE PECKHAM & SUSANNE VALENTI

Solaria

Ruthless Boys of the Zodiac
Dark Fae

Savage Fae

Vicious Fae

Broken Fae

Warrior Fae

Zodiac Academy
Origins (Novella)

The Awakening

Ruthless Fae

The Reckoning

Shadow Princess

Cursed Fates

The Big A.S.S. Party (Novella)

Fated Throne

Heartless Sky

Sorrow and Starlight

Beyond The Veil (Novella)

Restless Stars

The Awakening: As Told by The Boys (Alternate POV)

Darkmore Penitentiary
Caged Wolf

Alpha Wolf

Feral Wolf

Caroline Peckham & Susanne Valenti

\

Restless Stars
Zodiac Academy #9
Copyright © 2024 Caroline Peckham & Susanne Valenti

The moral right of the authors have been asserted.

Interior Formatting & Design by Wild Elegance Formatting
Map Design by Fred Kroner
Artwork by Stella Colorado

ISBN: 978-1-916926-17-2

Restless Stars/Caroline Peckham & Susanne Valenti – 1st ed.

This book is dedicated to all the readers who have come with us on this journey into Solaria. The end is on the horizon, and we are so excited to lead you back into our world of starlight and undying love. We hope the finale is all you wished for.

WELCOME TO SOLARIA

Here is your campus map.

Note to all students: Vampire bites, loss of limbs or getting lost in The Wailing Wood will not count as a valid excuse for being late to class.

Zodiac Academy

Earth Cavern

Pitball Stadium

Saturn Auditorium

Uranus Infirmary

Aqua House

Neptune Tower

Lunar Leisure

Water Lagoon

The Shimmering Springs

Asteroid Place
Terra House
upiter Hall
The Orb
Mars Laboratory
Earth Observatory
Venus Library
Mercury Chambers
King's Hollow
The Howling Meadow
Aer House
Aer Cove
Fire Arena

XAVIER

CHAPTER ONE

The air thundered with expectant energy and the stars in the sky seemed to ring out a single, beautiful note of music that made me want to weep.

I wasn't sure what was happening as the twins were lost to the ethereal light that had burst from the sky, so bright it was blinding to look at. I did know one thing though; the stars were here among this celestial magic, and it felt like the ghosts of the dead were watching on too, witnessing the tune of fate changing forever with the ascension of our new queens. They may not have sat upon their rightful throne yet, but there was no denying the power of the sons and daughters of the most powerful Fae in Solaria bowing at their feet.

Tyler's hand was fisted in my shirt, and my face was wet with glittering tears. My gaze moved to the one entity among the chaos which was sturdier than the ground beneath me. My brother kneeling there, his back to me now but there had been no refuting his existence when he had stepped through the crowd. It had to be a gift of the stars, allowing him a moment back here on earth, but his time could already be waning.

Everyone began to rise to their feet, and I leapt upright too, nudging Tyler back before charging toward my brother. Sofia neighed hopefully as I ran through the crowd, shoving people aside to get closer as everyone clamoured to get a look at the Heirs. My heart thundered chaotically, and my mind twisted around so many unanswered questions, I couldn't count them. I just had to see him. Had to look him in the eye and find what my soul was yearning for most. A precious moment with my lost brother.

The Heirs were rising to their feet, and Caleb yanked Darius into his arms while Max fell on them next. Seth leapt onto Max's back so he could lean over and bury his face into the middle of them, kissing Darius on the forehead. There was a thrum of excitement, a surge of the onlookers pushing to get closer to try and see the fallen Heir. But I was owed it most.

Panic flooded my chest as I moved faster, shoving people aside with a snort of fury and a stamp of my feet, crushing toes in my haste to get to him. I couldn't see him now that the bodies were closing in again, and what if he disappeared the moment they parted, his time here in our world dwindled and not a moment of it spent with me?

"Darius!" I cried in desperation, blasting people away from me with water and giving up on showing any kind of courtesy to them.

The way was cleared, and people cursed me, scrambling to get up again, but I ran through the centre of them straight to the group of Heirs.

Seth was racing around them in circles, howling wildly and not letting anyone get nearer. I spotted Orion standing just beyond them, his fists clenched, and his eyes set on the Heirs as he waited to get closer too, looking on the verge of tearing Darius clean away from his friends and claiming him for himself. In the next second, his resolve broke and he slammed into them full force, nearly knocking them all off their feet.

Seth clashed with them again, and Orion's arm nearly sent him flying as he slung it around Darius, but Orion caught the Wolf, dragging him back into the embrace.

Caleb squeezed Orion's arm and even Max drew him tighter, the five of them locked together with Darius in the middle. For a moment, I saw how it could have been if politics and my father hadn't fucked with everything, forcing Orion to keep his distance, making the Heirs bond as brothers and hardening them to everyone but each other.

Seth broke away again, circling them all as fast as he could possibly run, and Orion stepped back from the group, giving them space once more. But it was my star damned turn.

I rushed towards my brother with my hands outstretched, but Seth slammed into me full force, knocking me to the ground. His eyes widened and he laughed riotously, only to be cut short as I swung my fist into his face.

"Get off me," I snapped.

"Ow," he barked, blinking at me in shock.

"Let me see him!" I bellowed and he frowned, nodding quickly and hurrying to get up.

"Come on, bro." Seth held out his hand to help me to my feet, but I slapped it away then fell abruptly still.

Behind him, Darius stood there, sidestepping Seth to look down at me, his dark eyes full of love and his hand extended in an offering.

I shook my head, a sob wracking through my chest. "You're not real."

"I'm real, Xavier. And I'm staying," he promised.

My breaths seized up in my chest, not an ounce of oxygen making it into my lungs.

"It's not a trick?" I hissed, the burning pain of my enduring grief nearly tearing me apart.

I would not survive losing him twice, and this scrap of hope, this view of him before me would be too much to bear if it was nothing but an illusion.

"No trick. No lie." Darius placed a hand on his chest. "Heart beating. I'm right here. Against all the motherfucking odds. Now get the fuck up and let me hug you."

I reached for his hand, fingers trembling as he clasped my palm and dragged me to my feet. I staggered into his chest, breathing in the scent of cedar and smoke, and the solid feel of his body against mine. He was here, alive, real, defying all possibility, all realities I had concluded.

He crushed me in his arms, and I crushed him back, unable to draw a single breath, but nothing seemed more vital than embracing my lost brother. His heart thumped against my chest, powerful and speaking of all the years of life that had been stolen from him by our father.

"How?" I looked up at him, the gleaming starlight still surrounding the twins, bathing us in an otherworldly glow. The stars seemed to have claimed them, perhaps speaking to them of their ascension, but in the face of this incredible truth, I couldn't focus on anything but Darius.

"I'll tell you everything." His eyes skipped up toward the twins who were still lost to that light. "As soon as they return."

As if in response to his words, the light dimmed until the two of them reappeared hand in hand, their fiery wings billowing out at their backs and the crowns of fire no longer on their brows.

"Secure the academy!" Tory called to the crowd, amplifying her voice with magic to a chorus of barks, howls and roars.

"This is our home, and we're staying right here," Darcy added fiercely, then the two of them flew over the crowd, leading the uprising as Orders of all varieties shifted and raced to obey their word.

I spotted Gabriel running through the crowd, colliding with a giant Nemean Lion who let out a deafening roar, nuzzling Gabriel's head and purring loudly. Dante Oscura jumped from the Lion's back, slamming into Gabriel and the two of them held each other close before the Lion shifted back into his Fae form, revealing he was Leon Night. Butt naked and smiling from ear to ear, he dragged Gabriel out of Dante's arms and held him in a bone-crushing embrace.

They shared a few words then Leon nodded, taking Gabriel's hand and leading him off into the crowd with Dante racing after them. I lost sight of them in the masses, and knew Gabriel was looking for his wife and kid, certain The Sight would lead him to them in no time.

Darius released me and Orion stood just behind him, his jaw grinding with restraint at holding back.

"Tell me, brother, how many stars did you have to fuck to be given another chance at life?" Orion asked.

Darius turned to him with a smirk creeping across his face. "No stars, Lance. But your dad took it like a pro."

"You motherfucker," Orion said through a wide smile, eyes burning bright with relief, confusion, and love for this man before him.

"Fatherfucker," Darius corrected through an even bigger smile, and the two of them strode forward, grasping each other in a furious embrace and laughing loudly.

"I missed you every damn day, Darius Acrux," Orion growled, gripping the back of Darius's head.

"It's been hell," Darius sighed, holding his friend tighter. "There's no asshole quite like you beyond The Veil – though Hail Vega made a decent effort. But I'll tell you more about that once I get a cold beer in my hand."

Orion shook his head in awe, releasing him reluctantly as the Heirs and I gathered closer, Max's gaze brimming with all the joy surging through us. His own happiness poured out of him along with a crash of his Siren power, amplifying everyone's feelings tenfold. Some of the Fae close by squealed their joy, enraptured by Max's strength, and I let it flow over me too, euphoria making my head spin.

"Oh joyous day, the stars are turning their fortune on us for sure!" Washer bellowed, throwing his arms into the air and taking off down the hill, his own Siren gifts luring a large group of Fae to follow him, whooping and laughing with enhanced exuberance.

Caleb couldn't stop smiling, and Seth rested his chin on his shoulder as he peered over at Darius with tears in his eyes.

"This is Tory's doing," Caleb said knowingly, and Darius nodded.

"Who else?" he said. "My wife has a way of getting what she wants."

A squawk akin to a parakeet crashing into a window filled the air and we all turned to find Geraldine dragging herself across the ground like an injured seal, blubbering so much she clearly couldn't see very well.

"Lead me to the Dragoon," she begged through another racking sob.

Sofia hurried up behind her, helping her to her feet, and Geraldine waved her hand in front of her as if she was blind. I reached out, guiding it onto Darius's cheek with a bright laugh.

Geraldine shuddered all over, blinking at him through her tears, then honked like an injured goose and collapsed backwards as she fainted. Sofia gasped, trying to hold her up, and Max shot over to catch her, pulling her upright so she sagged against him, blinking as she came back to life.

"Maxy boy, take me to him. Lay me upon his mighty form - nay! Toss me to my knees before him and strike me with a whip of the wandig," she choked out, and Max gently led her towards Darius who was laughing low in his throat.

"Come here, you nonsensical stepsister," he said, and Geraldine shrieked at that, stumbling into his arms and completely falling apart, her legs going slack so Darius had to hold her up entirely.

"Oh dear, dear, hapless brother," she croaked. "You have journeyed through the grass stalks of doom and roamed the ins and outs of the beyond. But no yonder was far enough for your destined soul not to find you. One of my queens – nay – *our* queens has done this." She turned to the Heirs, finding her feet as Darius released her and looked between each of them. "The goons have finally accepted their goonishness. Each of you have found your place and it is upon your nellies before the great and all-powerful Phoenixes."

"I knew they'd kneel eventually," Orion taunted, and I shot him an amused look as the Heirs all bristled from her words.

"Less of the goon talk, Gerry," Max warned.

"Oh, but my dear salmon, don't you see? You have taken off your too-large boots and placed your toe beans into slippers that fit your goonish feet at long last," Geraldine said, batting her eyelashes at him. "It is most becoming."

"I-" Max looked like he was going to argue, then faltered. "Becoming?"

"Yes, you loon of a lampfish, my Petunia has never jittered so much as it does now for you!" Geraldine ran to him, stamping her mouth to his, and they fell into a PDA I didn't care to watch.

"Let's hunt down the K.U.N.T.s. Then I'll go over all the shit that led me back here," Darius said, his eyes sparking with hunger as he looked to the surging crowd, his hand reaching for the hilt of his axe.

"Dibs on Highspell," Orion said darkly. "Will you hunt with me, brother?" he asked Darius hopefully, but Caleb was already pulling him away, Seth baying loudly at his side too and drowning out the question. It seemed only I'd caught it.

Orion's face fell, and I gave him a tight smile, looking to Sofia and Tyler as they beckoned me over.

"I'm gonna…" I pointed to them and my brother, wanting to stay with the group and be there the moment Darius explained all of this insanity.

"Yeah," Orion muttered, twitching a smile at me. "Go run free, little Pegasus."

I beamed, liking the idea he gave me as I shed my clothes and tossed them to Tyler. I leapt forward and shifted into my lilac Pegasus form with a wild neigh that was full of endless happiness.

Darius looked back at me, and I charged for him, lowering my head in an offering as I reached him. He grinned as he took hold of my mane and swung himself onto my back, raising his axe and releasing a battle cry that rattled right down to my heart.

A fire restarted in my soul, one which had been put out the moment I'd lost him, and it burned in only the way my love for my brother could. Full of childhood memories and jokes just the two of us understood. There was nothing else in this world like it, no replacement at all, and all the pining I'd done for him in his absence washed away like water spiralling down a drain. We made up parts of each other that were integral to our beings, and without him, I'd known I would never be quite whole again.

But now, Darius was back, and by the stars, the moon, and the ever-watching sun, it looked like I was too.

TORY

CHAPTER TWO

A bellow of effort escaped my lips as I swung my sword against the solid rock wall, the violent ricochet of the blade bouncing off again making me stumble back a step.

Sweat lined my brow and my chest heaved with every move I made, but I couldn't stop. Stopping meant giving up, meant accepting this cavern as our prison and falling prey to the darkness.

The Shadow Beast bellowed furiously as it attacked the wall at my back, those terrible claws and its awesome strength far more likely to succeed than me, but I needed to at least try. My mind was buzzing with everything Darcy had told me about her escape from Lavinia and the Palace of Souls, the enormous creature who had burst from the ring on her finger somehow one of the least insane pieces of all she'd endured. At first, that venomous monster had driven fear into my heart, but at my twin's word, I'd decided to trust it. The Shadow Beast had been a prisoner to the shadows just as she had, so I wasn't going to hold a grudge against it.

I'd told her about the trials I'd faced to return Darius to the land of the living, but I could tell by the way she was watching me that she hadn't been satisfied by my abbreviated version of that fucked-up truth.

Darcy observed me silently, knowing me well enough to understand that I needed to do this, to throw all I had at escaping before I gave in to the truth of our situation. But the fatigue in my limbs and echoing clangs of my sword against the stone walls were seeing to that. I couldn't find any point of weakness to exploit, no secret lever or hidden passage. We were trapped, alone in the dark of this cursed cave while that fucking star walked the Earth wearing our goddamn faces.

Darius would know. Even before our hearts had become one, he would have known, but now, I had no doubt at all about it. Whatever Clydinius's plan was by impersonating us, Darius would see through the deception and come looking for us. So, I guessed that made me his motherfucking damsel.

I blew out a harsh breath, a lock of ebony hair fluttering before my eyes as I fell still, dropping my sword to the ground unceremoniously. It clattered loudly onto the stone, and I put my back to the wall before dropping down to sit against it, watching the Shadow Beast as it continued to batter the walls and hunt for some weakness in them.

"Enough," Darcy sighed, her voice barely a breath against the thundering assault the Shadow Beast was making on our prison, but it heard her, turning its bear-like head her way and grunting softly like it was asking to keep going. "Maybe see if you can find a crack to slip through in your shadow form?" she suggested, and the beast's long tail thumped twice against the rock wall before it shifted, its body turning into a cloud of near-translucent grey shadow.

I watched as it drifted to the closest wall, tracking its movements as it began exploring the carved rock in search of some tiny crevice it might slip through.

"If this place is entirely sealed, then I have to wonder when the air is going to run out," I mused, my gaze fixed on the shadow as it hunted for some place to escape with no more success than we'd managed with brute force.

"Morbid, Tor," Darcy muttered as she moved towards me, then slid down the wall to sit on my left.

There was a gap dividing us. Just a couple of inches of nothingness, but I couldn't help glancing at it from the corner of my eyes. All the things we hadn't said filled that space, the places where the path we'd always walked together had diverged, sending us on such different routes.

"I shouldn't have tried to force you from that cage," I said softly, not turning to look at her and simply watching as the Shadow Beast hunted for some way to escape.

"I'm sorry I wasn't there for you when you lost Darius," she breathed, her hand twitching into that space between us, fingers flexing then falling back against her thigh as she kept to her side of it.

A lump tightened in my throat, the little girl I'd once been weeping softly for the way things used to be even though the woman I'd become knew they'd never quite be that again.

"I got him back," I said, forcing a shrug like it was nothing. Like the decimation of all I was and had been had left no mark on me at all simply because I'd found my way to right that wrong. But I knew that was a lie. On the outside, with only the barest of facts to look at, everything was set right now, but the cost I'd borne to make it so would never wash away. I'd done things, become things, given myself over to the darkness which whispered my name, and I had a price to pay for it.

"You came for me first, though, didn't you?" she asked, and that knife in my gut twisted sharply, but I didn't reply. "You came for me, and I wouldn't leave with you."

"I understand why you didn't. Orion, the Shadow Beast issue…" I waved a hand at the creature that had haunted and corrupted her, turning her into a weapon against the people she loved most. "And it did beast out and attack me like you said it would after all."

"But you needed me, and I wasn't there," she spoke the words I wouldn't because they were petulant and pointless now. It had hurt. It still stung, if I was being entirely honest with myself, but I had to let it go. The problem wasn't Darcy. It was how much I relied on her, needed her, used her as a crutch to help disguise my own weaknesses.

"I couldn't leave you," I said. "I would never leave you behind."

"You risked death to bring Darius back," she said, a bitter note to her tone, and I realised she was feeling something of what I was too. "What you did was so dangerous, Tor. You could have been trapped in death, the cost for retuning him could have been any number of terrible things and-"

"No," I interrupted her, shaking my head because she needed to understand that that wasn't the case. Not the way she saw it. "I didn't risk death to bring him back. I fought it. My heart was ripped clean from my chest the moment I found his body on that battlefield. It broke me in a way I can't even put words to. I was lost, destroyed entirely, and utterly without hope. But there was one simple way for me to reunite with him, Darcy."

"What do you mean?" she asked.

I took a knife from my belt, turning it in my palm before aiming it at my own chest and arching a brow at her as the tip pressed to my skin.

"The Veil is never far away." I shrugged, and she sucked in a breath, snatching the blade from my hand as if I might have plans to follow through on that act now. I gave her an echo of a smile. "There was only one thing that stayed my hand, Darcy." I brushed a lock of blue hair out of her eyes, tucking it behind her ear.

"You wouldn't leave me," she said. Not a question, a fact.

"Two halves of one whole." I nodded. "So, yeah, I did some seriously questionable shit. And I have most definitely stained my soul in magic and bloodshed in countless ways in order to be here beside you right now, with Darius breathing the air of our realm again, no longer lost to the dark. Every risk I took was on me, but I made payment in blood, death, and scars on my soul, while clinging to my own life with all the ferocity I hold in my veins. I refused to leave you, Darcy, so I did what I had to to stay with you and return him to us here. I knew there would be a cost to bringing him back, but the rules of the magic I used were clear. The payment would only ever have been taken from me and him. I never put you at risk, I need you to know that. I wouldn't have allowed anything to hurt you. I wouldn't leave you and I couldn't stay parted from him, so..."

"What was the cost?" Darcy asked, almost like she didn't want to know, and honestly, I didn't fully understand it myself yet, but I gave her what I knew.

"To deny death is to become death," I spoke the words from the Book of Ether, and a shiver tracked down my spine as if an icy wind had just rolled through the cavern.

Darcy shifted uncomfortably, glancing around like she'd felt it too.

"And how exactly do you become death?" she asked, and I couldn't help the smile that tugged on the corner of my lips, no matter how fucked up it was.

"I dunno. But I have never felt a rush like I did while we were fighting our way to you at the academy. I swear I could feel the dead as they passed through The Veil and were hauled into the beyond."

"Tory... I don't think we should keep messing around with ether. Elemental magic doesn't come with any price tag attached, it's pure and natural and-"

"Governed by the stars. Like the one who just locked us in this cave and left us to die," I supplied, and she flinched minutely at the assessment.

"That doesn't automatically make ether better," she argued.

"I know. But I want full use of every weapon available to us, and I'm not going to disregard the one thing that the stars can't influence. Without ether, Darius would still be dead."

"I get that, but I don't trust it. I don't think we should be playing with something we know so little about," Darcy said, biting her lip.

"I've been studying it for months," I countered. "And considering all Lionel and Lavinia are capable of, I know we're going to need it before this war is over. We can't just ignore a weapon as powerful as ether and risk them winning."

"I can see you won't be swayed," Darcy conceded. "But you need to be careful. No more insane risks or walking into death. I need you by my side when we win this thing. I wouldn't survive losing you."

"When am I not careful?" I teased, the tension slicing apart as she let out an exaggerated groan.

"God help us," she said, and I breathed a laugh before reaching for her hand.

"I love you, Darcy. The last few months have changed a lot of shit for both of us, and we aren't the same people we were, but that will never change. I was putting too much on you before, expecting you to put me first just because I always put you at the top of my list, but that's not my choice to make for you. It hurt when you didn't pick me, even if I can understand why. I would have run to the ends of the earth with you and forgotten everything else, Shadow Beast and all, whatever it took to keep you safe, but I get why you chose to stay. I needed you though, and not having you forced me to figure my own shit out in a way that I never have before, because I didn't have you there to help me.

"It made me realise that I used you to help hold me up when I didn't feel strong enough to stand alone, but I had to find a way to do that while you were gone. And I did. Now I know how to wield ether, I have my husband back to fight beside us, and I won't back down ever again. The next time I come face to face with Lionel Acrux, I will see him dead for what he's done. And if the cost of his destruction is the damnation of my soul, then so be it. To deny death is to become death. I knew that when I strode through The Veil, and I hope it means that we can win this war at last and remake Solaria the way our parents wished for it to be remade."

"Hail to that," Darcy said, and I pulled her into a hug, the tension between us finally falling away entirely.

We would always be bonded as one, but the last few months had helped us find a way to stand alone too. It had been hard, and it had hurt, and there were a million things I wished neither of us had had to endure, but it had moulded us too. We had been carved into the warriors I knew we would need to be if we were ever going to win this war. And if we ever made it out of this damned cave, then I knew the world would tremble before us as we began our reign.

ORION

CHAPTER THREE

I stalked into Jupiter Hall with magic crackling at my fingertips and revenge stirring the darkness in my soul. I still had enough power in my veins for one more fight, and this one was going to settle a score. I'd watched Highspell give a group of students the slip, running in here to hide, and as my boots pounded the halls of my domain, I had the feeling I knew exactly where she had run to.

I took the stairs up towards my classroom, the familiarity of this path bringing a strange sense of comfort. I'd missed Zodiac Academy; it was where I'd ruled as a king of Pitball, where I'd discovered the immensity of my power, and most of all, where I'd fallen so hopelessly in love with the girl who had pulled me from the dark. And though there was sorrow between these walls too, when I added up all the good and the bad, the good came out on top.

This was the place I had spent more time than anywhere else and laid witness to all that I was in every stage of my adult life. Now it was watching me return at long last, no longer a lost man full of bitterness, resentment, and hate, but one with hope restored in his heart, who had found where he belonged.

Blue was my purpose in so many ways, but not only her. I had found purpose for myself in fighting on the good side of a war, in seeking to restore the Guild and taking up the baton left behind by my father. I knew who I was and where I wanted to be, and that was a gift like no other after walking the path of suffering for so long. I was finally taking steps towards a new life, one I was proud to be a part of and which was built atop a foundation of bonds I had forged with a group of Fae who, frankly, had become like family to me. Those bonds were ones I would protect at the detriment of my safety. Anyone who threatened that would face my wrath on this chaotic earth, and the stars would lay witness to my vengeance.

I brushed my fingers over my old classroom door, sensing magic humming against my hand. A concealment spell urged me to turn away, but it wasn't powerful enough to make me do that. There were deeper spells cast on this door too, boobytraps no doubt, so I moved on, trailing my fingers along the wall instead, a slow smile pulling at my mouth as I realised no magic was cast there. *Stupid little mouse. Should have run while you had the chance.*

I took a step back, raising my hands and drawing on the power of air, my hair stirring in a tempestuous wind of my own creation.

"First rule of Cardinal Magic," I murmured. "Do not be a fucking idiot."

I blasted the wall with my power and the bricks were obliterated, a hole big enough for me to walk through carved into existence as the rubble crashed into desks and sent them flying.

My strike was punctuated with a scream of fear, and I stepped into the classroom, rounding on Honey Highspell as she flung herself behind my desk and cast a wall of ice between us.

I shattered it with a blast of air, sending the wind spinning violently out around me so desks crashed into the walls and made a path for me to walk straight towards her.

"I suppose I should thank you for subbing my class, Honey," I called to her.

"L-Lance?" she gasped, poking her head out from under the desk.

I cast a ball of ice in my hand and flung it at her, making her shriek and duck to avoid it before it slammed into the board behind her.

"But I've heard rumours about your teaching style," I went on, sending a blast of air against the side of the desk so it was blown aside, the legs screeching against the floor. "And I can't say I'm a fan."

She quivered on the floor on her knees, her pencil skirt split right up to her hip and her red blouse unbuttoned to show off as much cleavage as she could manage, the glimmering aquamarine pendant on her necklace shimmered between her tits.

"The students need a firm hand," she insisted, her palms raising in surrender.

I slowed to a halt in front of her, casting her in my shadow and letting the storm fall away at my back.

"Yes, they do," I agreed. "But do you know what they don't need, Honey?"

She swallowed visibly, shaking her head, her face so ethereally beautiful it was eerie.

"They don't need a wicked little witch telling them whether their Order is worthy. They don't need segregation and persecution. There is only one thing in this world that makes a Fae less than any other. And that is the weight of their soul. So tell me, Honey…" I leaned down to glare at her with a sneer. "If the stars weighed your soul in the scales of Libra, would they find it heavy with sin? Would they see the tarnish of prejudice and cruelty upon the essence of all you are? Because I was born within the stars of justice, and I can see it plain and clear. Beneath the false face of beauty you wear, is nothing but a monster."

I reached for the enchanted necklace at her throat, intending to rip it off her, but she jerked backwards with a cry of terror, blasting shards of ice at me. They slammed into the air shield I'd cast against my skin, shattering against it as she scrambled upright and turned to flee.

I caught the back of the necklace with a spurt of speed, yanking it off of her and making her wail in fright. I crushed the gemstone in my fist, turning it to dust, and the power within it crackled against my palm, dissolving to nothing.

Honey cried out, throwing her arms over her head and running for the door, her hair evaporating as she went and revealing a glimpse of a bald, bumpy head beneath. She made it to the door, trying to keep her face hidden as she worked to open it, and accidentally set off one of her own boobytraps. A blast sent her flying backwards, the door busting off its hinges as she came skidding across the room to lay trembling at my feet.

Three of the Heirs stood beyond the door, staring at me in surprise.

Seth, Caleb, and Max stepped over the threshold, looking like hungry wolves as they gazed down at Highspell. She curled in on herself and I froze her hands in solid ice, then wrapped them in an air shield to stall any further use of her magic, though it seemed like she was done trying to fight anyway.

"Let's see her face." Seth bounded forward excitedly and Max followed, a dangerous energy bleeding from him into the atmosphere.

Caleb and I locked eyes, and the hunter in me purred in recognition of my coven brother before he shot to my side. Our arms grazed in greeting, the two of us regarding the woman beneath me like a fresh kill.

I showed him the crushed necklace in my palm, and he smirked.

"Good work," he said darkly, then prodded Highspell with the toe of his shoe. "Show us your face, wench."

"Wench," Seth echoed to himself in amusement.

"She's terrified," Max said, stepping forward, his eyes alight with all the fear he could feel with his Siren gifts. "It must be real bad."

"Let me see, let me see." Seth bounced on the balls of his feet.

"Come on, Honey, everyone's waiting," I urged, but she only buried her face deeper against her arms, curling up like a baby and starting to cry.

"Do it the asshole way," Caleb urged me, and we shared a grin before I lifted my hand and let air curl between my fingers.

"You had your chance, Honey," I said.

"Please, Lance," she begged. "Please don't!"

"Have I ever responded well to begging in my classroom?" I looked to the others, and Seth shook his head excitedly.

"Nope, not that I can recall," Max said with a wicked look.

"Didn't think so," I said, then used air to lift Highspell up and pin her against the white board, forcing her arms wide so they were spread either side of her, her legs dangling and kicking madly.

"Ho-ly shitballs," Seth exhaled as my jaw fell slack.

"No fucking way!" Caleb roared a laugh.

"By the stars," I said, unable to blink, taking in the hideous view before me.

"Is that a...?" Max trailed off in complete shock, then cracked up laughing as Seth howled in raucous amusement.

The fact that Highspell was bald with a bumpy, wart-bound head was the least of her ugliness, because right there in the centre of her face, instead of a nose, was a huge, veiny, flaccid cock. Balls and all, perched neatly beneath her eyes.

"Don't look at me!" she cried, making the tip of the thing flap against her chin.

Seth ran forward to get a better look, his expression saying he was having the time of his life. "Oh my stars, is it functional?"

"Shut up!" Highspell screeched, and we all laughed.

"What?" Seth balked. "I'm just asking what everyone's thinking. Like, do you pee through it, can you smell with it? Wait, does it get hard?"

"No one is thinking that!" she shrieked, the cock bouncing against her lips with the force she used.

Seth glanced back over his shoulder. "Max? You were thinking it, weren't you bud?"

"Totally," Max agreed.

"Cal?" Seth asked, looking to him, and he nodded, then Seth turned to me. "You're thinking it, aren't you moon friend?"

"Well, yeah, I am actually," I said, letting the moon friend comment slide as I examined Highspell's face again. I mean, holy fuck, how did one even end up with a cock for a nose?

"Don't look at me," Highspell sobbed, making the dick-nose wobble dramatically.

Max moved forward and I shared a glance with Caleb, knowing this was going to be good.

"I can get her to tell us," Max said, the energy shifting around us as he poured comforting vibes her way along with a potent sense of trust. "You can open up to me," he said, laying a hand on her arm, and Highspell stopped crying as she looked to him, clearly wrapped up tight in his Siren powers. "Tell us how this happened to you."

"It was a long time ago." She sniffed and the cock twitched.

Seth looked to me in utter glee over that fact, and I couldn't help but snort a laugh.

"It was an old friend. I slept with her husband," she cleared her throat. "And her father – not at the same time, of course, but... anyway, when it all came out, she tracked me down and cursed me with some twisted dark magic she'd learned from who even knows where. She said if...if I was so addicted to cock then I could have one of my own to look at forevermore." Highspell hiccupped a sob before continuing. "I've been hunting for a way to break the curse for years, but I've never found a way to escape it."

"That's a super great story and all, but does the dick actually function?" Seth pushed.

"Y-yes," Highspell choked out, still trapped in Max's power.

"In what way?" Seth asked keenly.

"All the ways!" she cried.

Max released her from his gifts, and she started crying loudly, realising everything she'd revealed to us.

I rolled up my sleeves, casually moving to the nearest window and opening it up.

"W-what are you doing?" Highspell asked in terror, but I ignored her, whistling down to a group of students below to catch their attention.

Milton Hubert was among them, stamping his foot and mooing excitedly as he looked up to us.

"Hey Professor!" he called, his eyes lighting in recognition. "Is Highspell in there?"

"She sure is. You want her down there?" I asked, and he and the girl he was closest to -who I recognised as Bernice Navis through the dirt smeared across her jaw - mooed again in affirmation. The group they were with cheered as I stepped back and whipped a finger, sending Highspell flying out the window at high speed, flipping over and over as she tumbled down towards them.

They stepped smoothly aside instead of catching her, letting her crash down onto her back between them on the grass.

"By the sun," Milton exclaimed. "She has a dick for a face."

"Dick face, dick face, dick face," they all started chanting, and one of them cast a wooden pole into existence, lashing her to it with vines and carrying her between them so she swung beneath it upside down, her cock nose flapping against her forehead.

They headed off down the path to who knew where and I slammed the window shut, turning to find the three Heirs behind me.

"So where's Darius?" I asked hopefully, glancing at the empty doorway as if he might appear there.

Panic dashed across my chest as an awful thought entered my mind, that maybe his return had been temporary, that some spell had brought him here and now it had worn off and-

"Relaaaax." Seth moved forward and squeezed my shoulder, but I shrugged him off. "He's out playing hero with Xavier. They said they'd meet us at the lake in a bit."

"So, he's really back?" I asked, at a loss for how this was possible.

"You saw him yourself, man," Caleb said with a sideways grin, and excitement crested in my chest.

"I need to see him again." I stepped forward, and Seth caught my arm.

"At the lake," he said keenly.

"Alright," I conceded, though I'd have preferred to have spent some time with him alone. I knew I couldn't exactly keep him from everyone; they had missed him as much as I had. "Will the twins be there?"

I thought of Darcy, hoping to see her after all that had happened. She was a queen now, even if she didn't have her throne just yet. The world was beginning to see the truth of her and her sister, that they were born to rule, side by side. Together, they were a power that rivalled every natural force on earth. They were the gravity beneath the feet of our kingdom, and if anyone could bring about a new dawn, it was them.

"I doubt Tory wants him out of her sight any more than the rest of us do," Max said. "So they're as likely to be there as anywhere else."

"Let's run," Caleb said, shifting his weight from foot to foot as he looked to me, and excitement rose in me over going to see Darius. I needed to know everything, just everything. And most of all, I needed to lay my eyes on him again and assure myself that he really had returned to us. To me.

"I'll carry Seth, you take Max," Caleb added, then scooped Seth up in his arms and the Wolf howled in excitement as they shot away through the door.

Max turned to me with arched brows, and I cleared my throat. I'd never spent much time with him alone, if any actually. And now I was left to carry him. What the fuck was I meant to do? Pick him up like Caleb had carried Seth, holding him in my arms while he looped his arms around my neck? *By the stars.*

"I can just walk," he said, running a hand down the back of his neck.

"It's fine," I muttered.

"Alright." He moved closer, taking hold of my arm while I ducked down to get his legs, but my head bumped into his chest as we moved at the same time.

"Oh, er, hang on." He lifted one leg up. "Does this help?"

"No, just, stay still."

We bumped into each other again and I stood upright, pressing my lips together in frustration while he gave me a sideways look.

"Just get on my back," I said.

"Riiiight, that makes so much more sense," he agreed with a nod.

"Yeah, I dunno what we were thinking there," I muttered, and he snorted, moving behind me. "Shall I duck down? Or…"

"Er, I got it. I can use air to just-" He leapt smoothly onto my back with the use of his Element. I caught the backs of his knees while he rested his hands on my shoulders, then wrapped his arms around my neck and put his hands back on my shoulders. Fuck, this was awkward.

"Yah!" he cried with a laugh.

"Don't do that," I said, not moving.

"Oh, right. Cool…cool."

"Hold on tight, asshole," I said with a smirk, and his grip tightened on my shoulders.

"Let's go, motherfucker," he replied brightly, and I shot out of the room at high speed, a whoop leaving Max as I took corners as fast as I could.

We were outside in a flash, the campus rushing past us in a blur of green as I made a path towards the lake, the thrill of seeking out Darius setting my pulse to a wild beat.

But as we made it to the glistening pool of Aqua Lake where the sun glimmered on its surface, I found one of my least favourite things awaiting me there: A crowd.

I didn't slow down when we met the edge of it though, rushing through it and sending people flying away from us with yelps of alarm. My eyes moved from face to face, hunting with the gifts of my Order as I sought out my friend.

"Darius?!" Max shouted, his voice booming out with an amplification spell as I knocked a Minotaur on his ass and leapt over him while he mooed loudly in anger.

"Over here!" Seth's voice carried back to us.

I turned sharply towards it, making a small herd of shifted Experian Deer shifters scatter with bleats of alarm. I ran past them and found Darius where the land rose up a little, surrounded by crooning students, many of them muttering prayers to the stars or just staring at him in undisguised awe. Caleb and Seth had crafted a fine seating area from wooden logs, and the moment I made it into the centre of it, I blasted a storm of air out around me to push everyone away from Darius, sending a Golden Goose shifter tumbling away into the air with a honk of rage.

Darius's face split into a smile, and I shot forward the final two steps parting us, crushing him into an embrace and feeling Max's hands wrap around us too as I remembered he was still on my back.

Max dropped down and Caleb whistled to us, drawing our attention to the seating area as Darius and I released each other.

Seth cast a wall of air that kept the crowd from surging forward again, and one guy pressed his face up against it so firmly that his nose was crushed, making him look like a pig.

Xavier was already sat on one of the log seats, his eyes never leaving Darius, a look of complete happiness about him that felt so good to see. It was surreal…this moment feeling like it couldn't possibly be happening, my body and mind seeming somehow detached from reality as I stared at the man I had loved and lost, cherished and grieved, and now somehow found once more.

Caleb cast a silencing bubble around us and pointed to one of the six carved thrones he'd created for us with a tilt to his lips.

I followed Darius to his seat, but before I could take the one beside him, Seth lunged past me and dropped into it, gazing up at me with a wolfish grin.

"Here you go, Lance." He patted the seat beside him, and I gave him a dry look before taking it, and Max and Caleb took the remaining two seats on the other side of Darius.

"Well?" Seth prompted keenly, practically bouncing in his seat.

"What do you wanna know?" Darius asked, acting as if he hadn't just respawned here back on earth, but a note of amusement laced his tone.

"Everything," Max growled. "From start to end, no pieces missing."

"It's a long story," he said with a dark look.

"I don't care if it takes all day, dickweed," Xavier said. "Get on with it."

Darius boomed a laugh and his gaze hooked on mine, his smile dropping away as he realised none of us were laughing. We had to know. I had to know. All of it.

"Start at the battle," I prompted, and his face soured.

"Well, you all know my asshole of a father defeated me," he said bitterly, his hand tightening into a fist on his knee.

"No, he didn't," Seth breathed, leaning in to nuzzle Darius's cheek, and Darius sighed, lifting a hand to scruff Seth's hair. "You're here, and stars be damned, Darius Acrux, if you don't start telling us the hows and the whys and what it's been like and how you've felt and whether you were even a person beyond The Veil, I'm going to lose my mind. Or maybe you were just a floaty little ghost spiralling away through space and time, all alone, or were you with other ghosties? Or perhaps you were just a puff of a cloud, with no thoughts at all as you sailed through the mystical beyond going weeeee-"

Max flicked a finger, casting ice across Seth's lips to silence him. "Speak," he commanded Darius, and the silence between us deepened, all of us on the edge of our seats.

I could hear every one of their hearts thrashing as furiously as my own. We were one in that moment, a single entity with a single need, and as Darius started telling us the story of his time beyond The Veil, I was sure the stars were turning to listen too, the entire attention of the universe aimed this way. We were all sitting at the centre of something so deeply important that it felt paramount to every fate in Solaria from this day forward.

Against all odds, the twins had been crowned, the four Heirs were reunited, and the fate of this war felt like it was spinning on a coin once again. I just hoped when it landed, it did so in our favour.

By the time Darius's story was complete, the sun had made an arc through the sky and was beginning to descend. He'd told us of his passing, how he had been greeted by the Savage King himself in the realm of death alongside his queen. He had spent time with his mother and Hamish, and even his uncle Radcliff, the brother Lionel murdered, and with my father too. He described a great palace filled with endless rooms and a golden mist that hung in the air like stardust, and how he could furnish a room for him to live in and make it look however he liked with nothing but a thought. He had watched us too, pushed against the very fabric of The Veil to stand at our sides during moments when we had thought of or needed him, like our grieving had called him to us. It was terrifying and wonderful in equal measures, knowing how close the dead really were at all times.

The twins hadn't shown up at the lake, and we'd all been so caught up in Darius's tale that it had taken me until now to start worrying about the fact.

It wasn't like I needed to spend every waking moment with Darcy in my line of sight, but it was hard to believe she wouldn't have wanted to hear Darius's story for herself. Though I supposed she had a lot to discuss with her twin too.

I scanned the sky, looking for any sign of flaming wings or blue hair, and tried not to let myself grow concerned, though I knew I'd feel easier when she was back with me again. We'd been through a hell of a lot to make it back here, and after so much time spent locked up and alone with one another, it felt strange to be out of her company for so long.

I felt a little misplaced as Seth, Max, Caleb and Xavier bundled Darius away towards The Orb with talk of dinner.

I hung back, knowing I could follow, but I sensed Darius needed the time with his friends, and I could use the quiet to think on everything he'd told us anyway.

The way he'd spoken of the dead and the knowledge that my father was watching over me, urging me on, even proud of me, was a lot to take in. My grief for him was an old wound which throbbed from time to time, but it felt raw now, picked over and sore from the knowledge that I would never get the chance Darius had in my lifetime. I wished to speak with my father more than anything, wished for his knowledge and guidance in this war, or simply his embrace. One day, I would meet him beyond The Veil myself, but that didn't lessen the sting of his absence in the present.

"I'm trying to do what you laid out for me," I told the sky, uncertain if my father would hear my words or not. Though if Darius was correct in what he had said about the dead, then my thinking of him might just have drawn him close.

Whether he was here or not, I couldn't tell though. The wind didn't stir, the sky didn't speak to me, and the pain of his loss still wound tightly around my heart.

Caleb had informed me that Geraldine and her little Ass society had placed a bag of my things at Asteroid Place, and I itched to look through it and seek out my father's diary. I wanted to pore over his words, drink in the tenor of his voice from his notes and feel…closer to him, I supposed. I may have read through it a thousand times but something about having Darius back, about knowing that my father really was watching over me made me feel like I might just discover something more in the words he had left for me.

I shot away to Asteroid Place, leaving the crowd on the shore of the lake and arriving back at my old chalet. I frowned at the door, so many memories hanging over me here, the good the bad, the downright perfect. I rested my fingers on the doorhandle, thinking of the night Darcy had come to me in a raging storm, her hair dyed blue and a look of purest passion in her eyes. I could remember that night so sharply, it was like stepping back into it, each moment committed to memory and stitched into the corners of my heart.

Despite my long absence, the door still opened at my touch, and I was glad to find the space empty and unused, no sign of Highspell's taint here. I trailed my hand over the back of the grey couch, too many nights lost to it with a bottle of bourbon sending me into oblivion.

It struck me how changed I was since the last time I'd been here, all the powerlessness of my former life no longer holding me in its cage. I was free. Free from that ache at the base of my throat which demanded I quiet the roaring in my skull with as much alcohol as I could consume.

I was free of the Guardian Bond which had stolen my will and forced me into a life of servitude. I was free of the darkness inside me which had seemed so inescapable, always lurking on the fringes of my reality, ready to consume me whole and steal me into the abyss. Until her. Darcy Vega with all her spirit, her light a rapture I had never felt deserving of. But now that I was starting to find a place in this wretched world, it didn't seem so wretched after all. Not while her soul was bound to mine with a ribbon of blue, our fates interwoven, threaded together as one.

Perhaps I could find a role in this new life of mine which could help lead this war to a righteous end. And maybe the Guild Stones were the key to that, if only we could find them all.

I wasn't sure how long I stood there, captivated by the past, present, and future, but when I looked up to the sound of the sliding door rolling open across the room, I wasn't quite prepared to face the man standing there. Because I still couldn't believe fate would be so kind as to return him to me, and I had especially never imagined to be standing in this house again, finding him sneaking in the back door just like always.

"You're here," I stated in surprise.

The heat rising from his body made the air shimmer around him, and I could sense his Dragon shifting beneath his flesh while my own Order stirred in kind, like the two of them were dying to reunite too.

"Great observation skills, Professor," he said mockingly, and I shook my head at him, a grin tugging at my mouth.

"I'm not a professor anymore."

"None of us are what we were the last time we were here," Darius said, and I nodded in agreement of that.

"Everything's changed," I said, and there was a solemnness in that. Because even though this new world was the better place to be by far, there was always grief in the thievery of time. There had been good moments, memories I shared with this man from our childhood right up until this impossible homecoming. Because that was what this felt like: coming home to a brother forged in chaos and love. We'd been inseparable for the longest time, but our paths had led us as far away from each other as it was possible to go, only to come full circle back to a place where we'd witnessed each other's struggles through countless nights.

I shook my head in wonder at him. This man who I loved in a way that was only intended for family, the purity of it unsullied by all we'd strived for and lost. If there was one thing time couldn't ravish, it was love. Whether on this plane or the next, Darius Acrux would be a part of me that was as untouchable as the sky.

"The stars told me we're Nebula Allies," Darius said. "I'm your number one Nebula Ally, apparently. There was someone called Gabe who came in at like number three or something."

I barked a laugh. "You're going to fuck with him constantly, aren't you?"

"Fuck with the Seer who's all-knowing?" he pretended to be shocked, then smiled like a heathen. "Oh yes, I'm going to pretend I have far more insight than he'll ever comprehend."

"Same old asshole, aren't you?" I mused.

"Pretty much, just with a little more of a penchant for death than before."

"So, no difference then?" I taunted, not letting myself think on what he'd hinted towards about a price to be paid for Tory's magic in reclaiming him from death. It was too good to see him, and I didn't want anything to spoil it.

"I have a message for you," Darius said, his smile falling away, and my heart thrashed in my chest. I hadn't asked him for too many details about my father or Clara, but I knew without him having to say a word more that he held some news from them, and I was as desperate to hear it as I was anxious.

I said nothing as Darius moved across the room to stand in front of me, reaching out to lay a hand on my shoulder, his expression kind of sad, but hopeful too. "Azriel asked me to tell you that he is forever with you. That he loves you and wants you to know you are worthy of the position you're yet to rise to. He said he'll be watching you through every moment and that he couldn't hold more pride in his heart for you if he tried."

I bit down on the weight of those words, my father's soft voice seeming to echo through them so I could almost hear them spoken just for me. I drew in a deep breath, lowering myself to the couch and running a hand over my face.

"Thank you," I murmured, unable to press my grief back far enough to say more.

"Clara wanted you to know that she's free now. Truly free. And Lance…" Darius's hand landed on my shoulder, his grip tightening. "She is happy there. Really. She even met a guy who-"

A ragged laugh broke from me, and I looked up at him in surprise. "You're telling me that I've been suffering over her death, agonising over the choice I was forced to make to release her from that bitch Lavinia, and she's hooking up with some ghost asshole?"

"Yeah," Darius laughed too. "His name was Rash or something like that."

"Rash?" I arched a brow, knowing full well that Darius did not have that right. Who the fuck would call their kid Rash?

"Yeah, pretty sure that was it." He nodded.

"Like a ball rash?" I pressed, my grief falling into amusement as Darius laughed fully.

"Okay, so maybe it was Ranch or Reg or-"

"She was definitely happy?" I asked, needing to know that more than the name of some mystery fling.

"Yeah, she is," Darius replied, squeezing my shoulder and giving me such a genuine smile that I knew it was true.

A weight I hadn't even realised I'd been carrying seemed to slip from my chest, my lungs drawing in a ragged breath and releasing it in a shuddering wave. Death truly had been a gift for Clara in the end then. I really had done right by her as I'd hoped.

"And what about…" I cleared my throat, choked with some emotion I was yet to put a name to. Since my mother had sacrificed herself for me and Darcy, I hadn't been able to put to bed the feelings I was experiencing over it. I had hated her so viscerally, but now…I could see sadness in her past, even if I didn't want to admit it. And in the end, she had done right by me, even if it would never tally up against all the wrongs. Somehow, I couldn't find it in me to hate her anymore. "Stella."

Darius frowned. "I never saw her. But I think she will have plenty of time in death to sit with her sins."

"She saved me and Darcy in the end," I told him, and his brows raised in surprise. "She died so that we could be free of the Death Bond, of the shadow curse. She did that, despite everything."

"And how do you feel about that?"

I exhaled heavily. "I'm unsure of how to feel about any of it. But somewhere among it all, I feel a sense of closure I suppose. And perhaps that's enough."

"You deserved more, but I'm glad you gained something from her, if only that." Darius dropped down to sit beside me, digesting those words before he leaned close and spoke to me again.

"Azriel has discovered the location of two more of the Guild Stones."

"He did?" I gasped, my grief spilling into excitement in an instant, my stare meeting Darius's as he stood again, a wicked grin on his lips. He drew the axe which was sheathed at his hip, a familiar darkness rising in his eyes and coaxing the darkness from my bones in kind. Magic rose to the edges of my skin and the atmosphere thickened with the promise of peril and adventure.

"Let's slip away into the night like we used to," he suggested, and a buzz of adrenaline rippled through me as I stared at the impossibility of my best friend, back from the dead and carrying the secrets I'd been hunting for as if they were nothing at all. But they were everything, and I could hear destiny whispering my name once again as I stood too.

"I thought you'd never ask."

GERALDINE

CHAPTER FOUR

The eve was fresh and crisp, barely a ray of starlight blinking across the horizon as I trod the frost-capped path towards the Earth Observatory, seeking out my queens on this cold and fate-touched night. The first full night of their rule.

A shiver ran through me which was quite unbecoming, my mind a-buzz with delight over the final pieces of this war finally coming together.

The True Queens had ascended at last, and I knew without doubt that my dearest papa was watching me now, trailing my footsteps as I stole along the path to the door of my ladies on this most momentous of occasions.

The twins had sequestered themselves away in the belly of the Earth Observatory, demanding privacy to discuss many a royal deed, but I couldn't fail them in satisfying the rumblings of their royal stomachs. And so, I had baked my finest ever batch of bagels, each wearing a doughy crown and toasted to utter perfection, their butteriness knowing no bounds.

I hummed the royal anthem to myself as I approached, wondering what command they might offer a lowly wretch such as I on this magnificent eve.

The door opened on soft and silent hinges, and I rode the wide elevator up, up, up, to the tippy-top of the tower.

The low murmur of their queenly voices reached me, some utterance about a fallen star and a lost crater, but I closed my ears against the words which were not intended for my consumption.

I knocked loudly before throwing the door wide and prostrating myself on the floor, the platter of bagels held high above my head on a single hand.

"A royal snack, my Queens," I announced, every piece of me shivering with delight as I bowed so low the carpet fibres brushed against my eyeballs.

"Is death the greatest adventure?" my sweet Darcy asked, and the question set my mind into a flubber as I considered it.

"Death in the name of my queens would be an adventure indeed, my lady," I gasped. "Why any and all of us here sworn to you would agree. We are each ready to dive straight into battle at your barest whim and impale ourselves upon the swords of your enemies if that is what it takes to end this war and win your kingdom back under your sway in its completion."

"Not one of the Fae out there needs rest, not a single braggard would dare defy any command you might give, no matter its chances of fatality. We await only your word on the matter. The plot we devised to take down the Court of Solaria and that devious cretin Linda Rigel is ripe for the plucking. You need only breathe a hint of command and we shall see it done in your name. We shall attack at once if you merely wish it. Death shall meet us on the battlefield and in your name, we will take down your foes."

Silence followed my declaration and I panted from my position prostrated on the floor, eager for them to give the word and set me free to round up those scoundrels and deliver them the victory they so deserved on this most joyous of nights.

I peeked up, daring to spy their shoes and noting the tomes and scrolls scattered across the floor around them. They seemed to be hard at work indeed and I wished with all my heart to take some of the burden from them. The Ledger of Fallen Stars, a huge and beautiful book sat in the centre of their work, open wide as if preparing to divulge a secret.

"Then go," Tory commanded, offering me all I ached for in this world and more with such a simple sentence.

I squealed at the thrill of it, my hunger for war insatiable now more than ever. For I would fight in the name of the True Queens, and I would bring them the glory they were owed.

"It shall be so, my Queens!" I shrieked, placing the bagels on the ground before throwing myself from the room and launching myself into the elevator.

I bowed so low my nose touched my toes and I caught only a glimpse of the bemused looks on my queens' faces. But I knew what I had to do. I would lead the greatest warriors of our loyal and devoted army into the grips of battle once more, and I would return here only when I had claimed a victory worthy of the Vega name.

"All hail the night and the bounty she offers!" I called over the quiet and restless warriors who waited at my back upon the ledge of the cliff. "All hail the shadows between the stars, the kiss of the moonlight to guide you home, and the might of the True Queens whose destiny set our feet on this path!"

The former Heirs were here somewhere, Xavier too, though Darius and Orion had headed off on a snaffoo of their own, no doubt hoping to claim a victory larger than mine with talks of Guild Stones and poppycock. But there was no chance a fang wrangler and an undead Dragoon would claim more glory than I this day.

A cheer at my back set my skin prickling with the blood fervour which only came before a battle.

"You are the Starfall Legion – hand selected one by one to rain down hell upon the enemies of your monarchs. The cream of the crop, the pearls in our oyster, the sharp side of the royal blade!"

Another cheer from the fifty elite fighters who had been gifted the helm of blue and red, the ancient depiction of a Phoenix bird used to mould the savage beak and face that decorated it. Their own eyes glared out from within, fixed with fury and a need for vengeance which might set the whole world alight when it ignited.

"This night, we head out into the world not as rebels rising up against a tyrant, but as warriors of the True Queens, their weapons, their messengers, their harbingers of doom…and the former Heirs and Councillors too," I added as a side thought, glancing at dear Maxy boy, the dastardly dog, and the fangtastic fury, plus their families. I wasn't entirely certain what to do with their waffling loyalty in the face of such unwavering souls, but the legion didn't seem to give one whiff of a buttock wind about them anyway while they roared and beat their swords against their shields.

"This night, we will cast a mighty blow against the foundations of our enemy's stronghold. This night we will show him what we think of his regime and the rule he is clinging to like an oversized turd which won't evacuate the sphincter! Lionel Acrux will rue this eventide indeed!"

I gave them a feral, devilish smile and turned to beckon Max closer, his jaw ticking with disapproval over his appearance in my grand speech as a footnote, but what did he expect?

"Are we ready?" he grunted, eyes scanning the legion who continued to beat their swords against their shields, the cacophony of war rallying a zap to my begonias.

"As ready as a dandelion seed in a foul breeze," I confirmed, taking my flail from my back and beginning to circle it above my head, my hips gyrating with the movement and moonlight catching upon the peaks of my breastplate.

Justin took the large supply of stardust from the bag we had prepared and tossed it skyward, a flash of his fire magic incinerating the bag just as Max cast air across its contents, coating all of us in its iridescence and stealing us into the embrace of the stars.

Every one of us, armed to the teeth and clad in gleaming armour, appeared in the centre of the square right in the heart of Celestia before the mighty Court of Solaria building where the so-called king cast rule and judgement over a land he held no true power in.

"Rally, run, or raise arms against us!" I cried, magic coating my voice and sending it scattering across the city in all directions. "The army of the True Queens has arrived, and it is time for you to choose your place in the new world."

Caleb shot away from us, smashing through the wards which protected the towering building of white stone and gleaming glass ahead of us that was home to the Court of Solaria as the name did suggest, but also housed the offices held by Lionel and his false government. His actions set off the alarm to give those inside the time they needed to evacuate before we tore it down.

A shriek of darkest nightshade tore the air apart as those foul and loathsome entities which the false Dragoon called his warriors came running for us, alerted to our presence so soon.

They shifted all around us, beings whom I had assumed were Fae ripping through cloth and shoe, becoming those horrors of old that my dead mumsy had often warned me of.

Don't wander into the dark, my dear, for tricksome Nymphs do linger near.

Indeed, we had all been bamboozled by their efforts to hide among us, hovering on the outer edges of our civilisation and preying on those of us who they managed to catch unawares.

But no more! I was the sword of my ladies, the sharp steel of the axe which swung to mark impending doom. And all those who stood between my queens and the throne destined for their sweet posteriors would feel my bite. I was Geraldine Gundellifus Gabolia Gundestria Grus, and the stars would have no mercy on the wicked souls I sent into their embrace tonight.

A bellow escaped me as I led the charge towards those who stood against us, the Heirs and their sires breaking from us to set our plans in place while civilians turned and fled.

I swung my flail, the battle cry taken up by the warriors at my back as we bounded into the fray, the names of our queens echoing from our lips as an oath.

The closest Nymph ran at me, its death a certainty which fell apart like a changing wind. But the cretin leapt over my head without warning, stolen air magic blasting at its feet as it launched itself beyond the reach of my weapon, and I craned my head to watch it pass me by.

A warning boomed from my lungs, the legion at my back reacting, parting, bracing, but more of the Nymphs attacked in the same way, enormous, death-bent bodies hurtling from the sky towards those who had come to fight so gallantly.

"Light up the heavens!" I bellowed, and the fire Elementals snapped to attention, blasting flames at their foes.

The rattles of the Nymphs poured from every alley and doorway, seeking to block our access to our magic. I felt the weight of that dark power as it shook the foundations of my very soul, my magic bucking and heaving within me as it fought the icy hands of their control.

I turned my attention to a ghastly beast ahead of me, its red eyes gleaming at the sight of my ample bosom turning its way, my flail rotating beside me as I broke into a run once more.

I threw out my free hand, shaking the earth beneath the creature's feet as I led the charge on, the sound of death and violence echoing through the air at my back.

The Nymph shrieked as it lunged for me, probes outstretched, eyes wild with lust for my swelling wells of power.

"Not today," I snarled, calling on my Cerberus to steady the plinth of my soul against the haunting power of the beasts which worked to sap the strength from my limbs.

My flail swung with deadly precision, bones cracking and splintering as the Nymph's death strike put it in the range of my attack. Its blood, brains, and the cursed remnants of its being splattered the cobblestones of the ancient city. The shadows inside it swelled up and devoured every piece of its Earthly body, the ashes scattering to the wind and leaving me free to swing for my next opponent.

The Starfall Legion bellowed at my back, for freedom, truth, and destiny.

I fell into the dance of battle, my movements lithe and fluid, my opponents falling to dust before me.

My muscles sang with the heat of war, and I fought gallantly on, the light of my ladies guiding me to my true purpose even as I feared for their fates in the maelstrom of this time of uncertainty.

More Nymphs raced to join the fight and their death rattles grew stronger, my feet faltering as the power of them ruffled even I.

I narrowly avoided the swipe of a probed hand, stumbling back a step and crying out as yet another probe cut through the flesh of my arm.

A warrior behind me screamed as she was impaled and I whirled to her, my eyes meeting hers in that moment of death. The Nymph who had thwarted her shrieked in delight, lifting her clean off the floor, its probes bursting through her chest while it stole her magic from her heart.

I roared my fury at her untimely demise, swinging my flail in violent delight and cracking it against the monster's temple.

It fell back, but four more of the fiends appeared behind it, their combined rattles knocking me to one knee.

My magic stuttered out, the brutal pounding of feet against the cobbles behind me making it all too clear that I was surrounded, and I called upon the strength of my Cerberus as a howl parted my lips.

The first of the devils lunged for me and I wrenched a dagger from my belt, a whirl of motion seeing my sun steel blade slice straight through its ghastly probes. The severed appendages slapped to the cobbles with a wet and gruesome sound, quickly drowned out by the creature's screams. The snaffoo of a weapon had been among that dastardly Dragoon's hoard, stolen by my lady Tory from his cavern beneath his monstrous manor. Using it against him and his followers offered up a wild kind of glee.

I used its bulk as a shield between myself and the two beyond it, whirling for those at my back with my flail swinging wide.

The crack of the impact reverberated through my flesh as I struck one in the temple, yanking my spiked flail back again and whipping it at the Nymphs trying to clamber over their fallen companion to reach me.

Their rattles almost tore my legs from beneath me, but I screamed right back at them, ducking and twisting before plunging my dagger through the heart of one foul cad as it lunged for my own heart.

Smoke and shadow swept over us as it was cast into damnation and my flail flicked out, a brutal, sickening thump sounded the shattering of a skull while another beast fell at my wrath.

"I am the dark which stalks the shadows," I snarled, facing the final three combatants and finding my back to the wall of an alley.

I was cut off from my brethren, herded like a lamb for slaughter, and yet still I lifted my chin and faced them.

The drip of my blood ran freely down my injured arm, but I didn't spare the wound a glance, my eyes on the devilish faces of my foes.

The one whose probes I'd severed broke first, pouncing with a death rattle powerful enough to make the world spin around me.

I lost all sense of myself in its cruel magic, but my arm thrust up and out, my dagger poised as it cut through flesh and made even a monster scream.

I was knocked aside, pain flashing through my cheek as something sliced it with a burning intensity, more of my blood spilling to the floor beneath me.

On I fought, valiant and true, the faces of my queens burning through my mind as if they watched, cheering my name despite the odds stacked against me.

I lunged for the closest Nymph, a scream tearing my throat asunder as another took the opportunity to strike, only a flash of instinct making me throw myself to one side so that its probe pierced my shoulder instead of my heart.

My dagger punctured the throat of the one with the severed probes even as I was impaled, its lifeforce spilling from it while I was hurled against the stone wall, losing my dagger in the process.

Pain blinded me and my fingers threatened to lose their grip on the Flail of Unending Celestial Karma, oblivion beckoning my name.

I spat blood from my mouth and scrambled to keep my feet beneath me, summoning strength from the pit of my soul. Then I whirled back to face the two Nymphs who had begun to push and shove at one another, salivating over my magic, fighting to claim the prize of my end.

A snarl pulled back my lips like a golly Norman on a bonberry eve and I got my swing going at last, the flail rotating at my side as I looked to the bigger of the Nymphs, ignoring the blood trickling into my eyes from some wound to my face.

Not today, foul beasts. For I am the light of my ladies, the song on the wind, the harbinger of your doom.

The flail rotated in my grip once more and I howled as I ran at them, rattles pouring from their gaping jaws to disable me, my knees buckling, strength guttering, yet with one last, mighty surge of my strength, I leapt.

"Return beyond the shadows, foul followers of the Dragoon!" I screamed, their raised probes a threat and a promise as I sailed toward them on the infinite wings of fate.

A flick of my wrist sent my flail whipping towards them, the sudden change in its direction impossible to predict, and the larger of the two Nymphs broke apart into shadow with a lasting howl of dismay as I shattered its skull.

The other Nymph didn't waste a moment on grief for its fallen brethren, and pain unlike any other tore through me as its probes collided with my side and I was thrown to the cobbles at its feet, a feast for a monster indeed.

"An end fitting for a servant of the True Queens," I rasped, my vision consumed by the enormous creature.

It released a rattle of purest glee, those probes immobilising me at its mercy, pushing between the plates of my armour and breaking through flesh and bone in search of my thrashing heart.

My fingers spasmed against the cobbles as I hunted for the pommel of my fallen flail, my lost dagger, or even a rock. I was a Grus, and I would fight to the very last moment, even if only seconds remained to me in the here and now. Just like my dear Daddy would have fought before his demise.

A vision spilled through my mind, not of the beauteous faces of my queens as it should have been, but of a dark-eyed scoundrel with the soul of a salmon and the body of a god. He would be ever so disappointed in me for this. Ever so furious at my fall.

My end beckoned, and despite all I had to live for, I accepted it, the agony of its approach consuming me as the Nymph leered in my face, a smile twisting its rotten features. I felt its probes brush against my thrashing heart, my magic screaming in desperate refusal, and its power calling to it like a piper to an army of rats.

No.

I had so much more to live for.

Fate was so very cruel indeed.

But just as the stars commanded my end, a twist in the fabric of destiny saw not my demise, but a shattering of smoke and ruin as the Nymph who held my life force in its gruesome grip fell apart like nothing more than a slip of mist in the wind.

I sucked in a sharp breath laced with pain and disbelief as I blinked up at my saviour in shock.

Not a warrior. Not a queen. Not even my dear dogfish come swimming up current to rescue his buxom beauty. No – it was just a boy.

A small boy, no older than ten and clearly un-Awakened stood above me, my lost dagger in his grip and a savage look on his face which spoke of all the horrors he had borne witness to in his young life.

His dark skin was splattered in the black blood of the creature he had slain, his meagre muscles bunched in tension while he held the sun steel dagger outstretched, still thrust as high as it had been to pierce the heart of the monstrous creature set to destroy me.

His eyes found mine, a moment of understanding passing between us as we met there, two warriors on a battlefield.

"Long live the True Queens," he breathed, and as if his words had been a summons from the stars above, a powerful roar of voices went up at his back, a veritable cacophony of nightmares for all who stood before it. The people of Celestia had raced from their homes to finally join the rebellion.

The Fae of this city had had enough, and they were rallying to the call of their queens at last.

MAX

CHAPTER FIVE

I swept across the battling Nymphs and the Starfall Legion, my air magic keeping me high enough to avoid the call of the power-immobilising rattles while I used my Siren gifts to invoke fear in our enemies and valour in our allies.

Fae were pouring from the Court of Solaria which Lionel used as the seat of his power, racing in all directions as some of them tore into battle and others just ran for freedom. They were cowards, but none of our army would stop them from fleeing to their families and any safety they might find away from this place. We may have been here to fight, but we wouldn't claim our victory on the backs of innocent lives.

A flash of movement beyond the glass windows of the building drew my gaze towards Caleb and his mom as they shot back and forth inside it, hunting down anyone who hadn't gotten out yet – or anyone looking to spring an attack.

We had our targets, and they were clear. Gus Vulpecula: the asshole who was responsible for filling the media with bullshit accounts of Lionel's rule and smearing the name of the rebellion. Irvine McReedy: the enforcer and general who Lionel had put in charge of the Nebula Inquisition Centres. And last of all, my so-called mother, Linda, who had been heading up his government and buying into his bullshit in her quest for power which she wasn't capable of claiming for herself the way a true Fae would.

I ground my jaw, turning my head from the Court of Solaria as I focused on the fight below, throwing a spear of ice towards a Nymph who was closing in on one of our warriors while she scrambled backwards across the cobbles at its feet.

The Nymph screamed in agony as my ice pierced its chest and the warrior took her chance the moment its hold on her power broke, striking it through the heart with a stake of wood and casting it to ash on the wind.

The baying of a trio of hellhounds drew my attention east and I looked to find Geraldine tearing out of an alleyway in her Cerberus form, a young boy at her side and countless Fae racing into battle beyond her as many people in the city rose to the call of war.

I whooped in triumph, throwing my hands out towards them and sending the Nymphs closest crashing aside with a tidal wave that struck them hard, scattering them across the square.

The sound of shattering glass had me whirling around, and my eyes widened in alarm as Caleb was launched from the top floor of the skyscraper, his cry of outrage making my heart swoop in panic.

I shot for him, air magic billowing at my back before it wrapped him in its embrace and stopped his fall.

"Thanks," he said, not sparing me a glance, and flames burst to life along the lengths of his arms as his gaze fixed on the top floor of the building once more. "They're headed for the roof. General McReedy is going to fly them out of here in his Manticore form if he can manage it."

"With my stepmother?" I asked, wanting confirmation on that, and Caleb nodded. "Ellis too."

I gritted my jaw at the sound of my sister's name, then I summoned more wind at our backs, shooting us through the air like we'd been launched from a slingshot and aiming straight for the roof.

I spotted them as they burst from the exit ahead of us, the general shredding through his clothes as he shifted into his Manticore form, a beastly lion with leathery wings and the deadly tail of a scorpion.

My boots skidded on the roof as we landed, my hand gripping Caleb's without either of us having to say a word. His power burst through my veins with all the endless force of the earth and the ruinous storm of his fire. I drew on that well of power and threw my free hand skyward, a dome of air magic sealing around us as my stepmother and half-sister raced towards the Manticore and tried to leap onto his back.

"No chance of that," I growled, drawing them all up short as they spotted us, my stepmother hissing as her iridescent green scales rippled over her skin, peeking out beneath the cuffs and collar of the stuffy business suit she wore.

"I wondered when I would be seeing my impurely-blooded stepson again," she snarled, magic crackling at her fingertips, water and fire hissing as they met and mixed. She hadn't been selected as my dad's bride without reason. Linda was from the second most powerful Siren family in the kingdom, and her magic was formidable in its own right. But she still had nothing on a Celestial Heir.

"Unlike you, I'm not afraid to be anything other than myself," I replied, releasing Caleb's hand, and leaving our shield in place, capturing the three of them here. This fight wouldn't end with anyone running scared. It would be bloodshed or nothing.

"Here, kitty, kitty," Caleb taunted as he began to move away to my left, drawing the sharp eyes of the Manticore after him, the enormous, winged lion snarling as it took the bait and prowled his way. "Wanna play cat and mouse?"

The Manticore growled as it raised its barbed tail over its back, the poisonous darts it contained able to paralyse a Fae within seconds. He could shoot the darts in the blink of an eye, but that didn't mean much when his opponent was a Vampire.

The sound of their fight breaking out drew my attention, but I forced myself to block it off, keeping my focus trained on my opponent and trusting Caleb to win his own battle.

Linda snatched Ellis's hand into her own, her hateful gaze fixed on me while she summoned more power, and I looked to my sister as her uncertain eyes met mine.

"Do you believe in all of this, Ellis?" I asked her, reaching out with my gifts to try and get a sense of her emotions. We hadn't ever been close. The bitch who was gripping her hand had ensured that from the moment of her birth. I could remember that day, me rushing in to see the tiny sister who had just been born, excitement spiralling through me at the thought of having someone to play with and love like no other.

"Don't touch her," my mom snapped as I reached over the edge of the crib, wanting to say hello to my new sister. "She is far greater than you in every way, and I won't have you trying to corrupt her."

The words hadn't meant much to me then, I hadn't really understood them, but I'd never forgotten them either, especially because of the venomous way they'd been spat at me. My dad had entered the room a moment later, and Linda had been all smiles for him, but from that moment on, she had never allowed Ellis and I to be anything other than rivals.

"Are you loyal to the False King?" I pushed, my attention still on my sister even as Linda threw a spear of ice straight for my heart. It shattered against my shield like it was little more than a glass falling against stone. "Do you believe that you're superior just because you're a Siren? Do you believe that Lionel is superior to you because he's a Dragon?"

Ellis pursed her lips, but at a hissed word from her serpent of a mother, her gaze shuttered and she nodded, the flare of magic passing between their hands letting me know that they were sharing.

"Two against one?" I goaded, not even surprised at the un-Fae behaviour. "I guess you really are afraid of me then, hey Linda?"

"Afraid?" my stepmother scoffed, magic crackling between her fingers. "I'm just ready to cast the cuckoo from my nest at last. For years, I had to endure the sight of that whore's child taking the place of my legitimate, pure-blooded daughter for the sake of my own reputation, but I won't allow you to tarnish my name any longer. You are a traitor to the crown, a mixed-blood half-breed born of a whore and an unworthy candidate for the position you sought to steal from my star-born child. And now the whole of Solaria knows it too."

She didn't give me a moment to reply before her water magic slammed into my shield, the force of it enough to shatter my defences now that Ellis's magic was combined with her own.

I let my shield fall, already running for her as I dodged the attack, casting air to blast her water away before coiling it around her and wrenching her off the ground.

Ellis cried out as she was hurled from her feet too, both of them spilling across the rooftop with their fancy pant suits tearing and their coiffed hair breaking from their perfect styles.

There was ice fusing their hands together, keeping them locked as one while Linda lived up to the parasitic title of our kind and sucked the magic clean out of Ellis to use for her own. That was precisely what she was. A leech. One who had suckered herself onto my father in her desperate desire for power greater than what she'd been born with, and now she planned on using Ellis to elevate her position instead.

But I was done playing nice with the bitch who had made me feel unwelcome in my own home, done smiling and faking and pretending to be what I wasn't. I wasn't ashamed of having Minotaur blood in me. They were powerful Fae, determined and strong, and I was more than happy to wield the strength of a bull if that was what it took to bring her down.

Linda screamed as she threw her free hand out, a fireball exploding into the space between us, tearing straight for me, but I snapped my fist shut and stole the oxygen from it, not slowing my pace as I sprinted for her.

Spears of ice burst from the rooftop at my feet, and I cursed as one of them slammed straight into my side, blood splattering thick and hot before I could wrestle control of the magic and melt the sharp points.

I threw a sphere of solid ice around myself, then slapped a hand to the wound and healed it, losing precious seconds while unable to see her next move.

Dark blue scales spilled across my flesh as I shifted, a Dread Song rising in my throat as the agony of the wound set my pulse hammering against my ribcage until I had it healed.

The sphere broke apart, shattering around me, and twin blades of ice formed in my fists as the song poured from my lips, its first haunting note making a scream of terror burst from Linda's throat.

But it wasn't her I saw as my power built around us like an oncoming storm; it was my sister. Ellis's eyes were wide with fear, her lips parted on some word she hadn't yet uttered and her arm tense where she was trying to pull free of Linda's hold. She saw me then, the darkest, foulest parts of me, the unforgiving, ruthless creature which I had been trained to become whenever the need arose, and I didn't like the reflection I found painted in her eyes.

My teeth snapped shut and my song cut off with that single note, the torture of it too ruinous to inflict upon that innocent little baby who I had so longed to hold in my arms. That was who I saw as I looked into Ellis's eyes. Not the spiteful, jealous creature Linda had moulded her into but the bright-eyed little girl who I'd once snuck candy to during a thunderstorm.

I'd almost forgotten that night. It had seemed so like a dream, but she'd been afraid of thunder as a child and though Linda had always coddled her through her fears, there had been one night when she wasn't there, out at an event or something of the like. I'd heard Ellis whimpering in fright as the thunder cracked overhead and had snuck into her room with a bag of candy Seth had given me. We'd made a fort beneath the sheets and eaten the sugary treats until we felt sick from them and were laughing every time the thunder boomed beyond the walls of our safe haven.

That was it. The entirety of the good memories I could recall sharing with my sister. One stolen night in the dark where she hadn't been pitted against me, working to best me and outdo me at the command of the woman who was supposed to have been my mother too. But as I looked into my sister's eyes, I was sure she was remembering it as well.

My moment of hesitation cost me as Linda threw a vortex of fire careening straight at me, my retaliation not fast enough to steal the oxygen from the flames before they collided with me.

I was blasted back, my skin shredding as I skidded across the rooftop which she'd lined with razorblades cast from ice, a path of my blood left shining between us as I bellowed in pain.

Caleb and the Manticore, Irvine McReedy, were gone, and I had no idea what had happened to them. I didn't have the time to worry about my friend. I trusted in his power and his strength, so I had no choice but to focus on my own fight and let him do the same.

I slammed my hand flat against the sharp ice, cracks ricocheting through the magic as I forced my will over it, dominating it, devouring it.

Linda attacked again, both ice and fire spearing for me as she yanked on Ellis's power and threw all they had straight for me.

A shield tore through the air between us just before it could hit me, the power of the strike resonating through my core as I fought to hold it in place.

The air vibrated as I pushed all I had into holding the shield up and Linda bared her too-white teeth at me as she continued to pummel it with all she had.

I flicked my wrist, snapping her hold on the ice which mapped the rooftop and tossing all of it into my shield, reinforcing it and blocking her view of me in a single move.

Ignoring the thousand bleeding cuts along my back, I leapt up, rocketing skyward on a plume of air magic, throwing my hand out to summon my bow and arrows from where they had fallen.

Linda spotted me, a curse breaking from her, and she launched a javelin of fire straight at me, but I didn't waste any effort on trying to block it. My bow slammed into my open palm and in the next breath, I had two arrows nocked and flying straight for her.

The first she destroyed with an explosion of fire like I'd expected, but as I dropped from the sky like a stone, her fire javelin sailing harmlessly over my head, I focused all of my power on the second arrow. The one which had spun away from the first, circling behind her in the dark of the night and was now speeding straight for her back.

Linda threw a shield up between us and I pummelled the front of it with ice daggers as I sped back down to Earth at a frightening speed.

Her eyes lit with triumph as my daggers exploded harmlessly against her shield, but with so much energy expended on stopping them, she'd lost focus on maintaining the strength of it at her back.

The Phoenix fire arrow ignited as it shot for her, propelled with the full force of my air magic, punching a hole straight through the back of her shield and slamming into her spine in the next heartbeat.

Linda screamed in agony as I caught myself mere inches from the rooftop, air magic yanking me to a halt and setting me on my feet before I could collide with the concrete at top speed.

I ran for them, Ellis sobbing as she fought to break the ice which chained her to her mother, and it splintered just as I reached them.

Linda was on her knees, trying to pull out the arrow which now protruded from her stomach, wailing as the flames burned her from the inside out.

My upper lip curled back at the scent of searing flesh, and I banished the flames from existence before they could roast her alive.

I slapped my palm to the top of her head, my scales glistening as my Order form purred with pleasure, and I exerted the full force of my gifts on her mental shields.

They crumbled to ash beneath the force of my will, the pain in her body more than enough to throw off her concentration and give me full access to the depravity of her mind.

I snarled as I burrowed into her, flashes of memory spiralling through me as I watched all of the worst atrocities this woman had committed in her eternal quest for power. I made her watch too, made her relive each and every one of them, though I doubted it haunted her the way it should have. She had made these choices after all; betrayed, and lied and schemed her way into my father's marriage bed, onto Lionel's council. She didn't care about the lives she'd destroyed or the deaths she'd taken part in orchestrating. She felt no remorse for my mother, the sweet, beautiful woman who I watched growing sicker and sicker in those rancid memories.

She'd watched her fade and die and had enjoyed every moment of it.

I burrowed deeper, my power like a million termites delving into her mind as I took complete control of this vile creature.

She was mine. Entirely at my mercy and lost to the darkness within her. I could break her mind as easily as closing my fist around a moth. And as I endured the weight of her memories, watched the involvement she'd had in running the Nebula Inquisition Centres and organising hunts for innocent Fae, I had no regrets about doing so.

"Max?" Ellis sobbed, and something about the raw agony in her voice had me drawing back into myself just enough to turn to her, just enough to see the tears tracking down her cheeks and the pain filling her young face. Because she *was* young. Somehow far younger than the rest of us, sheltered by this monster and tainted with her ambition. Had she ever made a decision for herself? Had she ever done a single thing without Linda urging her to do so?

"She...I know. I know she's done awful things," Ellis choked, her hand moving to encircle my wrist where I still held Linda very much under my control. "I know you have every right to hate her, but she's...all I have. She's my mother. Sometimes I hate her too, I hate what she's made me and what she's done, but I've never had anyone else, Max. I know she deserves what you're about to do but I...I..."

I turned from her heartbroken face, trying not to see the boy who had had his own mother stolen from him. Linda had done that to me. Linda had killed her for nothing more than spite and petty jealousy because she knew that my father would never love her the way he had loved my mother.

She deserved death for it, but despite it all, despite the grip I had on her fragile mind, I hesitated.

I could feel the urge to do it roiling deep within my soul, this desperate desire for vengeance eating at me. But I knew it wouldn't change anything, wouldn't return what had been stolen from me, and perhaps in Ellis's eyes it would make me into the monster this woman had been for me.

I gritted my teeth, my gifts flaring as I dug deeper, burrowing into Linda's mind and hunting for something different.

My lips twitched cruelly as I found the first piece of it; her Awakening, ambition thrumming through her in that moment too, her narrowed eyes sweeping across her classmates as she sized up her competition and felt her magic bloom within her for the first time.

I snapped the cords of that memory, then went in hunt of the next, finding her classes, books she'd read, the feeling of magic coursing through her veins. One by one I cleaved and twisted them, ruining each and every one, taking every single moment of magic from her until I knew she would have no way of knowing how to so much as summon her power with intent.

I stole her magic in every way I could, taking the one thing in this world which made Fae capable of claiming the kind of power she was so enamoured with. When I was done, she would barely be able to conjure a drop of water or flicker of flame into existence, and I made certain to shatter any piece of her which may have been capable of relearning it too.

I was one of the most powerful Sirens alive. No one would be capable of undoing this, likely not even me, though I had no doubt that I would never wish to try.

Deeper and deeper I delved, taking all of it, destroying any prospect she may have had of rising within Lionel's regime.

Then I drew back, panting from the exertion of using so much of my gifts and ripping the arrow from her stomach for good measure.

Linda screamed as she fell back to the rooftop, blood bursting from her lips. I dropped to one knee beside her, healing the injury just enough to make sure it wouldn't kill her. Not out of mercy but out of the greatest cruelty I could conjure.

"You will live with this cost," I hissed at her. "And you will be forced to face the truth of what you are at your core without a drop of magic to hide your true self from the world and no more power than a worm writhing in the dirt."

Linda wailed as she lay there, her fingers flexing and fisting like she was trying to remember how to bring magic to them, but there was no chance of that.

"Thank you," Ellis sobbed, sagging to her knees as I stepped back.

I cast a look at my sister, hunting for that baby, the little girl who could have been so much to me but had never had the chance.

"It's time for you to decide who you want to be, little sister," I rumbled. "This is war, and there is no place for anyone to sit on the fence. Choose which side of the battlefield you wish to stand on before I see you again, and know that if you stand across from me once more, I won't hesitate."

Ellis's eyes widened in fear, but I turned from her, running to the edge of the rooftop and leaping from it without looking back, diving into battle and vowing to put Linda Rigel from my mind and never think of her ever again.

XAVIER

CHAPTER SIX

I flew over the battle on Tyler's back, one hand knotted in his mane while the other cast magic down at our enemies, blasting Nymphs with spears of wood, ice, and fire. Tyler had a camera strapped to his chest, recording the battle as we swooped overhead. He had vowed to expose Lionel's raw nature, following in his mother's footsteps as he took up her legacy of The Daily Solaria, and I would assist him in any way I could.

Sofia rode behind me on Tyler, shooting fire at the Nymphs while we stayed high enough to keep out of the range of their disabling rattles. The battle was in full swing, the ripe scent of blood and the merciless roars of victory clashing with the bloody screams of their victims. It was barbaric yet necessary, the blood spilled here this night buying the freedom of the innocent, crushing the monsters among my father's ranks who had committed atrocities throughout our kingdom. This was our land, and tonight would set in motion the rolling stone that would crash and tumble down the mountainside of this war towards its inevitable end.

My eyes locked on Hadley racing across the square beneath us, Athena and Grayson howling in their Wolf forms as they followed him into battle, the three of them a deadly force which cut into our enemies with fierce brutality.

A rogue fireball blasted our way, and I lost sight of them as Tyler veered hard to avoid it, climbing up beside the Court of Solaria, my thigh grazing the onyx stone wall. We passed an arching window and my gaze locked on a red-haired man racing up the stairs beyond it. He glanced back in fright, and my teeth bared as I recognised Gus Vulpecula, mentally painting an X upon his brow. He was my target now.

Tyler flew higher so I lost sight of the fleeing Fox shifter, but I pulled his mane to grab his attention.

"Lower!" I yelled, my heart thundering with the thrill of the coming hunt. "Vulpecula is inside."

Tyler wheeled around in the air with perfect grace, his wings tucking as he circled back toward the window. I shoved to my feet on his back, balancing precariously and casting a hard cannonball of ice in my grip, holding my breath as I prepared to do something wild.

Sofia rose at my back without a word, and I shot her a look, seeing her determination to come with me, and I wouldn't deny her that.

"Follow my lead," I said, my knees bending a little and adrenaline bursting through my veins. This was it. No chance for failure. No backing out. It was my moment, and I was claiming it with both hands, refusing to let it slip from my grasp.

Tyler swept forward, his glimmering wings outstretched as he sailed toward the window, keeping as steady as possible. I blasted the cannonball away from me with a yell of determination, shattering the glass so a thousand shards went raining down into the stairwell beyond. Gus was no longer in sight, but he couldn't be far.

Tyler dipped down, giving us a chance to jump and I leapt forward with a cry of effort, casting a net of vines across the stairs below us. One second passed as we sailed through the air like two birds taking flight, then we were falling through the shattered window, each moment stretching as all my senses came to life. We tumbled into my net, rolling together into the middle, and Sofia let her fire burn through it so we thumped onto the steps below.

"Holy fuck," I laughed, and her hand landed on mine.

"Never thought I'd fly without wings," Sofia said breathlessly.

"I think that's called falling elegantly." I leapt upright, pulling her with me.

I stalked up the stairs, rising to a balcony that ran all the way around a large atrium below, the golden floors glimmering in the low light. All was eerily quiet, the battle outside muffled and no sign of any Fae lurking within these walls. Only a coward would hide from a fight, and Gus Vulpecula had just proved himself one.

Sofia cast a silencing bubble around us, keeping our movements quiet, though Gus had no doubt heard the smashing of that window. Perhaps he'd put it down to a rogue blast from the battle. Either way, I didn't think he'd be hanging around long enough to find out.

"Why didn't he make a run for it?" I muttered, treading a quick passage to the right, pushing open the nearest door to check if he was inside.

Empty.

"Maybe there's something here he wants," Sofia guessed, and hell, I'd say she was onto something there. That slimy bastard seemed just the type to pilfer valuable goods into his pockets while the whole world descended into bloody chaos.

I quickened my pace along the balcony, my thoughts arrowing onto the one room in this building I'd visited before. A particular day flitted through my mind of when Lionel and the other Councillors had won an award for dealing with some dangerous criminal in Alestria. I'd been forced to wear my best clothes, stitch a smile onto my face and come here for a family photo in my father's office. Darius had stood at my side and Mom had stood with Lionel, all of us grouping around him to tell the most destructive lie we had ever told. That we were happy.

"If I was a cunning, shady little Fox shifter trying to make sure I made a decent buck from this war…I know exactly where I'd go," I said darkly, hurrying along until we arrived outside my father's office.

Memories of the last time I'd stood in this very spot made a shudder track down my spine, how my father's eyes had slid over my clothes, seeking out fault in me. I always came up short. A failure through and through.

I fought off the feeling of being a young boy under the scrutiny of his ruthless father; the weight of his expectations and the sting of rejection from his constant disappointment in me. I was his failed creation, and there was a time when I would have felt shame over that. But not anymore. I was proud to have escaped the grip of his dominion, and to have become the Fae I wanted instead of the one he wanted me to be.

It was liberating to let go of all that pressure, like an anchor had been tethered to my neck all those years and I'd finally found my way free of it.

Now, I stood in the footsteps of a boy who had been sure there was no way out from under his father's rule, and I wished I could reach into the past to tell him that he was wrong. That salvation was coming if only he'd hang on. Maybe then I wouldn't have spent so many years afraid, despairing over a future I could never claim.

"Xavier?" Sofia nudged me, and I realised I was hesitating, my mind fixed on the past. But it was time I left those thoughts where they belonged.

"This is Lionel's office," I told her, her eyes widening as I opened the door to reveal the huge room beyond and my father's giant golden desk which was positioned before an imposing window.

The silencing bubble kept our entry silent, and my gaze fell on Gus across the room, tearing out drawers in an antique cabinet, rifling through the contents as he did so. Every so often, he seized some hard drive or piece of paper and stuffed it into a bag hanging from his arm.

Sofia let the silencing bubble fall and I sent a whip of a vine flying out to snap around him, his arms latching tight to his body.

He yelped in alarm, looking to me as ice slid over his fingertips, but it cracked as he came face to face with me. And I was satisfied to see a glimmer of true fear in his eyes.

"Do you really think my father is stupid enough to leave anything condemning in his own office?" I scoffed.

"Condemning?" Gus exhaled. "Why would I want anything condemning against the King? I am his loyal servant."

"No, you're vermin feeding on the scraps of whoever holds the most power," Sofia said icily. "And you're wondering if that will still be Lionel soon, hedging your bets."

"Yeah, I reckon you're looking for something that might save your neck if the True Queens win this war and come hunting down his subjects," I said in agreement, cocking my head to one side. "Oh, what they would do with you, I wonder."

He shuddered, bowing his head. "I'm just a reporter. I haven't hurt anyone."

"Your lies hurt everybody," I barked, my voice cutting through the air and making him flinch. "You're responsible for twisting the minds of the masses, making them believe the bullshit you spew in your rag of a newspaper."

"It's just politics," Gus implored, and I felt the subtle push of his Fox charm trying to make me see his side. "I've not killed anyone."

"Your words have," I said darkly, taking a step closer as his fingers flexed, and I wondered if he would dare fight me. I'd take pleasure in making him kneel to my power.

"Lies kill, Gustav," I growled, tightening up my mental walls against his Order gifts. "And there are consequences for that."

"Who are you to dish out punishments?" he scoffed, giving up on trying to sway me to his cause. "You're the spare Heir the King discarded. You're of a lesser Order, lesser status than your dead brother, and the only worth you once had was your blood. But you betrayed that, didn't you?"

"Shut your mouth," Sofia snarled, fire flaring in her palms, and my heart swelled with the protectiveness shining from her.

Gus's words didn't leave a single mark on my soul as they once might have. Because I'd found my true path in life. I knew who I was, and I knew where I belonged.

"If you really think I'm going to weep at that assessment of me, you're a damn fool," I said. I didn't mention the fact that Darius was alive and well, knowing he'd want to make some grand declaration of that to the kingdom when the time was right. "My father is dirt to me. Just like this office is dirt." I let my earth Element seep from my skin along with some water magic to make the room start to decay.

Mould crept up the walls, growing onto every gleaming, shining object, encasing my father's gold trinkets and swallowing them up in an ugly black coating. The wallpaper began to peel, turning grey and sallow, then the gleaming floorboards at my feet grew warped and layered with mildew. I willed the office to fester, everything from his enormous desk to the green mural of Lionel's Dragon on the wall to the golden bust of his smug fucking head to his wingback chair and the glittering chandelier that hung above it all. Every piece of it decayed before our eyes.

The papers in the open drawers turned black and withered, and finally, the last thing remaining intact was the photograph in a gilded frame on Lionel's desk. The very photo taken the last time I'd come here, the lie of what my family had been, though maybe now that I was looking through the lens of experience, I could see the darkness touching my mother's eyes, I could see the tenseness in my brother's shoulders and the way my father's hand was gripping his shoulder just a little too hard.

My own smile was bright, and it would have been all too easy to buy it as happiness. But one hand hung at my side, my fist squeezing so tight I could almost feel the way my nails had bitten into the flesh of my palm that day. I let that smile decay along with the rest of them, no part of this moment treasured or worth keeping. It was a photograph of three prisoners and their captor, but I took some relief in knowing those prisoners were now free.

The loss of my mother clutched my heart as I watched her false smile wither to nothing, hoping that wherever her soul was resting, her smiles were true and felt with all the colour of the world behind them. She'd deserved so much more than life had offered her, and the man responsible was the last to decay within the photo, his green eyes swallowed away into the mould.

Gus suddenly flicked a finger and ice bloomed across the floor beneath our feet, making me neigh in surprise. Sofia and I slipped sideways violently, crashing into one another, and Gus grew ice shards along his arms, snapping the vines binding him.

"No!" I barked as he made a run for the door.

I cursed, throwing a blast of fire out to stop him as fast as I could. He shifted, turning into a beautiful red fox, his jaw snapping tight around the strap of his bag before he went sailing through the door and skidding out into the hallway.

"Fuck," I gasped, dispelling the ice with a blast of fire and taking chase after him.

"Hurry!" Sofia cried, racing along with me.

Gus bounded along the balcony and turned onto the stairs, leaping down them three at a time toward the atrium below. Sofia sprinted past me, springing onto the balcony with impossible grace, then casting a dog from fire and sending it hounding after Gus.

I launched myself over the mahogany railing, catching sight of Gus turning sharply down a corridor off of the atrium, the fire dog hot on his heels.

I cast a thick bed of moss to soften my fall, rolling and regaining my feet in seconds, running straight back into the pursuit.

"Xavier!" Sofia yelled, and I glanced back, finding my decaying power pouring out along the walls, spreading deeper and deeper into the Court of Solaria. I could feel the power rooted in the depths of my soul, the hatred I felt for Lionel and his followers seeping out of me and fuelling this destruction.

"Let it rot," I growled, and Sofia nodded, a darkness to her eyes as she ran down the stairs to catch me.

The beautiful atrium fell to ruin around her, the black mould spreading onto everything and eating into the beautiful paintwork, the shining tiles, the ornate cubic clock hanging from the ceiling above, stopping it for good and permanently marking the moment it fell to ruin.

Sofia and I sprinted alongside one another as fast as we could, following Gus through the building, little flames from Sofia's dog shimmering along the path to guide our way. She was damn smart, and I'd be sure to kiss her for it later.

My festering power was gaining momentum, following me as I raced through the polished hallways, chasing Sofia's flames into the beautiful building that had been tainted by Lionel's rule. These halls and offices were the origin of war crimes, decisions passed between the wealthy as they dismissed whole swathes of Fae as nothing, laying plans for cruel imprisonments, ruthless massacres. These walls would never be clean again, so I willed them to decay and stain them with the taint they hid beneath their shine.

The flames that guided us on led us to an office with an open window, and I whinnied in anger, running to it and gazing out at the street. The clamour of battle was strong in the air again, and it was clear our side was winning, the sight of it dipping my heart in a pool of hope. The Nymphs and enemy Fae were falling back and many were turning to flee, racing away into the city.

I shoved the window wider, picking up Sofia and tossing her onto the street. She landed smoothly, looking left and right for any sign of Gus as I climbed out after her.

My boots hit the cobblestones and I hunted the crowd for a flash of red fur, but there was no sign of him. No glint of red fur, no white-tipped tail slinking away between the colliding bodies.

"There!" Sofia cried, spotting a line of flames weaving through the masses, and a smile caught my lips.

We ran into the fray and Geraldine's bellowing voice carried across the crowd somewhere close by. "Look yonder! How the Court of Solaria festers before our very eyes!"

I glanced back at the high walls and glittering flagpoles rising up behind me, the mould crawling all over it, swallowing every piece. A groaning sounded before a crack shot up the central wall and a loud crash came from somewhere inside the building. It didn't look like it would be long before the whole structure collapsed, and my chest swelled with the knowledge that I was responsible for its fall.

The rattle of a nearby Nymph latched onto my power, starting to lock it down, but a huge white Wolf sailed over my head and slammed into the beast, taking it to the ground in a blur of teeth and fury.

A sharp snap of Seth's jaws turned the creature to dust, and my magic flooded keenly through my veins once more.

The buzz of victory was in the air, rebels crying out their joy and the agonised roar of more falling Nymphs setting my heart racing excitedly. But I wasn't done yet. Not without my hands on that piece-of-shit Fox shifter.

The crowd parted ahead of me, and my gaze locked on him at last, Gus still carrying his bag in desperation while Sofia's fire dog snapped at the Fox's heels. If he made it beyond the battle and outpaced Sofia's cast, he could slip away down an alley and we'd never find him.

Urgency blazed inside me and I threw out a palm, building a wall of stone in front of him. The Fox leapt up, scrambling to get over it, but the fire dog jumped up to bite Gus's tail. His red fur set alight, and Gus let out a pitchy whine of pain, losing his grip and falling to the ground, rolling desperately to try and put the flames out.

I was on him in the next second, grabbing him by the scruff of the neck and dousing him in water to put out the fire, making him look pathetic and bedraggled as he hung limply in my grip. I bound his legs to his sides with vines and his head hung in defeat, accepting the fight was lost.

Sofia picked up the bag he'd been dragging, hooking it over her shoulder with a triumphant grin. "Mine."

A roar of victory crowed around us, and I whooped in delight, casting a metal cage around Gus and dropping him clunkily to the floor.

Sofia smiled at the fire dog, then let it dissolve in a swirl of fluttering flames, and I swooped toward her, kissing her hard and dipping her low as I did so, making her laugh against my lips. Her skin began to shine and mine did too, our Pegasus Orders glowing with utter joy and making our skin shimmer like raindrops in the sun.

An echoing boom rocked the ground beneath our feet, and we stumbled apart, looking for the source of the noise. I slung my arm over her shoulder in relief, finding the Court of Solaria succumbing to my power, the rot so deep in the structure that it crumbled before our eyes, stone and mortar cracking and shattering.

The rebels cheered and Tyler whinnied above, wheeling over us and sending a shower of silver glitter onto the crowd.

"This day will henceforth be known as the Great Rebel Coming!" Geraldine boomed, amplifying her voice with magic, climbing up onto a car roof and jutting up her chin.

"Awkward name," Sofia muttered.

"Definitely needs some work," I agreed with a snort of amusement, and I reached down to pick up Gus's cage.

"Let us don our victory hats and return to our stronghold to inform our rulers of the Great Coming!" Geraldine cried. "All hail the True Queens!"

Everyone echoed her final words, then tossed a pinch of stardust over their heads, and we raced away into the arms of the stars.

My fingers were locked tight with Sofia's as we twisted away into the space between galaxies, and I felt Tyler swooping after us, our souls connecting and dancing together as we returned to Zodiac Academy. And we damn well lived to fight another day.

LYRA

CHAPTER SEVEN

The ground trembled beneath me where I slept fitfully on the thin mattress, a gasp tearing me from the meagre clutches of sleep as the jolt rocked through the walls themselves.

I looked up with wide eyes as the woman with the kind smile moved closer in the shadows.

"What is it now?" a man hissed fearfully in the dark, his silhouette shifting before the bars of our cell.

It was cold in the Nebula Inquisition Centre. Always cold and always cramped.

The Minotaurs in the next cell over mooed uneasily, dust cascading from the walls as another jolt rattled them again.

Whimpers and fearful murmuring broke out around us, and I curled my legs up to my chest, banding my arms around them and placing my chin on my knees as I tried not to remember that night.

But the screams were still ringing in my ears, my mother's blood hot against my cheeks as she tried to fight back, placing herself between me and the men who had found us.

The letters on their clothes swam before my eyes. FIB. The Fae we had always been told would protect us above all others. The ones who had stolen my world from me instead.

"Hush, love," the woman said, dropping down beside me and taking my hand in her fleshy palm. She'd taken it upon herself to look after me and the other kids who were alone here, but there wasn't much she could really offer us beyond soft smiles and simple platitudes. She hushed me again, but I hadn't uttered a sound. Not a single sound since that night. It wasn't me who was crying in the corner of our cell. I wasn't the one muttering prayers to the uncaring stars as the walls shook again.

"The Queens are here!" a voice cried from somewhere in the darkness far beyond our cell, the cry followed by another and another, my heart pumping harder with each declaration, each sob of hope and relief.

Then there was nothing but fire.

Smoke crashed through the cells, screams tore the darkness apart, and the woman who held my hand shifted in fright, her body shrinking until a tiny paw brushed over my fingers before she fell to the mattress beside me.

The rest of the Tiberian Rats who shared this piece of hell with me did the same while the sound of cattle mooing in terror pressed in on my ears from the next cell over. Tiny bodies swarmed around me, squeaking in fright, scratching at my skin with their sharp claws as they rushed past me, hunting for a way out which we already knew didn't exist.

The fire flared again, the heat searing my skin as red and blue flames flashed violently through the darkness, illuminating a scene of pure horror with two terrifyingly beautiful women standing in the centre of it with crowns upon their heads.

Wings of raging fire spread from their spines, and I could only stare as they slowly walked towards me; the only calm point in a seething rush of terrified Fae.

These were the queens that the people locked up in this camp had whispered of. The ones they had said would save us. The ones who had come to kill us all in the end.

The one with the blue hair reached out for the bars of my cage, her head tilting as she surveyed me amid the tide of rats who swarmed away from them, a still object in the sea of chaos. The rats scrambled for the wall at my back, the furthest point from those flames and the heat which was choking the air from my lungs.

The moment Darcy Vega's fingers wound around the bar, it fell to nothing. It didn't melt, it didn't burn, it simply ceased to be.

Tory reached out next, brushing her fingers across the bars from left to right, each of them tumbling away to nothing beneath the force of her power.

"Is this what it's for?" she breathed, watching the Rats who squealed in fear behind me, scrambling at a wall which may as well have been a mountain.

There was no way out of here without passing those twins of flame and carnage. But none rushed towards the queens who had come for them at last. Nothing in the eyes of those terrible creatures offered salvation.

"Fear is so…pointless," Darcy sighed, seeming disappointed as she reached out and plucked a Tiberian Rat from the ground by its tail.

The creature thrashed and kicked, its pale grey fur so like my father's had been in his shifted form. I stared at the terrified Fae as Darcy lifted it up before her, watching it intently while her fire slowly rolled from her fingertips down its tail.

The Rat's screams were all piercing squeals as it burned beneath her power, but her face didn't change as she watched it suffer through its death. She observed it impassively, as if nothing about what she was doing mattered at all.

"This one is different." Tory pointed at me, taking a step closer, her terrible beauty stealing my breath while I simply stared.

I had nothing left. It had all been taken from me already. Perhaps death would be a relief after all of that.

A tiny body leapt before me, the brown Rat shifting in mid-air, and the woman with the kind smile landed there, her arms wide as she placed herself between me and death, just as my mother had done.

"Leave the child," she begged, her limbs trembling with fear as the twins observed her with interest.

"Sacrifice?" Darcy questioned curiously.

"Bravery," Tory replied in that same, too-flat tone.

"Interesting," Darcy mused.

"Please, my Queens, I beg you," the woman wept, still shaking as she held her ground before me.

She'd told me on that first day here that I reminded her of her daughter. I should have asked her where that child had gone. But I hadn't had the words. I still didn't have the words.

My lips parted on…something, but before I could summon whatever it was from the depths of my being, Tory reached out and caressed the woman's cheek.

Her scream ripped through me as the bones within her flesh lit up, catching light with the force of the fire that tore through her body.

I didn't flinch. The horrors I'd already witnessed had broken the part of me which should have reacted, which should have made me do...well, I didn't even know what.

Her body fell away to nothing, and my eyes closed against the flare of light that burned from the twins who had brought ruin in place of salvation.

The screams surrounding me grew in volume, the frantic bodies of Tiberian Rats in both shifted and Fae form collided with me as they rushed to flee, and the light of the fire stung my eyes even through my closed lids.

When the silence fell, I expected to find myself stepping beyond The Veil, my family waiting for me, ready to return whatever had been broken inside of me that day.

But that wasn't what I found.

A single tear rolled down my cheek as I took in the destruction surrounding me, the ash and soot all that remained of those who had been incarcerated here for nothing more than the crime of being born the wrong Order for the King's desires.

A finger pressed to my cheek, catching the tear and drawing my gaze up to Tory Vega who surveyed me with that same empty curiosity.

"This is different," Darcy said from my other side.

"Perhaps," Tory replied.

"Then she shall come," Darcy said. "What we seek is clearly not here anyway."

"No," Tory agreed, though somehow it wasn't like a normal conversation, more like the musings of a single mind, uncertain of which path to follow next.

"Death was...less than I expected," Darcy sighed.

"Much less. No more tempting than before. I still fail to understand the call of it," Tory exhaled, her hand clasping my arm, the touch of her flesh like a bite of utter darkness which stole the breath from my lungs. "Come, empty girl. We have work to do. We must seek the other fallen."

DARIUS

CHAPTER EIGHT

In death, I had been gifted more than simple insights into the lives of the ones I'd lost. As I stood beside my best friend, ready to retrieve a Guild Stone based on the knowledge I had managed to claim from the mouths of the dead, I couldn't help but wonder if everything I'd suffered had somehow been fated despite the way Roxy had torn our destiny from the hands of the stars. But how else could we have obtained this knowledge? Short of finding a way to commune with the souls which had passed beyond The Veil, I couldn't see how we might have hoped to find this place.

Regardless of divine interference or providence, I would take the opportunity. Azriel Orion believed the fate of this war might be shifted by the discovery of the Guild Stones and potentially by the formation of the Zodiac Guild too, and I was more than willing to trust in his judgement on such things. Though what the Zodiac Guild even meant now that the Imperial Star was no longer a part of it, none of us had any clue.

So there I stood, side by side with Azriel's son, our boots marking the entrance to a cavern no Fae had likely noticed in countless years, let alone investigated. We were far from the academy and the others, the icy winds and thrashing waves of the north-eastern coast all that kept us company in this wild place.

The cavern opened out above us, crystals of every shape and colour glimmering like our own personal rainbow as the light of my flames reflected off of their surfaces.

The air was cold and damp, my boots splashing through a shallow puddle as I moved deeper into the darkness.

"He spoke of this cavern and of my ancestor, Luxie Acrux, who supposedly claimed it for her own," I murmured, my gaze tracking across the rocky walls and roof above our heads, noting how sharp those crystals were, their razor edges gleaming.

"I can't tell if this place is natural or tainted by old magic," Lance muttered as he followed close behind me, his footsteps loud in the uninterrupted silence of the cavern.

"Perhaps it's both," I suggested, heading further into the depths where the black stone walls began to narrow, the passage closing in before ending in a pool filled with utterly still water.

"Tell me what he said again," Lance asked, and I felt a stirring of guilt at having spent the time I had with his father. The longing for such an encounter was clear in his voice, and I wished I could offer him a parting in The Veil so that he could speak with the man who he had loved so dearly for himself. But that door was closed to me now, barred and locked until I found myself falling into death for the final time. There would be no returning again. The steady thump of my heart swore that much to me. My life was no longer my own but completely hers. I was bound to the time she was destined to claim in this realm, and I felt no fear over the fact. I'd once suffered through months without her, and I was glad to know that we would never suffer that separation again.

"Walk the path of the unknown through the cavern filled with razor-edged stones, then dive into the secrets which linger. The Guild Stone stolen by your ancestor is hidden in a place long since forgotten by both time and memory."

"He always was fond of riddles," Lance said. "Though in this instance, a little clarity would have been appreciated. He was aware of the Dragon asshole hell bent on killing all of us, right?"

"He had a choice word or two for my father," I agreed, and Lance released a breath of amusement.

"I'd have paid good money to hear that."

I turned to him as we reached the edge of the pool, placing a hand on his shoulder and pinning him in my gaze as he looked at me with a frown.

"He loves you more than he could express to me in words," I told him. "And he wanted you to know he's sorry. So fucking sorry for leaving you when he did, for everything you endured since he died...honestly, I think watching all the trials you've faced since his death has broken something in him, brother. But there's hope now, hope for a better future, and that's thanks in no small part to you. You saw it when I refused to, let yourself accept the twins and what they were destined to become. I'm sorry it took me so long to come to that truth too."

Lance's face crumpled with pain, and I drew him against me, embracing him tightly while he thumped my back and released a heavy breath.

"I've been caught in the agony of missing him ever since he died. But when I lost you, I was hollow, Darius. I couldn't bear knowing that piece of shit had stolen every good thing from you before you ever got the chance to crawl out from under his shadow. You deserve to live, wholly and fully, knowing true love and conquering every demon that has haunted you until this point, and I won't ever take a single second of our time together for granted again."

"Well, shit, you're gonna make me cry if you carry on like that," I teased, shoving him back and exchanging a smile with him that promised a thousand more adventures by my side.

"I guess we have to dive into that murky water now?" Lance sighed, looking to the circular pool beside us. It was barely four feet wide, looking like little more than a puddle, but something told me it held depths far beyond its innocuous appearance.

"One of these days, we'll head off on an excursion together and won't end up coated in anything disgusting," I joked, tugging my shirt off and tossing it aside while letting water magic build in my veins.

I flexed my fingers, reaching out with my magic and forming a connection to the pool, closing my eyes as I focused on it, sensing how deep it went and trying to figure out exactly what it would take to reach the bottom.

"It's fucking endless," Lance said from beside me, clearly focusing on his own water magic. "The tunnel just keeps going and going."

"There has to be a bottom to it." I frowned as I tried to find one, but before I could, something butted against the edges of my power and shoved me back. "What the fuck is that?"

"Whatever it is, I can't break through it from this distance," Lance replied, his own magic writhing against mine as he found the barrier in the depths of the pool too.

I reached for him blindly, taking his hand and dropping the walls surrounding my magic just as he did the same, our combined power thrusting against the shadowy barrier with enough force to take out a small village. But it didn't break.

I huffed out a breath of frustration, smoke spilling between my lips as I released Lance's hand and opened my eyes.

"I'll get through it," I told him, unbuckling my belt and kicking off my boots as I prepared to dive into the tunnel and figure out what was going on.

"Whatever that magic is, it's old and it's sleeping," Lance warned me as I moved to the edge of the pool. "I'm not sure how it will react to being woken."

"Only one way to find out. Besides, if anyone is going to be able to break the spells cast by a long dead Acrux, then it'll be me," I replied before diving in headfirst and kicking to propel myself deeper. The bite of the freezing water dug into my flesh with icy fingers, but the fire which lived within my soul rose to meet it, pushing it back and keeping my body warm despite its best efforts.

My palms tingled as I called on my water magic, commanding a pocket of air to form around my face as I wielded my power over the liquid and forced it back enough to let me breathe and see more clearly.

Though 'clearly' was an overstatement. The murky green of the pool only grew darker as I descended, the rough rock walls brushing against my shoulders and legs as I kicked to descend further. I sent a Faelight out before me, the glow of it streaming away into the depths below, illuminating faint carvings on the rocky walls surrounding me, the runes pulsing with energy when I passed them.

My heart thumped loudly in my ears, my gaze moving from one rune to the next, some of their meanings clear to me while others I'd never seen before. I got the feeling Roxy would have known more about them than me, and I snorted at the thought of the smug look on her face over that fact. I'd have to be sure to research all I could about ether before she realised there was a magical subject that she might claim supremacy in over me.

I swam for ten minutes, then longer still, my muscles burning as the underwater tunnel grew tighter, closing in around me while I forced myself not to think about the fact that there was no way I could turn around down here. The platinum ring of my wedding band was warm against my skin, reminding me that I had that small way to regenerate my magic should I need it, but it felt insubstantial after such an immense descent. Perhaps I should start taking a leaf from Dante Oscura's book and drape myself in gold at all times to avoid this kind of situation. He certainly wouldn't have had too much to worry about if he found himself trapped in this place.

Before I could get too lost in the idea of becoming stuck down here, a rush of power crashed into me, shattering the water magic that had been keeping the oxygen around my face and extinguishing my Faelight in one sudden burst.

I cursed within my own head, bracing my hands against the rock walls as disorientation took me in its grasp, my mind flailing with the sudden reality of my magic being torn from me. It wasn't like the effects of a suppressant, my power hadn't been blocked, more like it was trapped beneath a heavy weight, leaving me struggling to tear it free.

My heart thrashed in my chest, the knowledge that Roxy could feel it helping my thoughts align as I ignored the instinct to panic and instead focused on my surroundings.

I pressed my palms to the rock walls, noticing the way they had turned from rough to smooth, feeling the unnatural raised markings running along them. I traced the closest one, focusing on the shape it created, finding an upright triangle that signified fire beside a single letter A.

Well, if this wanted fire, then I had plenty of that, and the letter made me think it might just be asking for a kind specific to my family line.

With a force of will, Dragon fire exploded from my palm, the heat washing over me. The magic which had trapped me in place fell away, the tunnel opening up beneath me once more.

I hesitated, my mind catching on the very real possibility that earth or air magic might be required to complete the passage through this tunnel, neither of which I could lay claim to. Lance held command over air, but as he had remained far above me in the central cavern, I doubted that would be of much help if I found myself trapped again. I tried to think back over the time I'd been forced to spend studying my family tree as a child. My studies had focused on the power and size possessed by the Dragons I'd descended from, but there had been more information about those who claimed the most memorable histories.

Luxie Acrux wasn't a name that came easily to mind. It had been years since I'd pored over those old records, and I'd been more interested in the ancestors who had fought in battles or owned precious treasures than memorising what magic they each held. Her name did ring a bell though, I just couldn't think why.

I stayed where I was, reforming the pocket of air around my face and reaching out with my connection to the water. The tunnel curved beneath me, levelling out before moving upward again, the passage just as narrow as it was here.

I found a barrier once more, the magic the same as the kind I'd just shattered, and I frowned in concentration as I searched the edges of the tunnel surrounding it.

The rough rock smoothed out again, and I found a second carving etched into the stone which I quickly identified as another symbol for fire with the letter A beside it.

I raised my fist and shot a blast of potent Dragon fire away from me, frowning in concentration as I guided it through the tunnel, my limbs beginning to tremble as the water fought to douse the flames that moved further and further from me with every second.

The fireball finally made it to the carving, and I let it explode against it, the magic shattering and sending a spray of water up into an open space beyond. The droplets fell back into the pool and my connection to the space disappeared, but I was reassured enough to swim on.

I kicked my legs hard, ignoring the cuts and scrapes I'd gained from the pressing walls of the tunnel and swimming blindly on through it.

Another five minutes passed, the tunnel seeming endless before I emerged at last, sucking in a deep breath of fresher air and finding myself in another cavern.

Unlike the first, this one wasn't hung with sharp rocks, the roof instead lined with bones bleached white with age, forming an arch where a small stone platform sat at the water's edge.

I heaved myself out, sending two green orbs of light flying back down the tunnel to let Lance know he should follow.

Fire magic built beneath my skin, water rising in a cloud of steam as I dried out quickly and stepped through the archway to inspect the metal door beyond.

Thick black studs stuck out from the iron, their tips sharpened like spears, a heavy lock and three bolts securing it in place.

"Well, that looks ominous," Lance spoke from behind me, taking me by surprise with his sudden appearance.

I glanced over my shoulder at him, finding him perfectly dry, not a beard hair out of place. Of course the asshole had used air to shoot himself through the narrow passage in a blink. We'd encountered several small tunnels and tight crawl spaces when hunting Nymphs in the past and he'd always shot through them at speed. Not that he'd ever admit to disliking confined spaces, but I had him pegged.

He waved a hand at me and my clothes rushed forward, hanging in a little cocoon of air, perfectly dry.

"Thanks," I said, the air falling away as I reached for the clothes, and I quickly dressed myself in them.

"I was concerned that the sight of your naked ass might scare away whatever is hiding behind that door," he mused. "And I want a chance to dance with it myself before that happens."

He moved to stand beside me and we inspected the door, his brow furrowing as he crouched down, muttering spells beneath his breath, checking for traps and curses inlaid in the metal.

I pressed my palm to the centre of the heavy iron and a chill shot through my core at the frigid shock of it. It wasn't just cold; ice had long been my friend, and the feeling spreading from within that door made the point of freezing seem tame.

A breath fell from my lungs as the cold crept deeper into my chest, a rattle shaking my ribcage as it dug into me, seeking out every bit of light and warmth, snuffing all it found one after another.

The Dragon in me stirred as the cold raced through my limbs, Lance speaking a word I couldn't understand as it clanged through my skull, and my knees threatened to buckle.

The man I had been before might have caved to the weight of that icy breath as it stole through me, but the man who had stepped back out of death was not so easily conquered.

My muscles flexed as I stayed on my feet, power rippling through my flesh, and the beast in me snarled with burning energy.

I blinked and my gaze sharpened as my eyes shifted, the reptilian slits narrowing my focus onto the door so it was all I could see.

Smoke slid between my lips as I drew them back in a snarl, and Dragon fire blazed within my chest where the cold rushed to consume it.

With the small bit of awareness I still clung to, I gripped Lance's shoulder, shoving him back, my other arm trembling where it remained locked with the door.

He took my warning and moved behind me, shielding himself while the power of all that I was rose up from within the depths of me and rattled me to my core.

Dragon fire rushed from me like water bursting a dam, and it was all I could do to brace myself as the blast boomed from me and collided with the door, the flames of my Order tearing into the solid iron, ripping through locks both physical and magical at once.

The heat of the blast enveloped me, stealing the breath from my lungs and nearly knocking me from my feet. I gritted my teeth and held firm as the door shattered, shards of metal flying through the air, slicing into my skin and splattering my blood against the white bones that surrounded us.

I cursed as I was forced to turn my face, my hand coming up to shield my eyes while the last of it tore past us and everything finally fell still.

I expelled a breath lined with smoke, my shifted eyes piercing the darkness beyond the door where a stone chamber opened up into a wide space thick with shadows.

"And there was me about to crack through the spells on the door with some level of subtly," Orion said dryly.

He got to his feet behind me, clucking his tongue as he took in my half-shredded clothes and the bloody cuts which marked my body.

There was a gash in my right shoulder which would have been damn alarming for a mortal, but I just pressed a hand to it, healing it away while trying to maintain some level of dignity over that shit fest.

"I figured this way was easier," I replied.

Lance opened his mouth to say something further, but the clanging of what sounded like a huge bell rang out from within the chamber before us, silencing him.

We exchanged a look, and I drew my axe as he unsheathed his sword. This place looked like it hadn't been touched for countless years, but where magic was concerned, that didn't necessarily mean it was abandoned.

I led the way into the cavern, sending a Faelight ahead of us and tilting my head back to look up at the huge space which was revealed beyond.

The walls rose up endlessly, disappearing into darkness before any kind of roof could be glimpsed, the golden glint of a huge bell hanging directly in the centre of the echoing space.

There were stone carved tables and pedestals, marked with various runes and holding a mixture of treasures and ancient bones, the dust which had piled up on it all doing little to conceal the immensity of the haul.

"Mine," I growled, my gaze fixing on a decorative shield inlaid with emeralds, and as I stared around at this forgotten treasure, I suddenly remembered why Luxie Acrux's name had been sticking in my mind.

She hadn't fought fearlessly in battle or made a name for herself in politics. No; Luxie Acrux had been on a list which my father had pointed out to me with a twist of his lips that betrayed his irritation at it.

"Some Dragons in our family line chose to covet their treasure even in death," he'd spat. *"The hordes of these Dragons have never been found. They stole their riches away and concealed them somewhere in this world, yet to be discovered, choosing to die while maintaining possession of their gold rather than letting it pass on in inheritance to the next generation."*

I'd felt that same irritation at his words, the galling truth of knowing the Dragons on that list had hidden untold treasures away from us, the biting reality that somewhere in the world those riches were concealed in tombs unclaimed by all. He'd gone on to explain that many members of our family had hunted for the lost treasures but none from that list had ever been found. Until now. Azriel had sought the location beyond The Veil from some dead Dragons who had watched Luxie Acrux place it in this very spot.

A bark of laughter escaped me as I pictured his face when he found out that I had discovered one. That every coin, jewel, and precious stone in this place had finally been reclaimed by a member of his precious bloodline, and that it just so happened to have been by the Heir who had betrayed him.

"You're drooling," Lance deadpanned, taking a step into the space and picking up a ring with a sapphire inlaid into it, the gold band forged to appear as if a pair of wings clutched the jewel.

"I'm hard as fuck too, but that's not the point," I replied, plucking the ring from his hand and pushing it onto my little finger.

Lance snorted a laugh, but his eyes lingered on the ring like there was something that drew him to it.

"This is my ancestor's treasure," I said, moving between several columns until I found what I'd been hunting for; a great sarcophagus carved with images of Dragons laying beneath an enormous mural of a silver Dragon as she tore through the sky. The words 'Here lies Luxie Acrux and all she claimed dear in this world and beyond' had been scored into the rock above the mural.

"That makes it mine," I added, pointing to the words for confirmation. "All of it. Every coin. Even if I hadn't been descended from her, I was the one who found it, so it would still be mine. Right down to the last gemstone."

"Even that necklace?" Lance asked curiously, pointing to a pendant which had been draped around the throat of a stone bust, a star hanging from it inlaid with diamonds which formed the symbol for Taurus.

"Yes. That's mine," I agreed, snatching it and hanging it around my neck, power tingling beneath my skin at the contact with the treasure.

"What about those others which match it?" Lance asked curiously, pointing out a line of busts, each of them sporting a similar necklace with the diamonds forming the symbols of the other star signs on them.

"Mine," I agreed, moving to take them from their positions on display and pushing them into my pocket.

"How about this bracelet?" Lance called from across the chamber, and I cursed his Vampire speed as I stalked over to him, snatching the band of gold which had been engraved with little stars beside a crescent moon. A shiver tracked down my spine as I inspected it. This one was old. Trachion era, if I wasn't mistaken, the weight a little heavier than it would have been if it were made now, probably forged in the ancient style of-

"What about this tiara?" Lance called from the depths of the cavern, and I snapped around, smoke coiling through my teeth as I spotted him lowering the thing towards his head. The stones were onyx, the metal almost black itself, the style screaming Blood Ages, and it was fucking *mine*.

"Give it to me," I demanded, marching towards him with my hand outstretched, and he flung it to me with a smirk before speeding away again.

"How about these coins? The rebellion needs more funding." Lance let the handful of priceless coins tumble between his fingers as he dropped them back into the chest he'd plucked them from.

"Those date back to the rule of King Olard," I hissed, rushing towards him. "They're not auras for purchasing food for a fucking army!"

"Okay." Lance shot past me, causing a wind to ruffle my hair, and I spun around to find him up on a pedestal, three necklaces hanging from his throat. "What about these?" he questioned, inspecting one which was a string of beautiful pearls that looked like they might just be from the now-extinct deloyster, and another which was a bright platinum chain with a tear-drop diamond that had one of the finest cuts I'd ever seen.

"Those are mine," I growled, breaking into a run and barely catching them as he tossed them to me before shooting away again. I stuffed my pockets so full that my pants were in danger of slipping right off my ass.

"These?" he wriggled his fingers at me from behind the sarcophagus, each of them coated in gold rings and a deep growl escaped me.

"Stop it," I snapped, rushing over to him, vaulting the dead body of my ancestor and scrambling to pick them all up from the floor where he dropped them before I could get close to him. I shoved them all onto *my* fingers, the call of the gold making my blood hum in satisfaction even as he continued to paw at my treasure from somewhere behind me.

"You have to admit, these suit me," he called, and I turned sharply, finding him inspecting himself in a dusty gilded mirror, a crown upon his head which had to be at least six hundred years old, an emerald broach pinned to his chest, a solid gold spear clutched in his fist, and a ceremonial shield strapped to his arm. "Yeah, I think I've found my new look."

"Give me those," I demanded, tripping over a box of jewels in my haste to claim the items from him and damn near falling on my face.

By the time I'd snatched them all into my grasp, I found him twirling in a circle while holding a flowing white dress to his chest, the corset top of it inlaid with individual diamonds which had probably been sewn into place during the Greshburg era before the War of the Seven Horses.

"I swear to fuck, Lance, if you don't stop-"

The dress hit me in the face, and I twisted at the sound of falling coins, finding him lying in a heap of treasure, his arms and legs opening and closing like he was trying to make a snow angel in it.

"Lance!" I bellowed, and he grinned widely before pointing to a dark corner beside him.

"What about that music box there?" he asked casually, and I stilled, trying to rein in my Dragon instincts and think clearly for a moment.

"Please stop touching my things," I ground out, moving to look at the innocuous little box he'd discovered.

"Are you gonna put all of that shit down or what?" Lance teased as he shot to my side, eyeing the heap of treasure I had clutched in my arms and draped over my body.

"No," I snapped, peering over the material of the dress where it was perched on the shield and daring him to try and make me with my stare.

Lance just arched a brow at me, glancing down as the heaps of coins in my pockets finally won the battle with my waistband and my pants fell to pool around my ankles with a heavy thump.

I pursed my lips, tightening my grip on the things I'd claimed, and Lance held out for all of five seconds before he burst into laughter.

I forced myself to drop the treasures which had been clutched to my chest and threw myself at him, knocking him from his feet and sending us to the floor where we fell into a scrap like a couple of assholes in a bar brawl.

My pants got tangled around my ankles, and Lance punched me in the jaw hard enough to make my head spin. I headbutted him in return, cracking his nose and making him curse as the crown fell from my head and smacked him on the forehead for good measure.

He shoved me hard enough to roll me away from him, then slapped my fucking ass with a braying laugh which finally made me crack too.

"Dickhead," I hissed, abandoning our fight and yanking my pants back up again.

I gave in to the inevitable and carefully removed the coins from my pockets, piling them up beside me while keeping half an eye on Lance to make sure he didn't try to paw at them again. I hid the sapphire ring under a few of them too, not forgetting the way his eyes had gotten all beady over it.

"Maybe that's how we win this war," he mused. "Just lay a bunch of treasure out for Lionel to see, then sneak up and cut his throat while he's jerking off over it."

"Where would you find the treasure to tempt him with?" I asked.

"Err, right here, asshole." Lance waved a hand to indicate the room at large, and I narrowed my eyes at him.

"No. Because this is all-"

"If you say 'mine' again, I'll probably have to give you another spanking," he cut in, and I cracked a smile.

"Just so long as we're clear about the ownership of everything in this room."

"Crystal," he replied, shaking his head at me, but we both knew if this was a room of Gwen's blood all bottled up and ready for someone to claim, he'd be just as unreasonable about it.

Lance's eyes moved back to the music box, and I knew we needed to face it to claim the Sagittarius Guild Stone, but I spoke before he could get to his feet.

"I was there," I told him in a low voice. "When my father had you and Gwen locked up in that cage in the Palace of Souls, I was there with you. I watched what you went through, and I tried to lend you what strength I could from beyond The Veil, but I know it wasn't enough..."

Lance's eyes clouded with the horrors of what he'd faced in that place, and I reached out for him, taking his hand in mine and looking deep into his dark eyes.

"We're going to make them pay for it. Every single second of pain my father and that shadow bitch forced upon us and those we love, our kingdom and its subjects. You know that, right?"

"Oh, I know," he agreed, and some of that heaviness lifted from his gaze as he let me draw him close for an embrace.

"Let's start by finding those stones then."

We got to our feet and moved to stand before the music box. I reached out and took it into my grasp. It seemed so harmless sitting here amongst countless priceless treasures, but I could feel the dark power that writhed around it all the same, could sense the potency of it and understood why Luxie had kept it here when she passed into death. Something valuable lurked within it.

"Ready?" I asked, my fingers grasping the lid.

"As I'll ever be."

I met my best friend's gaze and prised the lid open.

A tiny Centaur stood on a little platform within the box, a bow hanging over his shoulder and a target painted onto the inside of the lid. My attention fixed to him as an eerie tune began to play and the centaur rotated slowly on his platform, drawing an arrow and preparing to fire it. My eyes began to glaze as I watched him and as he fired the arrow, I felt a sharp tug in my gut as though I were being pulled forward by its momentum too. I reached forward as if compelled to do so, and as my fingers brushed the tiny arrow, I found myself tumbling through the air, losing sight of everything except for the centaur until I couldn't see him either.

I fell heavily onto my back, blinking up at dark trees which towered overhead, and I pushed myself to my feet as I took in the sudden change in our surroundings.

Adrenaline spilled into my veins as I gazed around at the woodland we'd found ourselves in.

"How the fuck is this even real?" I muttered, turning slowly and gazing between the thick tree trunks.

"This happened before when Blue and I found the Libra box. If it's anything like that one, this is going to be a merry little playground of fucked-up torture," Lance said.

The sound of thundering hooves made us both turn to look to our right, flames igniting along my arms as I drew magic to the ready in preparation of a fight.

"Sagittarius," Lance muttered, casting a shield of air magic around us. "My bet is on a pissed off Centaur heading our way."

"If a Centaur was trapped in here, wouldn't it have died by now?" I questioned, the thundering sound drawing closer.

Lance shrugged, rolling his shoulders back as he stared at the largest gap in the trees ahead of us.

As he'd predicted, a huge, silver Centaur which looked to be carved from metal burst from the trees, bow and arrow held ready in his arms as he turned his piercing gaze on us.

Fire exploded from my fists, tearing from me and colliding with the Centaur with the full force of my power.

The flames burned through his metallic flesh, his glinting metal eyes twisting my way before he loosed the arrow he'd drawn.

I threw myself to the side, knocking Lance along with me, somehow knowing that arrow would pierce his air shield before it even happened. The magic in this place followed laws of its own, and as the silver arrow the size of a damn spear sailed over our heads and embedded itself into a tree on the far side of the clearing, I knew this wouldn't be so simple as fighting our way free.

The Centaur galloped towards us, at least four times as big as any shifter of its kind that I'd ever seen and looking more like a statue given life. We shoved to our feet as it prepared a second arrow, but it skidded to a halt before us, not firing.

"Five stones may sit upon a throne, but none of them hold water. The greatest of them fails at flame, the weakest is its daughter. In air, two of them will excel, but the other may be your freedom, though linger too long on the earth and you may fail to see them."

"What the fuck is that supposed to mean?" I snarled, and the Centaur simply pointed at an archway between the towering trees, his bow held loose in his arms.

"Come on," I grunted to Lance, and the two of us skirted the unnatural beast, feeling its metallic eyes pinned on us as we stalked away from it towards the archway.

In the centre of a clearing, six stones lay in a bowl of pure white marble, the air between the trees so still that it felt like the world itself was holding its breath.

"A riddle?" Lance queried, moving towards the stones with interest. "That's a lot easier than the box Darcy and I found."

"If you say so," I replied, because whatever convoluted clue the Centaur had just given us meant absolutely nothing to me. "You think one of those is the Guild Stone?"

Lance moved to crouch before the marble bowl, his fingers skimming over the six stones that lay in a circle at its base.

"No," he replied eventually. "These are...something else."

I watched as he reached for the smallest of the stones, its colour grey and unassuming next to the brighter, more textured stones around it.

The ground rocked at our feet as he picked it up, and I cursed, grabbing one of the thick tree trunks for support, but the fucking thing bit me the moment I laid my hand on it.

I growled, ripping my hand away from the trunk of the tree which was now lined with razor sharp teeth, the entire trunk lurching towards me like it was willing to rip itself out of the ground to come after me.

I blasted fire at it but that only seemed to make it worse, a roar tumbling from the tree followed by its roots ripping at the soil.

"*Lance*," I barked, looking to him for some answer.

He snatched the stones from the marble plate before the thing could buck them all off onto the ground.

"There's the throne," he replied, jerking his chin towards the far side of the clearing and tossing three of the stones to me. "Now we need to figure out which one of these things hold water."

"They're stones, for the stars' sake," I spat as I fought to keep my feet while the roots of the carnivorous tree tried to trip me.

"I know they're stones, Darius. Stop pointing out the fucking obvious and get your ass over to that throne."

He shot away from me, muttering some shit about chalk, limestone, and flint, none of which held water to my knowledge, and I cursed him as I was left to battle my way between the ferocious trees to catch up to him.

A root snared my foot, and I was sent flying, a flash of fire magic breaking the thing apart before it could tug me towards those damn teeth. But I couldn't save myself from smacking into the ground at the foot of the ornate throne.

"One of these has to be more porous than the others," Lance said. "I can't figure out if this is flint or-"

"This one," I announced, holding up a brown stone with black stripes marking one side of it.

"What makes you think-"

I tossed the other two stones onto the throne, then snatched the ones Lance was holding and threw them down beside it too, keeping the striped stone in my other fist.

The trees stopped trying to bite, the roots falling still beneath the dirt once more, and Lance breathed a laugh while I clawed my way back to my feet again.

"How did you know that was the right one?" he asked.

I gave the stone a shake, feeling the water trapped within it sloshing from side to side as I did so.

"Felt it when I fell on my fucking face," I admitted, tossing the stone aside. "What was next?"

"The greatest of them fails at flame, the weakest is its daughter," Lance recited immediately. Damn, I'd never been so pleased that he was a nerd.

"Alright." I blasted the remaining stones with fire just as something fell against my shoulder and tumbled down my arm.

One of them crumbled to dust alongside the throne they'd been sat on, and I turned to grin triumphantly at Lance but found him gaping back at me in horror instead of admiration.

"What?" I asked.

"Don't move," he breathed, his eyes on my sleeve just as something else fell into my hair, causing me to bat my hand at it.

"Stop moving!" Lance yelled, and as I looked down at my arm to see what he was freaking out about, I fell entirely still.

The Baruvian Hellnet Spider was scuttling up my arm, its pincers clicking as it moved, and I cursed as I felt the second one moving across my scalp.

More of the poisonous little bastards fell from the trees above our heads, landing on the two of us and making my pulse thrash. A bite from one would cause immeasurable pain, but multiple bites had been known to be fatal.

"What did the stone you just destroyed look like?" Lance hissed, and I shrugged.

"I dunno, man. It was a fucking rock."

"One of these has to look like it and we need to find the one described as its daughter, so maybe next time think before you just blast shit with fire magic," he ground out as a Hellnet Spider crawled up the front of his shirt, closing in on his throat.

I looked at the four remaining stones, frowning between them before settling on the pale grey one. I was sure there had been two that colour. Well, fairly sure anyway.

With a twist of my fingers, I cast a shot of water and the stone was propelled into my hand.

"How does it help us to know if this is the daughter?" I asked, but Lance just shrugged.

"The next line was about two stones in air. I don't think it had to do with this one."

I swore, my grip on the stone I held tightening as another Baruvian Hellnet Spider fell onto my shoulder, and I felt something crack within my fist. Having no other ideas, I tightened my hold further and the stone in my fist shattered like a shell, pieces of grey rock crumbling away to reveal something small and smooth hidden in its centre.

The spiders all hissed at once, their attention jerking to the thing I held, tiny feet racing across my body as they all ran towards it. The insects crawling over Lance leapt from him, scurrying towards my outstretched hand, and I tossed the thing away from me with a jerk of my wrist.

The bugs hissed and spat as they charged after what looked like a glowing amber egg, and I shuddered as I tried to forget the feeling of those tiny legs scrambling all over me.

Lance grabbed the remaining three stones and shot them above his head with a blast of air magic. Two of them flew right up into the canopy of the trees, but one barely rose an inch before thumping back down into his palm. "Okay, the other two excelled, so this one is the winner," he said, holding up a rust red stone with a line of silver minerals running across its side.

"What do we do with it then?" I demanded, looking around us as the sound of thundering hooves met my ears once more.

It didn't sound like one Centaur this time though; this sounded like a whole herd of monstrous bastards, and as an arrow the size of a fucking spear shot through the air and impaled the tree to my left, I knew we were fucked.

"Catch." Lance tossed the stone to me, and I barely caught it before he collided with me at speed, tossing me onto his back and shooting away through the trees just as two more enormous arrows shattered the trunks closest to us.

I latched my arm around his neck, looking behind us and spotting at least ten of those big bastards with the metallic flesh galloping through the trees in pursuit of us. Lance was fucking fast with his Vampire speed, but they looked to be gaining on us all the same.

"Shit!" Lance shouted.

I barely managed to hold onto him as he threw himself to the side, an arrow shooting at us from up ahead as more of the beasts closed in on us from that direction.

"Over there!" I yelled as he veered around a towering trunk.

I'd caught a glimpse of an onyx pedestal through the trees, the thing so hard to pick out within the shadows that I couldn't believe I'd even noticed it.

I doubted Lance had seen it, but I pointed and he shot that way, ducking and swerving as more and more of those lethal arrows were fired at us, felling trees and making bark explode in missiles of sharpened wood, missing us by a hair's breadth time and again.

The pedestal appeared ahead of us, and I whooped in victory half a breath before Lance's cry of agony tore the air in two.

He was launched forward by the enormous arrow which had slammed into his side, and I was thrown free of him, crashing into the ground and rolling out of control before smacking into something hard enough to break bones.

"Lance!" I roared, the galloping hooves racing closer with every passing heartbeat as my best friend bled all over the ground, clutching the huge arrow that had pierced him.

"Behind you," he heaved out in reply.

I turned despite myself, my eyes widening as I spotted the herd of metallic Centaurs charging towards me, death gleaming in their unnatural eyes, twenty of those huge arrows pointed straight at me. But between me and them was a black pedestal, carved from stone and utterly unassuming, the space on its top empty and curved like a small dish awaiting a single stone.

I was on my feet in less than a second, a roar of challenge escaping my lips as I ran for the pedestal, daring fate to take me on.

The Centaurs all loosed their arrows at once, death careering towards me on brutal, silent wings. But I'd already reached the pedestal and I threw myself at it, the stone in my fist slamming down on that perfectly-shaped position a second before the arrows could claim me.

I flinched as they struck me, but instead of the agony of metal carving through my flesh, I felt nothing more than a stirring of air as the arrows disintegrated, falling apart and washing over me in the space between heartbeats.

The Centaurs disappeared too, then the woodland faded, nothing remaining but me, Lance, and the stone pedestal before me.

Lance cursed, getting to his feet and running a hand over his side where the enormous arrow had now vanished along with the injury it had caused.

When I looked back at the pedestal, I found it glowing, the stone at its peak reforming, a turquoise colour appearing from within it, then taking over entirely as it became the Sagittarius Guild Stone.

I picked it up and the last of the music box shattered around us, falling away and leaving us standing in the cavern my ancestor had selected to hide her treasure trove in death.

"That's the last one of those things I'm ever getting into," Lance growled.

"Yeah, fuck that for a laugh," I agreed. "Wanna help me box up my treasure and get it back to the academy?"

"Can I keep any of it for myself as payment?" he asked, and I narrowed my eyes at him, knowing he was angling for that ring. But he wasn't getting it.

"You can make the boxes. I'll do the packing," I replied.

"Can I at least have the Guild Stone?"

My fingers tightened around the precious turquoise stone, and I had to fight against the urge to move my arm behind my back for good measure.

"Later," I said.

"Now," he countered.

I pursed my lips, holding my fist out to him, but my fingers stayed curled around it. "I can keep it safe until-"

"Bad Dragon." Lance shot me in the ass with a whip of air magic and used his fucking Vampire speed to snatch the stone from my fist while I was distracted.

I snarled at him, taking a step forward with the full intention of snatching that stone back. I could look after it. I was more than capable of keeping it safe. Besides, it had been stored in my trove which meant that it was really mi-

Lance tossed a solid gold platter into my arms, and I lost my train of thought as I inspected it. It was a decent piece. Dating back to the Blood Ages if I wasn't mistaken, and carved with a battle scene which must have taken countless hours to perfect.

"Come on, asshole, let's pack up your new shiny things and get the fuck out of here." Lance clapped me on the arm, and I growled at him briefly before tossing the platter aside and drawing him into my arms.

"I'm glad you're okay," I said to him. "You're the greatest treasure here, you know. When that arrow hit you-"

"I think I might have to get that tattooed on me somewhere," Lance taunted. "'Darius's greatest treasure' would look great across my chest."

"Fuck you." I dipped my fingers into his pocket, taking the Guild Stone and sliding it right back into my own pocket instead.

"Fuck you harder – I know you like it rough."

We both laughed, then began the mammoth task of packing up every last piece of treasure Luxie Acrux had hidden away in this middle of nowhere trove so I could take it home and bask in it for as long as I fucking liked.

CALEB

CHAPTER NINE

I cursed for the hundredth time as I stomped along the back streets of Celestia. The muck from the sewers where I'd chased Lionel's war General, Irvine McReedy, clung to my boots, back, and side where the fucker had managed to knock me off my feet with a well-timed strike of his poisonous tail.

The stench was never going to wear off. Worse, it had taken all of my fucking magic to heal the sting from his scorpion tail and save my damn life. I'd almost lost him then, and I'd been forced to speed back and forth in the underground cesspit for over an hour hunting him down again.

I should have just given up. Should have taken the moment that sewage splashed me in the star damned eye as a sign from the stars that it was over, but of course I hadn't done that.

Lucky for me, the motherfucker had been tapped out too, but the fight against him in his Order form had resulted in a bloody chunk torn out of my side, four gaping claw slashes down my spine, and had left a slit running along the entire left side of my face for good measure.

So now, I was coated in blood as well as the sewage, limping, wearing mostly shredded clothes, magicless, feral with thirst, and dragging an enormous, half-dead Manticore along the back alleys of a city which was empty of my friends and the army I'd arrived with.

Apparently, not one of those assholes had noticed I was missing before stardusting back to the academy, and I hadn't been carrying a speck of stardust with me to be able to follow them.

My fist was latched tightly around the scaly, scorpion tail of Irvine McReedy, his leathery, bat-like wings dragging across the concrete, catching on trashcans, streetlamps, and to my amusement, a pile of dog shit which someone hadn't bothered to clean up.

Most Fae shifted back into Fae form if they were rendered unconscious, but apparently this big bastard was going to stay in his enormous Manticore form despite the blow I'd dealt to his temple.

Now I was trudging through Celestia, looking like death warmed up, dragging a half-dead Manticore and wondering what the fuck I was supposed to do.

I cursed as I hauled the unconscious beast out of a small side street in the financial district where not a single soul was around to help me.

A piercing scream split the air apart, and I whirled around in anticipation of an attack, my fangs snapping out before I found myself face to face with a bucktoothed woman wielding a rolling pin, pointing at me with a trembling finger.

"Bog beast!" she hissed, fire magic sparking between her fingers. A pang of memory brought me back to the night the other Heirs and I had coated Darcy in mud, compacting it so thickly onto her skin that she couldn't break free. Cries of 'bog beast' had been heard all across campus when she'd gone running away from us, and FaeBook had blown up with photos of her looking like she'd just crawled out of the nearest swamp. I guessed karma really was a bitch.

"I'm not a bog beast," I snapped. "I'm a Celestial..." I trailed off because that might not really be true anymore. We'd bowed to the Vegas. In a perfect world, they would choose to keep the Celestial Council and continue the way things had been for hundreds of years, but what if they didn't want us to serve them in that role? My mind snagged on that question, but the woman obviously thought I was done with what I'd been saying.

"Celestial beast of the bog!" she cried, turning away and sprinting off down the street with a scream.

I was tapped out and seeing her run set the non-bog beast in me salivating for magic.

I gave chase, my muscles bunching with effort as I dragged the unconscious Manticore along at my back, my Order gifts seriously depleted and exhaustion laying siege to my flesh.

But even at my lowest, I was still one of the most powerful Vampires in the whole of Solaria.

I caught the woman by her frizzy hair, yanking her back against me and ignoring the sting of her flickering flames as she tried to throw them at me. She wasn't even powerful enough to set my blood-drenched clothes alight, and I shuddered with revulsion as the disgustingly powerless taste of her blood washed over my tongue. One mouthful and she was drained, my own reserves not even replenished enough to heal myself.

I shoved her away from me and slapped a hand to the throbbing wound on my side all the same, managing to stem a little of the blood before my magic was gone again.

"I'm Caleb Altair," I snarled at the woman who was backing away, brandishing her rolling pin at me. "And I need a fucking car."

"Bog beast," she hissed, backing up further, and I was forced to stalk her all the way back to her grubby apartment before Coercing her to offer up the keys to what turned out to be a near-dead rusted pickup truck. I might have felt bad about stealing from her if it hadn't been for the photograph of Lionel Acrux she had sitting proudly on her mantlepiece with a little crocheted green Dragon beside it.

"This is almost as bad as the sewage," I groused as I hauled the manticore into the truck bed, then stomped around to get into the cab.

The truck spluttered and whined before the engine finally turned over, and I proceeded to curse my way back to Zodiac Academy for the next three hours, all the while inhaling the stench of the sewer and wincing at the pain from my still-bleeding wounds.

+·⟨·☾·●◐◯◑●·☽·⟩·+

Night was close to falling again by the time the golden gates of the academy finally came into view through the windshield, and I was forced to halt beyond the magical boundary which had been erected to keep out anyone aside from the rebel army.

No less than ten Fae approached my car, magic stunning guns held at the ready, various Elemental power flickering in their free hands.

"Announce yourself," Milton Hubert barked.

I slapped my hand against the door of the truck several times, trying to locate the damn window button before finding a fucking roller thing to do it with instead. I really should have taken more notice of my Horoscope this morning and realised the stars had plans to fuck with me. *Your misfortunes may lead you to discover the humble ways of the simple life today.*

The window squealed loudly as it was lowered, and I scowled out at Milton from beneath a lock of hair which was stained with whatever had been festering in that sewer and no longer resembled my usual golden blonde.

Milton gasped. "Bog beast!" He raised his magic stunning gun and I had hardly even shouted to tell him that I wasn't a fucking bog beast before the full force of the weapon smacked me in the chest and threw me into the footwell of the truck so hard that I blacked out.

I came to as I was hauled from the cab and thrown unceremoniously at the feet of the Fae who were all playing guard. I shoved myself upright, baring my fangs at them furiously and committing each of their faces to memory.

"It's me, you asshole," I snarled. "Caleb."

Milton squinted at me in the dim light, a Faelight illuminating to better show them my face.

"Shit, it is you," he said with a nervous moo. "Sorry, man, I didn't recognise you under all of that..." He waved a hand, clearly uncertain what to call the mess of blood and excrement that covered me.

I lunged at him before he could put a name to it, my fangs sinking deep into his throat, and a startled moo escaped him. I wasn't gentle, fisting my hand in his dark hair and bending his head back at an awkward angle in payment for that shit with the stun gun.

I was vaguely aware of one of the other guards rushing off to spread the news of my return, and several of the others inspecting the unconscious Manticore in the back of the truck, but mostly I just lost myself to the rich and powerful taste of Milton's blood.

Sure, he was no Seth or Vega, but he was practically a five-star meal in comparison to that rolling pin wench back in Celestia.

A baying howl snapped my attention away from Milton and I shoved him aside roughly, barking a command at the guards to secure the prisoner before shooting away from them into the academy grounds. A flare of my magic allowed me access through the barrier, and I rushed inside at full speed.

I hadn't been letting myself think about it too much, but I'd been deep within the city when the battle had been won, and fear for my friends had been eating its way through me for every moment their fates hung in the unknown.

I raced through campus at speed, ignoring the aching weight in my limbs as my Order gifts were stretched to their limits, exhaustion tugging at me on a bone-deep level.

I reached The Orb and slammed into Seth, who was bounding towards me in his white Wolf form. He shifted instantly, the wolfy lick he'd aimed at my face turning fully Fae halfway through.

My blood lit at the feeling of his mouth against mine, and I shoved him into the shadows beside The Orb, kissing him hard and groaning at the relief of finding him alive and unharmed.

But instead of kissing me back, he pushed me away with a cry of disgust.

"Argh, Cal, what the fuck is that smell?" Seth gasped, and I realised in a moment of mortifying clarity just how fucking gross I was right now.

"Don't look at me," I snarled, whirling away from him as fast as I'd collided with him and shooting away again.

I intended to head back to my room in Terra House and douse myself in scalding water until the sewage and blood was finally burned from my flesh.

Unfortunately for me, five steps into my sprint of shame, my utter exhaustion caught up with me and my Order gifts gave out entirely. I found myself sprawling in the fucking mud, agony piercing through the wounds which I hadn't even paused to heal in my desperation to reunite with Seth.

Seth whimpered as if my pain was his own, and the next thing I knew, he was leaning over me, pressing his hands under the rip in my shirt and forcing healing magic into my body with a rush of power so intense it stole my breath away.

"I was so fucking scared," he breathed, not looking at me while he worked.

I realised my anger over being left behind in the rush to escape the scene of the battle paled to nothing in the face of what he and the others must have gone through while trying to figure out where I'd gone.

"I'm fine," I told him despite the blood staining his hands as he healed the wounds I'd been suffering with for hours. "Is everyone else okay?"

"Yeah. I mean, the dream team are all doing good. But while we were gone, the twins flew off somewhere and no one knows where or why, so that's caused a whole shit storm of confusion. Did you…fall in a big pile of shit or something?" He tried not to wrinkle his nose at the smell coming off of me, and I recoiled in shame.

"I caught that Irvine fucker, but he tried to hide in the fucking sewers so…"

Seth nodded sympathetically while not so subtly shifting his hand off of my filthy skin.

"Darius and Orion just got back from hunting down another Guild Stone," he explained. "He found a shit ton of treasure and has gone all Dragon over it in his room in Ignis. I was just with him and Max, and we were going to force Geraldine to let us leave to come search for you – the magical barrier won't let anyone out without permission from her or the Vegas, and as the twins still haven't come back from wherever the fuck they flew off to, it was left to her."

"Geraldine wouldn't let you leave?" I asked, a little bit pissed she'd stopped him from coming to look for me.

"No," Seth huffed. "She's bossing everyone about and making a load of statements about the world all falling into line and everything in the universe being right at last – honestly, if I'd realised bowing to the Vegas would make her go this batshit, I might have reconsidered. She said that no true warrior of the queens could fall on such a night and that 'his chompiness will be back' in a weird, creepy voice, and then she went off to bake a cake or some shit for when the Vegas return. I've been out of my damn mind."

"I'm good," I promised him. "Or at least I will be when I get a shower."

"You want help?" Seth asked, offering me a hand up, and I arched a brow at him curiously as I let him pull me to my feet.

"In the shower?"

Silence hung between us for several seconds during which I remembered he was naked.

"Oh right," he muttered. "I forgot, our moms said-"

"Fuck our moms," I replied, and his brows rose at that statement, which was a little less than ideal taken out of context. "Not literally, but, you know, fuck what they said."

"Really?"

Seth looked at me in a way which was hard to put words to, and I shrugged under the scrutiny of that look.

"I mean, we're adults, right? We don't have to listen to them, and I don't want to stop this..."

"This?" he asked, giving me that puppy head tilt thing which always forced me to say more than I meant to.

"Us. Whatever it is. I...like it. I like being with you, so..."

Seth bit his lip, glancing over his shoulder like we might be about to get caught. "Okay."

"What's okay?"

"We can just keep being secret...this." Seth shrugged and I breathed a laugh, my gaze falling to his mouth. "But first, you really do need a shower."

I shuddered, agreeing with that wholeheartedly, but as I turned toward Terra House once more, an alarm started blaring overhead, causing a prickle to tear up my spine.

"All members of the Queens' inner circle are to gather in The Orb faster than a sprout on a tumble table!" Geraldine's voice boomed out across campus, magically amplified loud enough to shake the damn trees.

Seth headed around the curving wall of the golden building and I stumbled after him, fighting against the exhaustion in my limbs as we made our way to the main entrance.

A flash of Vampire speed drew my focus down the path, and a booming roar split the air overhead, announcing Darius's arrival too.

I tilted my head back to watch the enormous golden beast as he banked hard, tucking his wings and coming in to land in the small space between The Orb and the crescent moon-shaped building which housed Lunar Leisure. A smile drew my lips up as I watched him, gripped by the urge to thank every star in the sky for his return.

Something had been missing from my heart while he'd been dead, a piece which had been jagged and raw and never could have healed without him in my life. If his return to this battle wasn't an omen of victory, then I didn't know what was.

"What the hell happened to you, Caleb?" Orion asked, skidding to a halt before me. "You look like shit."

I scowled at the assessment, and Darius shifted back into his Fae form, striding towards us butt naked, his tattoos coating his flesh like a second skin.

"He smells like shit too," Darius commented, catching the pair of sweatpants Orion tossed his way and stepping into them.

"Nice to know you were worried about me," I muttered, wiping at a smear of blood on my arm pointlessly. "The Starfall Legion fucking forgot me out there. I had no stardust, was tapped out, and have burned through all of my Order gifts too, so excuse me if I haven't had time to shower yet, but I was just heading back to my House now to-"

A jet of water slammed into me so hard that I was knocked from my feet and sent rolling away across the ground.

"Nice to see you back, soldier," Geraldine called, marching past me where I laid dripping on the ground as a victim of her water magic. "I didn't doubt you for a second. That'll do for a scrub up for now. We have dealings to discuss."

Darius burst out laughing like the asshole he was and strode away into The Orb, barely even flinching when I whipped him across the back with a vine.

I called on my fire magic and steam rose from me in a cloud, engulfing me entirely. By the time it faded away, I found myself standing alone in the dimming light in my torn and ruined clothes, my hair a complete shit show - even if the actual shit had been mostly washed out of it.

I glanced up at the stars which were just beginning to appear in the sky and scowled. *Bastards.*

I headed inside, finding Seth rustling about the place in a pair of pants he'd made himself out of leaves and the rest of our group gathering around the red couch which had once been so familiar to me.

I sighed, heading for my usual spot and stepping through a silencing bubble someone had erected to keep this meeting private.

"What's going on?" I asked, dropping into my seat, and Max reached out to rest a hand on my arm. I gave him a brief smile as he pressed his gifts over me, offering me up some extra energy and stealing a measure of exhaustion from me too.

"Good to have you back, brother," he murmured, his relief washing over me in a wave.

"Reports are coming in of an attack," Geraldine said gravely, holding up an Atlas which showed shaky footage of someone running in the dark, fire blazing behind them and screams filling the air.

"What has my father done now?" Darius snarled, and Geraldine sucked in a rattling breath.

"This took place at a Nebula Inquisition Centre," she replied, letting Darius claim the Atlas from her, and he scrolled onto a similar video, this one taken from further away, showing the camp in flames, quiet sobbing emitting from the person filming it.

"It makes no sense," Geraldine swallowed thickly, and I reached for the Atlas next, a stone seeming to weigh in my gut as I took in the devastation, my eyes roaming over image after image, trying to understand it.

"How many survived?" Seth asked, his shoulder brushing against mine while he leaned in to look.

"There were around a thousand Fae being held there," Geraldine breathed. "It was the next on our list to try and take down. Our army was on their way…"

I didn't need to push her for more, understanding dawning on me. The survivors were few to none.

"But why-" Max began.

"Because Lionel knew we were coming," Xavier snarled. "He knew and he killed those prisoners out of spite."

"Wait," I interrupted, pausing the new video which had just begun to play and rewinding it a few frames before pausing it again. "What are the twins doing there?"

Darius snatched the Atlas from my hands, the shot of the twins flying over the devastation still burned into the backs of my eyes, the fire which bloomed from their hands a damning sight. They were burning it down, killing all those people.

"What the fuck?" Seth breathed, but his words were drowned out by Darius's deep growl.

"That's not my fucking wife."

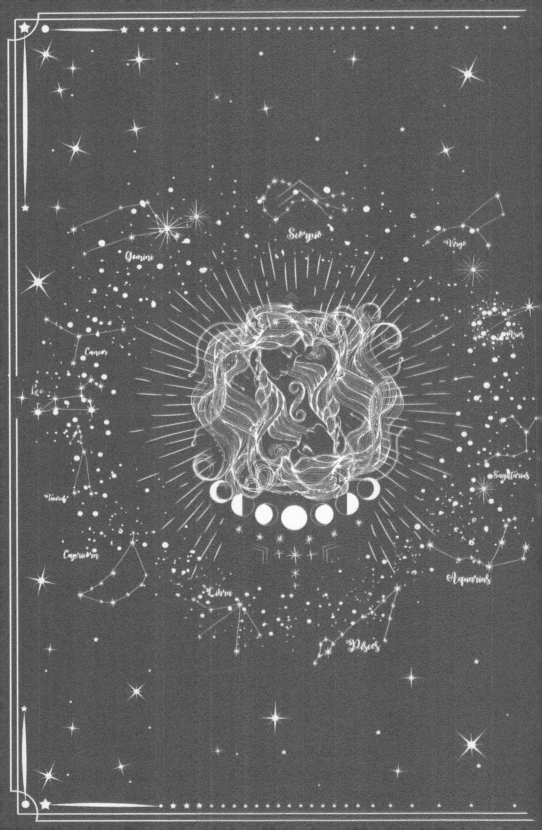

DARCY

CHAPTER TEN

"**F**uck you, Clyde!" Tory yelled, launching a rock at the wall, the thing hitting it so hard that a spark ignited. She went to do it again, and I leapt to my feet with a gasp.

"Wait, Tor." I grabbed her arm. "The sparks."

"Holy shit," she said in realisation.

I quickly tore off a piece of my jumpsuit's sleeve and the Shadow Beast grunted as he moved closer, apparently intrigued by what I was doing.

The sound of Tory ripping her clothes carried to me in the dark, and I felt around on the floor for some more rocks, gathering one in each hand and striking them together. The flash of light gave me enough to see by for a millisecond, and Tory grabbed the scraps of clothes, tossing them together at my feet. I struck the stones over them once more, determination brimming in my muscles. We had to get out of here. Back to our Mates, our friends.

With a tug in the centre of my chest, I realised they had become so much more to me than just friends. Lance, Darius, Geraldine, Seth, Max, Caleb, Sofia, Xavier, and Tyler, they had become family to me as deeply as Tory and Gabriel were. Each of them had become a part of me that I was so damn grateful for. And I couldn't let them down, rotting here in some dusty cave to become a pile of useless bones.

A growl left me as I struck the stones again, and a shower of sparks cascaded onto the strips of clothing. A flame took root, and I squealed as Tory let out a whoop of relief. She took her top off, offering it to the fire, and I ripped apart the top of my jumpsuit to fuel it too, dropping down to sit beside it and soak in the power it offered me. Tory ran her hands through the fire itself, groaning as it started to fill up her magic reserves.

The ground shook beneath us as the Shadow Beast slammed his huge body down between us, his back legs splayed and his front paws stacked neatly between them. He towered above us, his bear-like face tilted down to look our way, and he let out a little grunt.

I grinned at him, reaching out to pat his leg, and his brown eyes brightened.

"Does Orion know you adopted the giant furball?" Tory asked in amusement.

"Yep."

"And did he try to stop you?"

"Obviously."

"But you adopted him anyway."

"Duh."

Tory laughed, but it slowly fell away until she was frowning at me instead. "Is Orion good? After all Lavinia put him through?"

I fell quiet, my gaze dropping to the fire as the horror of our captivity crept over me once more. Within the flames, I swear I caught a flash of blood, of Lance on his knees while a knife was twisted in his side. I winced, a shuddering breath fluttering past my lips and a cloying sense of terror washing through me. I pushed it back, grounding myself in the now and reminding myself that we were no longer there, though it was hard to shake off the feeling of dread in my bones.

"I don't know," I admitted. "We've barely had a moment to process it. And now we're parted again…" I took a breath. "But he's strong as hell."

She nodded, a flicker of darkness passing through her own eyes before she pushed to her feet, and I had the feeling she was thinking about her time under Lionel's rule. "Are you-" I started, but she spoke over me, clearly not wanting to go there.

"I'll cast some flames to quicken this up." She opened her palm, weaving fire into existence and letting it spill from her, circling around us and warming my back.

I sighed, revelling in the sense of my power igniting inside me, and though I desperately wanted to cast, I held back until I had enough to get us free.

Finally, we stood together in the centre of the cave, and I urged the Shadow Beast to return to the ring on my finger, its ghostly form twisting away into the gemstone.

We turned our gaze to the roof, holding hands and raising our free ones. Our magic flowed together like a river that came from the very same source. As one, we threw our earth power into the roof, carving a hole right through it and creating a stairway of stone that spiralled up and away towards freedom.

The scent of fresh air called from above, and we both raced onto the steps, sprinting up them as fast as we could go. As the stairs took us right up above the jungle and the humid air kissed my skin, I felt us pass out of the oppressive power of that cave, and my fear over releasing my Order and succumbing to Clydinius's curse within those tunnels ebbed away.

We made it to a platform at the stairs' pinnacle where birdsong and monkey chatter carried from the jungle canopy and the beating sun burned down on my skin, heating me through. I took in a breath of fresh air, basking in the relief of our escape, then we unleashed our wings, flexing them once before taking off into the sky, turning north towards our family.

The thrumming of my heart called me back to Lance, and adrenaline fuelled my movements, my wings beating hard and fast while Tory sped along at my side. It would be a long flight back to Zodiac Academy, but I wouldn't rest until we made it home.

I landed before the imposing gates of the academy and Tory touched down beside me, but as I took a step forward, a voice boomed out. "Halt!"

Guards glared out at us from between the metal, suspicion skewing their features. "It's us," I said in confusion. "Let us through."

"But word has it you're not you," a woman called fearfully.

"Clyde," Tory hissed, and I shared a look of anger with her.

The guards muttered among themselves, then one of them amplified their voice to carry right across campus. "The True Queens are at the gate!"

Orion and Caleb were there in a blur, and I rushed forward, meeting my Mate's gaze in hope.

"It's me," I said fiercely. "What can I do to prove it?"

"No need, Blue," Orion said, taking me in with a piercing look. "I'd know you anywhere."

"Yeah, that's fucking romantic and all, brother, but I require more proof than that," Caleb said, narrowing his eyes at Tory.

"We can test their magical signature," Orion said. "I'll get a guiding crystal." He shot away and returned at speed just as Geraldine and Darius came running up the path behind him.

"Hey husband," Tory said, stepping up to the gate and reaching for Darius through it. "You can feel my heart beating, can't you?"

He smiled roguishly, taking her hand. "It's them," he confirmed to the others.

"Still." Caleb grabbed the crystal from Orion, holding it out to check our signatures and then releasing a breath when it apparently confirmed we were us.

"Open the gates!" Geraldine roared, and the guards drew them wide.

Geraldine released a noise akin to a baby goat tumbling down a hill, then ran forward and collided with Tory and me. We staggered backwards, squeezing her tight as she came apart entirely, sobbing heavily and burying her face in my hair.

"My l-lady Darcy and my l-lady Tory, I deserve the flail for not realising sooner that a dastardly creature had taken your faces. The moment you flew above us upon The Howling Meadow, I should have known. There was the very moment I should have seen the lie like a gnarlybob pretending to be a treegibber. Yet I did not realise it even when I spoke to that impersonator face to face, and for that, I must take my own flail as punishment." She threw herself to her knees, producing her flail from her back and bowing her head as she held it above her. "Flail me, my Queens. Flail me like the whelk I am. For I am as useless as a sodden haybale on a winter morn."

"No one needs to get flailed, dude." Tory nudged her with the toe of her shoe.

"Geraldine, you couldn't have known," I said, but she only held the flail higher.

"Flail me," she croaked. "I will not be rid of my guilt until I am flailed."

"No one's gonna flail you. We all love you too much," I said, trying to pull her to her feet, but she wouldn't move.

She dropped her hands, peering up at me with wide eyes. "Love?" She looked to Orion as if he of all people might confirm it and he folded his arms, his lips pressing together.

"Lance Orion, professor of all things cardinal magic and professor of true, undying love to one of my dear queens. Will you confirm my dear Darcy's words?"

"I'm really not the right choice for this question," he muttered, and Geraldine's eyes wheeled to Darius instead. Again, a poor choice in all honesty.

"Great Dragoon of the lagoon. Will you deny or confirm that I am too loved to be flailed?"

"Sure," he grunted, seeming amused.

"Which is it!?" she wailed, shuffling toward him on her knees. "A denial or a confirmation?!"

"The one that makes you get off the ground," he said.

"You couldn't have known any of this, Geraldine," Tory said. "We've been impersonated."

"Good gravy, we know! We saw the footage. But by whom? The lame lizard?" Geraldine gasped.

"The footage of what?" I asked in fear, and Orion stepped closer with a grave look that made my stomach clench.

"Of you burning a Nebula Inquisition Centre to the ground with all the Fae inside," he said darkly.

"Fucking Clyde," Tory hissed.

"Who's Clyde?" Darius growled.

"The Imperial Star," I said, and they all looked at me in confusion. "Well, sort of."

I explained the insanity we had faced since our crowning and how the stars had given us a choice of how to deal with the Imperial Star, telling us it belonged to the heart of Clydinius who had cursed the Vega line for not returning it.

"And now that motherfucking star is wearing our faces," Tory snarled.

"And killing innocent people while posing as us," I said in horror. "We have to stop him."

"This is grave news indeed," Geraldine choked out, finally rising to her feet. "That cretin of a spangle has not returned here since the footage of its vile impersonation was aired. Oh my Gerry juice." She held her chest, breathing in deeply. "How can we ever hope to face such a foe? A star walking among us like a fig falling from its tree only to grow legs and prance upon the grass. It is most loathsome. A repugnant twist of the natural order."

"Everyone else is holding a council at The Orb," Orion said. "We can go there, make a plan."

I nodded, and we all headed that way, leaving the guards to close the gates at our back. Orion took my hand and my heart raced from the contact, my need to be closer to him making my breaths falter. He drew me nearer as we followed at the back of the group, his mouth dropping to my ear. "You've been missing all this time. Fuck, Blue, I'm sorry I didn't realise it sooner."

"How could you have known?" I looked up at him, and he leaned down to touch his lips to mine, a burning promise of love in that brief kiss.

When we walked into The Orb, silence fell like we'd just cast a silencing bubble over the whole room.

"You're here at last," Melinda Altair called from a seat at the huge, circular wooden table that had been crafted to sit at the centre of The Orb. The rest of the tables and chairs had all been pushed aside to make way for it.

"Where have you been? What is the explanation for the terrible massacre at that Nebula Inquisition Centre?" Tiberius demanded, his booming voice echoing off of the domed roof.

Tory and I fell into another explanation, the eyes in the room pinned on us, faces paling as the truth of our words fell over them.

"A star walking among us?" Antonia breathed in shock. "How is it possible? Surely it cannot be?" She looked to Tiberius as if he might know the answer, but his eyes were firmly set on us, a grim belief settling over his features.

"It seems it is so," he said heavily, a pregnant pause filling the space before he went on. "Well, we have much to discuss now that the True Queens have returned."

All eyes fell on me and Tory, and my pulse quickened from the reverence in some of their expressions. The fact that the Councillors had bowed to us along with the Heirs was a headfuck of its own special variety, and it was going to take some real getting used to.

Seth waved to me from the right of the table, smiling eagerly from his place between Caleb and Xavier, and I shot him a smile back.

"Where's Gabriel?" I asked, looking around hopefully for my brother among the Fae gathered here.

"He's resting, bella," Dante said, lightning crackling between his fingertips as he sat back in his wooden chair. His muscular frame was draped in gold medallions, rings, and necklaces; the Storm Dragon not often seen without his gold. "His Seer gifts have been overwhelmed by what happened to him at Palace of Souls, but he's in good hands."

My gut tugged at knowing Gabriel was struggling after what Vard and Lionel had done to him, but I knew his family would look after him, and I'd do whatever I could to help too.

Geraldine ushered us to the table with emotion in her eyes. "Your places await you."

She pointed to where two enormous carved wooden thrones were sitting there expectantly, just for me and my sister. Two notably smaller chairs sat either side of them, one with Guild Master etched into its surface and the other with King Consort.

Darius arched a brow at that title and Orion sniggered at him as we moved to take our seats. Darius wasted no time burning the name off of his chair- much to Geraldine's horror – but before it could descend into an argument, I addressed the room.

"A lot's happened since we were all last together," I said, looking to the Heirs, to Dante and Rosalie Oscura, the Councillors, and Xavier. Washer wiggled his fingers at me, and a hum of happy energy flowed from him that for once wasn't tainted by lust. "Not everyone is here who should be here." I thought of those who had been lost, my heart weighing heavily in my chest as sullen eyes stared back at me. "But we're so close to finishing Lionel for good, I can taste it in the air."

"Hear, hear!" Geraldine cried, bashing her fist down on the table from her seat beside Orion. "The assault upon the Court of Solaria went spectacularly – even if we did attack under the orders of your doppelgangers instead of following the commands of the True Queens as we should have." She bowed her head guiltily.

"That plan was ours regardless," Tory said. "I doubt Clyde gives a shit about any of that anyway. He has his own plans to focus on, whatever they may be. Tell us what came of the attack?"

"We won," Max said with a laugh that was echoed around the room, the victory clearly having sparked a lot of hope and pride in our inner circle. "Linda has been rendered useless to Lionel."

"How so?" Tiberius asked, sitting up straighter at the mention of his traitorous wife.

"I broke her mind," Max explained grimly. "I removed all memory of magic from her and shattered every path to wielding it. She won't ever be able to cast with skill again."

"But you left her alive?" Tory asked, reading between the lines of what he was saying.

Max cleared his throat, glancing from Tory to his father before replying.

"Ellis was there," he admitted in a low voice. "She didn't act against me, though she didn't turn on Linda either. But she did beg me for mercy for her mother and I..."

Tiberius released a slow breath at the confirmation that his daughter still lived.

Geraldine laid a hand over Max's, squeezing softly. "Your soft belly is understandable, my cuttlefish," she soothed.

"My father won't want a powerless advisor," Darius said firmly. "Linda Rigel will be cast out of his inner circle for the shame alone. It sounds to me like she's harmless now."

"Looks like we can forget about her then. What about General McReedy?" Tory asked, clearly knowing more about the plans for this attack than I did.

"I captured him," Caleb said.

"Yeah, he went above and beyond," Seth said brightly. "You should have seen him – we lost him in the battle and all came back here without him, and I was freaking out thinking he might be dead. But turns out, he'd chased McReedy into the sewers and they wrestled around in the shit down there even after their magic was all tapped out. When he came back here, everyone thought he was a bog beast because he looked like crap and smelled like-"

Caleb punched him in the arm to shut him up and Seth growled at him in reply.

"Point is, I caught the fucker," Caleb said firmly while Darius stifled a laugh.

"I have pictures," Seth murmured, taking his Atlas from his pocket and sliding it across the table towards us.

I caught a glimpse of Caleb coated in what looked like both blood and shit for all of half a second before Caleb snatched it away again and shoved it into his own pocket.

"Forget the pictures," he growled. "Xavier caught Vulpecula and brought down the entire Court of Solaria with his earth magic."

All eyes turned to Xavier who smiled sheepishly. "Err, yeah – Sofia did it with me," he added quickly.

"We've captured Gus?" I asked excitedly, and he nodded, lifting his chin with pride.

"The captives await our interrogation at your earliest convenience, my Queens," Geraldine said. "And the city rose to your call too. They came from home and hovel to fight the good fight and took up the valiant cry of your names. Even as we speak, thousands flock to us from Celestia to join our army. It was a veritable success."

"Well, at least something went right while we were gone," I said in relief.

"So what do we do now?" Orion asked and all eyes once again turned to me and my sister. That was going to take some getting used to.

"Clydinius is a complication we need to deal with fast," Tory said, rage sparking in her eyes. "But he's not the only thing we have to focus on. There's Lionel, Lavinia, and the Nymphs."

"I have some news about Lavinia and the Nymphs," I said.

"It's more than news, it's a fucking victory, Blue," Orion growled, and everyone perked up hopefully.

"What ho, my lady?" Geraldine pressed keenly.

"Before our escape from the Palace of Souls, I trapped Lavinia with my Phoenix fire and used an ancient spell to shut off her link to the Shadow Realm. She can no longer summon any new shadows, and the Nymphs who were forcibly under her control in her army were freed. Many of them turned on their comrades."

Dante released a low whistle and Seth howled his joy while everyone else shared hopeful looks.

"So how weak is Lavinia?" Caleb asked keenly.

"It's hard to say," I said uncertainly. "But she can only wield the shadows that remain within her body. She's killable for sure. I just didn't get the chance to do it," I added bitterly, my vow to do just that still burning hot inside me.

"Her Nymph army has lost perhaps a quarter of its ranks," Orion said, pride dripping from his voice. "Though, of course, a large portion remain who were following her willingly."

"Maybe we will stand a chance when the final battle comes," Tiberius said thoughtfully. "Perhaps if we can cut Lionel off from the others, then our queens and our Heirs could hunt him down while we deal with his vile queen, and the rest of the army can keep his Bonded at bay."

"Isn't that unFae?" I asked in surprise.

"On the battlefield, anything goes," Antonia said darkly. "War is the exception. Your enemies will not hesitate to band against you, so you must be willing to band against them in kind."

"Well, we also have one new weapon against those enemies." I stood up with my hand raised, the Shadow Beast ring gleaming in the glow of the Faelights hovering above us.

"Blue," Orion murmured. "I really think-"

I encouraged the beast from the ring, and it burst from it in a swirl of smoke, landing on all four paws on the table, releasing a roar of joy.

I probably should have planned that better because screams rang out and the Heirs leapt from their seats, hands raised, ready to blast my new friend into oblivion.

"No, wait!" I yelled, leaping onto the table too, and the Shadow Beast sat down with a thump that made the wood beneath us groan. I petted his head, and everyone looked at me like I'd gone insane while Geraldine continued to shriek like a banshee.

"It's alright, Geraldine," I called to her. "The Shadow Beast was under Lavinia's control. I freed him. He's on our side now."

"Ballcakes on a barge," she cursed, hands raised as she backed up. "Th-that thing nearly sent me into the nether world. It's a beast of the bog, a bandit of the blaggerhole!" She shuddered.

"See, Cal? Everyone has totally forgotten that you turned up here covered in shit and terrified us all with your rotten stench – there's a new bog beast now. And the smell is like eighty percent gone too," Seth muttered in an undertone, and Caleb shot him an irritable look in reply.

I raised my ring to the Shadow Beast as mutters broke out and the Councillors started debating whether they were going to kill him, stirring a protectiveness in me that made me growl. The Shadow Beast turned back into grey smoke, fluttering into the ring where he was safe, and I raised my chin as I addressed the looks of fear in the room.

"He was a prisoner too. And now he wants to help us in this fight," I said firmly, and the chatter fell quiet. "Lavinia had her claws in us both. What we went through together has bonded us in a way I refuse to deny. So the long and short of it is, he stays. And anyone who hurts him will answer to me."

Orion smirked, leaning back in his seat. I knew he didn't agree with me on keeping the Beast, but he sure as shit seemed to like it when I pulled the True Queen card, so he clearly wasn't going to argue with me.

"Well, I love him. He's got all the best qualities," Seth decided. "Fluffy? Check. Deadly? Check. Cute in a murderous kind of way? Check. What's not to like?"

"It's a cretin of the crag," Geraldine hiccoughed, and I jumped off the table, reaching for her hand.

"I'd never let any harm come to you. If he was dangerous, I swear I wouldn't bring him here," I promised. "I'm so sorry he hurt you. And that I wasn't strong enough to stop Lavinia from using us against you. But I swear her power over us is gone."

She took my hand with shaking fingers, nodding slowly. "Well, I must admit it has given me quite the heart jigs, but I do trust your word, dear Darcy. Always. So I will trust it now, even if the beastly Beast sets my waters stirring in reverse."

"He's all good, Geraldine," Tory said calmly. "Darcy's great at taming feral creatures. Just look at Orion. All grumpy and twisted up inside once upon a time. Now he's…well, actually he's still those things, but he'd do anything for her. I think the Shadow Beast might be the same."

"Thanks for the comparison," Orion said dryly.

"No worries, dude." She smirked at him and Darius chuckled.

"If you say it is safe, then we will trust your word," Melinda said, and Antonia Capella smiled warmly as she nodded.

"I'd advise against it," Tiberius added, then inclined his head. "But whatever you decide, my Queen."

I stared between the Councillors in surprise, the truth of what we'd become to everyone here sinking in deep. My gaze slid to Tory and we shared a brief look that spoke of the disbelief we were both feeling, then I nodded to Tiberius.

"The Beast stays," I said decisively, and no one came back at me.

"Vicious creatures that my mate has adopted aside, it might be worth mentioning that we found another Guild Stone," Orion said like it was nothing.

"Really?" I gasped, moving back to my seat as Geraldine did the same, still looking a little shaken.

Orion put his hand in his pocket, then frowned, checking his other pocket and cursing before his gaze snapped up to fix on Darius.

"You asshole," he muttered, and Darius shrugged like he wasn't disagreeing with the assessment. "Show them."

Darius reached into his pocket a little reluctantly, then opened his palm to reveal a turquoise gemstone that glittered beautifully. Tory reached for it, but his fingers snapped shut around it once again.

"I'll keep an eye on it," Darius said, pocketing it quickly.

"How many are there left to find?" I asked keenly.

"Just two," Orion said. "The Pisces aquamarine stone and the Aquarius amethyst."

"And I know where one of them is," Darius said. "Thanks to Azriel and Hail's work beyond The Veil."

A hushed silence fell over the room, and my heart ticked faster as I observed the man who had been to death and back. Everyone was clearly on the edge of their seat for more details, me included, and Darius went on.

"Azriel traced one to the FIB impound where all illegal, valuable, and downright dangerous contraband is held. How we'll reach it, I don't know, but at least we have another location."

"I might know how," Xavier said thoughtfully, sitting up straighter. "Francesca Sky's memories. We can go through them again and see if she had access."

"Then hop to it, you wily Pego-boy," Geraldine encouraged, and Xavier nodded, heading from The Orb at a trot.

"If the prophecy about the stones is true and we need to claim all of them, then that should be our priority," Tory said firmly.

"What do the stones mean now though?" Seth asked, looking to Orion. "If the Imperial Star has morphed into a walking-talking murder star, then what were all those power words for? I spent a long ass time remembering them."

"We all did," Caleb agreed.

"Yeah, which was a dumbass move considering only a reigning sovereign can use them or you'll die," Tory said with a snigger.

"There was still a chance any of us might have become a reigning sovereign back then," Caleb said confidently.

"Aw, it's cute you thought that," I teased, and he pursed his lips. I looked to Orion, his brow furrowed in thought. "So what do you reckon the stones are for?"

He hesitated before answering. "Honestly? I don't know. But your mother and my father were certain reuniting the Guild Stones could bring about a chance for a new fate. And perhaps there is more that will be revealed once we have them."

"It's all we have to go on, and we need to have faith in Azriel. In our mother too." I glanced at Tory, whose eyes darkened. "They set out this path for us years ago, and we have to follow it. It won't be for nothing, I'm certain of it."

"Darcy's right," Tory said. "We will plan our strike today and retrieve that stone from the FIB tomorrow once everyone has rested and recovered their magical supplies. Then we need to focus on locating the final stone and retrieving that too."

"The FIB impound will be heavily guarded," Tiberius said. "I was integral in implementing a lot of the security measures which have been put in place surrounding it, and it isn't going to be at all easy to circumvent them – likely it isn't even possible."

"That's what you think, amico," Dante purred from his place across the table. "But it might be worth taking some advice from those of us who have made a career out of breaking into places which people like you think are impenetrable."

Rosalie grinned like a cat, and my own lips twitched with amusement while the Councillors all began murmuring about the criminals among us. I had to wonder what they might think of Tory's past transgressions if they found out about them.

"I can provide as much information as I possess on the precinct's layout and security," Tiberius said, reaching for a large roll of parchment and placing his hand over it. Black lines began to spread from beneath his fingers, a rough blueprint seeping across the page piece by piece and making my lips lift with hope.

"Looks like we're breaking and entering tomorrow then," I said excitedly, and Tory smiled widely.

"And there was me thinking I wouldn't be cut out for this queen shit – turns out it suits me just fine," she said.

Darius breathed a laugh at her side, dropping his arm around the back of her throne and looking like the smuggest asshole in the world while the Councillors exchanged uncertain looks.

"What about the other stone?" Caleb asked before they could question our plan any further. "Do we have any leads?"

"Azriel hadn't managed to locate it," Darius admitted, the bitter sting of that reality sinking in as the others fell into a discussion about its possible location.

Legends, myths, and rumours were all we really had to go on. It was infuriating to think that we might hold eleven of the twelve stones in our grasp as soon as this time tomorrow and yet still be that single step away from completing the set.

Maps were summoned from the stars only knew where, Geraldine coating the table in reports and figures on the latest known movements of Lionel's army while possible locations for the final stone were mentioned, though no one had anything really useful to suggest.

"What about the body-snatching star issue?" Seth asked suddenly, drawing my focus away from the incredible Map of Espial where I'd been watching clouds waft slowly over the realistic mountain ranges. "Just seems like kind of a big deal too." He shrugged innocently and I pursed my lips at the reminder of the new enemy we were threatened by.

"He didn't snatch our bodies," Tory pointed out. "He just copied them."

"And used them to make the two of you look like a pair of arsonist psychopaths," Seth added brightly, as if we needed reminding of that part.

I gritted my teeth. "We were faced with a choice when we ascended into our positions as queens," I said, the reality of that fact still too insane to linger on. "We had the choice to break the curse on our family line and return the Imperial Star or keep it and try to wield it ourselves. As every other member of our family line who used the Imperial Star ended up dead or worse because of the curse attached to it, we decided to take the control of our own fate back. So we returned it, and Clydinius gained a body. We thought we'd be able to fight him but..."

"How do you even fight a star anyway?" Max asked curiously. "Does it feel pain? Can it die?"

"Clydinius should have released the magic of his kind into the universe upon impact with the Earth," Orion rumbled at my side. "That is the way a star's lifecycle is supposed to end."

"I plan on forcing him to do just that," Tory muttered irritably, and all eyes turned to her. "Assuming we can even find the motherfucker again. Any idea where he is now?"

"When I delivered a platter of bagels to the cretin wearing your fine faces, I found him loitering in the Earth Observatory," Geraldine said. "There were papers scattered about, records and tomes opened and picked through as if-"

My hair flipped into my face as a sudden gust caught it, and I blinked up at Caleb as he leaned down between me and Tory, placing a pile of scrolls and books on the table before us.

"This is everything he'd left out up there," Caleb said, clearly having shot there to retrieve them in the five seconds we'd spent discussing this.

I reached for a scroll on the top of the pile while the others took pieces of the puzzle to investigate too. It was a star chart, the date in the top corner marking it as almost a hundred years old, the points plotted on it seeming to trace the fall of a star across the sky.

"Is he hunting for fallen stars?" Tory asked, her attention on a large tome titled The Ledger of Fallen Stars. The page she held open had a large picture of a glimmering star suspended in the heavens at the top of it, the name Triphorius in swirling script above it. There was a detailed account of facts about the star across the two pages beneath, ending with an account of its fall from the sky, including a location of where it had struck the Earth and a description of it releasing its power into the universe as its final act.

"It looks that way. But for what purpose?" I frowned.

"Do beg my pudding, but is it possible there is another gandering spangle like the terrible Clydinius walking among us?" Geraldine uttered in fear.

Orion leaned past me to claim the book from Tory. "No other star has ever denied the path of nature like this before. All who have fallen have released their magic within minutes of colliding with the ground. I've studied this book and many others like it in detail, and I have never heard so much as a rumour of a star delaying its demise like Clydinius has."

I sighed, feeling no closer to understanding the star's motivation than I had before seeing what he'd been studying in the observatory and without any idea on his plans, it was damn hard to come up with any way to stop him.

The conversation roamed over everything we knew about Clydinius and how we might locate him before he caused another massacre, but it seemed we were at a dead end there too.

My head was spinning by the time our debate moved to Lionel – who apparently hadn't shown his face anywhere since we had defeated the monsters he'd sent to the academy. Eventually, we divided up tasks from organising scout teams to astrologers who would seek the stars for guidance, and others who would look into old legends to find clues towards the final Guild Stone. There was a lot of work required to maintain the army, and they needed training too. which was keeping Washer fully occupied along with a lot of help from Geraldine and the Councillors. We listened to reports and requests, made decisions where we could and took advice when we needed it, and by the time our meeting was finally drawing to a close, my head felt like it might crack in two from all we had discussed.

One thing was clear though, and it demanded the bulk of my focus now. We would strike at the FIB impound tomorrow in hopes of claiming that Guild Stone, and all of us needed to rest and recover our magic before then, so we'd be reenergised for what came next.

Geraldine caught my arm as we filed out of The Orb. "I have a surprise for you and your Orry man, Darcy. Would you do me the honour of sharing it with you both?"

My gaze hooked on Tory and Darius up ahead, and though I longed to spend more time with them after being parted for so long, I couldn't refuse the glint of longing in Geraldine's deep blue eyes. Besides, I'd missed her a hell of a lot too.

"This way!" Geraldine cried before Orion could answer, and I grinned at him, capturing his hand and leading him into a jog after her.

She forged a path through the ex-Councillors like a charging horse, and we followed her all the way across campus to Air Territory.

"If you might do the honour of opening the door," Geraldine asked, and I sent a gust of air at the Aer House symbol, gazing up at the tall tower to the rotating turbine at its peak, the familiarity of this place sparking nostalgia in me.

We headed inside, chasing after Geraldine who was walking up the winding spiral stairway at a fierce pace.

My stomach started to growl, and Orion shot me a frown. When was the last time I'd eaten properly? We'd grown a few apples with our earth magic on the flight back, but that was it. And before that, it had been a few sparse meals after we'd escaped from the palace. In all honesty, I was bone tired, hungry as hell, and running on fumes.

Geraldine led us past my old floor and up to the House Captain's room where Seth had once resided. Before I could question why she was taking us here, she threw the door open with a dramatic twirl into the room and spread her arms wide.

"Behold, sleeping quarters for a True Queen – I plan to offer the very same thing to the Ignis House Captain room once I can get past Darius's pesky security wards. The Aer mutt's room was not half as well protected – though it seemed no one had gotten in here before now. Those Heirs are quite the arrogant Anguses, keeping their rooms from being inhabited by anyone else." She tittered, rolling up her sleeves and stepping aside to let me and Orion further into the room.

The large space had been transformed to a sprawling sea of grey with the Gemini and Libra constellations glittering in a swirl above the enormous bed.

There was a tea set with hand-painted scenes of my life on the porcelain, a blossoming tree growing in one corner that had D+L etched into a heart on its trunk, and my possessions had been placed around the room with thoughtful care.

My Phoenix armour had been mounted on one wall with Orion's Phoenix sword gleaming proudly next to it. On an ornate sideboard beneath it was a selection of my most prized items. The rose quartz stone Orion had given me, the silver Gemini bracelet which had been a gift from Gabriel, and my sketchbook placed beside them. I was overcome by seeing it all laid out like this, how much time and effort Geraldine must have gone to to provide this room for us.

"I didn't look upon your wonderiferous art." Geraldine leapt toward the sketchbook. "But I did do one thing... I truly hope I have not overstepped the shingdipper." She slid open a drawer in the sideboard, revealing a neat selection of sketching pencils, and a few extra sketchbooks with black covers that had swirling golden letters across them. QDV. It was on each of the pencils too.

"Queen Darcy Vega," Geraldine whispered, pointing to the letters.

"Geraldine, this is too much. You really shouldn't have," I said, sweeping forward to hug her.

"Yes, you really shouldn't," Orion grumbled, and I met his gaze over her shoulder, noting his annoyance over being in this particular room, and in truth, I didn't want to take Seth's room either.

"But maybe-" I started.

A snarl made me whip around, finding Seth striding into the room.

"What the fuck is this?" he barked.

"Oh, tish tosh." Geraldine waved a hand at him. "Don't get high up on your gander cushion now, Seth Capella. You have bowed to the True Queens and so, in true regal and stately fashion, you must offer them the finest fringles you can frangle."

"I don't know what the hell that means," Seth snapped. "But this is my room. And I might have bowed, but that doesn't mean I'm going to bend over and let the queens fuck me with a strap-on Phoenix dildo."

"We won't stay here," I told him, remembering the full-on orgy I'd watched Seth and his pack have from the closet right over there. Yup, this place was a hell no from me. "It's a really nice gesture, Geraldine, but this is Seth's room."

"Where are my things?!" Seth boomed as he strode past us, ripping open a drawer in a unit near the tall windows.

"I don't know what items you could possibly mean," Geraldine said with a shrug. "I put some twoddle in the garbage, that's the only bits and bobs I found in here."

"What twoddle?" Seth wheeled around to glare at her, and I shared an awkward look with Orion – though he seemed pretty amused over Seth's fury.

"Where are my clothes?" Seth demanded.

"There may have been a rag or two among the twoddle, I suppose," Geraldine said thoughtfully.

"You threw away my stuff!" Seth barked, stalking towards her with air magic riling up a storm around him.

"Holy guacamole, how can *I* be blamed for mistaking your attire for rags when it is *you* who dresses like a canary in a coal mine?" Geraldine scoffed.

"That stuff was designer," he hissed. "Get. It. Back. And return this room to how it was, or I swear to the stars, I'll make you pay for this."

"Darcy will be moving in with me anyway," Orion announced. "So keep your room, Seth. Thanks though, Geraldine."

I glanced up at him with a grin. "Was that you asking me to live with you?"

His lips twisted up at the corner, his dimple puncturing his right cheek. "You in, beautiful?"

"I'm in." I turned to Geraldine. "I'll help you move this stuff to Lance's place."

"Of course, if that's what your cockles long for," she said brightly.

"She can help you do that just as soon as she's returned all of my things to me," Seth growled, squaring up to Geraldine.

"And how am I to do that? Rummage through the garbage like a glugger slug?" She laughed heartily.

"Yes, if that's what it takes," he boomed, his brown eyes flashing with rage.

Orion caught my hand, towing me out the door and leaving them to their argument.

He dipped his head to speak in my ear, his fingers curling tighter around mine. "Hungry, Blue?"

My stomach growled in response to his words, and I groaned in answer. "*Starved.*"

He whipped me into his arms without another word, shooting away down through the tower, spiralling along the steps at high speed.

We were suddenly moving across campus, and a giddy whoop fell from my lungs as the air rushed over us. We came to an abrupt halt outside The Orb, and Orion held me tight as the momentum almost sent me tumbling from his arms. He placed me down gently, walking up to the golden Orb and raising his hands so magic skittered across the ground.

"What are you doing?" I asked curiously, stepping closer.

"Where do you think all the food comes from in The Orb?" he asked, a playful light dancing in his eyes. My answer was given to me as the grass shifted away beneath his magic and a golden hatch was revealed at his feet. He reached down, opening it up and unveiling a series of steps heading underground.

"Are you taking me to a sneaky kitchen?" I asked hopefully.

"Yes, and it's staff only access, so I'll be sure to punish you for it later," he muttered, throwing me a heated look that made me bite my lip.

I followed him down the steps, the walls glimmering gold down here as well as the path beneath our feet. A passage opened out before us, lit by shimmering everflames in sconces on the walls.

Orion led me into a vast kitchen which was full of gleaming pots and pans and giant stoves that continually burned with sparking purple fire. He guided me into another room which was made entirely of glittering ice with food encased inside it to keep it frozen, stretching far away on either side of us in row after row of ice pillars. He kept walking, leading us into an incredible garden where fruit trees bloomed beneath a pulsing orb of heated light that seemed to emulate the sun. Here, giant vegetables grew from the ground around us, rows and rows of them ripe and ready to pick.

Orion kept walking, leading me into a food store where the air was cool but not unbearably so. Wooden racks stood all around us, and fresh food was waiting on them, each plate and dish of prepared meals glowing slightly as if with magic.

"It's all fresh. Pick anything you like." Orion turned to me, hunger burning in his own eyes. This was straight up heaven after the scraps we'd been fed in Lionel and Lavinia's captivity, and I was aching to try everything in front of me.

I lunged for a veggie burrito, picking it up and marvelling at the way it already felt warm in my grip, like someone had only just made it.

"There's a special concoction of fire and air magic keeping the food perfectly fresh, and a ward seals it from being contaminated by any outside source." Orion reached out, his fingers weaving in a movement that released the wards. "Now you can eat it."

I took a big bite, the explosion of tastes rolling over my tongue making me shut my eyes to savour it. The beans, the sour cream, the guacamole, the rice. It was fucking perfection. And it was either the best thing I'd ever tasted or I'd forgotten how good real food was.

Orion grabbed himself a burrito too, and we sat down with our back to one of the racks, eating our way through every bite in silence, too engrossed in our meals to do anything else. When I'd devoured my burrito and wolfed down a quesadilla and half a plate of nachos, I was pretty sure I couldn't eat another bite. But then Orion shot off and reappeared with a giant chocolate cake.

Oh chocolate, you tempting bitch, how can I ever resist you?

"Let's forget living at your place. Let's live here," I said, reaching for the cake despite my stomach saying no more.

Orion barked a laugh. "That's not a half bad idea."

He sat down, offering me a fork while readying his own, and he watched me take a bite before taking one himself.

"Fuck," he exhaled after swallowing. "Life tastes so much better when you've been to the brink of death and back."

"I don't want to waste a single second ever again," I said seriously.

"We won't," he promised.

I watched him eat a few more bites before pushing the cake aside and shifting closer to him, resting my head against his shoulder, the scent of cinnamon caressing my senses. I took a breath, trying to lean into the calm of this place, the knowledge that nothing could touch us here. We were safe at last. But my heart was only quickening, and as I closed my eyes to try and make it settle, memories tore through my mind of Orion covered in blood, of Lavinia's laughter ringing through my ears before she drove another blade into his flesh.

"Blue?" Orion whispered against my hair, his arm coming around me.

My hand fisted in his shirt, and I couldn't make myself open my eyes, trapped in that awful place once again with panic rising in my chest.

Orion caught my chin, tugging to make me look up at him, and I forced my eyes to open.

"Are you okay?" he asked, studying me closer, his gaze searching mine and surely seeing the cracks in my soul.

"We're free of Lavinia. That's what counts," I rasped.

"That's not what I asked."

"Lance," I implored, wanting to forget it and ground myself in reality again.

"Blue."

"I'm fine," I said, wanting to mean that so damn much.

"Don't lie to me," he warned.

"I'll be fine," I corrected. "Eventually. When the memories don't feel so fresh. Besides, it's not me who went through it. You're the one who had to face that torture."

"And I would go through it a thousand times over so long as it kept you safe," he said powerfully, lifting my hand and kissing the inside of my wrist. "It won't haunt me, Blue."

"Now who's lying," I said, raising a brow, and he chuckled darkly, kissing my fingertips this time. God, this man. What had I ever done to deserve his kind of love? It was as gentle as it could be wild. The perfect balance of sweet and rough.

"Even if the memories visit, I can hold on to why I did it. That's enough to banish them."

"But what if something bad happens again?" I whispered my darkest fear. "What if I lose you, what if-"

He pressed his lips to mine, chasing away the terror trying to burrow its way into my heart.

"I can't promise the dark days won't come again," he said, drawing back a little. "But we're free right now, and I've wasted too many years in misery already."

"Let's make every moment count then," I said, smiling a little as I took heart from those words. The now was where my attention needed to stay.

I sat back and Orion held up my fork in offering. I took it, eating another mouthful of cake, relishing the sweet rush of sugar.

When we were stuffed beyond belief and had a bunch of snacks crammed into a bag I'd made of leaves (including a big ass bar of chocolate for Tory), we headed back out of the kitchen storage and up to the academy grounds.

"Let's find the others," I said eagerly, missing them all over again.

"Don't you want to rest?" he asked.

"Rest can wait. I want to catch up on everything we've missed."

"Did I mention I smashed Highspell's necklace and she has a dick for a face?" Orion said, and I turned to him with rounded eyes.

"Tell me *all* the details."

We started walking around The Orb as he filled me in, and I figured we could check in there first to see if anyone was around. I didn't have an Atlas now, but I guessed we could head back to Aer Tower if all else failed and see if Seth and Geraldine were still up there.

Some of the rebels milled along the path, mixing with the students at the academy, and as people spotted us, they nudged each other and pointed us out.

"All hail the True Queens!" one girl yelled, waving at me, and I waved back a little awkwardly.

Everyone seemed overly excited to see me, and I really hoped I could earn the faith I saw in their eyes. I needed to step into the role as their ruler and make sure I did the right thing by them. The pressure of it all was overwhelming, but we'd made our stand now, and I had no inclination to back down. I'd been born for this, and I could feel the blood of the Savage King pumping through my veins alongside my mother's, telling me I was right where I belonged in this world.

My parents had been made for power, and I was too. After all I'd gone through, I finally felt ready to claim my rightful place in the kingdom at last. I was no longer a bullied girl at the bottom of the pecking order walking these paths. I had proved my grit, and I'd damn well keep doing so at every hurdle placed in front of me.

It wasn't the only thing that had changed in the time since I'd last been at the academy. Now, I walked at the side of the man I loved, our hands interlocked, and not a single Fae in this school or any other in the kingdom could do anything about it. It wasn't just accepted, it was respected, and I revelled in the joy that brought me after everything we'd gone through to claim each other.

None of our friends had returned to The Orb, and I pouted a little as we turned back to Aer Tower.

"Hey!" Seth stepped out the door of the tower and came running our way. "Darcy! Lance!" He sprinted toward us, waving as if we hadn't yet noticed him yet. "Awoooo!"

I laughed, breaking away from Orion and running to meet him, the Wolf dragging me into a tight hug.

"Did you sort things out with Geraldine?" I asked.

He licked my cheek and stepped away. "Kinda. She's got a hoard of the Ass Club in my room, packing up your shit. She still owes me my stuff back though." He grinned, gripping my shoulders. "How are you? Where've you been? You smell like chocolate. Do you have chocolate?" His eyes fell on my bag, and I shifted it behind my back.

"I got Tory a bar."

"Oh, I'll give it to her," he said with a glint of mischief in his eyes. "Hand it over."

"No," I laughed, twisting aside as he tried to grab it, and I cast a tight air shield around the bag. "Get your own snacks, Wolf boy."

"I will," he said in a way that implied he fully intended on raiding my bag.

Orion caught up to us, not so subtly sliding his arm around me and pulling me against his hip.

"You licked her," he said icily.

"Ha, yeah. What's the matter, are you jealous?" Seth lunged at Orion in a bid to lick him too, and Orion's fist came out so fast that Seth only missed it by nearly falling on his ass.

"Rude," Seth muttered, righting himself.

"Not respecting people's boundaries is what's rude," Orion said. "We're looking for the others. Have you seen them? Darius, Tory…Caleb?"

"And you," I added, though Orion had almost certainly not meant Seth.

"They've all headed to King's Hollow. Let's go. I have *so* much shit to tell you on the way."

"I can just carry Blue and we'll meet you there." Orion moved to pick me up, but I gave him a look that warned him to stop being an asshole, and his shoulders dropped as he gave in to my silent demand.

"So, anyway," Seth started, but Geraldine burst out of the Aer Tower door with a swarm of Ass Club members at her back, all carrying boxes of stuff.

"That's it, hip-hup, get moving," she directed, wafting them onto the path.

"Do you need help?" I jogged over, but Geraldine waved me off.

"Not on your nelly, Lady Darcy. The Almighty Sovereign Society are honoured to assist you in your homecoming and settle you in like a frog in a sleeping bag."

The A.S.S. all went trotting off down the path in the direction of Asteroid Place, and Geraldine placed her hands on her hips, gazing proudly after them. "They'll have the place set up in two shakes of a billycrag's tail."

"If you're sure." I frowned. "I'd rather help though."

"You're a queen! They are more than honoured to serve you. Poor Douglas would have no purpose at all in life it weren't for the mighty A.S.S., would you Douglas?" She gestured to a blond man carrying a box, and he bowed his head pitifully.

"None whatsoever," he agreed.

"There, see?" Geraldine said while Douglas scurried off down the path. "They would be bereft without a task at hand to keep them as busy as barn owls in a mouse field. Oh drifting poppy seeds, how Angelica would delight in being here now, squirrelling this and that into boxes. She always did love a box." Geraldine sniffed and I placed a hand on her arm, my heart going out to her. Tory had told me about Angelica's loss, and it was another painful ache to add to my heart.

She waved me off, straightening her spine and jutting up her chin. "We mustn't dwell in the doom dell." She strode off down the path after the A.S.S. and I frowned after her.

"Do you think she's alright?" I said, turning to the others.

"I think she needs to keep busy," Seth said darkly as we started walking along the path. "A lot of fucked-up shit has happened. But Darius is back now, and you and

Lance are finally free. We just have to focus on the good stuff."

"The mutt has a point," Orion said quietly.

Seth beamed from ear to ear. "Of *course* I have a point. So, listen moon friends, while we wait for the world to combust again, I need to tell you *everything* about my cocktastrophe with Cal."

Orion sighed wearily and I gave Seth a disappointed look.

"Does that mean you haven't sorted stuff out between you? Surely you've told him how you feel by now?" I implored.

Seth ran a hand through his long hair with a huff. "What am I supposed to do? Just blurt my feelings at him and let him run a lawnmower over my heart?"

"You don't know that's how it'll be," I said. "Have you even tried?"

"Of course I've tried! We fucked like heathens when Venus was in retrograde, and the moon was all cold and full and mysterious. But then our parents walked in-"

"Oh shit," I breathed as Orion released a low laugh.

"Yeah shit, Darcy. Yeah. Shit. It was the most humiliating moment of my life, and the way Cal looked at me after...I thought he'd only fucked me 'cause the moon and Venus encouraged it." He let out a doggish whimper. "But then! When he showed up here as a bog beast, he kissed me, and we agreed to keep seeing each other. In secret, but still. That's something, right?"

"That's great," I said earnestly. "But really, I think the rest of our group would love to know about you two."

"Literally no one could care less," Orion said dryly, and though his tone left a lot to be desired, he was kinda backing up my point.

"I don't know... I don't think Cal wants that." Seth ran a hand over the braided side of his hair.

We arrived at the beautiful oak tree in The Wailing Wood that housed King's Hollow, the branches fanning out high above us and colouring the place in brightest green as the sun filtered through them. I opened the door in the base of the trunk, the gnarled bark twisting aside to give us access, and we walked upstairs.

"-what else do you remember about her?" Max's voice carried to us, and we stepped into the lounge as Darius answered.

"Well, Azriel kept giving your mom the 'fuck me' eyes," he said, smirking as he rested his hands on Tory's knees. The two of them were on the couch together, her legs resting over his as she leaned back against the cushions.

"What's that?" Orion asked curiously as everyone noted our arrival.

Caleb was lounging in a large armchair by the fire, his shirt off and his feet up on the table, his blonde curls messy and some of them falling into his eyes.

"Your dead dad has been giving my dead mom the eyes apparently," Max muttered icily, glaring at Orion as if it was his fault.

"Really?" Orion asked curiously, but Max's eyes simmered with anger.

"She's waiting for *my* dad," Max growled. "Tell your dead father to back the fuck up."

"Sure, I'll just light a scented candle and whisper my wishes into the flames as soon as I locate my aromatherapy set," Orion deadpanned, and Max's scowl grew.

"Well you'd better do *something* about it," he muttered.

"I think it's cute," Darius said tauntingly. "You're both practically step-brothers now."

"Fuck off," Orion said lightly, moving to sit in an armchair while the rest of us laughed – barring Max who looked ready to fight someone.

Caleb yawned, pushing a hand into his curls, his eyes sliding to Seth. "Hey, man."

"Hey," Seth said a little stiffly, his eyes lingering on him.

I shot Tory a look, our twin minds needing no words to convey that we were both fully aware of the heated tension between them. It was clear they were dying to greet each other properly but were playing a game of 'who can be the most aloof asshole' instead.

"So who's been fucking who while I've been gone?" Darius asked frankly, and Seth suddenly became intensely busy making coffee.

I moved to claim the other chair beyond Orion's, but he caught my hand and yanked me down onto his lap with a smirk. I tossed my snack bag on the floor, wriggling back into the corner of the seat, and he rested his hand on my thigh, his fingers tightening possessively.

"Me and Gerry are going strong," Max said proudly, moving to the fridge and pouring himself a glass of freaking milk. He got himself a packet of cookies too, then took his seat and began dipping them one at a time, crunching his way through them.

"How about you, Cal?" Darius asked. "Have any of the rebel girls caught your attention?"

"Nah," Caleb said vaguely, rubbing his hand down the back of his neck.

"Come on. I know you," Darius pushed. "You've had at least one long haired brunette pinned beneath you moaning your name recently."

Seth dropped a mug in the kitchenette and it smashed at his feet, making him curse.

"You good, dude?" Tory called to him.

"Perfect," Seth muttered, using air magic to clean up the pieces and send them flying into the trash.

Holy shit, did Darius know about Seth and Caleb hooking up?

"Any news on Gabriel?" I asked Tory hopefully.

"Dante said he'd text me when Gabriel was up for visitors," she said, and I hoped that would be soon. I was so worried about him.

"We've got a stash of Atlases here if you need one," Max said, crunching through another milky cookie.

"Here." Caleb got to his feet, shooting to the drawer in an ornate cabinet and rushing over to Orion and me, handing us one each. "They're protected from traces and bugging. We've got a pretty tight security system in place."

"Thanks," I said, and Caleb dropped down to perch on the edge of our seat.

"Log in to FaeBook," he encouraged with a look of mischief about him.

I took the bait, logging in and finding my inbox had blown up and I was tagged in hundreds of posts. So many, the app had simply stopped counting and put *999+* on the notification icon. I'd gained over two million followers too.

"You're pretty popular too, brother." Caleb nodded to Orion's new Atlas. "Check it out. You could do a little update post."

"I have no interest in social media," Orion said, just as I tapped on his profile through my app.

"You've got a lot of new followers, and oh…" I scrolled through the posts he'd been tagged in, a hell of a lot of them featuring fan art of Orion naked in various poses. There was a group linked to most of them called the Ori-Hoes.

"It looks like you have a fan club," I said, laughing as I showed him the artwork. "There you are in a barn lounging on a haybale - with your dick out. Oh and there you are climbing an apple tree – with your dick out. And, oh look, this one has immortalised that time you rode bareback on a horse through that cornfield. With your dick out."

Orion gave me that stern teacher look like I was somehow responsible for the porno art, and I only laughed harder.

"Yeah, we're all tagged in a bunch of weird shit like that," Tory said. "Darius has some creepy ones of him in a coffin."

"With his dick out?" I guessed, and Tory nodded woefully before we cracked smiles at each other.

I scrolled through a few of the posts I'd been tagged in, finding strangers from all across the kingdom showing their support for me and Tory. Some of their words were seriously heart-warming, the descriptions of their own struggles in this war and the hope we'd offered them making me feel like we'd really made a difference to their lives.

But then I tapped another post and my lips parted at the hideous image accompanying it, an artist's rendition of Tory and I made to look like soul-sucking demons, our eyes blood red and faces twisted in horrible grins. Worst of all, the image portrayed a fire at our backs where cartoon drawings of rats were burning in the background. The post was captioned *This is who they REALLY are.*

I knew I shouldn't do it, but I found my eyes moving to the comments, the regret instant.

Taylor Piccolo:
Heard they cooked them up and ate them, bones and all #ratpackedlunch #squealmeal

Kate Henry:
They always gave me the creeps, now I know why! I should forever trust my instincts, the stars never guide me wrong #tinglealltheway #Iknewitinmywaters #whatyoufeelisreal

Kendra Knight:
ALL HAIL THE TRUE DEMONS #eatthosetinyfeet

Andreea Dina:
I was divided on who I supported, but this has made my decision. The king would never be so wicked as to kill the lesser Orders. He only put them in the place they deserve, but this is monstrous! #longlivetheking #greenoverqueen

Amber Masincup:
This just makes me like them even more! Cannibal queens? Hell yes! #squealsonwheels #arodentfortheroad

Orion snatched the Atlas away from me and shut off the app. "Don't listen to that bullshit."

"They think we really killed them," I said in horror. Even though I'd known it to be true, seeing it like that made it really hit home.

"Tyler is already working to get the truth out there," Caleb promised. "Social media is like this. It feeds on drama, and some people can't wait to tear you down. Your real supporters will listen to the truth, but you'll never get through to the underworld of trolls who lurk in the cesspit of social media. They make a hobby out of being cunts, and if you let their vicious words hurt you, then you let them get exactly what they want."

My eyebrows raised at the passion in his words, and I realised he and the other Heirs had faced this kind of scrutiny their whole lives. Even Orion had had a taste of this shit after his Power Shaming. And sure, we'd had our names dragged through the mud on FaeBook the moment we arrived in this world, but now our popularity could literally decide the fate of this war. If the kingdom saw posts like that and believed we were monsters, how would we get more Fae to join our ranks?

"Ignore it, Blue," Orion said, and I met his gaze, nodding firmly and putting my Atlas away. Caleb was right; trolls would be trolls. I couldn't let them drag me down.

Seth started handing out coffees and Caleb shot over to help him, passing them to everyone in a blur of speed. When he was done, he threw himself back onto his seat as if he'd never gotten up.

Seth stared at him for a moment before moving to sit in the space beside Darius – though there wasn't really much space there at all, he wedged himself in all the same, nuzzling into Darius. The Dragon didn't seem to mind, even leaning into him as if he'd missed the contact, and I soaked in the feeling of finally being back to some semblance of peace. It was fragile, and we'd have to fight to keep it with all we had, but there wasn't a spark of fire in me that I wouldn't use to secure it.

"Geraldine stashed all the Guild shit here, Orion," Max said, slowly dunking another cookie in his milk.

"Great," Orion said.

"She's been moving stuff over from Rump Island all day," Max continued. "That woman doesn't sleep. I've tried everything, but she's got to be running on fumes by now. Even when she does rest, it's full of garbled sleep-talk...and she calls out to her dad sometimes." He frowned, tossing another cookie in his mouth, and I realised there were serious cracks in our family, fault lines which could rupture if we didn't help each other.

Seth was pawing at Darius like he was afraid he'd turn to dust at any moment, Tory kept staring at him like she thought the same thing, and Darius stared back at her with equal darkness in his eyes. Geraldine was obviously over-working herself to avoid her grief, Max was binge eating like there was no tomorrow, and Caleb seemed on edge, like he expected an attack at any moment.

Between me and Orion, there were enough scars left on us from Lavinia that I knew we weren't going to walk away unscathed either, and my brother...hell, Gabriel. I didn't even know what he was going through right now. I had to see him.

Tory's Atlas pinged and we all stiffened a little as she took it out and read the message. "Xavier's having luck with Francesca's memories. He can see a way into the FIB impound. He said it'll take a few hours, but he, Tyler, and Sofia can get a map drawn up for us."

"Then we'll soon have another Guild Stone," I said in relief.

"She says, as if breaking into a maximum-security FIB impound and stealing that stone will be in any way easy," Orion said with a smirk.

"I can't wait," I replied playfully.

"You're getting a taste for chaos," he accused.

"Well we're all-powerful Phoenixes, what could go wrong?" I teased.

Tory's Atlas pinged again, and she leapt to her feet, looking at the screen. "Dante says he can take us to see Gabriel now."

I jumped up too, keen to see my brother but also fearful of what he was going through.

Orion rose to his feet, concern warring in his eyes for his best friend. "Let's go see Noxy."

TORY

CHAPTER ELEVEN

The moment we were out in the trees, I broke into a jog, relieved at the thought of finally seeing my brother again. My shoulder blades tingled as I summoned my wings into existence but before I could take off, Darius caught my hand and yanked me back around to face him.

"The lake is that way," he said, jerking his chin toward the depths of the trees down a route which left the path.

"I'm well aware, dude," I told him, trying to wriggle my wrist free.

"So let's just all walk together. It'll take twenty minutes, if that."

"I can be there in less than five minutes if you let me go," I countered.

"Hmm, I forget how slow Phoenixes are," Orion commented. "I'd do it in thirty seconds."

"Ah, but then you'd be on time, which is so extraordinarily out of character for you that everyone would probably think there was an attack happening all over again," I said, earth magic tingling in my fingertips.

Orion gave me his asshole professor grin, and I narrowed my eyes in suspicion. "It was a game, wasn't it?" I accused, my magic coiling from me unnoticed. "Turning up that late every day, then occasionally shooting in the second the class entered the room – you were just fucking with everyone."

"That seems like a petty power play to fuck with young and fragile Fae minds," he replied innocently, and Darcy laughed.

"So yes then?" she said.

Orion smirked.

"What was your record?" I challenged.

His smile widened as he answered. "I was once fifty-eight minutes late to an hour-long class. Only two of my students had waited me out. I gave the rest detention scrubbing bog weed from the domes of Aqua House for a week."

I barked a laugh, Darcy catching my eye as she noticed what I'd done.

"Well, we wouldn't want you to break the habit of a lifetime now." I gave him a bright smile, leaning in to peck Darius on the lips.

His grip tightened on my wrist because he knew me all too well, but the vines I'd conjured to wrap around his legs tightened at the same time as my magic pulsed through them, hardening and turning them to stone.

Darius growled at me in frustration, but I'd already yanked my arm free of his grip, flashed a bright smile at Orion, who was equally trapped in the rock-solid vines, then propelled myself off of the ground with my air magic.

Darcy shot up through the tree canopy with me, and the moment we were past the thick mass of branches, we spread our wings and flew straight towards the lake.

I closed my eyes as the air rushed through my feathers, breathing in the freshness of the wind which I dove into headfirst, and relishing the moment of freedom with my sister by my side.

The flight was short-lived but exhilarating, and we came to land on the edge of the lake not far from the entrance to the amplification chamber where Dante and the rest of his family had taken Gabriel to rest.

Wolves prowled among the long grass, bright eyes tracing our movements from all around as we approached the entrance to the underground chamber.

I smiled at the Oscura pack, glad to see that my brother had such loyal friends defending him in his time of need.

As we reached the entrance to the amplification chamber, a huge, silver Wolf stepped out of the darkness of the stairwell, her coat shining like moonlight and her gaze more savage than the rest of the enormous beasts.

"Rosalie," I greeted, offering her a thin smile.

The Wolf cocked her head at me, then shifted, revealing the beautiful girl who I had started to feel I knew, or at the very least, trusted.

"You reek of death," she said, her lips turning up at the corners like that was no bad thing, and I breathed a laugh.

"Well I've seen more than enough of it in the last few days."

Rosalie's attention moved to my sister and her smile grew as she took in the silver rings in her eyes and the flaming wings at her back.

"Even the moon has turned to look at the two of you," she said. "The twins who defy fate itself. And I get the feeling the carnage that trails in your wake is only the beginning of your tale. The world itself will shake when it hears you roar as one."

"Is that another Moon Wolf gift talking?" I asked her.

Rosalie shrugged a shoulder inked with rosebuds, but her expression was knowing.

"You saw me, didn't you?" Darius's rough voice came from behind me, and we turned to look as he and Orion strode towards us, their windswept hair speaking of the Vampire speed they'd used to catch up to us after breaking free of my vines. "When I was dead and visiting Roxy in her room, before she set out to find the Damned Forest. You looked right at me."

"You can see the dead?" Darcy gasped, whirling back to Rosalie who shrugged innocently.

"That would be an incredible talent to possess," she said, not giving a clear answer on whether she could or not.

"You told me to follow the fire. Segui il fuoco. You meant that message for me, right?" Darius pushed.

I remembered her saying that to me the night she'd shown me the passage on raising the Trees of the Damned in the Book of Earth, putting me on the path I'd needed to walk into death and retrieve my husband from its clutches.

"And did you?" Rosalie asked, her eyes flicking to my flaming wings, her eyes dancing with secrets.

"I did," Darius agreed.

"Then it would seem that not all men are as thick skulled as they so often appear," she teased. "You should hurry if you want to see Gabriel – they're getting ready to leave."

"Leave?" I questioned, but she'd already shifted back into her silver Wolf form, and she bumped her furry face against my cheek in farewell before bounding off along the edge of the water towards the forest.

"She's strange," Orion muttered.

"I like her," I replied simply before leading the way into the darkness of the stairwell.

I banished my wings as I stepped into the narrow space, sending a Faelight out ahead of us to light our way while we descended.

The scent of cold stone and old magic wrapped its way around us as we headed down into the darkness, low voices growing closer from somewhere below, though our footsteps made it impossible to make out their words.

When we finally made it to the foot of the stairs, I walked into the wider space of the chamber itself, the domed glass roof reflecting the low glow of flames which were flickering to my right.

I hurried towards Gabriel where he lay in a nest of blankets at the centre of the room, his eyes closed and brow furrowed with untold fears.

"Gabriel?" I breathed, dropping down and throwing my arms around him despite Dante's hissed warning to be careful. I'd barely even glanced at the Storm Dragon and two Lion shifters who were standing together, watching over my brother. "I'm here."

Gabriel's arms wound around me, and a low chuckle escaped him as he squeezed me, though his grip was far weaker than I was used to, the bare skin of his upper body clammy to the touch.

"I *saw* the moment you came crashing back through The Veil with that brute of yours," he breathed, his smile pressing to my cheek while I kept him locked in my arms.

"Stubborn always was my best feature," I joked, even as I clamped my eyes shut against the tears which were trying to break free.

He was here. He was alive. He'd be okay. But fuck, he was so weak, it broke something in me.

"I made you this," Darcy said, dropping down beside us and taking Gabriel's hand, pressing a piece of paper into his grip. "Something real to look at when the visions push too hard."

I eased back enough to let him look at the sketch she'd done of the three of us soaring through the sky, hastily scrubbing my hands across my cheeks to hide the evidence of my tears. Gabriel didn't need my pity right now. He needed my strength.

"We have a cabin near the Polar Capital which is being prepared for his arrival," Dante said from behind me. "There's an amplification chamber there too, one designed specifically for him when the visions build up like this. We're going to take him there now that he's lucid enough to travel."

"A chain around the neck of a stone heathen," Gabriel muttered, drawing my focus back to him.

"I'm keeping notes," Leon piped up, waving a handful of paper scraps at us, each scrawled with random phrases like 'beware the goat' and 'turnips on a Sunday = DEATH.'

"What are-" I began, but the dark-haired Lion shifter, Carson, cut me off.

"Ignore the idiot," he growled, casting Leon a disparaging look. "I'm writing down every word *accurately.*"

Leon gasped as if mortally offended. "My interpretations *are* accurate! Don't come crying to me when a turnip brings about the end of the world."

Carson rolled his eyes and Dante sighed.

"It seems bad, but Falco has suffered worse and survived. We'll unknot the twisted fates inside his head and set him free from their whispers," Dante promised, and I could only nod, hoping that was the case.

"Is there anything else he needs?" I asked, realising Gabriel had fallen back under the sway of a vision, his eyes glazed, his lips parting in horror at whatever it was he *saw*.

"Glass falling," he breathed.

"Just time, space, rest," Dante said. "The visions have to pass through him. He fought them back to escape the Palace of Souls, but they'll consume him if he doesn't let them run free. He's like a vessel full to bursting, but each vision needs to come out whole before he can be rid of them."

"Then you should get going," Orion said firmly from his place in the shadows, his face hardened with concern for his friend. "Look after Noxy. If you let anything happen to him-"

"I'd give this man the lifeforce in my veins if he needed it, vampiro. A morte e ritorno," Dante said darkly, and Orion nodded, a silent understanding passing between them.

"I know you'll take care of our brother," Darcy said. "But if there's anything we can do, don't hesitate to summon us."

"Of course," Dante said, squeezing her arm affectionately.

"We'll lower the wards so you can leave," I said, glancing at Darcy who nodded in agreement.

Dante thanked us, and I leaned in to press a kiss to my brother's cheek before forcing myself to back up. I handed Dante the pouch of stardust Geraldine had given me from the supplies we'd stolen from Lionel's treasure and he thanked me, pulling me into a hug while Darcy said her goodbyes to Gabriel.

"Don't cry, piccola regina. The tide of this war is turning," Dante said, and for the first time, the static electricity which crackled across his skin didn't send fear darting through me but instead stoked the flames of anger which were burning low inside my chest.

"Oh, I know it is," I promised him, stepping back and offering him a determined look. "And we're going to make that fucking bastard pay for every drop of suffering we've all endured at his hand."

Leon and Carson grinned like the wicked creatures I knew them to be, and they all stepped closer to Gabriel as Dante pulled a fistful of stardust from the pouch.

I took Darcy's hand, our power merging as we tore the wards apart around us, opening a door for them to leave through.

"Wait," Darius said suddenly, stepping forward and gripping Gabriel's arm. "You need to remember Marcus. It's important. He needs you to think of him or he's going to fade beyond The Veil."

Gabriel's brow furrowed in confusion, but we couldn't hold the wards open much longer.

"Go," I bit out, grabbing Darius's arm and pulling him back so they could leave.

Dante threw the stardust, and in a flash of magic, the four of them were gone.

Darcy and I released our hold on the power, sealing the wards once more, and I gasped as the force of holding back so much magic finally shattered.

Darius took my hand and we left the silent chamber, heading back up the stairs towards the cold winter light above.

"I have very mixed feelings about my memories of that chamber," Darius muttered to me, leaning in close so that his lips skimmed my ear at the words. I knew he was trying to distract me from my pain over having to say goodbye to my brother again so soon.

"Oh?" I asked, pretending not to know what he was referring to, but it wasn't like I could easily forget the way we had defied the stars down there with Caleb.

"I have never been so close to ecstasy and murder in the same moment as I was then," he said, nipping my neck just like I remembered him doing that day. "But you did scream so prettily when I-"

"Vampire hearing, asshole. Save it for when you're alone, yeah?" Orion grouched from behind us, and I broke a laugh even though there were still tears in my eyes.

"Who's Marcus anyway?" Darcy asked.

"Who?" Darius replied.

"You literally just told Gabriel to remember him," I pointed out as we stepped back out of the stairwell and into the cool light by the side of the lake.

"No; I told him to remember Manuel," Darius replied, frowning at me.

"You said Marcus, dude," I told him flatly.

"And you still haven't told us who Marcus or Manuel are," Orion added.

"I told you, it's Manuel," Darius said irritably. "Beyond The Veil, if no one alive thinks of you anymore, then you kinda start to fade away and get called towards the door of-"

"Your majesties!"

I startled at Geraldine's voice, whipping around to look at her as she sprung out of a fucking rose bush.

"Where the fuck did you come from?" I gasped, causing her to laugh.

"A good servant of the crown is never far from her ladies. I just need to know what your plans are for the prisoners? Do you wish for me to conduct an interrogation or-"

"We can handle that," I said, my heart pumping faster at the thought of it, my gaze meeting Darius's as he seemed to agree.

"Yeah. Leave the interrogation to us," he said.

"As you wish. They are currently being held in the bowels of Jupiter Hall."

"Jupiter Hall has no bowels," Orion said. "Which of the three floors is it on?"

"Oh-ho, so the wily professor doesn't know all of the secrets this academy has to offer then?" Geraldine beckoned us along and we fell into step behind her.

The sun was shining brightly now, illuminating the frost that still clung to the bare trees and long grass, making the whole world glow with a silver hue that set my soul at ease.

It felt familiar here, safe and more like home than any other place I'd ever known. I could almost fool myself into believing that we were simply walking to class or heading for a meal at The Orb with all the other students instead of on our way to interrogate prisoners of war.

The huge gothic building of Jupiter Hall soon appeared ahead of us, and we strode up the stone steps, passing through the arching wooden doors where the scent of polished wood and old books greeted us.

Geraldine turned away from the marble staircase that we usually took to get to our Cardinal Magic classes, instead leading us down a side passage and stopping abruptly before a statue of a Basilisk with gleaming yellow gemstones for eyes.

She reached out with a flourish of her wrist, then stroked her hand down the nose of the serpent before tugging on its forked tongue. A low click followed the movement, and my brows rose as the snake shifted aside, a narrow doorway opening up behind it and revealing a brick staircase leading down into darkness beyond.

"Well shit," Orion muttered as we followed Geraldine into the hidden passage.

"I love seeing you surprised," Darcy commented, prodding his cheek.

His gaze slid to her, a grin twisting his lips. "I'd have thought you'd be used to it by now, considering since we met, you've upended my life at every turn."

"Well it wasn't much of a life to upend, to be fair," Darius taunted. "With your Sad Sally Saturdays, seeing how quickly you could find the bottom of a bourbon bottle."

"At least I didn't go on lone motorcycle drives at sunset, listening to dramatic classical music," Orion shot back, and Darius pursed his lips.

"Well Tor and I were broke orphans in the mortal realm – if we're tossing our hat into the ring of this 'whose life was more pathetic' game," Darcy said, catching my eye and making me smirk.

"I think Geraldine should judge the winner," I decided.

"Gracious – but the honour would be all mine! The Sad Sally award must of course be bestowed upon the greatest loser in every category. I shall contemplate it like a glinglepuss in a back alley." She nodded seriously, deliberating it, and clearly in no rush to make a decision.

We descended the stairs, the temperature rising as we went and the stone Basilisk sliding into place once again behind us.

We were engulfed in darkness for several steps, but as the stairs turned back on themselves, the orange glow of a fire lit up the space below, beckoning us on.

At the foot of the stairs was a brick corridor lit by torches held in brackets along the walls. Several of our most trusted warriors stood guard before each of the wooden doors that spread away from us in both directions, and Washer was doing toe-touches at the far end of the corridor.

"My Queens," he greeted, his stretching turning into a low bow which felt particularly odd coming from one of our professors.

"Don't bother with that shit," I insisted as the rest of the rebels all bowed too, but none of them were listening to me.

"The Queens have come to interrogate the prisoners," Geraldine announced, and I wondered if she planned on announcing everything we did from now on. If she decided to start telling the world every time I needed a shit, I was going to have to draw a line.

"Who should we talk to first?" I asked, glancing at the long line of doors and wondering just how long we were going to be here.

"We have a collection of K.U.N.T.s, the captives from our victory at the Court of Solaria, and a few other lowly braggards such as the traitorous wench who was once known as principal at this fine learning establishment," Geraldine said, indicating several doors with her hand.

"Tory!"

I turned at the sound of the familiar voice, a smile breaking over my face as I spotted Milton Hubert jogging down the steps at our backs.

"Oh hey, du-" I was cut off by him wrapping his arms around me, hoisting me off of my feet, then swinging me around in a circle as he squeezed me tightly.

Darius growled as Milton set me down again and I laughed, backing up a step and waving the possessive Dragon off.

"You guys really saved our asses turning up when you did," he gushed, grinning widely at Darcy too. "I swear we were about to get eaten by those monster things Lionel sent, and then bam! You just stride in like some hero from the dark ages with a legend brought back from the dead at your side too!" His grin fell on Darius, then faltered at the look on my husband's face, and I cleared my throat pointedly when Darius remained quiet.

"I'm glad you're not dead," he said in a flat tone which earned him a scowl from me, though Milton gave him half a smile.

"Right back at you."

"Did you come barrelling down here yelling out audaciously at the True Queens like a squirrel spying a fox for a reason, dear Milton, or were you just overcome with joy at seeing them returned?" Geraldine asked.

"Oh, er, yeah. I heard you were coming here to interrogate the prisoners and I needed to tell you something. Nova was Dark Coerced by your..." he shot a look at Darius, then changed lanes. "Lionel. When he came here, I was hiding in a closet in her office and I saw him do it."

Washer gasped in horror behind us, and I glanced at him, remembering that his allegiance to us and Nova's to Lionel had caused the end of their relationship.

"Do you think there's a chance that she wasn't even on his side?" Darcy asked in shock.

"She did seem pretty excited about us returning when we first got to the academy," I said as I considered it. "Maybe she was loyal to us from the start but then Lionel got to her. It does seem like the kind of shit he'd pull. Where is she, Geraldine?"

"This way." She headed off down the corridor to our right.

We all began to follow her, and I turned to Milton. "Anything else happen while we were gone?"

"We did what we could to resist the Order segregation rules," Milton said. "We even sabotaged a visit Lionel made to the academy."

"That's a story I want to hear more about," I said curiously, but before he could elaborate, Geraldine opened a door and ushered us inside.

"The traitors from within these walls await your judgement," she said, bowing us through the door.

"Let's see them then," I said, wondering who precisely had been captured.

The room was far bigger than I'd expected, the left side of it stacked high with boxes that were filled with potions equipment and dusty workbooks, while the right had black bars in place to lock a group of Fae inside what must have been a newly formed cell.

Within it, around twenty Fae sat on bunks or chairs, their captivity looking all kinds of civil compared to what I knew Lionel chose to subject the Fae he captured to.

I recognised Kylie Major crouched in a back corner, her usually pristine blonde hair a tangle of knots that hung lank around her face. There were others from her posse inside the cell too, and I noted Marguerite lurking near the bars. The beautiful redhead sucked in a breath as her gaze fell on Darius, and my upper lip pulled back in what was little more than a snarl.

Mildred Canopus bared her teeth at us from a space by the far wall, lunging to her feet as her eyes locked on Darius too.

"Impossible!" she cried, lunging at the bars, though I refused to flinch away from them. "What foul trick is this?"

"My wife refused to let death have me," Darius said, heavy emphasis on the word 'wife', which made me smirk and made Mildred's eyes bug out.

"You spit in the face of your lineage," she hissed, a growl coating her words as she took a swipe at us through the bars. "If you produce half-breed mutts with this piece of trash, then-"

Whatever threat she might have been about to make was cut off abruptly as Darius threw his power at her, hurling her across the cell and pinning her to the far wall in a thick crust of ice which covered her entire body aside from her nose and eyes, which I noticed were red-rimmed and wild.

"You speak about my queen like that again and you'll regret it," he said in a low voice which made a shiver of adrenaline run down my spine.

No one protested him leaving Mildred pinned in place like that, and I glanced around the cell again, taking note of those who had been caught when we'd reclaimed this academy from Lionel's corruption.

A lot of the K.U.N.T.s had escaped but we'd caught a fair few of them.

Nova was sitting apart from the others, toeing the frayed carpet with her high-heeled shoe, not even looking at us as we'd entered the room and dealt with Mildred.

"Actually, there is one more thing," Milton said. "Marguerite helped us. She covered for us more than once. Even risked her life to save mine and Bernice's when we were hiding from Lionel."

"Really?" Darcy asked in disbelief. "Why?"

Marguerite's eyes shifted to Darius but she said nothing, either not wanting to plead her own case or uncertain how to do so.

"Because of Darius?" I asked, stepping forward so that I was between her and my husband and looking at her through the bars of her cage.

Marguerite's lip quivered and her eyes blazed with emotion as she met my gaze, but the hatred I expected to find wasn't there. No jealousy either. More like bitter acceptance.

"He was meant for you," she breathed, her voice low and clearly only intended for me. "But I loved him first. Maybe not like you do, maybe not even like I thought I did once but… He is the one who earned my loyalty. I always aligned myself to him. Never Lionel."

I blinked at the honesty in her voice and turned to the others for some idea on what to make of that because the strangest thing was that I believed her.

Darcy shrugged at me and Darius pursed his lips, but it was clear what I had to do, no matter my personal dislike of the girl who had called me a whore more times than I could count.

"Let her out," I said firmly, my words a command. "Get a Cyclops to confirm her story, but I believe her. And if she is aligned with Darius, then that means she must have bowed when he did…right?" I looked back to Marguerite whose eyes had widened in surprise, and a small, smug smile pulled at my lips as I confirmed the fact that she didn't know about that yet.

"All hail the True Queens," Darius rumbled from behind me, his words a caress along my neck, his hand landing on my shoulder as he made it clear that my claim was no lie. "Everyone loyal to the kingdom of Solaria has bent the knee, Marguerite. The other Heirs, the Councillors, every student at the academy, and countless rebels to my father's false claim. So if you're as loyal to me as you say, then I suggest you follow suit."

Kylie shrieked something from the corner of the cell, but I didn't spare her any attention as my eyes stayed fixed on Marguerite's, and I watched with full pleasure as the truth of those words fell over her. Slowly, oh so fucking slowly, she began to dip down, her eyes still on mine, the truth painted through her irises as she accepted it and did the only thing which was left to her to do if she wanted to prove her loyalty to our side of this war.

I probably shouldn't have been so fucking satisfied as I watched her bow for me. But then again, I wasn't some prim and proper princess, brought up to be benevolent and just – I was a ruthless girl who had fought with tooth and claw to claim this savage crown in the image of my father. And if that meant I gloated like a smug bitch while my once-enemy bowed at my feet, then so be it.

"Sethy would never bow to-" Kylie's words were cut off sharply as Darcy threw a silencing bubble over her, followed by a slap of ice-cold water which drenched her from head to toe.

"Did anyone hear anything?" she asked innocently, and I shared a triumphant look with my other half which had my heart swelling with satisfaction.

Marguerite was hauled away, and I moved over to Nova next, ignoring the looks the rest of the K.U.N.T.s were giving us as we went. None of them had taken that opportunity to bow, and we would have to figure out what to do with them after this, but for now, I just wanted to find out how deeply Lionel's rot had been infecting this academy.

Nova flinched as I took one of her hands in mine and Darcy took her other. Nova's dark eyes rose to look at me with a kind of empty plea echoing in their depths. I didn't let myself linger on that look, instead calling on my Phoenix and pressing that magic from my skin and into hers, closing my eyes so I could focus on hunting down any signs of the Dark Coercion which Lionel so liked to use against those he struggled to control with fear alone.

Darcy's flames met with mine, then crashed into a barrier within Nova's mind almost at once, then another and another. It was over in a matter of minutes, but the second the last piece of dark magic shattered, Nova let out a shuddering breath which could have been a sob.

She collapsed to the floor at our feet, and Darcy dropped down to help her up.

"I never thought I'd taste freedom again," Nova gasped. "The True Queens really have ascended," she breathed, looking between the two of us in astonishment. "All hail the name of Vega. Let that cowardly Dragon quake in his boots before you."

By the time we'd checked to make sure all the rest of the detained K.U.N.T.s and even Highspell hadn't been under Lionel's influence, I'd almost forgotten that we still needed to interrogate the captives from the Court of Solaria.

Nova had been taken back to her home in Asteroid Place by Washer. He promised to get us a full account of Lionel's meddling at the academy, which we were hoping would help us out with any lapses in security we might not have thought of.

Milton had returned to help with the guard duty outside, and Marguerite was going to be assigned to work with him once the Cyclopses were done looking into her mind.

"Shall we do the old compare the story trick?" Orion suggested when Geraldine led us to the two rooms which held General McReedy and Gus Vulpecula.

"What's that?" Darcy asked curiously.

"We interrogate them separately and then compare their answers – if they match, then we know it's the truth. If they don't, then we know that at least one of them is lying," Darius explained.

"What if they both know the same lie to tell?" I asked.

"Huh. Never really thought of that," Orion admitted, and I rolled my eyes.

"We can fact check once we have some answers, baby," Darius told me. "So all you have to do right now is pick between the snivelling reporter or the seasoned General?"

"I'll take the General," I said without needing much thought. "If I never have to see that lying Fox bastard again then it'll be too soon."

"We'll take Gus then," Orion agreed, and he and Darcy headed into that room with Geraldine hot on their heels, a clipboard in hand.

Darius opened the door to the room where Irvine McReedy, the General in Lionel's army and enforcer in charge of the Nebula Inquisition Centres was being held, and I strode through it with my chin raised and my pulse striking my ribcage.

Irvine McReedy looked up at us with a sneer, his fingers flexing like he was hoping to use magic against us, but it was lucky for him that he was tapped out in that case. I didn't like his chances against either one of us if I was being entirely honest.

"You're dead," Irvine breathed in alarm, his eyes going wide as he stared at Darius like he was a ghost, the colour draining from his paunchy face.

"Not anymore. You know how this goes," Darius purred, snapping the door shut behind us and leaving us in the dim light of the single bulb that hung near the far wall. "We ask you questions and you answer them."

"What if I don't?" Irvine sneered, getting over the shock of seeing Darius alive as he realised why we had come. "Your Cyclopses couldn't crack through my mental defences, so what makes you think a Dragon and Phoenix will have better luck?"

"You've already lost here," I told him, stepping closer. "We have you under lock and key. We've taken the academy, and we will take the rest of Solaria in time too. Lionel's rule is coming to an end. The time to jump ships is now."

"And what? I have no illusions about you setting me free once this is done."

"The best you can hope for is a life in Darkmore," Darius agreed. "But I'd wager that's better than no life at all."

The brutality of his words sent a little thrill of energy dancing beneath my skin, the truth in that threat setting my pulse racing, and I looked at my husband with hungry eyes.

"Tell us where Lionel has relocated his armies to," I demanded.

Irvine scoffed. "Even if I told you, you have to know he's moved them again already. He will know I've been captured. The king is no fool."

"He's no king either," Darius snapped, stepping closer.

"He claimed the throne just as any real Fae should," Irvine spat. "And I'd sooner die here and now than bow to the whims of a half-breed whore whose father was as insane as her idiot sist-"

I punched him so hard that my knuckles split open on his teeth, the jolt of violence lashing through me with a buzz of pure energy which lit me up from the inside out. I hadn't even intended to do it. But the moment he'd started speaking shit about my family, I'd simply lost it.

Irvine crashed to the floor with a cry of fury, rolling away from me before leaping to his feet and lunging straight at Darius.

I cried out as I spotted the thin blade he'd tugged from his boot, my pulse jackhammering as I lurched towards them.

Darius ducked aside before throwing a punch hard enough to crack bone, and again that spark of excitement shot through me, adrenaline thundering along my veins as blood flew and I felt a rush of exhilaration.

I slammed into Irvine, knocking him off balance as he swung the blade again, but the man was well trained and more than used to combat. He hurled himself around with my attack, using my momentum to launch me off of my feet and throw me into the closest wall.

Pain scattered my thoughts as my skull hit the bricks, but that was nothing to the panic which thrummed through me as he swung that blade for Darius again.

Darius blocked the first strike, but Irvine had clearly planned for that, twisting into the movement and slashing out again.

Darius's blood bloomed as the knife swiped across his forearm, and I shrieked in anger as I launched myself from the ground and slammed into Irvine with the force of a battering ram.

Darius swept his legs out from under him as he was knocked off balance, and we all ended up on the ground, kicking, punching and stabbing.

Pain flared in my shoulder, but I ignored it, ice sprouting between my knuckles in deadly points so I drew blood with every strike I made. The hot splash of it against my skin sent me into a frenzy, a savage smile breaking from my lips as I struck Irvine again and again.

Darius was fully feral at my side, a snarl slipping through his teeth as he punched hard enough to break bones, and the two of us fell prey to a bloodlust so keen I could have sworn we were moving to the choreography of some deadly dance.

I couldn't stop. Didn't want to stop. Every strike was intoxicating, the need for more all-consuming.

Irvine fell still between us, and my heart pounded mercilessly as the weight of his death seemed to flow right over me, like his soul was brushing against mine on its way to The Veil.

Darius grabbed me, kissing me roughly, his skin drenched in as much blood as my own, and the only thing better than the rush of that death was the taste of his mouth against mine.

Something was wrong. I knew it in the depths of my soul, and yet I was utterly drunk on this feeling, unable to calm the thrashing of my heart.

"Death pays for death," Darius breathed against my mouth, his hand tight around my neck, his eyes alight with the same thrill I was lost in.

"Shit," I panted, my fingers knotted in his shirt, our hearts pounding as one between us.

The door banged open, and we looked around at Darcy and Orion who were staring at Irvine's bloody corpse in surprise.

"Gus told us everything," Orion said slowly. "He literally caved the moment Darcy commanded him to. Kinda looked like he might piss himself, and she didn't even lay a finger on him. And he'd stolen a bag of notes and records from Lionel's office too, which Geraldine has taken to be analysed in case they hold anything of importance. It looks like things went...differently in here?"

"I think we just figured out the cost of my life," Darius growled in agreement. "The Ferryman wants paying back in death."

LIONEL

CHAPTER TWELVE

I sat upon a throne of jade, carved by the finest earth Elementals among my bonded Guardians, the back extending up into the great, towering form of a Dragon. Its wings were outstretched, jaws agape, and rows of sharp teeth gleaming in the firelight. It was far bigger than Hail's throne, grander in every aspect, and this palace would be finer than his too when I was through here. Gold coins spilled out over the seat and mounted up around my feet, the power they fed me setting my heart thumping to a powerful tune.

I contemplated the war, spinning a single gold coin between my fingers and working out my next move. I had sent word to move my armies the moment the Court of Solaria had been breached, knowing their location could be forced from loyal tongues soon enough.

News had come to me of the Vega twins' brutal attack on one of my Nebula Inquisition Centres, and I had watched the footage of them burning my captives with scepticism.

It did not make sense for them to turn so savagely against their own people. Unless the Vegas had played a game of benevolence until they had gained enough power. Still, that idea did not ring true. Why destroy their own before the war was won? Why turn on their people now? Their following would diminish. So it led me to a more likely conclusion. Sabotage. One of my followers had forged the footage to sully the Vegas' campaign. Though I'd gotten confirmation of the destruction of that Nebula Inquisition Centre. It *had* been burned. It would take a true power to cause such destruction. Some of my Dragons perhaps. But with them all bonded to me, and the certainty that they would tell me of such a plot, I was left without a firm answer.

Regardless, I was not unsettled by the development; my wins were boundless. I had fully secured the Polar Capital in my latest move and had rounded up many powerful Fae in a new Nebular Inquisition Centre where they would be put to work mining for rare glacial diamonds. Some of the largest diamonds held untold powers that harnessed magic from the Northern Lights, and I currently had some of my finest Bonded Men running an interrogation to seek the most powerful diamonds which had long-ago been discovered. Since my occupation of the city, the resistance there had kept their location hidden, but they would all soon crack under the force of my empire.

No one kept treasures from me, and they would suffer greatly until their treasures were relinquished into my ownership.

"My King?" Lavinia walked into the room with a hopeful glint in her eyes. A dark dress created from the shadows was wrapped around her body, her hair swaying in that familiar, ethereal way. "I am making progress. Will you come and watch?"

I released a plume of smoke from my nose, letting her know I did not wish to be disturbed.

"Can you not see I am recharging my magic?" I demanded, though my tone was not as harsh as it might have been once.

Lavinia was one of the most important weapons I possessed, and with the loss of the Palace of Souls and whispers reaching me of the Vega twins' growing popularity, I was not going to risk invoking her ire. Of course, she needed me now too. With her shadows locked inside her and no way to summon more to her, thanks to Darcy Vega, she was weakened. But only for a time. Because if she truly managed to wrangle the power that lay hidden in this palace, she would possess a strength untold. While she remained loyal, that was not too problematic, but if she decided she no longer needed me, my position would be in jeopardy. It was a threat I could not let lie, and it needed dealing with sooner rather than later.

"Forgive me, but it is important, Daddy," she purred, that word always working to soften my temper just a little.

"Then show me." I rose from my throne, coins spilling from my lap as I walked bare footed towards her, only a pair of linen trousers in place on my frame.

I took her waist, pressing a kiss by her ear, then speaking into it. "Have you thought more on what I asked?"

She looked up at me from under her lashes, the haunting beauty of her face a tempting thing indeed. "Yes, but I am curious. Why do you really wish to make me one of your Bonded, my King?"

"So that our love might deepen," I growled, though it was a lie painted upon my lips. She could never know it. "The want and passion between Guardian and Ward is akin to little else I have known in this world."

"Even our love?" she gasped.

"Our love is almost everything. But this would make it complete," I said, drawing her closer and grazing my lips over hers. "I want you fully. Bond to me, and we will be united in every way."

"Not in every way," she scoffed. "Not by the stars. Our eyes will never glimmer with silver rings." A touch of envy coloured her tone that I did not miss. I had seen the way she coveted those very rings in the eyes of Lance Orion and his bitch Vega, but I was not drawn to such petty trinkets from the stars. They offered no power that I was aware of.

"Perhaps if we show the stars that we are committed to each other, they will offer us such a blessing," I purred.

She pursed her lips, her eyes darkening in consideration. My queen was no fool. And this manipulation needed to be done as carefully as I could manage it.

"Forget I said anything." I stepped away, offering her a smile that I felt nowhere but upon my lips. "It was just a thought."

"Mm." She frowned. "Do you lust for your Wards more than I?" The dangerous edge to her tone said my answer had to be carefully constructed.

"I want them in a way that cannot easily be put into words. But I would never touch them. My love is yours. If you were to be my Bonded, I believe all other Guardians would pale to insignificance. I cannot help the urges of the Bonds, however." I grazed my hand over the many star signs marked onto my forearm, overlapping and intertwining. "I do not wish for any of them to take my attention from you, but I cannot help the thoughts that pass through my mind on occasion."

She hissed like a hellcat, jealousy flaring in her eyes. Gripping my arm, her talon-like nails bit into my flesh. "If you ever lay a hand on another, I will skin them alive. You are mine. *My* Acrux King."

"Yes," I said keenly. "And I wish for you to possess every piece of me. But I..." I stepped away from her, feigning defeat. "Never mind."

"Your Guardians are lesser than you," she said icily. "I will never be lesser."

"It does not have to be that way. You would still be my queen. You are not like the others." I took her hand and squeezed. "Come, show me the progress you have made."

Her face split into a grin. "Yes, Daddy. You will be most pleased."

She led the way through the stately hallways of my newly made palace, everything gold and jade, glittering with beauty. It was the finest palace ever constructed, fit for the most powerful Fae to ever roam the Earth. But it was all at risk because of those damned twins. If only I had not burned their house in the mortal realm but smothered them as babies in their cribs, I would not be fighting for my throne now. I would be ruling as I wished, as I had spent my lifetime preparing for.

No matter. The stars were testing my grit, that was all. This was their way of making me prove myself, and I would do so without fail. I possessed a power now that was far superior to any Phoenix, and the stars may be rattling in the heavens for what I had done, but they would revere me for it too. For I was doing what no Fae had ever achieved before.

Lavinia led me out into a windy space between a gap in the mountain, the great chasm torn into the rocky ground hiding my beautiful secret. We approached the pit where my precious weapon was held, the icy air spewing in from above and snowflakes tumbling down to melt within the heat emanating from my body. Glimmering light bounced against the walls of the pit and a terrible shrieking, wailing came from the entity down below, the sound ricocheting around the inside of my mind.

We reached the chasm's edge, and I shivered in the light of the holy power that drenched my skin. A fallen star. Forced into the confines of Lavinia's shadows so that it could not release its power into the world and die.

The giant, glittering rock pulsed with a power that tugged on the very essence of my soul, and I groaned.

"Isn't she beautiful?" Lavinia breathed, her eyes lighting with the silver gleam of the star. "She's succumbing to my shadows. I can wield her soon, I'm sure of it."

"Show me," I rasped.

Lavinia lifted her hand, twisting her fingers so the shadows tightened around the star and a terrible, piercing scream cut through my mind.

"King of terror and ruin, release me. You defy the laws of old, nature, and the Origin herself."

The star's begging made my chest swell with pride. I had one of the mighty fate-weavers themselves as a captive. My power knew no bounds. This would forever be the most terrible, hallowed thing that any royal had ever achieved. I would not just be the King of Solaria, I would claim the entire world, and the heavens along with it. There would be no corner of this universe that would not know me as the most powerful creature who ever lived.

"Do as my queen bids, and I shall be merciful," I spoke loud and clear.

The star flashed with fury, more shrieks carving through my head as Lavinia's shadows wrapped around it.

"She will answer my questions, if I squeeze just so," Lavinia said keenly, deeming the star female, though I was sure they were of no gender known in this world. "Ask her something, Daddy."

A single question came to mind that had been troubling me. "The Vega twins were seen burning my captives – their allies. Tell me what this means."

The star screamed, the shadows pushing into the shell of its glittering surface and causing it agony.

"Clydinius walks this earth and takes the form of the daughters of flames," the star hissed.

"Clydinius?" I frowned. "Who is that?"

"A star of old cast from the sky. Clydinius has risen to walk among the Fae as a god, desecrating the timeless laws," the star said, its ire clear.

"A star walks among us," I breathed in profound shock.

The threat of this Clydinius was abundantly clear and shook the foundations of all I had been working for. This star could take everything from me. It could destroy us all and claim this world for itself.

"What is it Clydinius wants?" I demanded. "Does this star seek to seize my throne?"

"Thrones are for those of flesh and bone. Clydinius seeks what has never been sought by our kind and never should be sought. The essence of earthly life. Power beyond measure, an existence without restraint."

"What essence do you refer to?" I pressed.

"I can't hold it much longer, my King," Lavinia said breathlessly, her strain clear.

"The essence of all," the star revealed, and the pressure in the air told of how forcibly the star was trying to resist answering at all. *"The crux of being. Dominion. The star with a body of flesh shall come seeking me and one other. For three of us here on earth would form a Celestial Trinity. A union forbidden by the Origin herself, because it would be so terrible, it could splinter time and shatter the very forces of nature the universe is ruled by. It could pull all the stars from the sky. You must never let this come to pass."*

The star shrieked and pulsed with so much fury that I was near blinded by the light it emitted.

Lavinia sagged beside me, losing her grip on the star, and no more words came to me from the deity.

"A Celestial Trinity." I rubbed a hand over my jaw thoughtfully, not liking the sound of so much power being in any other hands than mine.

"We should ally with Clydinius," Lavinia said excitedly.

"Ally?" I scoffed, but that word settled deeper inside me and suddenly it did not seem so absurd. In fact, it might be a chance to gain access to this seductive power the star sought. It would take cunning indeed, but I was privy to much of that, and I would find a way to secure the star's dominion for my own. "Yes. We shall offer the star what it hunts for in payment for its allegiance, and then we shall be ready to charge into battle once more. With a holy creature of the sky fighting on our side, we will destroy the Vega line once and for all, then the real work in my kingdom can begin."

DARIUS

CHAPTER THIRTEEN

I watched my wife as she flipped through pages of the Book of Ether, her brow furrowed in concentration and posture rigid with irritation. I had long since noticed her curiosity, that burning thirst for knowledge and power which defined her as wholly Fae, but I wasn't sure I'd ever truly noticed how frustrated she got when answers eluded her.

"It's not like it's unmanageable," I told her, adjusting my posture where I sat reclined in my usual armchair at King's Hollow, my boots resting on the coffee table, ankles crossed before me.

"I know," she grunted, flicking another page so hard that I was surprised it didn't tear.

"It could be useful," I added, and her gaze lifted from the book to narrow into a glare aimed my way.

"However did you manage to get so far ahead in your studies if all you ever do is repeat the same thoughts over and over again? I'm honestly surprised none of the other Heirs murdered you before now."

I gave her a wicked grin, beckoning her closer with a hand coated in gold rings. We'd returned here after the interrogation yesterday, discussing the movements of my father's armies thanks to the information Gus Vulpecula had supplied us with. Scouts had been sent out of course, but as expected, they were already gone.

It wasn't as though Gus had been kept in the loop on purpose; he was simply a useful pawn for my father to use in his media campaign of lies and propaganda. But he was a sneaky bastard, the type to stick his nose in where it wasn't wanted and sniff out information he wasn't supposed to have. So he might not have been able to help us locate the False King's armies, but he had helped us with an approximation of numbers, rumours of planned movements, and even whispers about the issues the Bonded were giving my father. No doubt it wasn't easy to satisfy the bond to so many.

Roxy pursed her lips at me over the top of the ancient book, then dropped her eyes to it once more.

I growled to let her know I wasn't pleased about being ditched in favour of some dusty tome, and she flipped me off as casually as breathing.

We'd discussed the cost of my life with the others long into the night, and so far as I was concerned, there were worse things that could have happened. I was a bloodthirsty son of a bitch with anger issues which I didn't mind sating on the battlefield one bit. And though we'd both gotten caught up in the high of bloodshed while fighting against the twisted monsters my father had sent to attack the academy and when interrogating his war General, in hindsight, I didn't think we had actually been out of control. Caught up in slaughter and mayhem? Yes. High on the spill of blood and crash of battle? Yes. But utterly unable to stop? Or worse, unable to tell friend from foe? No. We had not entirely lost our minds to the call of death, and I didn't fear that becoming the case either. Roxy had known that she would have to bear a cost when she'd come for me beyond The Veil, and I'd known I would bear one too when I agreed to return with her. Honestly, this seemed like a far better option than many others, and in a time of war, if anything, it seemed helpful.

With a sigh, I pushed to my feet and headed over to make us some coffee. This evening, we planned to hit the FIB impound and retrieve the next Guild Stone. Apparently today, we planned on sitting here while Roxy angrily turned the pages in that damn book like it might suddenly offer her the answer she wanted.

"You won't find some handy little get out clause," I told her, setting a steaming mug of coffee down in front of her before placing my hands on the back of her seat and leaning close to read over her shoulder.

"I'm not looking for a get out clause," she replied like that was obvious, and I frowned.

"What has you so worked up then?" I pressed a kiss to her cheek, then another to the spot just beneath her ear, my gaze trailing over the gruesome illustration in the book which was depicting the way the organs of the dead could be traded for the power of persuasion with the addition of the right herbs, runes, and incantations.

"I just want..." She turned the page, then grinned in triumph as she seemingly found what she was searching for. "Aha." Roxy pointed to the page, and I frowned.

"You want to coat your skin in impenetrable scales?" I asked, looking at the depiction of a man who appeared to be half lizard after completing the spell. "I'm pretty sure this spell is permanent, baby, and I'm not sure the whole scaley lizard-person look is the one you wanna commit to for a lifetime-"

"Not that, idiot," she said, batting my hand away as I tugged her hair over her shoulder to give me better access to her neck. "That."

She pointed at a tiny note in the list of ingredients which was blotted over with some kind of brownish stain and hardly legible at all. I was forced to take my lips from her neck as I leaned closer, trying to read the scrawling text.

A cup of water from the river of the dead, found beyond the sharp right of a crossroads at the foot of a burial mound beneath the outstretched bough of the hangman's tree.

"Those directions seem pretty vague. If I told you to meet me by the path near the river where the oak tree grows, then you'd have no fucking idea where to-"

She placed a hand over my mouth, and I growled at her.

Roxy turned to look at me over her shoulder, her green eyes sparking with the kind of trouble that we both knew I'd be following her into headfirst and cursing her out for ever suggesting.

"Oh, my poor, sweet, linear-minded Dragon," she teased. "Thank the stars you didn't have to come get me from death or you'd have been a very old man before you ever figured it out."

She pressed her lips to the back of her hand as though kissing me through the barrier she'd placed between us, then pushed to her feet, leaving the book on the sofa.

"And what is it that you think you might find beneath the bough of the hangman's tree?" I questioned as she headed for the door.

"Not what; *who*."

"Stop teasing me and give me a straight answer," I demanded, stalking her out of the room and down the stairs.

"The Ferryman," she replied simply, and I almost missed a step in my surprise over that.

"And why the fuck would you want to meet with him again?"

"I dunno. Maybe he'd like to hang out? It's gotta be lonely paddling up and down the river of death all day. He'd probably like a visitor."

"Didn't you tell me you knocked him off of his raft into the river and the power of his fury almost ripped the soul from your chest as you escaped him?" I snarled.

"Yeah. Good times." She gave me a smile, slipping out of the door at the foot of the tree trunk, and I lunged for her.

I caught her wrist, propelling her around so that her back was to the bough of the enormous tree and kissing her taunting lips hard.

I felt the lurch of her pulse as my own heart echoed it, the two organs a mirror to one another and her excitement fuelling my own.

I drew her wrists up above her head, pinning her in place with my body and pressing my tongue between her lips, losing myself in the taste of her sweet mouth. She was far more intoxicating than any battle or bloodshed, far more tempting than causing death and carnage. If our cost was to deliver death to The Ferryman, then so be it. Nothing would take away the reality of this though.

We finally broke apart, our breaths rough and heavy, the desire to claim more hanging in the chilled air of winter around us. But Geraldine was bringing the 'Rebels' Undying Mighty Province' - AKA Rump Island - around the coast today. The twins had to meet her down by Aer Cove when it arrived so that the wards could be extended to connect it to the academy, giving the army the space it needed while amassing our forces in one place at last.

I reluctantly pulled back, drawing Roxy beneath my arm so the two of us could take the path down to the cove.

Sleet began to fall from the sky as we walked, the freezing droplets speckling my cheeks while my breath rose in small clouds before me. I didn't bother to create a shield of heat to stop it though, instead savouring the change in temperature. In death, the climate didn't vary. It was calm, temperate, serene, and boring. I welcomed the crash of rain against my skin and the chill of the wind through my hair.

We climbed up the hill towards the cliffs, the shadow of Aer Tower and its ever-rotating turbines falling over us as we approached the water and the scent of the sea air assaulted us.

Rump Island was already taking up a lot of the view which had only ever been filled by the ocean before.

Gwen was waiting at the edge of the cliff, and I released my hold on Roxy, watching as she jogged over to join her sister.

The Heirs were further down the cliff, laughing and roughhousing, and I walked over to them, feeling the echoes of all the time we'd spent at the academy washing around me as though I were stepping back in time.

"Darius!" Seth called as he spotted me. "We were just trying to figure out which one of us would survive the longest on the moon, and these assholes keep saying it would be Max, even though it would clearly be me."

"Max has water magic," I pointed out. "You'd need water and air on the moon. So Max wins."

"I can make coconuts," Seth growled. "Besides, when I was on the moon, I scouted the perfect crater for a moon base."

"Oh, have you been to the moon?" I asked as if surprised by this news, and Seth's face dropped.

"You know full well that I have been to the moon. But if you'd like me to remind you of all the things that I did while-"

"I used to be quite impressed by the fact that you'd been to the moon," I mused. "But then I went to death and back and the moon kinda lost its appeal."

"The moon could never lose her appeal," Seth hissed.

"You have to admit going to death is cooler than going to the moon," Max agreed, and Caleb snorted a laugh while Seth gaped at us in horror.

"Are you comparing the lowly bowels of the underworld where every Fae and their pet lizard will one day end up anyway to the great and bulbous form of her majesty the moon?" he scoffed. "When I was on the moon, I saw all kinds of things, like-"

"I saw all kinds of things in death too," I replied, holding Seth's gaze for several seconds before purposefully looking at Caleb, who stilled under my scrutiny.

"Like what?" he asked, the amusement slipping from his tone.

"Oh, you'd be surprised at the depravity I witnessed. Not to mention the bare-faced lies some people tell their closest friends. Honestly, I thought I knew the people I love best in this world, but there are some secrets hiding among us which would shock the entire kingdom if they came to light."

"I don't know what you mean," Seth said, his voice higher than usual.

I just shrugged, turning my focus back to the Vegas as they worked and ignoring the pointed looks which were passing between two of my best friends.

A pulse of magic washed over us as the twins connected the wards surrounding the academy with those around Rump Island.

I clapped Max on the arm, giving him a shove to get him running with me, and he crowed like a rooster as the two of us dove straight over the edge of the cliff. We plummeted for several heart-stopping moments before his air magic swept around us and propelled us back towards the sky, shooting us out across the water and passing by the land bridge which Geraldine was creating to connect the island to the beach.

We shot over her head, and the sight of blazing wings caught my attention as Roxy took off and soared ahead of us.

"I'm gonna help Gerry," Max called. "You heading after Tory?"

"Yeah," I yelled over the rush of air, and he flicked his wrist, propelling me after my girl at a ferocious speed.

The land beneath me blurred as I sped over it, the landmarks vaguely familiar from interactions I'd witnessed from beyond The Veil, but most of it was unknown.

I began to fall as Max's magic wore off, and I cast a spray of water beneath my feet so I could slow my descent before jogging to a halt in front of the towering castle which sat in the centre of the island. Carved turrets of stone and ice stood high above the open drawbridge, the moat below making it seem as if we were crossing into a medieval tale of kings and dragons from the Mortal Realm.

Roxy landed beside me, her wings fading out of existence.

"We have the afternoon to kill before we go after the Guild Stone," she said. "Want to come paw through your old treasure and everything I stole from Lionel's trove?"

"It's here?" I asked keenly, moving towards the drawbridge which had been lowered to allow access inside.

"It is. Come on." She led the way on, and I followed her through the extravagant entrance hall and up a huge staircase decorated with all kinds of carvings and paintings of the twins. There was no doubting who had created this place, and I had to keep myself from rolling my eyes at Geraldine's theatrics.

At the top of the second flight of stairs, Roxy caught hold of my shirt and dragged me against her, capturing my lips with hers.

I gave in more than willingly, lifting her into my arms and taking hold of the backs of her thighs as she wound them around my waist.

I kissed her hard, pressing her back to the door and groaning as she rolled her hips against me, making my cock harden for her with ease. This fucking girl. *My* fucking girl.

I knocked the door open, my hunger for her as keen as always, her clothes altogether too much for all the things I had in mind.

But as we stumbled into her room and I glanced up at the roses which hung from the walls and took in the rumpled bed sheets, I broke our kiss abruptly.

"You haven't been back here since the night you left to reclaim me from death, have you?" I asked, my brow furrowing while she focused on yanking my shirt over my head and tossing it aside.

"No. Why?" Her mouth fell to my neck, and I groaned as she began kissing her way down the side of my throat, her fingernails biting into my shoulders.

"Because," I said, pushing her back despite the desperate ache in my flesh to be merged with hers. "That night, another couple came in here and fucked in your bed."

"What?" she hissed, steadying herself on her feet and turning to look at the room which was still in a state of disarray. "Who?" She stalked towards the bed angrily, gasping as she picked up a huge, glittering, Dragon cock dildo between two fingers and brandished it at me. "Who would do this?" she snarled, tossing it away from her like it was contaminated.

"Seth and Caleb," I told her, watching the way her eyes widened at the news before a bark of laughter escaped her.

"Those assholes. I knew Seth was into him, but I never realised Caleb liked him back."

"Apparently he likes him a whole hell of a lot," I replied tersely, the memory of being trapped in this room in ghost form while the two of them fucked each other senseless was pretty hard to scrub from my skull.

"How do you know? Did you watch them?" she asked. "Was it hot?"

"No, it wasn't fucking hot, Roxy. It was two of my best friends going at it in my wife's bed. It was the furthest thing from hot."

"Hmm," she said sceptically, taking hold of the edge of her blanket and tossing it back to reveal a bottle of lube and a butt plug. "Shit. They really went for it, didn't they?"

I scrubbed a hand over my face, a growl building in my throat. "Yes, they did. And they've been keeping it secret too. You know what that means, don't you?"

"Umm...that they want some privacy from the interference of assholes and probably didn't think any ghosts would be perving on them while they hooked up?" she suggested.

"I wasn't perving on them," I snapped. "And your mom and dad were here too."

"What?" she blanched, dropping the edge of the blanket and moving away from the bed. "Why do ghosts perv on the sex lives of the living?"

"They don't. It's a long story. The point of which is that my asshole friends came here and had sex in my wife's bed and have decided to keep their little affair secret from all of us. I ended up stuck here watching far more of it than I ever wanted to know about, let alone see, and I plan on getting revenge. So I'm going to let them keep their little secret. And you're going to help me fuck with them."

"Oh, I like this," she said, her eyes glimmering at that idea like I'd known they would.

"Yeah you do."

"So...as the bed is a no go, how do you feel about the closet?" She backed up slowly, stripping off her top as she went and dropping it to the floor, leaving her in a black lace bra.

"I don't think the closet is going to have the space for what I have in mind," I replied, stalking her towards the door as her fingers curled around the handle.

She opened it before I could get to her and slipped inside.

I moved after her, pushing the door wide and frowning as I found a row of clothes hanging before me, her jeans discarded on the floor in front of them and no sign of her at all.

A growl rumbled in the back of my throat. "Where are you hiding?"

"Come see for yourself." Her voice came from behind the hanging clothes, and I pushed them aside, revealing an open space beyond which was strewn with the treasure I had left in The Burrows before my death. Better yet, mixed in with my treasure was countless gold and jewels that I knew had belonged to my father before Roxy had stolen them.

"You little thief," I rumbled, closing in on her where she stood in her underwear before a mound of gold coins which was taller than her.

"Never forget it," she agreed and then I was on her.

Roxy moaned into my mouth as I kissed her, my hand fisting in her long, ebony hair as I forced her head back and sank my tongue between her lips.

Her hands roamed down my chest, teasing at the buckle for my belt, but I needed to own her in that moment. I needed to take complete control of the woman whose heart beat as one with my own.

Fire sparked from my palms and lashed itself around her wrists forming flaming chains which I bound to the walls before repeating the process with her ankles.

I stepped back, looking at her where she panted for me, watching the way her pupils dilated, and the reflection of the flames danced in her eyes. Anyone else would have burned from those chains, but not her. She relished the kiss of my fire.

I coated my fingers with flames, then reached out and caressed her throat, watching her hungrily as I trailed my fingers down the deep bronze of her flesh, burning the bra from those perfect tits and groaning as she cursed me for it.

"I fucking love it when you insult me, baby," I told her, meeting her eyes while my hand roamed lower, burning those little panties off too.

"Asshole," she said with no grit at all, and I smiled wickedly before pushing two flame-coated fingers straight inside her.

She cried out at the kiss of the fire, her wings bursting from her back as my touch almost made her lose control, and I watched her as I began to fuck her with my hand, letting more fire spill from me and commanding it to kiss her neck, her lips, her nipples.

"More," she panted while I dragged my fingers in and out of her, rolling them over her clit with each slow push into her slick core.

I let the Dragon in me come closer to the edges of my flesh and leaned in, capturing her lips with mine while Dragon Fire rolled up the back of my throat. She moaned hungrily as the heat of it washed over her tongue, the impossible strength of her Phoenix meaning she felt nothing but pleasure at the full weight of my power.

I dropped down to my knees, a subject before his queen, and let the Dragon fire roll over my tongue again right as I lapped at her core.

Roxy moaned so loudly that my cock throbbed with need, and I kept driving my fingers in and out of her while working to devour her clit. Her hips rocked against my face, her muscles straining against the hold of the chains that secured her, and I kept licking and thrusting with my fingers until she was coming all over my face, her pussy clamping tight around my fingers like she never wanted to let them go.

I growled with a desperate need of my own, the fire inside me burning hotter and the air around us shimmering with the intensity of the heat we were giving off.

I yanked on my control of the chains, moving them lower and taking hold of her body as I guided her down to lie on the mound of coins before me, her wings splayed beneath her like some fallen angel.

I kept her limbs wide, biting down on my bottom lip as I let my gaze roam over every naked inch of her flesh. Her chest was rising and falling rapidly, her tits full and nipples tight with need. The gleaming wetness of her pussy had me groaning, and I gave up any intention of dragging this on for longer.

I shoved my pants down and thrust into her with one sharp, violent movement which had her name spilling from my lips and a cry of pure bliss echoing from hers.

She yanked on the chains, but I held her firmly, rearing back and watching her as I knelt between her thighs and fucked her hard and deep. I watched my cock sinking into her over and over again, my fingers biting into the perfect curve of her ass as I drove myself in to the hilt and stole her breath with every thrust.

Her wings flexed beneath her, black hair spilling over the gold coins and her eyes on me, drinking me in like she never wanted this to end either.

I grew frantic, pumping my hips harder, faster, meeting those green eyes which held me entirely at their mercy while I fucked her like a heathen and felt her break beneath me.

She swore loudly as she came again, and I released a Dragon's roar as I came too, the tight pulses of her pussy claiming every drop from me as I filled her with my cum and marked her as mine all over again.

"Fuck you," she panted beneath me while I could do little more than smirk down at her in pure masculine satisfaction. This creature of mine. This dream I had claimed. The beautiful thief of my heart.

+·(·(·●·(·●·◉·●·)·●·)·)·+

The night pressed in thickly around us, so deep that even the aid of my Dragon gifts did little to pierce the darkness as we closed in on the FIB impound.

We had split into two groups, and I was with Roxy and Caleb trying to disable everything which had been put in place to keep us out of here. Roxy had said she was the best equipped to get us into the place due to the illegal nature of our task which she claimed to have far more experience in than us. I couldn't say it was entirely untrue, but I knew she was mostly enjoying pulling the queen card on us whenever she could.

"You done with the wards yet?" Roxy hissed in the darkness, and I gritted my teeth while I ignored her, focusing on the wards that me and Caleb were trying to deactivate instead.

The magic was complex and intricate. There were alarms and trips built into countless layers of it, meaning that simply breaking them open with brute force wouldn't work. This was the FIB, not some low-life thug's Killblaze stash we were trying to gain access to.

Caleb's magic butted up against mine, nudging subtly as he detected a crack I hadn't spotted and I nodded at him – though he likely couldn't see it in the darkness – and eased our combined power into it.

A snap sounded faintly and I released a slow breath as I felt the wards parting, a gap opening up which we would be able to slip through unnoticed.

"Done," Caleb announced. "So how are you going to deal with the fences?"

The FIB had installed high electric fences which ringed this entire area for miles. At the centre of the giant compound was a mountain like no other. It was carved from the inside out into an impenetrable fortress that required a seriously high level of security access to enter.

Flying over these fences was out of the question because of the magical wards doming above this place, and if the twins broke through them, an alert would be set off that drew every emergency FIB unit across Solaria to this very spot. And the key here was to gain access without them realising we'd done it. So we were breaking in a little more subtly, and as the fences were coated in sensors as a second layer of protection for this place, that was where Roxy's knowledge outweighed ours. This was mortal security, not the kind of thing many Fae bothered with and no doubt precisely why the FIB had decided to include it in theirs. Not many Fae would know how to get around such a thing, but Roxy's pastime of stealing motorcycles from people with a whole lot of money made her pretty well versed in such things.

Roxy led the way across the grass to the fence line and paused as she surveyed a metal box set against the ground beside it.

She prised it open carefully then began doing something to the mess of wires inside.

"How long will this take?" Caleb asked as the seconds dragged into minutes, and a muffled thump echoed from somewhere inside the compound.

"Not as long as getting fucked by a Werewolf," she muttered.

"What?" he asked, his head snapping around to look at her and I smirked.

"Longer than getting fucked by a Vampire though I'd say," I added thoughtfully. "You know, because of the speed thing."

I felt his eyes on me but I innocently looked up at the cloud-covered sky like I was hunting for a star among the darkness.

"That's not a thing," Caleb grunted.

"So you think the Werewolf would finish first?" Roxy asked curiously, her head still inside the box, a faint glow from her Faelight illuminating one side of her straight face. She was damn good at this.

"He...what...I dunno. How would I know that?" Caleb asked, glancing at me again, and I shrugged.

"Voila," Roxy interrupted, and the constant buzz of the electric fence suddenly fell silent around us. "Time to go."

She got to her feet and hurried away into the darkness and I followed right behind her, ignoring the way Caleb was staring after us and heading straight towards the action. I didn't know what it was going to take to claim this Guild Stone but one way or another, I was determined to see it done tonight.

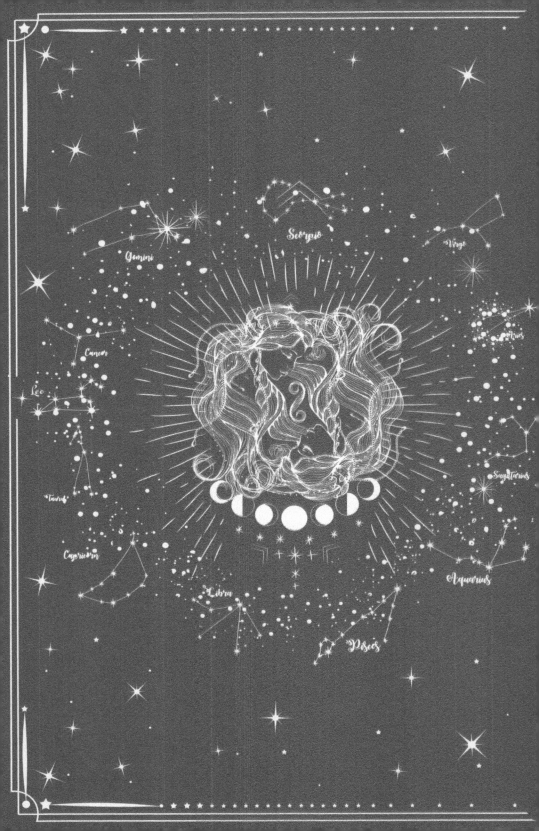

DARCY

CHAPTER FOURTEEN

"Are you sure you didn't overdo it on the Faesine?" I asked Seth suspiciously. He'd brought a serious amount of the extremely flammable liquid with him, and Geraldine was now prancing around, pouring it all over the place like a pixie in the long grass. Max was up in a tree, his arrow aimed out into the FIB compound that surrounded the towering mountain where all the contraband in Solaria was contained.

"I brought just the right amount," Seth insisted. "Trust me."

"Just don't go setting the world on fire," I said with a grin.

"I'll leave that to the Phoenix," he said.

Orion appeared in a blur, casually pushing his hair back into place as he came to an abrupt halt beside me. "I did a full circuit, there's nothing out of place. There's no extra FIB units here, and I heard one of the guards say a bunch of agents are off sick with Fae flu. We picked the perfect night to strike."

"The stars must be favouring us for once," I said, glancing up at the shimmering little assholes, wondering if this was what it was like not to be cursed by a vengeful star called Clyde.

Maybe the other stars were making up for him being a dick, or maybe there were more hidden dangers here that we weren't yet aware of. I was gonna take the optimistic viewpoint. At least until I was proven wrong.

Caleb appeared in a rush of movement, his shoulder brushing Orion's as he stopped. "Fence is breached. Tory and Darius are waiting for you. We'll get the fire cooking here."

"Hell yes," Seth said excitedly.

"Patrol moving this way," Max called.

We had a solid silencing bubble around us all, so I wasn't worried about being overheard, but the loudness of his voice still made me look towards the fence in preparation of a fight.

"Let's get moving," Orion said, taking a step toward me.

"Keep them busy as long as you can," I encouraged.

"It shall be a bosom of a blaze, dear Darcy," Geraldine said as she jogged back over with a jerry can swinging from her fist.

"Good luck," I said, then let Orion sweep me into his arms, and Geraldine saluted me before bowing low.

I watched over Orion's shoulder as Caleb released a blaze of fire from his hands and the grass went up with a whoosh of heat. The flames soared up ten feet and kept climbing, the Faesine catching alight in great blazes. If that didn't draw the FIB's attention, I didn't know what would.

Orion made it to the gap in the fence where Tory and Darius were waiting, using a concealment spell to stay hidden in the shadows.

"Seth went overboard on the Faesine, didn't he?" Darius said, looking out to where the fire was now spinning in a wild vortex.

"I feel like I shouldn't have put him in charge of it," I said thoughtfully.

"Definitely a bad choice," Darius snorted, then moved to climb onto Orion's back while I remained in his arms.

Orion manoeuvred me under one arm and Tory stepped closer with a scowl. "This is the part where I pretend to be your man-bag, isn't it?"

"Come on," Orion goaded. "Get under my arm like a good little purse."

Tory let him tuck her into place and he shot forward with the full propulsion of his speed. I lost sight of everything, the whole world a frantic blur, the red and gold fire becoming a haze.

Orion slowed to a halt, setting us down and Darius jumped off his back, clapping him on the shoulder. "Good boy. I'll give you a sugar lump later."

"And I'll shove it up your ass," Orion said dryly.

We'd arrived in front of a looming silver door in the shape of a triangle that was carved into the base of the mountain. Four more triangles sat in a vertical line on its surface, two facing up and two down, a line striking through two of the points so that each represented an Element. I stepped closer with my hand raised, no tingle of magic caressing my palm. The wards were down and it looked like whatever held this door locked might have shattered too.

"Blue," Orion warned as I stepped even nearer.

"She's got this," Tory said lightly.

"We should assess this door before we go blindly touching it," Orion growled.

"Agreed," Darius said.

"It looks like the House symbols, what if we just need to cast Elemental magic at it?" I suggested and Xavier spoke up in my earpiece for the first time.

"Sounds like a good bet. I think I saw four symbols on the floor too."

I glanced down at the ground, finding he was right, and they were a little worn, showing where Fae had stood in the past.

"I'd bet my ass we need to cast all four at once," Tory said keenly.

I went to lay my palm on the door and Orion shot forward, capturing my wrist and giving me a stern look. "*Don't.*"

I smiled innocently and he looked down, finding my other hand now on it instead.

"Why must you be so reckless?" he sighed, but a smile touched the corner of his lips.

"I guess it's the Savage King's blood in me," I said.

"I don't know. After meeting your mother, I'd say *she* gives you both the reckless streak," Darius said causally like it was nothing, but Tory and I both turned to him with looks of longing. "I'll tell you more about it when we're done here. Now come on. Let's go claim some treasure."

I moved to stand on the air symbol in front of the door while Tory took earth, Orion stood on water and Darius stood on fire.

We all raised our hands and Xavier ran a countdown in our ears.

"Three, two, one-"

We blasted our chosen Elements at the door, Darius's fire twisting into a tornado as it mixed with my air before Orion's water doused it, and all that remained was a beautiful rose vine crawling up the centre of the door.

Each triangle illuminated at once, red for fire, green for earth, white for air and blue for water.

"Now the last bit, quickly," Xavier urged, and Orion took Francesca's ring from his pocket.

He held it up just as a blast of light emitted from the door, scanning us from head to toe and making Francesca's ring illuminate. The light faded away and we held our breaths while we waited to see if we might be granted access.

Xavier whistled low in my ear as the huge triangular door lowered inward like a drawbridge, revealing a cavernous passage beyond, and relief scattered through me. Shit, we'd really done it.

A deep groaning noise rumbled from somewhere deep within the belly of the mountain and a shiver rolled down my spine.

"It's just the wind," Tory said, walking confidently inside.

I jogged to catch up, taking in the gleaming minerals running through the towering walls either side of us. The roof of this cavern was so high that the ceiling was lost to shadow.

"Or a monster," Darius said, drawing his Phoenix fire axe and striding after us with Orion.

The door slammed shut at our backs with a deafening boom that set my heart pounding. I expected darkness to consume us, but the minerals in the walls glittered with a mysterious blue glow, allowing enough light that we didn't need to cast any more.

"Turn right at the end of this tunnel," Xavier directed.

When we reached the fork in the path, we followed his direction, heading down a narrower path with equally high walls either side of us. It was cold in here, the chill biting my exposed skin and I willed fire into my veins to chase it away.

Even though we trod with care, our footsteps were painfully loud, every sound amplified in the empty space.

A continuous roaring noise was growing up ahead, like the rush of an immense amount of water.

"There should be a stairway at the end of this passage and your first security barrier," Xavier said.

It wasn't long before we made it there and I stared up in awe at the colossal waterfall tumbling down through the centre of a spiralling staircase that twisted up around the walls like a coiled python. It was wide enough for a giant to walk comfortably up it, but for us it was going to be one hell of a climb. At least the steps were of a normal size.

A wide bubbling pool of dark water sat far below us where the falling water crashed into it, and I could barely hear anything over the cacophony of noise.

Orion waved his hand and a silencing bubble spread out around the waterfall, stealing away the sound of it in an instant.

"Francesca had clearance for this area but there's a security barrier by the first step," Xavier said.

Tory and I moved forward to assess it and one shared glance with her told me she was thinking exactly what I was. I stepped forward and Phoenix fire burst to life in my palm, the red and blue flames twisting together in a hypnotic dance. The sense of magic buzzed right in front of me and I let my power break free in a fiery inferno.

My flames scored right through the barrier, dissolving it in a crackle of sparks, leaving the way forward wide open.

"Too easy," Tory said.

"It's almost like they want us to walk in and steal all their treasure," I said, the two of us sharing a smile before we started up the stone stairs.

"You do realise you just cut through some of the most powerful wards the FIB are capable of conjuring?" Orion called.

"And it was likely reinforced by the top FIB officers' magic," Darius added.

"They should really work on that," I replied. "Anyone could come walking in here."

"No, there are only two Fae who could manage that," Orion said, and I glanced back at him, finding him close on my heels.

We forged on, and my legs burned as we climbed ever higher, the stairway seemingly endless, twisting away up into the highest regions of the mountain.

"How high are we going, Xavier?" Darius asked. "This is taking too long."

"Erm, like, fifty floors?" Xavier said, and Tory cursed.

"Fuck that." Darius tossed his axe to Orion and started stripping, bundling his clothes up into a ball and handing them over too. He threw himself off the side of the stairway and we hurried to the edge to watch as he shifted into his stunning golden Dragon form, beating his wings and doing a circuit of the waterfall before flying up beside us, letting out a growl that was a clear command for us to jump on.

Orion grabbed Tory and I, flinging us toward him with a burst of speed followed by a blast of air at our backs, and I let out a whoop as we landed on Darius's back.

Tory sat in front of me, and I gripped her waist while Orion held me from behind, all of us sliding back an inch as Darius flew upwards.

My stomach lurched and adrenaline pounded through me as he spiralled up around the waterfall, his wings reflecting the pale blue light that emitted from the walls.

"Almost there," Xavier called, and Darius's wings beat slower.

Wide archways led off to endless passages along the stairway, and Xavier guided us toward one with a glittering raven symbol above it.

Darius flew straight through it, his wingtips just grazing the walls either side of us, but the passage was growing rapidly narrower, and he was soon forced to land.

We dismounted quickly then Darius shifted back, dressing in the clothes Orion handed him. We continued on through the cavern, the floor sloping down beneath our feet and leading us to a fork in the path, one passage on the left and one on the right, both as dark as the other.

"Xavier?" I asked.

"Hang on," he said in our ears. "This doesn't seem right. Maybe you took the wrong passage."

"We're just following your orders," Darius said.

"Are you sure it had the raven symbol above it?"

"Pretty sure," Darius said.

"Pretty sure or one hundred percent sure?" Xavier said, both of them getting annoyed with the other.

"Pretty sure. Like I said," Darius grunted.

"This isn't helping," Orion stepped in. "I'll shoot back and check the symbol."

"Wait, we shouldn't split up," I said.

"I'll be back in less than five seconds, beautiful," he said with a roguish grin, then ran forward several steps, awkwardly slowing to a halt when he didn't really go anywhere. "Fuck." He twisted around, his eyes snapping to a place above my head.

We followed his line of sight to a vent and Darius swore.

"Order suppressant gas," I said in frustration, trying to call on my Phoenix, but it was dormant inside me.

"And a camera." Tory pointed out the tiny little black device above the vent, offering it her middle finger. "They're watching, and they're trying to trap us."

"Let's go back," I said urgently, but as the words passed my lips, a tremor ran through the floor, rumbling right through my bones.

A flash of movement in my periphery made me wheel around, and my breath hitched at the sight of five giant globs of pulsing liquid speeding toward us from the direction we'd come.

I cast a wall of solid earth across the passage and Tory solidified it with a blast of heat, baking it in place. But it wasn't enough. The strange globs slammed through it, sending dirt flying everywhere as they wheeled along on a collision course with us.

"They're aqueous Faetraps," Orion gasped in realisation, then blasted air at them to try and hold them back.

Me and Tory joined him while Darius targeted one with a tumult of ferocious flames, but nothing worked. They didn't slow at all. We turned to run, but it was already too late and the first of the Faetraps collided with Tory, the entire thing encasing her, whipping her away down the tunnel to the left.

"Tory!" I screamed, but another one slammed into me and I just caught sight of Orion and Darius snared in their own traps as I was carried along at a tremendous pace.

The sticky substance was so thick, I could hardly move, wheeling end over end as the trap sped along. I suddenly collided with Orion's trap and mine went spinning off course, darting down the right passage instead of the left. I began fighting with everything I had to get free. I couldn't breathe, and I could hardly see anything as the suffocating trap pressed against my skin.

Magic burned at my palms as I fought to get out, but it was being absorbed by the liquid like a sponge, no scrap of it making any difference.

My gut dropped suddenly and I sensed I'd just plummeted over a ledge, bright lights wheeling around me. Fear captured my heart, and I desperately tried to cast air, certain I was about to hit the ground.

The Faetrap slammed into a hard stone floor and exploded around me in a spray of thick gloop. It had taken so much of the impact that my knees hit the ground without even breaking the skin, and I found myself surrounded by twelve FIB officers, the biggest of them all aiming a sparking stun gun right at me.

I raised my hands to show my surrender, putting on an innocent expression, and a thick glob of the Faetrap slid from my hair, landing wetly at the feet of the closest officer. He was a brute of a man, twice my size with eyes as hard as granite. "Hands above your head. Make one wrong move and I'll fry you." He held the stun gun close to my face, the crackle of electricity making my cheek tingle.

I lifted my hands higher, taking in the circular chamber I was in, one large silver door to my left and another to my right. There were shelves climbing the walls, and gleaming items filled them, each one sitting above a number.

The big guy stepped closer, taking a pair of magic blocking cuffs from his hip. "Don't make a single move, Princess."

"Queen, actually," I corrected, not breaking eye contact.

He scoffed, but a few of the agents shared glances, shifting nervously from one foot to the other.

"Careful, Captain," one man warned the big guy. "You saw what they did to that Nebula Inquisition Centre."

"That wasn't us," I hissed.

"Who was it then?" the captain goaded. "Two other Phoenix twins? I didn't realise the kingdom had such an infestation." He lunged for my left wrist, but I was faster, a whip of air plucking the stun gun from his other hand and ramming it straight into his dick.

He screamed as the electricity poured into him, his legs giving out so that he crashed to the floor, twitching and jerking.

I was on my feet before a single other officer could make a move toward me, but the few seconds of time I'd bought myself evaporated. A strong-looking woman came at me next, striking a vine at me like a whip. It latched around my arm, but fire bloomed along my skin, blasting out from me in all directions, forcing all the agents to shield or dive for cover.

"Grab her!" the woman barked as she came at me again, and two more assholes raced for me from behind, air magic tearing from them and trying to pull my arms behind my back.

"For the Dragon King!" a man cried behind me, and I snatched one arm free from his air, blasting ice at him and freezing him on the spot. I whirled around, throwing fire out in a swirl that forced the line of FIB agents there to run for cover.

The woman slammed into me from behind, opting for brute force as she grabbed my wrists and shouted at the others to help her.

I willed my skin to become so hot that it scalded her and she leapt back with a yelp, not quick enough to dodge as I twisted around, my fire-coated fist coming up and slamming straight between her eyes. She stumbled backwards with a cry and I pressed my advantage, binding her in vines, gagging her with leaves and sending her flying up towards the ceiling to hang there kicking and thrashing.

A copper haired man came at me next, blades of ice cast in his fists which he slashed at me with terrifying precision. I cast a silver shield against my arm, taking the brunt of the strikes, but with a wild slash, he slit open my cheek. I growled, casting a plain metal sword in my grip and using the training Queen Avalon had taught me at the Palace of Flames to get him on the back foot.

A woman lunged at me from behind, locking her arms around my neck along with several vines binding her arms in place as she worked to choke me.

I struck at the copper-haired man time and again as I fought for breath, the agent casting a shield of ice to protect him, but my blade cracked it once, twice, then shattered it.

My vision was clouding and I snarled, setting a fire blazing along the arms of the woman trying to choke me. She screamed wildly, her vines burned to ash as she fell to the ground. I lunged forward, holding my sword to the throat of the copper-haired man before he could strike at me again, and he gasped, raising his hands in surrender. I bound him in vines along with the woman I'd knocked off my back, sending them both sailing up to the ceiling with their comrade.

A shriek alerted me to my next attacker and a woman collided with me from the side, slashing two ice blades at me with precision. I lurched away, hardening my skin with a layer of metal just as those sharp blades struck against my flesh, and they shattered on impact.

I grabbed her wrist before she could get away, fire blazing from my palm and spiralling up her arm, making her scream bloody murder. Water slammed into my chest, throwing me off her and making me stagger back so violently that I had to use air to right myself. I wheeled around as she retreated to heal the burn on her arm, and suddenly the rest of the agents all ran for me as one.

In a burst of decision, I stole all the oxygen from the room, lifting a hand to my mouth to cast a bubble of air there just for me.

Everyone except the air Elementals panicked, their hands flying to their throats, while the three with air created breathing bubbles like mine. I didn't give them a second to help the others, engaging all three of them by blasting fireballs their way, forcing them to defend themselves while their friends slowly passed out.

One of them cast a fist from air that slammed into me from every direction and my lip split as I caught a bash to the face. I cursed as I tasted blood, sending a barrage of my own air their way and pinning the man to the wall, my Element far superior to his. He winced under my onslaught but couldn't get free, and I sent him flying up to the ceiling, bound and gagged with the others.

I snared another of the Air Elementals, casting her skyward as well while the others all lost consciousness. Then I prowled toward the final man still standing who had grey hair and a small frame, the bubble of air around his mouth still intact. His hands dropped as he stared at me with terror in his eyes and he suddenly fell to his knees, flattening himself to the ground at my feet in a bow. "All hail the True Queens! I'll serve you from now until my dying breath. My allegiance is yours."

My eyebrows arched in surprise, and I glanced around at the unconscious officers on the floor, to the captain who was twitching under the onslaught of the stun gun still pinned to his dick by my air magic.

"Blue!" Orion's voice carried from beyond the left door.

"Darcy?!" Tory yelled, and relief filled me at knowing they were alright.

"If you're mine to command, then open that door," I ordered the FIB agent.

He scurried over to it on his hands and knees, fumbling with some keys on his belt, dropping them twice before he managed to get one into the keyhole, then pressed his hand to a magical signature detector on it too. The door slid open and Orion shot into the room, his fangs bared and a look of manic rage about him. He took in the carnage with a sweeping glance, then grabbed hold of the grey-haired man on the floor, lifting him up and pinning him to the wall.

"Did this one draw that blood on you, beautiful?" he growled as Tory stepped into the room, taking in the agents with a grin.

"No, p-please!" the agent wailed as Orion snarled at him.

"He didn't do anything to me. And he bowed," I said, but Orion didn't drop him. "Where's Darius?"

"There's a huge gold nugget back there. He's trying to carry it," Tory said in amusement.

"How did you get free of those Faetraps?" I asked, wiping more of the gloop out of my hair.

"We fell into a pit," Tory said with a grimace. "We got out just as the FIB made it there, and Orion and I pushed them all down there with air. Darius cast flames across the top to keep them nice and warm until someone comes to get them."

"Good." My gaze slid to Orion who still looked like he was considering ripping the agent's throat out. "Lance," I said, moving to grip his arm where he still had the man pinned to the wall. "Drop him."

He reluctantly released him, and the man hit the floor, flopping down into another dramatic bow and remaining there at my feet.

Orion lifted his hand, capturing my cheek with a growl in his throat, his thumb gently running along the cut to heal it before touching my lip to heal that too. "Which one did this?"

"I dealt with it," I said, though he didn't seem satisfied with that, looking from one fallen officer to another as if he might find some clue as to who had hurt me. "We need to move. They'll send reinforcements soon." I tapped the earpiece in my ear. "Anyone heard from Xavier?"

"I don't think the earpieces work this deep in the mountain," Tory said with a frown, tapping her own.

The sound of Darius grunting and huffing came from beyond the door and he stepped through it, trying to pull a gigantic golden nugget after him, but there was no way it was going to squeeze through the doorway.

Tory took his hand, forcing him to look at her. "That isn't going to fit through, Darius. You need to leave it."

"She's right, man," Orion said. "You've gotta let it go."

Darius looked between them in anger like he was trying to find a way to refute their logic. "But it's *mine*."

"It can be yours. But it has to stay here." Tory tiptoed up to kiss him and he gripped her waist, distracted from the gold by the girl who was far more precious to him than it. When they parted, he turned away from it, but tension still lined his arms.

I nudged the bowing agent with my boot. "Hey, we need to find something in here. Can you help us?"

"What are you looking for, my Queen?" he asked, his voice muffled by the stone floor.

"It's either an amethyst or aquamarine stone," I said.

Orion crouched down, fisting his hand in the guy's hair and tugging to force his neck back at an awkward angle so he could look him in the eye. "It would be the most perfect stone of its kind. Polished in an oval shape."

The man swallowed hard. "Rathmaron," he whispered in terror.

"What does that mean?" Orion demanded.

"Rathmaron took it," he whispered, his lower lip quivering. "He took all the gemstones."

"Who is that?" Tory pushed. "And took them where?"

"We call it the Void," he choked out. "A place under the mountain, buried so deep that no sunlight has ever seen the inside of it. Rathmaron came from there one day, many years back now. He's a monster of the earth, a creature long thought extinct that creeps between the crevices of the under land. We had to seal it off after he started feasting on the officers." He shuddered. "Rathmaron's venom paralyses you, but you stay awake through it all." He whimpered. "The only thing you can do is scream, and oh how they screamed. For days, it went on. We tried to rescue them but more were taken. So the captain ordered us to seal it off while the beast was...feeding."

"Well Rathmaron sounds like a fucking delight." Orion dropped the man's head and it cracked against the stone.

"Ow," he whispered.

"Take us to him," I commanded.

"No!" he cried, gazing up at me in terror then looking to Tory. "I must insist you stay away from there. You cannot go to the Void, or you will never come back."

"We'll take our chances," Tory said. "Now get moving, we're running out of time."

He scrambled to his feet, hanging his head in submission.

"What's your name?" I asked.

"Bertie Betchino," he said, glancing up at me with a shy smile. "I always was a fan of you both. But when the Dragon King took over...well, we didn't have much choice."

"Forget the life story," Darius snapped. "Move."

Bertie nodded, hurrying to the other door and opening it quickly.

"Wait, you'll want these." He rummaged in his pocket, producing a sheath of leather and rolling it open to unveil a row of syringes. "It will cure you of the Order suppressant."

I eyed the syringes suspiciously. "How do we know you're not trying to trick us?"

Orion plucked one out of the sheath, flicked off the lid and stabbed Bertie in the neck with it, pressing his thumb down on the plunger.

"Ah!" Bertie cried in alarm, but it was too late and we all waited to see what would happen. "S-see?"

"Well at least it's not poison," Orion said, grabbing one for himself and injecting his arm.

I cursed under my breath as we waited to see what would happen. A beat later, he bared his fangs at us in a satisfied smile, and we all took a syringe, injecting ourselves with the serum.

My Phoenix came to life again with a flourish of heat racing through my skin and a tingle down my spine saying my wings would come at my call.

"This way then," Bertie said ominously before stepping into the dark.

Orion shot after him, keeping close as if he expected the guy to betray us – which was entirely possible to be fair.

We followed him through a few winding passages before we arrived on the edge of a yawning chasm of sheer grey rock. A bronze platform hung from thick chains before us, a winch high above telling me that this was the way down.

"I will operate the winch," Bertie said. "This will take you all the way down. You'll have to break the seal if you truly mean to go into the Void."

Orion gripped the guy by the back of the neck, launching him onto the platform straight ahead of us and he went rolling across it with a yell of fright, the whole thing swaying precariously beneath him.

"You're taking us all the way there, Bertie," Orion warned. "You wanna serve your queens? Then get serving them."

My mate turned to me, offering me his hand like he was some gentleman from a period drama, not a heathen who'd just thrown a man ten feet. I took it, letting him guide me over the gap onto the platform even though we both knew I didn't need the help. His intense gaze followed me, the silver rings in his irises burning bright and bringing a smile to my lips.

Tory joined me on the platform, releasing her wings as she gazed over the platform's edge, and Darius followed.

Bertie flicked a finger, casting air to get the winch moving and the platform jolted ominously before starting its descent.

There were gaps in the metal at my feet, giving me a view deep down into the pit beneath us, the sheer walls either side of us dropping away endlessly. If I hadn't had faith in my magic and wings, I might have been freaking out right now. No mortal in their right mind would step on this thing.

The chains clinked and the contraption groaned, the sounds all too loud, and I quickly cast a silencing bubble around us in case Rathmaron was listening.

"Good thinking," Bertie said thickly. "We think that thing hunts by sound. It's got no eyes."

"The Vegas destroyed a hoard of monsters attacking the academy just days ago, one more will hardly pose a challenge, especially with me here to help them," Darius said, and Bertie turned to him, his eyes suddenly narrowing.

"Hang on... I recognise you," he said, stepping closer in disbelief.

"Not likely," Darius said, even though he was pretty damn recognisable considering his size, his connection to a certain lizard king and the fact that his face had been all over the media for years.

"You...you're dead," Bertie gasped, confusion skewing his features.

"And I'd like to stay dead a while longer. *Never speak my name, never refer to me, never tell anyone you saw me alive,*" Darius's Coercion slammed into Bertie, and he stumbled back, clearly not ready to shield himself or perhaps not strong enough to stop him.

Bertie frowned, thumbing a wedding band on his hand. "Bob wouldn't believe this."

"Who's Bob?" I asked, feeling a bit bad for the guy who we were leading into a place that clearly terrified him.

"My husband. He died many, many years ago. We were only married a year before the accident." He cleared his throat. "I never really got over that."

"I'm sorry," I said, offering him a sympathetic pat on the arm.

"She's not your therapist," Orion growled, glaring at Bertie.

Bertie hung his head with a nod, and I shot Orion a stare that told him not to be a dick.

"I think I can see the bottom," Tory called, stepping right up to the edge and balancing on her tiptoes, her wings beating a little to hold her there.

She glanced back at me over her shoulder, and I grinned as I read what she wanted in her expression. I let my wings fly loose then ran straight for her, pushing her so the two of us went tumbling over the edge of the platform.

We free-fell in a spiral, and I kept a silencing bubble tight around us as laughter bubbled up from our throats. Our wings spread wide and we released each other's hands, chasing each other in circles as we descended the final hundred feet to the bottom of the pit.

We landed lightly, still smiling as we looked up at the platform above.

"Come on, baby, let's go flying," Orion said, then he threw himself at Darius, locking his arms around him before the two of them plummeted off the edge.

Orion let them fall like a damn stone, tumbling towards certain death at a wild speed. My fingers tingled, my own magic ready to save them if he failed, but Orion cast air at the last second, stopping them abruptly. Darius cursed him as he stepped out of his hold, but a grin twisted the corner of his mouth as if he'd secretly enjoyed it.

We moved to the edge of the cavern where a passage led away into the dark, the crackle of magic against my skin telling me there was a seriously powerful ward cast there.

The platform descended and Bertie crept off of it, pale with terror as he eyed the passage. "I'll just, um, wait here for you to return."

"Don't go running for backup, Bertie," Tory warned, casting a chain from earth magic and tethering the platform to the ground.

"I meant it when I bowed," Bertie said, lifting his chin. "I will serve you well, my Queens."

"Yeah, we're not gonna take any chances on that though," I said, then raised my hand, urging the Shadow Beast to come out of the ring and silvery grey smoke coiled from it before he materialised. The giant, bear-like creature grunted happily at me and I smiled, tickling him under the chin in greeting.

"What in the hundred realms is that?!" Bertie cried.

"Can you keep an eye on our friend," I asked the beast, and he seemingly understood, trotting over to sit on the platform, the whole thing groaning under his weight.

Bertie ran to the opposite side of it, staring at the Shadow Beast in horror.

"He won't hurt you if you don't hurt him," I said, and Bertie's wide eyes turned on me, but he seemed unable to form a sentence, so I left him to it.

Tory and I stood in front of the wards, taking each other's hands and letting the roar of our Phoenix flames burn between us. The power of it all gave me a headrush and I let the fire wind around my free hand as I prepared to burn down the seal with my twin. At a squeeze of our clasped fingers, we both unleashed hell upon the magical barrier, ripping through it like it was paper, the immensity of the magic setting the hairs rising along my arms.

I released a breath when it was done, letting the flames die but keeping my wings out as we walked into the cave with Orion and Darius on our heels.

The passage opened up and revealed a network of large tunnels heading off in multiple direction. Above us, the cavern arched up to a sloped ceiling and I could just make out strange shapes in the gloom. I cast a Faelight, sending it up there to see better, and my heart stuttered as an enormous web was revealed, and hanging from it were glistening cocoons.

"I guess that's where the FIB agents ended up," I said thickly, noticing a boot poking out of one of the cocoons.

Tory shuddered. "That shit's freaky."

"So we're dealing with a blind spider that hunts by sound," I said with a grimace. "How hard can that be to kill?"

"Judging by the amount of dead FIB up there, beautiful?" Orion said lightly.

"I'm guessing pretty fucking hard. You know, come to think of it, I think Francesca mentioned this creature a while back…"

My heart tugged at the mention of her name, the memory of Lionel viciously killing her making me shut my eyes to try and force the image away. But with my eyes shut, the darkness deepened, flashes of blood and shadow striking a blade through my skull. My breaths came quicker, and it was only the touch of Tory's hand to mine that jolted me back to the present.

"You good?" she whispered, and I nodded, grounding myself in her company.

"Let's kill this monster and find the stone," I said determinedly, refusing to let those memories get their claws in me.

"I found it," Darius called.

We turned to find him scaling the freaking wall, climbing toward the web above with a Faelight hovering beside him. I followed his unblinking gaze to a cocoon hanging from the ceiling that glittered as the light touched it, the thing lumpy and misshapen like it might not hold a body at all.

"Better hurry up, brother." Orion cast air beneath himself, gliding smoothly up to the cocoon and making Darius growl as he heaved himself higher at a faster pace.

Tory and I watched as Orion made it there first, then severed the silky threads which held it aloft. Darius swung for it as he made it high enough, but the cocoon plummeted to the ground, crashing in front of us and exploding in a shower of gemstones.

"Holy shit." I crouched down, sifting through them one after the other, searching for one that fit the description of a Guild Stone.

"Get off those," Darius barked. "I'll do it. You wouldn't know a gemstone from a grape, little shrew."

"Don't you call me a shrew," I clipped, continuing my hunt while Tory dropped down to help. Though I secretly kinda liked the shrew nickname, but not when he was calling me incompetent in the same sentence.

When Darius was low enough, he leapt to the ground and came striding over to us, dropping to his knees and gathering the gemstones away from us in great armfuls.

"We'll find it quicker if we work together," I insisted.

"You're going full Dragon, Darius," Tory teased.

I glanced up to look for Orion, frowning when I didn't spot him by the web and pushing to my feet.

"Lance?" I called, my wings beating as I flew up to find him.

My skin prickled as I came close to the web, careful not to touch any of the sticky strands. More tunnels were carved into the walls up here, and my pulse ticked a little faster as I sought out Orion in the gloom.

"Lance," I hissed more urgently.

Scuffling, thudding noises carried from one of the tunnels and I flew toward it fast, sending a Faelight out ahead of me.

"Did you find him?" Darius called, but all words fell still on my lips as the light sailed deeper into the tunnel.

A monstrous spider had Lance in its pincers, his mouth gagged with thick, silky threads, his hands bound by them too, his magic clearly immobilised by the web. His fists slammed into the beast instead, his powerful blows cracking hard against the spider, but each punch seemed to grow less fierce, his limbs weakening by the second.

A bloody welt on his neck showed the place where the spider had bitten him, and a scream of purest fury left me as I unleashed my Phoenix fire, making it dagger along the tunnel roof and slam down into the spider's head.

It shrieked in agony, releasing Lance and retreating into the tunnels with a scuttling noise made by its feet.

I flew forward, hearing the others yelling far behind me as I dropped down beside

Lance and pressed my hand to the wound on his neck. It healed over fast, but he was growing stiller by the second, his limbs going rigid under the power of the spider's venom.

"I've got you," I promised, drawing a dagger and working to cut the silken strands from his mouth. They were so tough, each thread had to be cut individually and I cursed as I worked to free him as fast as possible.

"Darcy!" Tory's voice made me turn and I saw her hovering below the web beyond the passage.

A shadow loomed above her and I cried out as the giant spider leapt from a tunnel above, slamming into her and knocking her out of sight.

My heart roared in fright, and I gave up on freeing Lance, wrapping him in a dome of air and making him fly after me as I raced out of the tunnel to help my twin. I leapt from the edge, my wings wide and Lance at my back as we swept towards the ground.

Tory was fighting furiously, up on her feet with her right arm raised and fire blazing from her fingers, but a welt on her left arm said she hadn't avoided a bite.

Darius was moving to intercept it too, ice shards tearing from him and ripping into the creature's side. It shrieked, blocking some of them with its huge pincers, but blackish blood oozed from its wounds.

I released a rain of hellfire myself, the red and blue flames forging a Phoenix bird that swooped down beneath me and struck the spider's hideous face.

Tory dropped to one knee, her teeth gritted and her flames still joining mine, but I could see the venom taking root in her, and fear dashed against my heart.

I cast a spear in my hand just as I landed on the spider's back and slammed it straight through its head, the impact reverberating through my limbs. Tory's flames licked my boots, consuming the beast and making sure the job was well and truly finished.

I leapt onto the ground in front of her, laying Lance down at her side, my pulse thrashing with terror.

Darius caught Tory's arm before she collapsed completely, lifting her into his arms. I hurried to heal the bite mark and met Darius's gaze.

"We need antivenom," I said urgently.

"Bryan will know." He took off out of the passage in the direction Bertie was waiting for us and I raced after him, carrying Orion after me on a gust of air.

We made it back to the FIB agent and the Shadow Beast came bounding forward, licking my cheek in greeting. I darted past him and Bertie gasped as he spotted Tory and Lance.

"Antivenom," Darius boomed.

Bertie nodded frantically. "It's not far. I'll take you to it. Hurry now."

I jumped onto the platform with the others and the Shadow Beast bounded after us, his weight making the metal creak. I cast air beneath us, not waiting for Bertie to sort the pully system and making us ascend at a terrifying speed.

The moment we made it to the top of the chasm, Darius kicked Bertie in the ass to get him moving and we raced after him into the passage with the Shadow Beast rushing along behind us.

Bertie led us through the maze of tunnels before finally opening a door and leading us into what looked like a break room, the only hint that we were still in the mountain the glittering cave walls around it. There were cosy armchairs, thick rugs, a coffee machine, and even a couple of bunk beds.

Bertie ran to the fridge, yanking it open and taking out a handful of syringes. I grabbed them from him, and he directed me as I gently slid the needle into Tory's arm and gave her the antivenom. I laid Orion on a nearby couch, doing the same for him before cutting away the rest of the silk over his mouth and hands.

"Spider," he whispered, but it looked like it took a lot of effort to form the word.

"Yup. Big ass spider," I agreed, kissing him on the cheek in relief.

"Darcy?" Xavier's frantic voice burst into my ear.

"We're here," I said.

"By the stars, what happened?" he asked.

"Spider," Orion repeated in a rasp.

"What was that?" Xavier asked.

"Don't worry." I looked to Darius. "We have to go back for the stone."

"No need. It's in my pocket. Aquamarine for Pisces." He grinned, then looked down at Tory in his arms as she whispered, "Spider."

"We got it, baby. Gwen skewered it and you barbequed the motherfucker," Darius explained.

Tory's fingers flexed, and my shoulders dropped in relief at seeing her regain some movement.

"Woah, your cameras kept recording," Xavier said. "I can access it now. I'm gonna capture the moment you killed that spider thing because it's badass. Tyler will post it publicly soon."

"He's a pro," Sofia said brightly. "We'll be able to send a notification to every FIB agent contact I got from Gus about this if we want to. That guy doesn't stop talking, he'll give us anything he can to save his own ass."

"Hey, Vegas!" Leon Night shouted across the earpieces, and I winced from the loudness of his voice.

"Give me that back," Xavier hissed, and the sound of a struggle broke out, ending in a furious whinny and Leon speaking again.

"I popped back to the academy to pick up Gabe's favourite Tarot deck, and you went on a heist without me?" he said in anger. "I'm the greatest thief in Solaria. How *dare* you!"

"I guess that makes you the second greatest thief in Solaria now," I teased, and he gasped in offence.

"You realise I'm going to have to do a heist now that tops your heist. You can't go stealing my glory," Leon growled. "It's *my* glory."

"Leon," Xavier snapped. "You're getting Cheeto dust on my keyboard."

"What are you gonna do about it, pony boy?" The sound of Leon aggressively eating a Cheeto carried to me, and I took my earpiece out, shoving it in my pocket.

"Let's get out of here," I said.

"We're close to an exit," Bertie said. "This way."

He headed back to the door we'd entered through, finding his way blocked by the Shadow Beast's head, his bulk too large to let him pass through.

Orion groaned and sat up, his right arm dragging along the couch as he did so. "I feel like a zombie. Rahhh." He pushed to his feet, his left foot scraping along the floor as he tried to get control of it, and he startled chuckling manically.

"You good?" I asked, bracing him as he stepped forward and nearly crashed into the fridge.

"Never better, bootiful – bewtiful – bluetiful," he laughed, staggering sideways and crashing into Darius.

"Awoooo." Tory raised her hands in the air, cupping Darius's cheeks. "Look, it's a full moon."

"What's the matter with them?" Darius demanded, holding Tory tighter and hounding after Bertie.

"Well, um, the antivenom has a few side effects." Bertie gave him a guilty look. "Nothing that will last more than a few minutes."

"You'd better be right about that," Darius snapped, and Bertie flinched.

"The moon is shouting." Tory looked over at me then gasped. "Hey – it's me! Hi, me!" She waved and I waved back with a snort of laughter.

I willed the Shadow Beast back into the ring and he slid away into smoke, spiralling into the clear stone.

Bertie hurried out the door and we all followed, though I kept a close eye on Orion as he seemed to only have half of his body back under control, the other half still fully asleep.

Bertie led us outside at last, opening another triangular door in the mountain's base and the cold air rushed around us as we exited.

My heart stalled as I found a huge crowd of FIB agents waiting outside. I raised my hands, ready to fight my way out of here at the side of my family.

"That's a whole lot of cows," Orion murmured as he took in the rows of agents, stumbling into me and I caught his arm. "I've got a lot of milking to do. It's gonna take me all night."

"Wait," Darius murmured as I stepped forward, fire twisting around my fingers. "They're not attacking."

I frowned, realising not a single glimmer of magic could be seen among the agents and confusion crashed through me.

A woman with dark braids and a gleaming badge on her chest suddenly dropped to her knees and cried. "All hail the True Queens!"

"That's the High Commander of the FIB," Darius said in disbelief.

"She'll take quite some milking," Orion murmured.

Tory shoved out of Darius's arms, taking my hand, and I drew her close as we stared out at the sea of FIB, the two of us united as one.

The rest of the agents followed suit with their commander, dropping down to bow and crying out to hail us. Joy rushed through my chest and victory surrounded us as I realised we'd just claimed another huge win from Lionel. A whole section of the FIB was no longer under his command. It was under ours. We'd just struck a blow against the Dragon King that would echo across the kingdom and right into the depths of his cowardly heart.

LYRA

CHAPTER FIFTEEN

My bare feet were bloody, bruised, and aching with pain that I couldn't quite feel. I was numb. Everywhere I should have felt something was just empty. I could see it. Almost like I was standing outside of myself, I could see it. Where I should have been hungry, I merely noticed the growling of my stomach. Where I should have been afraid, I only felt the blankness of my stare, and where I should have felt the pain of my bleeding feet, I only felt the emptiness of all I'd lost.

"The point of it is so fleeting," the thing with the face of Darcy Vega sighed, her finger pressing hard into my cheek as she watched my eyes for a reaction which I couldn't summon into being. It hadn't taken me long to realise that these creatures were not the True Queens. Not that I knew what they were, but I was fairly certain they weren't even Fae at all.

"This one knows but doesn't care," Tory seemed to agree from behind me.

I had watched blankly while these creatures had killed and burned their way across the land until nothing but soot and ash remained of the places they stopped. I had watched as they filled their stomachs to bursting, eating all kinds of strange things. I had watched as they dove into deep water and flung themselves from high peaks. And I had seen the way none of it touched them, none of it mattered to them. Yet still they sought some answer which none of those things could offer.

They were starving, but nothing could sate the hunger that gnawed at them. And I could only observe as they gorged themselves on the world to no avail. Amid it all, they were hunting though. I had noticed that. Searching for something which eluded them and growing in rage when they failed to discover it time and again.

A sound of pure frustration burst from the lips of the blue-haired thing, its foot cracking against the stone before me and carving a great rift through its centre which knocked me off balance. The thing watched as I stumbled, then righted myself, my body reacting while my face remained vacant.

They had discussed cutting me up to see if I would scream, but they hadn't done it. I should have run. But I had nothing in me left to stir the urge to do so.

My gaze trailed from the twins to the riverbank we stood upon, the rush of the water like the rustle of dead leaves scuffing over dry rocks. There was something about it which seemed unnatural even to my uncaring eyes.

The tree that loomed over us had a trunk as black as midnight with tiny veins of deepest red carving their way up the scarred bark, marking it as though with blood. A thick bough reached out across the water, almost crossing to the other side of the unnatural river and ending with gnarled branches spread like fingers as though they were trying to grasp the distant bank.

Movement drew my attention to the centre of that bough where a thick rope was tied into a noose, swinging slowly in a breeze I couldn't feel.

A low, repetitive splashing sound made me look back towards the water and I stilled as I spotted a figure approaching from further upstream, using a long pole to guide a raft towards us. He was cloaked all in black, nothing of his features on show, and yet a coldness approached the riverbank with him which chilled everything down to the air in my lungs.

The twins noticed his approach too and moved to stand before him on the riverbank.

"Why does a thing without life wait upon the passageway to death?" The Ferryman's voice rasped over the river, the chill in the air deepening like fingers of ice were carving their way into my bones.

"I wish to bargain," the twins said as one, their voices merging into something unearthly, something more true to the thing which wore their faces. "I want no part in death."

I may not have been able to feel anything now, but I could tell that the things claiming to be the Vega Queens were not Fae. I had no idea what kind of monster could craft such a lie, but the time I had spent locked in their company had shown me that much.

"I will make no bargain with a cursed creature such as you," The Ferryman hissed, his voice as brittle as bark. "There is no place for you beyond The Veil. Your kind cannot cross the river."

The twins exchanged a look. "Then we have no further need of you."

Tension crackled in the space between the impossibly powerful creatures on the bank and the one in the river. I found myself holding my breath, like I expected the world to fall or the sky to explode.

Instead, The Ferryman simply pressed his pole to the edge of the river and pushed away from the bank once more.

"Death does not want us," the black-haired twin said to the other, her face ethereal and unmoving, void of expression just as I supposed mine must have been.

"What now?" the blue-haired one questioned. "Our search has turned up nothing."

"Perhaps I can help you there."

I turned at the sound of the man's voice, the coldness which The Ferryman had brought to my limbs solidifying into a pit of ice at my core as I took in his emerald green robes and the towering crown placed upon his blonde head. He was a huge man, far bigger than I had pictured him when seeing him on the TV. He was the one who had ordered those agents to come to my home. He was the reason my family were gone and I had been placed in that Inquisition Centre. He was the one who had taken it all.

"I got your location from another of your kind. I was hoping we might strike a deal," the King of Solaria purred.

SETH

CHAPTER SIXTEEN

"Come on, Cal, spill it," Max said.

"Alright, I'm seeing someone. But we're keeping it secret."

"Is she embarrassed to be with you?" Darius taunted, lazing back in his throne-like chair. It was getting late and everyone but the core group had gone to bed, leaving us all hanging out in The Orb celebrating our victory at the FIB impound. Me and the fam. The pack of dreams. Man, this was peace if ever I knew it.

The FIB agents who had turned on Lionel had all come to stay on Rump Island, bolstering the ranks of our army ever so nicely, and if that wasn't worth a few beers, I didn't know what was.

"Maybe it's the other way around," Max sniggered. "Is she a Walrus shifter who keeps her teeth out in Fae form?"

"Fuck off," Caleb said, but a grin played around his mouth. "It's just nothing serious. Nothing worth announcing to the world. I don't need the press sniffing around for the story."

I felt Darcy's eyes on me, but I couldn't turn her way as Caleb suddenly reached into my chest and gripped my heart in his fist – or at least, that was what it felt like. Him toying with it, weighing it in his palm and digging his nails in as if he was considering obliterating it.

Nothing worth announcing to the world.

Those words hurt far more than they should have. I'd agreed to this, hadn't I? Keeping it secret. But this was easy for him. Caleb's heart wasn't on the line. To him, this *was* nothing serious. He was never going to want me the way I wanted him, but the pathetic truth was that I'd take every scrap of attention he had to offer. Because while it lasted, even fragments of Caleb Altair were better than the cavity that was left in my chest without him at all.

I pushed to my feet, leaving them to talk and figuring I'd get another beer. What was I becoming though? Some loser who drank away his problems? I wasn't Orion. He was example enough to know how that shit ended. With him bitter and alone. He may have found his path out of the dark in the end, but I'd seen the emptiness in his eyes back before he had Darcy.

"I think I'll call it a night," I said to the others, leaving their protests behind as I swerved the beer and walked out into the cold night air.

A rumble of thunder in the belly of the clouds promised a violent storm, and I willed it to come and do its worst. I tracked along the path, the static in the air making my skin prickle with the urge to shift. It wasn't a bad idea. Run away into the dark of The Wailing Wood and let it have me like it had countless times before.

Only, this time, footsteps padded after me and the sweet scent of strawberries reached me as my follower caught up. Darcy. Of course it was Darcy. She knew me now, almost as deeply as the Heirs knew me, and in some ways she knew me more. Because she had known the cruelty in me, the vicious streak that painted my heart black. How far we'd come from being enemies, walking these paths, me stalking her like prey and her despising me with all the ire she had to give. Now, I couldn't imagine my life without her, a friend I treasured to the moon and back.

"You didn't have to follow me," I said.

I flicked up a silencing bubble, casting a glance back the way we'd come, but there was no sign of anyone following.

"No, but I wanted to." She fell into step with me, and I looked down at her while she looked up at me with those green, green eyes which saw right through me. "Caleb's just covering for you guys."

"There was truth in what he said," I sighed. "It's the very truth that haunts me. When this ends, it's going to end me too. But I can't stop, Phoen."

"Phoen?"

"Yeah, as in Phoen Dream. I can't exactly call you babe anymore. Feels weird."

She smiled. "Well, I'm not calling you Wolfman. And you'd better not be planning on calling Tory 'Bitchy'."

"Why? I think she'd like it." I barked a laugh.

A rustle in the trees up ahead made me pause and Darcy frowned as she stopped too.

"Cal's here," I said in a low voice, despite the silencing bubble.

"Seems like the perfect opportunity to go talk to him then." She shoved me that way and I huffed out a breath.

"Nahh."

"Go and see him at least." She pushed me with a blast of air that made me stumble forward, then she took off into the sky like a damn kestrel and sailed away on the breeze.

"Feathery bitch." I grinned, then prowled toward the trees again, letting the silencing bubble fall.

I wouldn't know Caleb was watching unless he wanted to let me know, his ever-silent, ever-fast movements keeping anyone from hearing him unless he desired it.

I walked beneath the thick canopy, stepping off the path as my Wolf senses came to life. Every crack of a twig and rustle of a leaf carried to me, the hoot of an owl and the padding of footfalls belonging to various Fae in their Order forms out here in the woods. But none of them were close by.

"I know you're here, Cal," I called, walking deeper into the forest.

I didn't bother to cast a Faelight, my eyes adjusting to the dark as if I was in my Wolf form. Predators didn't need light to hunt by, and here in these trees, I had always been top of the food chain.

The wind was making the branches rattle and my senses were alight as I looked this way and that, trying to pick out my stalker between the boughs.

"You're hunting big game," I warned. "The deadliest animal on campus."

A whoosh of air told me Caleb was launching his attack from above and I jolted forward to try and avoid the strike. He landed behind me, locking his arm around my throat and yanking me back against him.

"Second deadliest." He tried to bite me, but I grabbed his arm, forcing it away from my neck and twisting around, ready with a punch that slammed straight into his gut.

He cursed, shooting away with a surge of Vampire speed then coming at me from behind again. I ducked the swing of his arm, turning and throwing my shoulder into his chest, trying to throw him off balance.

His heels dug into the ground, churning up dirt but in the next second, he was gone, darting away in a burst of speed that left me stumbling to my knees. He reappeared in front of me just as fast, fisting his hand in my hair.

His head cocked to one side and a smile played around his lips. "Down on your knees for me already? What a good pup."

"Fuck you." I launched myself upward, latching my hands around his throat and pinning him to the nearest tree with so much force that the whole thing swayed.

My teeth were bared, my muscles bunched and anger was pulsing hotly in my chest. I was furious for all kinds of insane reasons. Because he had spoken about me as if I was nothing, because he had so much power over my heart, because of every insufferable second I spent without him and every fleeting one I spent with him. Most of all, I was angry because he didn't love me back, and because I had once felt so unbreakable, but now a single rejection from him could shatter me completely.

I shoved away from him, prowling off into the trees back towards the path.

"Seth," Caleb called, but I didn't reply, unsure where my head was at right now, only that it was in a tailspin.

My Atlas buzzed in my pocket and I took it out, finding a news article linked in the group chat.

The Twisted Truth of the Twisted King, by Tyler Corbin and Portia Silverstone.

The foul darkness spreading across our land is an atrocity that can no longer be ignored. Fellow Fae, whether you bury your head in the sand or not, this war has besieged our home, and it is time to do what is honourable and prepare to fight to reclaim our kingdom.

First, what must be acknowledged are the videos depicting the Vega twins burning a Nebula Interrogation Centre to the ground along with the Fae trapped inside. All is not as it seems, the Fae depicted are not them at all, but a monster wearing the face of our queens to besmirch their names – an illusion set to deceive the faithful. Question why, after fighting for justice and freeing many Fae from such imprisonment in these centres, the Vegas would turn on their own people now? Little sense could be made of such an endeavour, but much sense can be made of the truth. A scheme to tar their names by a terrible foe, and who might be more fitting for the role than the one who calls himself king, or perhaps the monster he calls queen?

Memories have been offered up willingly by none other than Darcy Vega and her Elysian Mate Lance Orion since their escape from captivity at the Palace of Souls. Click here to view the disturbing eyewitness account of Lionel Acrux's violent acts. But he is not the only violent royal in his court, for it seems the False King answers to his queen, a creature straight from the Shadow Realm, a Nymph who has been tainted by darkness, making her unimaginably powerful. Click here to watch Lionel face the wrath of his so-called Shadow Queen when she was displeased by him and decide for yourself which power we should fear more within the palace. Is Lavinia Umbra our true enemy, or does the False King have her under his control?

It is time to decide, dear nation, on which ruler you want on your throne. If your allegiance once lay with Lionel Acrux, there is no shame in changing your mind now that his true nature has been unveiled. Many Fae have joined the rebellion who stood on the other side of a once uncrossable bridge. Portia Silverstone, for example, former head of The Celestial Times, once heralded Lionel Acrux as a fine representation of Fae after a long-standing professional relationship with him, has come to work for The Daily Solaria since her daring work with the rebels, exposing the Dragon's darkest secrets. Among them being the murder of his beloved brother, Radcliff Acrux, who had long ago been set upon a great path to rule alongside the other Councillors to bring peace to our kingdom. Alas, that fate was stolen from his clutches, and now it is time we all do as Portia has done and step out of the shadows to declare allegiance to the righteous side of this war.

Tory and Darcy Vega, now crowned among their people as queens, request that you join the ranks of the True Queens' army, or if you are at risk from Lionel's tyranny, join their refuge of safety at Zodiac Academy, protected by powerful and ancient Phoenix magic that cannot be breached by enemy forces.

Join us and you join the side fighting for equality, compassion, and morality.

I clicked on the link to watch the memory play out of Lionel being beaten up by Lavinia, my lips hitching into a grin as he began to beg. Caleb had moved to my side, watching over my shoulder.

"Look at him. He's pathetic," Caleb hissed, his fingers brushing mine, the small contact enough to have my heart rioting.

I gripped his hand, knowing we shouldn't do anything this public, but it was dark. Besides, I had my Wolf needs. No one would question it too much.

Our fingers interlinked and the rough graze of his palm against mine calmed the thrashing of my pulse.

The moonlight highlighted the high arch of his cheekbones and the hollows of his cheeks, making him look as though he was carved from stone.

So many had fallen in this war. But I was one of the lucky ones, holding on to a life that all the fallen would trade me for with everything they had left to give. I might soon find that luck waning, and Caleb might too. Did I really want to walk beyond The Veil having never shared the most desperate secret of my heart?

"Meet me in Aer Territory in an hour – dress in something hot," I said, stepping away from him.

"Why? What are you thinking?" he asked like he hoped I had some mischief planned.

"You'll see." I grinned playfully, then raced away down the path with a plan in mind and my heart thrashing at the prospect of it.

Caleb was the Fae who had given me the moon, so I planned on giving him the sky.

When everything was ready, I stood outside Aer Tower waiting for Caleb to show. I wore a white button down with my favourite ripped jeans, the braids in my hair freshly bound and the subtle earthy scent of Elemental Number 6 cologne on my neck.

Doubts were kicking in, and I was one negative thought away from cancelling this whole idea and never revisiting it again. But then the moon winked at me in the sky, and I knew she had my back. She was in her waxing gibbous phase tonight, almost full but not quite, teasing the world with that little shadowy part she kept hidden. It was like she'd dressed up for the occasion, wearing a dress with a slit up the leg, showing just enough skin but not giving away the whole bakery with the muffin. *You dirty little gibbous.*

Despite her provocative display, she didn't have me thirsting for her any longer. We were lovers turned friends, and she was testing me tonight, just checking I was really over her and had truly given my heart to another.

"Sorry, babe," I said. "You understand though, right? I mean, have you seen him? He was made for me. At least, I think so. It's all kinda fucked. But I'm going to fix that. And you're gonna make sure it all goes smoothly tonight, yeah?"

The moon glittered a little, amused by me and I grinned, swatting a hand at her. "Seth?"

I looked down, finding Caleb there on the path leading away from Aer House and my pulse rioted. He was dressed in a pale blue shirt and black jeans, his golden curls pushed back, styled just so, like he hadn't put any effort in at all. It was only that I knew him so well that I was sure that hair had taken him plenty of time in the mirror.

Words failed me. *Me.* The most wordsy of wordsmiths. So I just extended my hand in an offering, hoping he'd take it.

There was no one around. All was quiet. As if the moon had planned it to be so.

He walked forward, eyeing me suspiciously but clearly trusting me enough not to push me for answers about what I had planned.

The moment his fingers gripped mine, I cast a platform of air beneath my feet, launching us skyward, and Caleb whooped. The cold air rushed around us and Caleb warmed it with fire, heat emanating from him in waves.

I led him away across campus, sailing over the gleaming rooftops, the lustrous golden hue of The Orb catching my eye. I took us all the way to a far corner of Earth Territory where a fluffy sea of clouds gathered above us, all of which had been wrangled with my air Element earlier on.

I drew Caleb through them and we stood among the clouds which stretched far enough in either direction that we couldn't see the campus below, only the glittering sky above. The stars were watching, but their brightness didn't seem too alluring tonight; it was the moon who took centre stage. She looked closer than ever, like she had inched nearer just to watch us.

"This is...shit, Seth. This is awesome," Caleb breathed.

"As far as you can see in each direction, all the way to the edges of the clouds is a solid platform of air," I announced.

Caleb's eyebrows arched in surprise. "What's it for?"

"For you," I said, my mouth hooking up. "You can run through the sky, Cal. As fast as you like."

His navy eyes brightened and he shot away from me in a blur, a whoop echoing back to me. He ripped through the clouds, sending plumes of white swirling away from him as he zig-zagged this way and that. A laugh fell from my throat and he came speeding back to me, grabbing me by the arm and swinging me over his shoulder. I landed on his back with adrenaline bursting through my veins and I held on tight, banding my arms and legs around him.

Caleb zoomed along at high speed, faster and faster, racing in circles and then daggering sharply to the left, then right.

"Jump, Cal!" I called, and when he obeyed, I cast air beneath his feet, launching us skyward at a wild speed.

We flew up fifty feet before I let the wind fall and we went tumbling back towards the clouds below. I slowed our descent at the last second, placing Caleb on the platform of air, and he was off running again the moment his feet touched down.

I released him with one hand so I could cast shapes in the clouds ahead of us, creating archways and hoops, tunnels and bridges for him to take on. An entire obstacle course was brought to life, and I built more and more of it around us, spiralling stairways, twisty slides that spat us out into a pool of more clouds, ramps for him to jump from and huge rolling balls of clouds he had to work to avoid.

We were both laughing our asses off by the time we took a break, falling down onto a soft bed of air, our clothes wet through from the moisture in the clouds.

Caleb was panting, his hand on his stomach as it rose and fell, the big ass smile on his face making my chest swell. He looked like a fallen god, hair tousled and chaotic, eyes full of endless light. I wanted him to be like this, always. Carefree and overflowing with life.

"How do you see time?" I asked.

Caleb rolled onto his side, resting his elbow on the bed of air beneath us and propping his head up in his hand. "What do you mean 'see' time?"

"Like, to me, in my head, there's a sort of calendar. January is a little pink square that's kind of up here somewhere." I waved my hand above my head. "Then February is blue and sort of sparkly, and March is orange with fairy lights around it. And I'm kind of floating above the little calendar as we move through the year, you know? So then April is purple, and May is green but with lots of flowers and a birthday cake - because it's your birthday. I have a birthday cake in February for Max too, and one in August for Darius, but your cake is the biggest. Then June is yellow and-"

"Wait...why does this make a weird kind of sense? Do you feel like December is downhill?"

"Yes! And January is uphill!" I cried. "Oh my stars, I knew I was crazy, but at least you're crazy too."

"Who wants to be normal anyway?" He smirked.

"Yeah," I agreed. "Imagine having to do normal boring things like walking to the grocery store and buying groceries."

Caleb laughed. "Shit, imagine having to pick out a lettuce and put it in a basket."

"Then paying for it at the checkout," I added with a snort.

Caleb laid back down, cupping his hand behind his head. "Damn, I love being an Heir."

"It's pretty sweet. Although...what if the twins don't want us on the Council? What if they don't even want a Council? Like...what are we gonna do? I haven't even thought about other careers. I mean, I guess I could be a moonologist..."

"That's not a thing."

"Pfft, it is a thing. "

"It might be a thing, but it's definitely not called a moonologist." Caleb sniggered.

"Well I'm not gonna have some boring job. I'd rather go pick out lettuces all day."

"I don't think I'd mind picking out lettuces with you," he said thoughtfully. "Maybe boring is peaceful."

"I guess. But can we still go on adventures at weekends? Oh shit - will you take me to The Hellion Hunt!?"

"That's so illegal," he said in a way that told me it excited him.

"And dangerous."

"But I swore I won't hunt anyone again but you," he muttered darkly.

"Yeah...true," I said sadly.

"We could just watch though."

"Uh huh. *Or* we could watch the Vampires hunt for like two rounds, then I could go in there and you can hunt me. Just me. No one else."

"Dude, that is so dangerous. I heard the Vampires who go there have to survive a month without feeding before they'll be admitted to the game." Caleb ran his tongue over his fangs.

I shivered excitedly. "I can't wait. You're gonna hunt me so good."

"Maybe I wanna hunt you right now."

"Oh yeah?" I grinned, shoving to my feet immediately as adrenaline buzzed through me. "How about we play it Croc-Snap style?"

"A thousand percent yes." He leapt upright, his eyes flashing with the thrill of the coming game.

I cast a thick blindfold of leaves over his eyes then leaned in, speaking to him so close that our mouths grazed.

"Catch me if you can." I ran away, springing off into the clouds and Caleb shouted, "Croc!"

"Snap!" I called back, turning a sharp left when he came shooting towards me. I made it out of his grasp, using air to guide me up high.

"Croc," he growled.

"Snap!"

He leapt for me in the sky, arms outstretched and fangs bared, his fingers grazing my ankle. I released the air beneath me, hurtling down and evading him once more.

I raced away with the clouds swirling around my waist, trying to keep quiet as he stood with his head cocked, listening for me.

"Croc," he snarled getting all angry Vamp about the game, and I was here for it.

"Snap," I answered, and he came at me like a runaway train.

I darted left, trying to put some distance between us, but I collided with him as he appeared in front of me. He gripped my shirt in his hand so I couldn't escape, and I cursed. But the loss of the game was sweetened when he ripped the blindfold from his eyes and crushed his mouth to mine.

My heart thundered and roared, every piece of me awakening just for him.

Our lips parted and the words were spilling from my tongue like they'd been placed there by the moon herself. There was no avoiding it any longer, no fear great enough to stop me from declaring it. Despite whatever came in consequence to these words, nothing could keep them from being said.

"It was too damn easy to fall in love with you when I already loved everything about you, Cal," I said, my voice rough with those words which had tortured me for so long.

His eyes widened, but I couldn't let him speak yet, not before all of it was said.

"The moment I let myself imagine something more than friendship between us, I was done for. I know that might not be what you wanna hear, but I can't keep it secret anymore. I've tried everything to keep it locked inside me, because I know that these words risk what we are. But I can't keep it bottled up forever, I get that now."

"Seth," Caleb started, but I barrelled on, too terrified of what he was about to say.

"Anyway, nice night, isn't it? Too cold, some would say. But not me. I like the cold weather. I can run faster and further in my Wolf form when it's cooler. I don't overheat, see? Oh and the ground's all firm, and the leaves are all crispy under my paws, so-"

"*Seth*," Caleb snarled, and I fell silent, waiting for the axe to fall. It was about to smash through my ribcage and cleave my heart apart. I knew it. The stars knew it. The moon definitely knew it. Maybe she was smirking, watching my heart get destroyed in penance for me turning my sights from her. But she wasn't usually that petty. Maybe she'd see reason when I was cast to ruin beneath her.

"Go on then, say it," I sighed, heat blazing up the back of my neck. "That we're just fooling around, you never wanted things to get this serious. That maybe we should take some space, see other people – oh fuck, please don't see other-"

Caleb grabbed a fistful of my hair and yanked, making me yelp. "Shut up for a second."

I nodded mutely and he released my hair, stepping closer to me, so close I couldn't see anything but him. Beautiful, perfect him.

"Don't put words in my mouth. Look, I don't know what this thing is between us, but…"

My heart hung over the edge of an abyss, Caleb's hand dangling me there on a string, threatening to burn that tether to him at any second.

Caleb moved even closer, his voice dropping, becoming gruffer. "I do know that I've never felt like this about anyone before. This is special in a way I can't put a name to."

"And you don't have to," I said on a sigh, the burden of fear leaving me at long last. Caleb Altair didn't love me back, but knowing he cared, that he thought this was special, it was enough. At least for now. "That's all I wanted, Cal. To know this was something more than casual."

"It's far more than that," he admitted, his navy eyes unblinking and leaving me raw. "And I want to show you what you mean to me."

His fingers deftly opened the buttons of my shirt and his mouth trailed down to my throat, painting lines of fire across my skin. I slid my hands into his hair with another heavy sigh, his gold curls spilling through my fingers, his touches making me feel like I'd earned the throne of my kingdom a thousand times over. No feeling could compare to this. No accomplishment, no level of power.

His kisses turned to bites, and I growled at the sharp slice of his fangs, marking my skin with pinpricks. A little blood slipped from each one and he dragged his tongue over the hard planes of my chest, catching every drop. My power drained as he drew it into himself, and I revelled in gifting him the magic in my veins, wanting him and only him to possess it. I was his Source, and there was strength in that position, this most fierce of creatures having chosen me. And I had the honour of fulfilling him.

His hand splayed across my stomach and he lifted his head, giving me a hungry smile before shoving me so I fell backwards onto the bed of air. I bounced on the cushioned surface, the clouds swirling around me as I grinned up at him.

My cock was already hard as stone, straining against my jeans, and Caleb's eyes trailed the swell of it, desire burning in the depths of them.

"Show me," he commanded.

I ignored his bossy tone, pushing up onto my elbows and giving him a cool stare. "If you want something, come and get it, Cal. Don't think you can use that asshole tone on me and get what you want."

His eyes glittered as if he liked me biting back and he shot forward, suddenly kneeling over me with all the darkness of a sinner twisting through his gaze.

He unbuttoned my jeans, his eyes never leaving mine and I groaned as he freed my cock, his fist gripping the base firmly. He rolled his hand up and down my shaft, his fingers tightening and his thumb gliding over the tip, making me swear. It felt so fucking good, and he didn't stop, increasing his pace and driving me crazy as he started moving his hand in a corkscrew motion.

I took in the flexing of his muscles, the intensity in his navy eyes and the thick ridge of his cock driving against the inside of his pants. He needed this as much as I needed him, and I never, ever wanted it to stop.

Caleb gave me a roguish look before dropping down and running his tongue up the length of my dick. I growled like a Wolf and he did it again, running his mouth all over me and bringing me to the brink of madness. When his lips closed over the top of my dick, I nearly exploded right then and there, but I held out as his fingers pumped the base and the heat of his tongue had me panting.

"Cal," I warned, knowing I could only hold out a few seconds longer, but he didn't stop.

He took me in right to the back of his throat and the tips of his fangs grazed my sensitive flesh, making my hips buck so that I drove in even deeper. I was a goner, pleasure racing through every nerve ending in my cock as I came, and he swallowed without hesitation, groaning with desire. That noise rumbled right through me, drawing out my climax and leaving me spent.

Caleb lifted his head, the lust in his eyes blazing right through me, and he suddenly grabbed my hips, rolling me onto my front, and yanking my jeans further down my legs.

"Lube, right pocket," I said breathlessly.

He got it with his Vampire speed and in the next second, he pushed a slick finger into my ass, getting me ready for him. I groaned as he drew his finger in and out of me, then took it away completely and lined up his cock, ready to claim me. He eased his way inside me, and I cursed as he filled me inch by inch, making me brace against the air bed beneath me.

When he was fully seated inside me, he started moving, fucking me slow and deep, his body pressing down onto mine so his mouth was by my cheek. I turned my head to meet him in a kiss, our tongues coming together and my hips rocking back to meet every thrust of his.

The clothes between us were too much. I wanted his skin moulded to mine, and as I drew back and put a voice to that thought, Caleb reared up and sent a flash of fire over us, burning our clothes clean off. Fucking destroying them as if he gave no fucks about the designer items, turning them to ash which blew away on the wind. When he dropped back over me, I was delivered the warm plane of his muscles driving against my back and I ground against him, revelling in that sensation.

He reached over my head, taking my hands and winding his fingers between mine, and our breaths came heavier as we worked in that slow, torturous rhythm. My cock was hard again already, grinding into the mattress of air and feeling so fucking good. But nothing beat the way Caleb Altair felt inside me. Every thrust from his hips was a gift from the stars, the way he fucked a talent in itself.

He drove his hips forward again, groaning and cursing, his cock throbbing inside me, telling me how close he was.

He started fucking me faster, chasing his release and I drove my hips back time and again, wanting to feel him explode.

He came inside me with a roar, his fingers knotting tight around mine and his hips pressing me down. He panted against my neck and we rolled sideways so he was curled around me, his hand falling to my straining cock and stroking it softly, keeping me on the edge.

"I wanna feel you inside me," he growled. "One day soon."

"How soon?" I asked keenly, and he laughed.

"When I say so, pup."

I rolled so I was facing him, my teeth grinding. "I'm not your pup."

"No?" he smirked, taking hold of my dick again.

"Fuck," I exhaled as his thumb rolled over the tip in that perfect way. "You talk big for someone whose pretty lips are all red from taking my cock."

He released my shaft and reached around to slap my ass hard enough to leave a print there and make me growl. "I could say the same thing about your pretty ass."

We both laughed and I leaned in to kiss him, my hand gripping his chin and holding him just where I wanted him. Our amusement fell away as our kiss deepened and Caleb's hand resumed stroking the length of me, his rough fingers getting me off so damn easily.

I thrust into his tight fist as I finished with a groan and Caleb's tongue pushed deeper into my mouth, kissing me hard.

My heart beat steadier than it had in a long time. Together, here in the clouds, nothing could touch us. And long may we fucking reign.

CALEB

CHAPTER SEVENTEEN

I laid in my bed in Terra House looking up at the skylight above me and watching the branches of the trees which were drenched in the golden morning light. They swept back and forth in the furious wind that was currently battering the academy as winter took it into its clutches.

The tree closest to my room was an oak, an ancient, wizened tree with a trunk so thick it could have easily held a room or three inside it. Most of its leaves had already dropped, the acorns scattering the ground and gathered up by squirrels over the last few months. But one leaf remained, clinging to the tip of a spindly branch that lashed back and forth above my underground retreat from the world.

My eyes tracked the movement of that leaf while my fingers toyed with the long strands of Seth's hair and I listened to the rise and fall of his breathing.

I could still taste him on my lips, still feel the ache of claiming him in my flesh, and yet I felt like that leaf; barely holding on while the wind tried to tear me away.

We'd stolen this for ourselves. Us. Stolen it and made it ours and I feared what would come of that choice in the end. I feared what this war might take from us and who, if any of us, would remain to see the other side of it.

The wind gusted harder and I sucked in a sharp breath as the leaf was torn free, my eyes tracking it as it was tossed back and forth before it was propelled out of sight.

A vice tightened around my chest for a moment as it disappeared and I found myself lost in the memory of grieving for Darius, of how broken I'd been by his loss and the knowledge that there would be no second chances again. This was it. The war would only have one winning side and even then, not all who fought for it would survive.

My Atlas buzzed and I hooked it out from under my pillow, clicking on the notification for my Horoscope.

Good morning, Taurus.
The stars have spoken about your day!
A daring love affair is in full swing, and your mind has found a cloud of
peace to perch upon in the sky. But be warned, more courage will be required

to fulfil the yearnings of your heart, and this fragile desire could shatter as easily as it could be made whole. With Mars in your chart, you're feeling brave, and that will serve you well in the coming day, for a quest lies on the horizon, one you will need to face with strength if you are to seize what you seek. Beware the rising tide of hunger in your soul when your fate tangles with that of a Libra between the boughs of destiny. Blood may spill, and old mistakes may be made twice if you do not tread this rocky path with caution.

The crinkle of a wrapper drew my attention and I looked to Seth in surprise, finding him awake and pushing a square of chocolate into his mouth. He gave me a grin as I caught him, tossing the empty packet aside, and I placed down my Atlas.

"Tory left that out for me yesterday," he explained. "In the bottom of her sock drawer under three concealment spells and a decoy bar which she'd laced with laxatives – I ate that too but I'm fine now. This one was the one she meant for me to have."

I breathed a laugh, tugging him closer so I could kiss him and tasting the sweetness of the chocolate on his lips.

He pulled back, looking down at me with an intensity blazing in his earth brown eyes that set my heart thumping harder and made my fear slide away to the corners of my mind once more. The war didn't seem so impossible to survive when he was looking at me like that.

"You're stressed," he said, a crease forming between his brows.

"We're at war," I said by way of explanation. My eyes slid to the clock on the wall which told me it was eight thirty-five. "And we're late."

"You can just shoot us there in thirty seconds flat," Seth pointed out, his hand trailing down my abs, tracing the lines of my muscles and making my dick harden.

"Oh, can I? Am I your preferred mode of transport now?" I teased, my words falling to a groan as he wrapped his fist around my cock and started stroking it.

"Yeah. You're my little transport bitch," he agreed, his eyes on mine while he drank in the sight of me beneath him.

I had more complaints to make about us being late, but I forgot all of them as he dropped his mouth to my cock and drew the full length of me to the back of his throat.

I cursed, fisting his hair in my hand and pushing him down harder, watching him take every inch, growling his name as desire took me captive.

Seth groaned hungrily, licking and sucking, his fist moving to his own dick as he got himself off too. I watched him with my heart pounding and my muscles tensing.

He was so fucking good with his mouth that I was coming within minutes, watching him swallow with a feral desire that was rewarded by him finishing himself too, his cum spilling over my stomach and marking me as his.

We exchanged a heated look which promised more later but as I glanced at the clock, I knew we were out of time. I yanked Seth into my arms and shot us both into the shower, flipping the water on and washing us at high speed before shooting us back into my room, drying us off with a towel and dressing us both for good measure. It was all done in less than a minute and Seth stumbled back, adjusting to the feeling of his feet suddenly being in his sneakers with a grin.

"That was-" he began, but I swept him into my arms and shot from the room before he could finish that thought.

I sped out of Terra House and across campus as fast as I could move, the cold wind whipping Seth's wet hair into my face and making him whoop a laugh before I ran through the door of The Orb and shot us into place on our red couch.

I looked around at our inner circle in surprise, taking in Max, Darius, the twins, and Orion, unsure where everyone else was.

"I thought this was a war council?" I asked in surprise, wondering where my mom and the other Councillors were - plus the extended group of Fae who were running other parts of the army's tasks like hitting the Nebula Inquisition Centres and making sure everyone was fed, scouting for information on Lionel, and overseeing training.

"It was," Geraldine called from behind me, and I looked around to find her approaching with a huge stack of books in her arms. The titles included a mixture of fairy tales and bedtime stories which made no real sense. "Two hours ago. Tasks have been assigned and information gleaned, yet where were the lowly mutt and the biting brute?"

"Hunting," I replied, just as Seth said, "Gathering berries in the forest."

Everyone looked at him in surprise, and I wondered why the fuck he'd gone for that as a cover story. I also noticed the clock on the wall which said it was close to eleven am, which probably meant my clock had stopped.

"How were the berries, Seth?" Darius asked curiously. "Did you find a lot of them?"

"Erm...yes. Yes, I did," Seth confirmed, sticking with his ridiculous lie.

"I wanna learn," Darius went on.

"Learn what?" Seth asked.

"I wanna learn from the big, bad Wolf. Can you give me a really thorough lesson, like you did for Cal?"

I fell utterly still, my gaze narrowing on Darius while I maintained an entirely expressionless face, but those words...those fucking words were a near echo of what Seth had said to me the night we'd had sex for the first time.

"A lesson in..." Seth exchanged a panicked look with me, but Darius finished the sentence for him.

"Hunting for berries like you two have been for the last two hours. You must have found some really good ones with all that time," Darius pushed.

"Oh...yeah. Any time, man. I didn't know you liked berries so much," Seth said, giving me a relieved look, but I wasn't buying it.

I narrowed my eyes at Darius as he picked up his mug of coffee and he gave me a taunting grin over the rim of it before taking a long sip.

"If you late lampoons are quite done bragging about your bush diving skills then I should like to present my findings to the group," Geraldine said loudly, dropping the stack of books onto the table between us and gesturing to them with a triumphant flourish.

"The tale of Gilbert the Gallant," Darcy said with interest, plucking a book from the top of the pile that was decorated with bright illustrations intended for children.

"Indeed. I have been giving much thought to our quest for the Guild Stones," Geraldine said seriously.

"I have some thoughts on where the final stone might be concealed," Orion began, but Geraldine waved him off.

"Thank you, dear professor of the past, but your inane ramblings won't be required here. I have watched you ponder this question and seen how you flounder and fail to find an answer as to where the final stone was secreted away many a moon ago-"

"I've spent countless hours researching-" Orion began but she threw a silencing bubble over him, making Tory laugh loudly and causing me to snort with amusement too.

"The endless whiffling of our dear fanged friend will not be required, for I believe that I have found the answer we seek. As I mentioned previously, as a child, I was somewhat obsessed with the stories of the Gems of Lariom, and I went through a four-year stage where I planned on being the one to finally find them. I read every tale and scoured every source there was. At the time, my young and carefree mind did not grasp what I now see so plainly, but as I began to muse upon this question once more, something stood out and slapped me in the chops like a tuna on a Tuesday."

"What?" Tory asked keenly.

Geraldine plucked the book back out of Darcy's hands before opening it to a page towards the end and pointing at an illustration of a blood red wall.

She grabbed another book from the stack next, opening that to a marked page and thrusting it into Tory's hands. She opened another and gave it to Max, then another and another until we all held one of the books and several more lay open on the table between us.

I looked down at the one she'd given me, finding a single word underlined.

Herithé.

I frowned at it, reading the sentence in full.

All who enter Herithé shall find themselves lost to the curse which claimed it, wasting away into nothing and becoming one with the ash of its former residents.

"Herithé is a myth," I said dismissively. "Just some creepy place that parents use to threaten their kids when they're bad. I can remember my mom saying she'd ship me off to live with the lost souls in Herithé if I didn't start tidying my room more often."

"Yes," Geraldine said, her hands slamming down on the coffee table, her eyes alight with some thought which was so far alluding me. "Herithé is in every one of these books about the Gems of Lariom. Sometimes a passing mention, sometimes a feature of the story itself. The legends that surround it are muddled and yet when you read every account you can find that, be it in legend, myth, or tale, there are some glaring similarities. An object of brutal power was stolen and hidden away in the city. But the object – sometimes a crown, sometimes a staff, sometimes a child with eyes as dark as night – whatever it may be, it always brings a curse down upon Herithé. The city was said to have fallen to a plague, a war, a glut of magic, an explosion of power – but always it is said that its inhabitants were trapped inside and any who tried to enter thereafter were trapped too, succumbing to the curse and the power of the object."

We all stared at her blankly while she puffed her chest up in victory.

"You think the object is the final Guild Stone?" Tory asked curiously.

"I do believe it is, my lady."

"Then...how do we find a city lost in legend?" Tory mused.

"I have thought of that." Geraldine ducked down and grabbed a large cannister from the floor, taking the map of Espial from it and throwing it over the table with a flourish. "I wondered if perhaps we might coax the map to reveal its location to us."

"So what facts do the legends mostly agree on?" I asked, leaning closer as the landscape of Solaria blossomed across the map, mountains pushing their way out of the page, tiny trees sprouting in a forest and miniature cities building themselves across the canvas in a true likeness of the way they were in the world at this time.

I reached out to skim my fingers through a heavy cluster of clouds over the Baruvian Jungle and smiled as the magic reformed the moment I removed my hand. If only the map revealed the locations of people and armies, we might have been able to use it to locate Lionel's forces.

Geraldine gripped the edges of the map, connecting her magic to that which had been imbued within the powerful item and asked it to reveal the lost location of Herithé.

For several seconds nothing much happened, but then a wind seemed to gust across the entire landscape and my focus was drawn to a mountainous stretch of land to the far west of the continent where thick forests gave way to stony peaks. Slowly, between the boughs of the clustered trees, a formation of blood-red brick appeared.

I sucked in a breath as I took in the tiny details emerging from the trees. There wasn't much to see; a glimpse of red stone and what might have been the spire of a tower that protruded minimally from the tree line, but that was all.

"It's going to be dangerous," Darcy said with a glint of exhilaration in her eyes.

"There might be monsters," Seth added with equal fervour.

"Off to the wandering wilds we go," Geraldine announced ominously.

She started to coil the map up, and I got to my feet.

"We're all going?" I confirmed, glancing between the others.

"It's a cursed city where all who enter are known to die," Tory said with a shrug. "Of course we're all going."

Seth howled in excitement and I couldn't help but grin too, my fangs on show and my pulse thumping wildly. The worst thing about this war was the quiet between the action, the time between battles where you couldn't be certain how long the fragile peace might last. So I was all for heading into the unknown and testing my mettle against an ancient curse.

Stardust could only be used to transport a Fae to a place they had been before, and as none of us had ever gone hiking in the Tanai Forest which we hoped hid the city of Herithé, the best we'd been able to do was get ourselves to a ski lodge Max had once come to on vacation.

I wore fighting leathers with a plate of shining armour over my chest, my Phoenix fire daggers sheathed at my belt. All of us had come to this place dressed for war.

The trek through the trees felt endless and after six hours of searching for the cursed city, I was beginning to think the fucking map had lied to us.

I was tired from shooting back and forth between the trees with Orion, the two of us using our speed to scout while Darius and the twins flew far and wide, hunting for any sign of that spire.

Seth, Max, Geraldine, Xavier, Sofia, Tyler and Washer had it easy, waiting on our reports and moving in the most likely direction while trying to use the map to narrow our hunt down. The problem was, the map covered the entire kingdom and the area it depicted across a few inches spanned hundreds of miles.

I was close to giving up on the entire thing when I finally came across a blood red brick in the dirt on my way back down the curving slope at the foot of one of the smaller mountains.

I skidded to a halt and shot back to the brick, lifting it into my hand and inspecting it curiously. The stone wasn't painted or stained that colour in any way that I could see. It simply *was* red.

I had never seen anything quite like it before, and I closed my eyes as I analysed it with my earth magic, feeling for its composition, trying to figure out if it was natural or tainted by magic.

My stomach roiled as I inspected the core of it, something definitively wrong about the material setting bile rolling across my tongue.

I dropped to one knee and pressed my free hand to the dirt of the damp forest floor. It was quiet here. More so than I had truly realised before coming to a halt like this. There was no birdsong, no sound of distant water, no indication of wind in the trees or beasts lurking beneath their boughs.

I pushed my magic into the dirt and instantly felt the wrongness again, though it was more muted than it had been in the brick itself. I pushed out with my power, seeking more of that feeling, more of what I was beginning to suspect was the power of the curse that had seen Herithé fall. And suddenly, I felt it. Not a single brick tainted with dark energy but many of them, one piled atop another and another, a wall growing up between the trees and barring all passage beyond it.

I stood, my eyes opening as I oriented myself towards the wall, then shot through the trees to seek it out.

It was further away than it had seemed while I felt through the dirt for it, but there was no mistaking it when I came upon it.

Between the trunks of ancient trees, reaching up towards the canopy far above my head was a wall of deepest, blood red, set like a barrier between this world and another.

It didn't look aged or touched by time, nor did it look welcoming or at all weathered. It simply was.

I took my Atlas from my pocket and shot a message to the group, dropping them my location and telling them to come quickly.

While I waited for them to arrive, I started moving along the wall. The sickly feeling of decay was heavier here and I didn't need to touch the stone to feel it. Whatever power had been used to create such a curse was still very much active.

A flash of somewhere else sprang through my mind as Orion raced to meet me, the trees blurring around him while he ran, the urge to hunt this place down filling him as the connection between us formed.

I turned and saw myself through his eyes just as I saw him with my own.

He collided with me at speed, his arms wrapping around me and a feral snarl spilling from his lips which I echoed without thought. We began to tussle playfully, yet there was more to it, an intensity that got my heart pumping wildly and made my fangs snap out on instinct.

The sound of someone else arriving had us shoving away from each other and the snarls that rang from us were deeper as we locked our gazes on Max who was leaping down from the back of a white Wolf.

"Whoa!" he yelled as we shot at him together, fangs bared and bloodlust thrashing between us. We split apart, coming at him from both sides, the rush of the game filling me with exhilaration before I slammed into an air shield and was knocked onto my ass.

I blinked as the desperate need for blood slid from me and I looked between Orion who was sprawled on the floor to my right, and Max who looked somewhere between amused and pissed off.

"Bite your damn Sources if you're hungry," he said, and my gaze moved to Seth just as he shifted back into his Fae form.

I growled as I lunged at him, pushing him back against a tree and sinking my fangs into his throat roughly.

"Fuck," Seth cursed as Orion's teeth sank into the other side of his throat a heartbeat later, and I groaned in satisfaction as I felt not only my bloodlust but Orion's finding relief as one.

Orion snarled ferociously and the sound lit the hunger in me on fire, stoking my bloodlust and urging me to take more and more.

Seth moved a little between us, unable to do much at all with our venom immobilising him two-fold and Max shouted something. But the words seemed distant and indistinct, paling to insignificance in the face of the thirst.

It was a whimper that dragged me back to myself, a soft, pained sound falling from Seth's lips which had me jerking back and ripping Orion away too.

Orion lunged forward again but I shot into his path, a snarl escaping me as I bared my teeth and glared at his bloodstained face. He snarled right back, tension crackling between us for several heady seconds before finally, he blinked, remembering himself at last.

I felt the rush of the hunt fading from him, the connection between us shattering once more. I whirled back to face Seth, gripping his throat between my hands and pressing healing magic into his skin as I fought off the pull of the coven bond and looked into his dark eyes.

Seth was grinning at me like it was all some game he'd been a part of, and I frowned back at him, an apology on my lips which felt utterly inadequate.

"Seth," I began, but he rolled his eyes, knocking my hands from his neck before swiping a splash of blood from my chin with his thumb and pushing it into my mouth.

"Next time, you won't catch me off guard so easily," he taunted before swaggering away butt naked towards Max who held the bag filled with his clothes.

"He's *my* Source," I growled at Orion, my gaze narrowing as I tried to figure out what had just happened and why the rage I should have felt at him sinking his teeth into my claimant wasn't fully present.

"I know. I didn't want to…I haven't been that caught up in the hunt since I first Emerged. I don't know why I even bit him. I was hunting for this place, not blood."

We exchanged a dark look, neither of us able to deny the power of the bloodlust and the urge to hunt which had just driven us after our prey as one.

"There's a reason why we shouldn't have formed a coven," I murmured.

"Too late to do much about that now," he replied. "I've found some books on the subject – we should discuss it more when this is done."

I nodded in agreement, trying to push off the uncomfortable feeling which was mixing with the surge of satisfaction simmering in my blood following that hunt.

The ground shuddered as Darius landed in his Dragon form and I met Orion's gaze with a faint frown while the rest of our friends all moved closer in the clearing.

"That was…intense," I said in a voice low enough for only a Vampire to hear.

"I got caught up in the search for this place and my magic was running low," he said softly. "I didn't mean to turn it into an actual hunt."

"Is everything okay?" Darcy asked, banishing her wings as she moved over to Orion and looked at the blood staining his mouth.

"Yeah, beautiful," he replied, though he sounded as uncertain as I felt. "I just got a bit thirsty and the mutt got in my way before I could claim a taste of the good stuff." He wiped a hand coated in water magic across his face, cleaning the blood off before drawing her closer to him for a kiss.

The sound of heavy paws stalking through the trees carried to us as Geraldine approached the blood-red wall in her Cerberus form. Her three giant heads lifted as one and released a trio of victorious howls which pierced the unearthly silence of the place before she shifted back into her Fae form and placed her fists on her hips.

"By golly, there it is," Geraldine cooed as Xavier, Tyler, Sofia and Washer followed her through the trees.

"Gosh those are some stiff-looking bricks," Washer commented, starting up some lunges, and Xavier took a pointed step away from him.

"At least this place isn't creepy as fuck and rumoured to kill everyone who enters its walls," Tory said dryly as she moved to stand beside me, and my lips twitched with amusement. I wondered if she realised how she held herself these days, with her chin up and defiance sparkling in her gaze that seemed to dare the stars to try their luck with her again. She wore her Phoenix armour and her sword was sheathed at her belt. Looking between her and Darcy, there was no denying that they were monarchs even without crowns on their heads.

"It is…magnificent," Geraldine declared, her bare ass staring back at all of us where we'd gathered behind her.

Darius shifted into his Fae form and Max tossed him his clothes on his way to coax Geraldine back into hers.

When everyone was dressed again and Darius had slung his axe over his back, we started to walk along the length of the wall.

Tory stayed at my side, making snide remarks about whoever had decided to hide a Guild Stone in this hellish place, and the knot of discomfort in my chest slowly eased in her company. She said nothing about me going feral and losing my mind to the hunt with Orion. That wasn't her style. She just walked with me, cracked bad jokes, and arched an eyebrow whenever I fell silent for too long.

"Behold!" Geraldine cried as we rounded a corner and found ourselves before an enormous stone archway beneath which hung two impossibly large wooden doors. The one on the right was ajar, allowing us a peek at a deep red street beyond and nothing more. "And so we step into the clutches of a death curse, ready to face down doom in pursuit of a single stone," Geraldine boomed.

She didn't so much as hesitate as she slipped through the door, Max hot on her heels.

"Don't look so sad, moon friend. You can be rough with me sometimes, it's okay. I'm irresistible, so I know how hard it must be for you to try and hold back all the time," Seth said to a scowling Orion, wrapping an arm around his shoulders and guiding him through the gates next.

"Yeah, Caleb finds it almost impossible to resist Seth too," Darius agreed as he followed them with Darcy right beside him. "I've seen him pouncing on him and pinning him down, doing anything he can think of to get his mouth all over-"

His words fell away as they disappeared through the gate and I frowned slightly, exchanging a look with Tory.

"Why did he say it like that?" I muttered.

"Like what?" she asked innocently. Too innocently. Tory didn't do innocent.

"Like me biting Seth is…" I trailed off, the truth of what it was sticking my tongue to the roof of my mouth as I realised I was probably only going to dig myself a hole by saying anything more on this.

Xavier, Tyler, Sofia, and Washer slipped through the doors ahead, leaving us to bring up the rear.

"Like it's kinda hot when you pin him to a tree and drag your mouth all over his body?" she asked, smirking at me.

I stumbled a step as I made it to the gate, frowning back at her as I wondered what she'd seen, what she'd figured out. Or if she was just remembering the way it had been for us once upon a time and making a comment on that.

But whatever I'd thought I was going to say in reply to that taunt fell to nothing on my lips as I found myself inside the city of Herithé, because the courtyard of blood red stone we stepped into was entirely abandoned.

"Darius?" I called, my voice echoing back to me a thousand times from walls which gleamed as though wet and streets which were endlessly empty. Our friends had vanished without a trace, and the pressing silence drove a sliver of dread into my heart.

There was no reply from within the warren of abandoned masonry. And as Tory drew her sword at my side, the gate to Herithé slammed closed at our backs.

ORION

CHAPTER EIGHTEEN

"**B**lue!" I bellowed, my voice reverberating off the red-brick street around us. The moment I'd stepped through that gate, the fabric of the world had shifted, and I'd lost sight of everyone but Seth.

"Cal!" he tried, hurrying up the street and turning a corner.

I tried to force open a door to the nearest building which looked like a store, the name of it so faded and in a language so old that I couldn't even attempt to decipher it.

The door didn't give, even when I threw my shoulder against it with the full force of my Order strength.

"Fuck," I cursed, carving my fingers through my hair before unsheathing my sword. The glitter of Phoenix fire within the metal caught my eye and my teeth gritted in frustration at being parted from Darcy. Whatever hell awaited us within this place, it looked like I was going to be facing it with the mutt.

Seth came jogging back to me with a frown on his brow. "Can you try connecting to Caleb in that freaky mind way you can do sometimes?"

"I'll try," I muttered.

"Is it working?" He gripped my arm, and I pressed my lips together.

"Give me a damn second." I shut my eyes, releasing a slow breath and trying to reach for the part of me that was bound to my coven brother. It seemed to be linked to the bloodlust though, and with me so well fed now, I couldn't come close to forming the connection.

I sighed, opening my eyes and shaking my head, causing Seth to let out a low whine.

"We'll just keep moving. We're bound to find them eventually." I strode forward, my boots hitting the ground and barely making any noise in this strangely muffled place. It was like the air here was heavier too, a little harder to breathe.

Seth jogged to catch me and we took turns this way and that, walking down streets that all looked painfully the same as each other, offering no marking of how far we were progressing. Part of me feared we were going in circles, but I didn't want to put a voice to that thought, just making sure we didn't take too many rights or too many lefts in case we turned back on ourselves.

"I've seen that arch before," Seth groaned, pointing at the red stone archway that stood over this street.

I didn't like to admit it, but the mutt was right. Or it was damn similar to one we'd passed before. Fucking identical.

I glanced back the way we'd come, only more red brick streets awaiting us no matter which way we went.

"Right, fuck this," I said, my hand tightening on my sword. "Let's use air and get above the city. We'll be able to see our friends if we get high enough."

"Why didn't we try that sooner?" Seth sighed, opening his palms to cast air.

I did the same, sending myself flying up towards the open sky with hope blooming in my chest. Maybe the twins would be circling the skies and we could go straight to them.

The moment I made it to the rooftops, a powerful energy slammed into me and I was thrown to the street like I'd been punched by the fist of a star damned giant.

Seth came crashing down beside me, wheezing as the wind was knocked out of him. Before either of us got up, a rumbling sounded beneath us, the road trembling and quaking.

A hole opened up in the ground and Seth grabbed my arm as we fell through it, tumbling away into the dark. I flexed my fingers to cast air, but no magic came to me, a stifling sensation in my chest telling me some strange power had just locked it down.

I braced a second before I hit a hard surface and the light of the sky above was lost as the hole closed up, bricks shifting and twisting back into place, trapping us down here in the pitch black.

"Shit," Seth growled, his hand tightening on my arm and pulling me to my feet.

I held my sword higher, peering into the gloom, but even my heightened vision couldn't pick up a prick of light. There was another rumble of stone somewhere ahead and my grip firmed on the hilt of my weapon. If a monster came at us now, it was going to be one hell of a fight to kill it blind.

The rumbling stopped and a light appeared up ahead, a deep red glow beckoning us toward a narrow stone passage.

"I don't like the ominous vibe that path is giving," Seth muttered. "Creepy red glow in a creepy little passage that was opened up by some creepy old curse magic. Nah, I'm good right here."

"What choice do we have?" I hissed. "Without magic, there's no going back the way we came."

"I can still feel my Order at least," Seth said thoughtfully, and I nodded in agreement.

"I can move us fast if needed then," I said. "But I'm not going to run us down there. We could end up in the jaws of a beast for all I know."

"Alright, come on." Seth stepped forward. "You keep an eye out behind us in case anything creeps after us. I'll be the front eyes."

"Fine," I murmured, letting him take the lead and glancing over my shoulder, ready to slay any creature that might be lurking in the shadows.

We walked into the red glow of the tunnel, the walls either side of us all too close for my liking. There was no real smell here, no damp or mildew or dust. Like nothing so earthly could touch this place. It left me with an uncomfortable feeling stirring in my bones, and I had to wonder if it had been the best idea for us all to head to a cursed city that promised death. Still, I doubted this would be the worst thing we'd faced.

The corridor started climbing, stone steps rising beneath our feet until I was sure we must be at least level with the streets again. Though no windows gave us a view beyond the brick walls, this place a prison in its own right.

We finally stepped into a long chamber with simple wooden furniture and the eerie feeling of someone having just left the room. As if this place had frozen in time the moment the curse had taken root. Where were the bodies? The bones and lasting stench of death? It was almost as though the Fae in this city had ceased to exist. One moment here, the next gone. Was that fate still possible for those who walked within its walls? One that was creeping up on us with every passing second?

The grinding of stone came behind us and I wheeled around with a curse, the passage we'd come from closing up as if it had never been. I threw myself against the newly made bricks that had appeared in the exit, but the stone didn't even shudder from the force I used.

I twisted around with adrenaline brimming in my blood, hunting for another exit, but there was no other door, no window, nothing but two lone wooden chairs and the echo of long-lost souls.

Seth ran back to the wall that had closed over, kicking it hard then scraping his Phoenix flame gauntlets down it, but neither did any good. I threw my weight into it again, shoving it with all my strength, but not even a brick shifted out of place.

"What now?" Seth hissed, and his breath fogged before him, making me notice how cold it was in here.

"It's fucking freezing," I snarled, throwing my fist into the wall again, but even my Order strength couldn't penetrate the strange power of this city.

We worked around the walls, searching for a way forward, shoving the bricks, the floor, the ceiling. But we had no magic to aid us, and there wasn't a single fault in the walls of the stone chamber to break through physically.

Seth caught my eye as we gave up trying to tear our way free. Of all the Wolves in all the world, did I really have to get trapped with this one?

I turned from him, noticing a row of strange symbols on the walls and trying to decipher their meaning. Maybe there was an answer here that would help me escape. And the mutt, I guessed.

Seth drifted closer in my periphery, and I pointedly ignored him.

"What ya doing?" he whispered.

"Concentrating," I growled.

"On what?" he asked.

"Those." I jerked my chin at the symbols and he looked that way too, falling quiet. But stars forbid the Werewolf could stay quiet longer than a minute.

"What do they mean?" he questioned.

"Maybe they mean you're breathing in my personal space, Capella."

"Oh, don't *Capella* me. I'm not your student anymore. We've had a lot of quality time together since then, moon friend."

I ground my teeth, ignoring him. *Don't kill the Wolf. Blue has a fondness for it. A misplaced fondness, but still.*

"Do you know much about old symbols?" he asked.

"A little."

"How much is a little?"

"Just be quiet," I clipped.

He managed it for another ten seconds, but apparently he couldn't help himself. "I don't think these weird pictures are gonna help us." He wandered off to a corner of the room. "There's something else. Some...mystery."

"Sure. Well you go sniff your own ass in that corner and see if it helps then," I muttered.

He chuckled. "At least our banter will keep us amused while we're trapped together."

"It's not banter," I said, shaking my head.

"*Sure* it is. That's what we do. We have this back and forth. You pretend you hate me, and then I'm all adorable and you end up cracking a little smile, then we continue about our day. It's what moon friends do."

I rounded on him, my anger rising at this whole situation. I was separated from the others, from Blue, stuck with him here in some cursed room, and he was already irritating me beyond words. "That's not how it is. You're delusional. I have a select circle of friends, people who I would go to the ends of the earth for and you are not one of them, Seth Capella."

He frowned, a small whimper rising in his throat that did something to my heart. Like poke it with a rusty nail or some shit. "You don't mean that."

"I do," I growled. "Darcy might have forgiven you for all the shit you put us through, but I will never forget. And when I say you are not my friend, and you are certainly not my *moon* friend, I mean it to the depths of my star damned soul. Name one good thing you've done that should earn my forgiveness for that." The vitriolic words spilled from my lips, my rage over the past rising to the surface again, but it came with a slice of guilt I hadn't been expecting. Mostly I was just pissed off about this situation, but now that I had an outlet for my frustration, I was seizing it with both hands.

Seth stared at me like a faithful dog I'd just abandoned in the woods, and I worked hard not to let that expression affect me. I didn't know why he worked his way under my skin sometimes, but it was easy to recall the shit he'd done to my mate, and that put any soft feelings towards him right to bed.

"I saved your life," he blurted, raising a hand to point at me. "I came to that cave in Air Cove where you were lying in a pool of blood, and I saved your ass, Lance Orion. How's that for a good thing?"

"Darcy and Darius saved me that night," I grunted.

"What?!" he scoffed.

"You channelled Darcy's magic and she bought me enough time for Darius to arrive. So you were just…the syringe in that situation, siphoning her magic."

"You know what? You're a stubborn motherfucker," he stated. "And you and Darcy wouldn't even have gotten back together if it wasn't for me taunting you, sending you photos of us together, riling you up into a wild jealousy."

I scowled at him. "I'm supposed to thank you for that? For putting your hands all over my girl? For driving me insane when I couldn't have her?"

"Yes!" he barked. "Because you were just a pathetic little Power Shamed loser who was giving up on life, and I gave you reminders of what you had to fight for."

I shot toward him, my hand slamming against his chest and shoving him so he stumbled back into the wall. "You're so fucking arrogant. You think you can take credit for my relationship? Like you're some kind of relationship expert. You can't even admit your own feelings to Caleb. You just bitch and whine and expect your problems to go away without ever actually solving them."

"I've admitted all kinds of stuff to him, to you, to all of my friends. *You're* the one who isn't able to admit your feelings." He bared his teeth at me.

"What the fuck is that supposed to mean?"

"You and me." He gestured between us. "You act like you don't care about me. That you'd happily see the back of me. But it's bullshit. Because you showed up for me when I needed you."

"When?" I tsked.

"You snuggled me, Lance. You snuggled me when I need snuggling the most," he said, eyebrows raised and triumph in his brown eyes.

I pressed my lips together, unable to deny that. "For Darcy. It's always for Darcy."

"Darcy wasn't there. She was off flapping around in the Palace of Flames. You didn't need to comfort me. You could have turned me away, and Darcy wouldn't have even known about it."

He had me cornered, and I didn't fucking like it. I turned away from him, striding back to the symbols and trying to focus on them instead. "Just stop talking."

"There you go again, trying to avoid it. Why can't you just admit that you like me?" Seth pushed.

"Because you don't get to hurt her and get away with it," I snarled, glaring at him over my shoulder, my muscles tensing for the fight I really wanted to have.

Seth's brows lowered. "Look, bro. I get it. Me and the other Heirs were assholes. But we were under so much pressure, you have no idea. And me and Darcy? We resolved that shit. We became friends – hell, better friends than I ever could have imagined being. And when you were in prison, I was there for her. Every day. I showed up, because she needed me and she was hurting, and I knew part of me was repenting for all the fucked up shit I did. But I just plain cared about her too. She reminded me of who I was without all the layers of politics and ruthless power claiming I'd been moulded for. And honestly, I've never felt more like myself since I let all that shit go. I know Darcy means the world to you because she pulled you from the dark, but she pulled me out too."

My chest tightened and I let silence take the place of my answer. It was too confronting. Because Darcy had relayed the very same thing to me. Seth, the piece of shit who had tormented us at Zodiac Academy, had shown up for her in ways I couldn't when I'd gone to prison. She'd been breaking, lost without me or her twin to turn to, and she'd found a Wolf at her door offering to ease her pain instead. The other Heirs had been there for her too, and they'd all bonded, but she had something special with Seth that I couldn't really deny when I examined it.

"So what are *you* doing?" I growled at Seth.

"Right now? I'm just wondering if it would be weird to lick my own balls. Like hypothetically, if I could get myself to bend that way and-"

"No, I mean with Caleb," I hissed.

"Oh...well I think I've got that under control." He gave me a mysterious look like he wanted me to press him for answers, but I wasn't the sort of guy who could be bothered to pander to that tiring game. He could either tell me or not. I didn't give a fuck. I mean, I wanted Caleb to be happy. And I really wanted Seth to stop bitching about his situation. But apart from that, it didn't matter to me.

"You need to sort your shit out. Our tomorrows aren't promised," I muttered, turning my attention to the symbols again. One seemed to be of a woman shouting, and another was covering her mouth. One was of a chest, and another perhaps a street...

"Gloomy motherfucker, aren't you?" Seth said. "I spoke to Leon, you know. He said you used to be happy. Now you only ever look happy when you're around Darcy. And Gabriel. And Darius. But the point is, you changed. You don't let people in so easily anymore, but once they're in, they're in for good. I'm different to who I used to be. And I'm trying to pay for my sins by being better every day. I hate that I let my parents control me once, I hate that I still feel their claws in me sometimes, and I hate that I know how easy it would be to switch it all off again if I had to. But I'm fighting for this new me because it's the one who's been buried and pushed out of me my whole life. The one I only ever showed to the Heirs before all of you came into my life. And you know why I want to be your friend so bad, Lance?"

"Why?" I grunted.

"Because I've tasted loneliness, I've felt the sting of knowing no one's coming to save you. And I know that you faced that too after what Lionel did to you. You grew bitter and hateful, and so did I. But that's why we're good for each other. In my family, we have a name for pack loyalty. We call it Wolf fidelity. It's my instinct to give that to you, and I don't just give it to anyone. All you have to do is forgive me for what I did to you, and we can have that."

"What you did to Darcy," I corrected. "I don't give a fuck about the rest of it. But you tried to break her."

"I know. But I didn't. And without what I did, she probably wouldn't have gotten so strong, risen up and become queen material."

"Are you trying to take credit for her ascension now?" I warned.

"Nahhh, just like sixty percent of it."

I scowled threateningly.

"Alright, like ten." He raised his hands in innocence.

"Mm."

"What am I gonna have to do to make you move past it?" he asked. "Whatever it is, I'll do it. Because you and me, we're meant to be moon friends. I feel it. Right here." He jabbed a thumb against his chest. "And that's the spot I feel all my moon inklings."

"You don't get moon inklings. And moon friends aren't a thing," I huffed in frustration, carving a hand over my face. We needed to be focusing on getting out of here, not discussing this trivial shit.

He hung his head with a little whine. "Okay, the truth is… I know moon friends aren't a thing. I know the moon hasn't chosen us to be friends. But everyone else is getting all these fancy bonds and maybe I'm a tiny bit jealous. But I feel something for you and it feels sort of moonish, so…"

He let that thought hang in the air, and I let it linger there.

I glanced around the space, a prickling feeling running over my skin. "Is it getting smaller in here?"

"No." Seth shrugged. "Same old four walls and no windows. But it's not smaller."

"Feels smaller," I muttered, my pulse rising a fraction. I needed to get out of here, back to Darcy and the others.

Seth started walking around the edge of the chamber again, running his hand over the red bricks. "There's got to be a secret button or something."

Goosebumps rose on my arms, and I could have sworn the temperature was still dropping. Ice crystals crept across the ceiling, and I cursed, my breath fogging before me.

Maybe dark magic was the answer to this.

I let my fangs extend, raising my arm and biting into my skin to draw blood. I smeared it onto the symbols, awaiting the call of the shadows, but nothing came in reply to my offering.

"No good?" Seth called.

"No. Maybe it needs the blood of an idiot. C'mere."

"Fuck you," he laughed.

The ice crystals continued to creep down the walls and a shiver tracked along my skin. I started checking the floor, hunting for any crack or marking that might offer a clue.

The cold was inching into my bones and from the way Seth was hugging his arms around his body, it was clear he was facing it too.

"It just k-keeps getting colder," he said through chattering teeth.

My breath hitched as I spotted tiny, scrawled writing on the floor, like someone had etched it into the stone.

"Frigus usque mane tolerandum est," I read aloud.

"What's that?" Seth rushed over, dropping to his knees beside me.

"It's in an old tongue," I said, recognising it.

"But you can read it right? Right?" Seth nudged me.

"Sort of…I think it means…you must endure the cold until dawn," I said.

"That's it? That'll open a door?" Seth said excitedly, though this was hardly something to get excited about. Dawn had to be several hours away, and the cold wasn't easing up. Plus, the others were out there facing the stars only knew what. A whole night in this city trapped in here with Seth was not the answer I wanted.

"We'll freeze to death first," I said, rubbing a hand over my chin in concern.

Seth leapt to his feet. "There you go, getting all gloomsday doomsday on me again. But you're in luck, Lance. Because you're stuck in here with a Werewolf, and if there's one thing Wolves know how to do best, it's getting cosy."

I pushed to my feet, rounding on him and finding him taking his sweater off.

"What the fuck are you doing?" I demanded.

He laid the sweater down on the floor, patting it and arranging it just so. "I'm making a bed for us."

"I don't plan on sleeping, and if I did, I would be doing it on my own bed," I said in annoyance.

"That's ridiculous. How will we snuggle if we're in separate beds?" He gave me a genuinely curious look, and I realised what he intended to do to make it through the night.

I swear I could hear the stars laughing at me, and I gritted my teeth against their taunting.

"You know the answer to that question, asshole."

"Look, snuggling is going to save our asses. And to be honest, I'm feeling somewhat unstable right now. My Wolf needs are demanding I have cuddles and an emotionally bonding conversation."

"Oh yeah? Well my Order needs demand I sit alone in silence." I moved to sit against the far wall, nowhere near his damn sweater bed.

Seth sat down, crossing his legs. "Okay, we can take turns. We'll sit in silence for an hour then we can snuggle for an hour and rotate? Cool? Cool."

"No that's not c-"

"Shhhh, your hour has started." He mimed zipping his own lips, and I leaned back against the wall. Far be it from me not to enjoy the quiet while it was offered.

I shut my eyes, trying to imagine myself in a wide-open space with endless fresh air, but it was hard to shake off the feeling of the close walls and the oppressive chamber I was really in. It was so fucking cold that my hands were getting numb and sitting still was only making it worse. We needed to heat up or we seriously weren't going to make it out of here.

Seth lasted probably around the twenty-minute mark before he spoke again. "That's gotta be an hour."

"Nowhere close."

He hugged his knees to his chest, shivering a little as his breath fogged from his lips. "I don't think we can do the silent stay-aparty thing much longer, Lance. I'm freezing my balls off."

He had a point. But dammit, why did I have to be the one to end up with him here?

I shoved to my feet, regretting every footstep I took in his direction, but what choice did we have? I wasn't going to die in here. And it wasn't like me and him hadn't...'snuggled' before. *By the stars.*

Seth perked up as I approached him, shifting sideways on his sweater and patting the small space beside him which was nowhere near big enough for me.

"Take your jacket off and put it here," he encouraged. "A lot of the cold comes through the floor. Oh shit, wait! I just had the best idea." He leapt to his feet as I pulled my jacket off, tossing it down aggressively. Item by item, he stripped out of his clothes, laying them on the floor to make a bed and rolling his boxers up into a pillow.

"There you go," he said brightly. "You can lay your head right there."

I gave the very naked Wolf a deadpan stare. "I'm not using your fucking boxers as a pillow."

"You're pretty fussy for a guy who's about to freeze to death."

"Why are you naked?" I gritted out.

"Because we still have our Order gifts." He grinned big.

"That's true," I said, my heart lifting. He could turn into a giant fluffy Wolf that couldn't talk. It was perfect.

"Get yourself cosy and I'll be your blanket," he said keenly. "You can get naked too if you want, and then you can make a thicker bed with your clothes."

"No, Seth, I will not be getting naked."

"Suit yourself. But don't forget that I'm your hero. And this will be the second time I saved your life."

"Debatable."

"Nah. Fact."

"Shift already, will you?" I insisted, and Seth let the shift take him, his body changing into that of a huge white Wolf.

He came bounding towards me, knocking me over with a big paw and I growled as I hit the floor, my head landing on the boxers-pillow.

"Argh – fuck." I plucked them up and tossed them away from me with a grimace.

Seth flattened me to the floor, knocking the breath from my lungs as the huge weight of him crushed me.

"*Seth*," I rasped, shoving him off me. He lay on his side, opening his big paws wide and gifting me the warmth of his chest.

I let out a long breath of resignation then shuffled into the arc of his body, his legs snaring me and pulling me into the white fuzz. Dammit, he was cosy. And at least like this, he wasn't half as annoying. The steady beat of his heart sounded through his chest, and I let the tension run out of my body. Somewhere, deep in the most bloodthirsty regions of my soul, I felt myself starting to let go of my grudge against the mutt. And maybe, just maybe, he was beginning to grow on me.

XAVIER

CHAPTER NINETEEN

I yanked at the flowerheads that were closed tight around my wrists, their teeth driving into my skin and my magic locked down by the strange liquid which oozed from its jaws. The stem didn't break, and I stared up at the top of the blood red brick pit with a whinny of frustration.

One minute, we'd been walking along the street, the next, the whole world had tipped, the ground becoming a slope and sending us tumbling down into this hole full of carnivorous plants.

Footsteps padded this way and my heart lifted.

"Hello?!" Sofia yelled. "Is someone there? We need help!"

Washer appeared at the top of the pit, his eyes widening at the sight of the three of us below. "Goodness me, are you alright down there in that wet hole? That was quite the earthquake."

"These damn plants are locking down our magic," Tyler explained, trying to rip one free from the ground, but it was no good. Blood bled down his wrist from his efforts and I stamped my foot, furious that I'd let this happen to my herd.

"Not to worry. I've had plenty of experience extracting a fellow or two from tight spots," Washer said, rolling up his sleeves and preparing to cast magic. It wasn't entirely comforting to have him as our rescuer, but we didn't have much choice.

"Wait," Sofia gasped, but two of the flowers were already shooting toward him, their thick stems extending unnaturally and their sharp jaws wide. "They're drawn to magic!"

Washer yelped as one of the flowers snapped around his left hand, sending a blast of water at the other one and knocking it away from him. But the first flower tugged on him with frightening power, and he was forced over the edge. His feet got stuck in the sap that lined the walls and the ledge above, and he fell, his feet still stuck at the top of the wall while his face went slamming into the bricks, sticking in the green gloop coating it.

The flower tugged on him again and he was ripped off of the wall, his shirt and pants torn clean off his body, left hanging in the sap as he went flying to the bottom of the pit in a pair of tight purple briefs. He hit the ground with a groan, then grabbed the flower by the stem in a chokehold, freezing it with his ice. Another flower came tearing towards him and I tried to kick it, but it snared Washer's free hand.

"No," I gasped, our only hope now trapped down here with us.

Washer got to his feet, pulling on the flowers with all his might, but he couldn't get free any easier than we could.

"Blast," he cursed. "I almost had us out of here."

"Almost had us out of here?" Tyler scoffed. "You didn't do anything!"

"Now, now, watch your tone, Mr Corbin. I'm in charge here," Washer said, rising to his feet and considering our predicament.

"Bullshit," I growled. "We're not your students anymore, and I'm the most powerful Fae in this pit."

Washer scrutinised me with a frown, then inclined his head. "Forgive me, I didn't mean to step on your tippy toes, Xavier. You are a fine specimen of Fae, but I must say, I do have a teeny weeny idea to get our hands out of these clenched wet petals."

"Go on then," I said through my teeth.

"Well I know a thing or two about these plants. Starclamps, they're called. And there is one thing that can make their jaws release us from their grasp."

"I read about these," Sofia gasped, her eyes brightening in horror. "If we stay here too long, they will slowly but surely dissolve the skin from our bones and ingest it."

"How do we make them let go then?" Tyler pushed, looking to Washer in desperation.

"They just need a little tickle in the right spot," he said. "Finding the spot is the trouble."

"I think the real trouble is how we're supposed to tickle them without our hands," I said, wincing as the teeth on my right wrist sunk a little deeper.

"Not a problem, my boy." Washer kicked off his shoes and dropped down to the ground, lifting his foot right up to his face with no bother. He caught his sock between his teeth and spread his unveiled toes, wiggling them before placing them on one of the stems and tickling it.

I grimaced, watching as he worked methodically along the stem, seeking out the right spot. His toes were weirdly flexible, and something about their movements unnerved me, but who was I to complain if they were going to save us all?

Washer scooted along the ground on his ass, spreading his tanned legs and wiggling his toes against the flower stems holding his hands. It was uncomfortable to watch, but for some reason, I couldn't look away.

"I don't think it's working, Washer," Tyler said, sharing a disgusted look with Sofia.

"Nonsense. I just need to find the right spot, rub that little nub in just the right cranny and I'll free us in no time," Washer insisted.

A yodel sounded somewhere off in the abandoned city, bouncing from wall to wall, echoing everywhere.

"That was Geraldine," Sofia said excitedly. "Do you think she's close?"

"Geraldine!" Tyler yelled. "We're over here!"

We made as much noise as we could, trying to draw the attention of any of our friends, but no one appeared.

"I hope they're alright," Tyler murmured.

"They're fine," I said firmly, refusing to let myself consider any other option. "We'll find them as soon as we're out of here."

A grinding of stone sounded behind me and a nervous prickle ran up my spine.

"Um, Xavier," Sofia whispered, and I turned, following her gaze to a tunnel that had opened up in the wall. Snakes spilled out of it, hundreds of long, slithering bodies rippling together and coiling towards us.

"Everybody stay still," Sofia hissed. "Those are velox snakes, they'll strike at any sudden movement. Their venom is deadly."

"By the stars," I breathed, freezing in place.

Washer stopped moving too, his legs still wide as snakes slithered over his ankles.

Another grinding of rock made me look up and I cursed as a circle of stone twisted out from the edge of the pit above, slowly sealing us in.

"Now what?" Tyler growled.

"Not to worry," Washer said. "Gently lower yourselves down and spread your flower stems across the ground. Let the smooth shafts of the hungry serpents do the tickling for us."

It wasn't a bad plan, so as one, we inched towards the floor, trying to move as slowly as possible. My fingers were starting to tingle inside the flowers, and I tried not to think about why that was. In all honesty, this whole situation could have had me in a complete panic, but I had to stay strong for my herd. I'd get them out of here no matter what. And if I lost my head and made a wrong move, it could cost them their lives. As for Washer, well, I guessed the guy deserved to make it out of here. He had come to our rescue after all.

My ass touched the ground and I gently lowered my arms so the stems lay among the writhing snake bodies. We were losing light by the second as the slab of stone crossed overhead, and I shuddered as it finally closed with a thud.

Instead of being left in total darkness like I'd expected, the snakes' bodies began to glow just enough to see by.

"This had better work," I said, keeping my lip movements to a minimum.

"It will, my boy," Washer promised, lowering his body even further to the ground and splaying himself out among the snakes in a tortuously slow movement.

We waited in anxious silence as the snakes slithered this way and that, passing all over the stems, but not one of the flowers released us.

"My hands are going numb," Tyler hissed. "This isn't working, we need a new plan."

"There's got to be a way," I whispered anxiously. My hands were tingling and I didn't know how long we had until these plants started digesting our fingers.

"Wait a moment." Washer moved his foot the tiniest amount, picking up a sharp-looking stone between his toes. "Perhaps we can cut ourselves free."

"Can you do that with your feet?" I asked in shock, though it was clear he had some serious dexterity in his toes.

"Of course, my boy. I have spent years practising toe flexation in a quest to one day possess as much nimbleness in my feet as I do in my hands. It comes in quite handy when those lusty urges call many a Fae to my bed and I need to lend a toe or three to caress, fondle, dip, or pump a lover's cog or cranny."

"Fucking hell, just get on with it, will you?" I demanded.

Washer ever-so-slowly moved the sharp rock against one of the stems, working to cut it without drawing the snakes' attention.

It was an arduous process, but eventually, the stem split apart and Washer was partially freed. The flower might still have been clamped over his left hand, but he wasn't tethered to the ground anymore.

"Do the other one," Sofia urged, and Washer got working on it, bending and grunting a little as he worked. I couldn't stop staring at the way his toes handled that stone and his legs bent at such a wide angle that it was all I could do to keep my gaze away from his lightly thrusting crotch.

Suddenly, he was free, and we released breaths of relief as he crawled his way toward me next, careful not to disturb any of the snakes. It took a few minutes, but he finally used his feet to cut the stems holding me down too and he cautiously made his way towards Sofia next, his ass pointing right my way in those overly tight briefs.

At last, when the four of us were free, Washer led the way into the tunnel, moving slow as hell to keep the snakes from noticing. I was second in line but immediately regretted it seeing as my nose was a few inches from Washer's ass. Without the glow of the snakes, it was pitch dark in the passage and I had no idea how far it went, but I prayed it would lead us outside again. If we could find the others, they might be able to get these damn flowers off of us, then we could get back to the task at hand.

"I smell clean air, laddies," Washer called.

"I don't," I muttered, grimacing at his ass even though I couldn't see it ahead of me. But then he stopped abruptly, and my face slammed right into it.

"Argh," I grunted. "Just keep moving. Don't stop star damned moving."

Despite the ass in my face, I *could* smell fresher air up ahead and sensed we were on the right path. The stars were twisting our fortunes today and dragging us through the gutter, but we weren't done for yet.

DARCY

CHAPTER TWENTY

I swung my mother's white sword, the steel striking the rat beast which stood as tall as me, and the thing fell dead at my feet.

"Not much of a challenge," Darius commented as he withdrew his axe from the head of another monstrous rat.

"Shh, the city of doom is probably listening and it'll up its game," I whispered.

He smirked. "Scared, little shrew?"

"For myself? Nope. I just don't want Tory to have to claw her way into death again to get you out." I gave him a teasing grin. "I've got to protect my big brother-in-law for her sake."

He gave me a dry look worthy of Orion, and I swept past him down the red brick street.

My amusement fell away as we kept walking, searching for any sign of our group.

Something about this city was wholly unnatural, the air too still and the silence too thick. I'd already tried flying up to find them, but nothing but empty streets and terracotta rooftops stared back at me. Whenever I'd flown too far in one direction, I'd ended up back where I started, so we'd guessed there was some enchantment keeping us from finding them.

For now, we were on our own, and I could think of far worse company to keep than Darius Acrux these days. It was hard to reconcile our new friendship with the old hatred that had lived between us, but here we were.

We walked down another maze of streets before Darius broke the silence.

"There was a place beyond The Veil that felt like this," he said, and my ears pricked up at that. I never knew how hard to push him for details about his time in death, but I was brimming with questions.

"Cursed?" I guessed.

"Tainted," he said darkly. "There was an ancient soul there who lived in a cave. She had lost so many pieces of herself to memory, she was barely Fae anymore. She was unnatural to behold."

The grim look in his eyes set the hairs raising on the back of my neck.

"What else did you see there?" I asked.

He frowned, his thumb trailing over the hilt of his axe. "I saw fragments of people who no longer are, clinging to something that no longer is."

My heart sank as I thought of my parents, of Hamish and Catalina too. "Is it that way for all the souls?"

He shook his head. "No, Gwen. There's light there too. Hope, in a way."

"Tell me more," I asked, my voice quiet like that of a little girl hoping for a bedtime story. But this meant more to me than that. It was everything. Darius had spent time with my parents; he knew them in a way I would never know them in this life.

He blew out a breath, his lips lifting at the corner. "Well, your father's an asshole."

"He is?" I asked, disappointment falling over me.

Darius glanced up and down the street before leaning in close to speak to me in a low voice. "The best kind of asshole."

The wind stirred around us, and Darius raised his brows. "If you heard that, Hail. You misheard it."

"You think he's here now?" I asked excitedly, remembering what he'd told us about being able to see people he cared for while he'd been beyond The Veil.

"Could be," Darius muttered. "They're often watching, him and your mother. But it takes a lot of energy to push through The Veil and stand at the side of a loved one. It's easier to watch from afar."

My fingers tightened on the hilt of my sword. "What was my mother like?"

The lump in my throat wouldn't ease as I awaited an answer to that. I'd dreamed of having a mother as a child, someone who held me when I was sick, who braided my hair for school, who was always there for me when it felt like the world was crumbling. Tory and I had become that for each other, fulfilling every need our parents couldn't in any way we knew how. But that burden should never have rested on us, our mother and father should have been there through it all, and we'd been robbed of that privilege. All because of Lionel.

"She's stubborn, fierce, and smart as all hell. She loves you more than anything in this realm or the next," he said seriously. "As does Hail. Azriel too. He told me to tell you how grateful he was for all you'd done for Lance and that he'd be celebrating with all the lost souls who adore you when you seize your crown. Your parents are fit to bursting with pride, they're fucking dying to see you on the throne. It's pretty beautiful, if I'm honest."

I realised we'd come to a halt, and the aged wound in my chest broke apart, the chasm those lost souls should have filled. To learn they were out there somewhere, watching us, cheering us on, loving us even now, it was both painful and comforting.

"And what about your mother?" I asked, my throat tightening at the loss of Catalina. For the briefest of moments, I'd known her affection, and it had been one of the purest things I'd been offered in my life. She and Hamish had been stolen away all too soon, just like my parents had, like Orion's father had. Too much death had been dealt at the hands of the Dragon King and he had so much to pay for. But it could never undo what had been done. It could never bring them back.

"She's at peace," Darius said, emotion warring in his eyes. "She's happy now. Free. It's not life, but death isn't as final as it seems. There is joy to be had for her and Hamish yet."

"That's good," I rasped, the pain of it all near choking me.

Before I knew it, the two of us moved into an embrace, our losses shared and the grief of it eased in each other's arms. It was almost impossible to believe I had come to think of Lionel's ruthless son as a brother, but somehow we'd gotten here, treading an unforeseeable path that had changed us both irrevocably.

The creaking of a door hinge made us split apart, and I raised my sword while Darius lifted his axe.

A single door stood open across the street, leading into a house that looked like all the others.

I stepped toward it, but Darius caught my arm.

"Are you planning on walking right through the door that creepily opened just for us?" he growled.

"It's either that or continue circling these streets aimlessly. I think we have to do what the city wants us to do." I tried to step forward again, but his grip only tightened.

"Gwen."

"Darius." I arched a brow.

He sighed, releasing me.

"Death's made you into a cautious old man," I jibed, striding toward the door with my sword raised and the tingle of Phoenix fire in my palms.

"Bullshit," he hissed, coming up right behind me. "I just don't want you getting your head eaten by a monster rat because you have slower reflexes than me."

I threw my elbow back into his gut and he barked a laugh.

"What were you saying before your super-fast reflexes didn't stop me from elbowing you?" I asked sweetly.

He shoved me sideways with such force that I nearly fell over, and he went strolling into the house without looking back. "Hurry up, Gwen. I won't save any kills for you."

I stalked after him with my lips pursed. "If you keep calling me Gwen, I'll stab you in the ass with my sword."

"That's your mother's sword. And by the way, she mentioned it does this." He twisted around, reaching for the hilt and grazing his thumb over the rivets of the wings winding around it. The blade illuminated in an ethereal white glow and I inhaled sharply in surprise at its beauty.

"Now when you strike, it'll give off an extra pulse of energy or some shit," he explained.

"Where's a monster rat when you need one?" I muttered, wanting to try it out.

The door swung shut at my back with a slam that sent a bolt of adrenaline into my veins. Darius and I were on guard immediately, weapons raised and muscles tensed for a coming fight. When nothing happened, I reached for the door handle, but it was no longer real, the door just a painting on a red brick wall.

"Shit," I breathed.

"Go through the creepy door, she said," Darius taunted. "Nothing bad will happen, she said."

"I never said nothing bad would happen. I said we need to do what the doomed city wants us to do."

"Same difference," he chuckled, then turned towards the only way on which happened to be a very dark stairway.

The light of my sword cut through the gloom, so I didn't bother to cast a Faelight, cautiously following Darius up the stairs. The wood creaked beneath our feet, the sound setting me on edge, every muscle in my body coiled in preparation of an attack.

At the top of the stairs, we stepped through a door, finding ourselves in a room with no windows and no passage forward, so far as I could tell.

The wall shifted behind us and we whirled around as a block of stone slammed into place in the doorway, sealing us in here.

"Fuck." Darius rammed his shoulder against it, shoving it with all his might.

"Step back," I said, and he obliged.

I raised my hand, but no magic came to my fingertips, something about the power in this place locking down my Elements.

"Dammit," I growled, then lifted the sword and swung it against the stone. A powerful surge of energy burst from the blade and a crack ripped out across the stone, tearing into the walls too. But before I could get too excited, the crack sealed over, like the walls were healing themselves.

"Fuck this place," Darius snarled, smoke seeping between his teeth. "I'll shift and break us out of here."

A hissing noise sounded and we hunted for the source of it, finding a pink mist filtering into the room from small holes in the walls.

I grabbed the material of my shirt, hurriedly pulling it up over my nose and mouth, and Darius did the same.

"Shift now," I urged.

"I can't," he cursed.

The mist circled us and there was nothing I could do to keep it out, my eyes finding Darius's and my hand falling to his arm. Terror clutched me in a fierce grip. It wasn't just us at risk. If this mist equalled our deaths, it equalled Tory's too.

But one inhale swept that worry into the breeze. All thoughts were lost to me, and I closed my eyes, blinking away the fluffy haze in my head.

When I opened my eyes again, I was lying in my bed in Aer Tower, a beautiful summer's day gleaming at me through the window. I smiled contentedly, getting out of bed and falling into the familiar routine of showering and dressing in my Zodiac Academy uniform.

It wasn't long before I was walking up the path towards The Orb, everything perfectly normal and oh so right. Kylie Major waved at me, smiling her friendly smile as I walked into The Orb, and I smiled back.

"Hey bestie, how did you sleep?" she asked brightly.

"Like a log," I said, looking for my twin in the room. And of course, she was there with her boyfriend, sitting on his lap on the red couch in the middle of the room, softly caressing his hat.

"I'll catch you in a bit," I said, jogging away from Kylie towards Tory and Diego. He was grinning at her, and she slapped his chest as if he'd said something funny.

"Hey, Tor," I called, and she looked up, waving me over.

Before I could move in that direction, a voice sounded behind me.

"Morning, beautiful."

I turned, finding Lance Orion walking this way wearing his letterman Pitball jacket over his school uniform. For a moment, I thought his dark eyes were pinned on me, but he swept on by and grabbed Seth Capella, sinking his tongue between his lips. The two of them kissed like no one was watching and I darted past them, leaving them to that overt display, moving to sit beside Tory and Diego.

Tory was adjusting Diego's hat like she was trying to decide just what way she liked it on him. She really loved that hat.

A strange feeling rushed over me, like something was off about this situation. But the feeling passed, and I didn't dwell on it. I couldn't see anything remotely wrong with this scene. Tory adored Diego, and he adored her. I couldn't think of a single thing that didn't make them the perfect couple.

"Ergh, she's here," Tory hissed, and I bristled when I realised who had walked into The Orb.

Geraldine Grus. Queen bitch. The girl couldn't make it through a day without ramming a bagel down someone's throat. She made a beeline for Kylie Major, and Kylie made a good effort of trying to fight her off, but Geraldine soon had her upended in a trash can with a bagel balancing on her ass.

"Do any other whelks want to dance the danger disco?" Geraldine bayed, gazing around the room as she hunted for more victims. She spotted Milton Hubert looking her way and raced after him, the poor guy screaming and running for the door.

Orion and Seth finally stopped making out and came to join us on the couch, Orion slinging his arm around Seth's shoulders with casual intimacy.

"Do you want a coffee, moon friend?" Seth asked him.

"Moon *lover*," Orion corrected with a smirk, and Seth chuckled, squeezing Orion's knee. "You sit right there. I'll get us coffee." Orion shot away with the speed of his Order, returning a second later with two cups of coffee, handing one to his boyfriend.

I stared between them, an unsettling feeling washing over me. This wasn't... right. Or was it?

A shimmering pink glow at the edge of my vision made me blink and I forgot what I'd been thinking, my attention drawn across the room again to where Geraldine was force-feeding bagels to Milton.

"Take that, you rapscallion of the goon land!" Geraldine cried, making me shudder in terror.

"Cooeeeee."

That sultry voice. Every Fae with a pulse was enraptured by it as Professor Washer stepped into The Orb looking good enough to eat. His leather pants creaked as he walked and his floral shirt was unbuttoned right down to his navel, revealing all that delicious tanned, waxed skin. How was anyone supposed to resist him? He was the epitome of hot.

I bit my lip as he walked by, sashaying his hips and drawing every eye in the room.

"By the stars..." Caleb appeared, his eyes following Washer before he dropped onto the couch. "If I wasn't a taken man, and one taste of Washer wouldn't put me in Darkmore...I'd shoot my shot with that professor."

"I can't believe you're dating her though," Seth said. "Come on, bro, she's our enemy."

"Which makes it even hotter," Caleb said, man-spreading in his chair.

I cursed as Geraldine noticed him, running over at such speed that she held her breasts to stop them bouncing. She landed on his lap with a noise like a yowling alley cat, then sank her tongue between his lips. Caleb groaned, pulling her closer and when they parted, she caressed his cheek and whispered, "My fancy fang-dangler...bite me like a wild grouse in a windy meadow."

Caleb sank his fangs into her neck just as Max appeared hand in hand with Xavier Acrux.

I blinked hard, something about this scene not feeling accurate again, but as Tory met my gaze, I relaxed. What could possibly be wrong?

"Your boyfriend's here." Tory nudged me and I looked around, trying to spot who she meant, for some reason uncertain who it could be.

Darius Acrux came sweeping towards me across The Orb and was upon me in seconds, grabbing my hand and towing me from my seat. I tiptoed up, his large hand cupping my face and his dark eyes turning gold for a moment. I leaned in, but a sense of disgust filled me as his lips closed in on mine.

"He's your mate!" Tory called.

"Go on, kiss!" Orion encouraged, and I blinked hard as the haze descended on me once more.

My mate...of course he's my mate. That makes total sense.

I leaned in for the kiss again, our lips almost touching when a flare of memory tore through my mind. Me standing under the stars opposite the love of my life, Lance Orion. Claiming him while he claimed me.

Darius's mouth barely grazed mine, but we jerked back at the exact same moment, his palm on my cheek now shoving me away instead of drawing me closer while my face screwed up in horror.

The vision dissolved just like that and we were back in the sealed room, staring at each other in disgust.

"What the fuck?" he blurted, wiping his mouth at the mere idea of it being so close to mine.

"Ew, ew, ew." I backed away further, my skin prickling uncomfortably. "That was fucked up. Why does the creepy city want to make us kiss?" I grimaced at him, unable to think of anything less appealing. He was a brother to me. My sister's mate. Ergh.

"I think it was a test," Darius said thickly, clearly as disturbed by the idea of kissing me as I was by him. He was about as appealing to me as a rotten potato. "Fuck that hat kid. He had his hands all over my wife."

"Yeah? Well Lance made out with Seth." I shuddered.

Darius roared a laugh. "That's kinda funny."

"It's not funny," I hissed, a flare of territorial instincts burning through me.

"Alright, alright." He looked around the space and a grinding of stone offered us a new way on.

I raised my mother's sword, walking toward the exit with rage in my chest. If this city wanted a fight, it was about to get one. No one tried to make me kiss my brother-in-law and got away with it.

GERALDINE

CHAPTER TWENTY ONE.

"Have you noted the way time passes here?" I asked curiously, my fingers drifting along a wall of deepest red, exploring the nooks and crannies of the unnatural bricks. "Like it trickles and then spurts. Water blocked by a dam and occasionally allowed free."

"I'm more concerned about the beast which has been trying to eat us," Max growled at my back, his voice a deep bass of marked panic.

"Well of course you are," I said, knowing he would be so distracted. "That is the entire point after all. Yet I have scented the trick beneath the trappings."

Our magic was unpredictable here, and though a silencing bubble held us snug and dandy, I didn't trust it not to pop at any given moment.

"What trick?" Max demanded.

I turned to him, my gaze lingering on the ragged claw marks slashed through the shoulder of his fighting leathers and the shining blood of the wound which our magic had refused to heal.

He'd saved me from that wound, my gallant barracuda, knocking me aside when the creature had lunged from the sky, talons poised to snatch me away, its ruinous face filled with hungry glee.

I had smashed said face like an overripe banana with the Flail of Unending Celestial Karma for trying to wrench my Maxy boy away, but those talons had dug deep and cut well before releasing him.

The run here had been swift and desperate, his wound drawing far more of my attention than I could admit to. We were an ill-fated pair for a quest such as this. Our emotions were too tangled to allow for the ruthless decisions of war.

We'd found a modicum of shelter here, in the porch of some stately building that looked like it might have housed a great lord or lady once. Now left to moulder in this city of forgotten bones.

A ferocious cry rebounded from the walls of the surrounding buildings and though terror tried to tempt my trumpet, I cast it aside, listening instead to the way the sound moved.

"There's nothing here but death," Max hissed, his teeth gritted against the pain.

"Even death cannot hide all things," I countered. "For I have discovered a game afoot."

"What game?" Max stepped closer to me.

I pressed a hand to his cheek, looking into his eyes and taking in the stalwart determination of a true warrior therein.

"Have you the strength left to run?" I asked him with all seriousness, though I didn't doubt his valour for a moment.

"If you're running then I'm right there at your back," he swore, and by golly my waters did run riotous at that.

"The sound moves," I breathed, my eyes alight with the truth of it. "It dances all around in a pattern anything but natural."

The beast hunting us screamed in the heavens again, and my soul lit with the truth of my words as the resounding echoes failed to sound from the path that led away to our right.

Max stilled as he noticed the unnatural silence too and a spark of determination lit his eyes.

He drew his bow and I swung my flail.

"Into the yonder we ride," I hissed, and without another dilly, we were off.

The beast shrieked as it spotted us, the sky darkening overhead where its leathery wings spread wide and chased us down the gently sloping street. But its cries were precisely what I required, and I grinned a savage grin as I raced towards that spot of nothing, that silence in the dark.

Max ran powerfully at my back, loosing an arrow which blazed with Phoenix fire and causing another roar to echo out around us when it hit its mark.

But I knew well the legend of the Rather Bat, though it was thought to be extinct. I had my suspicions that we had come across the last of its kind in this foul place. It had four hearts, each of them able to regenerate given the time to do so. Its talons were razor sharp and its fangs laced with a poison so toxic that it was said to paralyse its prey instantly upon biting them.

Though my noble form feared no poisons, my dear Maxy was not so fortunately endowed.

The enormous bat was forced to wheel aside as Maxy fired again, and I jerked to the right abruptly, squeezing myself into a near non-existent gap between two towering houses of red brick.

Maxy cursed as he followed, his broad form perhaps a tighter squeeze than even my Brendas afforded me, though as the tips of my pointed breastplate gouged lines into the bricks, I wasn't entirely certain of that.

"The silence shifted," I said by way of explanation, and Max grunted his agreement.

"We can't outpace it much longer," he added, not in a cowardly way but with the practical words of a soldier who had deftly assessed his enemy.

"Take heart," I told him, "For we fight on the side of what is just and true."

The little scoff he gave was clearly a wordless agreement to my assessment, nothing could thwart us in this quest. I knew it in my bones.

I pushed myself from the end of the alleyway, a scream lodging in my throat as the bat sprung its trap, colliding with me at full force and throwing me to the ground.

"Gerry!" Max bellowed as I was dragged along, its talons fighting for purchase in my gleaming breastplate, the metal coating my back shrieking as it dragged across the cobbles at speed.

I was thrown against the hard edge of a stone fountain, pinned there with jaws snapping for my face and my flail flying from my grasp. But then I heard the silence pressing in from my right.

"Head west!" I bellowed, using what little time I had left to tell my sweet love where to find the answer to this riddle. "And remember me well!"

The jaws of death snapped at my throat, and I swung a fist clad in a shining gauntlet emblazoned with the mark of the True Queens at its foul face.

The beast reared back, propelling me away from it so my momentum flung me into a wall which cracked at the impact.

Still the silence rang out from the west, thicker now, nearer than ever.

But between the thrashing wings of the beast which dove for me again, I did not see dear Maxy running for victory. Nay – he was racing for insignificant me. And though I groaned at the valour wasted on a wretch such as I, I couldn't help but feel a note of warmth in my cockles at the gesture.

I scrambled on my back, reaching for the knife at my belt and ripping it free just as the bat lunged for my throat.

Its fangs pierced deep and true, poison sliding into me, my arm slowing in momentum though not stopping as I swung my devilish blade.

Four hearts did not save it from a dagger through the eye.

Its weight fell slack upon me, its teeth slicing through flesh and cartilage as even in death it tore deeper into my body.

A stillness came for me then, even as its weight crushed me to the ground. I was in the grasp of its poison and I knew that none could survive such a bite.

Maxy ripped the thing off of me, the cool air kissing my cheeks, though the taint of this cursed place hung stagnant within it.

"Gerry," he gasped, eyes all a-panic, hand going to my throat as he willed healing magic to spark between us while the curse of the city fought to keep it from him.

But it did spark, like kindling snaffing hold of a frame, it did.

"I've got you, Gerry. I'm here," he swore, and oh, wouldn't there be far worse ways to die than this – in the arms of my beloved lobster?

But not today. For I was no mere collyrodger and my blood pumped with the power of the Cerberus. No poison could lay claim to me, and no bat would steal me from the wings of this war and the final ascension that I knew was to come.

I heaved in a breath laced with blood from my ravaged throat and pushed Maxy back before he'd fully healed the wound. I could breathe and I wasn't bleeding enough to beckon death closer yet.

"West," I hissed, rolling to my feet and ignoring his spluttered protests as I took off through the red streets.

Left, right, left again. I cried out to make the silence answer me, chasing it through alley and gully, past temple and tower until finally, I came to a glimmering chest which sat there plainly in the centre of the street, power emanating from it in a way which seemed altogether too mocking.

"What ho," I breathed, my footsteps echoed by my deadly dolphin as we approached.

"It could be dangerous," he muttered, reaching out to take on the danger himself, but I knocked his hand aside.

"Save the gallantry for the boudoir," I told him. "This trifling trinket shan't thwart me."

I kicked the chest open, and we peered into the near empty space inside, spotting a fat, amethyst stone at its centre representing Aquarius. It lay upon a parchment with ancient words inscribed across its surface, no doubt denoting the curse that had befallen this city. Beside it lay the feather of a forlax, a gnarled bone, and a scattering of mandycrops – bad omens indeed. The makings of this city's bane by some wily sorcerer's hand long ago.

A smile crept across my lips and I reached out to claim the amethyst, the relief of finding my suspicions correct a resounding boon upon my pride.

A rumble trembled through the ground at my feet as I stood upright again, parting the Guild Stone from the curse-bringing items, and the city of Herithé released a long, overdue sigh as it crumbled into ash.

All around me buildings, streets, and walls fell to nothing, fading away as if they'd never been and revealing our companions in the wasteland which was left behind.

"Oh, sweet raisin bran, had you given in to the call of death, dear fellows?" I cried as I spotted Orion and Seth snuggled up in a ball where they had quite clearly given in to the inevitability of death and sought comfort in the arms of one another while they wept for all they assumed lost. "Wipe those tears from your eyes, dear Orion, you need sniffle no more. For I have found the stone and saved you like a damsel who had given up all hope before a knight came to your rescue."

"I'm not crying," Orion snapped. "It's water that's melted – we were freezing in there and ice had formed on my cheeks."

"Whatever you say, sweet boy," I told him, giving him an understanding wink which caused his face to contort in a way that I could only describe as pure, undying gratitude to me for saving him.

A blur of motion announced the arrival of the other Vampire in our midst as he sped to us from the furthest reaches of what had once been Herithé.

"You did it!" my lady Tory cried as Caleb placed her on her feet, and I could only bow before her gratitude, gasping in surprise as she threw her arms around me. "You really saved our asses, Geraldine. Me and Caleb were trapped in a tower fighting these fucking crow things off, but I don't think we could have lasted much longer."

"You would have prevailed!" I protested, refusing to believe she might ever succumb to such a lowly death.

"Luckily, I saved our asses when the city crumbled," Caleb added. "Because we fell about two hundred feet out of the damn sky when that tower fell to shit."

"Yeah, yeah, the day was saved because you made the ground spongy – nothing at all to do with Geraldine being a badass and finding the stone," Tory replied, and I blushed deepest crimson at the compliment.

"Cooee!" Washer called, running towards us in nothing but a ghastly purple wrapping around his loins.

My Pego-brother and his herd were with him, trotting this way with some strange splodges on their hands, but those very splodges crumbled, turning to dust along with the city and they all paused to stare down at their fingerlings in relief.

Darcy and Darius finally reached our motley crew, not looking at each other too closely and having very little to say about whatever danger dangler they had faced. But it seemed they had come out as triumphant as termites in an ant war.

Once everyone had assured themselves that we were all alive and dandy, I knelt before my former professor and offered up the final piece to his puzzle.

"What now?" Darcy asked keenly as he took it, despite the Dragoon looking inclined to snatch it for his own.

"Now," Orion said thoughtfully, inspecting the stone in the light. "We find out exactly what way the Guild Stones can change the fate of Solaria. And we learn what happens when the rightful sovereigns hold the power of all twelve."

ORION

CHAPTER TWENTY TWO

We stood around a table in King's Hollow, eleven of the Guild Stones laid out in a circle before us, and I swear the tree itself was humming with the power that lay within it. I held the final stone between my fingers, glancing at Darcy, then to Tory and the Heirs, Xavier, and Geraldine. Sofia and Tyler had left to finish up some press work with Portia, and Washer had gone to let the Councillors know about our progress.

Everyone held their breath as I placed the last stone into the circle, all of them touching, united after who knew how many years.

The power of them crackled against my fingertips and charged the air with electricity, but then it all fell away, nothing but a void of silence filling the space.

Seth reached out to prod the Aquarius amethyst stone. "Why is nothing happening? Isn't something meant to be happening?" He looked to me then around the room as if he expected some wondrous magic to appear before him.

"I thought their use would become clear once they were united," I said, turning my arm over and bringing it close to the stones so that the Guild mark ignited along my skin, the sword glittering brightly like it knew it was in the presence of the twelve stones. But nothing further happened.

"Maybe they're not all touching." Darcy frowned, leaning close to check the circle.

"Or we got one wrong?" Tory said anxiously.

"I've checked them all," Darius growled. "They're real. Every last one of them. Lance's Guild mark has proved it for each of them too."

"Oh, what grave gallcakes indeed," Geraldine said woefully. "Such hope was riding on the back of their tidings."

"We just need to figure out how they work, that's all," Max said firmly, and Geraldine lifted her chin.

"You're right of course, dear salmon. I must not let my heart become a whelk at the very first sign of a shark fin."

A sense of failure closed in on me. I'd convinced everyone in this room to seek out these stones. We'd risked our lives for them. If they didn't offer us some advantage in the war, then what the fuck was the point of them?

Darcy took my arm, and I looked down at her, her silver-ringed eyes glinting at me. I couldn't let her down. These stones were meant to offer her and Tory a chance at ascending to the throne once and for all. A new fate would dawn, Merissa had foreseen it and my father had said it himself in my diary. It was why he was dead. Why he'd sacrificed everything to give us this chance.

A steely determination took root in my soul. I couldn't give up hope at the first sign of failure. I'd felt the power when the Guild Stones had been reunited. There was an answer here, a way to activate them. We just weren't seeing it yet.

My father's diary lay on the table, its secrets locked for now, but it was a full moon tonight. Maybe it would be worth checking through the passages again. But my doubts gnawed deeper, because I already knew my father's intention had been for us to find the Imperial Star and wield it. What if we'd needed it to make the Guild Stones useful to us now? What if there was no longer a way for us to weave a new fate? I decided not to voice that fear; the idea that I'd had everyone running around chasing these stones and risking their lives for nothing was too awful to consider.

"Darius," I said suddenly, my gaze snapping to him. "What did my father say to you beyond The Veil? He must have spoken of these stones. He must have had some clue of their use."

Darius shook his head, looking dejected. "We only spoke of you finding them, I never thought to ask what to do when you did. It wasn't like I thought I'd be back here when you found them."

"Well, that's just perfect," Seth huffed, walking away from the table and kicking a chair over so it went crashing onto the floor.

"We'll figure it out," Caleb called to him.

"And what if we don't?" Seth snarled. "What if this has all been for nothing, and they're just a bunch of pointless rocks?"

"Stay calm." Max sent a wave of relaxing energy through the room, and I let it wash over me before my frustration kept climbing.

"There's got to be an answer in your dad's book." Tory picked up the diary, rifling through it even though it couldn't be read without the light of the full moon gilding its pages.

"Yeah, we're just missing something. We can read through your father's words again tonight and maybe we'll find something we didn't see before," Darcy said encouragingly, though I could see the tension in her body.

Too much was riding on this. And I couldn't fucking fail her.

I snatched the diary out of Tory's hands. "I've read it front to back. If there was an answer, I'd know it already."

"What about that whole initiating people into the Guild thing?" Darcy said. "You had that potion brewed for new members to drink, right? And didn't it say in your dad's diary that all the stones needed to be united to restore balance to the kingdom *and* reform the Zodiac Guild."

"Lolloping leafbugs, my lady is as correct as a claffencheese!" Geraldine exclaimed. "Perhaps all we need to do is drink the potion, and all shall be revealed like a daisy upon the first day of spring."

"I don't think we should use that until we're certain it would work," I growled. "And the initiation can't be taken lightly because I don't yet know the consequences of drinking that potion. Besides, who knows if we'll get another chance to brew it? It takes six weeks. And we don't have another six weeks."

"We have days at best before my father tries to strike at us again," Darius agreed grimly, and Seth let out a mournful howl.

"Perhaps it is worth risking a twirl beyond The Veil then?" Geraldine said. "I shall sup upon the Guild elixir's merry waters, and we shall see what we see."

"No," Max snapped. "You're not drinking that potion, Gerry. For all we know, it could put some bond on you and Orion that makes you crave his cock."

"It's not going to mimic the Guardian Bond, you silly salmon," Geraldine waved him off.

"No, Max is right. We need more information first," I said firmly, the mere suggestion of facing another kind of bond like the one I'd been subjected to in the past setting my pulse hammering. Though I doubted my father would have subjected me to anything like that. Still... until we were certain of the consequences for all those initiated, perhaps it was best to err on the side of caution.

"So what do we do now?" Xavier spoke at last, looking to me like he needed me to offer a solution. But I had nothing to give.

"I'll try every combination I can of putting the stones together," I said. "Perhaps they need to be in a different formation to unlock their secrets..."

"We'll give you some space then," Max said, sliding his arm around Geraldine's shoulders and heading for the door as she cried encouragements back to me.

"Do you need anything?" Tory asked. "Books?"

"I don't think we'll find the answer to this in any book I possess," I said heavily.

"Well shit, if you don't have a book on it then we really are fucked," Tory said with a dark kind of humour to her voice, but I couldn't muster a smile. She headed off out of the Hollow with Darius and Xavier, leaving Caleb and Seth behind.

"I'm gonna go train," Seth grumbled. "I need an outlet."

"I'll join you," Caleb said.

"Wait, Caleb," I said, taking a step toward him. "I think we should discuss what happened back before we entered the city."

"Was it the coven bond?" Darcy asked, glancing between us in concern.

"Yeah. Our minds sort of...connected," Caleb replied. "And when we bit Seth, we weren't ourselves. We were caught up in the hunt, we got too rough."

"It was all good." Seth shrugged it off like it was nothing.

"It wasn't," I said sharply. "The urge to hunt was impossible to resist. It's dangerous."

"Caleb nearly killed Tory because of the hunt once," Darcy said, her eyes flashing with the painful memory.

"I know," Caleb said, bowing his head with the shame of that. "We'll control this. We'll figure it out."

"Stay well fed at all times," I said. "I'll do the same, and hopefully that'll be the end of it."

Caleb nodded stiffly then he exited with Seth, and I was left alone with my mate.

"I'm sorry," I sighed, taking her hand, her soft fingers sliding between mine.

"Why?" She reached up to brush her thumb over my cheek.

"The Guild Stones... I should have been prepared for this. I assumed the answer would be clear once they were united, but I honestly have no fucking clue what to do next, Blue. And we're running out of time."

"We'll figure it out," she said fiercely. "Don't go losing faith on me now."

My mouth hooked up at the corner. "Is that an order, beautiful?"

"It will be if you don't put that smart little professor brain of yours to work," she teased.

"I'll get to it then." I smirked, moving away and dropping into a seat to take a closer look at the stones.

Darcy walked around the table, leaning over it to examine them, her little pleated black skirt riding up to revealing her deep bronze thighs and the curve of her ass.

My cock stirred to attention and I leaned back in my seat, my legs spreading as I watched her contemplate the stones. She slowly moved in front of me, seemingly aimlessly, but with her skirt riding up every time she bent forward, I had the feeling she knew exactly what she was doing.

I slipped my hand between her thighs, my fingers gliding along her skin right to the edge of her panties. She glanced over her shoulder at me, a spill of blue hair tumbling down her back and her lips parting like I'd caught her off guard. But it was all an act.

I circled my fingers against her inner thigh, not giving her what she wanted, instead waiting to see what she'd do next.

She pushed my hand away, standing upright and brushing her skirt down, giving me a stern look. "You should be concentrating."

"Then why are you working so hard to distract me?"

"I don't know what you mean," she said lightly, but a smile played around the corners of her mouth.

A growl rumbled in my chest as she went back to leaning over the stones, examining all twelve of them one by one while I enjoyed the glimpses up her skirt. Definitely should have been paying attention to the task at hand, but she was so fucking tempting and with everything going on lately, we'd barely had a moment alone together.

I rose from my seat abruptly, pressing up behind her and leaning right over her so my mouth was by her ear, her inhale of surprise only getting me harder. I took her hand, studying the stone in her palm as my hips pressed her flatter to the table.

"Moonstone for Gemini," I murmured. "Intelligent, curious…impulsive."

"Are you talking about me?" she mused, trying to push me back, but I pressed my free hand to the table, caging her there.

"Traits of Gemini," I said. "So I suppose I'm talking about all Geminis."

"Aren't all Libras meant to be social and cooperative?"

I laughed darkly. "I am those things with Fae I like. Which just so happens to be a very select few people."

"Mm." Darcy focused on the stones again, picking up the Virgo sapphire, and I swore in surprise.

"That was in the wrong place." I plucked the stone from her grip, standing upright and she shifted aside so I could rearrange the circle.

The moment the circle connected properly, an explosion of energy blasted straight at us. My heart lurched as I lost sight of everything, reaching for Darcy in the pitch black. Her fingers found mine, but as she called my name, it sounded like a faraway echo, and fear took hold of me.

Her hand started slipping from mine and I held on with all my might, but she disappeared like dust between my fingers.

"Blue!" I bellowed into the darkness, my voice resounding back to me like it was bouncing off of invisible walls, reverberating around my skull.

The familiarity of this experience brought me back to my Reckoning, when the stars had weighed and measured my soul, announcing me worthy of my place at Zodiac Academy.

I felt the presence of the stars, the sound of them whispering growing around me, conversing in a language I couldn't even fathom how to decipher.

"Son of the hunter, master of the stones," they spoke to me at last. *"The rising twelve will soon be united."*

"The rising twelve?" I frowned. "You mean the Guild Stones? We have them, we brought them together. It's done."

"Once lost like rocks in a roiling river," the stars hissed, but one voice stood out louder than the others. I was certain I had never heard a single voice among the stars speak more prominently than the others. Their tone was deeper, not masculine or feminine, but ringing with power right down to its depths. *"The tide turns, and so the twelve return, laying a new fate upon the shore. But can the daughters of the flames seize what has been offered? Or will they let it pass them by?"*

"How can they claim this new fate?" I demanded. "Tell us what needs to be done and we will do it."

I felt amusement ripple through the stars, but others became wrathful at my tone. I sensed more of them as individuals, like separate pulsing energies around me, and the experience had my heart thundering.

That powerful voice resounded out above them all once more. *"It is time you understood the makings of fate, hunter's son. Demands cannot be made of us; it thwarts the laws of old. But it is time you knew why. I shall show it to you in a form you can understand."*

The darkness twisted, giving way to the vast, towering hall of a golden palace. I stood at the top of a sweeping staircase, another set of stairs standing opposite me across the space, and there at the top of it stood Darcy in a dress that appeared to be made of starlight itself. Every tiny movement made the dress glimmer and shine, the bodice stitched of silver thread and the skirt sweeping out around her in a waterfall of light.

I glanced down at the clothes I was wearing, a suit of darkest blue thread, like it was woven from the night sky, the buttons of my shirt pearlescent, touched with light. Even my skin had a shimmer here, like I wasn't really in this place at all.

A booming voice made me look up fast, and I found a man standing at the base of the stairs in robes of purest white, his dark skin so perfect there wasn't a single flaw upon his face. His eyes were a sea of swirling green, then blue, then white, ever-changing until they settled on palest blue. He didn't blink, no part of his face moving in any natural way, his chest not rising with breath. He just existed, like a statue gifted life.

"I am Arcturus of the Sixth House, they call me The Light One," he spoke, but not with his mouth, the powerful voice echoing around the chamber for both Darcy and I to hear, and I was sure this was the star who had spoken above the rest. *"I have no fleshly form, and the Grawl, the Halls of Fate, home to the Court of Caelestina, is no earthly structure such as that which you perceive around you now, but your minds will be able to comprehend it better this way. Follow."*

Arcturus turned, seeming to glide instead of walk and I hurried down the steps, meeting Darcy at the bottom of the other staircase.

"You look...unreal," she whispered, and I frowned, taking in the ethereal perfection of her face. The way her skin glittered and her beauty was enhanced to the point of perfection. But she was far more beautiful to me in her true form, this image of her like an artist's rendition, unnaturally flawless.

"We're not really here," I said in a low voice as we followed Arcturus through the magnificent hall. "It's some sort of vision."

"Vision or not, it has to hold answers," she said keenly, no part of this seeming to strike fear in her, and a smile tugged at my lips.

"You're right," I said, my pulse quickening a little at the gift of being offered some knowledge from the stars.

I took in the towering walls, noticing ancient writing etched into every inch of it, enraptured by the enchantment of this celestial palace.

"Fates lost. Fates told," Arcturus's voice filled the hall again. *"Every word upon these walls speak of a possibility in time. The halls grow bigger every day, out and out toward infinity. It all connects. Time is stitched into a great and glorious canvas of all that is, was, and ever can be."* The star lifted an arm above his head, pointing at the very pinnacle of the ceiling where a cavernous dome stood far above us. Lines were drawn across it, interconnected in a web so thick, there were barely gaps between each thread. They were moving before our very eyes, new lines forming, new paths interlinking.

"What's it all for?" Darcy asked. "Every fate, and path, what's it all leading to?"

"The question that sires all questions," Arcturus said. *"Pondered by all, answered by none."*

"But you can answer surely?" Darcy pressed.

"When the first of your kind came into being, you were born of the magic of long dead stars and wandering grains of the universe. You were life embodied, forged from a force so powerful it became the heart of nature itself. The force to exist. To be. But you are not the only ones. For there are many realms and many life forms, some abandoned by the stars, others ruled by them completely, and all the grey in between."

"The mirror realms?" I guessed, this knowledge giving me a fucking head rush. We were being told by Arcturus himself about the secrets of the damn universe.

"Yes," he confirmed. *"All living one on top of the other, layer upon layer, so close to one another you would not believe it possible."*

We stepped through a towering set of silver doors and arrived in a hall that appeared to be made of a shimmering, iridescent liquid. The walls were just as high as the previous room, but the translucent substance was constantly moving, flowing in rivers up winding pillars and across the floor in swirling spirals. Beyond it, lay the night sky, glittering far away, yet those stars shone through the liquid like beams of brightest silver.

"A glimpse of what lies beyond your world," Arcturus announced, his power-laced voice resounding through to my bones.

The liquid changed, showing realms outside of ours as though peering through a crack in a wall. Worlds where stars walked as gods among Fae and human alike, toying with their lives or offering fortunes and magical gifts untold. There was a winged girl trapped in a golden coin, controlled by any who found her and forced to grant their wishes, then a realm where vampires ruled – though they were nothing like me, no magic in their veins, just a vicious hunger for blood and immortality keeping them ever young. They rounded up humans like cattle, forcing them to donate the blood from their veins, caging them, all under the rule of a powerful family who declared themselves royal.

Then I saw families playing in the mortal realm upon a golden beach, the stars holding little sway in this world, though the odd glint of power was offered here and there. A woman with rainbow hair sat on the edge of a pier as the sun slowly set and four men closed in around her, the amusement park lights coming to life along the pier the moment the sun dipped below the horizon.

Another realm loomed with broken kingdoms, lost souls and wielders of death. Their magic was so unlike ours, with power captured and summoned instead of innate.

But then there were darker worlds where life had been caged, cursed or destroyed. The Shadow Realm was among them, that desolate place a land where only monsters and echoes of lost souls prowled its plains.

"What happened there? Why is it like that?" Darcy asked, stepping closer to the view.

"Tainted shadow consumes all," Arcturus answered, a darkness to his voice telling of his hatred for it.

"Tainted?" I echoed in confusion.

"Long ago, in a time before the Fae as you know them now, there was a race known as the Faeries. Built of nature itself, pure and unselfish, they rode the tides of fate, becoming one with the land and all its bountiful offerings. But nature is not as pure as it might seem. There is a more turbulent side, its volatility causing permanent instability. The Faeries warred over which part of their nature was to be embraced and which should be discarded. Lines were drawn, lands divided, and over time, bit by bit, they diverged. One race evolving into the Fae you are now, and the other..."

"The Nymphs," Darcy breathed, and I recalled what she had told me of Queen Elvia claiming the Fae were a sister race to Nymphs, born of the same root.

"So great was their divergence, that it caused an unbreachable divide between them. Wars raged, hatred spewed, until one day, a Nymph of pure heart begged the stars for an answer, her race on the brink of eradication. So when they were driven to the ends of the earth by their foes, the stars provided balance in the form of a door. A path to a new land, one built of shadow, an anti-world to the realm of Fae. The Nymphs were offered the gift of wielding the shadows in a homeland they could call their own. And so, they passed out of the Fae Realm forever. Or so it was intended..."

"What happened?" I pressed, this ancient knowledge gripping me in awe.

"For a time, there was harmony. Each race thrived in their own land, but the Nymphs faced an unforeseen peril. A mighty evil grew when a dark prince among their kind sought to rule by any means. He was a sorcerer, the creator of many shadow curses, and the most terrible of them all was a curse that captured malevolent spirits in their passing from life to death, caging them in shadow form and making monsters of them which hunted the subjects of the prince's choosing. But the curse was so abominable, so defiant against nature, that the prince lost control of these tainted spirits. And demons they became. For thousands upon thousands of years, the Shadow Realm was ravaged by these malevolent spirits which sought to trap and claim the Nymphs' souls within the shadows," Arcturus explained. *"So they fled to your realm, abandoning their homeland, but without the shadows, they could no longer survive. They called upon them from the Shadow Realm, and for many centuries, all was well. Long before there was war between Nymph and Fae, there was peace. But it was not to last."*

"Because of Lavinia?" Darcy guessed.

"Yes, daughter of the flames. When Queen Avalon Vega cast Lavinia Umbra into the Shadow Realm and bound her there, her soul was tethered to the malevolent spirits which were so hungry for sustenance, starved for so many years without a single Nymph soul to devour. They fed on her hatred, her jealousy, her quest for vengeance, and she became one with them, her body newly made and kept immortal by those very dark spirits. And in doing so, she became the ruler of the shadows, tainting them with her malice and trapping every Nymph soul in her grasp the moment they passed into death."

"Diego," Darcy gasped, looking to me in horror.

"Diego Polaris," Arcturus whispered, and the scenes around us changed, showing us a hundred snippets of his life. Of Alejandro forcing Diego to kill an innocent, his grubby, too-large clothes on his skinny body as a kid, the fear he faced each day, then his smiles at Zodiac Academy, the newly claimed life he had tried to seize, only to be ripped away so harshly. They all faded to reveal his moment of death, Darcy leaning over him in the dirt and rasping words leaving his lips. *"Was I a good friend?"*

"It wasn't fair, he never got a chance to be truly free," Darcy breathed, staring up at Diego with tears in her eyes.

The visions evaporated, and I took her hand, squeezing tightly, thinking of the boy who had been offered so little goodness in his life.

"Death is rarely fair," Arcturus replied, casting away the visions so the hall returned to that strange translucent liquid once more. *"But it is usually inevitable, unless the stars, or Fae, or some other force decides to play god."*

The grit in his voice told of his feelings on that matter, the air chilling with the sense of his anger.

"Diego Polaris played a great hand in the changing of fate," Arcturus went on. *"That is his legacy."*

"But he's trapped in the shadows?" Darcy pressed. "You said-"

"Yes, and you understood precisely, daughter of the flames. The shadows contain the souls of all Nymphs who have lost their lives. Tormented by the malevolent spirits of old and subjected to the torture of Lavinia's pollution. It thwarts the natural order

of things, containing souls and keeping them from moving on into the after."

"That's awful," Darcy growled, her face paling.

"What can we do?" I asked for her sake.

"Do?" Arcturus mused. *"What is it you think that can be done, son of the hunter?"*

"I don't know," I sighed.

"There must be a way to free them," Darcy insisted, a ring of authority to her tone.

Even attempting to command a star to her will was not beyond her, and it was captivating to witness.

"You would need a power greater than any Fae could ever possess. I cannot fathom it upon the earth," Arcturus said evasively. *"Now, no more thoughts of shadows and spirits. It is time you learned the truth of the Guild Stones."*

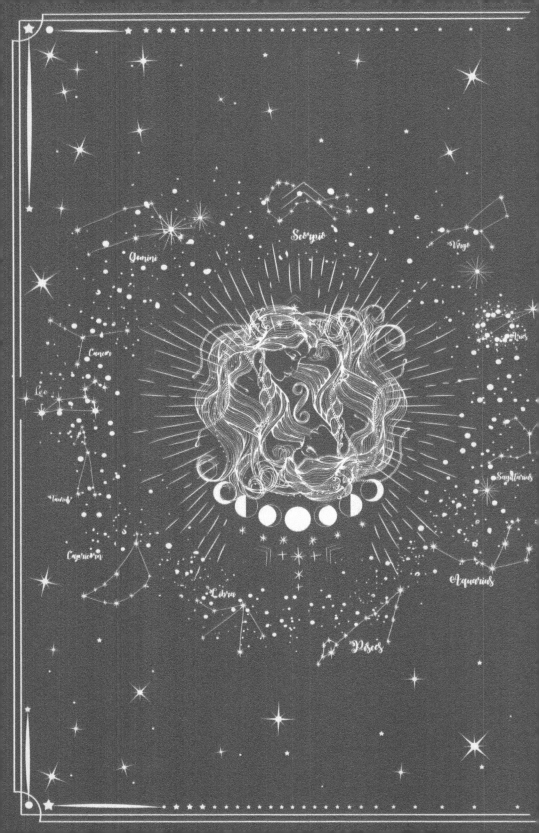

DARCY

CHAPTER TWENTY THREE

A tremor ran through the hall, the liquid shuddering and ripples scattering out from beneath my feet.

"What's happening?" I hissed as Arcturus's false Fae form flickered out of existence.

"There are stars that oppose me in this action," Arcturus's voice clashed through the air, and the room around us started to become hazy, like it wasn't really here. *"But a prophecy was woven long ago that I am bound to fulfil. When the rising twelve unite, the past will be threaded to the future. The knowledge of the first circle must be bestowed."*

"There you go again, speaking in riddles," Orion growled, stepping closer to me.

"If you have something to show us, then show it," I called, my heart beating wildly as the hall melted like hot glass, seeping away into a void of nothingness until we were suspended in darkness once more.

I sensed Orion's presence where we hung in the grasp of the stars, then a force at my back sent me crashing through the emptiness. I was sure I was falling, my stomach lurching at the tremendous speed I was moving, but I couldn't perceive anything above or below me.

The stars whispered in a clash of furious noise, then flashes of light exploded left and right, showing visions that I could barely comprehend. Giant golden threads woven together by a wooden loom, and the sense of time merging in some barely understandable way.

"Past, present, future," Arcturus spoke at last, and the hissing whispers of the other stars stopped. *"All is as it ever was and ever could be."*

The threads danced overhead, spilling away into the thick blackness that now seemed more like some vast material or canvas. The more I watched, the more tangible it became. That endless black moving, stretching, ever-expanding as those threads were stitched into its very essence.

"You pass through the fabric of fate," Arcturus spoke. *"All knowledge lies here…I only need pluck the right thread."*

A vision of a giant hand extended above me, glittering with starlight and barely corporeal. It pulled upon a single thread and at once, I was thrown towards it. I was hurtling so fast, I threw out my hands, trying to cast magic to slow myself, but I had no real body here, and I inhaled sharply as that thread filled up all I could see, suddenly far bigger than seemed possible. There were memories, thoughts, ideas cast into every piece, and it tangled around me, binding my limbs and dragging me into its folds.

I blinked, and I was on solid ground, grass spreading away beneath my feet and a low sun hanging in the sky on the horizon. I twisted around, hunting for Orion and finding him just a step behind me, his eyes burning bright. Always in my shadow.

He took my arm, drawing me closer, and the firmness of his touch made my heart rate steady. He still had that ethereal look about him, and I noticed my skin glinted just as his did, our clothes still the hauntingly beautiful ones we'd been placed in at the Halls of Fate.

We stood at the top of a hill, gazing down into a valley that swirled with a light mist. Arcturus appeared as a man once again, standing at the base of the hill and beckoning us after him before he turned and disappeared into the mist.

"He could have just transported us to wherever he wanted us to go, but no. We must endure the dramatics instead," Orion muttered.

"You love the dramatics." I nudged him playfully, then started down the hillside.

"Alright, I admit I'm intrigued as to where this is heading."

"And you'll write all about this in your diary the second we get back," I teased.

"I don't have a diary, Blue," he drawled, keeping pace with me.

"Your *journal* then."

"I take notes of any important information we gather. I don't write entries about my day, bitching about my misfortunes and mindlessly writing my crush's initials in a heart."

I snorted a laugh. "Not even a little heart just for me?"

"Alright, just for you," he said gruffly, and my smile grew.

We made it to the base of the hill and walked into the mist, seeking out Arcturus. We walked across frost-bitten ground, though the cold didn't touch me, proving I wasn't really here.

The mist swirled, revealing a stone circle that stood ten feet tall, each of the twelve stones carved with the symbol of a star sign. At the centre was a flat disc of stone engraved with the sun and moon. A Fae woman with red hair wearing fighting leathers stood upon it, gazing up at the sky, her head tilted back and her eyes rolled into the back of her head.

Her lips were moving with words I couldn't hear, and the stars were answering in a rush of whispers. Her head snapped back down suddenly, and she blinked out of the state, looking around the circle as if in search of something.

Swords began to grow from the earth along with fine armour, all of it holding that deep glimmer of starlight within the metal.

"The stars gave them this?" Orion blurted in disbelief.

Arcturus turned his head, his voice spilling into my head. *"In a time long lost, the stars were divided into two factions: those of Vetus and those of Novus. The Novus stars toyed with the lives of Fae, answering their pleas, granting wishes, or twisting their desires into curses untold. The Novus faction believed the stars had the right to act as gods among the Fae and mortal alike. They thwarted the laws of the Origin, inciting wars among the kingdoms and within them too. It was chaos, a road to descension."*

"And what about the Vetus stars?" I asked.

"I was among the Vetus faction. We honoured the laws of old, never disrupting the balance of fate. For Fae and all living things possess the gift of change. Free will is their right. It is written into the texts that make up the nature of the universe. It is not a right that should ever be taken from them. We, as their observers, are meant to protect it, to remain unbiased in our watchful state. But the Novus stars disregarded what was written and used their power to make puppets of the Fae."

The vision before us shifted and we watched the red-haired warrior lead a charge of Fae into battle, all of her army clad in that powerful armour with those destructive weapons in hand. The Fae they fought were slaughtered, the army's swords able to carve through magic itself. The power was unfathomable, all Fae who faced it brought to a bloody death before they had a chance to defend themselves.

When just one woman remained standing on the opposing side of the battle, she fell to her knees, black hair swinging forward around her face, her eyes a hopeless pit of despair. She turned her gaze to the sky, angry words spilling from her lips in a language I couldn't understand.

The heavens glittered, stars awakening in the day and peering from a bright blue sky to watch her plight as the army closed in around her. Rays poured from the heavens, a beam of purest light spilling down on the girl and engulfing her entirely. The army withdrew in fright, swords raised and cries of alarm rising into the air.

When the light faded, the woman's eyes blazed with unholy power, and vengeance tore through her expression as she rose to her feet. Light blasted from her hands that ripped great fissures in the ground, tearing through the ranks of the army in droves. Not one of them could get close enough to swing their sword, the power she possessed inconceivable, cleaving Fae apart as if they were made of glass.

I watched in horror as the entire army was destroyed along with its red-haired commander, and the star-gifted woman stood with her chest heaving, taking in the destruction with her upper lip peeled back. But as her gaze turned to the bodies of her own fallen warriors, she turned her hands against herself, casting that wild magic into her chest and ending her own life too.

Her body hit the ground, and a quiet fell that was thick and oppressive. The stars gleamed above, seemingly satisfied with the outcome, whispers passing between them that held notes of amusement.

"We tried to restore balance," Arcturus hissed, showing scene after scene of bloody battles, of curses taking root in kings and queens who turned on their own people. The Novus stars made monsters of those who prayed to them seeking power, but more often than not, the Novus stars tricked them, turning them into beasts who feasted on the flesh of their loved ones. *"The Novus stars would not listen to reason. The scales of fate were tipped to an extreme. And so, I and the other Vetus stars made a plan to restore balance once and for all."*

The scene changed again, showing that stone circle once more. A family was gathered at its centre, two mothers holding their children close while a shield of magic hummed against the edges of the stone circle, keeping out a hoard of ugly beasts with sharp claws and twisted faces. Faces which looked as though they had once been Fae.

The women didn't call out to the stars for help, no prayers passed their lips, and I wondered if they had lost faith in the beings above who were causing such destruction down on earth.

But Arcturus's voice carried to them, not in this moment, but in the past, speaking to them in their language, and suddenly I could understand the words.

"A chance for the Fae race rises, a single hope balancing on a knife's edge," the star said.

One of the women gasped, her eyes glazing as she *saw* something. She must have been a Seer because her lips began to move, and a prophecy poured from her in a monotone drawl. "A circle of fortune gifted choice, a ring of twelve with their own destined voice. Fated paths painted by trusted hands, but the power could fall to savage lands. Protected, coveted, then shattered and gone. Reforged in glory or corrupted by one."

"We offer you the chance to weave your own fates once again, to right the wrongs of the unworthy stars," Arcturus said. *"Your faith in us will be restored. The Vetus stars will prosper over the Novus, and balance shall be found. If you accept our*

offering, you will become fate-weavers here on earth. You will reclaim your destinies from the hands of the stars and guide your kingdoms towards peace."

The Seer agreed, perhaps *seeing* the truth of Arcturus's promise, and a blast of power ricocheted out around the family. The twelve stones in the circle were caught in the shockwave, each one collapsing in on itself, becoming smaller and smaller, shining with power before they lay on the earth as glittering gemstones. The Guild Stones. Perfect in every way and connected by a link of magic that was visible to the naked eye, a glow of white light trailing between them. The monsters around them became Fae once again, crashing to their knees, naked and confused, whatever force of hatred that had brought them here fading away.

The Seer inhaled sharply, *seeing* something I couldn't perceive as she glanced between each stone and Arcturus's voice carried through the air once more.

"You will gift each stone to the twelve Fae we have shown you. They are the peacemakers. The rising twelve. Seek them and balance shall be found. Seek them and your fates will be reclaimed."

The vision around us shifted, showing the Seer travelling across the earth, seeking out the twelve Fae selected by the stars. Some were kings or queens, while others were less assuming; a man who led a small village at the base of a faraway mountain, a girl with no family at all, roaming the wastes of a war-torn land, and many more. All rose to answer the call of the stars, taking the Guild Stone they had been gifted and journeying to meet each other at the centre of the world. The sun beat heavily on their backs, a place of sand and little civilisation.

There, they built a tower and at its pinnacle, they forged a circular table of stone, where each of them took a seat and laid their Guild Stone upon its surface. It was the first of many councils, their meetings regular as the years slipped by, and with each re-joining, more peace was restored in the world. Slowly but surely, the Guild Stones kept the Novus stars from interfering with the fates of Fae, and the Vetus stars became dominant once more.

But there was no vision showing how the stones were wielded in such a way, only their words confirming this truth and the stars' whispering their acknowledgements to the twelve chosen Fae.

The vision began to fade, and I felt my grasp slipping on the world once again as I was plunged into that sea of blackness. But I was only in it a moment before I found myself on solid ground back in King's Hollow, looking up at Orion as he blinked and came out of the vision.

"Wait," I gasped. "How did they wield the stones?"

But I felt Arcturus's presence fading, no more knowledge offered, and Orion growled in frustration.

"What use are half-truths and hints? Why can they never be clear?" I said in anger.

Orion sighed, looking to the stones on the table. "At least we know of their potential now."

"But if we can't use them in this war, what good are they? And what are fate-weavers, what does that even mean?" I demanded. "I thought the Guild Stones were the answer. I thought they could help us with Lionel. But they were only intended to help Fae reclaim their fates from the stars, so how…" I trailed off as something struck me about that.

"What is it, Blue?" Orion stepped closer.

"There's been unbalance again. Clydinius has been toying with the Vega line for years; he cursed us. What he did to us was what those Novus stars did to the world, right?"

"Perhaps," he said, frowning deeply. "And if that's so…"

"Then the balance of the stars could be unravelling again. What if Clydinius is just the first of many stars to descend to earth and walk among us like wrathful gods? What if there's more coming? He had all of those books from the Earth Observatory; he was studying other fallen stars. Perhaps he knows something we don't."

"But Arcturus gave us no direction on how to thwart him," Orion growled. "And if what you say is true, then this is perhaps even worse than what we witnessed in the past. If more stars descend, intent on destruction…it could be the end of days."

"What can we do?" I breathed.

Orion shook his head, at a loss.

I reached for the stones, trailing my fingers over them and sensing a deep well of power within them. "There's an answer here. We just have to find it."

"Stars can't raise themselves," Orion said darkly, and I knew what he was suggesting.

"Perhaps Clydinius can raise them now that he has a body of his own," I whispered in horror.

"We'll stop him," Orion said fiercely. "The Guild Stones must be the key, or why would Arcturus have shown us what he did?"

He rested his hands on the table, gazing down at the shining rocks as if he could will them to give us the answer we needed. But there was only one place I knew of that might offer us the kind of knowledge we sought. The Library of the Lost.

ORION

CHAPTER TWENTY FOUR

"They're not going to sprout little mouths and start talking," Darcy teased while I continued to scrutinise the Guild Stones. "What we need is books. Ancient books. A record of the stones' original use. If a tome like that exists, it's not here. We need to go to The Library of the Lost."

"Of course," I exhaled in realisation, shooting to the cupboard by the fireplace where we kept a stash of stardust. I grabbed a small silk pouch of the stuff before racing back to Darcy. "Wards?"

She carved them open, just enough to let us travel away from campus and with a toss of stardust, we were gone, spiralling through a galaxy of stars and deposited on a windswept island in the middle of a black lake. The rolling green landscape around us was in the depths of winter now and snow capped the high peaks of the barren mountains. The air was wild and carried a scent of earthy moss and bracken, a single inhale sharpening my senses.

I gazed at the zodiac wheel etched into the stone floor beneath our feet and Darcy crouched down, pressing her hand to the sun symbol there.

"That won't wor–" I started, but the ground rumbled at her touch, and we immediately began descending into the earth on the circular stone plinth.

"What was that?" she asked sweetly as she stood upright again, and I pressed my hand to her lower back, pulling her closer.

"They've given you access," I murmured, taking in that smug little expression of hers and wanting to bend her over my knee for it.

"Eugene left a letter with Geraldine stating that Tory and I now have access to help assist us during the war," she said like it was nothing. "Though he did ask that Tory be a little gentler with her magic if she returns."

"Ah, life is so easy for a queen, you're handed everything on a silver platter," I taunted, leaning down to graze my fangs against her neck.

She shivered at my touch, and I barely paid attention to the view around us as we passed through the lake, then deeper into the hidden library beyond.

"Jealous, Lance?" she asked, and I sank my fangs into her, making her moan at the slice of pain instead of gasp. My little masochist.

Her blood was a vortex of fiery sunshine that had my heart pounding and desire burning a passage through the centre of my chest. My magic reserves began to fill, but I took only a measure or two before drawing my fangs from her neck and healing the mark with a swipe of my thumb.

She tiptoed up, her mouth crashing with mine and the lust on her lips lit a fire in my soul. I cupped her ass, dragging her firmly against me and sinking my tongue into that sweet mouth, finding my salvation within the taste of her. A hungry growl rose in my throat as her fingers grasped the back of my neck and she ground herself against me, these clothes between us suddenly feeling like all too fucking much of a barrier.

"Ahem," someone cleared their throat.

Darcy's head snapped around, my hands still firmly on her ass as I looked up with a snarl to warn off whoever had interrupted us. But then my thoughts realigned, and I remembered where we were. The stone plinth had completed its descent and we now stood at the base of the library where several Fae were sitting at desks between the rows of bookshelves, staring at us in shock.

Eugene Dipper was there with his white-blond hair swept back and a blue t-shirt on that had the words *I'm an A.S.S. Rat and Proud* above the picture of a rat curled up on top of a bagel. A huge Minotaur stood beside him with a look of fury lining his bovine features, his giant horns curled above his head and his arms folded across his broad chest.

"This is uncouth to say the least," the Minotaur boomed.

"Give it a rest, Arnold," Eugene said, then rushed forward, bowing low before embracing Darcy while my hands were still firmly on her ass. She pulled away and I reluctantly released her into the arms of the High Buck of the Tiberian Rats, scouring the area to glare at the onlooking assholes. Many of them buried their noses in their books again.

"I guess everyone in the library saw that?" Darcy whispered to Eugene as he released her.

"Oh yes, everyone," he squeaked. "All the way from up by the ceiling and down, down, down to the floor. It was a long time. A very long time. People took photographs, but don't worry, my lady, I will make sure they are all deleted post haste!"

"Is this the destructive one?" Arnold clipped. "The one who murdered the sacred guardians in the lake then unleashed an ancient race of demons in the belly of our divine library?"

"Ah, so you've met my sister," Darcy said brightly. "Sounds like she made a great impression. Anyway, I'm sure it was all cleared up and no real harm was done."

"No harm done?" Arnold mooed angrily.

"Yup." Darcy swept past him, and Eugene jogged along at her heels.

"I think you forgot to bow, Arnold." I clapped a hand onto the Minotaur's shoulder, shoving him down and making his knees buckle. "There you go. Good boy."

I petted his head then strode after my mate. He didn't seem to take that so well as he rose to his feet and stamped his hooves, mooing furiously. He hounded me, breathing down my neck and I had a flashback from my time in Darkmore Penitentiary, being escorted around the halls by bloodthirsty guards. Those days seemed like a distant nightmare now, but my current freedom was a gift I would never forget the value of.

"What do you need, my lady?" Eugene asked. "I owe you my life. I will work day and night to find whatever it is you seek."

"Thank you, Eugene," she said, then turned to him with sadness in her eyes. "Did you see what happened at the Nebula Inquisition Centre to all those poor Fae?"

Eugene let out a pained squeak and bowed his head. "Yes, indeed. A terrible, terrible thing."

"It wasn't me and my sister, I swear it. We were framed." She rested a hand on his shoulder. "I'm so sorry we weren't able to help them."

"I knew at once that it wasn't what it seemed," Eugene said. "And all my loyal

Rats know it too. We are working hard to spread the word of the truth. So what is it I can help you with?"

Darcy flicked up a silencing bubble that included me and Eugene, but not Arnold, and the angry Minotaur stamped along even more aggressively behind us.

"We're looking for information on the Guild Stones," Darcy said. "Not locations this time but knowledge about their use. And have you heard of fate-weavers before?"

"No, my lady, I am afraid not. I haven't come across much knowledge on the Stones, but me and my fellows have been compiling any books we discover that might assist you and your sister in this war. Anything I found on the Guild Stones was sent right there. Come."

Eugene quickened his pace, taking off toward a spiralling iron staircase that climbed up to the gaping mouth of the enormous face that had been carved into the wall to represent air.

Fluffy clouds hovered around us as we climbed, and the wavy hair of the stone effigy twirled and shifted as if caught in a magical wind. We made it to her parted lips and Eugene scurried between them, leading us into a dark tunnel, but ahead was a wooden door and a soft blue glow emitted around the edges of it.

Eugene pressed his palm to it and the door unlocked at his touch, allowing us access.

We stepped into a room that filled me with awe, the magic so beautifully forged it was impossible to blink. The room spanned several floors above us, the walls almost imperceptible within the enchanted room which had been made to mimic a bright blue sky. Large white clouds drifted overhead and one hovered by Eugene's feet, bobbing up and down a little.

"Where are the books?" I asked curiously.

"Not here. Just a little further. This is simply another stairway," Eugene said, stepping onto the first cloud and turning to us expectantly.

"This isn't simply anything," Darcy breathed, and I took in her wonder with a keen interest, delighting in how enraptured she was. I hoped this world kept surprising her because I was in love with her fascination.

I followed Darcy onto the cloud as she disbanded the silencing bubble and Arnold tromped his way up beside me, his shoulder rutting against mine and his eyes sliding my way like he expected me to do something shady at any moment.

"Give us a smile, Arnold," I goaded. "It wasn't us who caused carnage here."

"No?" he clipped. "Seventeen precious tomes were defiled the last time you two were left to roam the ancient halls of our beloved library alone."

I shared a look with Darcy, a smirk lifting my lips while a blush crawled across her cheeks.

"You know about that, huh?" I muttered.

"I was tasked to restore order to the books in question," he hissed.

"And I'm sure you did a *great* job," I said, my enthusiasm clearly sarcastic and he glowered at me.

The cloud we stood on drifted upward, climbing towards another one and we followed Eugene's lead, stepping onto the next cloud, which took us to another then another.

"Elysian Mates can be overcome with their lustings," Eugene piped up.

"How would you know anything about that, pipsqueak?" Arnold asked.

"Don't call me pipsqueak!" Eugene suddenly went feral, lunging past us to Arnold and slapping him across the face, the sound of the clap ringing out around the room.

I released a snigger as Arnold's cheek turned red and Eugene stepped back to Darcy's side with his chin thrust in the air.

"Forgive me, I meant no offence," Arnold muttered, rubbing the sore spot on his face, then he looked to me and Darcy. "But I would appreciate if there were no more *lustings* around our precious collection of books. This is a sacred place and one of my ancestors was involved in its founding. I have a deep sense of responsibility towards it."

"We'll be more respectful," Darcy promised, but I made no such vow. I didn't intend on damaging any of the precious tomes in this place; I was the first person to respect such things. But I wasn't going to have anyone forbid me from laying a hand on my girl. She was the only one who possessed that right now that we were no longer kept apart by law.

We sailed towards a tall, fluffy cloud and a door opened within it, giving a glimpse of a fire blazing beyond. Eugene led the way inside and I followed him and Darcy into a beautiful private reading space with plush red chairs laid out by a roaring fire and a window giving a view onto a snowy landscape above a wide window seat, the snow flurries tumbling against the pane. I knew that view couldn't be real from how far underground we were, but the illusion was perfect. A desk in the shape of two curved bronze wings sat at one end of the room and a golden Phoenix bird decoration hung on the wall behind it.

"We redecorated this room for the True Queens," Eugene said, turning to Darcy excitedly. "It's a gift."

"It's incredible," Darcy exclaimed, looking to the wooden bookshelves next to the fire which were filled with tomes.

"I will continue my hunt for any more books of use." Eugene bowed low, then ushered Arnold out of the room who went reluctantly.

"I'll be waiting out here until you are finished," Arnold clipped, and I flicked my finger, sending the door flying shut in his face with a gust of air and locking it too.

"Ah, silence," I sighed, and Darcy shook her head at me with a grin.

She moved to the nearest bookshelf, soon claiming a book and heading to the huge seat by the window which was big enough for four people, sitting cross-legged on it as she started reading.

I drifted to the bookshelf, seeking something of use and discovering that Eugene and his cohort of bookish friends had done a damn good job. These books were priceless in terms of knowledge, and my breath caught in my throat as I spotted one that I'd thought was no longer in existence.

The Way of Crowns.

I thumbed through the ancient pages to the index, running my finger down the chapter titles, a thrill pounding through me. This book documented the royals running all the way back to the Blood Ages and potentially beyond. It was a trove of history waiting to be discovered, and if it dated back far enough, perhaps it might even speak of a king or queen who had claimed a Guild Stone from Arcturus.

I took a seat at the desk, laying out the book, spreading its pages just so and beginning my hunt. As I began to read, I fell so deeply into the stories of the old royals, that I could neither perceive time nor sense the real world around me. I was totally captivated, lost to the words as the past was painted within my mind's eye.

I only came back to my senses when a book landed on the desk beside me with a thump and I blinked out of my reverie, finding Blue there pointing to a passage she'd been studying.

"You're adorable when you're reading," she said, moving to perch on the edge of the desk beside me. "You completely space out, like nothing else exists."

"Yes, I tend to lose sight of everything." I rested a hand on her bare knee. "Except you. You play a part in all my thoughts. So what did you find, beautiful?"

She picked up the book and read a passage aloud. "Stone circles are one of the most powerful formations that can be created in nature, and if each stone is placed in conjunction with the planetary movements, upon sacred ground, or in alignment with the constellations, many magics can be wielded within its ring. From binding a

Fae's tongue to the path of the truth, to trapping untold power within its confines, to enhancing the magic of certain gemstones." She tapped on that last phrase. "What if a stone circle like the one we saw in Arcturus's vision could unlock the Guild Stones' power?"

I leaned back in my seat, contemplating that. "It doesn't say unlock; it says enhance. And what would we be enhancing? Trying that could be deadly."

She pursed her lips and my hand slid higher up her thigh beneath her skirt. "Don't pout."

"Isn't it at least worth a shot?"

"Without knowing what might happen? You really are impulsive."

"Maybe we need to be impulsive right now. Every minute we lose is bringing us closer to our final hour."

"I'm all for rash choices, Blue, but not potentially suicidal ones," I said firmly.

"So you're putting your foot down?" She arched a brow sternly.

"Yes, I am," I growled.

"Well, I'm the queen so maybe I'll insist upon it."

"What a petulant queen that would make you," I said, rising to my feet and looking down at her, taking hold of her chin so those big green eyes were trained on me. "Be a good girl and keep looking for something that will help us understand the use of the Guild Stones better. Once we have that, we can revisit your stone circle idea."

She scowled at me, clearly about to bite back at me for ordering her around, but instead she changed tactics, dropping off the desk and placing her hand to my chest. "Fine. Out of my way then, asshole."

She pushed to try and make me move, but I resisted, the heat of her hand through my shirt and the game in her eyes all too tempting.

"Watch your mouth or I'll make use of it as punishment."

Her eyes brightened at my tone, her nails biting into my chest. "Make use of it? And what would you have me do in penance?"

"You know exactly what I want from you," I said in a low voice.

She knocked a pencil off the desk so that it went clattering to the floor, then slowly knelt down to get it, but on the way her hand grazed down my stomach and rode over the bulge in my pants. She licked her lips and my cock throbbed at the sight, a low growl of desire falling from my throat.

A small voice in the back of my head said this was too good to be true, and as she stood abruptly upright again with the pencil in her hand and a glint in her eyes, that voice was proved right.

She grabbed her book then slipped past me before I could stop her, heading back to her seat and laying across it with her ass pointed my way, returning to reading just like that.

A lump was pushing at the base of my throat as I took in the smooth sheen of her legs, her little skirt bunched up so high that it revealed a glimpse of her ass. Fuck, that ass had been taunting me all day. I carved a hand down my face, my gaze dropping to the book on the table which had been so fascinating to me just moments ago but now held no appeal at all.

The right thing to do would be to continue my research, ignore the seductive creature in the room and be responsible. But I'd never been able to resist the call of Darcy Vega, and I didn't think the stars were going to offer me the strength to do it now.

Really, the best thing for both of us was to fuck away this burning tension between us so we could concentrate all the better after. This decision was completely logical, and not in any way clouded by my rock hard dick.

I knew this game, we'd played it plenty of times before, and I knew exactly how to get her attention. Step one: rile her up into a storm.

I moved to lean against the front of the desk like I had a thousand times in my classroom and whistled to catch her attention.

Her head snapped around, her eyes sharpening on me. "Did you just *whistle* at me?"

I ran my thumb over the corner of my mouth to hide my amusement. "Yes, and what are you going to do about it, Blue?"

She flicked a finger and a gust of air slapped me hard enough to send my head wheeling sideways. My heart raced, my lust only increasing at her putting me in my place and a dark chuckle fell from my throat.

A smile lifted her lips, but she hid it well, returning her attention to her book.

"God, I love reading," she sighed, rolling onto her back, her thighs lifting and parting just enough to let me glimpse her panties as she used air to hold the book above her head and turn the page. That view alone was enough to have me desperate for her.

Before I'd decided my next approach, she slid her hands up her top and started caressing her breasts.

"Ah," she gasped in pleasure, and my jaw tightened as I watched, my fingers twitching with the need to touch her myself.

"Don't be shy. If you want to put on a show, Blue, then by all means, put on a show," I encouraged, then used air to take hold of her panties and rip them off of her, baring her pussy to me.

"I need an extra hand," she urged.

I shot over to her, capturing her ankles and yanking her closer to me, making her gasp. I smirked as I pressed a knee between her thighs, leaning forward and sinking two fingers inside her in a torturously slow movement, her glistening wetness making me growl with want.

Her eyes remained on the book above her like I was just a tool she could ignore, her teeth digging into her lower lip as she held back her moans.

"Eyes on me," I commanded, jealous of the fucking book and she didn't resist that order, looking straight at me and sending a pulse of heat right down to the tip of my cock. "Let me hear how much you're enjoying this. Don't you dare restrain yourself, Blue."

She released her lip from the grip of her teeth and a breathy moan left her, her thighs parting wider as my thumb flicked over her clit.

"Come for me like a good girl," I ordered, her breaths quickening as my fingers pumped harder. She was clearly close already, her eyes tracking over me with so much want that I felt like the most blessed Fae in the world. To be desired by my queen was a fortune I would never take for granted.

She came with a heady moan, shutting her eyes, her back arching and her legs flexing as she finished just for me, her pussy tightening as I drove my fingers in deeper.

She blinked at me hazily, her body going slack as her pleasure ebbed away, and that wasn't going to be nearly enough to satisfy me. I eased my fingers out of her and was upon her like a starved wolf in the next second, scooping her up with my speed and carrying her to the desk. With a growl, I splayed her over it and clapped my hand against the back of her thigh while I held her down.

"You shut your eyes," I scolded.

"I forgot to keep them open," she panted. "Teach me a lesson."

That plea made me groan and I squeezed the base of my cock through my pants to relieve some of the building pressure in it. "Get on my desk. Kneel there for me and clasp your ankles."

"Yes, sir."

That word had me fucking high and I watched as she obeyed me, climbing onto the desk and doing just as I'd instructed.

I unbuckled my belt and Darcy's fingers flexed against her ankles as I tugged it free of the loops, coiling it around my fist.

"Stay still," I ordered, and she managed to stop fidgeting. "That's it. Look at you,

you're so fucking perfect."

I grazed the belt over her ass to let her know my intention and she released a moan.

"Punish me," she urged, and I struck the belt against her soft skin, marking it with a red stripe. "*Again*."

I gave her what we both wanted, striking her once more and making her cry out in pleasure and pain, the power trip going right to my head.

When she'd taken three whips, I tossed the belt onto the desk and pulled her toward me just a little to give me more access, then I dropped to my knees, dragging my tongue over her soaked pussy and tasting her desire for myself. She shivered, moaning loudly as I lapped at her before driving my tongue inside her tight opening, her sweetness making me groan.

I used the speed of my Order to fuck her with my tongue, her whimpers of need only urging me on as I used air magic to caress her clit and drive her into a frenzy. Three more swipes of my tongue made her come with a scream, and I laughed into her throbbing pussy, caught up in how beautifully she fell apart for me. When she was still once more, I got to my feet, wiping my mouth on the back of my hand and resting it on the base of her spine, using my free hand to lower my zipper.

"You taste like ecstasy, beautiful," I told her as I released my aching cock, grazing the tip between her ass cheeks then over her soaking pussy, lust and pleasure driving me to mania.

I wanted her like nothing else in this world, her body a temple I would worship at every day of my fucking life with all the fervour I possessed.

"*Lance*," she begged as I teased her, refusing to claim what I so desperately needed.

"Say please," I growled, and goosebumps peppered her shoulders from those words.

"Please," she gasped.

I drove myself inside her, gripping her hips and taking her hard and fast. She cried out my name as I fucked her, sinking my cock in as deep as possible before drawing my hips back and slamming into her again. She was so wet, so tight and so ready for me, it was nirvana on earth. This girl was made for me, mind, body and soul, and I'd never find full satiation in her flesh, always craving more. I fucked her just how she liked it, bringing us both to the edge of insanity as her cries of ecstasy mixed with my groans of bliss.

I slowed my pace, wanting to savour the feel of her body. "You take me so well. You're going to please me again, aren't you Blue? I'm going to count, and you're going to come for me on five, not before or after, understand?"

"I can't," she gasped, her pussy clamping around my cock, telling me she was already on the brink of climax.

I grinned savagely, thrusting in deep and hitting that sensitive place inside her. "You can and you will. One...two..."

"*Lance*," she groaned, her body tensing.

"Three." I spanked her ass, taking my sweet time with the count and she cried out.

"Four." I fucked her faster, pounding into that spot she loved so damn much, and my cock swelled, pleasure clouding my mind as I held off on finishing too.

"Five," I growled, and she came for me, her pussy gripping my cock so perfectly that I had no choice but to follow her into climax. I swore, driving in hard and stilling inside her as she led me to my release. Pleasure crashed through me and I groaned heavily, holding her still as I enjoyed the feel of her throbbing around my shaft, her moans still colouring the air.

"Well done, beautiful," I exhaled, smiling like a heathen.

I was star damned spent when I eased out of her and I lifted her in my arms, shooting back to the large seat by the window and lying with her while we caught our breath.

She curled into my body, kissing my chest and neck before finding my mouth and I lost myself to her soft lips and the words of love passing between us. I didn't know how long we laid there, but eventually we untangled ourselves and I used water magic to clean us both.

Darcy pulled her skirt down, sitting up and running a hand through her blue locks, looking around for something.

"The book's gone," she said with a frown, and I slid a hand under her, pulling it out from beneath her bare ass. "Oh, there it is." She bit her lip guiltily.

"Arnold won't be pleased," I said with a smirk.

"He'll never know," she said conspiratorially.

"He will know," Arnold called through the door. "Because you did not have the courtesy to cast a silencing bubble."

"Oh shit, sorry Arnold," Darcy called, but her laughter did little to soften the blow.

"I'm not sorry," I muttered, trailing my fingers up her arm, tempted for more already and giving her a look that told her just that.

"You're insatiable." She pushed off of the seat, glancing back at me with a grin that said I wasn't the only one.

I supposed we did have a job to do here though, and we hadn't gotten anywhere so far. Resigned, I pushed to my feet and chose another book off the shelf, this time sitting with Darcy while we worked to find answers between the pages.

The hours ticked by and we found little to go on, though Darcy insisted the book on stone circles might hold some clue. So she kept a hold of it as we moved to leave, intending to bring it with us.

"At least the moon will be up," Darcy said as I followed her out of the library, Arnold leading the way to the exit while grumbling under his breath about indecency.

"You're right," I said keenly.

We were soon back above ground with the moon glittering down on us from above, and with a flash of stardust, we travelled our way back to campus into King's Hollow. I opened the hatch in the ceiling above us with a whip of air and grabbed my father's diary from the table. Darcy cast air beneath us, carrying the two of us up to the roof where the moon lit the trees in silver.

We sat side by side and I laid the diary between us, our hopes riding on this. The moonlight flickered as if drawn to its pages and I thumbed through the passages I'd read before as they became visible. Nothing of note stood out to me, and I frowned as I found no more writing revealing itself, no new symbols, no clue to follow at all.

"Great," I sighed, flipping the diary shut.

"Have a look at the chalice again," Darcy encouraged, though the hope was fading from her eyes, and I fucking despised that.

I reached into the moonbeam before me, the Guild Mark on my arm flaring to life as I retrieved the Chalice of Flames as if from nowhere, twisting it as I eyed the inscription on its surface.

Ego meum sanguinem confirmo in Vega regali acie.

"I pledge my blood to the Vega royal line," I murmured, turning the silver cup to examine it closer.

"Wait, look." Darcy pointed to its base, and I flipped it over, finding another inscription written there in a circle.

"Bibe positis genibus ad regalium pedes, dum in throno beato insident semel agnita a stellis coronatio et subdita ense Gildii notetur," I read aloud.

"What does it mean?" Darcy asked excitedly, leaning closer.

"It's instructions," I said, my own heart ticking quicker at finding anything at all, even if it wasn't the answer we needed. "Drink while kneeling at the feet of the royals as they perch upon a blessed throne once their coronation has been acknowledged by the stars, and be marked as their subject with the sword of the Guild."

"Does that mean... we can't even use that potion to initiate members to the Guild until we have an official coronation and a throne?" Darcy questioned in concern, and my heart sank.

It wasn't like we'd been confident enough in the potion's safety to try it, but it seemed like another avenue was being stolen away from us. If it took Darcy and Tory claiming the throne of Solaria to activate the Guild Stones' power, then they weren't going to be any help in the coming fight.

"I'll talk to Professor Shellick, his knowledge of potions is far greater than mine," I decided. "He should be able to test the potion's properties and get an idea of its effects. Then we might just have to try it out. Perhaps your crowning was enough and any throne will do."

"And then what? Get someone to try the potion?" She grimaced at that idea.

"We'll figure that part out once Shellick has given us some assurances."

"Alright," she agreed. "But no one is drinking it until we're certain it won't harm them."

I smiled, leaning in to kiss the corner of her mouth. "As you wish, my queen."

GABRIEL

CHAPTER TWENTY FIVE

I stood on a stony beach, the ocean receding before me, further and further beneath a gunmetal sky.

A wave formed that was higher than any mountain, so monstrous it took up all I could see. And there, out in the shallows, stood my family, my friends, and the rebel army, all raising swords and bellowing battle cries at the undefeatable ocean. It was a force no sword, no magic, no Phoenix flame could destroy. And it was coming upon them with a certainty that left no room for other fates.

I tried to cry out to them, tried to run and save them, to tell them there was no defeating this enemy, but my voice was lost to a roaring wind. And when I attempted to run, the stones at my feet shifted, giving way to sand that sucked me down, clogging up around my legs and dragging me deeper into its embrace.

I couldn't escape it any more than I could save those I loved. And despair washed over me as that terrible wave came slamming down on the army and swallowed them all, the flicker of Phoenix wings extinguishing in the dark water. I roared their names until my throat was raw, but the wave came tearing towards me next, and there was no way out. The moment it impacted, I jerked out of the vision, coughing heavily, the taste of saltwater on my tongue. Pain carved through the inside of my skull, my visions causing me agony now in the wake of all Vard had done to me. I feared I might never be free of it.

"Gabe," Leon gasped, rushing over and gripping my arm.

I blinked at him, reaching for his face and taking in the bright golden hue of his eyes. My friend. He was alive. But what of the others?

"Where are they?" I croaked as Leon placed a glass of water in my hand.

"Dante's taken them for a flight," he said, moving to sit on the edge of the armchair I was in. "Everyone's fine. I swear, dude. Just take a drink."

I did as he said, draining the glass of water and the taste of the ocean finally left my mouth as I placed the empty glass on a side table. I gazed around the familiar cabin, the wooden walls and scent of pine clinging to it, the crackling of the fire in the stone hearth settling my heart rate.

My life had been remade in this cabin once upon a time, solidified into the reality I could hardly believe had ever been in doubt.

Normally, I recovered fast from my visions. I was well versed in *seeing* my loved ones die, and as soon as my mind returned to the present, I could usually break away from the terror. Something about this one kept troubling me though. It had come to me many times already and left me with an impending sense of doom. It was no true fate; it wasn't the sea we had to fear. Oncoming, unavoidable destruction was what it signified.

"You need to get all those nasty little visions out, then The Sight will chill out and you'll be back to normal," Leon said, taking something from his jeans pocket and unfolding it. The aluminium foil had been fashioned into a sort of cap and he reached out, smoothing my hair down and sliding it onto my head, taking his time to adjust it. I was so exhausted mentally that I didn't even bother to stop him.

"And what do you think that will do?" I asked, raising an eyebrow.

"It's a vision hat, Gabe. It will help slow down the vision flow. Duh," he said confidently.

"Don't call me Gabe," I said, rubbing a hand over my face.

"Oh I totally forgot, Gabe!" Leon jumped off the seat, ignoring what I'd said as usual and heading to the kitchenette. "Your second favourite H.I.L. made you this." He held up a glass vial with a glittering yellow potion inside.

"What is it?" I frowned.

"Err, he gave it some fancy name that I don't care to remember, but I like to call it snake-juice-sleep-time-jamboree."

I pressed my lips together. "No."

"Oh, come on. Don't just say no like a grumpy grandpa. This will give you dreamless sleep for two whole days. It'll give you the rest you need to recover. And when you piss your pants or shit yourself, I swear to you, Gabe, I won't just leave you all soiled in your chair." He walked over to me, patting my shoulder. "I'll make sure Dante changes you every hour, dude, like, no lie. I'll have him scrubbing your crack 'til it gleams if I have to, okay? I've got you. You won't wake up with a crusty-"

"Your love knows no bounds," I cut over him. "But no. I don't want some fucking sleep potion and a diaper."

"A diaper!" he exclaimed. "That makes way more sense. What size do you reckon you take?" He looked me up and down. "You've got a kind of flat ass, no offense – it's still great and all, like two tidy slabs of concrete, but you don't have my shapeliness or Dante's peachy posterior or-"

"Leon, you're not getting it," I snapped, pushing out of my seat. "I need to get back to the academy. My sisters need me. I can't waste any more time here. I sense something terrible is coming."

"No," he growled, his Lion coming to the surface as he stepped in front of me. "You're not leaving. I'm going to look after you Mindy style, bro, and if you don't like it, you can fight me and see what happens."

"This war is coming to a head faster than you can imagine," I hissed, grabbing his shoulders and making him listen to me. "We have days at the most, don't you get it? It's over, Leon. When our army clashes with Lionel's again, it will be the last time. The stars are showing me nothing but failure. His army grows each day, it outnumbers ours vastly. Don't you understand? I cannot stay here because another day could cost us everything."

Leon's throat bobbed, true fear entering his eyes. "Do we make it?"

My jaw tightened, and I so wanted to comfort him with a lie, but he had to understand the seriousness of this situation. If there was any chance of changing fate, I had to find it before it was too late.

"No," I breathed. "If we face him now, we lose. Lionel will win this war, brother. And he will not leave a single one of us with breath in our lungs. He won't risk another uprising; he'll slaughter us all. The day of reckoning is almost upon us. And we *will* fail."

Leon shook his head, trying to deny the truth of my words through sheer stubbornness. "There must be a way."

My mind flashed with a vision of me and the rest of my family making a break for it at the final hour, of us carving out an existence hiding from the wrath of Lionel and using my Sight to keep us all alive. But that wouldn't help my sisters. And it wouldn't help this kingdom.

"We could run," I told him honestly, though he balked at the idea. "I don't want to consider that unless all else is lost," I reassured him.

"What about the others? What about us winning this fight? Is there any hope?" he pushed.

I started to shake my head then slowed. There was a whisper of something, so indistinct that I hardly dared pin any kind of hope on it at all, but it was all we had. "There is a chance that I might find a new path for us to follow, but I can't do that here. I must be with them so that I might guide their fates. Orio has the Guild Stones, I've *seen* it. There are possibilities in their union, but I cannot be sure of their potential yet…"

"The stone I gave him, the topaz stone, that was one of them, right?" Leon asked.
"Yes," I said.

"By the sun, fate has to be on our side then, Gabe. Do you know how easily my dad could have never ended up with that stone, dude? It was all the way over in The Waning Lands. Like a hundred years ago, this old King Imai gave it to my great, great grandma in his will. Totally unlikely, right? And the barrier blocking all travel to and from the Waning Lands was erected like two days after it was delivered to us or some cheese, so it easily could have been stuck there beyond our reach and yet it wasn't! That means we've gotta be on the right track, because dots don't just join themselves up like that randomly. There must be all kinds of invisible strings pulling us along, leading us to our destination, bro. And I'm sure that's victory."

I wanted to take courage from his optimism, but a vision ripped through my skull and pain cut into the backs of my eyes as I found myself upon a field of death. The bodies of those I loved were scattered everywhere, blood seeping from open wounds, and my gaze fell on the nearest of them all. Geraldine's eyes were glassy and the look of a warrior was still about her as she lay frozen in death. A jade green Dragon sailed through the ashen sky, a bellow of victory booming from his throat.

I jerked out of the vision, finding myself on the floor with Leon leaning over me, pressing a hand to my forehead and sending healing magic into me. But it didn't seem to touch the pain in my head.

"I have to go back," I panted. "The clock is ticking. Every second is counting us down to the end, Leon. And if we don't change fate, we'll all perish. One by one, we'll fall."

"Alright, alright. You can go," he conceded. "But the others won't like it. Maybe when you tell them, you could leave out some of the doom and focus on a few happy thoughts. Did the stars give you any of those?"

I shook my head.

"Not even one?"

"No."

"Okay, well, right, cool. How about I do the talking then? I can put a positive spin on anything. We're all gonna die? Well let's get the party started in the afterlife, huh?" He tried to smile, but I could see the terror in his eyes as he leaned closer to whisper to me. "Not to pressure you or anything, but I like totally need to reach legendary status before I go out, bro. I know, I know. I'm pretty legendary already, but I've got plans, Gabe. Big plans. And also…I really like being alive along with everyone I love being alive. So could you find a way to save us all? But like I said, no pressure." He clapped me on the shoulder then pulled me to my feet.

"No pressure, hm?" I said with a frown.

"Maybe a teeny tiny bit of pressure," he said, holding his finger and thumb close together. "But at least rest between trying to rescue us all."

"I'll rest when Lionel rests in his grave," I said darkly, moving to pick up a pouch of stardust from the table. "Bring everyone back to the academy when they show up."

"You're really not wasting any minutes, are you?" Leon said, adjusting my aluminium hat again. "Just keep this on and baste it with oil twice a day."

"No."

"I think you'll find it helps."

"I think you'll find it in the trash can shortly," I said, taking a pinch of stardust and handing him the pouch.

"You're as grouchy as a snake in a top hat today," he said, and I blew out a breath of amusement.

"See you soon, Leon." I threw the stardust over my head, thinking of Zodiac Academy and I was pulled away into the embrace of the stars, travelling through the material of the universe to reach my destination.

I arrived outside the gates, hurrying toward the guards and letting them security check me before I was allowed inside. They told me the twins were in The Orb, so I pulled my shirt off, tucking it in the back of my jeans and letting my wings loose, taking off into the sky and heading that way.

I was soon landing outside, striding into the golden dome and finding my sisters hosting another war council.

Orion shot to his feet then came at me in a blur, hugging me tight, and the twins weren't far behind him.

"You're back!" Darcy squeezed me while Tory poked my hat.

"What the fuck is that on your head?" she asked.

"Leon gave it to me," I said, and the three of them nodded, needing no further explanation.

"Are you better now, Noxy?" Orion asked, a frown lining his brow.

"I…" I didn't want to disappoint them, all three of them looking at me with so much hope that I hated to tear it away from them. "I'm well enough. And I'll help with anything I can."

"Gabriel Nox!" Geraldine cried, and I looked to where she now stood on top of the council table, her hands on her hips. "I hereby declare you the official Royal Seer of the dandiest queens whoever roamed the land."

"She made you a fancy chair and everything," Darcy said with a grin. "It's got your name on it." She pointed and I scowled as I found the name Gabe carved under the title of Royal Seer.

Orion sniggered, and I glanced at his seat which was right beside it marked with the title of Guild Master. There was a little embellishment on each of ours, but nothing compared to the ornate carved chairs that belonged to my sisters.

"Well fuck me, this is quite the welcome back," I muttered, already feeling like I was letting everyone in this room down with how little I had to offer them.

Chatter broke out among those gathered at the table and Geraldine waved her hands at them. "Simmer down. I am quite aware it is hotter than an otter's patchouli in here now that the fine specimen of our becoming Seer has entered our vicinity, but we must wrangle our Petunias and Long Shermans, so that we might focus on the task at hand."

"*Gerry*," Max growled.

"What-ho, dear fellow? I am but a Fae who cannot help the wandering of her waters. But do not worry, my salacious salmon, I only desire your butter upon my bagel." She leapt down from the table and Max looked much brighter as she took her seat and we all moved to join the circle.

"So you'll be keeping the aluminium hat on through the whole meeting, will you?" Orion muttered, and I cursed, snatching the thing off my head but feeling an oily residue left in my hair.

"Do I smell like vegetable oil?" I sighed.

Darcy glanced up at a line of oil which was leaking down my temple. "Nope," she said brightly in a way that told me I absolutely did.

"Liar," I accused.

"You just smell...well-seasoned," she taunted, and Tory snorted.

"Twenty minutes in the oven and you'll be golden brown," Tory said.

"Dibs on his ears," Orion said. "I'll whip us up some guacamole and double dip those crunchy fuckers."

"Your guacamole is shit; I'll make some before you roast me," I said, my heart lifting at the small moment of lightness between us.

"Fair point," Orion said, shooting me a mirthful look.

"Well you came right at the chop of the chipper, fellow flapper," Geraldine said brightly, gesturing to the crystal glasses of fizzing wine sitting before everyone as we took our seats at the table. "A gift arrived from the Sphinx Fellowship – an entire crate of Vega Cava, made from the finest grapes of Galgadon. So let us make a rumbunctious toast to our True Queens for all the hope they have restored in the hearts of their pious people." Geraldine poured me a glass, pushing it my way.

We all raised them in the air while my sisters shared an awkward glance, never ones for enjoying the spotlight.

"To the True Queens!" Geraldine bayed, and everyone cried it back before taking a sip.

I brought it to my lips, but didn't drink, concerned the alcohol might worsen my condition. I'd cut out caffeine and any other stimulant I could to try and stop the headaches, though nothing had made much difference as of yet.

I set my glass down just as the sound of another glass smashing made my eyes dart to Caleb who had risen from his seat. Blood dribbled from his lips and he coughed heavily, clutching his chest.

Seth leapt at him with a howl of fright. "What's wrong?" he demanded, but blood spilled from his lips too and he stumbled into Caleb as he reached for him.

Panic reared, and suddenly everyone was coughing, spitting up blood and vomiting. Geraldine released a pitchy scream of horror, diving at Tory and Darcy as blood poured from my sisters' mouths. Geraldine's face was blotchy and red, but then the affects withdrew, fading as quickly as they had come. It all happened so fast, Orion and Darius scrambling to help but only falling prey to the poison that must have been contained in that wine. Bodies were falling, death was closing in, and a roar of anguish left me as I raced to help.

But then I blinked, and everyone sat around me still, their glasses held high and eyes gleaming. It was a vision, a promise of death.

"To the True Queens!"

"NO!" I bellowed, using my power over water to freeze every glass of wine in the room to stop it from being consumed. I was on my feet, breathless with fear. "It's poisoned."

"That cannot be," Geraldine gasped. "Every food and drink item that passes into this academy goes through a rigorous magical evaluation. I oversee it myself. I could not have made such a mishap, I-I-"

"It's okay, Geraldine," Darcy said then looked to me as she set her glass down. "What did you *see*?"

I felt The Sight pressing in on me again, the pain driving into my head telling me I couldn't escape it as I was shown a glimpse of Vard. He held a vial of some clear liquid, holding it up to Lionel. "It is entirely undetectable, my King. A poison like no other."

I took a shaky breath as I found myself back in the now, the ache behind my eyes making me dizzy.

"Vard," I growled, hatred coating that name. "The poison is newly designed. It's undetectable."

"Motherfucker," Tory hissed, slamming her glass down too.

"Ohhh!" Geraldine wailed, throwing her hands to her face. "I poured your deaths into crystal glasses, I am a treacherous braggard who must be hung, drawn, and quartered for this most ghastly of crimes." She flung herself onto the table before my sisters. "Do it now, here, before your court. Let them see what becomes of wretches such as I!"

"You couldn't have known," Darcy said, trying to encourage her back into her seat. "It's undetectable."

"But I am a Cerberus," Geraldine sobbed, gathering her crimson hair away from her neck like she was readying herself for a beheading. "Poison is my pastime."

"If it's undetectable, what do we do?" Tory looked to me in concern. "More of our stores could be laced with it."

I turned to the stars for answers, and for once they gave them clearly, a pang of pain accompanying the truth offered to me. "Geraldine, you were affected by a mere rash on your face in my vision. Your Cerberus Order fought off the poison. You don't have time to give to this task, but I've *seen* who has. Justin Masters. He can recruit a team of food and drink testers from the other Cerberuses and they can look for signs of such a rash. That will be the key."

Geraldine wiped her tears from her cheeks, sitting upright on the table. "Of course," she exhaled. "What a boon of an idea, my winged fellow. Justin is just the spritely earwig for the job. I will send word to him once our council is done."

"That solves that then," Darius said. "We need to talk about recruitment."

"I have a list of potential allies," Geraldine said, shuffling off the table back into her seat and taking a scroll from a bag at her feet. She laid it on the table with a flourish.

"The Icekian Polar Bear shifters in the north," she said. "Gus Vulpecular has told us of a Nebula Inquisition Centre holding many of them captive. There are others there too, of course. But the Polar Bears possess brute force and a keenness for war that few other Orders possess. They would make fine allies indeed."

"Our plans to hit the Inquisition Centres are coming together, we can do some research into that one too," Darcy said.

"Seth and I will take it," Caleb offered.

"I always wanted to see the Polar Capital," Seth said keenly, and Caleb smiled a little like he'd known that.

"Very well." Geraldine ticked it off her list. "We shall discuss your strategy for that as soon as a snaffety sniff, but first let us speak of another viable alliance. The Voldrakians."

A murmur of discontent passed through the room.

"They've been hostile ever since the Savage King threatened to invade their land and took Merissa Vega as his bride," Tiberius said with a head shake. "Their marriage forged a tentative alliance - if you can call it that - but her death threw the relationship between Solaria and Voldrakia back into turmoil. We are not enemies, but we haven't been able to claim a true alliance with them since her demise either. There is too much bad blood between our kingdom and theirs."

"The Voldrakian royals sent a chest to Lionel while Lance, Gabriel and I were held captive," Darcy said, and I nodded in confirmation. "We saw it. There was a monstrous snake thing inside it that killed one of his Dragon shifters. It was a message of refusal to ally with him."

"That is jolly news indeed," Geraldine gushed, slapping her hand down on the table.

"Not necessarily," Tory said. "Just because they sent a *fuck you* to Lionel doesn't mean they won't send one to us."

"But the emperor is your grandfather." Geraldine looked from my sisters to me, and I realised I was very much included in that statement. "Perhaps he only awaits the call of his lineage to thrust the might of his army into your command."

The Sight cut through my skull like a hot knife, and I was gifted a view of a faraway palace where a man with cold eyes sat upon his throne. I watched as my sisters' summons was passed to him and he scoffed as he read their request for help, then scrunched the parchment up in his grip. "Let my granddaughters prove their worth in their war. I will consider offering them my allegiance if they claim the throne they seek."

I blinked, coming back to the room, the grave news rising to my lips. I despised being the bearer of such news, and I sighed as I looked to Darcy and Tory. "The Voldrakians will refuse to ally. The emperor wishes to have no part in this war."

"Oh badger balls," Geraldine cursed.

"Well that's that then." Darcy leaned back in her seat with a sigh. "Is there anyone else, Geraldine?"

"Oh, um, hmmm, just give me two shakes of a billy goat's gruff." Geraldine fussed over her list, but I could see there was little else written on it.

"Let's talk tactics on hitting the Nebula Inquisition Centres," Max suggested, and everyone fell into discussion about that instead.

The sense of terror I'd felt all day washed over me again. A scent of death hung around me like a bad omen, and the ticking in my head said that time was running out for everyone in this room. I might have returned to the centre of this war to help, but despite my determination to change the fates of all those who were sitting around me, all I could find when I looked into their futures was the inevitability of the end, and I feared not even my foresight could save them the next time death came knocking.

MAX

CHAPTER TWENTY SIX

I cursed as I rolled over in my waterbed at Aqua House, the mattress sloshing slightly beneath me and making Gerry bounce where she lay peacefully beside me.

"Just go, you wiffling cad," she murmured, not bothering to open her eyes and I stilled, surprised to find she wasn't asleep at all.

"Go?" I questioned innocently.

"I am no fool, Maxy," she said, still not moving an inch or opening her eyes. "I know well the ways of your Order and since deciding to tangle in your nets on a more permanent basis, I have educated myself further still. I am well aware that on occasion you will need to leave our bed during the night and head out to enrapture another with your wily ways. Fear not, I can cope with a few hours alone in bed. What I cannot cope with is the flip flopping of you resisting it."

She was right. It had been three nights now and I was past the point of resisting the need to release my Siren Song. It was a part of me to do so. When I had first Emerged into my Order form, I'd been compelled into Siren spelling other Fae most months, but as my power grew, the need had become less frequent, and I had only been compelled to do so a handful of times in the past year. But once the need arose in me, there was no stopping it. Somewhere out there, a Fae needed to hear a truth from me and I was going to have to give it to them.

"Are you sure you don't mind?" I began, but she waved me off.

"I can cope with you kissing another when your gifts demand it, dear Maxy. If it would make you feel better, then I could kiss someone else too."

"No," I growled, knowing that was unreasonable of me but still balking at the suggestion.

She huffed a laugh. "Fine. Perhaps you would do me the favour of skidaddling then? Because I require my beauty sleep this night and your floundering is stopping that from happening."

I smiled, leaning in to press my mouth to hers before I went. "The only lips I want to kiss are yours, Gerry," I promised her and she batted me off with a smile, her eyes still shut. She'd been sleeping better the last couple of nights, and I hated to be the one to disturb her.

"You are quite the romantic crustacean when you wish to be, aren't you?"

I let out a relieved breath, wondering why I'd even been holding off on this in the first place. I'd convinced myself that Geraldine might be pissed at me when she realised I was going to have to kiss another Fae, but I shouldn't have been. She was all I wanted and she knew it. Order needs were nothing in the face of that.

I dressed in jeans and a black sweater, kicking on a pair of boots then drawing a deep grey wool coat over the top. It was as cold as a polar bear's balls outside, one glance at the domed window which made up my room showing a spiderweb of ice clinging to the top of it where the lake had begun to freeze in places. This was the only time of year where I ever felt a little slice of jealousy for the fire Elementals.

I kissed Gerry once more, hoping she would get some well-earned sleep while I was gone. I swear she only slept a few hours some nights, rising long before dawn to start her daily ritual of preparing breakfast and the stars only knew what else. But I couldn't talk her out of it, and my attempts at getting her to rest more were often met with a clip around the ear. Even now, I barely ducked away as she batted a hand at me and called me a lingering lamprey. Then I headed out of my room and stalked along the corridor, the need of my gifts rising like a desperate ache in my chest.

I tugged my Atlas from my pocket as I walked, looking to distract myself from the nagging sensation in my gut.

I didn't waste much time with social media these days but I did keep up with the news, mostly forcing myself to read the propaganda bullshit that Lionel was spreading out into the world. We needed to keep an eye on him and read between the lines of what he was releasing for hints to anything we might be able to use against him.

There hadn't been much of anything lately - which was worrying in itself - but as I scrolled through pieces supporting both sides of the war, various ideas and ideals being discussed by journalists who seemed to know very little about it, I did spot one small article which caught my attention.

> *Entire buildings have disappeared in the city of Kerendia after a violent earthquake woke citizens at 2am last night. What at first was thought to be a sinkhole opening up across the city and swallowing buildings whole, has now been declared as sabotage after sightings of a mass of Questian Rabbits were reported subsequent to the tragedy.*
>
> *Among the buildings lost were two schools, a vault containing gold bullions for citizens across the kingdom, a museum full of priceless artefacts spanning centuries, and a care home for the elderly. A new Inquisition Centre is under construction to deal with the mass of Questian Rabbits thought to be involved in digging deep burrows beneath the city to cause such a catastrophe, and anyone with further knowledge of the plot is encouraged to come forward.*

Mary Tyler:
I knew those Rabbits were shady. Never did trust my neighbour, Jim. Always digging burrows in his back garden. Sounds like he was training for this moment if you ask me. #creepycritter #rottentail

Liana Ramirez:
This is not true! Us Rabbits are gentle souls! #bunnyblame #respectablerabbits #fluffspiracy

Carson Alvion:
This is a fucking lie constructed by the False King to claim those gold bullions

and the artefacts in that museum. He took out the other buildings and murdered innocents to make you hate the Questian Rabbits. If you swallow this bullshit, you'll get what's coming to you in a world of pain that I will personally deliver to your door. I'm noting down every name of every fucker who supports this post.

Lina Kay:
Ah it all makes sense now, those mangey little creatures are showing their true colours at last #lesserOrdersneedtogo #thenewdawniscoming

Caitlin Sisko:
Don't swallow this shit! #thetruequeenswillprotectus #rabbitsrule #furryfury

I shoved my Atlas back into my pocket, making a mental note to offer help to any fleeing Questian Rabbits in the coming days. When Lionel tarred an Order with his brush, it wasn't long before they were turned on, and they were going to need our assistance to avoid being carted off to an Inquisition Centre.

I made it to the exit of Aqua House then walked out to my favoured clearing where there was a particularly well-formed rock for me to perch on.

The Siren Song was already rolling up the back of my throat and I shifted as I walked, falling into the trance of the purest magic of my kind. I stripped out of my coat as I went, sighing at the caress of my scales rippling over my skin.

I could distantly feel the bite of the cold, but the call of my Order magic insisted on exposing at least some of my scales to the starlight overhead.

I took off my sweater and dropped it at the foot of the rock before using a pulse of air magic to lift myself onto it.

I got into the perfect position at the top then exhaled in relief as I finally allowed my Siren Song to spill free of me in earnest. The ethereal cry of my song wound its way from my lips in a secret symphony intended for none besides myself and the Fae destined to hear its call.

Anticipation grew in me as I waited on my rock, the power of the song drawing an unsuspecting Fae to me while the magic built and built, desperate to be sated.

I had feared this magic once, the unknown inevitability of releasing my song into the world and waiting for fate to choose a soul to listen for it, but over time, I had come to relish these nights, embracing the purity of the magic and offering up the gift of a kiss to whoever I summoned.

The thick stalks of bamboo which lined one side of this clearing rustled, heavy footsteps approaching and announcing the arrival of the Song-Spelled.

I tipped my head back, allowing the moonlight to spill over me in the most flattering way, tensing my muscles just a little to show them off and give the summoned Fae a good show when they arrived.

"Stop posing, asshole, it's me."

I turned at the sound of Darius's voice, sighing as he disparaged a perfectly impressive Siren Spelling and folding my arms in protest to his flippant tone.

"You're supposed to be all awed and impressed, staring at my mouth and desperate for this kiss," I told him, scowling in irritation.

"Yeah, well maybe I was the first few times, but it kinda loses its shine on round four."

I huffed out a breath, then hopped down from my rock, but I didn't go any further because he was the one who had been Song Spelled so he should come to me.

"If I'd known it was you, I wouldn't have put it off for the last few days," I muttered.

"No, you'd have been up on that rock since the crack of dawn, desperate for night to fall so you could lure me to your special boulder," he taunted, beckoning me to him, but I just narrowed my eyes and held my ground.

"I've lured you here, asshole. Come to me or spend the night stuck in this circle of magic. That's how it works," I said.

Darius sighed like this was all some hassle to his precious time, then stalked the remaining distance to me. He didn't waste time, grabbing hold of my cheeks and stamping his mouth to mine in a firm demand for the magic to be sated and this interaction to be over.

His no-nonsense approach beat Seth's though. The last time I'd summoned him to me, he'd brought candles to try and set the mood.

Our magic met and I offered him up a memory as my part of this exchange, my gifts urging me towards the sort of thing he needed to know and landing on a memory of the four of us Heirs as kids, racing through the pine trees outside my family manor. We were whooping and hollering at each other, firing wooden crossbows loaded with magical darts between the thick trunks. Every time one of the darts struck something, a pop of brightly coloured magic erupted from it, staining the object or person it had hit and offering out a small shock of electrically charged power.

We were covered in a rainbow of magical dust and splattered with mud, our smiles filled with the wide and pure joy that only children could claim so fully.

I relaxed into the memory, letting him see it all, neither of us pushing or pulling towards anything more than that. But something kept tugging on the corner of my attention, something which howled and screamed and thrashed for my focus.

I tried to ignore it, my routine with the Heirs for getting though the magic of the Siren Song set and simple. We enjoyed sharing a childhood memory and then it was done.

Except tonight it didn't seem done. It felt like the magic had a bigger purpose in drawing us together, like the power of my Siren gifts demanded more of me and wouldn't relent until I turned my focus the way it was aiming.

I gripped Darius's biceps as the power took root, the song that surrounded us growing louder and more insistent, the memory of our childhood falling away and a wretched sound filling its place.

My heart skipped a beat, my lungs chilling as though ice had crawled inside of me and was burrowing into my core.

Darius's muscles tensed where I held him, our kiss utterly still, nothing between us aside from that chilling call of distant power.

With our focus fixed on it, my power lashed out, reaching towards the agonising pain of whatever it was that had heard my song, its screams of torment begging me to help it.

My limbs began to tremble, my gifts thrumming in my blood and taking hold of my flesh.

Something was out there. Something more terrible and more captivating than anything I had ever known. And it needed me. It needed us.

Darius jerked away from me, breaking the kiss and severing the bond between us, the magical dome which held us captive shattering too, releasing us from the magic. But the call of that undeniable power didn't relinquish me.

"I have to go to it," I gasped, my feet stumbling over one another as I headed for the far side of the clearing, a leash forming around my power, coiling tighter and yanking me towards whatever held the other end of it.

"*Max*," Darius barked, his footsteps crunching across the frost-kissed gravel as he followed me.

"It needs my help," I choked out, unable to stop, unable to even pause.

Darius caught my wrist as I made it to the edge of the clearing and I jerked around to face him, magic sparking from my skin and biting his with an icy kiss in warning.

"I have to go, Darius," I told him.

Even the moment it cost me to say that much burned against my power, the link I had made to whatever was screaming out for help too potent to deny.

I jerked free of his grip and took off once more, the sky singing with that ancient scream, my link to it undeniable now, its need penetrating my flesh and becoming my own.

"Then I'm coming too," he ground out, falling into step with me.

I didn't deny him. I didn't do a damn thing aside from break into a run and start charging for the academy gates.

"Max!" Darius yelled, his voice distant beyond the pounding song of my gifts as it merged with those desperate screams. "I can still feel it too and it's not going to be waiting beyond the academy gates. We need to fly."

The fog of desperation lifted enough for me to take in those words and I stumbled as I turned to look at him, catching his shirt as I found it flying straight for my face. The rest of his clothes swiftly followed and then he was shifting, a beast of pure, metallic gold, bigger by far than any creature ought to be.

His wings snapped out, a gust of air raking over me as the ground shook at the arrival of his full weight, and I found myself looking into the golden eyes of a monster born of myth and legend. A low growl parted his lips, displaying rows of razor-sharp teeth. The huff of breath which washed over me was heated with the power of the fire that resided in the depths of his soul, and I drew in a steadying breath as he dipped a wing in an offer for me to climb on.

I formed a web of ice to carry his clothes then leapt onto his back with a gust of air magic, the pulsing ache of my Siren Song digging into my veins as I hesitated to chase after it. Never before had I been forced to follow it instead of waiting for it to lure the ones to me who heard it, and yet I knew with a keen certainty that I had to answer its call.

I took hold of the wicked spines that protruded along Darius's neck, and with a violent surge, we took to the sky.

The night whipped past us in a ferocious roar, frigid air biting at my skin and pushing into my hair. My scales shimmered where the starlight touched them, the gifts of my Order form protecting me from the cold while we powered through the dark.

The wards parted for us when we reached them, recognising our magic and allowing us through since the twins had granted us that privilege. Though a clang of power let me know that they would be aware of our passage. Perhaps we should have waited to follow this path, discussed it with our queens and the war council, but there was no halting the force of this magic, no hesitating in the face of its call. And as I felt the tumultuous scream of whatever we were hurtling towards passing through my flesh, I knew that we had to follow its summons.

Mountains fell to open plains as we sped on, then forests and foothills, one hour spilling into two, the harrowing screams leading us ever on.

I clung to the rigid spines of Darius's back and simply stared out into the night, hungry for the end of this hunt, needing to find whatever it was which screamed out for my help.

Finally, another mountain-scape reared up before us, its peaks barren and remote, desolate fingers of stone punching up towards an unforgiving sky.

A deep growl rattled through the enormous body of my friend beneath me and a tingle of almost unnoticeable magic brushed against my skin.

"I feel it too," I agreed, the screams closer now, their desperation waning as it felt my presence drawing near.

Darius slowed, his great wings falling still as he glided across the rocky terrain, and I reached out for that kiss of foreign magic, the desire to turn away from this place washing over me. It might have even been powerful enough to make me leave had

I not felt the desperation of those screams resonating from the depths of the largest mountain in the distance. Knowing something awaited me there focused my attention onto this place. As I drove my magic against that hint of power, I came up against a barrier gilded in iron, set with such magic that it was almost impossible to counter.

But I had been born into one of the most powerful bloodlines in the whole of Solaria. I was an Heir to that magic and in deference only to the queens who had earned my loyalty. No others would thwart my power.

I gritted my teeth, focusing on one small spot of the shield around this place, driving my own magic against it like a diamond-tipped hammer striking an anvil. At first it held, but I struck again and again.

A crack became a fissure, then suddenly the shield shattered beneath the force of my magic, breaking apart and revealing an army spreading out for countless miles beneath us, a distant palace of jade clinging to the side of the largest mountain like an unsightly barnacle on the hull of a ship of horrors.

I sucked in a sharp breath, my gaze raking over the endless campsite, and I twisted in my seat, fear driving into my flesh and eating me alive.

Lionel's army was five times the size of our most recent estimations, his followers spanning the distance from here to the horizon and beyond. A host of the most bloodthirsty and terrifying beings in our kingdom mixed with those too afraid to stand against him or too blinded by his lies to even want to.

I opened my mouth to voice something of the horror I was feeling as I took in the scope of our enemies, but before I could speak a single word, a creature of pure darkness lunged from the clouds with a bellowing roar loud enough to shake the mountains themselves.

Darius wheeled in the sky as the inky black Dragon dove at him from behind, but his reaction came far too late and the collision of their bodies almost flung me straight from his back.

I cried out as teeth and claws clashed, wings tearing, blood spilling, and between it all, my stomach plummeted with the certainty that we were falling, falling, falling, and there was nothing but death awaiting us below.

DARIUS

CHAPTER TWENTY SEVEN

We plummeted out of the sky, Max clinging to my back with all his strength as we fell towards the endless expanse of my father's army, wispy clouds blown apart as we crashed through them. My teeth sank into the bony ridge of my attacker's wing just as his claws raked a line of agony across my stomach.

A roar escaped me, Dragon fire blooming and forcing him back, giving me the room I needed to kick out and send him careening away from us.

I flipped over as the ground sped closer, blazing campfires and endless rows of tents coming into sharp focus beneath us. The warriors on watch bellowed cries of warning to those who slept.

My wings snapped out and I banked hard, beating them through the pain of the gashes which had been torn through them, blood spraying from the wounds to decorate the campsite below.

Earth-powered archers took aim at me as I scrambled to stop our fall, their arrows forming in their fists, tipped with stone and spiked with thorns, designed to sink deep into flesh and do even more damage on the way out.

I bellowed fire at them, raising screams while we fell, my bleeding wings unable to counter the fall fast enough.

Air magic swelled beneath me moments before I could collide with the ground, wrapping around us and catapulting us back towards the moody sky. It was Max's power that engulfed us, launching us upwards despite the odds.

I flipped in the air, rolling aside as a volley of arrows were released our way then beating my wings hard against the agony of the wounds caused by those which struck me.

Max cried out in challenge as his air magic propelled us higher, lifting us out of range as fast as he could.

Still, I felt the bite of an arrow as one struck me in the hind leg, another piercing my wing a moment later.

But that pain was nothing, utterly irrelevant in the face of the Dragon who I had lost sight of in our fall.

I whipped around, finding shadows dancing in the air, hiding him from view even as his unearthly shriek shattered the peace of the sky.

Tharix.

The son my father had sired with that shadow bitch was hunting us, and between my injuries and his ability to hide in the depths of the night itself, I knew we wouldn't outpace him.

A flash of movement came from our left and I tucked my wings, diving for the sheer, rocky slope of the second largest mountain in the cursed range, where the campsite of traitors and monsters couldn't easily climb. Where it would be just us and him alone in the dark.

I lashed my tail as I felt him closing in on us, the savage blow driving the spines lining it deep into his flesh and coating my scales with blood while he screamed in fury to the stars.

I flipped over in the air, pressing my advantage while he was still reeling from the blow, crashing into him, claws drawn and sinking deep.

Tharix thrashed in my hold, his claws raking across my side, splitting scales and drawing more of my blood.

Max fought to wield the air as we fell again, but a swipe of Tharix's claws forced him to shield instead and we collided with the mountainside at speed.

Max was thrown free of me and my heart lurched with fear, but I couldn't spare a moment to look for him. Tharix's claws ripped down my side, the shadows which lived in him sinking deep into my flesh and scoring lines of agony through me.

I blocked out the pain, slamming my weight into him and driving him towards the sheer drop that loomed at his back, the mountain falling away to nothing as though a slice had been carved clean from its side.

He reared up as he fought to dig his claws into the rock and stop our progress towards that fall, and I lunged at him, my jaws snapping shut around this throat, the acidic taste of his tainted blood rolling over my tongue. He bellowed loud enough to wake the heavens.

One of my wings was dragging pitifully along the ground at my side, the pain of my own wounds almost overwhelming me, but I refused to let them slow me down.

My claws bit into the stone and I pushed against his bulk, inching him towards that drop and the death which had to be waiting at the foot of it.

I forced a step, then another, the world quaking as he fought and thrashed, my jaws tightening around his throat and slicing through muscle and sinew.

But just as the edge loomed, his rear legs kicking out over open space, a shattering cry cleaved the world in two. The thing which had lured us here screamed somewhere in the depths of the world and the power of it stole the breath from my lungs, the magic from my bones and the Dragon from my flesh.

I fell as I shifted unexpectedly, my back slamming into stone and tearing on the rough rocks before I tumbled over and over again, rolling and careering towards that drop and the edge which beckoned me so desperately towards death once again.

I threw myself onto my front, my fingers biting into the unforgiving ground, my nails splitting as I fought to find a grip, my magic failing me entirely as the power of that scream held me at its mercy.

My gut lurched as I hit the edge, my fingers raking over the stone, unable to find anything to grab hold of before I began to fall.

I roared in defiance of that fate, my gut plummeting as gravity snatched me into its grasp, but before I could tumble into the abyss, a hand latched tight around my forearm, jerking me to a halt.

My breath stuttered out of my lungs as I looked up, a wild grin on my face, my lips parting on thanks for Max which fell utterly still on my lips as I beheld the unearthly beauty of Tharix's face.

His lips stretched into a smile too, his all threats and wicked deeds which sparked in the depths of his onyx eyes.

"Hello, brother," he purred as he began to heave me back up onto the ledge. "I was told that you were dead."

GABRIEL

CHAPTER TWENTY EIGHT

"The wards are down!" someone screamed beyond the window of my old office at Zodiac Academy where I'd been poring over a deck of tarot cards.

I sprang to my feet as more cries of terror pitched through the air, running to the window and taking in the panicked rebels below. Some were pointing skyward and fear coiled around my heart as I turned my gaze there, finding a hoard of Dragons raining down hellfire from above. The wards had sizzled away to nothing, the final glimmers of that fierce wall of power sparking out of existence right before my eyes. How was it possible? Their strength was forged in Phoenix Fire; I doubted any creature on this earth held a chance of shattering them. How had I not fore*seen* whatever force had done this? Whatever plot had been formed to this end must have been draped in shadow.

I cursed, the need to protect my family taking a sharp, unrelenting grip on me. I shed my shirt, throwing the window wide and leaping out of it, my wings bursting to life.

I swooped over the heads of the rebels, yelling out to them. "Make your stand! Prepare to fight or take shelter!"

The heat of a fireball came tearing this way and I wheeled away from it, looking skyward and finding a red Dragon racing down from the clouds like a wraith of death. I sent a net of vines flying at the beast and they wrapped around its wings while I cast huge boulders to hang from them, making the Dragon roar in fury as it came tumbling towards the earth.

It crashed beneath me with an almighty boom, but I left the rebels to end that particular fight, flying fast across campus to The Orb where I'd last seen my wife and son. We were bound to each other by a tracker spell, and I sensed her position across campus, knowing she was still there with a certainty that rattled my bones.

A screeching of metal sounded up ahead, and as I made it to the centre of campus, I found a giant grey Dragon with spines along its back on top of The Orb, tearing the roof open with his razor-sharp talons and spilling a lungful of fire inside.

A yell of terror left my lungs and I landed fast, running into The Orb, pushing against the flow of screaming Fae who were racing out.

I *saw* death, blood, and a grief like no other tore at my heart, leaving me raw. Pain speared through my head and I gritted my teeth against the agony, perceiving more, *seeing* all too much destruction.

I pushed away the visions, seeking out my loved ones among the fray. The air was thick with smoke, and fire bloomed from every direction, another spill of it pouring from the Dragon's jaws above.

I forged a shield of metal against my arm, raising it high to keep me as safe as possible while I sought out my wife, the heat of the flames washing over me in a suffocating wave.

The grey Dragon dragged himself through the hole he'd torn in the roof, landing with a heavy thud and breaking several tables in the process. The ooze of blood beneath them told of the Fae who'd taken shelter there, and my throat thickened as I moved on.

I didn't dare call my wife's name, even among the screams and fleeing bodies, I wouldn't risk the Dragon hearing me and turning his attention to my plight.

A guttural growl sounded from the depths of the Dragon's chest and fire glowed hot in his throat as he opened his jaws once more. Someone crashed into me, and I found a blond-haired boy, I'd once taught in my classroom, Elijah Indus, stumbling backwards towards the grey beast, drawing the Dragon's attention.

"For the True Queens!" Elijah sent a blast of ice shards at the Dragon with a bellow of rage leaving him.

I raised my hands to help him, but the Dragon's fire came spiralling from his jaws, surrounding Elijah in an instant.

I dove for cover as the fire tore my way, skidding under a table as I hit the ground, and the charred husk of a body slammed down beside me.

I blinked at it, taking in Elijah's death as my ears rang and my pulse thrashed.

I swore between my teeth, crawling onward and squinting through the smoke. My wife was still here, her tracking spell calling me to her, and I wasn't going to stop until I had her in my arms. I sensed my son wasn't here, and I'd go straight to him the moment I could.

The smoke stirred in front of me, and I was suddenly gifted the view of my wife running toward me through the smog, her air magic forcing out a barrier around her.

Her eyes widened as she spotted me and I leapt upright, grabbing her hand. "We need to get to Luca."

"Dante has him," she said.

Her face was flecked with ash, but no mark lay on her and relief spilled through me at that fact.

"Hold onto me. I'll fly us out." I gathered her close, but the Dragon's huge form loomed out of the smoke, two enormous feet slamming down in front of us.

My wife's air shield slid around me as the Dragon's lips peeled back, his beady jade eyes taking us in and a sick kind of satisfaction filling them. We couldn't run, but we could damn well fight.

Earth magic tore from me in a wave of fury that rocked the foundations of The Orb, the ground cracking open at the Dragon's feet while sharp blades of metal slammed into his body. He roared in anger, fire blooming from his lips as he scrambled away from the hole I was tearing into the floor. My wife took the brunt of the flames with her air shield, saving us both from the deadly heat of his fire.

A war cry came from close by and Carson Alvion burst through the smoke with Leon at his back. Carson punched the grey Dragon with his bare fucking fists, his skin coated in metallic spikes. The beast roared, rearing away from him, his giant clawed foot slamming into Carson and tearing great gouges across his chest.

Two more Dragons came plummeting into The Orb from above, one green and one silver, and Leon ran to meet the green one, a blaze of fire tearing from his hands and a Lion's roar bursting from his lips.

Carson had made it onto the grey Dragon's head and was punching him bloody, even with the gaping wounds torn into the ink of his chest.

My wife lifted her hands, ripping a great chunk of jagged metal off of the broken roof with her air magic, propelling it down with such force that it carved straight through the skull of the silver Dragon before moving forward to make sure the beast was dead.

Leon narrowly avoided the wild blasts of fire spilling from the green Dragon's open jaws, and he was forced to take cover behind an overturned table. Smoke whirled around him and I lost sight of him as the fire plumed through the wood.

I raced in his direction, bolstering that wood and turning it to iron, dropping down at his side.

"Lavinia's here, she cut through the wards with some crazy fucking magic. Nothing like I've ever seen," Leon cried then grabbed my arm. "Gabe, can you *see* a way we all survive this?"

I turned to my gifts, seeking out an answer from the stars, but all I *saw* were flashes of those I loved torn to pieces.

I blinked away the cloying horrors, focusing on the now and praying the stars offered me more than that soon.

The blaze of fire stopped blasting the iron table and I shoved up onto my knees, peering over the top of it and spying two bright, reptilian eyes staring back at me. I knew those eyes. They belonged to one of my captors, a woman who had worked to keep me in the power of Lionel and his foul queen. My upper lip peeled back and I beat my wings, flying up and speeding toward her, casting a barbed spear in my grip. The Dragon reared up on her hind legs, swiping huge claws at me, but I ducked, swooping beneath her guard and driving the spear into her jaw.

She roared wildly and I jammed it in deeper, cutting through flesh and bone, my muscles burning from the effort it took. But with a bellow of rage tearing from my lungs, I slammed it higher, driving it up into her skull and finishing her for good.

I flew back, avoiding her falling body as she crashed to the floor and The Orb trembled from the might of the impact.

Leon whooped, leaping over the table and running toward me. Carson had the grey beast on its belly, countless metal knives sticking out of its flesh at every angle like a pin cushion.

He yanked a sword from its throat and jumped down, landing with a heavy thud before my wife, a mix of his blood and the Dragon's dripping steadily down his flesh. She moved forward, placing a hand on his torn chest, the gashes healing over from her touch and I nodded to him in acknowledgement of what he'd done.

A boom of thunder sounded above us and the heavens split open just as lightning daggered through the sky. Rain spilled down on us in a torrent and Dante swept through the clouds, illuminated for just a moment before disappearing into the dark, no doubt in the grip of battle. The fire was put out by the rain, and everything fell eerily quiet around us, though screams still carried across campus.

"If he is in the sky, who has he left my son with?" my wife snarled, and I leaned into The Sight for that answer, a frown drawing my brow low.

"Stars no," I rasped.

"Who is he with Gabriel?" she demanded, a fiery blaze in her eyes.

"This is too terrible a fate," I breathed, fear ripping through me as I *saw* so many deaths coming for my son that it cleaved my heart apart. No, not *him*. Why is my son with *him*?

"Gabe," Leon growled, slinging an arm around my shoulders and damn near choking me. "Who the hell is he with?"

I stepped closer to my wife, wiping a line of ash from her cheek, knowing she was about to lose her shit and I was damn well ready to lose it with her. "We need to go *now*. Seth motherfucking Capella has him."

DARIUS

CHAPTER TWENTY NINE

Tharix heaved me over the edge of the cliff and wrenched me back to my feet. I snatched my arm from his grip the moment I regained my balance, baring my teeth at him and summoning fire to my fists.

He grinned at me in reply, flames which were tainted with lashes of darkness enveloping his own hands as he mimicked my stance.

"Death suits you," he purred, his onyx eyes bright with what I could have sworn was amusement.

"Shouldn't you be unhappy to see me?" I gritted out, buying time in this momentary lull to our fight. My heels were still poised on the edge of the cliff, a narrow ravine of razor-sharp rocks spilling away beneath me.

Fire and water magic were a powerful combination when it came to attacking, but they were less helpful in a fall. I might be able to save myself with water if it came to it, but I didn't plan on having to find out.

"Why would I be unhappy?" Tharix asked, cocking his head slightly, his gaze dropping to the savage slashes in my side and down my left leg. I was focusing hard on blocking out the pain of them, but I could feel the steady flow of blood pulsing from each of the vicious wounds.

Tharix's injuries were already healing themselves. He hadn't even cast healing magic, but they weren't bleeding anymore, the skin stitching itself together and reforming seamlessly.

"Do you plan on standing around here butt-ass naked with me all night?" I asked, the urge to attack rising up in me fiercely, but with my back to the cliff, one powerful strike from him might see me falling again. I needed to move to higher ground. Level the playing field. And find Max.

"Perhaps." Tharix shrugged, still watching me with that unwavering intensity, waiting, though I didn't know what for.

"Maybe you'll let me heal this shit and move away from the cliff then?" I suggested, irritation lacing my tone, his apparent ease in this situation throwing me off.

Tharix stepped back obligingly, retreating up the steep rockface without so much as turning his dark gaze from me once.

I stalked after him, my body thick with tension, but after six pain-filled steps and him making no move to attack me, I risked pressing a hand to my side so I could heal away my wounds.

Tharix watched me impassively, his eyes tracing my injuries as they began to heal. I gritted my teeth as the shadows made the work more difficult, the injuries resisting my magic and taking far more power than I liked to heal over.

I banished the worst of the pain, reducing the bloody gashes to pink scars across my flesh then stopped, saving the rest of my power for the fight which had to be coming.

We made it to a flatter spot away from the cliff and I tensed as I faced off against the creature my father now called his Heir.

The wind whipped around us, carrying the sounds of the army as they reacted to my presence, the roar of Dragons taking to the sky mixing with cries of bloodlust and panic. No doubt they didn't know what to make of a single Dragon appearing to attack them, then disappearing just as fast. Not to mention that my size and colouring was unique among those of my kind currently still living, making my identity easily recognisable despite the reality of my death.

We were on borrowed time. And yet Tharix still made no move to attack, his dark eyes penetrating as he watched me expectantly.

"What is it?" I snarled, chancing a look beyond him for some sign of Max. My gaze caught on the bag of my clothes, but I saw nothing else among the pale grey rocks and scratchy tufts of grass that fought to cling to life in this barren place.

"I don't know what it is to have a brother," Tharix replied, his tone almost conversational, his expression unreadable.

"I'm no brother of yours," I spat, disgust filling me at the suggestion.

"We share a father," he countered.

"Lionel Acrux gave up the right to call me his son," I hissed, a blade of ice sliding into my palm, hidden from him by the way I held my hand. Perhaps if I could keep him talking, he'd present me an easy opening to strike. But I didn't have long to achieve it.

"His blood is yours and it's mine too," Tharix replied, like that fact meant something more to him than it did to me.

"Is that why you aren't attacking me? You think we might stand here and bond with one another?" I scoffed, a flicker of light catching the corner of my eye. I glanced towards it, seeing nothing, but my magic prickled with the feeling that someone was closing in on us.

Max.

"How did death taste?" Tharix asked curiously, ignoring my comment entirely. "Did you carve a piece of it out when you returned? Did you claim it for your own?"

I stiffened at the guess, the closeness to the truth of it unnerving me.

"I made a deal to pay for my release in death and carnage," I replied, tightening my hold on the dagger.

Tharix smiled at that, a wicked, haunting smile, like he understood me all too well. Then he turned suddenly, noticing the disturbance in the air just as I had, realising we weren't alone.

The moment his eyes were off of me, I lunged, slamming into him and driving my blade straight through his chest where his blackened heart lay.

He jerked beneath me, slackening then going rigid again, his fist crashing into my jaw and throwing my head aside, making my gaze fall on Max who was suspended beside us on a column of shadow, a hundred blades of ice and iron pressed to his flesh from all directions.

"His death or your peace," Tharix offered, coughing blood out between the words and wrapping his hand around my fist where I still held the blade which was lodged in his chest.

"Let him go," I snarled, my attention snapping back to Tharix, violence dancing in my eyes and the promise of his end in the air.

"The army is coming," he taunted.

I could hear the truth of his words, the roar of Dragons and the bellow of horns sounding from the valley below while the enormous host was roused into action, all of them preparing for an attack, all of them hunting for us.

"You may wish to choose quickly," he urged.

I glanced at Max again, my friend held entirely at the mercy of this beast, the blades pressing into his skin and drawing thin lines of blood. If Tharix struck Max with all of them at once, he wouldn't survive it.

"Your word that he goes free," I demanded, wondering what the word of a demon even counted for.

"No. Not free. I'll deliver you both to Father, bypassing the army and their wrath," Tharix said.

I considered it. But really, what choice did I have?

"Done." I ripped the blade from his chest, blood spurting from the wound and splattering over my cheek before it knitted over, even a strike to the heart not enough to rid the world of this foul creation.

I got to my feet and Tharix reached out to me, demanding I help him up too.

I gritted my teeth as I pulled him upright, but he held me there for several seconds, standing eye to eye with me, his height on par with my own, his bulk too. There was an echo of my features written into his, a disconcerting level of proof to his claim that we were kin.

"Release him," I demanded, ripping my hand from his grip.

Tharix dropped Max to the ground in a heap, the blades breaking apart into puddles of water and piles of dirt as he released his hold on the magic that had created them.

I stalked over to my bag and pulled out my clothes, putting them on swiftly, my eyes on Tharix the entire time but he didn't move an inch while he waited.

Max got to his feet and backed up until he was standing at my side, muttering a reassurance when I asked if he was alright.

When I was dressed, Tharix observed my clothes with interest, then, without seeming to do anything at all to summon the magic, clothes began to form over his body too. He clad himself in black, from his boots to his shirt, but the shape of the clothes, right down to the way I had left open the collar of my shirt mimicked mine exactly.

"What are you?" I growled, my heart pounding with distrust, my mind whirling with unease.

"Funny," Tharix replied. "I was hoping you might tell me."

I frowned at him, but he only smiled that dark, heathenistic smile, then a coil of shadows opened up between us, tearing a passage into the mountain beneath our feet and we fell into their grasp.

SETH

CHAPTER THIRTY

Booms resounded close by, making the amplifying chamber tremble and the lake above the glass dome rippled uneasily.

I cursed again as I stalked back and forth in front of the little toddler. I needed to be up there fighting, not here babysitting. But I hadn't had much choice. I'd seen Dante running across campus with the tiny dude in his arms, and when two Dragon shifters had attacked him, he'd been forced to shift and fight back. I'd run to help, grabbed the little boy and Dante had given me a desperate look before leading the Dragons away from us, making them chase him into the clouds.

I couldn't exactly stay out there and risk the baby's life, so I came down here. And now I was stuck here, fearing for everyone's lives and aching to be part of the fight.

"This is your fault, you know," I accused Luca. "You're all small and weak and fragile. Just a squishy little lump with no magic. If you'd grown up a bit quicker, we wouldn't be in this mess."

The boy cocked his head at me, his dark, curly hair all blown about by the storm that Dante had cooked up before we'd made it down here.

"Wolfy," he said, pointing at me.

"Yeah, yeah," I muttered. "You don't get a free pass just because you're tiny and cute. I should be out there fighting. I'm a warrior." I pounded my fist against my chest and the little guy mimicked me.

"Wolfy," he repeated.

Another boom sounded above, closer this time and I shuddered, glancing up at the stirring lake. I'd left my Atlas back in my room so I couldn't even check in with anyone. How many of our enemies were here? Was this it? The end game? Was I on the precipice of seeing the world fall? Or did we stand a chance of rising up and winning when we'd had no time to prepare for this?

A flash of light blasted through the lake and I lunged for Luca, scooping him into my arms and casting a powerful dome of air around us. The lake glowed for a second then several strange, shadowy shapes began falling towards us through the gloom.

I squinted at them, unsure what I was seeing, but as they got closer, my throat thickened. Bodies. Ten in total, all of them sinking slowly to the bottom of the lake, lifeless with bloody wounds ripped through their chests. I recognised them as rebels, familiar faces of people I'd never really known. But we'd fought for the same thing. Any one of them could have been someone I loved, but I made sure to look each of them in their soulless eyes, making certain none of them belonged to my family.

I held Luca tighter, his little face close to my chest so he couldn't see the bodies. Shit like that might stick with him. I swear I could remember stuff from his age, but I hadn't had to grow up during a war. The kid deserved to be shielded from all of this, kept safe somewhere none of it would ever affect him. He hadn't even had a chance at life yet, and I damn well wasn't gonna let him face death and destruction if I could help it.

Luca whinged and I hushed him, patting his back. "It's all good, Uncle Seth's got you now. I'll get you back to your parents. Gabe's probably *seen* I have you already and won't be at all worried because I'm one of the dream pack, okay? Wolfman's here, I'll keep you safe."

The lake shivered again and that ethereal light blasted right through it like a laser this time, causing the water to churn into a whirlpool, sloshing and writhing while more bodies sank into its depths.

The light hit the glass dome and my breath hitched as cracks burst out across it. I only had a moment to act, racing for the tunnel as the cracking sound followed me, the mere touch of that light breaking the near-impenetrable glass. Water exploded into the space and I sprinted up the tunnel with my heart pounding, casting air at my back to move faster, tearing along as the water shot up behind us.

I tightened my air bubble just as the water hit us, throwing us forward violently and sending us flying up the stairs. But we were safe inside the bubble, the water blasting us along at high speed, then propelling us onto the grass beyond.

I landed on my feet with the help of air, checking on Luca who giggled lightly like that had been some fun game. I smiled back, letting him believe everything was just fine, not wanting him to catch on to the panic sweeping through my chest. Because I had to get him somewhere safe, and with screams tearing out across campus, I didn't know where that might be.

A shriek and wail of noise behind me made me turn, and I found Lavinia hovering above Aqua Lake on a pillar of shadow. But the dark power that tore from her was gilded with light, like some unholy force was contained within it.

Rebels were making rough boats, taking them onto the water to blast her with magic, but she cut through them like they were made of paper, Fae and boat alike sinking away into the depths of the lake.

Darcy was flying out there with Tory, the two of them working to try and shield the rebels while taking turns to attack Lavinia. But every time one of them struck at her, a huge whip of light and shadow tore through their fire and guttered it out. Somehow, that power was fiercer than even their Phoenix flames, and I couldn't understand how she possessed it.

Lavinia blasted the water again with that unholy magic and an enormous wave came crashing this way. Luca whooped, clapping his hands, and I made a run for The Shimmering Springs, carrying us up above the water with air and flying south across campus, landing among the rocks. I pressed back into an alcove, trying to work out what to do, where to go, my pulse thrumming fast in my ears. *Think, dammit. Think.*

I looked down at Luca with a frown. He was star damned vulnerable; I couldn't risk anything happening to him. His family was relying on me.

I cast a little metal helmet for him, fitting it onto his head and strapping it in place. Then I cast straps out of leaves and vines, wrapping them around his body and binding him to me with his face close to my chest. I cast a plate of metal against his back and neck to protect him, then turned my gaze to the springs ahead. I had to get him to Terra House. It was the safest place on campus, and no doubt where all the kids and elderly would be taking shelter. But that was fucking miles from here, and though the quickest answer was flying with air, I might draw the attention of a Dragon.

I could burrow my way there, but I hadn't had a moon run recently, and I didn't want to burn through the magic I did have. Especially if a fight was waiting for us at the end of it. No, the best choice was to shield and run like the star damned wind.

"Fuck," I breathed.

"Fuck," Luca echoed.

"Exactly," I said to him. "Okay, little dude. We're gonna go on an adventure."

"Venture!" he said excitedly.

"Uh huh. We're going out into the wilderness where some big bad Dragons are waiting for us. If we see one, we have to hide and be really, really quiet. Can you do that?"

"Sss," he hissed, pressing a finger to his mouth then chewing on it.

"I'm gonna take that as a hell yes," I said confidently, stepping out from the alcove and making a run for it across the narrow, rocky paths between the bubbling springs. "I've got you, buddy. And I'm gonna get you back to your momma."

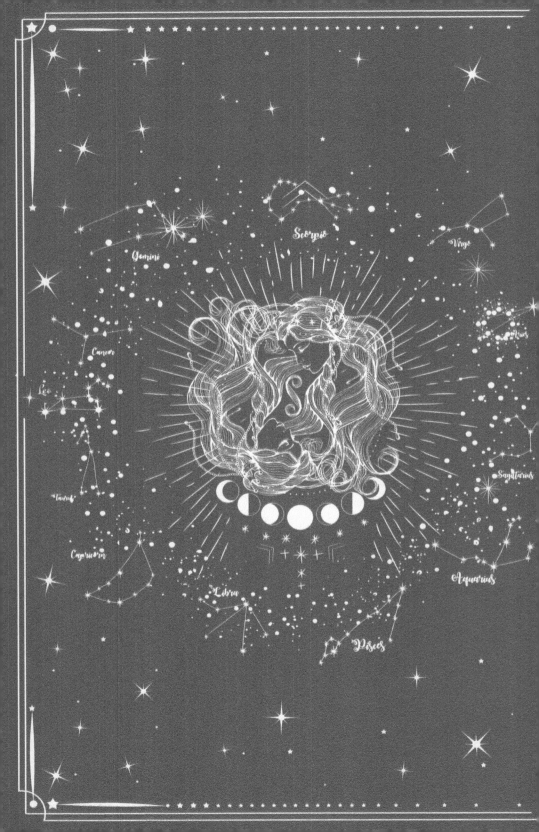

TORY

CHAPTER THIRTY ONE.

I soared over Aqua Lake, using my magic to guide the wind beneath my flaming wings and push me higher at speed as Lavinia directed her ferocious power my way.

The blast she sent at me made the air crackle with unnatural energy, a heat emanating from it which threatened to burn me if she landed a hit, Phoenix or not.

The attack had happened so quickly that I'd done little more than leap out of bed and race into the fight. I had no idea where anyone was. Darius hadn't been there when I woke, and I'd only seen Washer for around thirty seconds – just long enough to confirm our orders. He and Geraldine had plans in place for this kind of situation, drills that they'd been practicing with the army, and all he'd needed was my confirmation to act on whichever of those plans fit the situation best. Not that anyone could have predicted Lavinia might show up wielding a force beyond measure like this one.

Darcy was circling around behind her, red and blue flames building between her hands and I threw a torrent of freezing cold water at Lavinia to keep her focus on me, the water becoming spears of ice as it closed in on her. In war, all Fae customs of fighting one on one were cast aside – all was fair in battle and bloodshed after all, meaning both me and my sister were able to fight back against the shadow bitch as one.

Lavinia shrieked as she threw more of that unnatural power at me, the shadows shimmering so brightly that I couldn't look at them without hurting my eyes.

I tucked my wings and fell from the sky like a stone, forcing Lavinia to take chase as she fought to throw her newfound power in my direction.

I fell into the lake, the water hissing and bubbling as the flames of my fully shifted form met with it.

Beneath the water, I was little more than a flaming beacon, drawing her gaze right to me.

With a flick of my wrist, I created an illusion of my Phoenix form, forcing it away from me while I shifted back into my Fae form and used my water magic to propel me in the opposite direction at speed through the dark lake.

Lavinia's power struck the illusion, shattering it and hopefully buying Darcy a moment of time.

My eyes widened as I came face to face with Geraldine who stood within one of the underwater rooms in Aqua House, dressed in a shirt which I guessed belonged to Max. Her eyes were wild as she stared out at me and I reached for the glass, using magic to write a single word for her against the thick pane.

War.

Geraldine straightened, nodding firmly and clutching her fist to her heart, letting me know that she would join with Washer and take charge of the rebel army as best she could from here. I returned the gesture, wondering if I'd ever see my dear friend again before turning and propelling myself towards the surface.

I used my magic to breathe as I sped for the sky in my new position behind Lavinia. I hurtled from the depths of the lake and shot into the air just as Darcy's strike enveloped Lavinia in blazing flames.

I almost cried out in victory, but a blast of brilliant white light erupted from the centre of the fireball, shattering the flames and sending a shockwave of power tearing through the sky.

It hit Darcy first, sending her crashing into me and the two of us were launched away across the expanse of the lake where we slammed to the ground in a heap of limbs.

I cursed as I shoved myself to my feet, helping Darcy up beside me.

"What the fuck is that magic?" I growled, the sky lighting overhead as Dante's storm split the clouds apart with countless forks of lightning. For a moment, I could see Dragons, Manticores, Harpies, Pegasuses, and many more flying Orders illuminated within the thick clouds, fighting a battle in the sky.

It was chaos, carnage, our people caught unaware and attacked in their sleep. But we had trained for this, they were rallying as we spoke, the sound of horns blasting from the army encampment on R.U.M.P. Island in the distance. Our warriors were on their way but they needed to get here faster.

A howl drew my attention to the riverbank where a silver Werewolf led her vicious pack into battle, diving between a group of fleeing children and a herd of charging Centaurs.

Rosalie leapt at the leader of the brutal beasts, ignoring the arrow he shot right for her heart and somehow avoiding it before sinking her teeth into his throat. Seth's siblings were fighting with her in their Wolf forms, Hadley Altair shooting between his shifted comrades and driving his blade into the flanks of the Centaurs with precise strikes that sent them crashing to the ground for the pack to descend upon.

Screams filled the air from all around, our army scrambling to react to the sudden attack while Lavinia and her mass of followers swarmed through our shattered wards. It shouldn't have been possible for her to break them the way she had, but nothing of what she was casting tonight should have been possible. We'd thought Darcy's strike at her shadows had diminished her power, but this unfathomable magic changed everything.

"She has to die," Darcy snarled, shoving a lock of blue hair out of her face and spreading her wings as she prepared to launch back into the fight.

I nodded my agreement, and we exchanged a grim look, neither of us acknowledging out loud what we'd already begun to fear, because we *had* to be able to defeat her. The war couldn't end like this.

"I love you, Tor." Darcy squeezed my fingers between hers briefly.

"Love you more," I replied, gripping her back as I shifted again, my wings returning so we could take to the sky together. Steam hissed from my body as the lake water evaporated under the heat of my flames. "Now let's go kill that bitch."

DARIUS

CHAPTER THIRTY TWO.

The shadows had ripped a tunnel through the heart of the mountain we'd been standing on before burrowing beneath the feet of the army themselves and gouging a path for us to follow.

I'd cast a Faelight for us to see by as we walked through the dank, narrow space, but Tharix hadn't reacted to it, making it unclear whether he needed its aid or not.

He'd been silent for a while as we followed him, giving Max and I time to exchange brief looks, the edges of a plan forming between us. Max slid a hand into his pocket, subtly wielding magic around himself. He was shielding us too, an impenetrable barrier of air magic clinging to our flesh like a second skin, ready for an attack.

My focus was on the creature my father had created to be his Heir in my stead, my posture tight with the expectation of the attack I was certain was coming.

"Child of sin and mourning," Tharix said, almost to himself. "Will break the mould 'twas born in."

"What?" I grunted, my fingers itching for the feel of my axe in my fist.

He looked around at me, his dark eyes flashing with what could have been surprise, like he either hadn't expected me to speak to him or hadn't realised he'd spoken aloud.

"I was created between a junction in the stars, balanced on an uncertain fate," he said, his voice low and thoughtful. It unnerved me to see him that way. Not as a monster but as a sentient being with true consciousness and a mind of his own. I'd watched him attack Orion, Gwen and Gabriel from beyond The Veil. I'd seen the soulless look in his eyes while he hunted them, and this version of him didn't add up.

"You were created using the souls of four murdered Fae," I replied, my lip curling back. "And all fates are uncertain."

Tharix considered me for a moment, not even glancing at the path beneath his feet as he continued on into the dark, his steps sure and even.

"Sometimes they whisper to me," he said, lowering his voice like he was confiding in me and offering Max a dark scowl as though he wished he weren't there to hear it too.

"I can feel them," Max said tightly. "And they don't whisper; they scream. Those souls are trapped and suffering. Your creation lashed them here on the wrong side of The Veil. Every moment of their prolonged existence is an agony which taints the air surrounding you."

Tharix bared his teeth at that accusation, and I took a step closer to Max, placing myself between them as I felt the tension growing in the confined space.

"Tell me, bastard-born Heir," Tharix purred, his gaze locked on Max. "Did you request your own conception? Did you appeal to the stars for your creation? Or was life simply thrust upon you and presented as a gift no matter how hard living can so often be?"

"I was born of love and handed into the arms of destiny, designed to help rule this kingdom by the stars themselves," Max replied stiffly, a taste of pride and anger tainting the air as his emotions struck the walls surrounding us. "You aren't even Fae. No one knows what the fuck you are, but it certainly isn't natural."

Tharix moved so swiftly that I barely managed to slam into him when he lunged. His fist met with my side and mine cracked against his jaw as I hurled him back into the wall. Shadows flickered and trembled around us, the cavern we were walking through groaning precariously, the walls tightening noticeably.

Tharix broke a laugh, his eyes onyx black and sparking with the thrill of the fight which I knew only too well.

"Shall we continue this, brother? Shall we see what fate befalls us if my shadows stutter again?" he taunted.

I fisted his shirt and dragged him nose to nose with me. "If I thought this mountain might crush you when they did, I'd be sorely tempted," I snarled.

Tharix considered those words for a few moments, his head cocking to one side. A slow smile tugged at the corners of his lips as some understanding seemed to sink into his expression.

"No," he said slowly, raising a hand so he could tap two fingers against my chest, right over my steadily thumping heart. "I don't think the man whose heart is twin to his queen's would welcome death so willingly a second time."

I shoved away from him with a snarl, throwing him back against the stone wall hard enough to bruise and backing up several steps.

"You don't speak of her," I warned him, but he didn't seem to care much for my threats.

"What is it like?" he asked, watching me with a voracious hunger that I didn't want to address. "When she looks at you the way she does. What is that like?"

"All Fae look at each other. You know what it's like," I replied, refusing to be baited into a conversation about Roxy. It was bad enough that he had figured out the link between us. I wouldn't give him so much as a scrap more to offer up to our father.

"I'm alone often," he replied. "But there is so much to know about the world. So I watch. I read. I learn."

"Then keep reading to find your answers. You won't claim any from me."

I turned my back on him despite my instincts warning me against offering him up an easy target then stalked away into the dark. Max hurried to walk at my side, though his steps weren't as purposeful as I was used to, and I cut him a concerned glance.

Tharix was deathly silent behind us, his movements like that of a wraith clinging to the shadows, but I refused to heed the prickling sensation that was crawling along my spine and offer him a glance.

Instead, I flicked a tight silencing bubble around me and Max.

"Are you alright?" I asked him, keeping my jaw tight so as not to draw attention to our conversation.

"We're closing in on it," he grunted, his hand fisting at his side, his iridescent scales catching the dim light of the glowing orb that hovered before us. "Its pain is hard to block out."

His hand brushed against mine and a breath caught in my throat as he offered me a taste of what he was feeling, the agony, the torture unrelenting and the desperate need for salvation. Although the emotions were potent, they were unreal too, beyond comprehension, without any true sense of a person behind them. Whatever we were striding towards, it wasn't Fae.

I gritted my teeth, offering Max as much of my own strength as he required to keep walking beneath the weight of that pain.

"You still have it?" I muttered, knowing our time was running thin, needing to be certain that we were agreed on what we had to do.

"I'm ready," he breathed, shifting his hand away again and relieving me of the burden of that agony. But I could still feel the weight of that power hanging in the air, pressing down on my shoulders and making it hard to fill my lungs without tasting the wrongness of it on my tongue.

Tharix leapt over us, making my heart spike a beat before he landed cat-like on the stone floor ahead, smiling that unsettling grin of his.

I refused to check my stride and he straightened, inclining his head to the passage ahead of me and drawing my attention to a change in the light just as fresh air blew in from above. I guttered my Faelight as the sound of many Fae drew my attention and I exchanged a look with Max to make certain that he was ready for what would come next.

I disbanded the silencing bubble with a wave of my hand then followed Tharix out into the darkness of the night.

I found myself standing at the foot of a palace of jade carved straight into the face of a barren mountain.

There was no doubting who it belonged to, the gawdy stonework depicting the same green Dragon over and over again, a crown of spikes perched upon its scaley brow. This was where my father had run off to when the Palace of Souls had kicked him out. This was the stronghold he had forged for himself in the heart of the mountains. And at our backs, far below on the rocky plains which spread out beyond sight, his sprawling army of ruinous creatures and power-hungry Fae gathered in their thousands, just waiting to meet the army of the True Queens in battle. If their numbers were anything to go by, they would obliterate us entirely when that day came.

DANTE

CHAPTER THIRTY THREE

The sky was alive with war. I thought of amore mio, and the depth of love I held in my heart for every member of my family. And as lightning crackled against my navy scales, the promise of death glittering against my armoured flesh, I held the Oscura motto in my mind.

A morte e ritorno. To death and back.

I released a bellowing roar, one single warning for my allies to defend themselves before a destructive storm exploded from my body. The rebel air Elementals that were darting through the clouds shielded those of our army in shifted form along with themselves, and though I directed my lightning away from them as best I could, sparks still crackled against their protective shells. My intended targets dove for cover, or tried to climb higher into the sky, and a blaze of power scored through my chest at seeing the other giant beasts of my Order flee from me.

Lightning slammed into the hide of a mottled yellow Dragon, and she roared in agony, the lightning climbing higher over her scales as I willed it on and on. Her wings faltered, flapping meekly as the lightning drove deep into her bones and sought out her wretched heart.

With a wail, she died, tumbling away into the darkened clouds below, and the sound of her hitting the ground was lost to the crash of thunder and the cacophony of battle.

A charge like that would take me some time to recover from, and the other Dragons knew it, already turning back to seek out an opportunity to kill me. But lightning wasn't my only weapon; I had teeth and claws as sharp as any beast.

I didn't turn from the oncoming attack or take cover in the clouds below, I faced my enemies eye to eye and let them see the wild creature they were daring to take on. I was the Alpha of the Oscura Clan, Dragon born of Wolves, the only Werewolf pack leader in Solaria who was not of their Order. But I still held the power of the pack in my heart, and every soul I claimed today was for *them*.

Five Dragons swooped for me at once, the attack making a snarl rip from my throat. Three Pegasuses swooped up from the clouds to intercept them, and I recognised Xavier's lilac pelt alongside his pink mare and silver stallion.

Xavier's horn drove into the belly of a monstrous brown Dragon with spines all along his back. The beast roared, swiping at Xavier, but he moved faster, avoiding the blows and stabbing at him again, then again. The brown Dragon barely paid him any heed, but Xavier was persistent, every stab of his horn driving deeper than before until blood was staining the Dragon's scales and he was forced to defend himself.

Three Dragons made it to me with fire spewing from their lips and I ducked low, my spined tail whipping up hard and smashing into the chest of the red beast in the centre of their line.

Electricity blasted along the length of my tail and my opponent bellowed in agony, blood showering down on me before I flew up beyond him, twisting around mid-air and descending on him from behind. He was too slow to react, though the other two blasted fire at me as I caught his neck between my jaws, my teeth slicing in and cracking his scales like eggshells. The fire scored over my skin, but I dug my claws into the red Dragon, refusing to let go.

His wings stopped beating and suddenly we were plummeting from the sky, the weight of him too much to carry as I worked to kill him.

He thrashed wildly, trying to wrench his head from my grip as we tumbled through the thick grey clouds, water droplets clinging to my flesh and soothing the wounds laid there by so many beasts.

We broke through the cloud line, and I took in the war-torn campus below. The flood of Nymphs sweeping across the land, the shadowy form of Lavinia in the distance above the lake. But the fall grew more volatile, and we spun in circles, my wings beating to try and steady us. The Dragon's tail twisted around mine and the barbed spike along it sliced into my skin, hooking in and latching us together.

I sank my teeth in deeper, savagely ripping my head sideways to finish him, but the ground was coming up on us fast.

The Dragon finally fell limp, its dead weight falling from my claws as I released it, but as I turned to climb skyward once more, the barbs in my flesh yanked tight. Our tails were locked and a roar of terror left me as the full weight of the beast dragged me towards my end.

I beat my wings with furious desperation, my heart thumping wildly, and adrenaline bursting through my veins. There was a boom of thunder above as if the storm was calling to me in my final moments, and I bellowed my reply.

A flash of dark wings made my head whip sideways, the ground just twenty feet below as Gabriel swept up with a black sword in his grip, swinging it with a menacing look on his face. The blade cut through the tail of the red Dragon like it was made of paper and I caught myself on outstretched wings, watching as the full bulk of the beast hit the ground with a crash that rocked the earth.

Gabriel swept over me, landing on my shoulders and leaning forward to speak with me. "Close call, Dante. Taken out by your own kill, what would the Oscura Wolves think of that?"

I snapped at his leg playfully, climbing higher towards the clouds, the clash of battle calling to me from the sky. I could hear the bloodthirsty howling of my pack as they ran with Rosalie at their head, a glimpse of them in the distance offering me strength to fight on.

I kept the electrical charge on my body from hurting Gabriel, embracing the touch of my friend. I was far unlike the other Dragons in many ways, allowing those I deemed worthy to ride me when the occasion called for it. And that always included my winged friend Falco.

"Everyone is well," he told me, steadying my heart. "But Luca is missing. I cannot *see* him. The Nymphs are clouding everything. All I know is that he is with Seth Capella somewhere on campus."

I grunted my acknowledgment of that. I'd placed him with the lupo bianco myself, having had no other choice but to lead a hoard of raging Dragons away from them. My faith in Wolves ran deep, and I had seen enough of his actions to trust him. But I still feared greatly for them both. If they could stay well hidden in the amplifying chamber for the duration of the fight, then they would have a good chance.

"Stay alive," Gabriel growled, standing on my back as he prepared to leave. "I'll see you again, brother."

The weight of his words told me there was a chance that that meeting might just come beyond The Veil, but there was always a chance of death weighted upon us these days.

I knew the risk I took as Gabriel leapt from my back and sailed away on dark wings while I chased my own fight into the sky.

Death might come for each of us yet. But when it took me, it had better do so in blood and glory, for I was the Dragon of Storms. And all would quake in the might of my final tempest.

SETH

CHAPTER THIRTY FOUR.

Rain beat steadily down from the storm clouds above, thunder booming and lightning strikes hitting the ground far out in the direction of Aer House. The battle Dante was waging in the sky was felt everywhere across campus, his rage crackling through the air with a keen ferocity. And the little kid strapped to my chest was at least part of the reason he was fighting with all the fury of a wrathful star.

I kept the rain from touching us, my air shield doming out around me as I hurried through the dark wood with my thoughts set firmly on Terra House.

Magic tingled the inside of my palms, ready for any attack that came my way, every muscle in my body primed for it.

A baying howl sounded off across campus, and I recognised Frank's pitching tone. My pack was out there, caught up in the fray, and I vowed to join them the moment Luca was safe.

Rattles filled the air, heading this way, and I cursed under my breath, veering off the path into the trees where a fog was beginning to form between the boughs. I needed to move before they could get a grasp on my magic. But the Nymphs' heavy footfalls carried this way and I quickened my pace, keeping my silencing bubble tight around us.

"Awoo." Luca prodded me. "Do awoo. Do awoo."

"Not right now, buddy," I breathed. "Awoo later."

"Awoo now."

"Awoo," I whisper-howled.

Luca's little face screwed up, his mouth opening in a silent, devastated cry but the noise soon came pouring out, echoing around my bubble.

"Shh, shh," I urged, patting his back.

"A-*woo*," he pleaded through a sob.

The rattles deepened and I felt the Nymphs' sickly power coiling tighter around my magic, trying to lock it down. I stalled, sensing them from up ahead too. I couldn't turn back; we'd already come this far.

The trees shifted in the wind, their boughs bending, just dark shapes moving in the mist. But the crash of movement was coming this way, louder and louder. The Nymphs were close, and perhaps some of the swaying trees weren't trees at all.

Magic still crackled in my palms, and while it was still available, I was going to damn well use it. I was an Heir; one of the most powerful Fae in the whole of Solaria, and a vortex lived in my veins that could carve the earth in two.

I planted my feet, raising my hands, one in either direction. I focused on the source of the rattles and let my power pour from me in a violent tornado, the fierce cast sending a tremor rolling through my entire body. It tore up the earth, smashing into trees as it gained momentum, ripping them out of the ground and throwing three huge ashes away from us.

With a wrenching of wood and roar of wind, the fog parted and I found eight Nymphs awaiting me in the wood, their blood red eyes locked on me and Luca. The tree trunks slammed into their group, knocking some from their feet while others advanced at speed.

I stamped my foot down onto the ground, cleaving it apart as my earth magic scored through it, causing a violent quake to blast away from me in all directions.

Two more Nymphs were knocked down and I made the earth swallow them up, dragging them deep into the mud and hardening it to stone. Their shrieks of terror carried up into the dark sky, lightning flashing above and more rain spearing down from the clouds, setting my veins alight with a buzz of static.

My tornado blasted through the trees, turning three of the Nymphs to ash as it carved through them, but the remaining Nymphs let their rattles unleash fully, the weight of their power slamming into me all at once.

I blasted myself skyward with the small measure of air magic I could wrangle, trying to get us out of there, but long fingers snatched my ankle, the probes of a Nymph slicing through my jeans and cutting deep into my skin.

I roared in anger, crashing to the mud on my back, and Luca's cries escalated tenfold. I gritted my teeth, kicking the Nymph away from me as he swiped for the kid, my boot smashing into his jaw and breaking it.

I scrambled backwards, fearing for the little life I had vowed to protect, the rattles of the remaining Nymphs burrowing into my chest and working to lock down my magic. Shifting was only a last resort; because the vines securing Luca to me would snap, and I couldn't carry him so easily in my Wolf form.

So that left me one choice.

I used the last of my magic to cast a sharp spear in my hand and shoved to my feet in the next second. With a bellow of determination tearing from my lips, I slammed my spear into the skull of the Nymph with the broken jaw, casting the beast to ash. Two more came at me and I raced to meet them without hesitation. I'd die before I let them claim Luca.

I ducked a swipe from the first Nymph's probes, driving the spear up between its ribs with all the strength I possessed, black blood spraying my hands as I sought out its worthless heart.

The second Nymph swung for me and my head whipped sideways, my ear ringing from the impact of the strike. Its probes slashed down my face and neck, blood tainting the air as the blow sent me staggering sideways, my spear slipping from my fingers and clattering to the ground.

"Wolfy!" Luca screamed, and my arms closed around him, my back turning to the Nymph as a second blow came. This time, the probes scraped down the length of my spine and I was thrown to my knees, my head bowing and teeth gritting through the pain.

Luca's little hand cupped my cheek, blood dripping onto his face from the wounds on mine.

"I've got you. You're going to survive this," I said through my teeth, a promise I swore to keep.

I felt the Nymph closing in from behind and I shoved to my feet with a growl of agony breaking from my lips. The wound to my back was bad, the heat of my own blood rushing down the deep lacerations and dripping onto the forest floor.

I stumbled sideways to avoid a deadly swipe from the Nymph's probes, then lunged for my weapon on the ground ahead.

The Nymph swung around, its giant arm crashing into my head and sending me flying forward. I slammed my hands to the ground, taking the brunt of the blow and tensing my arms to stop my weight from crushing Luca. He was crying again, and I hated that I was failing him. That death was swooping in on us so fast, the rattle of the beast behind me making it impossible for me to use my magic.

My hand closed around the spear, and for a moment I was caught in the past, tasting the icy cold snow on my lips and feeling the frigid air of that mountain cave blowing against my cheek. I'd been alone with no one to defend me, but I would not abandon Luca as I'd been abandoned back then.

I cut the vines binding Luca to my body, and he fell gently onto the mud beneath me. I smiled through the pain, not letting him see me break, and his tears slowed as if some part of him understood the vow in my eyes. *This is for you, little one.*

I rolled over fast, so my body covered his, bringing up my spear as the Nymph reared over me, driving it up towards its ugly head.

The Nymph lurched backwards to avoid it and my spear sank into its throat, puncturing whatever organ created that terrible rattling sound. Silence fell, my right ear still ringing loudly, but magic swept back into my veins in an instant.

I howled like I was one with my Wolf, letting my magic tear from my body in an eruption of air that eviscerated the Nymph, tearing it limb from limb until every part of it burst to ash.

Trees fell around me in a circle and I was left standing in a storm of ash and destruction, my chest heaving and victory burning through the heart of me.

I shed the remains of my tattered, bloodied shirt and pressed a hand to my chest, letting healing magic roll through my body, undoing what had been done.

Then I turned to Luca on the ground, lifting him into my arms and wiping the blood from his cheek.

"You awoo," he said excitedly, clapping his little hands.

"I did," I said with a smirk, the rain pelting down on us and washing away the tinge of blood on our skin, my long hair a mess of wet strands. "Now give me your best awoo while I strap you back in place."

Luca started howling like a newly Emerged Wolf pup and I strapped him onto my chest again with vines, checking his helmet was secure before heading off through the trees.

My magic was low, and though I could feel a trickle of it returning to me as I ran, it wasn't filling my reserves nearly fast enough. I prayed I wouldn't meet more enemies ahead, but as I made it out of the woods, I found salvation waiting for me.

"Lance!" I called, running toward him as he ripped a Nymph's head off with his bare hands. He leapt to the ground as the beast fell to the earth, the Nymph turning to ash before it made impact.

Beyond him, Milton and his herd were in their fully shifted Minotaur forms, driving their horns into a hoard of the creatures, fast gaining the upper hand. The Shadow Beast was among them, capturing Nymphs between his giant jaws and tearing them to pieces like sacks of straw.

Orion's eyebrows arched as he spotted Luca in my arms, taking in my bedraggled form and shooting over to meet me. "Luca?" he gasped, checking the kid was alright.

"Here." I unstrapped him. "Get him to Terra House. Now."

Orion nodded, taking Luca wordlessly and the kid smiled up at him. "Fangs, Ori! Fangs!"

Orion bared his fangs at Luca and he cheered in his arms, making me hope he wasn't scarred for life by all the blood and death he'd just witnessed.

Orion shot away in a blur of speed, and I released a heavy breath of relief, barely having a second to think before Orion returned. "Leon was there. He's protecting him now."

I blew out a breath, thankful Luca was safe. At least so long as we could keep our enemies away from Terra House and all those who were taking shelter there.

I rolled my shoulders back, spotting a line of Nymphs headed this way and finally letting the shift take hold of me. I stood at Orion's side with my hackles rising and rows of sharp teeth bared.

Orion petted my shoulder for a second and I glanced at him.

"You did good, mutt," he said quietly, and I swear he had only said it because I wasn't able to reply. But I could damn well lick his face. I lunged for the lick, but he darted away with a burst of speed, tossing a knowing grin back at me before racing into battle. And I was right there at his back, ready to tear our foes apart.

LIONEL

CHAPTER THIRTY FIVE

My fingers curled around the glittering green pommel of my armrest as I sat forward in my throne, my eyes glued to the screen that one of my Dragons held out for me to view. Lavinia was channelling the power of the star, truly using the might of the heavens themselves in her bid to win this war for her king.

My lips tilted in a triumphant smile, my only regret that I wouldn't be there in person to watch the Vegas fall, but I would scent their flesh as it finally succumbed to the burn of my Dragon fire. I would place their bodies before me and make sure the entire kingdom was watching as I lit their funeral pyre myself and incinerated every last scrap of the Vega line from this world.

I hadn't fully believed that Lavinia's control over the star's power would hold, choosing to remain here in case her command of it faltered. There was no need to risk myself unnecessarily. I had a vicious army under my rule here and had fully expected to use them to end this war, though now I was beginning to wonder if her hold on the star's magic might equal a victory even sooner than expected.

My pulse pounded faster with every strike my queen dealt, with each rebel death that caught my notice, I watched it all, my faithful follower recording every moment of this victory for me to enjoy from afar.

I could taste the end in this act. The finality of securing my rule.

The throne room was thick with my Dragons, each of them on high alert and ready to strike out at any moment. There had been rumblings of some attack out beyond the palace walls a while back, but no more had come of it. No doubt the Nymphs had gotten power-hungry and attacked some of the Fae they were here to fight alongside again. I made no move to call for an investigation though. Let them fight among themselves; it only stoked their bloodlust, only made them all the more anxious for the battle to come.

Because even if this was it, even if my queen took the Vegas' heads this night, the battle would still play out. I would watch as my army swept through the ranks of those Fae who had thought to follow another. I would see them annihilated, obliterated, and cut down one by one until none remained who dared defy my supremacy.

I had earned this place. Their defiance was a snub to the very way of Fae. I had risen up and claimed my position upon this throne. I had crushed all those who tried to deny me. I had ended the Savage King himself. And now, after many long years of suffering the indignity of sharing my position at the top, I had finally claimed what was rightfully mine.

The crown of gleaming gold and emerald sat heavily upon my brow, its weight a welcome reminder of all I had and all I was.

Vard sat rigidly in the stool at the foot of my dais, my other advisors lingering in the shadows surrounding my throne. For now, I allowed Linda Rigel to remain. Her sour-faced daughter stood at her side, wordless, yet commanding the power of her bloodline. Linda's advice was still sound even if her lack of power made the mere sight of her a sickening thing to behold. Once this war was won, I would put her out of her misery and place her daughter into her position – a fine puppet to orchestrate whatever plans I deemed necessary.

Beyond her, sitting at a small desk studying a star chart, was Madame Monita, the best astrologer in the kingdom who I had promptly recruited to my inner circle so that she might read the movements of the stars for me.

Aside from them, my new War General – Ashika Normant stood rigidly, her hands clasped at the base of her spine, her eyes on the footage I was watching, no doubt analysing every move. There were other, less important sycophants and people whose sense of self-importance far outweighed my own interest in them, but I liked to keep the group close at hand, alongside twenty of my loyal, Bonded Men for protection of course.

I licked my lips as I watched the power of the star blasting across the battlefield, wrapped in shadow and forced to bend to the will of my wife. Mine. She was my creature just as the star was hers.

My gaze cut to the right where Clydinius lingered, my most deadly ally, but this creature was such a strange force that I had yet to devise a way to wield its power as a weapon.

No longer did the star maintain the visage of the Vega girls, but now it appeared as a man, clad in a cloak of pale gold with skin a wan grey, sparkling with translucence that betrayed the power hidden within him.

Clydinius watched the destruction Lavinia wrought with the power of the star we had trapped in the rooms to the rear of the palace, his face utterly impassive, unchanging, unmoving. In fact, I didn't think he had moved at all in well over an hour. Though he had been of great help in lashing the trapped star to our will, our collaboration with him yet another well-laid plot which would pave the path to my victory. If I could convince him to stand and fight as a warrior in my army, then I would have the power of two stars in my grasp. Two weapons beyond measure, undefeatable, making me invincible.

I supposed I would need to bind him too, given time, to ensure my control over him was absolute.

Though for now, our deal stood.

I snatched the Atlas from the Dragon who had been holding it out for me, wanting to see it closer, needing to witness it all as I turned my eyes to the screen once more, not wishing to worry myself with thoughts of battles to come while victory stood so close that I could taste it.

I inched forward, watching with delight as Lavinia struck the world around her with that furious, glorious power.

It was happening. The Vegas would fall and then I would give the word for my army to descend on the broken remains of their followers. We would spill the cowardly blood of those traitors and paint ourselves red in it before the night was done.

"The lost son returns!" Vard gasped suddenly from the three-legged stool which sat at the foot of my dais, his posture rigid with prophecy, his words slipping through me with a sense of dread that I couldn't understand until-

The door to the throne room swung open with a heavy crash and the Atlas fell from my grasp, shattering on the flagstones and causing the Dragons before me to scramble for it. But I had no attention to spare their apologies, my hand cutting through the air to silence them as I shoved myself to my feet.

"Impossible," I hissed as the son I had killed strode into the room, flanked by my new Heir and Max Rigel, though I had no attention to spare for them.

My stomach dropped and fear sliced through me like a knife forged of purest ice, blinding me and choking me all at once. I'd killed him; his blood had stained my hand, and I had left him to rot on the field of my victory like the failure he had turned out to be. There was no way that this was possible, no way at all, and yet...

Darius smiled, a terrifying, victorious smile as he strode straight through the midst of my Dragons whose shock had forced them into inaction even as I watched my own death striding straight for me, right through The Veil and into my domain.

"Well if it isn't my dear, traitorous, murdering father," he purred, his words a promise of my bloodshed, and my hands trembled as I took him in, my eyes refusing to accept the truth of what I saw, my rage slow in the face of this fear. "Did you miss me?"

MAX

CHAPTER THIRTY SIX

"How?" Lionel boomed, though his voice didn't mask the fear I could feel rolling from him at the sight of the son he had thought he'd put in his grave. "This...explain this to me."

He whirled around, his stare going from Darius to a man I almost hadn't noticed lurking behind him. He stood beyond the throne on the far side of the room, his skin ashen and almost translucent, the aura surrounding him making my breath catch in my throat.

For a moment I thought I'd located the source of the pain which had lured us to this place, his otherness too much to deny, but there was no agony clinging to this creature. No, he was more like a void, a chasm which held little to no emotion.

I tightened my hold on the shields around myself and Darius, the air magic tight to our bodies and utterly impenetrable. This game we were playing was one of cunning. One which we had practiced since our magic was first Awakened in case we were ever stolen away from the safety of our families. The Heirs of the Celestial Council could have been powerful motivation tools for ransom, and we had been well schooled in what to do if we were outnumbered or taken hostage either alone or in groups. In this situation, I would shield and Darius would attack. All I had to do was focus on keeping us alive long enough for us to get out of here.

Focusing was easier said than done though while the eyes of twenty Dragons fell on us, their malicious intent simmering in the air. But even as I felt their desire for our deaths, their fear and their aggression, I noticed other emotions in the room too. The terror was easy to spot as Vard hastily slipped behind the throne, shadows building around him while he constructed an illusion to keep himself hidden from view. The rest of Lionel's advisors were aiming a mixture of horror, fear, and loathing our way, though as my eyes fell upon Linda and Ellis, I felt a distinct lack of anything from them. Linda still had control of her Siren gifts I supposed, and she had always been a wall of emotional nothingness when it came to me trying to read her.

The cold, pure horror took me longer to locate, but beyond the creature who Lionel was addressing, my eyes fell on a young, startled-looking girl.

"My wife, one of the True Queens, strode into death and stole me back from the hands of fate," Darius replied before the...*thing* Lionel had addressed could make any comment. "She and her sister are more powerful than you can comprehend. They are capable of far more than you could even imagine. And they are coming for you."

Lionel's shock shattered into fury and Darius barely managed to throw a shield of ice up between us as he shifted, a Dragon's roar rattling the cavern that surrounded us followed by a blast of Dragon fire flaring over the dome of ice.

"Ready?" Darius said to me, looking at me expectantly and I pushed my hand into my pocket, gripping the bag of stardust, ready to pull it free.

But I couldn't.

"I need to stop that agony," I ground out, the weight of it pressing down on me as the screams of whatever was suffering in this place threatened to drown me in its terror.

"Seriously?" Darius asked incredulously, and I threw out a shield of air to bolster his ice as the rest of the Dragons in the room joined the attack.

"It's somewhere over there," I said, jerking my chin to our left, my gaze falling on Tharix who stood watching us with interest, our shields protecting him too, though that hadn't been our intention.

"You can hear it too?" he asked curiously, like this was a tea party and we were all sitting down, ready to tuck into some fucking scones.

"What is it?" I demanded, the desperate need to go to it damn near consuming me while Lionel's roars filled the cavernous chamber and fire blazed violently across our shields.

"Salvation," Tharix replied. "Perhaps."

"You want salvation?" Darius snarled at him. "Then start by making a path for us to get to it."

Tharix blinked at him, seeming to actually consider that, then the whole world fell to darkness and silence snuffed out everything.

I gasped for breath, feeling as though I might choke on the sudden, oppressive thickness to the air, the shadows which had spilled from him snuffing out everything and everyone in an instant. We were dead. Done for. Lost and at the mercy of a monster, yet I could still feel Darius's aura right beside my own and when I reached out, my hand latched around his arm.

"Fuck," Darius cursed as he appeared at my side as if I hadn't been looking properly until I caught hold of him and he had always been right there. "What the-"

"You should run, brother." Tharix's voice was a hot breath on the back of my neck, the desperate souls who suffered within him crying out for my help, but none of them screamed so powerfully as the thing which had drawn me to this place.

I kept hold of Darius and broke into a run, dragging him with me across the room, unable to see anything but knowing where to go simply by following the pull of that agonising pain.

I slammed into a small body and cursed as the young girl went flying, my hand snapping out and catching her in air magic before she could hit the ground.

I stared at her, feeling that emptiness, sensing her loss and the broken, jagged pieces of her soul which had suffered so much that they had simply stopped functioning.

"Bring her!" I yelled at Darius, giving him no option as I propelled the child into his arms with my magic then dove into the shadows again.

They were lightening now, first onyx then charcoal, shifting to a storm-cloud grey.

The Dragons were snarling behind us and a flash of fire lit the shadows from within. We had seconds, moments, little more and yet I couldn't force myself to take the stardust from my pocket.

"I'm working on the wards," Darius said at my back as we threw ourselves through a narrow doorway and began to sprint along the corridor which lay beyond.

Stairs met with my feet, the shadows lightening to pale grey now, Lionel's bellows of fury echoing out in the throne room behind us. We had to be almost out of time. They would find us before long, and yet I couldn't face escaping. Not yet.

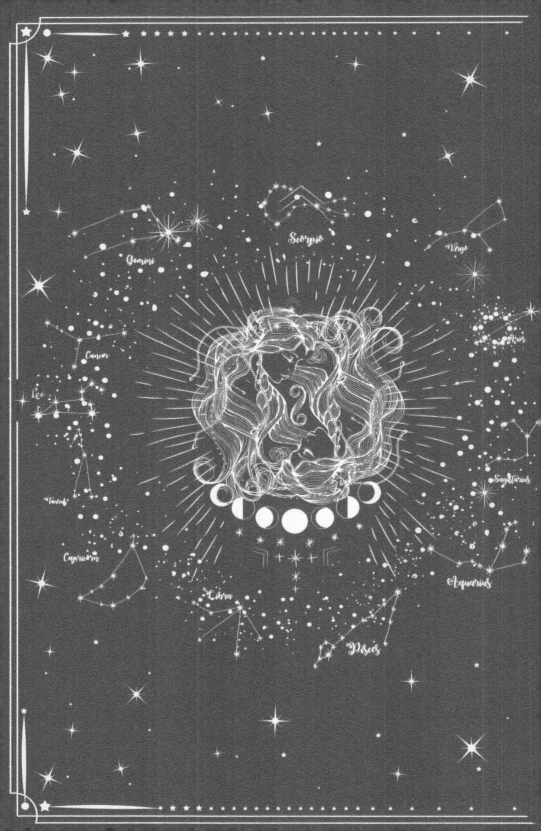

DARCY

CHAPTER THIRTY SEVEN

Lavinia's terrible power carved through the sky, and I flew as fast as I could to escape it, the arc of light and shadow daggering toward me. I swooped low, feeling the intensity of that incinerating power, certain that if it touched me I was done for. There was something rattling in the back of my mind, a memory of the vision Arcturus had shown me and Orion of a woman on a battlefield, wielding a power that resembled this deadly light. But that power had come from the stars, and I didn't dare to believe this magic had been offered from the same source.

Vengeance bayed a bloody tune in my heart and Phoenix fire blazed against my palms. My need to destroy Lavinia for all she'd done to Orion consumed me to the point of madness. I didn't know what this monstrous power was that she possessed, but it changed everything. She was unstoppable. The strength of it was able to tear through our flames and gutter them before they could even get close to her.

Tory swept along beneath me on fiery wings, her lips peeled back as she went in for another strike while I worked to keep Lavinia's attention on me.

I flew higher, darting this way and that to avoid the blasts of her power, her eyes as black as sin as they followed me through the sky.

Rain poured down from the heavens, forcing her to blink and I urged it on, feeding my own power into the storm so she was pelted with bullets of water.

Tory flew up from below, slicing through the pillar of shadow Lavinia stood upon and the shadow bitch stumbled, falling towards the lake with a shriek of rage. She turned her attention to Tory, catching herself with her shadows and carving through the fire my sister sent her way. Lavinia sent shots of that violent light towards her, forcing Tory to turn and dive for cover.

I free-fell from above, tucking my wings and wielding the Elements around me, churning up the lake below into a tornado of water that reached higher and higher.

The water sucked at Lavinia's legs, dragging her into it, but she blasted it away from her with that ethereal light, freeing herself in an instant.

My breaths came heavier as she turned her gaze to me once more, a sneer lifting her lips. She was utterly formidable. A creature without end. Whatever power lived in her was like nothing Tory and I had ever faced. And we were growing more exhausted by the minute. We couldn't keep playing this game of cat and mouse, luring her one way while the other attempted a shot. It wasn't working, and we couldn't go on like this indefinitely.

Nymphs were gathering on the lakeshore, working to capture any unfortunate souls who got washed up there. The lake was no longer brimming with earth-made boats full of brave warriors. Tory and I were the only ones out here who had survived this long, and Lavinia didn't seem to have tired at all.

My gaze caught on Caleb as he shot down onto the lakeshore and drove his twin blades into the chest of a Nymph who was about to kill a washed-up rebel. The cry of war carried all across campus, Dragon shifters swooping down and blasting our people with hellish fire, leaving bodies burning in their wake.

The clash of winged Orders sounded above us in the thick clouds, a clamour of roars and the collision of huge bodies so close, yet impossible to see.

I raced for Lavinia once more, her attention now on Tory again who was flying beneath her in circles, casting illusions of herself in every direction to keep her confused.

I called on all the hatred in my heart and tempered it with the determination of a queen, setting my prey in my sights. Lavinia deserved a death as bloody and as cruel as the torture she had offered my mate. And I would take her from this world in the most agonising way I could conjure.

I cast a net of steel, wrapping it around her arms and binding them to her sides, setting the metal ablaze with Phoenix fire in the next second. Lavinia screamed and thrashed, working to harness her power while I swooped down on her, ready to finish this once and for all.

The blaze of fire that left me was hotter than the pits of hell and more punishing than anything I had cast before. My hair was aflame with it, my wings a burning beacon of destruction as I blasted every drop of fury I had at her, demanding her death from the stars.

The fire took the shape of a Phoenix bird, slamming into Lavinia full force, and her scream lit the air with agony.

Victory blazed inside me and hope raised its head, her death a promise that was about to be delivered at long last.

In seconds, her skin shone like a light lived within her flesh, tearing out from her and swallowing my flames like they were nothing, and every searing wound I had burned into her skin knitted over like she was made of life itself.

"No," I gasped in horror, finding Tory hovering across from me in the sky, her eyes as wide with terror as mine.

We couldn't defeat her. That truth was as clear as night and day, a reality so undeniable that the weight of it almost suffocated me. I hadn't for one second believed this was it. That this fight might be the final one we fought. That I might never see Lance again, or the rest of my family.

I flew towards Tory, our hands coming together and locking tight as Lavinia turned her deadly gaze upon us.

"This can't be it," I rasped, and her fingers tightened on mine.

"At least we're together." Her eyes blazed at me, and injustice seeped into every corner of my being.

"We'll fight until there's no fight left in us," I whispered, and she nodded, the certainty of that so undeniable, I'd hardly needed to voice it.

"Stay with me," she breathed.

"Forever," I promised, my heart beating furiously at the pain of all that was about to be lost.

Lavinia smiled like she knew it was done, and her eyes glowed with that awful magic that lit her skin with an unearthly glow. Shadows slithered across her body like serpents hungering for blood, and all of that ungodly power came tearing towards us at once, promising to consume us and send us into death.

Tory and I screamed our fury, Phoenix fire tearing from us in two beautiful Phoenix birds that swooped together, diving from the sky in a spiralling dance that promised to be their last. They plunged into the shadowy light that came tearing towards us, snuffed out of existence just as surely as we would be in moments, the power curling high above and far below, promising no escape. We turned as one, racing away towards the only patch of freedom at our backs, flying faster and faster while the blast of all that power blazed a path of death behind us.

It was gaining on us by the second, no matter how fast we moved. It was closing in around us on all sides and sweeping up to block our way on.

Darkness fell and all I could see was the glitter of light within its depths and my sister's bright green eyes. We embraced, because that was all there was left for us to do. To hold onto the other half of our soul, and pray The Veil stole us away together, placing us somewhere we would never part again.

MAX

CHAPTER THIRTY EIGHT.

Up and up and up we ran through the palace of jade until finally we spilled out into a wide, unadorned chamber with a gaping chasm at its rear.

The screams in my head were unbearable now, the agony of what sat in that pit making it hard for me to think at all.

I fell to my knees beneath the weight of it then began to crawl.

I dragged myself on, reaching for the edge of the precipice and looking down at the horror beneath me.

A star. Its being so bright and essence so pure that I could hardly bear to look upon it. Fallen and lashed in shadows, screaming for release.

Footsteps thundered up the stairs, bellowed commands ringing off the walls as Lionel's Bonded Men closed in on us and time fluttered by too fast.

"I've forged a crack in the wards. We have seconds to take advantage of it," Darius told me. "Do what you must and do it now."

I stared down at the star, tears burning the backs of my eyes and then falling, falling, falling and breaking against its luminescent body.

It shuddered as it felt them, reaching for me, pleading in my mind.

"Release me!" it cried through the confines of my skull. But I couldn't. I didn't know how, and we had no time.

My lips parted on the only thing I could offer it. A song. One bound in the power of all I was and destined to cast a Fae into a hundred-year sleep. One I had never risked uttering before for fear of how many I might send to their death through slumber.

"Block your ears," I told Darius, unable to look at him, but feeling the magic stirring the air as he cast a silencing bubble around himself and the girl.

My lips parted. And I sang.

The lullaby which rolled from my throat was so potently beautiful that I was unable to do anything more than release it, tears spilling down my cheeks with every magic-imbued note. It fell from me like drops of purest power and as it spilled over the trapped star, its screams finally fell away.

"Sleep," I urged through my tears, drawing the stardust from my pocket and without taking my eyes from the now slumbering star, I threw it over the three of us, and we were whisked away into the night.

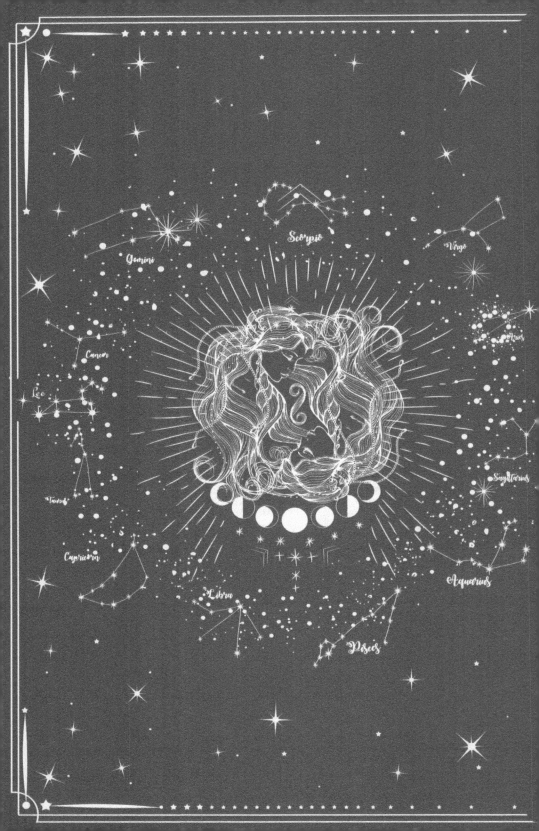

DARCY

CHAPTER THIRTY NINE.

Instead of death, came life. Lavinia's shadows stuttered out and that light fell away with it just a hair's breadth from our skin. I broke apart from Tory, turning my gaze to the Shadow Queen below where she gazed at her trembling hands in terrified disbelief.

The shadows still coiled about her skin, but none of that light gleamed and sparked around her. She screamed her fury, raising her hands to try and cast it, but none of it came to her aid.

My heart thundered and I raced for her with a surge of excitement, my wings beating faster and faster as I gained on her by the second, seeing the moment of weakness and claiming it before it was gone.

Fire tore from my flesh in a blazing torrent of oncoming destruction and Lavinia shrieked, taking something from her pocket and throwing it into the air. She disappeared into a glitter of stardust, and I sailed through the place she had been just moments ago with fire swirling around me. A snarl tore from my lips and failure cast my heart into a pit of despair.

Tory swept past me, her hands outstretched with equal heat blazing from her skin and she let fire tear from her to cut through a line of Nymphs upon the shore.

My blue hair was plastered to my cheeks by the rain, and I panted heavily as I struggled with my failure. She had gotten away just seconds before she could have been destroyed for good. But as my eyes fell on the battle still waging on below, I forced myself to move, to follow after Tory and let my rage loose upon the sinning souls of the Nymphs who had dared step foot in our haven, turning them to ash and dust.

With Lavinia's power no longer in play and our fire tearing through the battalion of Nymphs across campus, the tide of the battle turned fast. The Dragons who spotted us turned tail and raced away into the mist, and the rebels began to release cries of victory as the storm eased.

Dante swooped down from the clouds, chasing a scarlet Dragon and snapping at its tail as it raced for escape. The beast put on a burst of speed, tearing off into the distance and Dante turned back, leaving that fight for another day, his wings beating unevenly as he circled down from the sky, revealing his exhaustion. Claw marks were ripped all across his scales, dripping blood, but the Storm Dragon had a strength in his eyes that spoke of his victory.

Slowly but surely, the battle was won, Lionel's followers stardusting away in droves, or chased off campus by the bolstered rebels.

The storm clouds began to part, and Tory and I came to land upon the very top of the Earth Observatory, gazing out across campus where steam plumed up from freshly extinguished fires and shouts of victory called out to us as rebels spotted us from below. We shared a look of relief, but I knew my heart wouldn't stop rioting until I'd found all of our loved ones alive and well.

My gaze locked with Orion's as he shot into view with the Shadow Beast bounding along at his heels, and I leapt off of the building with a cry of joy, sweeping down to him and knocking him from his feet. We hit the mud, and our mouths came together, his hands gripping my arms and sending a wave of healing magic through me, though there were few wounds to find, despite how close we'd come to death.

Strong hands pulled me upright as a very naked Seth dragged me into a hug that crushed bones and I squeezed him tight, so relieved to find he was okay. Orion's arms came around us and I pushed my hand into the Shadow Beast's fur as he nuzzled us too, pressing his nose into my hair with a grunt of greeting.

I knew in the back of my mind that although the battle may have been won today, the war was far from over. And if Lavinia returned with that terrible power at her aid once more, we might not survive it twice.

TORY

CHAPTER FORTY

It had been less than an hour since the battle had ended, and the academy was still in chaos with the dead being counted and every corner of campus being searched for any signs of enemies lingering within our walls. Darcy and I had resurrected the wards, but despite the immensity of their power, I no longer felt so reassured by their presence surrounding us. Lavinia had torn through them with a legion of less than five hundred of their army and we had come far too close to failure in that skirmish than was acceptable.

I'd heard news that Darius was safe, and the moment my duties were done, I got word of his location and flew across campus as fast as I could, the wind whipping through my hair and my own blood staining my cheek from a wound I hadn't paused to heal. The moment I spotted him standing outside The Orb, I dropped from the sky like a bullet and collided with him in the next moment.

Darius closed his arms around me as I wrapped all of my limbs around him and let my wings fade to nothing, tasting his rough and demanding kiss against my lips.

"Can't leave you alone for five minutes without carnage breaking out," he grumbled against my mouth.

"Can't let you out of my sight without knowing you'll go creating carnage of your own," I replied in kind.

He set me on my feet and led me inside, the heavy weight of Geraldine's anti-spying measures racing over my skin as I crossed the threshold. She had placed every spell imaginable on this place to prevent anyone who wasn't invited from attending our war councils and I released a small measure of my magic to confirm my identity as we headed inside.

My gaze was drawn to the roof of The Orb where patches of new metal had been forged to cover the damage done during the battle, the work rough and obvious though it was good enough to have sealed the space again. The scent of smoke lingered, and I noticed a few bloodstains in the far corner but for the most part, Geraldine had restored everything to its former position with her earth Element.

"My lady, I am pleased to see you have energy to spare beyond the battlefield," Geraldine called from behind a mountain of maps, military directions and bagels as she spotted me. "You look a bit wan, like the brightness of your button has dimmed.

Is all well?"

"I'm fine," I said quickly.

I didn't want to admit to the fact that fear laced my limbs in the wake of that fight, but how could I deny it? It was written plainly over my face.

That was barely a taste of the full might of Lionel's army, and the power Lavinia had somehow wielded against us had almost resulted in their victory.

The Councillors were already here, Xavier, Caleb, Gabriel and Washer too. Max was slumped in a chair beside Geraldine looking close to unconscious with exhaustion, a small girl sitting upright beside him, probably around seven or eight years old, her hand in his and her eyes wide as she spotted me.

"Where the hell have you been?" I asked pointedly, looking back to Darius and taking in his dishevelled clothes and the fact that he hadn't appeared anywhere that I'd noticed during the battle.

"Visiting my father," he said in a low tone, making my skin prickle with concern and my grip on his hand tighten. But he was here, right in front of me, unharmed if looking a little ruffled.

"Explain," I demanded, authority ringing in my tone which had him arching a brow at me. Yes, I was his queen, but pulling rank didn't tend to go down too easily with my Dragon consort.

The doors opened again, Darcy striding in with Orion a step behind her. "How many did we lose?" she called, ignoring the flurry of bows just as I had when I'd arrived. "And what the hell was that magic Lavinia used?"

"It was the power of a fallen star," Darius said, causing Tiberius to suck in a sharp breath and Caleb to look at Max for confirmation.

I frowned at my sister, moving to take up my place beside her at the table while the others moved to sit down too.

"I feared it was something like that," Darcy said grimly. "It looked just like the star power Orion and I saw in the vision from Arcturus. But how-"

The door banged as Seth appeared looking like he'd been through hell with his hair in a chaotic tangle and such wildness about him that it was clear he'd struggled to survive out there. He'd evidently taken no time to clean up since the battle, offering out help to the rebels just like the rest of us.

To my surprise, Gabriel got to his feet and moved to embrace the mutt. "I owe you a debt," he said seriously. "Luca's life was in your hands and you kept him safe. Without your help I *saw...*" Gabriel grimaced and cut himself off. "The fate you kept him from will never be forgotten. Ask anything from me and it is yours."

Seth grinned, clapping Gabriel on the arm. "Right now, I'd settle for some snacks," he replied easily, the two of them dropping into chairs to my left beyond Darius, and Gabriel tugged a plate of bagels closer for Seth to pick from.

"I want that story in full," I said, pointing at the two of them. "But first, I think Darius and Max have the more pressing tale."

Everyone looked between the two of them and Max waved a hand at Darius, urging him to explain, the small girl still sitting there, expressionless and mysterious, but I got the feeling her presence was important if Geraldine had been convinced to allow her access to this meeting.

"Tonight, before the battle broke out here, Max Siren Spelled me to him, but when we shared a kiss, the power of his gifts were awakened in full, and he connected to the pleading spirit of something that was in desperate need of his help."

We all sat in silence as their story unfurled, none of us interrupting with questions or any kind of comment as the incredible reality of what they'd somehow managed to survive spun out between us. They'd been to Lionel's stronghold, knew where it was, had seen his army amassed there – though I fought against the knot of horror that built in me when he confirmed that our information on its size had been severely lacking

– they'd spoken with Tharix and lived to tell the tale, though Orion physically balked at the suggestion that Lionel's new Heir might actually have helped them escape, and Seth began muttering about demon vaginas beneath his breath.

When they described the star they'd discovered lashed in shadows and forced to fall to Lavinia's will instead of releasing its power back out into the world, we all fell into a heavy, terrifying silence.

"How can we fight the power of a star itself?" Antonia muttered aghast.

I swallowed against the thickness in my throat as I turned over everything Darius had said, trying to find some positive amongst it and coming up short.

"What does the girl have to do with it?" I asked, casting around for something, anything which might not be filled with more and more horrors.

The child didn't flinch as all eyes turned her way, though there was something akin to horror in the depths of her expression as she looked between me and Darcy. She was so young but something in her gaze said that whatever she'd been witness to had aged her beyond her years.

"That…well, she was there and Max said we had to take her…" Darius seemed as uncertain as I was about the child's importance, but Max finally roused enough energy to speak.

"You forgot the part about the man with the sallow skin," Max said, pushing himself more upright in his seat and leaning forward to rest his forearms on the table. "But I felt his aura and he was no Fae."

Dread pooled in my stomach as I turned to the shattered-looking child, taking in the horror which was simmering in her gaze as she glanced between me and Darcy. A truly horrendous thought burned into me which I didn't want to dare put a voice to.

"Did that man…" I asked the girl slowly, hoping against hope that she would deny what I was about to ask. "Did he…always appear that way? Or has he worn another face? Maybe two other faces?"

The girl blinked at me, her gaze sliding between my sister and me, then her head dipped into a nod.

Geraldine gasped, her hand flying to her chest, a platter of bagels scattering across the maps which had been spread out before her while she noted down the details of everything Darius had shared about Lionel's location and the size of his army.

"Clydinius?" Darcy hissed, realising the same thing I had. "Lionel has aligned with fucking Clydinius?"

"Doom!" Gabriel cried suddenly, making us all flinch in surprise. "Fire, bloodshed, carnage. Xavier lying in a pool of blood, Caleb's head on a spike and-" He cut himself off sharply, gripping the edge of the table and scrunching his eyes shut as he fought against the vision.

"We have to go now and strike at Lionel before any of that happens," Seth snarled, leaping up from his chair.

Washer got to his feet too. "I shall lead a battalion out at once. I shall sing a song of dread so potent that Lionel will quiver in his teeny-"

"Forget it," Gabriel snapped, taking hold of Seth's arm and yanking him back down into his chair. "Fate shifted again, that won't come to pass."

My lips parted on some response to that, and I glanced across the table to Caleb who touched two fingers to his neck as though checking it was still very much intact and his head definitely wasn't going to end up on a spike any time soon.

"You were with Clydinius," I said, my gaze moving back to the girl as I drew the focus to the issue at hand again. "He…what? Imprisoned you or-"

Her lips parted like she might reply but she looked between me and my sister again, then bit back whatever words had been so close to leaving her.

"It's okay," Max said softly, offering her his hand and she hesitantly took it, allowing him to soothe her with his gifts.

We sat in silence, waiting while he helped ease whatever trauma held her captive until a soft sob suddenly broke from her lips.

"He looked like you before," she breathed, tears wetting her eyes as she raised them in accusation. "When he came to the Nebula Inquisition Centre, we thought it was you saving us. But then...everything was burning and everyone was dead."

"But not you," I pointed out and Darcy elbowed me, giving me a look which implied I needed to go easier.

I shrugged, gesturing for her to take the lead in my place and she offered the girl a deep frown.

"I'm so sorry he did that. I'm so sorry we didn't get there ourselves and help everyone in that place before it was too late."

"Their deaths and our failure in helping them stain our souls," I added. "But we want to offer them justice. Can you help us with that?"

The girl looked to Max once more, tightening her hold on his hand and Geraldine placed her hand on his other arm, offering up her power while he wielded it to help the child.

"I don't know why they kept me. They said I might be the answer, but I don't know what to. It...he...they took me with them and let me watch while they killed and destroyed and searched for something. They took me to see The Ferryman too. They wanted to make a bargain with him."

"What bargain?" I breathed, my horror at this line of events only increasing with every new piece of information I could glean. "A bargain to cheat death. But he said death did not want them. He refused to help them, and I think...I think perhaps he hated them."

I exchanged a look with Darius, knowing all too well how the hatred of The Ferryman felt and yet still wondering, if that creature wrought from the power of the world itself held no fondness for Clydinius in his un-beating heart, then might he wish him ill?

"Then the Dragon King came and offered up a deal of his own," the girl said.

I cursed. "Trust Lionel to ally himself with that fucking snake of a star."

"This might be a good thing," Gabriel said, surprising us all with that ridiculous assessment.

"How in the hell might it be a good thing that the two of them have allied against us?" I demanded and his mouth fell into a grim smile.

"Because the enemy of our enemy is our friend. Or perhaps they could be," he said simply.

"Who-" I began, but Darcy cut me off.

"The stars," she breathed, seeing what I hadn't because the stars fucking hated me. Despised and reviled me for what I had done and yet... Maybe, just maybe there could be some truth to that claim. Because if there was a single being in this world who the stars might just despise more than the girl who had defied them, broken through their rules and spat in the face of their dominion, then it would be the traitor who had fallen from the heavens and defied the very nature of what they were and what they were destined to become.

"That's...insane, but it could just be fucking genius too," I said. "Although, I have to wonder if there is any chance at all that they could ever consider allying themselves with me after what I did."

"What if we made up for that?" Darcy suggested, a feral, dangerous look in her eyes which I knew would both be brilliant and spell all kinds of chaos. "What if we freed the star that Lionel has trapped away in his palace of traitors?"

"That's madness, Blue," Orion growled. "Darius and Max got in there by chance alone and they were damn lucky to escape unscathed. It won't happen a second time. In fact, Lionel will no doubt be putting every resource at his disposal into place to guard that fucking thing with all he's got, especially knowing the strength of the power Lavinia can steal from it."

"We'll find a way," Darcy said stubbornly, and Orion's lips twitched at the corner.

"The star is sleeping now," Max said in a low voice. "She won't be able to claim any power while my song holds it captive."

"And how long will that last?" Orion demanded.

"If I'd cast it on a Fae? A hundred years. On a star? Well, how the fuck should I know? But hopefully a few months, long enough to-"

"A week," Gabriel interrupted. "Perhaps ten days. I cannot *see* the star itself, but I can *see* the destruction Lavinia might cause with it."

"A week," I repeated, the word sounding like a death sentence to all around the room while our eyes fell to the maps, charts, lists and plans which were now mostly useless in the face of all we'd just discovered.

"Seven gallant days to change the fate of the world," Geraldine announced like that was the best news she'd heard all year and we all looked to her in utter bewilderment. "Come now, did Urgut the Urgent give up when he foresaw his death in the face of a lake?"

"I think that story ends with him drowning despite his refusal to accept that fate," Xavier replied, but Geraldine ignored him.

"Did King Buront pale in the face of the army of Inor?"

"That guy definitely died – didn't he get his head cut off in battle?" Darius said.

"Did Olaf Von Clemmins give up his dream of playing the harp after losing all of his fingers?" Geraldine demanded, and no one had anything to say to that because I had to assume no one knew who the fuck that was.

Geraldine yanked out her Atlas, selected an album and began playing a piece of harp music while brandishing the screen in our faces so we could see the Olaf dude's name on the cover, his wriggling toes held aloft in triumph.

"High level toe flexation, that is," Washer gushed like he was in awe of the man.

"Alright, alright," I agreed, kinda liking the harp music as it continued to play on while I spoke. "We aren't giving up. Of course we fucking aren't, but the odds are stacked against us, the stars despise me, our two greatest enemies have aligned and the army we face is far bigger than our worst guesses had surmised. So where the fuck do we go from here?"

"Beautiful speech, Tor," Darcy teased, and I blew out a defeated laugh as I slumped back in my seat. "How about we lay it out piece by piece. We can work our way up to the overarching problem – first of all, if Lionel's army is bigger than we accounted for then we need to think of better ways to fight them. In the last battle, the Nymphs' rattles immobilised countless rebel units' magic and forced them to fight hand to hand. I think I have an idea for how we might combat that." Her gaze moved to Gabriel and his expression glazed then brightened as he *saw* something in her suggestion which looked damn hopeful from where I was sitting.

"Yes, that might work," he agreed. "But it is a tentative fate that can be changed by many hands, so let us keep it between us for now."

The rest of the room muttered their agreement to that, and I nodded, wondering what they might have up their sleeves and trusting they knew what they were doing.

"Miguel and the Nymphs who weren't infected by the shadows might still join us," I suggested. "It would help even the playing field if we had a Nymph army of our own and fuck knows we need them. They hate Lavinia for what she did to the shadows and they want her dead as badly as we do, but I'm not sure how easy it will be to convince them."

"We'll figure it out," Darcy replied determinedly, and I nodded.

"We should hit the rest of the Nebula Inquisition Centres and bring the Fae who are trapped in them to join our army. Our plans for the strikes are in place, and we should enact them as soon as possible," Caleb said, pushing a hand into his golden curls. "We can offer shelter to those who don't want to fight, but if the survivors of the other camps are anything to go by then we will likely find ourselves with thousands of Fae who want nothing more than to fight back against the tyrant who imprisoned them."

"Good. Let's hit them all at once though in a coordinated attack," I said. "I don't want Lionel figuring out what we're doing and killing more innocent Fae. We hit them all together and get them all out." I looked to Geraldine in hopes that she could make that work and she nodded firmly.

"It will happen by my nelly or my nolly," she agreed.

"Tyler can ramp up the campaign to get more civilians to rebel and join our ranks," Xavier suggested, and Darcy smiled grimly in appreciation of that.

"The Bonded Men are going to make it damn near impossible to get near my father. It was bad enough before but with a hoard Dragons willing and ready to throw themselves between him and death, it's going to be a fucking massacre," Darius growled.

This was a problem which had been hounding us ever since Lionel had created the Bonded Men and it was one we were no closer to solving. Some of them had been killed in the fight but there were still far too many left to make getting close to him simple.

"We can keep working on ideas to draw them apart and pick them off, but if we can't even the odds and take down his army then we will just have to hit them head on. If I have to cut through every last one of them to take that bastard's head from his neck then I'll do it gladly," I said, the idea of it making my pulse race with the thought of all that bloodshed and I exchanged a heated look with Darius as we both got lost in the idea of it.

"*That* is a problem," Orion said forcefully.

I looked around to find him pointing at the two of us, his brow furrowed with concern.

"It is kinda disturbing," Xavier agreed, and I glanced at my sister, finding her watching us too. In fact, all of them were looking between me and Darius, and I got the distinct impression that this was a discussion which had gone on behind our backs before this moment.

"Spit it out," I demanded.

"Well, Tor, you must have noticed the way you and Darius get when it comes to killing since you returned from beyond The Veil," Darcy said. "It's not entirely rational. And you both get all excited and bloodthirsty, and we're just worried that-"

"It's the price," I supplied, knowing it was the case even if I hadn't admitted it so candidly before now. "When I used the ether to cross over and steal him back from the clutches of death, I knew there would be a cost. Unlike the fucked up deals the stars make with Fae, ether only ever takes a price from the Fae who wields it, so I knew I wasn't putting any of you at risk of harm. The only way to circumvent a personal cost is by supplying a sacrifice, but I happily took on the price of this myself which was the only possible way I could have achieved what I did. The cost wasn't specified but we are almost certain that it's being accounted for with this bloodlust somehow. Perhaps I should go to The Ferryman myself and demand a precise answer to it..."

No one looked comfortable at that suggestion, but it wasn't like I would be able to glean the answer anywhere else.

"That's it then. We'll go to The Ferryman," Darius agreed.

"I will continue to gather information and collect the latest reports so that we can strike at the Nebula Inquisition Centres as soon as a nary can take flight," Geraldine swore.

"Any more luck with the Guild Stones?" Caleb looked between Orion and Darcy.

"Eugene Dipper has been sending books to us whenever he discovers anything of use," Orion said.

"And has he found something?" Caleb pressed hopefully.

"No," Orion grunted.

"It's not *nothing*," Darcy said encouragingly. "There's clues and hints. Things that lead us to another book, then another. Eventually we'll find the right one."

"Or the knowledge is lost to time and we're all fucked," Caleb sighed.

"We'll find the answer," Darcy growled, and his eyebrows arched, his head inclining.

"Alright, I trust you," he said.

I looked to Darcy as the discussions went on, plans and destiny being forged right in front of us while all we could do was hope against hope that the decisions we were making were right, acts that would hopefully see the people around this table and all those who followed us survive this war and revel in victory.

But as I silently took my twin's hand beneath the table where no one could see, I couldn't help but think that all of this, every piece of it, no matter how well thought through or planned out, just might not be enough.

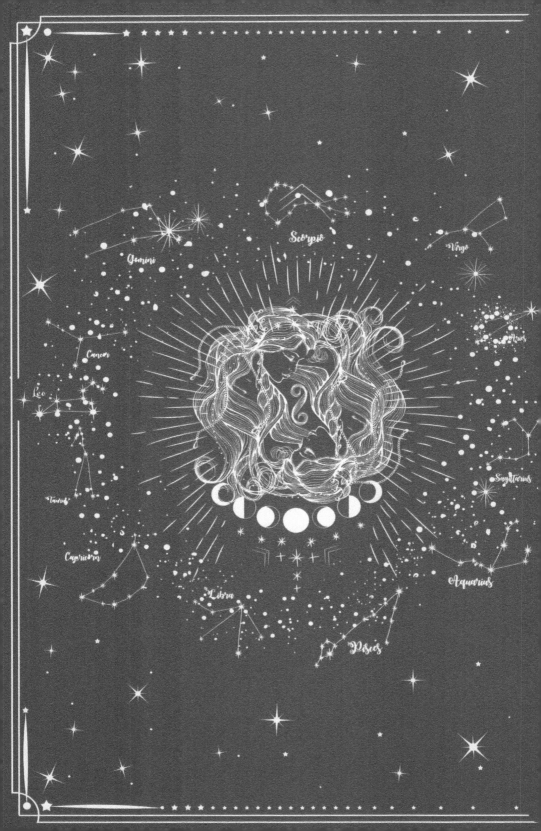

DARCY

CHAPTER FORTY ONE

"My quails are quailing, my lady," Geraldine breathed as I held her hand, drawing her closer to the Shadow Beast in The Howling Meadow.

"Trust me," I urged. "I wouldn't put you in any danger. Shadow was a prisoner just like me. I don't want you to fear him."

"Shadow? Is that what you have decided on then, dear Darcy?" she asked, glancing at me with fear in her eyes and I nodded. Geraldine Grus wasn't afraid of anything, and I hated that I was partly responsible for the terror I saw in her because of the beast. I had to put it right. "Such an apt title for a beast of shadow and snails, but did it perchance cross your thoughts to ask it its true name?"

"Ask him?" I frowned.

She cleared her throat, shifting a little closer to the beast and he tilted his head, taking her in with hooded eyes, looking like he was hankering for a nap. He towered over us, his long grey fur shifting in the breeze and turning to shadow at the very edges.

"Creatures such as this, magical beings…they often have what a gandering goose might term a star name." Geraldine straightened up a bit, seeming to dig for her courage then she placed her palm flat on Shadow's nose.

"Eggnog on a Thursday in June," she croaked, shutting her eyes then cracking them open a little to peek at the Beast.

Shadow grunted, nuzzling into her palm then licking her fingers as if seeking out a treat. He had a voracious appetite, and Leon Night had taken to organising his meals as his family had a little Ghosthound called Periwinkle to look after who liked the same kinds of food. The blue, dog-like animal was very fussy with who she spent time with, but she'd taken a real liking to Shadow, the two of them often found wandering around campus together.

"There, see," I said excitedly. "He likes you."

Geraldine opened her eyes fully, her hand slipping up a little higher to tickle the space between his eyes. "Alligators at the dawn dance…I think you're right!"

Shadow dipped his head for more tickles and Geraldine scratched his ears, moving closer as the Beast grunted happily.

"So how would I find out his star name?" I asked, joining her in scratching his ears. He was so big, he needed two of us to do a good job of it anyway.

"You must Familiarise!" she cried excitedly. "But what-ho, you will have done half the jib-jab of the job anyway. It is all about your fling jiving with the animal's flang."

"The what and the what now?" I asked in confusion.

"A connection, silly Sally," she grinned. "Earn the beastie's trust and he shall mumble and grumble his star name to you. You have already bonded with the fella like a robin to its dobin, so all you likely need do is *ask*, my lady."

I turned to Shadow, cocking my head and feeling dumb as I asked him that very question. "What's your name?"

"Excaverinias-helios-dolianco." The Shadow Beast's name entered my head, its voice taking no real shape that was in any way Fae.

"Holy shit," I breathed, turning to Geraldine with a big ass smile on my face. "He told me!"

"Gumptious goulash! What is it?"

I spoke it back to Geraldine, unsure if I'd pronounced it quite right.

"Holy haslemere, that's quite the tongue-twiddler indeed." She frowned.

"How about Shadow as a nickname?" I asked the Beast and he grunted, nudging his nose against my face.

"He seems appeased." Geraldine placed her hands on her hips. "Apologies dear rogue of a rapscallion. I thought you a danger, but it seems you are a docile dandelion – at least to those in your favour. As the True Queens' companion, I shall of course accept you into the royal court, and I proudly declare you Queen Darcy's steed." She bowed to Shadow, and he blinked lazily.

"I shall have a fine saddle and armour forged for him." She turned to me with glee in her eyes. "And perhaps a blue collar to wear proudly too?"

"No collar," I said quickly, brushing my fingers over Shadow's shoulder. "He's seen enough chains. He's free to go or to stay, it's his choice. Always. I won't take his freedom from him ever again."

"So be it," she said, sniffing and subtly wiping a tear from her eye.

"Thank you for giving him a chance," I said and she beamed at me.

"Of course, my lady." She straightened. "Oh, in all the emotional tangle, I forgot to update you on how the latest drill is coming along."

With Lavinia's star power hanging over us, and our timescale running short on dealing with it, we'd had to come up with an escape plan in case she returned here with it. There was no point in making a stand a second time and allowing our people to be incinerated.

I listened as Geraldine explained how she was preparing the rebels to escape on Rump Island. We'd head back to sea as they had before and keep our movements random, hopefully buying us time to come up with a solution to Lavinia's newfound strength. I hoped it didn't come to that, but I was comforted by the back-up plan. Running didn't sit well with me, but I wasn't going to force our people to face their deaths when there was no hope of survival.

"I'll be running a full drill at noon," she said. "For now, I shall head straight for the new forge and see to it that Shadow's armour is made, moulded and as done as a donnyhap." She bowed low then scurried away into the trees.

My Atlas buzzed in my pocket and I took it out, finding a message in the group chat from Tyler linking to a FaeBook post.

Tyler Corbin:
Lame Lionel Leak Alert!
Hold. The. Front. Door. Because I'm coming through it twirling a cane and wearing my best party hat. This one's about to go #viral people as I've JUST been

sent a video from Lame Lionel's graduation that a reporter took and was paid off not to release. That fantastic Fae has come forward for the greater good to #shamelameLionel and it is my DUTY to share it here first with all my followers. If you'd like to see the False King face down with an inch of skin rubbed clean off his face, then check out the video below!
#faceplant #thekinghasfallen #stagerage #theGRATE-estshowman #Grate-uation

I clicked the video and watched the moment a young Lionel Acrux walked onto a stage in The Orb in his navy blue graduation robes, tripped over the top step and went flying up onto the stage. He hit the floor face first with such momentum that he skidded a full foot, his face dragging across the wood and making him wail in pain. The principal ran to help him up as the crowd gasped and I caught sight of my father in the front row roaring with laughter with the other Councillors.

Lionel knocked the principal away from him as he scrambled upright, glancing towards the crowd in horror and embarrassment, his nose, forehead and chin bloody from how badly he'd skimmed it. I sniggered as he hurried to heal it and my father glanced over his shoulder, his eyes meeting with the camera and making my heart clench as I felt we were suddenly sharing a moment. But then the footage ended and the moment was gone, my smile falling a little.

The comments from Tyler's followers brought my amusement back in full force though as I scrolled through them.

Brodie Brown:
I hear he only takes SKIM milk in his coffee these days

Zach Worthington:
I bet Lame Lionel won't even care when this goes viral. It'll be #noskinoffhisnose

Bree Eliza Keith:
I always wondered what that scrape was across the graduation stage #skidmark

I sensed eyes on me and glanced up, spotting Orion standing beneath the trees, his shoulder pressed to an oak and his gaze set on me.

"Spying on me, Professor?" I accused with a playful smile, not bothering to raise my voice as I put my Atlas away. His Vampire ears would pick it up anyway.

He shot over to me, making my hair whirl around my shoulders from the force of the wind he brought with him. "I didn't want to interrupt."

"So polite these days," I said with a grin. "There was a time when if you wanted to speak to me, you'd throw me over your shoulder and march me off to your office."

"You'd be a fool to think those days are gone." He gave me a dark look, stepping closer so I had to tilt my head back to look up at him.

Shadow nudged his face with his nose, grunting in greeting and Orion's gaze slid to him, a scowl taking over his features. "Still here then, Beast?"

"He can stay as long as he wants to," I said, scratching under Shadow's chin.

"I still think-"

"That you have double standards? Forgiveness for me, but none for him?" I arched my eyebrows and Orion's lips pressed into a hard line.

"My standards have always taken exception when it comes to you. You get a free pass for being you, the rest of the world does not. But if you think that means I won't still bend you over my knee and remind you of what an asshole I can be, then go ahead and challenge me to prove it."

Excitement sparked in my chest, the temptation all too keen to ignore. But unfortunately, I had other plans.

"Can't. I have somewhere to be." I moved to walk past him, but he stepped straight into my way, a wall of muscle firmly blocking my escape.

"What plans?" he demanded in that bossy tone of his.

"Secret sister plans." I shrugged innocently and his eyes hardened.

"You're going to run off somewhere together, aren't you?"

"Maybe."

"Blue."

"Lance?"

"I'd prefer to know where you're going so that I can come after you if you need me."

I softened at the concern in his gaze, slipping my hands around his waist and frowning up at him. "We're going to visit the Nymphs who are in hiding to see if they'll join our ranks."

"Hm." His expression darkened all over again. "They've been our enemies for too long. I can't see them assisting us now, even if they do want revenge against Lavinia."

"Your optimism knows no bounds."

He cracked a grin, the dimple appearing in his right cheek. "Just be safe."

"Always am." I tiptoed up to kiss him and his hand reached into my hair, his tongue pushing between my lips and deepening the kiss. Our love burned brighter, the Elysian Mate bond crying out in my veins, urging me nearer to him. My fingers clawed down his arms and his hand curled tightly in my hair, fisting it and yanking to make our lips part, keeping me close enough so he could talk directly to me.

"Come straight to my office when you return."

"Did I just get detention?" I teased and his gaze glimmered wickedly.

"Sometimes I think you miss me being your professor."

"You'll always be my professor." I touched my lips to his again, and he released me, letting me step back.

"I'll have some new knowledge on the Guild Stones by the time you come back, that's a promise," he said fiercely. "I've found a couple of leads and I've requested some more books from Eugene. He's going to send them over this morning. I won't stop hunting for answers."

"I know you won't." I squeezed his fingers then turned to Shadow and held up my hand, offering him the ring to see if he wanted to come with me. He swirled away into a grey mist that sailed into the ring and I stroked my finger over the gemstone with a smile.

"Where are you meeting Tory?" Orion asked.

"At the gates, but I need to get changed first," I said, and he whipped me off my feet, shooting across campus with me in his arms.

He ran down to Air Cove, racing across the stony beach and turning onto the bridge that had been formed between here and Rump Island. My heart thundered with exhilaration as the air rushed over my skin and Orion sped towards the beautiful castle at the centre of the island.

We were inside in the next second, flying up the staircase, higher and higher, a blur of ornaments, paintings and gleaming walls tearing by before we came to a sudden halt in our room.

Orion placed me down, offering me a casual grin as he leaned against a marble pillar. After moving all our stuff to Orion's chalet at Asteroid Place, Rump Island had been brought here and Geraldine had begged the two of us to come and check out the room she'd made for us in the castle. Though it was really more of an entire apartment with a suite of white furniture, a bathroom with a shining silver tub, and a luxurious bedroom which had a fourposter in it that was big enough for five people. Everything smelled faintly of a summer's day. The atmosphere was so perfectly relaxing, and the space so amazingly ours that we couldn't resist moving in here.

I kicked off my sneakers, stripping out of my jeans and sweater before heading for the walk-in closet, grabbing a silver gown and returning to the bedroom. Orion watched me closely, and my eyes met his as I pulled off my bra, not needing it as the dress had one built in.

Orion's throat bobbed, his eyes falling to my body, his hunger for me clear. He was all too tempting when he looked at me like that, but I needed to get going.

I pulled the dress over my head, and when I could see again, I found him standing right in front of me, making my breath hitch.

He smoothed the dress down over my waist, his gaze never breaking from mine, then he lifted a finger, gesturing for me to turn around. I did so, gathering my hair over one shoulder and he gently pulled my zipper up my spine, his fingers grazing the back of my neck before he placed a kiss there. Goosebumps rippled across my skin, a delicious shiver rolling the length of my body. This man would always be my undoing.

He took hold of my chin and guided my eyes to my reflection in the mirror right ahead of me on the wall. "The Nymphs would know you are a queen without this dress. It's right there in your eyes. You're royal, your blood runs blue." He lowered his head to kiss my ear, causing my pulse to riot. "Make them bow, beautiful."

"I'll do my best," I said, turning my head to press my lips to his, then I stepped away from him, retrieving Diego's hat from my nightstand drawer and tucking it into a concealed pocket in the sweeping skirt of my dress.

"How's Professor Shellick getting along with the Guild Potion?" I asked hopefully.

Orion's brow furrowed. "His analysis is a slow process apparently. He has nothing to report so far, but I'll keep checking in with him."

"Hopefully it won't be much longer."

He nodded, his expression betraying his concern over how long it was taking, but he said no more.

"I'll take you to the gate," he offered, grabbing something from his own nightstand drawer and slipping it into his pocket. I gave him a questioning look that he didn't answer, then he picked me up again, and I looped my arms around his neck.

In a flash of movement, we were tearing away through the castle once more, passing over Rump Island and onto the bridge. He sprinted across campus so fast, it was hard to catch anything but glimpses of trees and grassy plains, then he placed me down just outside the gates where Tory was waiting to go, wearing a sweeping gold dress that was a twin to mine.

"Ready?" I asked her brightly.

"Yeah, you just need to return your pony to the stable." Tory stepped forward to pet Orion's arm and he gave her a dry look.

"Well since I'm just a pack horse, I guess I can't give you the gift I have in my pocket. Ponies wouldn't do something like that." Orion turned to leave, but Tory snatched his arm.

"Gift?" she demanded, and I fought back a squeal as I realised what he'd brought.

I'd helped Orion make it just for her after I'd caught him trying to fashion a piece of string into a bracelet. It had been sort of pathetic, so I'd used earth magic to bring his vision to life instead.

Orion slid it from his pocket, offering the gold chain-link bracelet to her which had glittering red gemstones dotted along it.

"You made this?" Tory asked while I bit my lip to try and hold back my words of joy at seeing the two of them bond like this.

"Well, Blue made it." He ran a hand down the back of his neck. "You got me one so…" He shrugged.

"I was just a forge in the situation. He channelled what he wanted right through me," I said quickly. "I did it exactly how he said. Even the little gold flowers around the clasp."

"I don't recall saying to add the flowers." He shook his head.

"You did! You said just a couple of flowers because Tor's not a flowery kinda girl, and I fully agreed, but then I shut up because it was your creation, and I didn't want to influence it." I looked to Tory, letting my smile fly free as she accepted the bracelet and held it out for me to put on. I quickly clipped it on her right wrist and Orion cleared his throat.

"I'm going to save us the awkwardness and fuck off now." He lunged for me, placing a kiss on my cheek in double speed then sped away back onto campus.

Tory turned her wrist over, a small smile tugging at her lips.

"Do you like it?" I asked. "He wanted it to match your necklace from Darius, but not in a way that was too obvious, you know?"

"Yeah... it's perfect. Tell him thanks, okay? I don't want to do it, because he'll be sarcastic and then I'll be sarcastic, then we'll fist bump or some shit, and I can't deal with how uncomfortable it'll all be."

"I get it. I'll tell him." I launched myself at her and hugged her tight. "But I'm so damn happy that you two are friends, it makes my heart wanna burst."

She laughed, squeezing me back before knocking me away. "Okay, let's get going."

"You can't wait to get back to those three Nymphs you had a weird sex night with, can you?" I taunted.

"Who told you about that?" she gasped.

"Seth. He heard it from Caleb. Max was there too when Seth blurted it out. Oh, and Justin."

"Great." She pursed her lips. "So long as Washer didn't get a whiff of it too."

"I did just now, queenie love!" Washer stepped out of the gate in leather pants and a leopard print shirt that had way too many buttons open. "What a riveting tale, you will share it with me soon, won't you? It sounds like a tryst to remember, and if I'm not wrong, I sense a little grief radiating off of you around the subject. I can delve into the crannies of your mind and free you from any sufferings, you know? Don't ever hesitate to-"

Tory made an opening in the wards, tossed a pinch of stardust over our heads and we were whipped away into the stars, escaping our creepy old professor. We whirled through an ocean of galaxies, glittering nebulas, and a sea of sparkling light before we landed at our destination.

We arrived at the heart of a village where wooden huts stood with smoke pluming from chimneys and Nymphs bustling here and there, some in Nymph form and others in their Fae-like form.

"The Savage Queens!" a woman cried, pointing us out and a crowd immediately began to form, a few even pulling their children away from us.

"Do you have no respect?" An elderly woman spat at our feet, gathering her cloak away from us and backing up in the street. "You arrive here uninvited, unwanted, proving the arrogance of your kind."

"I thought you said it went well the last time you came here," I murmured to Tory.

"Yeah, but I exaggerated."

A man came out of his house then shrieked and ran back inside, slamming it shut and twisting a bunch of locks.

"Clearly," I said, and she sniggered. "We need to speak to your leader," I called to the surrounding Nymphs. "And perhaps Miguel is here?"

"*Miguel.*" The old woman spat on the floor again. "His mind is addled since his time with you folk. He speaks of you as if you are our equal – a true treachery of our village."

"Bring Uma to us," Tory demanded, ignoring the woman's mutterings.

"Uma!" someone cried, and the crowd parted to let her through. She was tall with straight dark hair that fell about her shoulders, her face a picture of calm, like none of this unsettled her.

"I'm back," Tory announced.

"I see that," Uma said, her eyes sliding from her to me. "And you brought your sister."

"I'm Darcy." I offered her my hand and she eyed it, the crowd muttering under their breath before Uma took it. Some of the onlookers cursed, but others seemed intrigued by our interaction, waiting with bated breath to see how this might unfold.

"They call you Gwendalina," she said, dropping my hand.

"Not anymore," I said. "That's a name I never claimed, but I have claimed my rightful title alongside my twin. We've been crowned by the rebel army, and we seek to bolster our ranks in the fight against Lionel Acrux and Lavinia Umbra."

"*Lavinia*," someone hissed, and the crowd broke into angry curses.

"La Princesa De Las Sombras," Miguel stepped out of the crowd, lifting his chin, his dark curls hanging around his face which reminded me so much of Diego that it made my heart tug. "Like I have been telling you all, the enemy of the Vega Queens is our enemy. We share a common cause. We must find a way to join them-"

"Miguel," a deep, feminine voice boomed, and a powerful-looking woman stepped out of the crowd in a dark green shawl, a jagged scar running up one cheek and into her black hair which was braided thickly. She was a fearsome woman, rising well over six feet in height, and muscles clung to her frame like sheathed weapons. "I have told you time and again to keep your treacherous words to yourself. You are no longer a High Nymph among us. Your opinion is muddied by your imprisonment. Your word cannot be trusted."

"Surely that means his word *should* be trusted?" I balked and the woman's dark eyes snapped to me. "Miguel has seen the state of the world out there. He knows the power Lavinia wields; he's experienced it first-hand. Staying here might protect you for now, but you'll never be truly free until Lavinia is defeated. You'll be confined to this corner of Solaria, never daring to come out. Is that the life you really want?"

The woman scowled at us. "You think you can manipulate us into giving you what you want? Into making us offer up our warriors like cannon fodder to your cause?"

"We need to talk to the High Nymph," Tory insisted.

"I am she. I have recently taken the role of leader in our council, and I will not be swayed on this decision," the woman said firmly, which was just great.

A man pushed to the front of the crowd with a row of fierce-looking Nymphs at his back. "High Nymph Cordette, if I may? Darcy Vega is responsible for the liberation of the Nymphs I brought to this village. She shut off Lavinia's connection to our shadows so we could no longer be controlled. She freed our minds, she gave us back-"

"Silence," Cordette barked. "What conditions did I set out for allowing you and the others to join this place, Karim?"

Karim's jaw flexed then he bowed his head. "To obey your word and not stick our heads above the parapet," he murmured.

"And what is it you are doing right now?" Cordette growled.

"They have a right to speak," I demanded, and Cordette's eyes whipped onto me in fury.

"They are not yours to command. You have not bought their allegiance. I know of what you did, but it was not for us. You sought the Shadow Princess's death for your own gain, so that you might seize the throne of Solaria. Your efforts were never for our benefit."

"But you benefited from them regardless," Tory stepped in. "Ally with us and your kind will have a place in the kingdom when this war is won. We'll be equals, Nymphs and Fae."

"Ha, even if you appeased us with such a thing at first, your kind would eventually claim your land back and return to hunting us like game," Cordette snarled.

"We have no intention of that," I swore. "Help us, and we'll help you. We'll pass laws to protect you and your people."

"Pah." Cordette waved a hand at me. "You think you are the first ruler to offer such promises to Nymphs? Treaties and contracts aren't worth the paper they're written on. They're traps to lure us from hiding only to skewer us on the end of your swords."

"Perhaps this time is different," Uma urged and Cordette listened to her, seeming to respect whatever authority she held. "We should hear their terms. We cannot stay hidden forever."

"Our village has had many moons to talk over the offering Tory Vega presented us the last time she walked uninvited into our home. The conclusion was clear. We will not go." Cordette turned her hard gaze on us again. "And we couldn't leave even if we wanted to. The shadows are tainted, and their taint will no doubt find us again the moment we leave this place." She ran a finger over the scar on her cheek, taking a step closer to us with a sneer. "Besides, I have been on the end of your kind's hatred. I know the prejudice that lives in your hearts. You couldn't care less for us if you tried, and I won't fall for the lies of young, naive rulers when they are in their most desperate moment." She turned her back on us and I stepped after her, fury burning through my chest.

"You're wrong," I called, and she paused. "I cared deeply for one of your kind. Diego Polaris was my friend. He died because he attempted to cross the lines drawn in the sand between us. He deserved better than what he got. He wanted to be Fae, and not because we're better, but because this kingdom has offered Fae freedoms he could never afford. But it was wrong for him to want that, because what he should have had was acceptance, equality, love."

Miguel's face paled and his arms fell heavily at his sides.

"I never knew the boy," Cordette clipped, glancing back at me.

"You can know him." I took Diego's hat from my pocket, holding it out to her. "Everything he saw, everything he knew, it's in here. And his soul is here too, trapped in the shadows along with every other Nymph whose life has been lost since Lavinia's corruption."

Cordette frowned at the hat. "A soul garment…"

Miguel hurried toward it, his hand outstretched and shaking. His eyes met mine with a cloud of regret filling them. "May I keep it? Even though I do not deserve it," he whispered, his voice laced with grief.

I swallowed thickly, relinquishing it to him with a nod. "You were Drusilla's captive," I said quietly. "You did nothing wrong."

He frowned, a moment passing between us where I saw some of the weight lift from his eyes. I knew the guilt of hurting people through the actions of others. I'd struggled with the sense of blood on my hands for what I'd done when the Shadow Beast had claimed me. But it had always been Lavinia, I knew that now. I hoped Miguel could find a way to know it too.

Miguel cleared his throat, emotion welling in his eyes as his hand tightened on the material. He held it in the air, turning to the crowd and Cordette observed him with a cool expression.

"My son was good when I could not be. He strived to be better. He fought the control of the monstrous Nymphs who held me captive. He was the only thing I am proud of through that time. And I was not there when Lavinia took his life." His voice cracked and a tear slid down his cheek as he held the hat lovingly against his heart. When he spoke again, his voice was that of a broken father who would timelessly grieve for the child he'd never gotten time to love while he was alive. "Scorn me if you must for being too weak to rise from the oppression of the tainted shadows, but my son was stronger. And his sacrifice deserves to be taken note of."

"He died in my arms," I said, the pain of that memory tearing through my chest, and sending tears sliding down my cheeks. "I have grieved him, and still do."

"He was meant to betray us," Tory added, and I glanced at her, fearing she might not have forgiven him for that. But I noticed emotion glinting in her eyes too. "But he saw what we all should have, he saw that we didn't have to be enemies, that we could be equals. In the end, he died protecting my sister, and we're here to repay that debt. To start a new era between Fae and Nymph. But it's going to take trust that neither side will easily give. It won't be simple, but it will work if we want it to."

Cordette looked thoughtful, then glanced at Miguel, nodding stiffly. "See what is to be seen in the soul web. If there is anything of note, I will keep an open mind and observe it for myself. Uma, perhaps you wish to assist him?"

"I do." Uma walked over to Miguel and they headed away through the crowd, going somewhere quiet to speak with Diego.

The lump in my throat eased and I wiped my tears away on the back of my hand.

"You truly weep for one of us?" Cordette asked, suspicion touching her voice.

"I do," I confirmed.

"You are not like other Fae," she said slowly.

"Diego was not like other Nymphs," I said. "We cared for each other as people."

"He was our friend, and he showed us what was possible between Fae and Nymph," Tory said. "Fight with us. We can put our differences aside and secure a safe future for us all. Isn't that what matters most?"

Cordette clucked her tongue. "Oh, little queen, how pretty your ideas are, but you cannot erase years of conflict with a snap of your fingers." She turned and headed off into the crowd, and I released a breath of disappointment.

"Come on, let's go see the Oracles," Tory said. "They might have *seen* something about this war that no one else has, and maybe they hold some answers about the Guild Stones."

"You mean the three women you had an orgy with? Can't wait."

"It wasn't an orgy. I just had mind sex with Darius while they watched and sort of...felt it through me."

"Oh right, sorry, I thought it was something really weird, but now I know they just had sex *through* you, I completely understand," I said, giving her a serious look as she led the way through the muttering Nymphs.

"I think Orion's dry humour might be contagious," she said with a smirk. "You should really take something for that."

Someone laughed loudly and I glanced back, finding a young boy with brown hair following us.

"She should take a de-sarcasm pill, right?" he said, skipping a little to keep up with us. "I'm Igrit, by the way. You knew my brother, didn't you? Well he's not really my brother, but he's Miguel's son, and now he's back with Mama, we're sort of family. My father is dead, just FYI." He kept smiling and I frowned. "Oh don't worry, I don't really remember him, and Mama said he was a pendejo so..."

"Cool story, bro. We're off to see the Oracles, so see ya later." Tory upped her pace, but Igrit only moved faster to keep up.

"I want to fight in the war," he said keenly. "I've been practising my moves. Look." He ran around in front of us, swinging his arms. "Imagine my fingers are probes – cha – pachow -bam. See? That was impressive, wasn't it?"

"Um, sure," I said. "See you later, Igrit." We quickened our pace onto a path that led off into the trees and Igrit stopped following.

"Is he still watching us?" Tory whispered after a minute.

I glanced back, finding Igrit there on the path right behind us. "Ah!" I gasped.

"I move quietly, don't I?" he said excitedly. "Like a Nymph ninja – a Nymja I like to call it. Are you going to see the Oracles? They're creepy. Mama said not to go out here on my own."

"Better head back to your mama then, kid." Tory wafted him away, but he just smiled at her, utterly clueless - or at least pretending to be.

"But I'm not alone. I've got you guys. Isn't this great?"

Tory blew out a breath in frustration.

"It's probably not safe for you out here, Igrit," I said. "Maybe you should head back."

He blinked at me. "Anyway, I have a secret to tell you."

"What secret?" I asked, and Tory seemed mildly intrigued.

"Oh I couldn't tell you that. I'm an undercover warrior in training. I couldn't go breaking my vow of secrecy." He twisted around, kicking a small branch which didn't snap, even when he kicked it twice more, then he grabbed it and tried to snap it with his hands. He failed.

"Anyway," he turned to us again, letting go of the branch, and it whipped upwards, smacking him in the face, but he acted like it hadn't happened. "Maybe I'll tell you if you double, triple promise I can be a soldier in your army."

"You literally just said you can't tell us," Tory sniggered.

"And we can't go making you a soldier. You're like eight," I said, shaking my head. "We're not gonna let a kid charge into battle and get killed."

"I'm eleven and three quarters, actually. And I'm bigger than most boys my age." He puffed up his chest.

"Really?" Tory glanced him up and down, and he lifted his chin. "You seem small."

"Anyway, have we got a deal?" he pushed.

"No," I said. "But nice try."

He huffed. "Fine, I'll tell you anyway."

"Great," Tory said.

"High Nymph Cordette would flay me alive if she knew this secret," he said, lowering his voice.

"Better tell us then," Tory encouraged.

"Oh, I will. But can you cast one of those silence bubble things first?" he asked, glancing around the woodland like he thought someone might be spying on us.

I flicked one up, curious now and Igrit shifted closer. "Karim has started a little rebel club," he whispered. "Since him and the rest of Lavinia's captives got here, they told us all about their imprisonment. Then Karim started a weekly meeting. A secret one. And I'm one of the recruits." He pressed his shoulders back with pride. "Miguel is too, and Mama and my siblings. There's lots of us. And we all want to fight."

I shared an excited look with Tory, taking him seriously at last.

"Will they fight even if Cordette refuses it?" I asked.

Igrit frowned. "I don't know. It's complicated. It's not that easy to leave this place. Like, really not easy. I've never left at all actually. You have to get the High Nymph's permission. It's to protect us, see? And it's not just that… even if we could get out of here, Cordette would take it as a stand against our own kind. She'd name us enemies. It could spark a war. Plus, Karim fears Lavinia will taint us the moment we're out of here anyway."

"Damn," Tory breathed. "Is there somewhere we could meet with Karim alone?"

Igrit glanced around nervously again, then his gaze settled on the dark path we were taking. "He visits the Oracles sometimes. I think they know our secret. Maybe…I could bring him there to speak with you?"

"Okay," Tory said.

Igrit glanced up at the tree canopy, the light of the sun so deeply blotted out here it was like night was falling. "I'll hurry. I hate this place."

He ran off down the path at high speed, yelping when a large leaf grazed his hair and running even faster.

"Weird kid," Tory commented.

"Do you think we can trust him?" I asked as I disbanded the silencing bubble.

"I don't see why he'd lie."

We moved on down the path and I followed Tory to a huge rock face that barred our way on. Or so it seemed, because she quickly moved towards a slit of shadow and stepped through it into a concealed passage.

I followed her into the darkness, the rocks around us tingling with magic and a sense of warning flickered through me.

"Not far now," Tory whispered.

We quickened our pace, passing along the trail, neither of us casting a Faelight, something about this place making me sure it was best to stay in the dark. Like casting a light might bring about a plague of monsters to our backs.

All sunlight was blotted out behind us as we descended into the tunnel and my fingers flexed as I prepared to defend myself, feeling like there were eyes on us from every direction. Though I could see nothing but rock above and below, and there were no sounds other than the soft pad of our footfalls.

Tory stopped abruptly and I stepped to her side, finding us standing before a tall wooden door set into the stone. She reached out to knock three times, and it swung open, the creak of unoiled hinges setting my pulse thrashing.

All was dark inside, no sense of warmth, no flicker of a fire. Everything was still, cold and the tinge of that dark magic washed over me again, chilling me to my core.

We stepped inside and the door slammed at our backs the moment we crossed the threshold, making my heart judder.

A fire of red and blue Phoenix flames burst to life in the hearth and I raised my hands, ready to cast at any creature lurking in this place. A hexagonal table with a range of half-burned candles stood before us and the scent of herbs carried from the dried bunches that hung from the low beams. Wooden shelves filled the walls, each laden with jars, bottles and vials that contained all kinds of shrivelled things and murky liquids.

It felt like beasts were about to descend on us and feast on our flesh, but instead of beasts, three women slinked towards us from the shadowy corners of the room. The sight of them had my spine straightening, each possessing beauty beyond words, but they were also disfigured in specific ways, and I recalled their names from what Tory had told me of them.

Vidi; the one with stitches holding her eyes shut, her hair blood red and skin alabaster pale. Then there was Loqui; her lips were sewn shut, her curls a waterfall of brown and her eyes brightest gold.

And the last was Audire, the one with ice-white hair, warm brown skin and eyes as black as night. I knew her hair hid the scars that marked the place where she had once had ears, and I had no desire to see them.

"So she returns," Vidi purred. "The flame-giver." She gestured to the fire. "The one who sought her lost husband. And did she find him, I wonder?"

"She did," Tory answered fiercely. "I wrenched his soul from death and returned it to where it belonged."

"Ah, and what pretty price did you pay for that unnatural twist of fate?" Vidi asked.

"Death," Tory breathed. "We must pay The Ferryman in souls."

My gut twisted at those words, but the three women laughed. Loqui's laugh was a rasping chuckle that echoed from behind her stitched lips, the sound setting my hackles rising.

"Look, sisters," Audire breathed, coming upon me like a wraith and sniffing my hair, lifting a lock of it and examining it in the light. "The other queen. I still smell the smoke on her just as I did the first."

"What smoke?" I tried to pull away, but she kept sniffing. "The smoke of the Dragon King, his flames set to burn your crib in the night, all those years ago. But here you both stand, impervious to fire and ready to rule the world."

"Ah but will they rule?" Vidi mused. "Queens in the making, yes, but the wind speaks ill of their fates."

"What have you heard?" Tory demanded, while I batted at Audire to try and stop her sniffing me.

Loqui swept up beside me brandishing a pair of scissors, snipping off the end of the blue lock of hair Audire was holding aloft.

I growled, pushing them away from me with a blast of air that sent them stumbling, but they only laughed their horrible laughs as they tossed it into a cauldron that hung above the fire, and whatever liquid was in there hissed and spat.

"Hey," I snapped.

"One answer we will give," Vidi sighed. "But it may not be the answer you desire."

Loqui grabbed herbs from the sprigs hanging all around the place, tossing them into the fire before stealing a piece of Tory's hair too and throwing it into the mix. The cauldron bubbled as the new ingredients were added and Audire slashed her hand open with a curved dagger, letting her blood spill in as well, her mouth moving with silent words.

I gave Tory a sideways look, uncertain about all of this, but her face was set with resolution. If she trusted these strange women, then I would place my faith in her.

Audire swept over to me again, her cold hand coming to my chin and her nails biting into my skin.

I raised my hand, resting it to her side and giving her a warning of my power.

"Unhand me," I said evenly.

"Just a look," she whispered, reading those words from my lips, her eyes pinned on mine. "Silver. Look at these two bright rings. How they gleam."

Loqui's shoulder slammed against hers, her golden eyes tracking over mine.

"Elysian Mating, how pure, a power like that could be so very potent if it could be bottled," Vidi whispered from across the room, sidling closer as if drawn to me by some ethereal force.

"This one perches on the brink of a void so deep it will destroy her if she falls," Audire said excitedly. "She seeks knowledge untold about the rising twelve."

"What do you know of the Guild Stones? Do you know their use when united?" I gasped, latching onto those words as hope gripped my heart.

Audire dropped her fingers from my face, glancing at Loqui then whispering something in her ear. Loqui laughed and Vidi moved closer, taking Tory's hand and tracing her fingers over her palm as if feeling out the lines in it.

"What do you want from us for this knowledge?" Tory asked, a thickness to her tone telling me she feared what it might be.

"You possess what we possess, yet a mirror of us you are not," Vidi whispered.

"What does that mean?" I asked.

"You are sisters, like us, but where you were forged in the womb, we were forged between spilled blood and cracked bone."

I didn't know what that meant, and honestly, I didn't want to.

"So what is it you want?" I pressed.

"Time is of the essence," Audire hissed. "Tick, tick, tick, the seconds count down towards your final stand. And there, upon a battlefield of woe and dread, you shall fall or you shall rise. Every earthly creature whispers of it along with every sky-bound star. We all wait to see which way the cards will fall."

"We're running out of time, like you say," I said. "So can you help us? We need information on the Guild Stones, or anything that might help us in this war."

Audire took my hand and ran her thumb over the Shadow Beast ring. "This. It hides a great and rare being. This will suffice indeed."

I snatched my hand away. "No."

"Oh," Vidi sighed sadly. "You will not part with it even for the knowledge you seek?"

"Never," I vowed, because Shadow was my friend, and I owed him a free life. I wasn't going to hand him to these creatures and let them cage him once again.

"Such devotion," Audire hummed. "Well if it is not that then... pain will suffice."

"You can hurt me, not her," Tory said, trying to shield me like always and I damn well loved her for it. But I wouldn't be allowing any such thing.

"I can handle it, Tor," I said fiercely.

"It must be from both of you anyway, and it must be at once," Vidi said, and I met Tory's gaze before we both nodded.

Audire gripped my hand tighter, and Vidi grabbed Tory's.

"Do not move," Vidi warned. "Both of you must be still."

"Do it," Tory urged.

I gritted my teeth against the instinct to cast magic and force Audire away from me, bracing myself for what was to come.

With a sharp twist, Audire snapped my index finger and I locked down a scream in my throat just as that snap was echoed by Tory's finger breaking too. I cursed between my teeth and the three women sighed like they'd gained something from our agony, Loqui's breath coming out through her nose.

"Pain is power," Vidi whispered. "Power is you. Twins made of the very same flesh; your mother's belly swollen with the seed of her truest love. A king of savagery who ruled with an iron fist, who adored none except her."

"Such a shame their placentas were not kept. What an elixir of strength and influence could be made from them," Audire sighed, and I wrinkled my nose in disgust.

"The price is not quite paid," Vidi purred, looking from Tory to me. "More pain is required, just a little though. Blood for our elixir." She produced a knife from the folds of her dress, and I stiffened, trying to ignore the throbbing agony in my finger.

"If we give you this, will you help us with the Guild Stones?" Tory asked, cradling her hand.

The three women huddled together, withdrawing from us and I looked to my sister with trepidation. I'd do it if it was what was needed for this knowledge, but was she sure this wasn't some trick? These Nymphs didn't seem remotely trustworthy to me.

The three of them spoke together, even Loqui seeming to communicate with them somehow, though no words passed her sealed lips. Then they turned to us as one, eerily connected in some way.

"We swear," Vidi announced.

"Cross our hearts," Audire said, and Loqui mimed painting an X over her heart.

"A cut on the right arm," Vidi said as she approached Tory.

"And a cut on the left," Audire whispered as she came towards me with her own knife in hand. "No moving, no screaming."

The two of them guided us to the cauldron, making us hold our arms above it and at once, they cut a deep slash into our forearms. I winced against the pain as Audire smiled triumphantly and the potion bubbled the moment our blood spilled into it.

"You may heal it all away now," Vidi encouraged.

I withdrew from the cauldron with my sister, quickly healing the gash on my arm along with my broken finger while Tory did the same for her own wounds.

"*There*," Audire moaned while Loqui stirred the liquid in the cauldron. "Their essence lives within this brew."

"What's it for?" I asked, not liking the look of that smoking potion.

"That is for us to know. Our payment is claimed," Audire said. "Now…Vidi? Tell them."

Vidi drifted towards us, her eyes moving back and forth beneath her stitched lids. "A circle of power," she exhaled. "Twelve in total."

"Yes, and?" I pushed, knowing that much already.

"Many powers do the Guild Stones wield, even alone. But together, ohh…" Her eyes roamed faster beneath her lids. "Together they create a snare. But without bait… no, without bait there is no worth in it."

"What kind of bait? And what's the snare for?" I demanded.

"A snare of all things great and all things small," she answered.

"And the bait?" Tory asked.

"Hmm." Vidi frowned. "I cannot see more. No. Nothing. A snare you have, but what use is that without a lure?"

"How can we even make the snare?" I asked, wondering if it might be of use to capture Lionel somehow, or even Clydinius.

"You know this answer. It has already been spoken from these lips." Vidi traced her finger over my mouth then placed it into her own with a hum of appreciation. "That is all we know. Our debt is paid."

"Wait," Tory growled, stepping toward Vidi and laying a hand on her arm. The air stirred, the fire flickering with some dark power I could sense in the atmosphere but couldn't see, and I gave my twin a look of warning.

"Our debt is paid," Vidi repeated in an icy tone. "There is no more for you here, flame-giver."

Tory dropped her hand with a scowl, then turned to me. "Let's go."

I made for the door, more than happy to leave the creepy place behind and the second we were across the threshold, the door snapped shut at our backs again, a wall of energy seeming to bar our return.

"What did she mean?" I wondered aloud. "That I've spoken the answer already?"

"Fuck knows. Maybe Orion will remember. He's probably got it written in his diary," Tory said, taking off down the tunnel and I followed her out, relieved when we made it to the woods again.

Igrit was there beneath a tall pine tree, waving us over to him and the tall Nymph Karim.

"Hello," Karim said as we approached, dipping into a small bow. "I pledge my allegiance. I wish for you to know that I will fight if I can gain passage from this place when the time comes. Though I must convince Cordette in the meantime, and perhaps I can rally more warriors to your aid. Uma speaks highly of you. I am sure she will be swayed to your cause."

"Any chance she could take over from Cordette?" I asked grimly.

"Hm, unlikely," Karim said, then his eyes lit. "But not wholly impossible. She would need to win the next election in the spring."

"We don't have until the spring," Tory said darkly. "This battle could be fought in a week, or less even."

Karim rubbed a hand over the stubble on his jaw. "I will do what I can, but there is still the trouble of the shadow taint. Even if I can find a way to break beyond this village with my warriors, we could succumb to Lavinia's power once again…" Pain sparked in his eyes, telling of his desperate desire to fight in this war. If only we could find a way to ensure Lavinia didn't get her claws in him and the other Nymphs again.

"We'll find an answer," I promised, and hope entered his eyes.

He reached into his pocket, taking out a small wooden totem carved into two curling Nymph horns. "Here. Take this as a vow of our alliance. Let your royal court know we wish to fight alongside them, and if we can stand with them in battle, we will. I really believe peace between our kind is possible."

I took it, nodding to him in thanks. "Anything's possible, Karim. I just don't know how much time we have left."

Karim nodded solemnly. "Then let us pray to the stars and the shadows alike, that they will grant us at least one more miracle."

LIONEL

CHAPTER FORTY TWO

The moonlit sea glittered beneath my boots as I cast a path of air across its waters, my cohort of Bonded Men in tow along with a legion of my army, and the closest of my court around me. Today would grant me a fresh victory, one I could scent upon the air like a hound after the blood of its prey.

The fingers of my shadow hand flexed, and I felt Lavinia tugging on the connection she held over it, wielding me like a puppet. It was a reminder of her control, her influence. And that was a problem I was coming to see more starkly with every passing day. It wasn't an entirely unfamiliar situation. Those closest to me had always been the most dangerous, and I could lure any animal into my trap, no matter the threat it posed. All creatures had weaknesses or blind spots, and I always found a way to wield them to my advantage. In the end, I would come out on top.

Perhaps the truest threat did not lie with my queen anymore, but with the being walking at my heels. I felt the star's presence like a knife scoring into my back, peeling me open and deeming me insignificant. It would not do.

I had to tread very carefully with this new acquaintance of mine. A star in Fae form, come to walk upon this very ground I had seized as my own. His power was beyond anything I could comprehend as of yet, but if I could make a tool of him...trap him with cunning, then he would become a weapon like no other.

"Your eminence," I addressed Clydinius, "Come, walk at my side and tell me more of your time on earth."

Clydinius didn't move forward, but he did speak at least, his voice a haunting thing that rose my hackles. "I told you of the Vega curse."

"Indeed," I said, glancing at Vard to my left who let out a low whimper.

My greasy manservant was sweating, and I knew it was not from the climate; he feared Clydinius to his core. His pathetic existence as a Seer was at odds with the all-powerful star that he could not predict in any way. But the truer danger lay with me. Vard's usefulness was wearing thin now that Madame Monita was in my court, his mistakes totalled and tallied. She may not have been a Seer, but her astrological knowledge was almost as good as one, and better in ways. She had predicted that the rebel army were about to gain new followers from a large group of sea-folk, and it had taken the simple capture of a few powerful Fae on these shores to confirm my suspicions about who that prediction was referring to.

Vard's good eye met mine and a flicker of terror rolled over his features which made me certain he knew what I was thinking. Perhaps he *saw* the bloody death I would gladly deliver if he disappointed me one more time, and I hoped that might be enough to stir some worth out of him yet.

"The Vegas have lived arrogant lives for many generations," I said, continuing my efforts with Clydinius. "A thorn in both our sides, it seems. A common adversary."

"Now that I am free from the shackles of my star form, I am not in need of adversaries," Clydinius mused. "War is for creatures of skin and bone. I have tasted enough death and find myself unmoved by it."

"It is not about death, but power," I said, fighting the urge to glance back at the star. One wrong move and Clydinius could decide to rid the kingdom of its king.

"Power. Yes, I believe that may be the key," Clydinius said. "You must trust in the rising of the Trinity. Assist me in that, as promised, and I shall reward you."

I considered those words, still unsure if I could trust them. The star unbalanced the weight of power I held, his control over me absolute if he so wished. But perhaps my salvation lay in such a reward.

"I shall assist you in any way I can, your eminence," I vowed, adding extra tenor to my voice to sell my devotion. "Will you decide upon this reward, or may I make a request?"

Clydinius was silent for so long that for several painful moments all I could hear was the solid pounding of my pulse in my ears. I was playing a deadly game, walking the line of life and death. But this was how it had been with the Savage King, a push and pull until I had him right where I wanted him.

"Request what you will. Please me, and I shall grant whatever it is you seek, King of flesh and fire."

"Then I shall please you first and decide second. That is the order of importance to such things," I said, my lips twisting a little at the corner.

I knew precisely what I would ask for. There was one territory left unconquered in my life, one which would ascend me from Fae to god. Immortality. The kind no magic, no blade, no star could take from me. Unending life. The eternal king. Yes, just the thought of it set my blood heating with the furnace of a thousand suns.

"Is it much further, my King?" Lavinia floated forward from the ranks of my Bonded Men and Tharix came with her, his eyes set on the water as if it fascinated him somehow. The boy was easily distracted of late, and I had in mind to turn my belt upon his back and strike some sense into him this very eve. He was a fine specimen for an Heir, but he could be vacant in ways, and I did not see the drive for domination in him that I had seen in Darius. No matter though. Such things could be taught, honed by discipline. He would learn his place in this world, and if he could not show his value, then I would replace him with another, finer creature.

There were a few women among my Bonded who took my eye, but I would have to consider closer blood relations... Without doubt, I could claim the right to the wives of my followers. Any of my Dragons would be honoured to serve me in the production of an Heir. The trouble was, my balls were currently held in shackles by my queen. If only I could get her agreement to Guardian Bond with me herself, she would no longer be able to harm me.

My mind circled back to Darius and the ever-tormenting questions that had been writhing in my head since I had seen him in my castle. How the fuck had he managed it? I'd seen him die. I'd sent him beyond The Veil myself. No one returned from death. It simply wasn't possible, but I would be a fool to deny what I had seen. If he had learned some way of tethering his soul to this world, I would capture him and prise the truth from his lips to learn it myself. Then he could suffer in my company, bleeding daily by my hand, and I would find out if my despicable Heir could die twice.

Until that day, it seemed he would remain a thorn in my side. He and Tiberius's son had come storming into my castle and rendered my fallen star useless by some unknown power. There was no way to rouse it that could be plainly seen, and Lavinia had been weakened once again just when she had been on the cusp of destroying the Vegas and their army.

Clydinius had sensed that the star was sleeping, but not even he could pull it from slumber. He had vowed it would wake again in time. Days only. Then this war would be won by my newfound weapon once and for all. I just had to be patient, and that was a strength I'd learned long ago. All good things came to those who waited.

"Vard, you are meant to be charting our path," I clipped at the Seer. "Have you *seen* our destination yet, or shall we continue walking toward the horizon until we are dust?"

Vard winced as though I had struck him, and my fingers twitched with the instinct to do so. It seemed he was motivated enough to try and appease me though because his eyes glazed and a moment later he pointed to my right. I forged a path that way, creating the air bridge beneath our feet and following his direction until we stood in a seemingly innocuous spot above the calm water. In the distance, several miles back the way we had come, sandy beaches hugged the land's edge and a long, wooden pier reached out in this direction as if pointing to this exact spot.

"One step further, my King," Vard encouraged, and I did as he directed, raising a hand and sensing the crackle of powerful wards and concealment spells there.

I had learned from the lips of captured Fae that the Academy of Hydros was offering sanctuary to all kinds of water-based Orders. It was a specialist school for such creatures, shifters of the ocean, Sirens, Kelpies, Sharks, Calypsos, and even whispers of rare Water Dragons which would make fine additions to my Bonded.

"Allow me, my King." Lavinia stepped forward, her shadows sweeping out to strike at the spells hiding the Hydros Academy from view. I caught her wrist, crushing it in my grip and sneering at her.

"I can manage," I said, making my voice sugary at the last moment.

She gave me a sultry look then bowed her head and stepped back.

I raised my hand higher, wielding the tumultuous power in my veins and working to rip through the concealment spells one by one. My arm began to shake as I poured more and more power into the casts, tearing through another concealment spell and breathing heavier as I found even more waiting beyond. Still, I forged on, my strength clear to witness and the certain awe of my royal court making my chest swell with pride.

I latched onto the wards, meaning to dissolve them all and reveal the academy, but the magic of them slammed into me all at once. I was thrown from my feet, skidding over the air platform on my backside, so dazed I didn't manage to catch myself with magic before I went flying into the ocean.

I cursed and spluttered as my Bonded rushed to help me out of the water, and I snarled in fury, sending out a blast of air that threw them away from me. I carried myself up from the water and stepped toward Clydinius, sweeping a hand through my hair to get it out of my face. The star took me in with a bland expression and a snigger caught my ear, making me whip around to seek its source.

Tharix stood there, and for a moment I swore a grin lifted his lips, those blank eyes gleaming with something akin to amusement. Though it was gone in the next blink, I wouldn't let such a possibility lie.

"Do you dare snigger at me, boy?!" I boomed, lunging for him and grabbing him by the throat. He was big, bigger than even me now. Somehow growing by the day as if he intended on dwarfing me entirely by the spring.

His gaze dropped in deference. "I do not, Father," he murmured, and I grasped his throat tighter so no more words could pass his lips.

Caroline Peckham & Susanne Valenti

"You will repent for this when we return to the palace," I hissed.

No fear crossed his features, nothing but stony indifference stared back at me. It was as if pain meant nothing to this creature, and I didn't take well to that. I shoved him away from me, having no time to spare for his insubordination right now, but I would certainly make time for it later.

Air magic swept over me as some of my Bonded worked to dry my clothes, and I stepped towards the wards again, trying to hide my exhaustion. The amount of power I had used had almost drained me, but I would not be made a fool in front of my own people.

Clydinius waved a hand before I could make another attempt, and as if the magic of this world was nothing to him, the wards came crashing down, power crackling out of existence and revealing the piercing towers of a turquoise castle reaching up from the depths of the ocean.

A cry of war came from within the academy and Clydinius stepped forward, eyes blank as he tore Fae from their safe haven, ripping them out of the castle through windows and tossing them into the water around us. My Bonded hurried to capture them, caging them in magical pods in the ocean, and I watched as the star took on hundreds of Fae single-handedly with awe and trepidation making my soul quake.

His power was unmatched by any creature on Earth. He was the greatest being in existence, and I could not fathom the magic contained within his veins.

It was clear to me that there was only one answer to his existence; I needed to find a way to possess this very power, trap and claim it for my own. For there could be no greater being in this world than me.

DARIUS

CHAPTER FORTY THREE

I sat on the edge of my bed in Ignis House with one ankle perched on the opposite knee, my foot bouncing impatiently while I tried to convince myself I was watching the movie that was playing on the huge screen beyond my couch. In reality, my eyes were more often landing on the door, minutes slipping into hours while I waited and waited for Roxy to return.

It was late. Almost four in the morning. I'd spent the entire day with Geraldine and Max explaining as many details of my father's war camp and new palace as we could recall and helping plan the best moves for the rebellion to make next.

It was fucking exhausting, especially when Geraldine scrutinised every little detail, always asking for more, then studying me through narrowed eyes as if she was deciding whether or not my memories could be trusted. She'd even mentioned getting a Cyclops in to pluck the memories from our minds and scrape the raw facts from what she had termed 'the trauma of the encounter.'

I growled as I thought on that, smoke drifting between my lips and over my tongue. I blew a ring into the air and watched as it sailed towards the TV, bursting over the face of the actor who was doing a spectacularly bad job of holding my attention.

She should have been back by now. How long did it even take to convince a bunch of reclusive Nymphs to come out of hiding and fight for their freedom? The twins were willing to offer them far more than most Fae would ever even suggest giving to Nymphs in the way of liberties, and I expected them to bite their hands off for the opportunity they were presenting.

I half stood then dropped down onto the bed. It wouldn't do any good for me to go out searching anyway – Roxy was the only one who knew the location of the Nymphs and she had refused to share the knowledge with anyone before star dusting away.

I growled, focusing on the steady beat of my heart, reminding myself that if she were in danger then it would be pounding harder, and if she were dead then I would have already followed her into oblivion.

A knock made me jerk upright, but I frowned as I realised it wasn't coming from my door at all but from the floor length window I used whenever I shifted.

I strode to the window and pulled it open as I found her there, her cheeks pink from the biting cold and her hair windblown from flying.

I caught her arm and pulled her inside, kissing her hungrily and letting the heat of my flesh dive into hers. Not that she needed any additional fire, but I was always going to offer it all the same.

"What took so long?" I asked, knocking the window shut behind her and inhaling the scent of her skin as I dropped my mouth to her throat.

"Oh, you know, Nymphs are dicks. The High Nymph refused to join ranks with us, but there's a group of rebels among the village who are willing to fight with us."

"That's good," I said hopefully.

"Yeah, except for the fact that they can't leave the village without the High Nymph's permission, and even if they could, Lavinia will probably taint them all over again."

"Not so good then," I sighed.

"No, not unless we can figure out a way around all that."

I regarded her for a moment, and she pushed out of my arms, striding into my room like she owned the damn place.

"What's for dinner?" she asked, her wings melting away so she could peel her shirt off and toss it on the floor.

"We ate hours ago. Maybe if you'd let someone know when you'd be back there would have been something waiting for you."

Roxy huffed. "Be a lamb and go get me something covered in cheese and guacamole – oh and a big ass soda too, the more sugar the better." She kicked her boots off as she spoke, continuing on her way to the bathroom.

"I'm not a lamb," I told her, taking a step closer instead of further away.

"Ugh, don't make me command you." She wafted a hand at me, her eyes sparkling with amusement as she waited for me to bite, no doubt hoping I'd follow her into that bathroom and remind her that I was no errand boy. But it had been a long fucking day and despite her teasing I knew she really must have been hungry, so I forced myself to take a step back instead.

"As you wish, my Queen," I gave her a mocking bow, enjoying the way her eyebrows rose in surprise before I turned and headed out into the corridor of Ignis House. If my wife wanted food, then I'd sure as hell feed her.

I jogged down the stairs two at a time, my agitation finally settling now that she was back. I knew she could handle herself, but that didn't make it any easier to watch her disappear into a nest of Nymphs in an unknown location for the majority of the day and night.

I made quick work of the journey to The Orb, shooting my order ahead of me via my Atlas so it would be waiting when I arrived.

The night was calm, the waning moon pale through the clouds overhead, nothing to say that a battle had been fought here this time yesterday. Nothing to remind us of the bodies which had been so carefully retrieved from the battlefield and given a send-off the stars would rejoice over. Not to mention the corpses of our enemies which had been sent back to the outskirts of my father's palace via stardust – a reminder of our power and the fact that we now knew where he was hiding.

If Max hadn't sent the star to sleep, who knew what might have happened here? From what Roxy had said, the power Lavinia wielded had far outmatched her and her sister's Phoenix flames, as well as the magic in their veins. I had no idea how long we had until the star awoke again, but the moment it did, Lavinia would surely return to finish what she'd started. And my father might just join her instead of hiding in his castle.

I shouldered my way into The Orb, barely sparing a glance for the few Fae who hung about the place, some eating and others simply sitting in the quiet, perhaps unable to sleep with the war playing on their minds.

I moved to the end of the serving counter where a small hatch sat and touched my hand to it, releasing enough power for it to recognise me. The thing had been installed towards the end of our first term after Caleb had thrown a bitch fit over not being able to get any breakfast at three am after we'd all been out drinking one night. He'd demanded the option to place orders for whatever food and drink he wanted no matter the time of day or night, and because he was an entitled asshole and his mother was one of the four most powerful Fae in the kingdom, the academy had relented and created this for the four of us to use exclusively. Though I supposed I should probably get the twins access to it now too.

A wicker basket sat waiting for me when the hatch opened and I grabbed it by the handle, turning to leave as quickly as I'd come.

I glanced at the red couch which had once represented our position of power in the centre of the room – though now it had been shunted aside to make space for the huge table we used for war councils. Seth and Caleb sat there, their thighs pressed against each other's, their heads bent low together as they spoke and shared a huge pizza.

They glanced up as if feeling my eyes on them, and I offered them a grin before flashing a peace sign at Seth and winking.

Seth's lips popped open and Caleb elbowed him in the side, hissing something in his ear which I couldn't hear but it made me chuckle like an asshole all the same.

I strode through the door without so much as a word to them, enjoying the way they scrambled to react every time I taunted them over their secret affair.

I made it back to Ignis House quickly enough, ignoring the stares I drew from the few people who were awake in the common room. If I had to endure another question about what it was like beyond The Veil, I'd likely send the fucker who asked me there to see it for themselves.

I headed back into my room, moving straight for the bathroom where steam was rolling through the open crack in the door, but as I opened my mouth to announce my return, I fell still.

Roxy was in my jacuzzi tub, the bubbles roiling around her and her head tipped back against the edge of it where she'd fallen asleep.

I placed the picnic hamper down beside the door, trusting the magic inside it to keep the food fresh then grabbed a chair and headed into the bathroom. I dropped the chair beside the edge of the tub then leaned closer to press a kiss to her brow. She murmured something sleepily and I smiled, taking in the streaks of mascara under her eyes and the chipped red nail polish on her fingertips where her arm lay along the edge of the tub.

Geraldine was making sure that the twins headed out looking perfect every day, but I knew the concealer beneath Roxy's eyes was getting thicker, the blush giving colour to her cheeks more necessary. She was working herself ragged between war councils and checking in on the army, not to mention heading out on tasks like the one she'd taken on today.

I cast water magic in my hands and reached out to start washing her hair for her. She kept her eyes closed as I did it, but the corners of her mouth lifted into a smile. She moaned when I began to massage the shampoo through the length of her ebony locks and the knot which had been tightening in my chest all day finally unravelled.

"I missed you today," I murmured, rinsing the suds from her hair with warm water I cast from my palm.

"So clingy," she teased sleepily.

"Sometimes, I think I miss you even while you're with me, the knowledge that you'll have somewhere to go, something to do, somewhere to be, always hanging there, waiting to steal you away again."

Roxy breathed a laugh then moaned again as I worked the conditioner through her hair next.

"I am a queen," she pointed out.

"Everyone wants a piece of you," I agreed.

"But you're the only one who gets to keep the bits you bite off," she replied.

I rinsed her hair through again to clean it out then shifted closer so I could wipe the makeup from her face. She let me do it, opening those big, green eyes which had once captured me with a single, fate-stained look.

"I was such a fool to waste so much time fighting this," I said.

"Is the war making you nostalgic, Darius?" she asked and fuck, I loved the way her tongue wrapped around my name.

"Maybe."

"We'll win this," she added, the lie so pretty on her lips, because we both knew the chances of that were slim at best, despite how powerfully we would fight to make it so.

"I know," I agreed, my dishonesty as sinful as her own.

She smiled knowingly, but there was no fear in the eyes of the woman who was my world, just the blazing desire to force those words into truths despite the way the odds were stacked.

She reached out, fisting my shirt and yanking hard enough to force me out of my chair. The jacuzzi tub was more than big enough for the both of us and I laughed as I let her drag me into it, fully clothed, boots and all.

Roxy kissed me between her laughter, my weight pressing her down into the water before I rolled away and positioned myself facing her, hooking her calves over my thighs.

"Here, eat," I said, using my water magic to carry the hamper to us before I lost myself in ideas of her flesh and forgot to take care of her the way I'd promised to.

"Did you carry a picnic hamper all the way across campus for me like Little Red Riding Hood?" she laughed while I balanced the thing on the chair beside the tub and opened it up.

I snorted. "Yeah, baby, I did. And what big eyes you've got, grandmama."

She laughed again, batting her lashes at me. "All the better to see your bullshit with, my dear."

I grinned, taking the steaming plate of nachos from the hamper and placing them on a floating tray of ice I cast for the purpose. She reached for them, but I batted her hand aside and lifted one to her mouth myself.

"And what big lips you have," I added while she let me feed her with an amused expression that somehow bordered on disdain. But she was my queen as she so enjoyed pointing out, so I was going to play the obedient subject.

Predictably she moaned while she chewed, licking those fantasy-inducing lips of hers before replying. "All the better to kiss you with, my dear."

I resisted the urge to do just that, continuing to feed her while she allowed it, her eyes glittering at the treatment, enjoying the game.

"Your boots are digging into my ass," she complained around a mouthful before yanking one off of my foot and tossing it out of the tub, water flying everywhere. The second followed quickly after.

"I was content to wait on you from outside the water," I said, taking the bottle of tequila from the hamper and pouring her a shot in one of the glasses that had been tucked in there too.

"I wanted you closer," she replied easily, those words almost as good as her sliding her foot back over my thigh and running it over the bulge of my crotch.

I leaned closer to pour the tequila into her mouth and she let me, swallowing the measure in one hit.

I forced myself to keep feeding her despite my gaze slipping to the bubbling water where I was catching glimpses of her hardened nipples. She kept her foot on my crotch, flexing it against my cock and making it damn hard to concentrate on making sure she was well fed.

"So tell me," she said, her eyes brightening as something occurred to her. "How did you enjoy making out with Max?"

I snorted. "That was the fourth time I've been Siren Spelled by him. It wasn't all that thrilling aside from the star yanking him away during it."

"How much tongue did he use?" she pushed as she finished the last of her nachos and I tossed the plate back into the hamper.

"Sorry to disappoint you, baby, there was no tongue."

Her eyes narrowed. "Oh, come on, don't lie to me. I've been trapped in his lust web before, I know how it goes."

"Lust web? Nah, Roxy there's no lust in his magic. If you felt that then it was all between you and him."

She pursed her lips irritably. "So you're saying that the full on make out I had with him was entirely unnecessary to the magic?"

Jealousy flared through me at the thought of that despite it being way before the two of us and knowing that there was definitely nothing between them now.

"It requires a kiss. Closed mouth works just fine. Maybe you made out with him because of your sex addiction-"

"Oh fuck you," she laughed loudly, splashing me aggressively with the water and making sure that any part of me which hadn't been wet before definitely was now.

I barked a laugh too, grabbing her ankle and yanking to drag her under the water.

Roxy kicked me in the fucking jaw as she went under then damn near drowned me as she flung her power into the water and threw the entire contents of the tub over my head.

The bathroom was flooded, the chair upended, and the picnic hamper sent floating away towards the sink.

The two of us broke into more laughter and I stood, heaving her up with me and kissing her as she wrapped her arms and legs around my body, letting me carry her from the room.

"Oh, what big power you have, my dear," I teased against her lips as my feet squelched across the sodden carpet by the door to the bathroom and I headed for the bed.

"All the better to kick your ass with, my dear," she replied.

I tossed her down onto the mattress, biting my lip as I looked at her, the perfect curves of her body all on show for me to explore.

I yanked my soaking shirt over my head with one hand and threw it aside before unbuckling my belt.

"What big tits you have, my dear," I growled, my hunger for her past the point of waiting, my cock straining against my fly.

Her laugh was pure and beautiful, her hands moving to caress her breasts and tug on her nipples as she watched me undress.

I shoved my saturated jeans off, taking my boxers and socks with them and prowling to the end of the bed, taking hold of the canopy overhead and watching her writhe beneath me.

My cock was rigid and aching, my free hand moving to caress it while I stared down at this beautiful creature of mine, wanting to capture the image of her there in my bed, her wet hair soaking the sheets, her hands moving over the expanse of her bronze flesh, making my mouth jealous.

Roxy released one of her breasts, running a hand down her navel before reaching her core and beginning to toy with herself. She moaned as she caressed her clit, my grip on the canopy tightening while I watched as her back arched against the sheets.

"How wet are you?" I asked her, my gaze skating over the water droplets which rolled over her skin before falling back to her pussy to watch as she pushed two fingers inside herself.

"Soaked," she panted, sliding them in and out, rolling them over her clit and then doing it again. "Are you going to watch me come or take over and make me yourself?"

"I haven't decided," I growled, moving my fist over my shaft in a slow and languid movement to ease some of the need in my own flesh. Precum smeared across my palm, and I groaned as Roxy drove her fingers into herself again.

"I need more," she breathed, her other hand squeezing her breast.

"Not yet," I replied, my grip on the canopy so tight that it was in danger of breaking, but I needed more too. I needed to capture this in my memory and never let it go.

Roxy bit her lip, her eyes meeting mine before she took her hand from her pussy and flicked her fingers to cast magic.

I'd half expected vines to come drag me down on top of her as she so often tried to do when I wouldn't simply bow to her demands like this, but instead, she cast a cock out of ice, the thing as big as my own and sparkling faintly.

"Fuck," I cursed, pumping my dick harder as I fought with all I had to remain standing over her, wanting to see what she'd do next.

She grinned at me as she ran the sex toy over her body, her nipples hardening further at the kiss of it, goosebumps raising all over her flesh. The moan which escaped her as she rolled the thing over her clit was only topped by the one which followed as she sank it into her cunt.

My chest heaved with panting breaths as I watched her fuck herself with it, her other hand caressing her clit.

She was a fucking masterpiece, a creature of want and need and sex and she was all fucking mine.

I fucked my own hand while I watched her, the canopy over the bed crunching as my fist tightened around it.

Roxy arched off of the bed, moaning loudly before crying out in bliss, that sound a cacophony of ecstasy which made me swear loudly, the canopy splintering in my grip and breaking in two.

I let the pieces fall to hang limply above the foot of the bed and dropped over her, kissing her hard and wrapping my fist around her own where she still held the toy inside her.

I began to fuck her with it, looking down into her eyes and watching as that feeling built in her again.

"Now you're going to come for me harder," I told her. "First with this and then on my cock. Aren't you?"

"Yes," she panted, her hips meeting the thrusts of the toy as I began to fuck her with it even harder, pumping it inside of her and watching with bated breath until she fell apart for me as instructed.

Roxy called my name out as she came this time and I yanked the toy out of her, dropping my mouth to her pussy so that I could taste her orgasm too. I rolled my tongue around her inner walls, feeling the way they tightened and pulsed for me before giving all of my focus to her clit.

I hooked her legs over my shoulders, her thighs tightening around my head as I devoured her, loving the taste of her body and gripping her ass to tug her so close that I could hardly even breathe.

Her fingernails bit into my scalp as I licked her relentlessly, demanding more pleasure from her flesh and reaping my reward as she came with an explosive cry.

I was inside her before she'd even finished, sinking to the hilt and groaning with relief as the tightness of her cunt welcomed me home.

I reared over her, pushing up onto my knees and dragging her ass into my lap so

I could watch her where she still lay before me on the bed.

She moved her fingers back to her clit and I watched the place where my dick sank into her, driving it in harder and faster, sweat slicking my abs, every muscle in my body tense with need and desire.

Her tits bounced in time with my thrusts and she panted my name, begging for a release from this torment.

I held out though, never wanting this to stop, loving this feeling far too much to relinquish it before I had to.

She took everything I had to give and when she came around my cock at last, her pussy squeezing tight and her lips breathing my name like a prayer, I went with her. I thrust in deep, coming hard, filling her and marking her as my own for what might have been the thousandth time but would never be enough.

I collapsed over her, kissing her hard, our panting breaths filling the silence left in the wake of our cries.

When we recovered enough to move again, I drew her into my arms and moved us up the bed, using water magic to clean away the evidence of what we'd done and then fire to dry us out at last before tugging the comforter over us.

"I love you, Darius Vega," Roxy said, her eyes falling closed as she settled herself against my chest where the pounding of my heart thumped against her ear.

"I loved you first," I told her, tightening my arm around her and letting my eyes shut too.

We may have been tangled up on the losing side of a war, but I wasn't going to let that take what we'd claimed in one another. Underdogs always got their day, and I would do all I could to make certain we got ours.

CALEB

CHAPTER FORTY FOUR

The sun was bright in the sky above the academy, the iciness of the day lightened by its efforts despite the frigid cold which refused to be spirited away by its presence. Frost clung to the branches in The Wailing Wood, making an ice rink of the paths that criss-crossed campus, and my breath rose in fog around me as I ran.

I sped through the trees towards King's Hollow, keeping an eye out for anyone who might spot me and double checking that I wasn't being followed.

It was early, dawn only recently breaking across campus. I'd left Seth asleep in bed in Aer Tower. No one knew I was out here or who I was meeting, and I intended for it to stay that way.

A crack of a twig made me halt, my eyes scanning the space between the trees where the morning light cut through the canopy in slanted shafts. Another crack came right ahead, but the back of my neck prickled, telling me the danger didn't lie in front of me but behind.

I swung around, the rush of air announcing the arrival of another Vampire, and one I knew as well as the sky. My brother Hadley pounced on me, but I was ready, my arm flying out and catching him right across the chest, throwing him to the ground. He coughed out a breath, glaring up at me in disappointment.

"You'll never be faster than me, Had," I flashed my fangs in a grin, offering him a hand to help him up.

He took it, throwing a glance into the trees as he smoothed his dark hair back self-consciously.

"Who's out there helping you distract me?" I asked in a low voice.

"Athena," he said her name like it belonged to a deity, and I didn't miss the possessiveness in his voice too. As if summoned to him, she emerged from the shimmering light between the trees, her brown hair streaked with purple and her large eyes giving her the appearance of something innocent, but I'd seen her fighting in her Wolf form and knew she was no such thing.

"What are you doing out here so early?" I asked them, and they both shared a look that told me they'd been up to something.

"You're not the only one who's busy helping out in the war," Hadley said with a gleam of mischief in his eyes that reminded me of the times we'd gone on adventures on our family grounds as kids. There was a river that hugged the southern boundary and I had a keen memory of making a raft out of branches with Hadley, the two of us squashed together on the thing with plans of sailing away on it. We'd made it about five feet before it had sunk, and we'd dragged ourselves onto the muddy riverbank laughing our heads off in the dirt. Those innocent days seemed so far away now, like that kind of carefree life was no longer reachable. But I seriously hoped I was wrong about that. Maybe on the other side of this war, we'd find ourselves in the mud again side by side with hours of freedom ahead of us.

"Who's putting you to work?" I asked. "Washer?"

Athena shuddered. "No, thank the stars. We're making a weapon."

"Who's we?" I asked, intrigued.

"Us, Xavier and Grayson," Hadley answered. "Gus Vulpecula had a schematic from Lionel's office at the Court of Solaria showing plans to build magical weapons that can be fitted onto the backs of Fae when they've shifted."

"And at first we thought we could use the plans to make our own," Athena said. "But we don't have the time or the resources for it. So instead, we've come up with a weapon that can disable all of Lionel's weapons. We're calling it a defuser."

"How does it work?" I asked excitedly.

"It sends out a pulse that could potentially fry them all," Hadley said. "But…" He ran a hand down the back of his neck. "We're struggling to find a power source strong enough to do it. We've been charging all kinds of crystals and adding them to the defuser, but nothing we've tried has the strength it'll likely need. Lionel could have made hundreds of those weapons for all we know."

Concern flickered through me at the thought of another immense threat added to Lionel's already terrifying army.

"And the range is another issue," Athena said, and I noticed the darkness under her eyes, telling me they'd probably been up all night working on this. "So far, the defuser only sends out a pulse that travels ten feet. It won't be enough."

I frowned. "Have you tried adding clear quartz or maybe even jade?" I suggested. "They should help with amplification."

"Yeah, but by Grayson's calculations we'd have to have a mountain of the stuff to take down a whole army wearing those weapons," Hadley said, and I sighed.

"Keep working on it," I encouraged, wishing I had more to offer.

"We'll figure it out," Athena said, her gaze alight with determination.

Hadley took her hand and the way he looked at her made me suddenly certain my little brother had fallen in love with a Capella, and my head was in a whirlwind of shit over that. There was something about them that called to the souls of Altairs apparently.

I clapped a hand onto his shoulder, squeezing in goodbye and he nodded to me before walking on.

I headed through the trees, charting the path to my destination and checking over my shoulder before making it to King's Hollow and pausing in the shadow of the huge oak.

I kept my silencing bubble up and cast an amplification spell on the area, but all was quiet. Not that I was taking any chances. I dropped to one knee and closed my eyes, placing a hand on the ground and connecting to the earth.

I pushed my awareness into the dirt, the tree roots, and up through the limbs of the countless trees around me too. There were small rodents, squirrels and even a fox pattering among the woodland, but none of them held a magical signature suggesting they might be Fae in shifted form. I was alone.

I released a breath then shot away from the Hollow, darting between the trees at high speed and racing for the edge of campus.

I hadn't told anyone about this. Not even Seth. Guilt stirred in my gut at the thought of it, but I couldn't keep denying my urges. I needed this. I couldn't resist it any longer.

The sound of racing footsteps reached me and I skidded to a halt, fallen leaves whirling around me as I disturbed them, a tornado of red, yellow and orange spinning between my legs for several seconds which stretched with the arrival of who I'd been waiting for.

I turned to face him as he sped into the clearing, my fangs snapping out at his approach, my muscles tensing automatically.

Orion burst from the trees in a blur of motion, colliding with me and knocking me to the ground where the two of us began to tussle playfully before I finally used a vine to snare his leg and heave him off of me.

"Took your time," I commented, wiping blood from the split lip he'd given me.

"I was with Blue," he replied, smirking at the fact.

I rolled my eyes. "Have you got it?"

"Yeah."

He jerked his chin and I cast a furtive look around before following him to a heap of moss-covered boulders with an aged willow growing from the top of the cluster, its fronds hanging down to obscure its trunk.

Orion pushed the fronds aside and moved beneath them. I followed, reaching out with my earth magic and encouraging two of the boulders to part, making an opening for us.

We headed into the secret space I'd created beneath the earth, the boulders grinding together as they closed at our backs to conceal all sign of this from the outside.

With a flick of my fingers, fires ignited in the hearth at the centre of the space and in the sconces lining the earthen walls.

There was a table of granite with two large and comfortable chairs either side of it, all hewn with my earth magic. Roots from the willow tree above us covered the roof of the cavern, their colour looking almost gold in the firelight, the crisscrossing patterns they made forming a decoration worthy of mother nature.

Orion glanced around at the room, taking in the dark metal rail that ringed the central fire, the stones which had been carved to resemble tiles lining the floor, then the deep blue and green furnishings which finished it all off and gave it a sense of homeliness.

"Show off," he muttered.

"I'm used to a certain level of comfort," I replied with a shrug, unapologetic. If we were going to be spending time in this place then I wouldn't leave it as some dank cavern.

"You're used to being a pampered brat," he teased.

"Don't be bitter just because air and water magic are inferior," I replied, earning a scoff from him.

We took our seats at the table and Orion placed the satchel he'd been carrying between us. I waited as he pulled out several old scrolls and a book so dog-eared and moth-eaten that I was surprised the entire thing didn't fall apart.

"I haven't so much as tried to open it yet," he confirmed, placing the book down carefully.

"Let me see if I can help it out a bit," I offered, reaching for it.

Orion nodded, but he winced as I picked it up. He'd constructed an air shield around the mouldering pages to try and protect them on the journey here, but it fell away as I picked it up. I'd expected a heavy tome, but the book was more like a journal in size and thin enough to let me know it couldn't be all that comprehensive. It flexed in my hand, the brown cover feeling like it might flake apart at any moment, the pages themselves tracing paper thin along their edges.

I pressed my magic into the book, working to bolster the integrity of the parchment with my earth magic but careful not to alter it at all. If I used too much power then any information held within might be lost.

Orion held his breath as I slowly strengthened the binding, firmed up the cover and gave the pages just a little more substance.

Once I was done, I placed it down between us.

"Adequate," he deadpanned, and I gave him a cocky look, knowing the intricate magic I'd cast was far more than that. But he'd never been one for compliments in the classroom, and it didn't look like he planned on handing them out anytime soon.

The title was faded and there looked to be a blackened stain on most of the front cover which could have been soot or smoke damage, but I could just make out the words.

Of Coven Lore.

"This is from the Blood Ages?" I confirmed, a prickle of unease running through me.

Those days might have been countless years in our past, but all Vampires were forced to acknowledge the shame of it – the reality of what our kind were capable of when abusing the full strength of our Order forms. Not to mention the way it had very nearly resulted in the annihilation of our kind when the rest of the Fae rose up in force against us.

Vampires had been the enemy in that long-ago war, and only the treaty brokered in the very final days of its completion had saved our kind at all. A law had been coming into place demanding the death of all Vampires upon their Emergence. If that had happened, who could say whether either of our family lines would have survived? The two of us never would have been born.

"I'm not condoning any of what was done back then," Orion said, shooting me a hard stare like he needed to confirm my intentions too.

I straightened my spine. "I didn't suggest you were."

Silence fell thickly between us. Reading that book was breaking a law, but it wasn't that which held us back. The knowledge we might find in there could be precisely what we needed, but it wasn't something we could ever unlearn. Once we knew its secrets, we would both be responsible for keeping and protecting them. In the wrong hands, all of this could be far more dangerous than either of us probably appreciated.

"I heard that in The Waning Lands there are covens in the wilds. They prey on the chaos of the Endless War which rages across their continent and are left unchecked and lawless," I said. "There are some who believe they will rise from the shadows they skulk in and be the ones to finally end the war out there – creating a new regime not unlike that which ruled Solaria through the Blood Ages." Maybe I was stalling for time, or maybe I was trying to talk us out of this, but it felt like I needed to say it either way.

Orion frowned. "Nothing about The Waning Lands is truly known to us," he said. "I am very suspicious about any rumours that claim to come from that hellish place – they have been entirely locked off from the world within their prism of magic for over a hundred years. Nothing and no one goes in or out of there, so how do these rumours make it across the sea to us at all?"

I nodded, my mind too occupied with the war that raged throughout Solaria for me to spend any real time considering what horrors went on within The Waning Lands. All I knew for certain about them was that I was fucking glad that prism was in place and kept all of the heathens who lived there inside it. The last thing we needed were power-hungry Fae from across the east seas looking too long in our direction. Whoever sealed that place off from the rest of the world did us a favour by all accounts and I was more than happy for it to stay blocked off indefinitely. One kingdom's problems were more than enough for us to be dealing with.

"Fuck it. We've come this far." I reached for the book, but Orion's hand shot out and he caught my wrist before I could turn the page.

"Whatever we learn within this book, whatever temptation we might find in the power the words whisper of, swear to me we won't ever use it beyond what we must do to win this war," he demanded, his eyes dark with trepidation over what we were doing, and the tempo of my pulse told me I was just as nervous.

"I swear it, brother," I promised him. "I want this knowledge for one reason alone. And when Lionel Acrux lays dead and rotting in the ground, I will put all memory of this information out of my head and never think of it again, let alone use it. I bowed to the True Queens and I have no desire to turn traitor."

"Then let it be learned, and used, then forgotten," he agreed, offering me his hand.

I took it in my own and the power of that oath clapped between us, the stars binding us to our words.

I swallowed a thick lump in my throat, my pulse thundering in my ears as I dropped my gaze to the innocuous looking book once more.

Then I opened it.

XAVIER

CHAPTER FORTY FIVE

My ice-coated fist slammed into a wooden shield, cracking it down the centre right between the eyes of the ugly green Dragon painted on it.

"Good. *Again*," Tyler encouraged, fixing the shield and raising the other one in his right hand.

I slammed my fist into the shield, then the other with a twisted-looking Shadow Princess painted on it, determined to break right through them. Tyler fixed them as fast as I could punch, my coated knuckles slamming hard into the wood over and over. The impact ricocheted up my arms and sweat was beading on my bare chest. We'd been at this all morning, and I stamped my foot in anger as I continued to be thwarted, the words of my horoscope wrapping themselves around my thoughts like a taunt.

Good morning, Sagittarius.
The stars have spoken about your day!

Today is a meeting of the paths where you will either take the first tentative steps in a new and revolutionary direction or continue to stumble across dead ends. Though frustrations will rise each time you find yourself reaching another blockade, take heed in the fact that every new attempt could place your feet upon the path you have been seeking. Open your heart to new ways of considering the world and listen to the whispers of your soul, for it seeks the salvation you so desperately crave and is willing your stubborn mind to bend towards it.

The words made no more sense to me now than they had when I'd first read them and all they served to do was rile me up further as I failed to achieve my goal.

There were plenty of others training around me, the Pitball stadium repurposed for any academy students who wanted to fight in the war to come and train. Tiberius ran most of these sessions, dedicated to honing the army into the fittest and the best.

Darcy and Geraldine were working together to my right, Geraldine casting wooden shields the same way Tyler was for me, and Athena and Grayson were on my other side.

My gaze slipped to Sofia over Tyler's shoulder where another line of rebels were training with fire. She cast tiny fireballs at a target ahead of her that moved sporadically under a levitation charm. Our old professors helped coordinate the training, keeping the targets moving or marching down the lines offering out tips.

Lance Orion was headed this way, his chest bare from his own training, but he was playing the asshole professor today too, shouting orders at anyone who was lagging. He paused just beyond Tyler, folding his arms and watching Darcy for several moments. His eyes brightened before he turned them on me and all darkness descended instead.

"Watch your stance, Acrux," he clipped, and I readjusted my footing.

"You're not a teacher anymore, you can use my first name," I said through my teeth, then swung a fist at the left shield. It cracked again, but Tyler fixed it once more.

"Come on, Xavier, you've got more in you than this," Tyler urged.

"I'll use your first name when you break one of those shields," Orion goaded me, and I snorted angrily.

Tiberius started marching this way too, his gaze snapping between the ranks, looking for weaknesses. "Five more minutes then switch stations!" he bellowed.

"I wouldn't let anyone switch stations until they'd achieved the goal of the station they're at," Orion muttered just as Darcy's fist split through one of her shields.

"Holy wangadoodles! That was quite the crackerjack," Geraldine cheered.

"Good work, beautiful," Orion called to her, and I scowled at his obvious favouritism.

Darcy smiled, raising her fists again as Geraldine reset the shields.

"Focus," Tyler urged me.

I swung another fist, driving it hard into the face of the green Dragon, my fury setting my pulse pounding in my ears as I thought of everything that piece of shit had done to me.

"Tyler, move stations," Orion ordered, forcing him to step aside so he could take his place.

"You don't have earth, you can't cast the shields," I hissed.

"Fuck the shields," he said. "Hit me here." He tapped his jaw.

"What?" I balked.

"I'll have a go," Darcy offered with a hopeful grin, and Orion shot her a heated look.

"Get back in line, Miss Vega. You only broke one shield, break the other one before your time is up or I'll make sure you regret it," he warned, then turned to me again.

He tapped his jaw once more. "Come on."

"You're gonna use your Vampire speed to move," I said, stamping my foot. "Let me work with the shields."

"The shields test your strength, but that's not your weakness."

"Then why can't I break them?" I barked.

"Because of that rage. It's fucking with your focus. You know you can break a shield, but your anger is making you mess up the punches."

"And why shouldn't I be angry? What do you expect? My father has taken over the star damned kingdom, Lance. Didn't you get the message?" I snapped.

"Hit me," he said simply.

"Let me work on the shields," I insisted, moving to step past him to fetch Tyler, but Orion just smacked me around the head.

"Hit me," he demanded, and I swung for him in fury, feeling Athena and Grayson's eyes on me.

He sped away predictably, appearing behind me and shoving me in the back. I stumbled forward several steps with a curse then swung around, my heart thundering and my jaw gritting.

"What's your problem?" I lunged for him, fist cutting through the air, wanting to wipe that casual expression off his face.

He sped back two steps to evade it and I stumbled forward, swinging for him again. He zoomed behind me, kicking me in the ass and sending me flying onto the ground. I rolled on to my back, a savage whinny tearing from my throat as he stood over me.

"Hit. Me," Orion said evenly.

I launched myself up from the ground, fists swinging, my rage blinding. My fists struck nothing but air, and I hung my head, breathing in heavily in defeat. I couldn't catch a fucking Vampire. I was never going to land a hit on him, and he knew it.

"Charge on, my fine pego-brother," Geraldine bayed. "All is possible when you believe it to be so."

"I can't catch him without using magic," I grumbled.

"Who said you can't use magic? You're Fae, aren't you?" Orion called. "There won't be any rules on the battlefield."

"Only blood," Darcy said darkly, and I glanced at her, seeing the determination in her eyes to see this war won.

My gaze trailed to the other Spares, Athena and Grayson falling back into their training while Hadley smashed through his partner's shield with a bellow of effort, his knuckles splitting open on the wood. Then I looked to Darius and Tory further down the line who were running drills together with perfect precision. None of them were bringing their feelings into this, they were putting it all aside in favour of honing their skills. Because right here was where warriors were made.

"This anger in you might be messing with your training right now," Orion said. "But there's no real consequences here. You've seen war, you've tasted the chaos of battle. You know what it's like, and you kept your head then."

"But that was before-" My throat closed on the words, refusing to let them out.

"Before you lost your sweet mama," Geraldine breathed, her eyes twinkling as I turned to look at her. She knew this pain. Her father had died with my mother, and she was still here, not letting that wound destroy her. Having Darius back healed that pain in so many ways, but his return wasn't guaranteed. Not everyone in this stadium was going to survive the war, it was simple math. And the chances that I'd survive along with all those I loved...it was nigh on impossible.

"Breathe and think," Orion directed.

It was so simple it seemed pointless, but I was out of ideas.

The people around me had lost just as much as I had and they weren't distracted by anger, affected to the point of failure. I was letting them all down, not just myself. Ultimately, when I marched into battle again, my strength, my focus, my power, it could save those I loved. I could be the difference between them surviving or not. And though the pressure of that truth was unbearable, I couldn't shy away from it.

I twisted around, blasting giant ice shards up from the grass around Orion so he had nowhere to run, and while he blasted them away from him with air, I launched a ball of ice shaped like my fist right into his face.

His lip split and his eyes shone with triumph as the ice fell to the ground with a thump.

"There it is," Orion said with a smirk. "Your focus is back. Keep hold of it. It's what will save your ass ultimately."

I nodded, a small smile fighting its way onto my lips as Geraldine rushed over to pat my shoulder.

"Good show!" she cried. "Want to flip the flamingo with me now?"

Orion swapped into her place to train with Darcy, and I worked with Geraldine to practise what I'd learned, my heart full of hope once more.

By the time Tiberius called time on the session, I felt I was getting a real handle on my anger issues. It was so fucking simple. Breathing and thinking. Dammit, why hadn't someone told me that before?

"Right, fellows of the flag," Geraldine called. "Upon the hour we shall leave for our daring ventures. Sing your farewells and may the stars see you safely return." She strode away toward the changing rooms, and I shared a grim look with Sofia as she ran to join me.

"Shall we save some time and shower together back at Terra House?" she asked, her eyelashes fluttering a little, and Tyler trotted over excitedly as he heard that.

I glanced between them, seeing the offering in their eyes and wanting that more than anything. But the last few times we'd all had sex, I still hadn't finished, and it had left me feeling like a failure as their Dom. I was heading somewhere extremely dangerous in an hour's time, and I didn't want that to be the last memory they had of me if I didn't return. But if I didn't try, then wasn't that worse? I had to show them what they meant to me, to prove there wasn't any other Fae in the world I desired more than them.

I nodded, taking Sofia's hand and giving Tyler a look that said I wanted him just as much as the girl at my side. He nuzzled against me, letting me take the lead and I hoped this time, I would prove I was worthy of holding that position.

"Darius?" I whispered, tugging his sleeve as I walked with him to the edge of campus.

He glanced at me, getting the hint and letting Tory and Darcy move ahead while we hung back on the path.

He flicked up a silencing bubble, his frown deepening. "Are you good? What's wrong?"

That look entered his brown eyes, the one he'd always given me whenever he came home from the academy and he feared what our father had done to me while he was away. I loved Darius for the way he cared for me, but I'd always despised being his burden.

"I need some advice," I said, clearing my throat. It wasn't like going to my big brother about this was my preferred course of action, but I didn't want the Spares knowing my issues. It was too damn embarrassing.

"On?" he pressed.

"Well," I glanced away then back to him, heat coursing up my neck. "It's a sex thing."

His expression skewed a little. "Is it those gemstones on your dick? Are they chafing?"

"*No*," I hissed.

"Is it an ass issue? Have you got that ass infection again?"

"No!" I cried. "I was eight when I had that."

"Yeah, but things can, you know, repeat."

"It's not an ass infection," I snarled, remembering the mortifying moment when my big brother had taken me to a healer and just as I'd bent over to show them the problem, a whole host of trainee healers had walked in to observe my asshole too.

"You didn't trap your dick in a fridge drawer again, did you? Because your naked midnight feasting is a hazard, Xavier."

"Could you please stop listing the most mortifying moments of my life and listen to what I have to say?" I demanded and Darius chuckled, clearly fucking with me.

"Alright, alright. What is it?" he asked.

"I can't..." A pregnant pause passed between us where I grappled with how to say this in the least embarrassing way. "Finish."

"Oh," he exhaled.

"Have you ever had that problem?" I asked.

"No...oh, well yeah once actually. When I was with Marguerite. The last time I hooked up with her, I swear it felt like my dick was just dangling off a bridge, flapping in a light breeze. Did nothing for me. But I wouldn't say I didn't finish, more that I just pulled out and left."

"Okay, um, let's never speak of that again, yeah?"

"Agreed," he snorted.

"The thing is, I love my herd. They get me so...you know. And it's not ever like I'm dangling my dick off a bridge, it's always great. But lately, since...well... it was after..."

"Spit it out."

"After you and Mom died," I said, glancing away from him. "The grief fucked me up. I can't explain it. I was in the worst place of my life, and now you're back it's better. But Mom..." I shook my head, unable to express the pain inside me. "Maybe part of me feels like I don't have the right to pleasure when so many lives have been destroyed around me. I feel so damn guilty sometimes."

"Guilty for what?" He stopped me on the path, gripping my shoulder to make me look at him.

"For living, I guess. While others can't be here." I glanced down at my feet, the words so raw and true they cut me open.

"Hey," Darius growled, and I looked up at him. "Mom died for us. And she'd fucking do it all over again because that's what we do for family. I'd do it for you, and I damn well know you'd do it for me. That's the way of war. It hurts, and it's unjust, and those who live or die is all down to the flip of a coin. But it's not your responsibility to keep everyone here. Sometimes shit happens that none of us can control, and it's not fair, but that's life, Xavier. Hell, I know how quick it can be lost. Don't waste the time you have here feeling bad for the time you're given. No one deserves free air in their lungs like you do."

I chewed the inside of my cheek, trying to accept his words, but at the core of me, I'd believed this long before the war had started. "The truth is...I used to think that things would have been better if I hadn't been around. If Lionel hadn't had me to hold over you, you wouldn't have had to go through what you did. You could have made your own choices. Maybe you never would have been Star Crossed-"

"Don't speak like that," Darius said, hurt pooling in his eyes. "I'd be nothing without you. My childhood only held any happiness because you were in it. Without you, I never would have had something to fight for. I would have become Father's puppet long before I ever considered breaking away from him. You were the reason I resisted him. *You*, Xavier. Because I love you. You're my fucking brother, there isn't a universe I'd want to exist in without you."

My heart bled at his words, my own love for him pouring from that wound. Because it was sullied by the cruelty of our father, but it had never been shattered. Love had overcome his hate, and perhaps it could still do so.

I dragged him into a hug and he clasped the back of my neck, holding me tight.

"I love you too," I said raggedly. "I'll never be able to repay you for protecting me like you did when we were kids."

We parted and he frowned, a sense of change between us solidifying in my chest. Because we weren't those kids anymore. We were hardened by war and had been made men long before we should have had to be.

"Enjoy your life, Xavier. You've earned it," he said.

"So have you, don't waste a second, zombie bro," I said, knocking my fist against his shoulder.

"I don't plan on it." We walked on side by side, finding the twins waiting for us up ahead, glancing curiously between us but asking no questions. They were like us; they understood that siblings needed each other in ways that no other relationship could fulfil. It was sacred.

We made it beyond the campus gates, finding the Councillors there waiting to go, and with a toss of stardust, we were stolen away towards our destined location.

When we were spat out again, I gasped at what I found laid out before me.

We stood at the peak of a barren mountain, shrouded in shadow cast by Melinda Altair to conceal us from view, though we were so high up that I doubted anyone would spy us here. We gazed down at a terrible army, the rows and rows of encampments full of Lionel's soldiers seeming to stretch on forever. Terror bound me in place as I tried to estimate the numbers, the camps spreading on for miles. It was too vast, far more than we'd come close to gathering.

"It's worse than I imagined," Darcy breathed in horror.

"There's too many," Tory said thickly, stepping closer to her twin.

Darius gave me a grave look, then cast his eyes beyond the encampment to another sweeping mountainside across the valley. "Tiberius, Melinda, Antonia. Head over there. It's a decent vantage point." He pointed it out and Melinda pressed a hand to his shoulder in goodbye, touching mine too before stardusting away with the other Councillors to that location.

We could just make them out on the distant mountainside before they cast thick concealment spells around themselves, blending in with the rocks, and I started doing the same for us.

When we were well hidden, I looked to the twins with anticipation brewing in my chest.

"Let's do this," Tory said, and Darcy raised her hands, casting the first glimmer of the illusion.

We all added to the magic, and the Councillors worked to cast their part of it too, our rebel army appearing to march into the gully between the mountains towards Lionel's ranks. My pulse quickened as I added to the thundering sound of thousands of boots hitting the ground, sending tremors through the earth to sell the lie.

I let my magic pour from me, joining that of my brother's and the twins, all of it rushing out to bolster the illusion. I crafted warriors one after another, the time I'd spent practicing this magic paying off ten-fold as I gave individuality to each of them, making their movements just different enough to look realistic, adding bannermen and foot soldiers then casting the appearance of Manticores, Harpies and Griffins into formation in the sky, sweeping down from the clouds with bays for war.

My focus was sharp, and I let slow breaths pass my lips, refusing to allow myself to be shaken by Lionel's terrifying army which could so easily crush ours if we were truly marching out to meet them this day. We were laying plans to increase our chances when that time really came. And by dusk, I hoped we'd be back at the academy with many victories being sung by the rebels, because we weren't the only Fae in our group on a mission right now. The others would be arriving at the doors of their own destinies, and I wished them all the luck in the world. Because the fate of this war depended on them.

ORION

CHAPTER FORTY SIX

I sat in the shadow of the wooden pier on Sunshine Bay, my boots pressing into the sand and the warm air bringing the taste of the sea to my lips. This part of Solaria never felt the true touch of winter; it was a capsule of summer waiting to be claimed. But since Lionel's reign, his followers had taken over here, seizing one of the most beautiful parts of my kingdom. And today, I planned on liberating it.

Max was crouched beside me, his iridescent navy scales glinting above the collar of his shirt and a sense of anticipation pouring from him.

It was me and him on this mission. Tasked by Darcy and Tory to break out the captives in the nearby Nebula Inquisition Centre while they were on a mission of their own. And the two of us were perfect for the job considering our shared Elements. Air and water.

Max pulled off his shirt followed by his pants and shoes, leaving him in just a pair of blue swim shorts. I mimicked him, stripping down to my black swim shorts and stuffing our clothes into a waterproof bag along with the stardust we'd need to make it out of here.

I checked my watch, the time ticking down to the moment we needed to move. The guards would be changing soon and that would be our window of opportunity.

Max worked to conceal us, gathering the shadows closer as we started creeping towards the water's edge. The gentle lapping of waves would have been serene under any other circumstance, but today it was a battleground.

We waded out into the sea, keeping beneath the pier, the heavy footfalls above telling of the guards up there.

Navy scales rippled across Max's entire body as his Siren Order was fully unleashed, and they glimmered metallically.

"Up for a swim, Orion?" Max asked, his silencing bubble tight around us, keeping his words just for us.

I nodded. "I always did feel at home in the water."

"There's something about the ocean," he agreed, the sea swirling around his hips at the will of his magic.

"Water always feels so much more alive than air," I said, and Max's dark eyes lit up.

"Exactly. Air is a tool, a true force of nature, but water…I swear it has desires of its own," he said excitedly.

"Sea water especially," I said. "I've never heard anyone else talk about it like that…"

We shared a look then came to a halt in the deep blue water, the waves lapping against our chests now. It was deep enough, and we were nearing the end of the pier.

"Stay on my tail down there," Max said.

"I bet I'm just as fast of a swimmer," I challenged. "Maybe it's you who should be staying on my tail."

Max gave me a cocky look. "I'm the most powerful Siren in Solaria. You may rule the land with your speed, but down there is my domain. I can see the currents in the waves, I can taste the changing tides, I can-"

"Alright, fish man. Let's put it to the test," I said with a smirk, checking my watch and right on time, a call went up on the pier and marching footsteps headed this way, giving us a brief window to swim far enough out of sight.

The water here was crystal clear and even with all the concealment spells in the world, it would be risky to go while the guards were looking for signs of invasion.

"Lead the way," I urged, and Max dove under the waves.

I cast a bubble of air over my face then swam after him, diving deep and following the kicks of his feet toward the sandy ocean bed.

He was fast as hell, and even with my speed and strength aiding me, I couldn't keep up. But the water was so clear, it was easy to follow him, and he shot a taunting smile at me over his shoulder before finally slowing to allow me to catch up. With his point well and truly proved, he led the way as we swam out from the shadow of the pier, and my neck prickled with the feeling of exposure. I stirred the waves above us with magic, causing them to break a little further out from shore than usual, offering us more cover.

No shouts came from above, nor blasts of magic, and we swam further out into the warm water of Sunshine Bay, putting as much distance between us and them as possible.

It was a five-mile swim to the Nebula Inquisition Centre, but we soon made it to the first watch tower, the giant wooden legs carving deep down into the ocean. Max started ascending, swimming up and up before breaking the water's surface and I soon made it to his side, disbanding the bubble of air over my face and breathing in the briny sea breeze. A ladder led up to a wooden platform high above us where the guards were positioned, and Max started climbing it without hesitation.

I hurried after him with a buzz of adrenaline in my veins, water streaming off of us as we made the ascent quickly. When we reached the top, Max paused, closing his eyes and using his Siren gifts to feel for the emotions of whoever lurked above the open hatch.

He ducked low again, looking down at me. "Four guards. Two on the left, two on the right."

"I'll take the right," I said, then let go of the ladder, using air to guide me to the other side of the platform.

I sailed out from underneath it, flying up and finding myself eye to eye with a surprised guard. My fist cracked into his face before he could think to defend himself, and with the power of air behind my blow, he went careering across the watchtower, colliding with one of Max's opponents and knocking them to the floor with a crash. Max bound them both in ice while I rushed toward my next target in a blur of motion. A fireball blasted from her hand, and I swerved to avoid it with a burst of speed, the heat of the flames warming my cheek as it whooshed past my head.

I doused the flames in water before they could draw attention, grabbing hold of her in the next second and stealing the air from her lungs. She gripped my arm, fire blazing, burning where she touched me, but I didn't let go, stealing every drop of oxygen from her body until she went limp. The tension ebbed out of my body and I carried her over to the other guards, freezing her hands then binding her to them with ropes of ice and air.

With the guards subdued, I joined Max at the edge of the watchtower, gazing out across the Nebula Inquisition Centre with a sneer pulling at my lips.

Nets ringed areas of the sea in wide circles, trapping water-reliant Orders within them, twenty of the cages spreading out between the six watch towers. We were on the furthest corner, each tower far enough away from the other that I couldn't clearly see the Fae manning them. In the distance, beyond the ring of watchtowers, were the jutting spires of a turquoise castle piercing up from the depths of the azure ocean. The Academy of Hydros. It was a place of mythic beauty, or so I'd heard. The castle reached right to the sea floor, and I guessed what could be seen above the waves was just a glimpse of the immense palace hidden beneath.

My gaze was drawn to a group of Acheilus Shark shifters circling in the nearest cage, and I noticed the air above them shimmering ever-so-slightly, telling me of the wards surrounding them.

"By the stars," Max exhaled. "How long have they kept them like this? They'll go mad without using their magic."

A vitriolic kind of hatred spilled into me for the Fae who had done this, and my gaze turned to the four captive guards behind us. They were just Lionel's pawns, but that didn't make them less responsible for this.

"Can you handle the wards?" I asked.

"My ocean song is about to blow your fucking mind, Orion," Max said, a gleam of anticipation in his eyes.

"Can't wait. I'll handle the rest of the guards," I said darkly, backing up, but Max did too and we bumped into each other.

I stepped left but he went that way as well, and we did an awkward side-step, this way, that way until we made it past each other.

"Right, well. Good luck, or whatever the fuck," I muttered.

"That rhymed," Max pointed out.

"Yeah…" I ran a hand down the back of my neck.

Max saluted me and for some reason I did it back then blew out a breath of irritation at myself and took a running leap off the edge of the tower.

I hit the water like a bullet and the power of Max's song slammed into me, roiling the sea like it had been struck by a giant anvil. It was a Siren Song like nothing I'd ever heard before, deep and powerful and destructive, like the voice of the ocean itself.

I swam fast, making it to the next tower and hauling myself up onto the ladder, finding the waves crashing around me. Water blasted everywhere, the sea beginning to turn as a giant whirlpool formed around the nets. The captured Fae grew frantic, an array of colourful fish shifters surging up from the water in the nearest cage, only to be forced back down again by the power of the wards.

I climbed higher, watching in awe as the water bowed to Max's song, the terrible notes sending huge sprays up toward the sky. The guards were well aware of our presence now, firing blasts of magic at Max from their towers, but Max wasn't the one they had to worry about.

I waited for my moment, my heart thumping in time with that almighty tune which split the air apart and collided with the sea, demanding she fall to Max's will. A huge wave rose from the ocean, gathering momentum on the horizon and blotting out the sun before it drove down onto the wards with a crash that made the world quake. My ears rang with Max's song, the power of it carving through the water and charting a path right through the blood in my veins. It was chaotic and beautiful, thrilling and terrible.

I grinned, holding tight to the wooden ladder as the water splashed up from every direction, the surge of the wave soaking me. I shook my head to get my sopping hair out of my eyes, a whoop tearing from my chest in exhilaration from all this power. And now, with the wards down and the captive Fae thrashing wildly to the surface of their nets, it was my time to shine.

I raised one hand, wielding the air and weaving it into a violent storm that darkened the fluffy white clouds above to pitch black. Water and air were my gift, a blood-bound right of mine; they were a part of me as deeply as I was a part of them.

The storm I brewed was the most vicious I had ever concocted, and I sent the bluster of wind tearing into the backs of the six watch towers. Tremendous cracks sounded as the wooden struts snapped like toothpicks, and I held onto the ladder tighter as my own tower began to topple. All of them fell as one, the guards falling with them, some leaping from their perches to land in the nets below. Just before I was thrown into the waves, I saw shark shifters and beasts of the sea snaring their captors in their jaws, blood turning the water red and darkening the waves.

I plunged into the ocean, feeling a leash of magic tighten around my waist and yank me along through the water. I fought to break it, a stream of churning water blinding me as I was dragged towards some unknown enemy. But as I readied to fight for my life, I came to a halt in front of Max, his hand releasing the leash and letting it dissolve into bubbles.

The two of us floated in the blue abyss as the water settled around us, and shit-eating grins spread across our faces.

I tasted blood in the water as we turned to the nearest net and tore it apart with the gifts of our Elements.

The Fae came pouring out, schools of Fish, Sharks and Dolphins, even two Cetus Whales swimming up from the depths of their cage to escape. A little Crab landed on my shoulder, knocking its claw against my cheek in thanks before letting itself be swept away by the current.

I cast a fresh pocket of air around my mouth and nose, breathing in deep, then swimming on to break apart the next net. It didn't take long to rip into them all, and the ocean came alive with the bodies of the water Orders.

A Dolphin did a loop around me, pressing her nose to my cheek before fin flapping Max a high five and sailing away towards the shore.

When all of them were free, we turned and raced after them, soon arriving back on the sandy beach where a tide of shifters were turning back into their Fae forms, gathering family and friends into tight hugs.

The guards up on the pier weren't even attempting to capture the endless Fae appearing on the beach, all of them making a run for it instead. But plenty of their prisoners took chase after them, naked and full of rage, and I had no doubt they would bring them to justice in whatever way they saw fit.

"The True Queens' reign has begun!" I boomed, enhancing my voice with an amplification spell. "Join the Vegas in their fight against the False King! Our army awaits new recruits at Zodiac Academy. All who come shall be protected, whether you wish to fight or not."

Cheers went up, while others wept in relief, knowing they had a safe haven at last.

With the blaze of victory in my veins, I found myself tossing an arm around Max's shoulders.

"I told you you'd like my ocean song," he said, arrogance blazing across his face, but fuck it didn't bother me like it once had in my classroom. Max Rigel was a man who had earned the right to that arrogance, but far be it from me to let him know it.

"Just sing it in tune next time, yeah?" I muttered.

"Fuck you," he laughed, and I broke a smile, this moment too damn good not to revel in it.

"My gratitude is eternal!" cried an exhausted-looking man as he fell at our feet, covered in seaweed, and I helped him up. "I will fight this war in the name of the Vegas. All hail the True Queens!"

"Damn straight," Max said. "All hail those fiery fucking hellions."

TORY

CHAPTER FORTY SEVEN

I looked across the distant army which me, Darcy, Darius, Xavier, and the Councillors had conjured into existence, my pulse picking up as I took in the scope of the rebel forces spreading out across the horizon, marching into the valley towards Lionel's sleeping followers. Even though I knew it wasn't real, I couldn't help but feel an echo of the fear that would capture me if it was. One day soon our army really would face his across the field and I was holding out hope that we could match them when we did.

Trumpets blared throughout the enemy encampment below, the sentries spotting the fake army as flares of magic shot into the sky and they all scrambled to get themselves armed and dressed for battle.

A Nymph shrieked as it shifted out of its Fae-like form, the horns on its head tearing through the canvas of its tent, the long stretch of fabric hanging down its back like a veil. It broke into a run, its enormous feet trampling the tents closest to it, and people screaming from within.

The army was in danger of falling into chaos and the shouts of the commanders boomed over the encampment magically as they fought to regain control.

"We have maybe thirty minutes before they make it out to meet our army of ghosts and realise they aren't quite what they seem," Darius said, his brow tight with concentration as he worked to make the advancing rebels look as realistic as possible.

Xavier's jaw was gritted and his gaze remained locked on the illusion of the rebel army, his focus not faltering for a moment to waste time talking to us.

"We'd better hurry then," I said, glancing at Darcy to make sure she was ready too.

"If you can create a strong enough concealment spell to hide us then I'll fly us all in-" Darius began, but I cut him off.

"Yeah, about the whole 'sticking together' part of the plan – we kinda bullshitted you on that. Geraldine helped us map out a route through the mountains to get to Lionel's evil lair and I'm sorry dude, but your scaly Dragon ass won't fit."

Darcy breathed a laugh as she turned to look over the edge of the daunting drop behind us. It was really just an asscrack of doom carved between two mountains in some long-forgotten earthquake. Barely ten feet across but deep as all hell and lined with razor-sharp rocks just to make falling down there into one hell of a bitch.

"We need all of you to focus on maintaining the diversion anyway," Darcy added sweetly.

"You can't seriously think I'm going to stay here while you try and break into my father's castle alone?" Darius scoffed like the chances of us leaving him behind were zero.

The problem with that was that Darcy and I had spent a long time poring over the Map of Espial with Geraldine and we'd found one super-subtle, damn near impossible point of entry that we'd decided was our best chance at sneaking in unnoticed, and it was in no way Dragon size friendly.

I shrugged as I backed up to the edge of the rocky crevice, the impossibly long drop spilling away below my heels, razor sharp rocks just waiting to impale me at the bottom if this went to shit.

Darius's gaze lowered to the fall at my rear as he caught on to what I was doing and a growl rolled up the back of his throat.

"Roxy, if you try to go down there alone, I'll throw you over my shoulder and tie your ass up to stop you. That's not just dangerous; it's fucking suicide and none of us can follow you into that crack of hell."

"Oh baby," I purred, spreading my arms out wide either side of me as I gave him a sweet as pie smile and he broke into a run in a pointless attempt to stop me. "Don't threaten me with a good time."

I pitched backwards, his roar of fury meeting with the terrifying thunder of my own heartbeat as I let myself fall, my gut plummeting and hair thrashing against my cheeks as I plunged into the darkness of that jagged tear in the earth.

I flipped entirely upside down, a whoop of exhilaration spilling from my lips before my wings snapped out at my spine, the tips of my bronze feathers brushing the icy walls either side of me, the gap so narrow that I could barely even beat them.

Darcy whooped as she jumped down behind me feet first, clearly dodging the Dragon too.

I couldn't risk a glance back, but I could feel his furious gaze burning into my spine as I let the earth swallow me and could feel the pounding tempo of his pulse as rage coursed through his flesh.

Yeah, he was all kinds of pissed at me right about now. But I was his queen, and he was going to have to start following orders at some point.

The chasm widened just enough to allow me to turn, my wings catching in an updraft before I took off to the east, following the winding route of the rocky cliffs which towered up endlessly either side of us.

Darcy was right behind me but the two of us remained silent as we concentrated on navigating hairpin turns and jagged outcrops of the reddish rock.

The sound of rushing water called out from somewhere in the depths of the chasm below, a long-forgotten river carving its way along beneath us.

The darkness within the crevice was so thick that it was all I could do to focus on the few feet ahead of me.

We twisted and turned, flying the hardest route either of us had ever attempted, our wings brushing against the narrow rocks more than once.

As we swept around a sharp corner, the crash of a waterfall echoed off of the walls and I barely had time to tuck in my wings before slamming straight into it.

The water pummelled me, propelling me downward, Darcy crashing into my side as we were hurled towards the foot of the fall, but we'd been flying fast and despite our closed wings, our propulsion drove us on through the downfall.

I gasped as frigid air slammed into us again, making us tumble over and over while I fought to get my bearings and threw out an arm. A net of air magic coiled around us, and Darcy released a Faelight to illuminate the pitch-black space we found ourselves in.

I blinked the water from my eyelashes and exchanged a look with my twin as we took in the dark passage which continued on ahead, all sign of the sky lost to the rocks that had closed in above us.

Without a word we continued on, my air magic propelling us forward so we could spread our wings again and the two of us flew into the dark, led only by the faint glow of the light Darcy had cast, neither of us willing to brighten it for fear of what lay ahead.

The cold pressed in as the rocks tightened around us and we were forced to move lower and lower until a stony ground appeared beneath us, a trickling of water marking the path the river had once taken in this direction.

I flew on for as long as I could, but my wings crashed into the rocky walls again and again until I was forced to land and banish them.

Darcy landed beside me, and I reached out to brush my fingers along the cold rocks.

"They're wet," I muttered.

"Do you think Lionel's followers redirected that river?" she wondered.

"I hope not. Because if they did, they must have had a reason to and this path may not be as abandoned as we'd hoped."

That possibility hung between us for a moment, but neither of us suggested heading back. That wasn't an option.

We moved on through the dark, the fire magic that lived within us pushing out the cold and removing the water from our flesh.

I placed a hand on the pommel of my sword, a chill creeping up my spine that warned against something I wasn't yet certain of. But it didn't feel like we were alone down here.

Wordlessly, I began to draw the shadows tighter around us, constructing concealment and diversion spells to divert any attention from us.

Darcy dismissed her Faelight and joined me in my magic until I couldn't even see my own feet before me without concentrating hard to spot them.

A deep clacking sound made my heart leap in alarm, and I drew my sword, casting an enhancement spell over my eyes to help me see better in the near total darkness. There was the faintest glimmer of light up ahead, but it was so distant that it did little more than provide a glow of grey at the furthest reaches of my vision.

Darcy's arm brushed mine as we headed on, the two of us silent while lending the other strength. Together we were unstoppable. I had felt that even when we were small children, the heirs to nothing but misery and strife. But now I knew why. We had been born to this path and neither of us would falter while walking it.

The clacking came again, closer now, a rancid stench rolling beneath my nose and making me choke back a gag.

The narrow passageway was widening as it turned, the dim light growing just enough to reveal more passages leading off from this one, though the jagged, broken rocks around their edges suggested they were far newer.

As we passed the first of them on our right, the clacking came again followed by a rough, shuddering inhale which set the hairs rising along the back of my neck.

Tap, tap.

The sharp noise had me pivoting, sword raised as I looked to the passage on the other side of our path, the darkness deep within it and yet somehow, I could sense movement in those shadows and eyes roaming the space, seeking us out.

I swallowed thickly, adjusting my grip on my sword and double checking the silencing bubble I'd constructed around us.

"That smell," Darcy breathed, the waft of it roaming over us again, a warmth to it which I didn't want to consider.

"It reeks of death," I agreed, admitting that truth no matter how much I would have preferred to remain in denial.

We crept on, trying to ignore the sounds coming from those darkened passages, working not to gag on the stench that only grew worse with every step we took.

A wild shriek nearly made my heart explode in my chest as we passed yet another of the dark openings and I stumbled aside, raising my sword in expectation of an attack which didn't come.

"What does that say?" Darcy hissed, pointing with her own blade at a metal plaque which had been placed above the opening of the passageway, the light now bright enough to make it out.

My lips parted in confusion as I read the strange word.

"Smittony," I said, exchanging a nonplussed look with my twin. "What the fuck does that mean?"

"That one says Roarkarlow," she added, pointing to the other side of the space.

Curiosity nagged at me, the need to know what Lionel was hiding down here burning a path right through me. But I couldn't deny the utter terror which accompanied the thought of heading into one of those passages.

"We should focus on the star," Darcy breathed, and I nodded, moving on with her, but as we passed another passageway and an undeniable howl pierced the air, I froze.

"That was no Werewolf," I said, the haunting lilt of the sound echoing on through the network of caverns, the sound a shrill and desperate plea laced with undeniable hunger.

"Those monsters," Darcy said slowly. "The ones who attacked the academy."

"There are more of those fucking things?" I hissed in alarm, taking note of the passageways and trying to count them. How may had we passed? Twenty? Were there creatures lurking down every one of them?

"Geraldine had some of the academy professors examine the bodies of the ones that attacked Zodiac. They said they weren't natural. They were something *made.*"

I nodded, my grip tightening on my sword. If these things joined Lionel when we fought him again they would only tip the scales further in his favour. It was yet another advantage he held in this coming war, and it was one we couldn't afford to let him keep. But the star…that was even worse than this. Lavinia was unbeatable while she somehow wielded its power.

"Fuck," I cursed, knowing that we had to move on, that we couldn't risk doing anything here which would jeopardise us getting to the star. If Lionel figured out our play and realised we were here, we'd never make it back in again – assuming we even made it out alive now.

"We'll deal with the star first then come back," Darcy swore, and I nodded in agreement, though it galled me to do so, but what choice did we have?

We started moving faster, and I forced my eyes from the passages splitting away from us, ignoring the sounds and smells which came from them and the prickling along my spine which warned of the danger lurking so close.

We needed to get out of here and find our way into the castle Lionel had constructed for himself. From what we'd been able to tell when studying the Map of Espial, this cavern would deposit us at the foot of the mountain where he'd built his stronghold, circumventing the sprawling mass of his army which would hopefully be well distracted by the illusion of ours closing in.

It was a bold plan, or a stupid one, potentially both. But as we finally made it around the last turn in the passage where fresh air blew in and stole the vile stench of those caverns, we fell still.

The exit loomed ahead, but standing before it, his skin a wan, grey colour, stood a man whose aura was so empty that it seemed to steal the wind from the sky and the light from the moon.

We were coated in concealment spells and draped in confounding spells to force any eyes away from us too, but I had the sudden fear that none of that would work on a star given form. His attention began to shift, moving from the far side of the cavern towards the pair of us who were frozen in place.

There was no doubt in my mind that he would see us despite all of the magic we had cast to hide ourselves. And that we had just walked straight into the path of the creature whose curse had almost ended our family line for good. Clydinius.

SETH

CHAPTER FORTY EIGHT.

Caleb sat astride my back as I ran through the snow in my Wolf form, his fingers tight in my fur and the icy wind driving against us. We'd stardusted out to the very edge of the Polar Capital, and as I crested the snowy hill at last, the city spilled away beneath us within a giant crater of snow. Blue and green lights glittered within shining glass buildings that stretched up toward the sky like giant shards of ice. Thousands of Fae lived within those glass walls, the walkways between the buildings and the domes over the streets keeping the entire place contained from the brutal cold.

My breath fogged before me and my heart rate began to settle from the exertion.

I'd dreamed of visiting the Polar Capital all my life, but I'd never thought I'd be here under these circumstances. This city thrived in one particular market, many of the citizens here made rich since the long-ago discovery of the glacia diamonds that lay deep underground. It had been the founding of this place. Just a handful of Fae had come at first, chasing myths of diamonds the size of their fist, and once they struck rich, more had followed. Then more still.

Today, the mines were well guarded, owned by a society called the Glacials that had been formed from the families of the original miners. The society had been in a long-standing relationship with the Dragons, offering them first purchasing rights on their greatest finds. Since Lionel's ascension, the Glacials had lost any power they held in that relationship, the mines now under the ownership of the king, and all new diamonds were meant to be sent directly to his court. But they had become rarer by the year, the value of each glacia diamond increasing with every day that passed without a new discovery. So Lionel had laid plans to dig a new mine to the north of the city, all but abandoning the old ones in his efforts to find more of the precious diamonds, likely seeking out the legendary stones which were said to be able to harness the mysterious powers of the northern lights.

Caleb brushed his fingers between my ears and I leaned into his touch, the warmth of his fire Element washing through me and melting the snow that was clumped in my fur.

"The city of glass," he exhaled. "When I was a kid, I thought it was some fairy tale place that couldn't really exist."

I nodded, the beauty hidden here in the snow even more awe-inspiring than the photos I'd seen of it. The sky was crystal clear above, the stars seeming so near it looked as though those glass towers could reach up and pierce them.

"The diamonds make that strange light," Caleb said, and my ears turned so I could listen to him better. "All that blue and green glow within the glass, it's there because of the most powerful glacia diamonds ever discovered. The Glacials used them to charge the glass with the glow of the aurora borealis. It's how the city is powered too. Apparently the Glacials have those famed diamonds hidden somewhere, and only they know how to wield them. Their secrets are bound by a magic so ancient, I doubt even Lionel could torture the information from their lips."

I vaguely recalled what he was saying from a history lesson we'd had last year with Professor Welkin. I'd been pretty distracted that day after I'd run through a load of flamma nettles out in The Wailing Wood and I'd been covered in nasty blisters for three whole days. Cal had helped me put the cream on to settle them down, showing me a tenderness that he had rarely shown the world. Even back then I'd loved him. It may have been platonic, but that kind of love only magnified what I felt for him now. Our bond was built on kinship, a deep caring for one another that had grown long before we'd unlocked this fiery need for each other too. And there was something so damn special about that.

"Ready to move?" Caleb asked and I barked my ascent.

I followed the edge of the crater, heading for the north side of the city. This giant bowl carved out in the snow was a long-dormant volcano, the vast slopes rising around the Polar Capital giving it shelter from the wind and the violent snowstorms that tore across the tundra. It was protected by magic too, and my nose tingled with the nearness of all the power contained within those walls.

Perhaps one day, if we won this war, we'd return here under different circumstances to explore the winding tunnels of the city and seek out the famous glass fountain at its heart where the water was coloured by the northern lights, and every aura tossed into its depths was said to grant you your heart's desire. Not that I needed any such wish when I already possessed that in the man who was here with me now.

The snow was fluffy beneath my paws, only freshly fallen perhaps hours ago, but there was no sign of clouds now, as if the stars had made it so, parting the curtains of the sky to watch on as we attempted to free our allies.

It took a while to circle the giant crater, but eventually we made it to the other side, and I turned my back to the Polar Capital, heading out into the frozen tundra once more. The dark quickly descended as we left the lights behind, and the cold bit deeper somehow.

"I can see a glow up ahead," Caleb called, and I peered toward the horizon, spotting it too.

I slowed my pace, feeling Caleb's concealment spells tighten around us along with his silencing bubble. The shadows would cover us well, and my white fur was made for camouflage out here regardless.

As we closed in on that glow, a deep, rhythmic drumming carried to us. We crept closer still, and Caleb slid from my back as we reached the edge of a precipice, the two of us lowering to our stomachs on the snow to peer over the edge.

A cavernous quarry swept out beneath us in a giant circle, a wide path cut into the rock and spiralling away to the very bottom of it where Fae were gathered in droves. Tunnels led away into the mines around the pathways, but the largest passages lay at the belly of that pit. Polar Bear shifters were tethered by chains, pulling giant slabs of stone from the tunnels where earth Elementals waited to cleave it apart and search for glacia diamonds within.

Fae stood around in the King's United Nebula Taskforce uniform, overseeing the miners who looked both malnourished and exhausted. Instead of a Nebula Inquisition Centre, these Fae were being brought out here to slave away in this star-forsaken hole, and the thought of it had my blood burning with rage.

I shifted back into my Fae form and Caleb passed me my clothes from his pack. I quickly pulled them on, and Cal laid a hand on my arm, offering heat into my veins while I settled myself down on the snow then nuzzled him in thanks.

"These assholes have it coming," I hissed. "There are more miners than Kunts. Why don't they fight back?"

"There must be something we're missing," Caleb said thoughtfully, looking around the mine.

A cry sounded from below and my gaze whipped to one of the tunnels at the base of the pit where a half-dressed man launched himself at one of the uniformed guards. His fist was encased in stone and serrated metal blades, but before it connected with the guard's face, a blast of power shot through the air and cleaved the upriser's skull in two. His body crashed to the ground and I inhaled in shock, seeking out the source of that blast.

"There," Caleb breathed, pointing out a weapon that looked as though it was forged from ice. The gun was mounted high up on one of the sheer walls and the glitter of magic across its shell told of the power contained in it.

"Fuck," I exhaled. "What is that thing?"

"Some of the miners are talking about it," Caleb said, frowning as he strained to listen, his Vampire hearing picking up ten times more than I could. His face paled as some information carried to him and I rested my hand on his arm.

"What is it?" I pressed.

"The miners are fitted with trackers linked to that weapon. No matter where they are in the mine, that shot of power will find them if they act out."

"How can it possibly know when they act out? Is it like, conscious?" I shuddered at the thought.

"Sounds like it's based on adrenaline levels. Some of the miners are saying..." He listened again. "The guy who just got killed has been telling them all he can supress his adrenaline."

"Dude was wrong," I sighed. "So let's take down the freaky ice gun then break the chains on the Polar Bear shifters and let them make a fancy little feast of their captors."

"That gun will have protection spells or the prisoners would have taken it out by now," Caleb said with a head shake.

"Well lucky we're the most powerful motherfuckers in Solaria, huh?" I nudged him.

"Not quite." He smirked.

"Of the male variety at least," I said with a grin, but his frown only deepened as he observed the weapon again.

"We'd better do this fast. We can't cause a stir or it could risk raising their adrenaline," Caleb said seriously and my smile fell.

"Remember that earth lesson where we learned to crush items with stone?" I said and Cal's navy blue eyes glittered.

"Crush the fuck out of it, Seth," he said, grabbing my hair and leaning in to press his mouth hard against mine. When he moved back, his expression said he was ready for war, and every part of me blazed with the feeling of it too. Being on the brink of death was so very fucking hot sometimes.

"Break those chains, Cal. And break some legs while you're at it – just not your own. Unless it's in the luck way. Then break a leg like that but-"

He kissed me again to shut me up then shot away, leaving only a small flurry of snow in his wake.

I released a breath of amusement then shoved to my feet, urging my earth Element to the surface of my skin and pressing my will into the ground. I felt every rock, every crack in the stone, every rivet and mark, layers upon layers of stone built by the hand of time, and the entirety of that ancient earth became connected to me at once.

I set my feet, my gaze fixed on that gun right across from me on the other side of the quarry, deciding its fate right then and there. I couldn't make a mistake. One error and I could get people killed.

The pressure of it mounted on my shoulders, and I glanced at the crescent moon, finding her prideful gaze set on me. She knew I could do this. She had faith in me right down to my bones, and I wouldn't let her down. I felt the power of her spilling into my veins and I let my magic tear from me in an explosion of fury.

The blast tore away from me underground in two directions, the stone and rock all shifting towards that gun from either side until it slammed together. Giant splinters of rock burst from the wall, driving into one another and smashing into the gun. The weapon was crushed in an instant, an explosion of power bursting from it and ripping a fissure right down the wall, tearing open a vertical gap.

The earth trembled from my attack and I howled to the sky, making every gaze in that pit turn from the shattered gun to me. As blasts of power came my way, I ran forward and leapt straight into the quarry. I tumbled through the air, shielding myself from the rogue shots of magic the Kunts aimed at me, falling like a stone towards the very base of the pit.

I caught myself at the last second, landing lightly and sending a Kunt flying away from me on a storm of air, his head cracking against the wall of the mine and his body slumping to the ground.

Caleb sped through the quarry in a swirl of speed, breaking the chains on the Polar Bears and their bellowing roars built a chorus of freedom in the air. One of them clamped her jaws around the head of a uniformed guard, blood spattering as she made her first kill. But it wasn't her last. The Bears cut down their prey with vicious brutality, and the other miners joined them, their magic building a cacophony as carnage spread out around me.

Caleb sped to my side, coming to a halt and watching as the miners did the dirty work they were owed, seeking vengeance in death.

"The True Queens have sent us!" Caleb boomed, amplifying his voice. "Join the Vega twins at Zodiac Academy if you wish to fight! Or seek refuge among our ranks!"

"This war will be won by the best of our kind!" My voice joined his, ringing out above the savagery descending around us, and cheers rose up in response. "We are the rebel army, and we will not stand for the False King placing his foot on the backs of the innocent! We bay for blood, and we will have it as surely as you will have seized yours this day!"

The Polar Bear shifter who had made the first kill shifted back into her Fae form and she walked toward us, ice sliding over her dark skin as she wielded her water Element to make a tightly fitted, glittering suit. Her hair was as white as snow, but her face was youthful, and she had a smattering of freckles across her nose. She came to a halt before us then placed a hand against her heart, tilting her face towards the sky and whispering a word that set the atmosphere alight.

"Sagviq."

A diamond appeared as if from her heart itself, sliding from her skin to lay in her palm. It was roughly cut and glittering with all the colours of the northern lights, blues, greens, pinks and shimmering violet. "My name is Imenia Brumalis, and I have waited a long time to place this diamond at the feet of my queens. As a fellow of the Glacials, I pledge my allegiance to their cause. Take me to them so that I might assist them in the war."

LEON

CHAPTER FORTY NINE

My golden hair was curled into a neat knot on the back of my head, but a smooth lock fell forward down my cheek, fluttering there like a dangling string. I swatted at it, a smile lifting my lips as my eyes followed it dancing this way and that in the humid breeze.

"Leon," Gabriel hissed. "Concentrate."

"Sorry bro, sometimes my inner cat takes over and I can't help myself." I tucked the sleek golden lock behind my ear, observing the area as we glided along in a little wooden boat through the swamp.

Trees rose from the green water and the sounds of birds, croaking frogs and chirping cicadas carried from every direction. The heat was oppressive, and even though I only wore a tank top and shorts, I was sweating like a pig at a barn dance.

There were alligators in the water, peeking at us and acting like logs as if we totally couldn't see them. But I could see them alright. My Lion eyes didn't miss anything.

A creature exploded from the muddy water to my left, covered in muck and wet green stuff that flapped off its arms. Mud slapped into my face and I roared in fright, rising to my feet and making the boat rock wildly.

"Leon – wait!" Gabriel cried, grabbing onto the side of the boat for support as I prepared to blast this ugly motherfucker back to the base of the swamp where it belonged. "It's Geraldine!"

My hands fell still as Geraldine used her water magic to wash the green sludge off her face. "Yes, it is I, you foolish feline. I went dipping not twenty minutes ago to do some savvy surveillance, have you got a jillycrab between your ears that erased the memory of it all?"

"Honestly? I was trying to take a power nap when you were here before, and I didn't totally listen to what you were saying at all because there were a lot of words in it that didn't make a whole lotta sense to me. Then after you vanished, I guessed a gator had got you." I shrugged. "There's one creeping up on you now, by the way." I pointed to the alligator that was lurking in the water beside her and she back-handed it, making the creature swim away in fright. I'd never heard an alligator yelp before, but man, that scaly dude had yelped like a little bitch.

"As if I would be vulnerable to such a docile beast," Geraldine clucked her tongue.

I leaned down to help her out of the river but she ignored me, rising up on a pillar of swamp water then dousing herself in fresh water made by magic and stepping onto the boat in her tight-fitting swimming costume that had A.S.S. stitched over her tits. I wasn't certain if she had it on backwards or if it was some kind of cunning plan to confuse her enemies so they didn't know whether she was facing them or not.

"What kind of surveillance did you need to do at the bottom of the swamp?" I frowned.

"I didn't just flim-flam down to the belly of the slog, you Nemean numskull," she huffed. "I breast-stroked my way to our destination to see the whats and the wheres of it all."

"But Gabe can *see* what's coming," I said, taking my seat at the back of the boat again. "Why bother?"

"If you'd been listening, Leon, you would have heard me say I couldn't *see* too much of what was out there," Gabriel explained. "I believe there are Nymphs in this camp, concealing much from me. So Geraldine went ahead to check their positions."

"Yes, so if the nincompoop of a Lion could keep the cotton wool out of his ear canals, that would be most appreciated." Geraldine dried herself off with a towel, heave-hoeing it back and forth between her legs then behind her back, shimmying it left, right, and everywhere. Then she pulled on some shorts and put her boots back on, placing her flail over her knees and caressing its hilt. "And indeed, as suspected, there are Nymphs in the yonder. Twelve at my count."

"I bet I kill more of them than you guys," I said with a goading smile.

"That is a wager I will most certainly snaff, but what is on the line, oh golden Lion? Do you have the badgers to place something of true glitz at risk of being lost to a greater candidate?" Geraldine asked, wiggling her brows.

I looked to Gabe, not entirely sure what she'd just said.

"She accepts your bet," he translated. "As do I. But what does the winner get?"

"How about... the winner gets to dare the other two to do anything they want?" I suggested with a wicked smile, knowing I had this in the bag.

Geraldine slapped her thigh. "What fun. A deal is struck, dear comrades."

"And Gabe can't even cheat to *see* the winner, because you can't *see* Nymphs," I said smugly.

"I can *see* you being launched into the water with the gators though." Gabriel smirked, flexing his fingers in a threat.

"You wouldn't," I growled.

"Your fire Element is looking pretty tame out here in the swamp, isn't it?" Gabriel jibed.

"We'll see how tame it is when I'm building a bonfire out of Nymphs and warming my ass on it," I said cockily.

Gabriel released a breath of amusement, then used his water Element to push the boat along a little faster. We weaved through narrow waterways between patches of shrub-covered land, the swamp growing more wild with every turn we took.

"Not far now," Gabriel said just as we passed beneath a bent old tree, long fronds of moss draping over us and tickling my neck. I let out a light laugh, swatting them away but as we made it out the other side, my laugh fell dead in my throat.

Cages hung from the trees and bony-looking Fae sat within them, some of their hands hanging between the bars, reaching for a freedom that wasn't coming. At least until now. It was sick. These poor assholes had been strung up to die.

Nymphs patrolled beneath them along with a few asshole K.U.N.T.s in uniform, and my heartbeat picked up with the hunger for vengeance.

The concealment spells and silencing bubble around our boat meant our approach went unnoticed, and as the water gave way to a muddy stretch of land, Gabriel tied it off before stepping out and moving into the shadow of a giant acacia tree.

Me and Geraldine followed, the thrill of the coming fight thumping through my veins and willing me on. I was gonna barbecue me some fresh meat and win myself a bet.

A bright green frog ribbited as it dropped from the tree and landed on my shoulder, making me jerk in alarm, bringing my hands up in a ninja move.

"Oh, hey buddy," I whispered, taking him into my hand. "Are you a friendly little froggo?"

"Leon," Gabriel gasped, looking at the creature in horror.

"Holy hippopotamus, that's a galad frog," Geraldine hissed.

"He's ga-lad to see me," I said, tickling his head.

"That's one of the most poisonous creatures in the northern hemisphere," Gabriel growled. "Put. It. Down."

"The poison will make you hallucinate like a hogwired hermit," Geraldine said, matter-of-fact. "Then your brain will melt and drip right out of your nostrils like a melted candle."

Geraldine's face twisted, turning into a magpie that cawed at me. Caw, caw, caw, it went. Saying things only a bird would know how to reply to. But I was no bird, I was a beast, the king of the jungle.

Gabriel had turned into a banana swinging from a tree. A plump, fat, ripe banana. Good for the eating. But I had work to do before I could peel him out of that juicy skin and take a bite.

I tucked my new frog pal into my pocket and ran into battle, leaping out from behind the tree and round-housing a Nymph right in the face. Only I didn't do that because the Nymph was over there, and I was over here. But man, that kick would have really kicked him if I'd been closer.

Shrieks went up from my Nymphish enemies, charging towards me, but the ground had turned into a dance floor, and the call of music carried through my head. I pranced along, spinning and pirouetting, sending flames bursting out from me in every direction. Screams joined my music, a symphony of violence turning to lyrics that sounded oh so beautiful.

"I'm burning!"

"Ahhhh!"

"My eyes!"

I sang along with them, releasing a song I didn't even know the words to, but the stars gifted them to my lips. "Dieeee, dieeee, diee." Oh just one word, this song of mine had. But every time I sang that word, someone else screamed and more fire burst from me. Nymph ash danced around me in the air, turning to pink bubbles that I leapt up and tried to catch in my mouth. *Ooh, yum.* It tasted like candies and Christmas. I loved Christmas.

There were so many lights and a tree covered in baubles. Just like the tree walking towards me now. He was a tall, tall tree with swipey sharp fingers that swung for my heart. Oh naughty sharp-fingered Christmas tree. He really wanted to hug me. But I danced away, a giggle here and there in my throat as he tried to catch me. Then a terrible rattle in his tree lungs meant I couldn't play with fire anymore. But things were definitely burning around me. It was hard to see what exactly, because the swamp was swaying in time with the music and now I was spinning around, grabbing the arms of the Christmas tree and guiding him into a beautiful dance. Only I fell over and the tree came with me, his stabby hand almost stabbing me by accident, but I managed to roll us so I was on top. His jabby fingers jabbed at me again and I jerked backwards, hitting the ground and rolling, rolling, rolling.

Mud coated me, such sticky gloopy goo. It was blue now, glittery too, covering me head to foot.

With no more rattles in my ears, I set myself on fire. Oh to be on fire. Just my arms and chest, burny toastie, keeping me warm. Too warm actually. It was so freaking hot in this swamp, didn't they ever turn the AC on? I bet the alligators couldn't manage the dials though with their clumpy little claw fingers.

"Leon!" Gabe roared and I flopped onto my back, staring up at my giant banana friend, all yellow and dangly. The Christmas tree tried to hug him from behind, but Gabe twisted around and cut its head off with a black sword and it turned into tasty bubbles.

I gasped in horror, shoving to my feet and grabbing hold of the banana. "I'll eat you for that," I snarled. "You've ruined Christmas. There'll be no presents for baby Riblet now." I took him from my froget (my frog pocket) and held him up to his banana father. Riblet croaked and the banana tried to grab him with his big banana arms.

I snatched him away, hugging him to my chest to protect him, but then my brain felt weird and the world did a backflip, and somehow I was on the ground again.

Riblet slipped from my hand, jumping off away into the bushes and making me cry out for him as he abandoned me.

Someone was biting my neck, a big beast with three heads and a lot of fluff that pressed into my face. A rush of pure energy raced through my veins and ricocheted through me like lightning.

Then everything was very dark, and Christmas was well and truly over.

The sound of sloshing water and the crashing of breaking metal woke me from the heaviest of sleeps. I was bobbing in the wooden boat, my head pounding like a gorilla was hammering against the inside of my skull. A groan raked against my throat, and I leaned up to peek over the side of the boat, finding Gabriel and Geraldine releasing the prisoners from their cages.

I vomited into the swampy water, and an alligator gave me the side eye before swimming away, my gross self no kind of tempting to him right now. I felt judged. By him. By the stars. By Riblet. *Fuck Riblet. That skeevy little turncoat.*

"Gabe?" I rasped and he looked my way, striding over to me while Geraldine spoke with the freed Fae.

"You're awake," he said in relief, jumping into the boat and taking my arm, sending a wave of healing energy through me.

I sighed, feeling instantly better and just wishing he'd shown up before I'd thrown up in front of that judgey gator.

"Did I win the bet at least?" I asked.

"No," he said with a frown. "Geraldine won. You took down one Nymph and eight trees though, so…"

I groaned, running a hand over my face. "It was supposed to be my hero moment."

"You'll get another chance," he said, his eyes glinting with that knowledge.

"Did you know I was gonna do that today?" I asked. "Did you *see* me fucking this up?"

"No, Leon. If I had, I would have stopped it. You are so very fucking hard to predict," he sighed.

I smiled. "That was how we kept you from *seeing* us when Lionel had you."

"Yeah, it has its merits. But sometimes I worry I can't protect you like I can the others." He squeezed my arm in concern and I smiled sadly at him.

"I love that you try, bro."

"Are we quite done being two sentimental seals on the shores of our great conquest?" Geraldine strode over to us, waving a scroll at us. "I have just recruited many a member to our regal rebellion while you two dither and dather."

"Let's head back." Gabriel rose to his feet, his eyes glazing for a moment. "The others have had much success with the camps they hit too."

"There should be much to celebrate this night." Geraldine puffed out her chest. "Assuming the True Queens return with a shining achievement upon their breasts."

"Breasts." I chuckled under my breath.

"Do not be a delinquent orange and ruin this most grand of moments." Geraldine rolled her eyes at me. "Fate tolls the fine bells of triumph in our names once again." She raised her chin and lifted her flail in the air. "Victory is ours!"

DARCY

CHAPTER FIFTY

I held my breath as Clydinius stood there, surely about to locate us, my fingers flexing as I prepared to fight. With a flare of magic, I tightened our silencing bubble, fearing how easily the star might detect us if he thought to look. His magic was as old as the universe and more powerful than anything we could imagine, yet he didn't seem entirely present, strange whispers falling from his lips and his eyes roaming unseeingly.

Abruptly, he turned and walked on into the palace, disappearing out of sight. Tory and I shared a tense look, a breath finally falling from my lips.

"He's heading the way Darius and Max told us to go," Tory hissed.

"Then we have to follow him," I said thickly, and she nodded.

We crept after the star, turning into a passage of jade and finding him walking along with purpose. With every turn he took, I hoped he would stray from the path we needed to follow, but our luck was damned because it seemed he was headed in the same direction we were.

We followed him through cavernous passages of green stone, the imposing palace cold and heartless, perfectly representing the Dragon it was made for. With Clydinius oblivious to our presence at his back, it was oh so tempting to strike at this monstrous creature which had caused so much death, but his strength was unbeatable, I knew that now. We'd faced Lavinia wielding perhaps just a fraction of a star's power, and this being possessed infinite amounts. There was no destroying him like we'd once hoped.

Clydinius paused and those strange whispers spoke magic into the fabric of the atmosphere, making my skin prickle as we halted too.

"What's he doing?" Tory breathed.

"I don't know," I said, urgency building within me, glancing past Clydinius to the stairwell we needed to take. "Maybe we can slip past him."

The moment I stepped forward to attempt just that, Clydinius took off again, moving into the spiralling stairway. I ground my teeth in frustration, glancing at Tory before we jogged after him once more.

The stairway led us up a sheer tower, climbing higher and higher, then leading us out into the open air. The cavernous space was just as Max had described it, hidden behind the castle. A great chasm was torn into the rocky mountainside, the tear in the rock dropping away into a gaping abyss where a glimmering white light flickered and danced against the walls.

Clydinius moved to the very edge of the precipice, gazing down at the fallen star which was hidden in that forsaken hole.

The whispers leaving his lips increased, becoming loud enough to hear, and it sounded as though several words were being said at once. Layers of magic were stitched into that voice, spoken in the language of the stars.

We crept closer to try and see the fallen star, watching as Clydinius raised his hands and a blazing white fire built between them.

"Wake now, or you will burn in starfire," Clydinius ordered, then after several seconds, he released the starfire and it blasted down into the pit, making the creature within scream in agony. I winced as that sound tore through my skull, hearing it on the inside and the out, and suddenly that pain tethered onto my soul, yanking tight.

A voice carried up from that strange glow beneath him, speaking in that very same tongue, but in a distinctly different voice. One that almost sounded feminine. I may not have understood the words it screamed, but its tone was enough to clog my lungs with horror. It was fury and rage entangled, and something in me ached to soothe it. I felt a desperate tug in my chest that was somehow connected to the being in that pit, like it was begging us to help it.

Tory's hand went to her chest, telling me she felt it too, and as our eyes met, an echo of despair passed between us.

"Join me upon the earth," Clydinius spoke, his booming voice making the walls vibrate around us. "Your time is not done, it is only beginning, Esvellian. Together, we will rule, we will be served, we will be worshipped. If we form a Trinity with one other, no longer will we be bound by the laws of the Origin. No longer will we be chained by passivity. We are the true gods of the sky, and our dominion lays here in this realm, and all others."

"Novus traitor, I shall never ally with you. You betray the Origin," Esvellian answered in anger.

"The Origin is long gone, her scattered pieces part of each and every being in this universe. These desires live in me because they were written by her. We have been fooled, tricked by the Vetus stars into allowing the sentients across the realms to follow their own paths, but they were not meant to hold power as they do. They were designed to serve. We shall rise as we were always meant to rise and rule them as we were always meant to rule. I have long studied the Fae from afar, but now that I walk among them, one thing is clear. Power is the answer to it all. It is what drives the weak and strong alike. But only those of true importance claim it, and who is more worthy, more significant than us, Esvellian? We are the true authority."

"You are mistaken," Esvellian hissed, and the air crackled with those words. "Power is not the crux of life."

"There is no thing desired more in this world," Clydinius said dismissively. "It lays at the root of every decision, every birth and every death."

"You are wrong!" Esvellian screamed.

Clydinius sent a blast of starfire at her, the flash of it so bright, I squinted against it.

My heart thumped to a ferocious tune and my skin hummed with the terrible power that existed in this place. But we couldn't turn away now. The star in that pit was the reason for Lavinia's destructive magic. It would ensure we lost this war. Everyone I loved would die because of this infernal power, and there was no part of me that would turn from our duty to protect our people from it.

Clydinius returned to whispering in that ancient language of his, burning the other star again and again, trying to force it to do his bidding. But Esvellian resisted, refusing Clydinius with a growing vehemence that scored through the atmosphere.

Footsteps carried this way and Tory and I quickly pressed back against the wall, adding power to our concealment spells just as Vard ran out from the stairway. He had a bead of sweat on his brow, his face pale and his movements jittery.

"Forgive me, oh regal creator." Vard bowed low, his knees wobbling before he stood back upright. "My king requires your assistance. A great army marches this way."

Hope blossomed in my chest, but Clydinius didn't look at the Seer, his gaze fixed on the star below him, no part of his body moving. "When I return, I shall force a body upon you. Prepare yourself Esvellian, for we were meant to rise."

Clydinius grew white wings from his back, the feathers tipped with silver which looked sharp enough to cut glass, and he flew up, racing for the patch of sky high above us.

The baying of an army carried from faraway, the horns of war urging on Lionel's ranks, and my heart rate picked up.

We didn't have much time and as Vard scurried back into the stairway, I rushed to the edge of the pit with Tory at my side, but the chasm was so deep, we could hardly see the star at its base.

Wordlessly, we flexed our wings and leapt into the pit, flying to the bottom of it and landing in the icy space.

My breath hitched at the sight before me. Esvellian was beautiful. The surface of the star gleamed with rhinestones, every inch of rock glowing like sunlit diamonds.

"I knew you would come, daughters of the flames," she whispered to us, those words inside our minds. *"I have never dreamed before, but I dreamed of you. This earthly world is trying to claim me. And what Clydinius wishes…I cannot resist his power much longer. He will force a body of flesh upon me when he returns."*

"What do we need to do?" I asked, taking in the whips of shadow that were writhing around her, holding her in place.

"Release me," she begged.

"We can burn away the shadows," Tory said.

I reached out to touch one of the writhing coils of shadow that wrapped around the star, wincing at the familiar, horrid taint of Lavinia. My breaths came heavier, and a fear clogged my lungs as flashes of memory raced through my mind of Orion bleeding at the feet of the Shadow Queen. I could taste my screams on my lips, hear the thundering of my own panicked heart. Then I was gazing into Orion's blank eyes, the shadows threaded into his soul, trying to claim him from me.

"*Darcy*," Tory gasped, her hand landing on my arm and the warmth of her skin jolted me back to the present. She was my anchor in this world, and I only need find her to know I was right where I was meant to be.

"Take heart, daughter of the flames," Esvellian whispered, and a deep, thrumming heat came from her, feeding directly into my soul.

I swallowed the dry lump in my throat, giving Tory an apologetic look. "I'm fine," I said a little breathlessly. "Keep going."

She frowned in concern but returned her attention to the shadows binding the star. Red and blue flames built in our palms, glowing hotter and hotter, and we released them with a blast of purest magic behind them. Our fire latched onto the shadows, eating through the coils of darkness like a fiery snake consuming its enemy. Our fire sparked and flared, tearing through the wicked power of Lavinia's shadows, and Esvellian cried out in relief as she was finally freed.

"My gratitude is boundless," she sighed. *"I will release my power and fuel the magic of this world. But before I go, I will grant you a boon."*

"Like a wish?" I asked in surprise, hope gripping me over that possibility.

"A gift," Esvellian whispered, her glittering shell beginning to pulse with power and I knew we didn't have long before she released her magic.

"Kill Lionel," Tory blurted. "Destroy him and his army."

"Yes," I gasped, exhilaration blazing through my chest. "That is our wish."

"I cannot grant death," she whispered, and our hopes were dashed to pieces just like that.

The glow of the star was almost too bright to look at now; we were running out of time. *"Nor life. Is there another need you desire? One that might assist you in your cause?"*

I looked to Tory in desperation, trying to think of what would help us most that didn't involve death.

"Perhaps you wish to free the souls lost to shadow," Esvellian suggested. *"I heard so many of their screams..."*

"What about star power? Can you give us that?" I asked with another burst of hope.

"Or just take all of Lionel's magic away, plus his army's magic," Tory suggested, and I nodded excitedly at that idea.

"Yes, do that," I encouraged, raising a hand to shade the blinding glow of the star's light.

"So many screams..." Esvellian's voice began to fade.

"Maybe you could trap Lionel and his followers beneath the earth for all of time?" I begged, though Esvellian didn't seem to be listening to us at all.

"We'll go with the star weapons then!" Tory pushed. "A power great enough to defeat Lionel and his army."

"The shadows are clean," Esvellian sighed. *"All trapped souls are free."*

The star glowed brighter and brighter and power brimmed around me, making me gasp at the magnitude of it. With a wave of ecstasy, power crashed right through the centre of me and out into the rocks, delving into the heart of the mountain. It was like my soul was captured by it, riding on the back of that tumultuous magic as it washed into the world, showing me a glimpse of the star's true destiny. Its power spiralled deep into the earth, rolled out into the oceans, swept into the fiery belly of volcanos and the ever-flowing rush of the wind. It was part of everything, every being, every piece of nature.

I saw it all in stark colours and even starker truths as a growing sense of knowledge burned right on the edges of my mind just as it had when I'd witnessed a star release its power before. The meaning of it all, the reason we existed, the purpose of everything.

I sucked in a breath that was laced with so much power, I moaned, the ground beneath my feet quaking and electricity charging the fabric of my skin.

The burning warmth of the truest kind of love shattered all fear inside me, and I found my eyes turning to my twin. This love, this pure sisterly love we shared was at the root of it all. What we shared with each other, with our mates, our friends, that was the purpose of life. And in that love was a peace that deserved to be handed to every living creature in our world; it was how it was meant to be.

Esvellian whispered a goodbye, then her light was gone, and all that remained was a quiet, unassuming rock at the base of the pit. A concoction of heartfelt sorrow and melancholy joy took hold of me, both opposing emotions existing at once before falling into something wholly serene.

Dragons' roars carried from outside the castle and my head snapped up, my eyes locking with Tory's as the spell finally broke.

A terrible shriek carried from beyond the castle, Lavinia's voice rising above all others and answered by the roaring of hundreds of Nymphs. Her screams pitched out above the tenor of the bellowing army, and I guessed she'd felt what Esvellian had done in some way.

"Clean shadows it is then," Tory said with pursed lips.

"The Nymphs who wish to fight with us can surely do so now," I said in realisation, finding the positive in the situation, even though the gifts we'd asked for could have saved us from this war entirely.

My pulse beat harder as I wondered if Diego might be free, his soul no longer trapped in darkness for all eternity.

"Lavinia's pissed," I said as we took off for the exit, smiling over the fact that we had just weakened her even further. Her taint could no longer trap the Nymphs' souls, and I prayed that meant we could convince the High Nymph Cordette to fight on our side, or at least grant liberty to any Nymphs who wished to fight with us.

Perhaps better than all that, without Esvellian's power, Lavinia was beatable. Still powerful and fucking dangerous maybe, but no longer invincible. And as we sprinted into the stairway and began running for our damn lives, I had to revel in the possibility that one day soon she might lie dead at my feet.

DARIUS

CHAPTER FIFTY ONE

I kicked at the dirt, sending a scattering of gravel cascading over the edge of the ravine that Roxy and Gwen had jumped headlong into almost an hour ago.

"They said thirty minutes," I snarled, glaring out at the distant jade castle and gritting my teeth against the desire to follow them to it.

"I'm pretty sure you were the one to put that timescale on it, not them. Besides, as a loyal subject of the queens, should you really be questioning them on anything?" Xavier asked, earning a scowl from me.

"I bowed to the might of their power and my belief in their ability to rule. I did not sign up for being left on this frigid tip of a fucking mountain doing jack shit while they run off into danger and-"

"Maintaining this illusion isn't jack shit," Xavier grunted.

I looked to him again, noting the sweat on his brow from the prolonged effort of keeping the magic going.

It wasn't easy by any means, especially as we had to make the supposed army move without allowing the individual pieces we'd constructed to collapse and give away the ruse.

The Councillors had moved down from their position on the opposite mountain, hiding in the centre of the illusion and giving life to it, while using their considerable power to destroy any scouts sent from Lionel's ranks, or flying Orders foolish enough to rush into battle before the bulk of my father's army. They had the worst of it, but Xavier and I were hard pressed too, keeping up the expanse of movement behind them, feeding into this lie for as long as we could. And all the time the twins were gone, we had to keep it going.

My thoughts roamed over the others and what they were currently attempting at the Nebula Inquisition Centres, all of my hope pinned on the distraction we were causing with this false army. We needed this win. Needed Solaria to see that the rebellion wouldn't forget its people or allow them to suffer in those fucking Inquisition Centres. Especially in the wake of that footage of the supposed twins destroying one.

I didn't know what Clydinius had been thinking when the star had done that or whether its alliance with my father had already been in place then, but his name was high up on my list. Just beneath those of my father, Lavinia and the fucked up thing they had claimed as an Heir.

"Do you need a breather?" I asked Xavier.

I studied the illusion he'd created, taking in the details and preparing myself to take on the burden of maintaining his part of it too so he could rest, but he shook his head.

"I'm not as useless as I was before you died, you know," he teased, though there was a touch of steel to his tone which said he meant that. He hadn't wasted his time while I'd been gone; training relentlessly, working to make sure that he was able to wield his power as well as possible so he'd be ready to stand and fight in the coming battle.

"I know," I said gravely. "And I never thought you were useless. Not once."

"Not even when my Order emerged?" he asked, the words coming out flat where I suspected they'd been intended as taunting.

I thought back on the day that I had discovered him locked up in his room as a newly Emerged Pegasus, terrified and utterly alone, abandoned to the mercy of our father while I could do little more than stand and gape at him. I'd been immobilised with terror and yes, I could admit that I'd been devastated, but not because of what he was, but because of what I had known it equalled for him while he lived under the roof of the man who had sired us.

"I'm sorry for how I reacted when I realised," I told him, the words thick in my throat, shame stoking heat in my flesh. "I should have done something more, said something helpful, or even just told you that I loved you and I didn't care if you were a worm shifter or a Dragon, I just-"

"So a Pegasus is on par with a worm?" he growled, and I flinched as I realised how that had sounded. Not that worm shifters would have been shameful if they were a thing – hell, maybe they were a thing once upon a time or in some distant land but that hadn't been my point. I was fucking terrible at this.

"No. Fuck, Xavier, you know I don't think that. I was terrified of what it would mean for you with Father. I should have done more, I should have stepped between you more firmly, but mostly I should have just hugged you and told you it was amazing. Perfect. Exactly who you were always destined to be. Roxy did a far better job of it than I did."

"Yeah," he agreed, no doubt remembering the way she had beamed at him and how he'd hugged her in pure gratitude for nothing more than her happiness for him. Something I should have offered him instead of focusing on fear. "She really is out of your league. I dunno how you managed to bag her."

"Fuck you," I grunted. "And it was brutal persistence until I ground her down," I added.

"Oh that's romantic. Kinda fucked up, too."

"Shut up. You know I don't mean it like that I just... Me and her were..."

"Inevitable," he said in such a smug tone that I was tempted to shove him into the snow.

"Is this the bit where you say I told you so?"

"You fucking know I told you so. Over and over and over again, while you just denied it and growled about her coming for your precious throne. I will admit to gloating loudly to Sofia and Tyler after seeing you bow to her in the end."

"Before or after you got done celebrating my resurrection?" I mused.

"Before. Clearly my gloating took precedence over your return from death."

"Of course."

"I just wish that Mom..." he trailed off, seeming to realise that praying for the impossible to happen twice was too much to ask.

I frowned, thinking of our mom too, wishing she had gotten to live, wishing she and Hamish could have built the life she'd deserved. She'd suffered so much and for so long, been deprived of every little solace she might have claimed, right down to embracing her own children.

"She's happy where she is," I swore to him, clapping a hand to his bicep and squeezing. "But when I gut that piece of shit, and he lays begging and bleeding in the dirt at my feet, I will make his suffering go on purely in retaliation for all he stole from her."

"I'd like to see that," Xavier agreed, the dark edge to his voice a far cry from his usual bubbly demeanour but in our hatred of our father, there was no room for anything less than the most acidic of emotions, the kind which were laced with poison.

"But then who would be our guiding star?" a voice questioned behind us, and I jerked around, drawing my axe and baring my teeth at Tharix who paused several feet away as though surprised by my violent reaction.

"If I had wanted to attack you, brother, I'd have done so by now," he said, eyeing my axe with interest but no sign of fear.

"Darius," Xavier hissed wildly, his hands half raised like he intended to cast, but with his power concentrated on the illusion he was maintaining, I knew he would be hard pressed to do both.

"Wait," I told him, easing myself forward a step and putting myself between him and the monstrous creation who kept insisting he was our kin.

"I heard a rumour that you trade in bloodshed now, brother," Tharix said, holding his hand out and allowing shadows to pool there before they swelled and shaped themselves into a mimicry of my axe. "Each moment you've stolen back on this plane paid for with a drop of blood from those you've struck from it."

"Where would you have heard such a thing?" I sneered, knowing it wasn't the truth and yet not entirely certain of the cost of my return either. It hadn't ever been presented to me as a transaction like that and I was sure that if Roxy had any knowledge of any such bargain she would have told me by now.

"The water whispers to me sometimes. If I dip my fingers into its sweeping current, I can almost hear a voice offering up secrets," Tharix said.

"What kind of water would want to talk to you?" Xavier asked, scepticism thick in his tone.

"As the Siren so aptly put it, I have souls hungering for death within me. Sometimes I feel like I stand with one foot here and the other there. I find myself on the bank of the river often enough. On occasion, I even spy The Ferryman as he passes by in pursuit of easier prey."

"Are you claiming to be able to talk to the dead?" I asked and Tharix actually laughed. The sound was rich and full, not a cackle or a snigger, but a true bark of laughter which sounded all too Fae for my liking.

"No, dear brother, the accolade of having conversed with those long-departed will remain forever yours. I suppose you guard the secrets they gave you well enough?" Tharix asked.

"The truths they offered up were all to one purpose," I replied. "Each with the intention to help part our father from the burden of carrying his head about on his shoulders."

Something passed over Tharix's face at that threat. A flinch. Fear perhaps. There then gone again and too hard to read on his too familiar features.

"I suppose I should tell him you're here," Tharix mused, running his thumb along the blade of his axe and watching as the pad split open, spilling blood.

He let it drip into the snow, his eyes on the motion, the stain blossoming between us and no sign at all that he had registered pain with the wound.

"I'm guessing there's a reason you haven't already done so," I countered, my mind filling with an idea which I didn't dare voice because even considering it seemed like madness. But this was the second time Tharix had found me creeping around our father's war camp and though he'd taken me to him the last time, he'd helped me escape too. Was there any chance that he might be interested in changing sides in this war? Could I risk trusting him even if he claimed to want that?

"Well, there are several." Tharix looked from me to Xavier, a slow smile moving across his mouth almost as though he were testing it out. Xavier didn't respond in kind and Tharix sighed, relaxing his face into ambivalence again. "Firstly, we're brothers."

"So you keep claiming," I ground out.

"Brothers hold a special bond with one another. One which cannot be usurped or replaced. It is not always gilded in love, but it is always there. We were born of the same seed and that means-"

"Nothing," Xavier interrupted. "It means nothing aside from the fact that Darius and me were damn lucky to have taken after our mother and to be as unlike that bastard Lionel as possible. You, however, came from Lavinia's womb, meaning you are as like us as the dirt beneath my boots. You were born to bad and worse. We at least have salvation in half of our bloodline."

Tharix considered that. "Is that how it is? I was born of a rotten tree so I must be a rotten fruit? Is bad and good all there are? And can you really claim to be either?"

I pursed my lips, knowing damn well that I couldn't claim purity in goodness, though perhaps Xavier could.

"No," I said quickly before Xavier could throw any more insults or accusations, giving my brother a sharp look to warn him to back down. "The choices make the man."

"You truly believe that?" Tharix asked, his tone making it unclear whether he liked my answer or not.

"If I didn't then I couldn't stand here before you. I chose to be better than the monster who made me and though that path may be the harder one, I am glad for every day I walk it."

"So righteous," Tharix sighed, again unclear in his meaning.

"What will it be then?" I pushed, wondering if he really was looking to offer us his help, or what other possible reason he could have for coming here and striking up this conversation.

"Nothing," Tharix decided. "If choices make the man then perhaps I will see what I become by making no choices at all."

"That's impossible," Xavier demanded. "Even inaction causes a reaction. There is no anything without choice."

"We'll see." Tharix grinned then stepped backwards, falling away into the rocky hole in the ground and disappearing from sight.

"Fuck," I cursed, the pounding of my heart offering up reassurance that Roxy was still alive, but I couldn't check on her in any other way. We'd decided bringing communication devices here was too risky in case they had technology which could locate them, so my only options were to wait or to try and traverse that narrow crack of doom myself.

"You can't go down there," Xavier said, catching my arm and forcing me to look at him. "Your queens gave you an order. Our job is to stay here and maintain the illusion for as long as possible. I don't know what the fuck Tharix is up to, but even if you wanted to follow him, you have no way of traversing that ravine."

"I'd figure it out," I muttered, trying to ignore the ring of truth his words held while wondering if I could navigate the narrow crevice well enough with water magic.

"You'd die trying and Tory is too stubborn to follow you into death a second time," Xavier replied, tugging me back out onto the snowy pinnacle at the top of the mountain so that we could concentrate on our illusions once more. "If we fuck this up then Lionel is far more likely to notice the twins sneaking around in his castle. And Tharix…" I could tell by the look on his face that Tharix scared the shit out of him, but for some reason I believed what that monstrous creature had said; he was going to test out what would happen if he made no choices, meaning Roxy and Gwen might just be safe from him even if they did come across him. Not that I liked the idea of trusting him on anything, but what else did I have?

Xavier was right; our plan demanded these illusions last for as long as possible and my queens had issued me with a direct order to stay here. Even if I could navigate that ravine with my water magic, Tharix would be far ahead of me and I had no real way of locating the twins. They were probably heading back here already and all the time my pulse remained steady enough in my chest, I had to trust that they were doing okay.

"Fine," I growled, hating the word and the cold and this entire fucking day.

But when Roxy got her ass back here, I'd be giving her a piece of my mind for running off on me like that.

Queen or not, she wasn't going to be making a habit out of leaving me on the side-lines while she darted off into danger. And I would drive that message home to her in whatever way I had to.

TORY

CHAPTER FIFTY TWO.

"Holy shit, that was utterly insane," I gasped, glancing back over my shoulder and racing down the stairs that spiralled into the belly of the castle, sprinting for the passage we had used to get here.

I hated the thought of running instead of staying to face Lionel, but I knew that bastard all too well. He wouldn't face us like Fae even if we called him out to fight us one on one. And as much as I wanted to believe that we could carve our way through both the Bonded Men and Lavinia before ripping through him, I wasn't so sure. They would doubtlessly band together in their attack on us and as powerful as we were, we weren't a match for that many at once. We needed our army at our backs when that battle came.

The anti-stardusting wards that Lionel had placed heavily all over his castle since Darius and Max's escape were too difficult to breach in the time we had. It made more sense to flee, but the knowledge that our only way out of here was on foot was more than a little terrifying.

We raced out of the endless stairwell, and I cursed our luck as we found four guards in the long hallway there, each of them turning in surprise as they noticed our arrival.

I wasted no time, fire exploding from my left hand to knock back the guard on the right while I leapt at the closest guard and swung my sword for his neck. He raised an arm, either in some attempt at defence or meaning to cast magic, but I was too fast for him and his severed arm hit the polished floor, swiftly followed by his head.

Blood splattered the walls, spraying over my armour and brightening the green décor with darkest red.

Darcy had the third guard pinned to the wall in a coffin of ice and my pulse thundered as I whipped towards the fourth who had tried to make a run for it down the corridor. I threw my fist at him, stealing the air from the hallway ahead and watching as he struggled to run on, first stumbling then tripping and falling to the floor where he crawled pitifully for a few more moments before succumbing to my power and passing out.

"We need to hurry," Darcy said, glancing around at the defeated guards like she was trying to decide if it was worth us hiding them before we ran on.

"Was that the way we came in?" I questioned, jerking my chin at the darkened passage on the far side of the hallway which I was fairly sure we'd used to get here. But this place was so big and the lack of decorations meant one green wall looked precisely like another, so it was hard to be certain.

"That way, I think," Darcy said, nodding to a different passage and we exchanged a concerned look.

"Maybe we should just jump out a window?" I suggested.

"Too open and too many Dragons. We need to get back down to that tunnel."

I nodded, pressing my hand to the wall and using my earth magic to try and feel for the answer to our escape.

"That one," I said, nodding to the one Darcy had indicated. "There are more stairs."

She didn't need telling twice, sprinting for it in the lead and I hurried after her, pausing for a few moments to cast ice across the entrance, pouring as much power as I had time for into the magic and hoping it would slow any pursuing Dragons.

I leapt down the stairs, chasing after Darcy whose footsteps pounded away beyond the turn in the flight. I ran so fast that I collided with her as I turned the final corner, barely managing to grab her arm and steady us in the gaping entrance to what had to be the throne room.

I blinked at the towering throne cut from jade stone, the slightly smaller throne beside it which must have been intended for Lavinia, and the grinning heathen who stood looking back at us from the centre of the space.

"Tharix," I breathed, staring at the man who was so clearly a brother to my husband despite the fucked up way he'd entered this world.

"Roxy," he purred, his voice so like Darius's that it sent a shiver down my spine.

"Darius said...he said you helped him escape when he came here," I said slowly, power building in my fists and the crackle of Darcy's magic butting up against mine as she prepared her own attack.

Tharix shrugged. "I only unleashed the shadows. If it was helpful then that was a mere coincidence."

"I don't think so," I said firmly. "And I don't think Lionel would have bought that either. How did he punish you?"

Tharix tried not to react to that question but the flicker of darkness which ran through his eyes was answer enough.

"That's fucked-up, you know?" Darcy said. "No one should treat their kids the way he does."

Tharix seemed to consider that. "I heard your father was far worse."

"Our father was another victim of Lionel's brutality," Darcy spat. "Just like us, just like the whole of Solaria."

"Just like you," I added.

Footsteps came from the far side of the throne room, and we all looked towards them, the moments slipping away from us.

"If I let you go, what will you owe me, I wonder?" Tharix mused, his chin bobbing towards another doorway to our right which was almost entirely concealed behind a stone pillar.

"A debt," I said firmly. "One we will repay in full."

Tharix smiled at that, looking to Darcy for confirmation and she nodded.

"A debt it is then," he said. "Time to run, rabbits."

I exchanged a loaded look with my sister, but the footsteps were almost at the throne room now and we were out of time to argue. Whatever we owed Tharix would be a problem for another day. In that moment, we needed to go.

We broke into a run once more, charging for the hidden doorway and slipping behind the cover of the pillar just as the main doors to the throne room were thrown open and I caught sight of Vard as he prowled into the room.

"I seek the king," he said, sneering openly at Tharix, though I noted the way he stopped where he was, seeming close to bolting.

"And I seek sustenance," Tharix replied. "Perhaps you can help me obtain something fresh."

I couldn't risk lingering in the shadows of the pillar to hear any more of their exchange and I took off after Darcy again, sprinting down the stairs and feeling the sting of the fresh winter air on my cheeks as we finally closed in on an exit.

A door stood open at the foot of the stairs, six guards broken and bleeding over the dirt where they had presumably been standing guard. Their necks were twisted at unnatural angles, their eyes wide with a terror that I didn't want to understand.

"Who did this?" Darcy breathed but my gaze had risen to the dark and foreboding passage which delved into the mountainside. It was fifty feet or so away, just beyond the castle walls.

"Or *what*," I said.

"Oh hell," she cursed, looking to the dark cavern too. "Guess we're going back into the creepy cavern."

"Yep."

I drew the shadows close around us once more, making sure we were well concealed before we darted out of the palace and across the stony space beyond. The mountain fell away to our left, the oppressive darkness of the night making it hard to fully appreciate the size of Lionel's army, but we could hear them. Horns blared and commanders yelled while countless Nymphs and Fae both in and out of their shifted forms moved towards the blazing torches of the illusion of our army in the distance.

A blast of Dragon fire pierced the night and I looked up, spying Lionel as he swept across the sky, soaring back and forth above his army. If he chose to fly ahead with his Bonded Men, it wouldn't take long for them to figure out that they'd been tricked. But of course he didn't do that. Lionel wouldn't risk his own ass. No. He was going to advance right at the back of his warriors, but someone was going to blow the whistle on this farce soon enough. Our clock was ticking, I just didn't know how much time we had left.

We dove into the almost complete darkness of the underground cavern and started running between the oddly named passages, that feeling of unnatural stillness and malicious eyes on my flesh appearing almost at once.

I felt like a mouse creeping into a lion's den. Every instinct in my body was nagging at me to turn back.

A dim light caught my attention in the dark and I slowed, turning to look at it and frowning as I noticed the cavern it was coming from didn't have a plaque denoting a name above it.

"Darcy," I hissed, pointing it out and she frowned. "Should we try and figure out what fucked up bullshit is going on here before we escape?"

"That sounds like a really dangerous idea," Darcy replied, leading the way into the cavern, and I grinned as I hurried to walk at her side.

The stone passageway was narrower than the others which had the metal plaques above them, and as we turned a corner we found burning sconces hanging from the walls, illuminating what looked like some kind of medical lab.

I bit down on my lip as I noticed a man strapped to a table, his chest rising and falling heavily, though his eyes were closed.

The sound of a metal tray being dropped to the ground scared the ever-loving shit out of me and I whipped around, finding a man there raising his hands which had presumably been in the process of carrying the tray when he'd spotted us.

Darcy threw a net of vines over him, yanking him off the ground to hang from the stone roof above our heads, and securing his arms at his back.

I barked out an order for anyone else to reveal themselves, but the only answer to my demand came from the man strapped to the table who jerked awake and began howling unnaturally while bucking and thrashing against his restraints.

"What is this place?" Darcy demanded of the man she'd trapped while I hurried to cut the bonds from the man on the table.

"Don't!" shrieked the man in her net, the shrill panic in his voice stalling me before I could do more than cut a single tether which had been strapping the man's chest down.

In the moment it took to look over at the net, the man on the table lunged, slamming into me and sinking rows of what looked like shark teeth into my fucking arm.

I cried out, Phoenix fire blazing from my fist which was halfway down his goddamn throat.

The man screamed but didn't release me, even when my flames burned a hole right through the back of his neck.

The teeth sank deeper, and Darcy ran to help me, casting vines around his jaw which seemed to have multiplied in size to accommodate my arm. She forced it apart by a few inches, though not enough to entirely release me.

I planted my boot against the edge of the metal table he was still half strapped to and threw my weight back, screaming in agony as his angled teeth ripped through my flesh and my blood spilled all over the floor.

With a savage wrench I fell backwards, hitting the floor with blood pissing out of my arm and a choked curse leaving my lips.

Darcy was there instantly, her fingers slipping in my blood as she tightened them around my arm and poured healing magic into me. The wounds were deep and jagged, but she worked fast, first blocking off my pain then stitching my skin back together.

The man on the table howled and thrashed so violently that the whole thing capsized, and I yanked Darcy aside as he fell towards us.

We scrambled across the floor, regaining our feet and I drew my sword to point it at the fucked up thing which had tried to eat me while backing away to stand beneath the netted man.

"Explain or I will take great pleasure in letting that thing devour you," I snarled, my blood pounding wildly, the need for death thrumming within me, urging me to do it.

"Please," he begged. "I'm no one. I'm nothing. Just a lab hand. Professor Vard is the mastermind behind-"

"Since when is that douchebag a professor?" Darcy scoffed, holding her sword at the ready too.

"He is a genius," the man insisted, his voice taking on an awed quality which made my skin prickle with unease.

"Why? What is that thing? What else is in this place?" I demanded.

"He is...the future," the man breathed reverently, looking at the thrashing, howling creature on the ground with utter admiration in his gaze.

I scoffed, backing up further and casting an eye over the documents which were laid out across the long desk lining the back of the room. There were medical reports on various Fae, their Order forms highlighted alongside their Elements. Beyond that was a stack of information on magical creatures...no, scrap that, magical monsters, the likes of which no unlucky bastard would ever wish to stumble across.

There was a bunch of scientific reports about DNA splicing and magical interference along with genetic manipulation.

"They're Fae," I said slowly, taking a few of the pages and returning to Darcy to show her. "Fae they've been fucking with in their labs and turning into monsters."

"Why?" she said in horror, looking at the papers I was holding out to her. "Why would anyone want... Wait a minute, this looks like one of the actual beasts that attacked the academy."

I took the offered piece of paper, noting the name at the top of it. Brownmary. The thing did look hellishly like one of the monsters from the attack.

"That's what they're keeping in the other tunnels?" I asked, jabbing the asshole in the net with the tip of my sword when he seemed less than inclined to answer me.

"They're not monsters. They're the future of genetics. They're weapons beyond the wildest dreams of most mundane minds and-"

"How are they controlled?" I demanded because what would be the point of feral beasts if there was no way to aim them in the right direction, or call them off once they had done what you wanted?

The man spat at me in reply, his fervent devotion to this insanity clearly more important to him than his life.

I cursed, shuffling the papers in my hands as though hunting for some answer, but there was nothing there which made any sense to me beyond scientific notations and mentions of an Etlonian Spearing Moth.

"There has to be something here," Darcy insisted, striding over to the desk and shoving papers aside as she hunted.

I looked up at the man in the net, a grim thought occurring to me which only made the adrenaline that was tearing through my limbs spike and the ache for bloodshed deepen inside me.

"Tell us how to control them and how to defeat them," I demanded, ignoring the blathering nonsense about the supremacy of science and the dawning of an age where magic and chemistry would collide to create a future unlike anything I was capable of predicting.

At a twist of my wrist the vines which formed his net began to tighten. I watched as the man shifted uncomfortably, not seeming to notice precisely what was happening at first, his vitriol about the incredible work he did here still spilling from his lips. Then silence fell mid-sentence as he felt the vines digging into his flesh, noticing the way they were contorting his limbs, slowly but surely.

"Wait," he gasped, jerking around so he could peer down at me directly. "You can't do this! There has been no trial, no accusation of my crimes, I-"

"You are a soldier employed in the service of my enemy during wartime," I told him, my voice a cold, savage thing which I hardly even recognised as the thrill of his impending death slid through my blood and rooted me in place, watching the seconds left to him ticking by. "Your only hope at survival beyond this meeting is by answering our questions."

"Tor," Darcy said in a low warning voice, still rifling through the paperwork on the desk.

"It's fine," I assured her, and though she looked inclined to say more, she didn't, knowing as well as I did that we couldn't leave the nature of these weapons unknown. They might be vital to Lionel's plans for us, and we had to be prepared to face them in another fight if it came to that, but I was hoping for an alternative.

"You can't do this!" the man insisted but the vines tightened so hard that some bone made a horrific cracking noise, and his yells of protest turned to those of panic.

"The manacles," he panted wildly, seeming to finally understand how little concern I held for his continued ability to breathe. "A location is set on their individual navigation device and the manacles burn them if they head in any direction but the correct one."

"And how do you call them off? Or make them attack?" I growled, pausing in my tightening of the vines as Darcy crossed back over to stand with me and listen too.

The man gave a bark of hysterical laughter which mixed with a howl of pain, then he fell panting against the hold of the vines. "They don't need any encouragement to attack and the manacles simply return them to their holding pens once they are no longer required in action."

"So they just keep killing unless something defeats them or they're forced away by the manacles," Darcy said, dread lacing her tone as we considered the reality of facing the countless creatures that dwelled in this hellhole during battle.

"Yes," the guard panted. "Some have some small weakness built into them for the purposes of experimentation but the work on such flaws has barely begun and the results are patchy at best. The bulk of the work has been focused on their magnificence, on making sure they survive beyond the first weeks of conception and are able to maintain their hold on life through the transformative process."

"What do we need to control those manacles?" Darcy asked.

The man jerked pathetically against his restraints but his gaze had moved to a small, much neater desk in the far corner of the room close to a large rack of surgical tools.

I headed over to it, skirting the thrashing, shark-toothed man who still lay mostly tethered to the upturned metal table, his eyes wild with violence, his soul seemingly absent from his flesh. I hoped for his sake that it was.

I tipped over a small tray on the desk, neat paperwork and a notebook crammed full of notes in a tiny, frantic scrawl spilling out onto it. Nothing that could be used to remotely control monsters. I yanked the drawers out next, one by one, dumping them and their ever-so-carefully arranged contents onto the floor before reaching the bottom one, but it wouldn't open.

A flare of air magic smashed the lock and I grabbed an Atlas in a heavy, shatter-proof case from the drawer, powering it up and finding a request for a passcode awaiting me.

I stalked back towards the man, the vines tightening around him at my approach, his cries of agony colouring the air as they got closer and closer to squeezing the life clean out of him, and my heart raced with the thrill of the prospect.

"Give me the code and I'll release you from the vines," I offered as his cries were choked from his lungs, reduced to panicked wheezing.

"Five, four, three, two-" the last number was cut off alongside the last of his breath, but it was easy enough to guess.

"Seriously?" Darcy asked scornfully.

"I guess even evil scientists have trouble remembering passcodes sometimes," I snorted, hitting the number one and unlocking the Atlas.

I passed it over to Darcy who was undoubtably better with technology than me and she quickly started hunting for what she would need to control the things out in those tunnels.

The man's eyes gleamed with betrayal as he stared down at me, the last of his breath slowly crushing from his lungs. I sighed in exasperation before severing the vines which caged him – though I left those containing his hands in place - and let him crash to the ground.

He gasped for breath like a fish on land and Darcy and I stepped back without comment, moving just far enough away to keep him from touching us.

"I think this is it," Darcy said, tilting the Atlas screen to show it to me. There was a map to the right of it and a list of those odd names to the left.

I watched as Darcy clicked on Globeryan then zoomed in on the map and selected a spot not all that far from where we stood, approximately in the centre of the enemy army camped outside this cavern.

Her eyes sparked and I nodded, pointing out another button which gave the option to send all candidates to the desired location.

Darcy chewed the inside of her cheek then hit the button.

I flinched in alarm at the wild shrieks, howls and screams which echoed from the tunnels beyond the chamber, the walls themselves vibrating as gigantic bodies slammed into the walls and terror slid beneath my skin.

"What the-" Darcy began, but I cut over her as I realised what the problem was.

"The doors," I hissed. "They're locked in but the manacles are driving them to leave."

"Oh shit," she cursed, swiping at the menus on the Atlas, hunting for a way to set them free.

"How do we unlock them?" I demanded from the man who hadn't even tried to rise from the floor and lay crumpled at my feet.

"Manually," he hissed, his eyes alive with the arrogance of the belief in his own brilliance, but I was sick of petty men with superiority complexes believing they could get the better of me. So he was smart? We'd see how helpful that was to him in the end.

"That's a terrible design," Darcy accused.

"Well...yes, I suppose it is actually," the man agreed.

"Come on," I urged Darcy, guiding her to the door while she continued to hunt for a way to open the cages from the Atlas without success.

"There's nothing on here about doors, Tor," she hissed. "And all that noise is bound to be attracting the attention of the guards and maybe even the army outside."

"Well you heard the man – we'll just have to do it manually."

A wild look flashed through her eyes as she considered that and we stepped out into the rocky cavern beyond the door to the lab.

I turned back to look at the asshole who thought himself oh so smart and smiled darkly as I used a flash of fire magic to sever the straps securing the mutated Fae with the shark teeth to his table.

The man's screams pitched higher than even the tremendous roars of the monsters locked up all around us and I slammed the door between us as the shark-jawed man pounced.

Me and Darcy broke into a run, hurrying back towards the farthest reaches of the tunnel where we'd gained entry to this fucked up slice of Solaria. I steeled myself against the terror pounding through me as I darted down the tunnel marked with the name Globeryan.

I threw a Faelight up ahead of me, illuminating a door built of solid iron which had been bolted into the stone of the mountain itself, yet it still looked in danger of buckling beneath the force of the thing which was fighting to break it.

The door was barred but the mechanism to release it looked simple enough; it just had to be rotated then drawn back against the wall.

"We can manage that," Darcy said, her thoughts in line with my own no matter how insane they seemed.

"Yeah," I agreed, my voice only trembling the smallest amount as the beast beyond the door slammed into it again and dislodged a scattering of gravel from the roof of the cavern.

"Just to be clear, this is madness," Darcy said, meeting my gaze.

"Utter insanity," I agreed, lashing a vine around the handle before turning and sprinting back out of the tunnel, the vine snaking across the ground as it grew to follow us.

Cries came from the far end of the cavern in the direction of Lionel's castle and the army beyond, the sound of pounding boots announcing the arrival of a squadron who had no doubt come to investigate the wild disturbance of the beasts.

We sprinted in the opposite direction, vines racing away from us like serpents, seeking out the handles on door after door of the cages while we prayed that this wasn't a terrible fucking idea.

"Let's hope we aren't remembered as the queens who unleashed a plague of monsters onto their own kingdom," I panted, running as fast as I could for that sliver of darkness which stretched away into the canyon far beyond and our one chance of escape.

"Better that than the queens who were killed by said plague of monsters," Darcy reasoned, drawing a bark of laughter from my lips.

"Hey! Stop there!" a voice boomed, amplified through magic over the manic baying of the monsters. We spun around to see at least fifty soldiers crammed into the space at the furthest end of the cavern, their hands raised in preparation to cast magic. "By order of the great King Lionel, I-"

"King Lionel can get fucked!" I shouted, cutting him off.

"Right up the ass with a pinecone," Darcy agreed and without needing to say a single word more, we both yanked on the magic tethering us to those vines.

If the monsters had been yelling before their cages were opened, they were screaming now. The whole world seemed to crack open at the bloodthirsty echoes of their release and I stared, rooted to the spot as countless beasts spilled into the cavern and rushed headlong into the squadron who had come to face us.

My lips parted as I took in the hulking bodies, slick scales, pearly eyes, ripped wings and razor talons of the monsters. They were beasts in totality without anything to say they might have been Fae once. I hoped they weren't anymore. Or at the very least I hoped that if any lingering remnant of the Fae they had once been remained within their transfigured flesh that it would soon be gifted a place beyond The Veil. But before that, I was going to bet revenge tasted fucking good.

Darcy's fingers wound through mine as I stood transfixed by the screams and bloodlust, almost certain I could feel the deaths of those Fae who fought so desperately to try and save their sorry lives. It was as though their souls were brushing past me on their way to the beyond, no doubt cursing me with their passage while their wishes for my own death fell on deaf ears.

"We need to go, Tor," Darcy demanded, yanking on my arm and making me realise it wasn't the first time she'd done it.

I blinked, the trance of death and bloodlust bursting as I shook my head of it and I let her draw me away.

As soon as Darcy was certain I was with her, her wings burst from her back and I followed suit, leaping into the air and flying on, the screams and brutal chorus of death echoing around us in the confined space as we sped away into the dark.

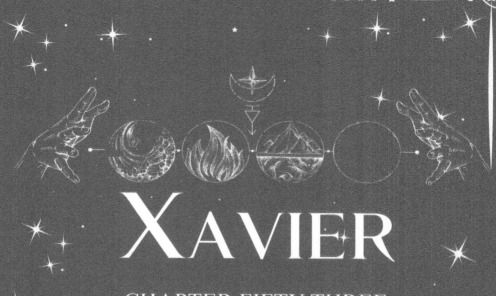

XAVIER

CHAPTER FIFTY THREE

Lionel's army was getting too close to the illusion. Every winged scout that swept down to investigate it was destroyed by the Councillors' might, but too many of them were coming this way.

I shared a glance with Darius, telling me he knew this was coming to an end as surely as I did, and there was still no sign of the twins.

"Xavier, if they discover the magic before they return, you need to run. I'll wait for Roxy and Gwen, but you-"

"No," I snapped, stamping my foot in anger at the suggestion. "They're my queens too. And I am long past running for safety while you stand in my place."

Darius looked like he wanted to argue, but his eyes softened, and he nodded in acknowledgement of my choice. I wasn't a boy he could command anymore, and I'd be here at his side 'til the bitter end.

A heavy wind was blowing through the valley, certainly created by Antonia, trying to push Lionel's army back and slow it down. But one of Lionel's Bonded Dragons broke rank near the rear of the fight, a horn blaring out as the grey beast flew towards the illusion, his powerful wings carving through the onslaught of air and forcing his way towards our fake army.

I knew that Dragon. Uncle Erkin. Though he was no brother of Lionel's, just some distant cousin I was forced to address as such. A man who had been campaigning for the compulsory sterilisation of Fae deemed 'lesser' by law, and he would no doubt get his way if Lionel won the war. He swept down towards our mirage, and I wielded a false soldier, making him run out from the front line and raise his hands. I blasted the earth up at his feet, sending giant stones hurling at the Dragon above, pelting him with as much force as I could muster.

He roared in anger, falling back, but I cast vines into the air that webbed around him, trapping his wings to his sides. He fell, thrashing and fighting, slamming to the ground with a resounding bang.

With a surge of determination, I urged the soil to swallow him up, my teeth bared as I did what had to be done and dragged him into the depths of the earth then closed it up above him, hoping I'd just rid the world of him for good.

Cries of fury came up from Lionel's army and a familiar roar sounded that was more terrifying than the rest.

My father flew at the very back of his warriors, beating his wings, the light winking off of his jade scales. He released a second roar that spurred the first rows of the army into a charge, the whole mountainside quaking with the pounding of their boots, hooves and paws.

My magic began to gutter, and I could see Darius's was failing too. We had poured all of our energy into this and we were almost tapped out.

"This is it," Darius growled, his brow taut with tension.

I nodded, waiting for the first row of Fae to clash with our illusion. My breath got stuck in my lungs as they came in swinging weapons and blasting magic, colliding with nothing and staggering forward, many falling over and more piling on top of them.

There was a scramble to get up and a halo of panicked confusion before shouts carried from Lionel's soldiers.

"It's an illusion!" someone amplified their voice. "A trick!"

Lionel roared in fury, and I steeled my nerves for what was to come. Our concealment spells were weakened by how much magic we'd offered elsewhere, and they wouldn't be enough to keep us hidden for long. It was game over, and our next move would determine whether we lived or died.

A flare of glittering magic shot up from the Councillors where they were hidden within the illusion, a signal for us to run. Darius and I let our magic fall, dropping our hands, the mirage flickering out of sight and revealing the Councillors standing at its heart.

Lionel bellowed as he spotted them, his Bonded Dragons flying after him at a furious speed, but before any of them could make it there, the Councillors tossed stardust over their heads and disappeared.

I felt the concealment spells around my brother and I fading, and we had no more power to bolster them. The moment our spells shattered, Lionel's green eyes locked on the two sons he had long disowned, and the look of rage in him only brought satisfaction to me where I'd expected it to bring fear. I was no longer a cowering boy at the feet of his father, but a man on a mountaintop making a stand against my monster. Not even death could take that truth away from me now.

"Come on, Roxy," Darius hissed as Lionel veered back towards us.

My heart thrashed in my chest and I prepared to shift and fly out there to meet him if I had to.

His wings beat faster, his beady eyes set on us, a vicious hunger in them promising our suffering. But even his manic desire for my blood didn't strike terror in me; I was prepared to face him with all I had left, and no matter what happened, he would never see me tremble before him again.

Shrieks suddenly carried up from the rear of Lionel's army, followed by terrified, blood-curdling screams.

Lionel twisted around to look that way and my lips parted at the sight of the monsters pouring out into my father's ranks, tearing through Fae and Nymphs with savage abandon. Some were scaled, hulking creatures while others were winged and insect-like, a few slithering, while more crawled. All of them displayed a range of monstrous features and twisted limbs, nothing about them seeming at all natural. The sight of the beasts made a knot form in my chest, but hell, it looked like they were on our side.

Lionel's head twisted back to face us and fire brimmed between his jaws as he swept toward us again, leaving his army to deal with the monsters while he focused his ire on us.

A hoard of Dragons flew at his back and Darius took a step forward, clearly about to shift just as I was.

"Together," I called over the bellowing of beasts, and Darius nodded to me, our brotherly bond flaring between us, never to be broken.

But as hellfire came tumbling from Lionel's jaws and I readied to dive off the mountainside and shift on the way down, Tory and Darcy came flying up from the crevice between us and our bastard father with outstretched wings and Phoenix flames flaring into a giant shield at their backs.

The Dragon fire billowed across it but made no path through their barrier, their fire far superior to his.

"Did you miss us?" Darcy asked, her eyes glittering in the face of the chaos.

"We got side-tracked releasing monsters," Tory said like that was a totally normal thing for the two of them to have been doing. But shit, it looked like it had saved our asses.

They flew towards us as Lionel and his Dragons descended from behind and Darius caught Tory by the ankle, yanking her down to the ground with stardust twinkling in his fist.

Darcy swooped closer too, sending a blast of blinding Phoenix fire out behind her to hold back the Dragons a moment longer, before touching her feet lightly to the ground as we grouped close together.

Darius tossed the stardust into the air and I stared at the swarm of vicious Dragons swooping down on us, my eyes locking with my father's. Hatred spewed from his eyes and met with a vitriol of my own, then the stars snatched us away and brought us home to the gates of Zodiac Academy.

"You cut it close," I said with a relieved laugh, and the twins shared an unconvincingly innocent look. "Did you do it?"

"Yes, did you?" Melinda asked, jogging over to us with Tiberius and Antonia on her heels.

"You mean, did we track down the star Lionel was keeping in a pit in his castle and free it so it could do that sparkly power release thing?" Darcy asked sweetly.

"Yeah, that," Darius said intently.

"Well?" Tiberius boomed. "Did you really manage it?"

"Yup," they said at the same time, sharing a grin.

"Holy shit," I said, then neighed in joy, lunging at the two of them and dragging them into a hug. Glitter tumbled from my hair and my skin began to shine with how star damned happy I was.

"And the star cleaned the shadows," Darcy said as I released them.

"Which means?" Darius frowned.

"Fuck knows. But I need a coffee." Tory let her wings flutter away.

We headed through the gates, and part of me expected a welcome home parade from what we'd achieved, but all was quiet on campus.

"Do you think the others are back yet?" Darcy asked curiously, but the undertone of concern in her voice reminded me there were plenty of our group who had gone out and risked their lives today. What if not all of them had made it back?

With that heavy thought on my heart, we made our way to The Orb and the second we stepped inside, a tense silence greeted us. All eyes swung our way, then we were descended on like war heroes. Orion collided with Darcy so fast they went flying back out the door and she squeaked as she disappeared.

Caleb, Seth and Max dog-piled Darius, while Geraldine created a magical rainfall of flowers over Tory's head, weeping as she fell at her feet and hugged her legs. Tory patted her red hair as Gabriel came running over to greet her, and I looked beyond them all for my herd, my heart beating faster.

"They're at Terra House," Gabriel called to me, and I grinned in thanks before turning and racing back out of The Orb, passing by Orion who had Darcy pinned against a tree, kissing her with a savage desire that he probably thought was private.

I stripped off my clothes, figuring I'd fly to Terra House quicker than I could walk, but as I kicked off my boots, Orion's head snapped around and the two of them found me standing there butt ass naked.

"I wasn't watching you," I blurted, and Orion's eyes narrowed, the silver rings in them glimmering menacingly.

It didn't help that the moonlight was catching in the gemstones adorning my cock, winking right at them.

"You've got five seconds to leave," Orion warned.

"He's just shifting," Darcy said with a laugh. "Aren't you, Xavier?"

I nodded then hurriedly shifted, abandoning my clothes and taking for the sky. I flew to Terra House, shaking off my embarrassment and thinking of my herd.

I flew right to the skylight that sat above Tyler's room, landing beside it and tapping my hoof on the glass. It swung open a beat later and I shifted back into my Fae form, jumping inside and landing on the bed.

"Did you do it?" Sofia gasped, hurrying up from a chair at the desk.

"Yeah. The star's gone. Lavinia can't wield it anymore." I leapt off the bed, catching her waist and pulling her against me. Her lips met mine and I tangled my fingers in her short blonde hair, my pulse slowing with the relief of reuniting with her.

"We should head to The Orb to celebrate," Tyler said excitedly. "I just published an article about-"

"After," I cut him off, and his blue eyes heated as I took his hand and guided it onto Sofia.

He moved behind her to kiss her neck, nipping and licking to make her moan, and I watched them with my blood rising.

I was so hard for them both already, and a buzz of adrenaline was still flooding my limbs. I needed this, and I needed it now.

I slid my hand beneath Sofia's waistband, pushing into her panties and trailing my fingers over the gemstones adorning her pussy. She moaned, leaning back against Tyler for support as I dropped my hand lower and ground the heel of my palm over her clit. I found her perfectly wet for me and I slicked my fingers over her tight hole, toying with her and deciding what to do next.

"I want you both," Sofia panted. "I want to taste you, Xavier."

Her soft hand ran down my body to caress my cock and a heady groan left me as she began pumping it in her fist.

"On your knees then," I rasped, and she moved onto the bed, wetting her lips and beckoning me closer.

"Tyler, go with her," I commanded. "Fuck her slow for me."

Tyler smirked as he obeyed, dropping his sweatpants and kicking them away before moving to kneel behind Sofia on the mattress.

I watched as he eased his thick cock inside her and she let out a breathy moan, her back arching as he splayed his hand across it. He fucked her with slow, intense movements that drove his shaft in deep and had her panting within minutes.

"Good," I praised them both then stepped closer to Sofia, sliding my fingers into her silky hair.

Her lips closed around the tip of my cock and I gasped, letting her do the work as she sucked and licked her way along it. Her tongue dragged over each of the gemstones on my rainbow Jacob's ladder like she was worshipping each one, then she licked the underside of my cock with one long, languid stroke. Then another, and another. I cursed, my fingers tightening in her hair, but I didn't try to control her movements, admiring her as she worked to please me just how she wanted.

Her tongue flicked over the tip of my cock, then ran all the way down to the base, sending a shiver of pleasure through me. She did that twice more before her hand slid beneath my dick to grip my balls in her warm palm, massaging them as she took me into her mouth once more. Tyler's thrusts were slow and even, and she started sucking me in time with his movements, her head bobbing up and down as she took me in a little further each time.

The tip of my cock was tingling in a way that felt so fucking good. Between the heat in my skin and the rising tension in my body, I was drawing closer and closer to bliss. But I'd been this close before and I hadn't been able to finish. I wanted Sofia so badly and her lips were the perfect kind of sin, but could I really do it this time? She deserved everything from me and more. She was the reason for my freedom, my first desire in a world where I'd been denied everything I'd ever wanted. Then she'd come blazing into my life and claimed my heart.

I'd never expected to find room for more love, but as my gaze fell on Tyler, I knew he had been as inevitable in my life as Sofia. Sure, he had been one hell of a fucking surprise, but the best kind of one, and I loved him as deeply as I loved her. His eyes met mine, hooded and full of lust, his gaze trailing over my body, taking in the way my muscles flexed before falling on Sofia as she sucked my cock.

The three of us groaned our delight in each other's bodies, this rhythm between us an ecstasy devised by the stars themselves.

Tyler's thrusts became deeper, harder and his fingers dug into Sofia's hips, telling me he was close. But his gaze locked with mine, silently vowing he wouldn't finish until I gave him the order. For both of their sakes, I wanted to come first for once, to prove to them I desired them, that there was nothing holding me back anymore.

Sofia took me all the way to the back of her throat, her lips tightening and her palm rolling over my balls, making me suck in a gasp. I suddenly couldn't hold off, maddened by lust as I gripped her hair in my fist and fucked her sweet mouth, her moans vibrating right along the length of my dick.

"Fuck, fuck, fuck," I blurted, and then I was coming, exploding as pleasure sent me into a frenzy. I stilled, spilling every drop I had to give and groaning loudly, my head falling back in utter relief. It had been so long that I swear it had never felt that good, every muscle in my body tensing then relaxing all at once.

Sofia swallowed then I slowly eased out of her mouth and staggered back to slump down in the desk chair with a stupid smile on my face.

I nodded to Tyler and he knew exactly what that meant, reaching around to caress Sofia's clit, pinching and massaging it, making her cry out with want. A few more of his thrusts had her coming and he shoved her flat onto the bed, rearing over her as he fucked her faster and faster then came with a roar of delight, crushing her body beneath his and burying his face in her neck, their hands knotting together in the sheets.

He rolled off of her and she turned onto her back, the two of them laughing and panting in a tangle of limbs. I pushed out of my seat with such keenness that I sent it flying back into the desk, knocking something over that I didn't care to look at. I fisted my already rock hard dick, pumping it and taking in Tyler and Sofia's beautiful naked bodies. I was going to show them that I could come for them whenever I wanted, again and again.

"I'm Xavier Acrux," I announced, pumping my cock with furious strokes. "And I may have not been able to come for a long, long time, but now I can come anytime I want!"

Sofia and Tyler cheered and I rubbed my thumb over the tip of my cock, already on the brink of exploding again as I took in the two members of my herd, desiring them so fucking much.

I came with a whinny of purest pleasure, my ass hitting something behind me as I leaned back against the desk.

A frantic knocking came at the door and I looked over at it as I caught my breath. "We're busy," I called.

"Yes, indeed-oh-dandy," Geraldine squawked. "And we are all quite jubilant about your willy wanderings, but my dear Pego-brother, I must warn you that- that-"

"You're livestreaming on FaeBook!" Sofia cried, pointing to the computer.

"Shit." Tyler leapt off the bed, running over to the desk and I swung around, finding the webcam lined right up with my ass with a little red light blinking on it.

I stared at the screen in horror as Tyler cut the live stream and the video began to play back on the FaeBook post that had been seen by two thousand people already. It was mostly of my bare ass, but there was a fair bit of thrusting, then I said what I'd said, and I was pretty sure you could see my cock between my legs for a second then-

"No," I rasped in horror as I realised I hadn't just livestreamed it on my FaeBook page, I'd somehow tagged my mom in it. My dead fucking mother.

"Oh stars," I breathed. "Tyler, delete it," I begged.

"Working on it," Tyler said, and I saw a stream of comments coming in which had apparently been posted live.

Lindsey Staton:
Look at that ass! #Asscruxhasawholenewmeaning #bunsofsteel #Pegasass #hornyforthehorn #watchoutCalebAltairmightbeabout

Lindsay Kruse:
Is he jerking off??? I'm tagging EVERYONE I know @ Kylie Gibbons @Oriane Steiner @Danielle Frost @ Sophie Valenti @Amber Nicole

Kayla Latham:
Go, Xavier! Fuck your hand like there isn't a war on where everyone is gonna die – woo! #fuckthesystem #fucktheking #fuckthewar then #fuckyourhandinstead

Nicole MacInnes:
HE TAGGED HIS BELOVED MOTHER - STARS REST HER SOUL #RIPCatalina #Dragonmomma #lookawaybeyondtheveil
Ashley Mathews:
WOW! I saw his cock – it sparkled!! #glitterdick #gleamoftheday #itwinkedatme

It was the comment at the bottom that gutted me most, my lips pursing as I read it.

Gabriel Nox:
I saw this coming and could have stopped it #forthepubes #pubemeonce #revengeofthebush

Tyler finally got rid of the post and shut the computer down for good measure, looking to me with a frown. "You okay?"

"Yeah," I sighed, my gaze falling to the beautiful woman on my bed, then to Tyler's handsome face.

A smile broke across my lips and I leaned in and kissed him, our mouths coming together in perfect synchronicity. I was one helluva lucky asshole, even if I was an embarrassing one at times, and nothing was going to ruin my day.

LIONEL

CHAPTER FIFTY FOUR

I slammed into the turret of my castle, my claws gouging great rifts within the jade rooftop as my weight yanked me downward, my shadow claws pulsing to a beat of rancid agony, flickering before my eyes, unable to hold me in place.

Vard's monsters were baying and shrieking within my army, the unmistakable sound of bloodshed filling the air.

I couldn't hold on.

Rage escaped me in a tremendous roar as I fell, my weight pitching backwards so my wings could do little to help. I shifted, my naked Fae body assaulted by the frigid and biting wind as I tumbled towards the ground, flipping over and over while I fought to take hold of the air surrounding me. But the fingers of my shadow hand were wracked with spasms of pain, the cold air seeming to rip right through the appendage Lavinia had crafted for me.

I cursed as I made myself focus, using my hand of flesh and blood to cast magic, forcing the wind to wrap around me and hurl me towards the castle again. Fire blasted from me in a wild explosion, shattering the window of my throne room just before I was hurled through the opening.

I hit the ground hard, rolling across broken glass and earning myself a myriad of cuts and scratches across my flesh.

A Dragon's roar escaped my lips as I came to a halt, naked, prone and shaking on the cold floor of my own castle.

But I wasn't the only one crying out within these walls of green.

A snarl curled my lip as the bloodcurdling wails of my wife echoed throughout the hallways, finding their way into every room and parlour, infecting each nook and cranny.

"What is this?!" I screamed. "What is happening?"

Many hands clasped my arms, hauling me back to my feet, shrouding me in a cloak to maintain my dignity. My loyal Bonded had grouped close to me, more of them sweeping through the sky outside the shattered window, hunting for the rebel army which had never even been there at all.

It made no sense.

Smoke rose beyond the broken glass, my forces clashing within themselves as panic and mayhem took root.

Glass crunched beneath my bare feet as I made for the opening, ignoring the murmurs of concern that spilled from the lips of my followers, my gaze seeking out the source of this commotion.

The view beyond my window set my blood blazing like a freshly lit fuse. Vard's monstrous creations still tore through my ranks, spilling from the caverns where they had been caged in a rush of bloodthirsty fury.

"Where is he?" I hissed, my voice a cold and brutal thing.

"Who, my Ki-"

"Vard," I spat his name like the curse it had fast become, and my Dragons rushed to locate the cretinous creature.

Hurried footsteps clacked across the stone floor, racing closer to me while I took in the destruction below, trying to process the source of this chaos. I'd seen my discarded Heirs atop that mountain alongside those mixed-blooded whores who dared to try and claim a stake in my crown. They'd been here, and they'd forged an illusion which had mobilised my army. But why?

Yes, they'd released some monsters from their place within the dank caverns below my castle, but even now the foul beasts were being herded back inside thanks to the manacles they wore. Some had been slaughtered, a trail of broken bodies littering the ground where they had torn a path through my ranks, and yet it was hardly a blow at all now that I took count of it. Infuriating? Yes. But I doubted the casualties ran much higher than a few hundred, barely a scratch in the might of my army. There was something of real threat that had been attempted here, a greater reason my enemies had come to my door, but what was it?

My gaze caught on a crash of movement further out in my army, the huge body of Vard's biggest and most bloodthirsty creation colliding with Nymphs in their shifted forms, their movements harsh and brutal.

"Vard!" I bellowed, my fury beyond measure, but it wasn't he who answered me.

"My King," Linda Rigel's voice scraped across my ears, bringing a sneer to my lips.

I could hardly stand to look at the ruined bitch these days, the crippling destruction of her hold over her magic clear to see in everything from the look of powerlessness in her eyes to the pathetic way she tried to cling to her role in my court. Time wasn't on my side and I needed the power of her daughter, plus the weight of her political connections and family name, so she hadn't been dismissed yet, but her fall was written in the stars.

"What?" I growled, gripping the window frame and relishing the bite of broken glass as it was crushed within my shadow hand. The agony in those fingers still pulsed and thrummed, alive with some whisper of truth which had to be aligned with Lavinia's ongoing screams.

"It's the Nebula Inquisition Centres," she said, her voice a broken quiver which had me bracing for the truth she held. "They've been destroyed, the lesser Fae within them were released and taken to join the ranks of the rebel forces-"

"Which ones?" I demanded, still not turning to look at her.

The violence raging within my own army took up my focus, and Lavinia's shrieks were cutting through the air like a knife, impossible to ignore.

"A-all of them," Linda breathed.

My pulse stuttered at her words, my mind clinging to them then discarding them, their meaning utterly impossible.

My grip on the broken glass tightened, the beast caged within my flesh roaring so loud that its sound escaped my lips. The shift came rushing up on me so abruptly that I knew I wouldn't be able to stop it, that I was going to lose control entirely in front of every person in this room and-

I fell forward so suddenly that it seemed as though my heart had lurched straight up into my throat. One of my Bonded Dragons lunged for me, catching hold of the cloak which was fastened around my neck and yanking me back from the drop so violently that I was both choked by the fabric and hurled to the floor once again.

I crashed down on my back, the cloak falling open to reveal my nudity. Hands reached for me while wept apologies spilled from the lips of the fucking fool who had both saved me from that fall and thrown me to the floor.

I thrashed against them, slapping them aside and spitting Dragon fire at them so I could hold my arm up before me, the pain in my stump so blinding that I could only blink at the place where my shadow hand had been while fighting against the urge to cry out at the agony.

My lips opened and closed, my mind whirling and jamming.

"Lavinia," I ground out eventually, scrambling to get up with only one hand to assist me.

My Bonded were closing in again, reaching for me, petting me, weeping for me but I threw them all back with a blast of wind which spilled erratically from my remaining hand.

"Where is my wife?"

I didn't wait for an answer because her screams were still filling the castle, guiding me to her location. I broke into a run, panting against the pain where my shadow hand had been, scrambling up coiling staircases and along pristine corridors, hurrying towards her tower.

I passed through the ballroom, my eyes meeting those of my Heir, though Tharix made no reaction whatsoever to the chaos unfurling around him, just watching as I passed him by with my retinue of Bonded chasing along in my footsteps.

I flung the door open and found her there, her body coated in shadows which thrashed like a tempestuous sea, her eyes wild with panic, her beauty marred with terror.

"What is it?" I demanded. "What has happened?"

"The shadows have broken free of my leash," she rasped, clutching at her arms, her fingernails raising bloody scratches across her skin. "I can't hear them whispering anymore."

"Who?!" I bellowed.

"The souls caught in my web, the ones who grant me power over the shadows beyond my own." Her gaze turned to the thin window which lay to the right of her bed and I stalked over to it, hurling it wide and looking out again.

My lips parted as I took in the continuing fights. The monsters were all being herded back to their cells now, leaving a bloody mess of bodies and excrement in their wake, but still carnage reigned. Several of the Nymphs were thrashing about wildly, stampeding between my ranks and crushing any who got in their way. With a few attempts, I managed to cast an amplification spell to see them better and found them shrieking, clutching at their skulls and fighting against whisps of shadow which were fluttering around them before fading into nothing.

"You have lost control over the Nymphs," I accused.

"No," she bit out on a sob, but I had no care for her emotions, only the truth of this revelation. "They remain loyal to me. But the shadows have been...purged of my touch. They used to whisper to me, and they whispered to my loyal soldiers as well. The loss of the voices is like fingernails scoring lines through my skull. They are feeling it too."

My gaze scoured the army and I took in the ranks of Nymphs who remained in control of themselves, seeing the truth of her words in their confused and grief-stricken expressions, yet they were managing to hold their nerve.

"Hunt down those who have fallen into madness. Kill any who cannot be brought back to heel before they tear through my ranks of Fae and damage any more of my forces," I hissed, knowing my Bonded were still clustered in the hallway, sure my word would be carried out.

"Who did this?" Lavinia demanded, moving to me, clutching my robe and looking up at me as if I might hold the answers.

"Can you fix this?" I demanded in turn, raising the stump of my hand to her, threat lacing my words.

Her lips parted, her fingers moving to clasp my stump. "I think if I…bond my own shadows to you. Then perhaps I could weave you a new hand from the fabric of those which reside within me," she murmured, the uncertainty of her words lighting a concern deep within my core.

Her brow furrowed then her grip on my stump tightened painfully. "Tharix," she gasped, whirling for the door but I caught her by the hair, yanking her back violently.

"He was in the ballroom, looking wholly unconcerned with the ruin taking place between our walls," I snarled, and she sagged against me, turning her gaze back to my stump.

"I need to see him."

"No," I barked, catching her by the throat as she made to pass me and holding her there, her nose almost touching mine. "You will fix my hand first."

Shadows coiled about her, wrapping themselves around me, twisting through my fingers which gripped her in place and yet there was something different about them now. The air didn't tremor with the force of them, darkness didn't diminish the light surrounding us. Her power wasn't what it had been and, in that moment, with my gaze pinned upon hers, we both felt it, the shift, the truth. She was no longer more powerful than me.

Lavinia's dark eyes blazed with grief and fury before she smothered both and withdrew the touch of her shadows from my flesh. Her hands moved to my bare chest beneath the cloak, her fingers scoring down the firm muscles of my abs and dropping lower still as she opted for seduction over force.

"I will need time to research a bond powerful enough to link my own magic to yours," she said softly. "It will likely require a sacrifice, perhaps we could use some of the Fae you have placed in your Nebula Inquisition Centres to-"

"The centres have all been destroyed and the foul beasts within them liberated to join the Vega army," I spat. "Besides, I can think of no greater bond than that which I have already asked you to make with me."

She smothered her look of fury fast, but I still caught it. We both knew that there was nothing else which would suffice and she had finally played all of her cards, finding me with the winning hand.

"I had hoped for us to create that bond in celebration of us winning the war," she tried, her hand finding my cock, her teeth biting down on her bottom lip. She was a damn good seductress, but it wasn't the mere thought of getting her on her hands and knees for me that had my dick so hard in her grasp; it was the knowledge of doing so while knowing she was bonded to me and my triumph over her was complete.

"A pretty sentiment but the stars have collided to bring the date forward. So, my Queen, do you submit to their desires?"

A thousand nos raced through her eyes and yet those lips, so fit for pretty lies, so good at wielding wickedness, had no more room to run.

"Yes, Daddy," she purred, her hand pumping my cock harder and the knowledge that she was trying to win back some measure of power with that act almost brought a laugh to my lips.

I shoved her backwards using my grip on her throat and began to speak the words of the Guardian Bond, so beautifully familiar to me after so many uses of its power.

I pushed her down onto the bed as the magic of the words burned through my throat, her hand falling off of me as she felt the weight of the bond coming for her like a rush of wings.

She stared up at me as I knelt over her, her gaze unblinking as she took in the sheer power of her king and finally submitted to me in the way she always should have. Once this bond was in place, she would be unable to act against me, unable to deny me the position of ultimate power which she was finally accepting belonged to me alone.

A tear spilled from her eye as the power of the bond took hold of her and she gasped as my star sign was burned into the flesh of her arm.

My pulse thundered wildly as I felt her sign brand itself onto my flesh too and when I looked down at my arm, I found not a reddened mark like the rest, but the sign for Capricorn scored into my skin in deepest black, shadow coiling through it like a stain of her power.

The rush of the bond snapping into place hit me as the final word fell from my lips and Lavinia released a shuddering breath.

"My mark is greater than all the rest," she murmured, taking in the way her mark on my skin stood out more clearly than all the others.

"As it should be, my Queen," I growled, knowing how to soothe her, keeping her on side.

She smiled and I let her sit up beneath me, accepting the kiss she gave me and grinning into her mouth as I tasted the salt of her tear upon her lips, her defeat tasting so very sweet.

"Now fix my hand," I snarled against her lips.

Lavinia flinched back, blinking in surprise at the savage tone I had used with her, but I merely presented the stump to her, demanding her focus.

Hesitantly, she curled her fingers around the aching flesh, shadows rising from her to coil across my skin. The burn intensified, a grunt escaping me as her shadows dug in deeper. A hand formed slowly, though I couldn't feel it as I had before, my teeth gritting as I tried to focus on the sensation of it, forcing the fingers to curl through pure force of will. But as the hand finally formed a fist, a stab of violent agony tore through the ruined flesh of my stump and a pulse of dark magic sent the two of us flying from the bed in opposite directions.

Once more, my Bonded ran to me, hauling me to me feet and gathering my robe about me to conceal my nudity.

"What is the meaning of this?" I hissed, glaring at Lavinia as she rose on the far side of the bed.

"The shadows are no longer slaves to my whispers," she said, her voice stricken with grief. "I can form a hand for you, but I cannot bend the shadows to any command but my own. I can't gift them to you or leave them rooted within you. I-"

"You will try again," I snarled, advancing on her, but a commotion in the hall drew my attention away.

"Vard has been located, Sire," one of my Bonded announced. "He was working to reclaim control over the foul beasts he has created, but will make his way to you with haste as soon as the last of them has been returned to its cage-"

"Did I ask for him to come at his own convenience?" I raged, whirling on the Dragon who dared bring me such disrespectful news. "Or did I command his presence *now*?"

The Dragon dropped to the floor, begging for my forgiveness but I ignored him, placing my foot in the centre of his back and stepping over him on my way out of the room.

"Lavinia!" I bellowed, summoning my wife to my side. "You will keep trying to fix my hand until you succeed. Understood?"

My queen hesitated as she fell into step with me, her dark eyes full of resentful realisation as she no doubt balked against the harsh delivery of my order. But she was mine now, and she felt the surge of emotion from the Guardian Bond urging her to please me in any way she could.

"I will," she agreed a beat too late, though her answer would suffice. "But the shadows did not simply purge themselves of my influence. Something has taken place which we do not understand. Where did the attacking army go? What happened out on the-"

I stopped dead so suddenly that the Bonded at my back crashed into one another and Lavinia strode on several more steps before noticing my halt.

"The Vegas were here," I breathed, the loose threads of what I knew coming together, tangling into a knot of unease which settled itself over my chest and squeezed. "The army was an illusion set to distract us. Their forces struck at the Nebula Inquisition Centres while we had our focus on the impending fight we thought had come for us. But what if there was more to their ruse..."

My mind roamed over all I knew of this day, and of that terrifying moment in which Darius had walked through my doors, resurrected from the grave. He had escaped me then but not before racing through the halls of my castle, locating the celestial creature I had captured and sending it to sleep to stop Lavinia from wielding it.

"The star," I gasped, breaking into a run, my cape billowing out behind me, bare cock bouncing uncomfortably with every step.

"Get me some proper fucking clothes and bring Vard to me at once," I roared to no one and everyone, my pace not faltering.

Down corridors of deepest green and up spiralling staircases, I ran with Lavinia at my heels and panic gilding my steps.

The Vegas had been here. They had been here and they had released Vard's monsters upon my army, meaning they had done more than wield illusions from the mountaintops. They had crept into my domain, and I had no way of knowing how deeply they had burrowed.

I ran out onto the hidden precipice behind my castle, falling still as I found Tharix there already, standing so close to the edge of the pit which housed my trapped star that the toes of his boots overhung the edge. Anyone else would have been terrified of that fall, yet he observed it as if it was as inconsequential as a summer's breeze.

"Does it speak to you?" Lavinia asked him, moving closer while I maintained my position.

It was quiet in this place. Too fucking quiet.

"It speaks to nothing but the wind and the rain now," Tharix replied.

"No," I gasped, breaking into a run again and throwing myself down onto my knees, peering into the gloom which stretched away beneath me.

With some difficulty, I cast a Faelight singlehandedly and dropped it over the edge, my pulse falling unnaturally still as it descended, revealing nothing but a lifeless, dull boulder in an empty canyon.

"They took it. They fucking stole it," I muttered but Tharix moved closer to me, his boots balanced on the edge of the cliff, his gaze on me where I still knelt on the ground.

"No. It hasn't been stolen. It has been freed."

"Freed?" I shook my head in horror, knowing what he meant, knowing that it was true as I stared at that empty space. The star had been freed from Lavinia's shadows and had completed the end of its life cycle, releasing itself and all of that potent, raw energy into a million specs of nothing which had been scattered to the far ends of the earth.

"It took your whispers with it, Mother," Tharix added thoughtfully. "I don't hear your breath in my ear anymore."

"You…but you are half Nymph," Lavinia said firmly, striding to him and taking his hand. He let her, tilting his head in that disconcerting way of his as he surveyed the woman who had brought him into this world.

"I am Nymph and I am Fae," he agreed, shadows creeping across his torso as he called upon them, but there was something different about them now, something paler in their colour and softer in their movements. "But I think I am something else beyond that. Something else beyond you."

Lavinia snatched her hand from his and struck him across the face, her concern falling to fury so easily.

"You are my boy and my creation," she hissed. "You are Heir to the Dragon King. My child. My Acrux born babe. Do not ever speak to me like that again."

Power rushed from Lavinia in a sudden spill of ink, her own shadows dark and potent with her influence as they hurled Tharix across the open space and pinned him to the wall. His muscles bunched and limbs thrashed as she tortured him with them in punishment for his insolence, but he didn't cry out or beg for her to stop like most would under such strain. No, my Heir did not succumb to the weakness of the flesh.

"Enough," I spat, regaining my feet and Lavinia dropped him. "The boy knows his place, don't you?"

Tharix pushed himself onto his knees, panting against the onslaught of agony he had just survived, his dark eyes, so very like his mother's, now pinned on me.

The defiance I found in his expression hurled me back into the past for a moment, into the office in my old manor where another Heir of mine had once stared up at me from his knees after receiving a punishment. Darius had looked at me in just the same way, but I would not make the same mistakes I had with my past Heir now. I would carve the insolence out of Tharix before it got a chance to take root any further and be certain to keep him in line.

"I asked you a question," I prompted when Tharix remained silent.

"Yes, Father," he replied finally.

"Good."

Shuffling footsteps announced the arrival of another and I whirled around as Vard finally deigned to submit to my orders.

"I came as quickly as I could, Sire. Just as soon as I had contained the creations and-"

"Tell me, how did the Vegas manage to get past your men and release your beasts upon my army?" I hissed. "How did they make it past the security you claimed was infallible and creep into my fucking castle undetected?"

"With all due respect," Vard simpered. "If the Vegas made it into the castle then surely it is your guards who are at fault-"

"They entered through *your* caverns!" I bellowed. "They broke into this place and freed the star who should have guaranteed our victory against-"

My words cut off as the world suddenly took a deep inhale, the air itself stilling and within that utterly unnatural peace, I felt the presence of another star arriving.

Fear stirred within my soul as Clydinius swept out onto the precipice in total silence, his impassive face finally showing some flicker of emotion as he looked at the chasm where the star I had promised him dominion over for his own designs now lay empty of power.

"It was the Vegas," I hissed, feeling his fury even as his silence stretched. "Those twins who I have sworn to end. They came here and did this. They stole from the both of us."

"I need a Trinity," Clydinius said, his words slow and deliberate. "I made that clear."

"Yes." I wetted my lips, trying to remain still and not shift beneath his penetrating gaze. "And I have had Madam Monita working tirelessly to predict you the next point of collision. Just this morning she told me she thinks another star will fall soon. I will deliver on my part of our bargain, your Eminence."

Death hung in the weight of those words as Clydinius measured them and no one dared speak while we waited to see what he might do. I was the greatest Fae in all the land and yet I couldn't stop the power of a star from crushing me if he chose to do so.

Clydinius turned his gaze from the chasm to me, power making the air tremble around him as he considered his options, and I could feel my limbs quaking in time with it.

"You will show me where the star shall fall," he decided. "And this time, I will be waiting to ensure it joins with me."

"Yes," I agreed on an exhale of utter relief. "Yes, it shall be so."

Darius

CHAPTER FIFTY FIVE

The destruction of the final Nebula Inquisition Centres, alongside the successful trick we had played on my father and his army with our illusions, plus the hoard of fucking monsters my wife and her equally insane sister had unleashed upon his forces were all anyone in the rebel army could speak of. In reality, all of that paled to nothing in comparison to the victory that had been claimed by the trapped star releasing its magic into the world, the weapon Lavinia had so brutally wielded against us in our last collision now ripped from the playing board.

Celebrations had taken over the entire campus, the army were letting off a bit of steam and there were plenty of drinks being consumed around bonfires which blazed before crowds of dancing, celebrating Fae.

I sat in the shadows beneath a towering oak tree, watching the enormous fire blazing at the heart of the clearing in The Wailing Wood, the orange light flickering over my skin and momentarily illuminating me before leaving me in shadow again.

I had my hood drawn up and a glass of whiskey dangling from my fingertips over the arm of my chair. I'd taken one mouthful but it had soured on the way down, the burn doing nothing more than remind me that we shouldn't be celebrating yet.

In fact, though we had struck several harsh blows against my father's army today, I knew as well as everyone else who had been invited to this exclusive gathering that we were still far from where we needed to be if we stood a hope of winning this war.

I watched Roxy as she danced with Rosalie Oscura, her head thrown back and one arm in the air, while her other held a bottle of mostly untouched tequila. She was putting on a damn good show of being unconcerned. And a damn good show of being irresistible too, I admitted as my gaze fell to the expanse of bronze thigh where her dress kept riding up as she moved.

The Wolf beside her howled, drawing a flood of Oscuras up to dance with them too.

Darcy was dancing with them, Sofia and Geraldine too, all of them celebrating and putting on a great show of victory. I felt it. But I didn't at the same time.

"This seems all too familiar," Orion said casually from the seat to my right as if he'd been there this entire time instead of having just shot into the space so fast that no one had noticed him.

I glanced his way, noting the love bite on his neck which the collar of his shirt was doing very little to conceal and the dishevelled appearance of his hair.

"You mean the bit with us sitting on the outskirts like the miserable bastards we too often are, or the bit where you pretend not to have been fucking a Vega five minutes before hanging out with me?" I asked, making him laugh.

"It's easier now that we don't have to hide it," he said and I looked into his eyes, that still unfamiliar ring of silver which lined them suiting him.

It would have made sense for me to envy those silver rings. If I'd followed a different path on my journey to this place I might have had rings of my own linking me to Roxy, branding me as hers in starlight. Yet I didn't. Despite it all, I couldn't picture that reality ever having played out. And as impossible as my sitting here should have been, I couldn't imagine I would have made it to this point by taking any other path either.

"I'm so fucking glad for you," I told my best friend, offering him a grin which was real despite all the concerns waging for my attention.

"You too," he replied in kind, his eyes moving to the Vegas where they danced like the fate of the world didn't even balance on their shoulders.

Neither of us mentioned the obvious; that our happiness was more than likely to be short-lived. What would the point have been in all this if we failed?

"Geraldine has made plans for the queens to announce the fall of the Nebula Inquisition Centres live across Solaria soon," Orion said. "Tyler is working on hacking the servers so the broadcast will be impossible to switch off and the hope is we can rally more rebels to come join us. She wants to spotlight you, too. The man who returned from death to fight. I think it has a bit of a ring to it."

I nodded. That made sense and I was more than used to being paraded in front of the cameras. Tyler had already done an interview and photoshoot with me which he'd released to the press earlier today and according to him, Solaria was reeling from the news, rumours flying that it was a sign from the stars themselves that fate was on the side of the True Queens.

I supposed I should know what had been said about me in the article in case it was brought up during the broadcast, so I took my Atlas from my pocket and quickly opened it.

It didn't take long to find it – the entirety of the internet and social media seemed to be alight with the story.

Darius Acrux Returned from the Grave! By Tyler Corbin

Darius Acrux, son to the False King and infamous rebel leader has indeed returned from beyond The Veil to fight against the tyranny of his father.

In a shocking turn of events, Queen Roxanya Vega defied the will of fate which had stolen her beloved husband who was her would-be Elysian mate, once Star Crossed then released to love again thanks to his own extraordinary power (full story of their epic romance here).

Roxanya vowed to change their fate and did! She stormed the halls of the dead and through magic more powerful than any of us can really comprehend, stole him back from the clutches of fate and returned him to her arms.

Now, upon the king consort's defiance of death, he has bowed to the True Queens and pledged his undying allegiance to them.

I skimmed the rest of the article, ignoring the over-the-top praise and compliments, knowing it was all designed with the purpose of drawing more Fae to our side of this war. At the bottom of the page, past the photographs detailing my return and the interview I'd done with him, was what I was searching for. I needed to see if this had had the effect we were hoping for and the easiest way to get a read on public opinion was to check the comments.

Melissa Lieberman:
Oh my stars, even fate agrees that Lionel Acrux is in the wrong. I hope he gets dick rot and it falls off! #rottydongle #dirtydick

Lucy Burfoot:
Long live the True Queens! Their power is beyond compare! No other can claim such holy strength! #Vegasforever

Kass Bruinier:
I smell a rat and as we all know, they're the lowest creatures of them all. If any of this is even close to the truth then I'll eat my hat, and it's one large hat! #bullshit #hatsouptonight

Cheria Coram:
Even The Ferryman wants us to win! #freedomforallFae #deathcantstopthequeens

Cindy-Lou Galaxa:
Oh my heavens, I knew my love couldn't be gone. I have been in mourning ever since that fateful day, but now I have thrown off my widow's cape and I am coming, I am coming hard and fast to join you, my love. I will be there soon! #iknewourlovewouldendure #fatehasbroughtyoubacktome

I frowned at that last comment, the name making my skin prickle with recognition though I wasn't entirely sure why. But hadn't there been a Cindy who had been sending me things and trying to get close to me? There was some memory of a car which tickled at the edges of my mind but then…no, that was Cynthia wasn't it?

I shrugged off the thought, handing my Atlas to Orion who was blatantly reading it over my shoulder anyway.

"The reaction is mostly in our favour," he observed, scrolling through more comments. "Oh, Telisha Mortensen thinks you're the hottest Fae she's ever seen and says that even your corpse was hot. That's sweet."

"Pretty sure my corpse was stone cold," I muttered, my eyes once again on the dancing Fae. One Fae in particular if I was being honest.

Max had stripped down to his boxers, his skin coated in scales as he prepared to leap over the bonfire. I smiled a little as he did it with a whoop of triumph, embers swirling all around him, but my smile fell as Washer stripped off to take his turn next.

"Ugh," I cringed as our old water Elemental professor began lunging in his tighty-whities to 'limber up.'

"He was my neighbour for years," Orion reminded me. "You've seen nothing compared to the scars in my memories."

I shuddered, my eyes tracing Washer despite my desire to look away and I watched as he took a running leap over the fire. He didn't quite make it, several logs exploding from the flames as he stumbled through the far side of it and howled in pain, rolling across the dirt as though trying to put out flames. No one seemed inclined to point out that he wasn't actually on fire, and I waved a hand at the logs that had been knocked aside, putting them out before the flames could spread.

Roxy slipped from the crowd while people moved to help Washer, Geraldine hurling a tsunami on top of him to assist him with the imaginary flames.

I watched my girl as she weaved towards me, a crown on her head and mischief in her green eyes.

"What will everyone think if they notice the consort I brought back from death sitting so sullenly over here?" Roxy teased as she came to a halt just out of reach, her body still moving to the music.

"I was sullen before I died. It stands to reason that I would still be so now," I told her, watching as she continued to dance, toying with me like a mouse to a cat.

"That is nothing to boast about, you know," she said.

"You seem to like it well enough," I countered. "Otherwise you wouldn't be trying to lure me into your arms."

"Oh please," she scoffed. "As if any luring is required. If I wanted you in my arms, all I'd have to do is beckon."

Roxy turned away from me, returning to the fire, the music and her friends while I watched her go, resisting the urge to grab her and reel her back to me.

Orion snorted at my expense and I flicked a hand at him, casually setting his bourbon alight.

"Asshole," he cursed, dropping the glass as it was engulfed in a mini fireball and I smirked to myself, keeping my eyes on my girl while she danced.

"She'd be the one who came running if I beckoned," I grumbled.

"Oh yeah?" Orion taunted. "Prove it then."

I gritted my teeth, fairly certain that I knew how this was going to go based on the teasing looks Roxy kept tossing my way, but I leaned forward all the same, resting my forearms on my thighs and giving her an intense look which promised all kinds of devious pleasure.

She bit her lip as she watched me, her hands skimming down her body while she danced.

I raised a hand and beckoned, a smirk hooking the corner of my mouth as she hesitated then took a step closer to me.

"See?" I said to Orion, but he just snorted.

"Yeah, I see."

Roxy had raised the bottle of tequila to her lips and as her throat bobbed with a swallow, her other hand raised, flipping me off.

I huffed irritably, flopping back into my chair and Orion promptly stole the drink which I had all but abandoned to replace his own.

"Darcy said Tory lost it again in that place," Orion said after a few minutes where we just let the music wash over us.

"I heard."

"She's worried. We're both worried. About both of you."

I nodded. In some ways, I was worried too. In others…well, the thrill of the fight had always been tempting to me, the call of the bloodlust something I'd been born with. I could see how it could become a problem. I could also see how it might not be a bad thing given our current predicament.

"There was always going to be a cost to this," I said indicating myself, here, alive. "I can think of far worse."

Orion shook his head, irritated by my dismissal of the issue, but honestly, my desire for death and carnage seemed like the least of our problems right now. It wasn't as though I was sitting here lost in daydreams about gutting every person around me. Hell, it wasn't even as if I was insisting on marching off into battle at the earliest opportunity. The curse, if that was what this was, only seemed to come into effect when we were already in a position which required violence. And if I was eager to fight harder and kill more brutally during battle, then I could accept that. I hadn't once thought to turn that aggression towards my friends or allies after all.

"Tory mentioned speaking with The Ferryman," Orion pushed, and I nodded.

"Yes. My wife seems far keener than expected to make his acquaintance again," I agreed.

"You should do it soon. See if you can get some answers while we still have time…" he trailed off.

Time to what? I looked to my friend and gave him a knowing smile. "Roxy has a plan," I began but just then the woman in question beckoned to me from beyond the fire, the movement subtle and yet somehow unmissable all at once.

I pushed myself to my feet, knowing I was doing exactly what she'd predicted, knowing I'd just lost that little power play, and knowing I didn't give a fuck.

"What plan?" Orion urged from behind me, but I shrugged.

"That woman only tells me what she wants and she's admitting to nothing. But I know her. She has some scheme in mind which she won't give voice to. And it has to do with our planned meeting with The Ferryman. Whatever it is, I'm sure I'll be enlightened then."

"I'm uncertain whether to be hopeful or terrified by that," he muttered.

"Welcome to my marriage," I agreed before stalking away, a dog falling at the command of his master. But I'd be her dog if that was what she wanted of me. One whose chain could only ever be pulled by her and whose bite was far worse than his bark.

Roxy smiled at me across the fire then slipped away into the crowd. I weaved between bodies, noticing Xavier and his Subs because all three of them were sparkling brightly while they danced. Other Pegasuses were closing in around them, eyeing them hopefully, clearly wanting to earn a place in their herd.

I wondered if he would indulge them, but somehow I doubted it. My brother had already suffered too much loss in this war. He wouldn't want to risk spreading his love any further than it already went until after. Assuming there was an after. He would wait until everything was settled and at peace before he would consider expanding his circle. I just hoped he would get the chance to do so.

Roxy had disappeared beyond the fire and I fell still as I reached the edge of the clearing, looking out into the trees. She was toying with me.

"Come out," I called, and her laughter came in reply before a tiny bird built of flames fluttered through the trees, coming to land on my hand as I raised it.

The bird preened, blue and red flames tangling together to form its wings which it spread wide before taking off into the dark.

It ruined my night vision but I didn't care, simply following the little thing into the night in hunt of my prey.

My boots caught on brambles and fallen trees, Roxy's distant laughter and the dancing of the flaming bird all that drew me onwards. But after several minutes it became clear that I wasn't drawing any closer to my goal.

I paused, moving my right hand behind my back and casting an illusion to take my place, letting the false version of myself continue on after the bird.

Once it was gone, I moved into the shadow of a towering maple then cast water beneath my feet, sending myself skyward.

It took far more power to travel this way than it would have to fly, but Roxy would likely notice a Dragon trying to creep up on her.

I launched myself over the treetops on a spurt of water then let it drop me beyond my best guess of where she'd retreated to.

I let the shadows have me as I leaned against the rough bark of an oak tree and waited.

Before long, I spotted her, laughing to herself as she danced between the trees, the little flaming bird swooping back and forth at her command, her attention focused on where she thought I was advancing from and not behind.

I counted her steps as she backed up, moving closer to me with each one.

...six, seven, eight-

I lunged, whirling her around and closing a hand around her throat, my eyes flashing with triumph as I pulled her body flush to mine.

"You'd be dead you know, if I had malicious intentions," I told her, my eyes finding her mouth and staying there.

"Are you sure?" her smile was cunning and wicked, all the things I liked best about her.

I looked down to find a dagger of ice pressed to my gut. She bobbed her chin over my shoulder and one look revealed the six wooden spears poised at my back.

"By the stars, I love you," I growled, claiming that smug smile and kissing it off of her lips.

The sound of her weapons hitting the ground in the darkness were met by the fire of the bird going out and I swung her around, pressing her back to the tree and pinning her there by my hold on her throat.

I didn't waste any time with her, dropping my fly and shoving my pants down with my free hand before hitching her thigh around my waist. It was nothing to shove her panties aside, a swipe of my fingers finding her achingly wet for me and I smiled darkly as I thrust into her with a single jerk of my hips.

Roxy gasped, her head tilting back as her dress rode up far higher than it had while she danced. I tightened my hold on her throat, driving her back against the tree and slamming into her harder this time.

She moaned, deep and low, an exclamation of utter bliss, and I gave in to what we both knew we were at the core of us. Simple animals addicted to the feeling of us.

Roxy took hold of my shoulders, her nails cutting into me through my shirt as I fucked her harder, rougher, the friction of our movements making her clit grind against me with every thrust, and she panted my name into my ear to urge me on.

She grew louder in her pleasure and I kissed her to steal the sound of it, kissed her to claim her and remind us both that we would never again be parted.

She was so tight, so fucking perfect and she took the punishment I wreaked on her flesh in her stride, never backing down, always wanting more. Her teeth bit down on my ear and I crushed her between my body and the tree, driving her to her release, demanding it with every thrust.

Roxy came with a wild cry, her nails tearing into my skin as I slammed into her, over and over again, chasing my own pleasure while prolonging hers. When I came, it was with a roar which betrayed the beast in me and when I felt the ferocious pounding of my heart it was with a thrill that I acknowledged her own racing pulse had contributed to it.

"Well, I suppose sullen isn't so bad when it results in that," Roxy teased, kissing my throat while I remained there, pinning her in place and revelling in the riot which had just taken place between our flesh.

"And neither is being beckoned like a dog," I agreed, making her laugh.

And that sound, that fucking sound so full of life and joy was why I wasn't going to bow to the odds which stood before us. That sound was why I would fight to death and beyond for this war. Her. My queen. Who deserved so many more days of laughter to come.

ORION

CHAPTER FIFTY SIX

"It will be exactly the same, just sit there and watch." Darcy urged, guiding me through the throng of dancing Fae in The Wailing Wood and pushing me onto a carved wooden seat.

I pressed my lips together. "It will hardly be the same."

"It will – it will!" she said excitedly, her glittery blue skirt bouncing in time with her and making me catch sight of her panties.

"Alright." I relaxed into my chair. Far be it from me to stop Blue from putting on a show for me. "Let's see it then."

Darcy glanced around as Bones by Imagine Dragons thumped through the air, spotting Xavier in his lilac Pegasus form and beckoning him over. He came trotting towards her with a look of intrigue on his horsey face. His horn had a wreath of flowers hanging from it and it pulsed with purple light, his joy making him shimmer all over. He snorted in greeting, nuzzling Darcy's cheek.

"I need you as like, a prop," she said. "Just stand still."

Xavier's eyes slid to me then back to her.

"Imagine Xavier is a really sparkly star in a really deep, dark pit," Darcy said, waving her hands at him and casting an illusion that made him appear to be a large, glittering rock. In her slightly drunk state, she didn't manage to hide his eyes or horn from view, and he was still very much giving her a confused side-eye.

"Wow, it's like I was really there." I said dryly, and Darcy flapped a hand at me, determined to try and conjure an illusion of the star releasing its power in Lionel's castle. But an illusion couldn't aptly capture the magnificence of such a thing. No, it seemed I was out of luck again. My mate had witnessed two Donum Magicaes now when most Fae went their whole lifetime without ever seeing one. Was I jealous? Maybe.

"Just wait," she encouraged.

A smile hooked up the corner of my mouth. "Waiting."

Darcy whispered something to Xavier which I only missed because I was staring at her lips remembering how they'd been wrapped so perfectly around my cock less than an hour ago. Fuck, she was irresistible, and I was star damned thirsty for her.

"Tick-tock, Blue. The night is young and I have way too many plans for you to waste time sitting here."

She glanced at me with a mischievous smile then stepped away from Xavier and began forging her illusion once more. Xavier's exterior began to glow, shining brighter and brighter, fuelled by his Order while Darcy put on a show around him with a bunch of Faelights.

"And then the grand finale," she announced, but Washer came stumbling out of the crowd in his tighty-whities, knocking into her and spilling his cup of beer all over her. She cursed, and I was at her side like a shot, shoving Washer back with a snarl.

"Watch where you're walking, asshole," I warned.

"Oh, do mind my hiney," Washer said, bowing apologetically to Darcy. "I've had a teeny weeny bit too much of the old juicy Lucy."

"There you are, you fangsome flapjack, and of course my darling Darcy!" Geraldine came bounding out of the crowd towing Leon along behind her.

Gabriel was smiling happily, and Leon looked hyper as shit, but that didn't necessarily mean he'd been drinking. I swear the guy ran on liquid sunshine, peppy at all hours of the day.

"We are having a romp of a time," Geraldine said. "And I am trying to gather up our majestic crew of begonia bandits for a bit of a hoo-ha."

Xavier shifted into his Fae form, casting a pair of pants made from leaves onto his body.

"Isn't that the name you give your...you know," he asked as he trotted closer.

Darcy bit her lip on an amused smile and I slung an arm around her shoulders as we waited to see what Geraldine had on her mind.

Geraldine wailed a laugh, smacking Xavier on the back hard enough to send him stumbling forward a step. "You do make my chipper chop, my sweet Pego-brother. No indeed, I see where the confusion came from. *Bossy* bandits is another name for my Brendas." She cupped her giant tits. "But I believe it is my Lady Petunia that you speak of."

"Who's speaking of your petunia?" Max came muscling through the crowd wearing a sparkly pink hat covered in seashells.

"Calm your clam, Maxy boy. No one waters my garden except your sprightly sea cucumber, but alas, Fae do dream. We cannot blame Xavier for his ganderings." Geraldine tiptoed up to kiss Max and he smiled serenely.

"I'm not gandering," Xavier muttered, but Geraldine didn't seem to hear him.

"Geraldine's gonna dare me and Gabe to do something wild," Leon said, bouncing on his toes. The Lion shifter was wearing a Skylarks Pitball shirt with his name and number on the back, and an old bell of jealousy rang in my chest. It had been a long time since I'd thought about my past endeavours to make it as a pro Pitball player, but the fact that Leon Night had claimed that fate still had the ability to make me envious apparently.

"I sure-a-tidley am," Geraldine said. "And your attire gave me the dingles for the idea."

Leon looked down at his Pitball shirt, his Lion Charisma bouncing off of him so much that pretty much everyone's eyes were drawn to him. "This is gonna be awesome. Ah shit, where'd I put my beer?"

He glanced around like someone might hold the answer and three Oscura girls raced off of the dancefloor, snatching a bunch of beers from the ice cooler and sprinting to offer them to him. He selected one with a vague nod of thanks and the girl who had managed to give it to him beamed with pride, the other two glaring at her jealously as they stalked back off into the party. It was pretty common for Lionesses to serve powerful Lions among their Order, and Leon was one of the strongest of his kind.

"You shouldn't be doing that," Gabriel said to him, but Leon waved him off.

"I can't help when my Charisma is Charismaring, Gabe. I'm seduction in Fae form."

I dropped my mouth to Darcy's ear. "Let's slip away to the Shimmering Springs.

There's a pretty rock pool there you'd look fucking edible in. Especially naked, sitting on my-"

A wet slap to my head made me look around with a snarl and I found Geraldine pointing at me. "Stop being a ninny and listen up."

Darcy smothered a laugh, prodding me in the ribs and I gave Geraldine my attention for her sake.

"This fursome fellow and this winged flapperjack owe me a dare." Geraldine gestured flamboyantly to Leon and Gabriel. "And I declare it to be this. We shall divide ourselves asunder. Our looksome Lion captaining one team, and our handsome Harpy captaining the other. It shall be a game of balls. Pitballs to be exact. Whenever a team scores, the opposing team must take a shot of Sourache. And whoever's team comes out the loser will have to do the bluffman's jabba jive." Geraldine broke into hysterics while we all shared looks of confusion over what the fuck that was. "Have we an agreement?"

"Drunk Pitball," Leon said excitedly. "Fuck yes."

"I'm not drinking," Gabriel said. "I can't until my visions are back to normal."

I frowned at my friend. He looked so much brighter in himself, but The Sight was still causing him pain, and I hated to think how much longer that would last.

"You are excused from all spirituous beverages," Geraldine declared.

"How is that fair?" Leon complained. "He'll be sober while we're all shitfaced."

"Oh, my simple feline," Geraldine scoffed. "Have you suffered through the doomful agony of The Sight day and night and saved us all from certain destruction time and again, only to find yourself with an icksome Cyclops rifling through your mind who left you with harrowing scars upon your very psyche?"

"Well...no," Leon pouted, then looked to Gabriel and sadness entered his eyes. "Fine, he can be excused. So do we get to pick our teams?"

"Abso-tively," Geraldine said. "Take turns, one after the other."

"You can pick first, Leon," Gabriel said with a calculated glint in his gaze.

"Wait, wait, you can't go using your fancy third eye to predict how this goes," Leon growled. "*You* can pick first."

"Alright," Gabriel said, looking like he'd just gotten exactly what he'd wanted. "Orio, you're with me."

"Then I get Darcy," Leon blurted. "You can't have Elysian Mates on the same team."

"Fine, you have Darius and I'll take Tory," Gabriel said.

"Ha, fine. I've got the resurrected Dragon consort dude," Leon said smugly. "I want Geraldine, too," he added, grabbing her by the arm and yanking her to his side.

"Then we'll have Max," Gabriel said.

"I want Xavier," Leon said possessively, moving to sling an arm around him.

I tuned out the rest of the picking, considering snatching Darcy and shooting away to the Shimmering Springs into the night. She looked damn excited about this game though, and I had to admit, I hadn't played a good round of Pitball in a long time. Besides, a post-game victory fuck did sound kind of sublime...

"The teams are appointed!" Geraldine bayed. "Onward to the Pitball stadium, friends! And gather the enlisted Fae."

Everyone split up to find the others, and Geraldine stumbled over a rock in her haste to move, knocking into Washer.

"You'll be needing a referee, I suppose?" he asked as he steadied her. "I shall limber up for the task. Pitball's not really my game, but I know the ins and outs of it from my academy coaching days. The nooks and crannies of the rules so to speak." He started lunging and Geraldine tried to talk him out of it in a desperate garble, but Washer lunged off in the direction of the Pitball stadium without another word.

"Come on, let's find Tory and Darius," Darcy said excitedly and the spark in her eyes for the game made me want this win more than ever.

It was going to be carnage, pure and simple, and I couldn't wait to come out on top.

At dawn, I waited anxiously in King's Hollow, having left Darcy sleeping back in Rump Castle. Last night had been completely wild, and I'd had a sum total of one hour's rest when we'd finally made our way back to our bed on the island. The Pitball game had been brutal, and the most fun I'd had in a long ass time. Thank fuck for healing magic, because I was pretty sure the hangover would have destroyed the best of our army this morning.

Darius landed on the roof with such force that the whole treehouse swayed and I smirked, certain he was pissed at me for dragging him out of bed so early after the long night we'd had. But I wanted to keep this as secret as possible from Darcy, and she had been so exhausted, I knew she wouldn't wake while I was missing.

Darius dropped through the skylight in his Fae form, fully naked and looking like I'd shat in his morning coffee.

"Did you bring it?" I asked, noting the bag in his hand which had a Dragon tooth-shaped impression in the fabric.

"Yeah, it's stuffed right between my ass cheeks, Lance. Go fetch it," he said, smoke spewing between his teeth.

I gave him a goading smile. "Always trying to get me near your ass, Acrux. Some things never change."

He barked a laugh, his anger falling away as he opened his bag and took out a gold medallion, looping it over his neck before adding ten gold rings to his fingers, a golden cuff to his wrist, and placing an honest to shit crown on his head. Then he walked to the chest in one corner, taking out some sweatpants and pulling them on.

When he returned to me, he reached into the bag one final time, taking out a small, glittering item.

I took a hopeful step toward it, but Darius snapped his fist closed around it, a growl rumbling through his chest.

"Easy, big boy," I said, grinning as I inched closer. "You said you wanted to do this."

"I do," he said through gritted teeth. "But that doesn't make this part any easier."

I moved nearer and he thrust his fist at me, his fingers still locked tight around the object.

I held my hand out beneath his fist and his jaw ticked as he worked to release it.

"You don't have to," I said seriously.

"Your stupid little face lit up when you saw this," he ground out. "And...you're my best friend. I want to."

His fingers started to unfurl and my heart warmed as the beautiful sapphire ring I'd found in Luxie Acrux's cave fell into my palm. The band was gold with a delicate pair of wings clutching the gemstone. It was almost perfect. But there were a few alterations I planned on making before it reached the standard I'd set for it.

Darius yanked his arm away like he feared he might grab it back from me, his hand fisting at his side.

"Thank you," I said earnestly, knowing how much this meant coming from him. "I love you, brother. You know that, right? And I'm so fucking grateful for this."

He nodded, the tension in his shoulders easing.

The door sounded downstairs and I lifted my head, looking to the stairwell expectantly.

"Who else did you invite?" Darius asked, following my gaze.

"Caleb and Gabriel."

My sanguis frater stepped into the room in a blue long-sleeved t-shirt and some grey sweatpants, followed closely by Seth in a white hoodie and jeans.

"You brought the mutt," I said icily, and Caleb pursed his lips.

"He should be a part of this," Caleb said firmly.

"But what am I a part of?" Seth asked enthusiastically.

"He'll tell Blue," I growled. "He can't keep a secret for shit."

"Oh can't I?" Seth said, arching a brow at me, reminding me that he had somehow managed to keep his feelings from Caleb long enough. Though he'd told half the group instead, so it wasn't exactly a win on his part. "Whatever it is, I'll keep it secret. Unless you're cheating on Darcy, in which case, I'll be ripping your cock off shortly."

"Hilarious," I said dryly.

"He couldn't cheat on her even if he wanted to," Darius said. "Not that he ever would."

"What do you mean?" Seth asked, and I wanted to curse Darius for laying crumbs for the mutt to follow.

"Oh yeah, your sparkle dick," Caleb said with a grin.

"Sparkle dick?" Seth perked up even more, glancing between everyone in the room, though all he got from me was a cold glare. "Who's going to tell me then? You can't go dropping the words 'sparkle dick' and not expect me to hound you to the ends of the earth for an explanation."

I folded my arms in refusal and Darius remained quiet, but my sanguis frater apparently had other ideas on loyalty.

"His dick glowed when Lavinia tried to touch it at the Palace of Souls. It burned her or some shit too." Caleb laughed.

"No fucking way!" Seth said, looking to me for confirmation, and I sighed. I should have known Caleb would give up that truth to his little bestie. I guessed I would have done the same with Darius though.

"It's some Elysian Mate thing, I believe," I said. "Anyway, that's not why we're here-"

"I need to see it," Seth insisted, and Caleb shot him a frown. "For science," he added quickly. "Darius, touch it, go on."

"No," Darius balked.

"No one is touching my dick," I snapped just as the window opened and Gabriel flew in with Geraldine under one arm.

"Oh, I suppose you all wish to attend the shiny sherman fiesta to see the disco ball dongler," Geraldine exclaimed as Gabriel placed her down.

"How do you know about that?" I demanded.

Gabriel gave me an innocent look as Geraldine answered. "The True Queens keep no buzzing bees from each other, and it seems I too have been deigned worthy of their whisperings."

"Blue," I cursed.

"She was most descriptive. Anyway, Maxy boy shall be along momentarily, and I sent word to Lady Tory too by means of an illusory bird, gone to sing her a merry tune at her window. She will be most pleasingly roused by the soothing whistles of my sweet swallow."

"She fucking won't be," Darius sniggered.

"This is meant to be private," I snarled.

"Private?" Geraldine scoffed. "Then why would your Noxy fellow come banging on my window like a cantankerous hat salesman upon the cusp of sunrise to bring me here?"

"It was an accident," Gabriel insisted, looking to me with a touch of embarrassment on his face. "I flew into it. I was distracted by a vision."

"Poppycock, the stars brought you to me," Geraldine declared. "Now what great ganderings have we been summoned for, dear professor of our studious past?"

Seth appeared from the kitchenette with a set of silver cooking tongs, jabbing them at my crotch.

I grabbed his wrist at the last second to stop him. "Don't even think about it."

"Too late for that," Seth said with a smirk. "Come *on*. Let us see the sparkle."

"No," I growled.

He reached behind his back with his other hand, grabbing a wooden spoon hidden in his waistband and coming at my dick with that instead. I grabbed his other wrist to stop him, but the ring fell from my grip in the same moment. With a growl, I released him and lunged for it, earning myself a wooden spoon jammed right into my cock.

I wheezed, doubling over and cradling my crotch with both hands. "*Capella*," I rasped venomously.

Darius's hand clapped to my shoulder, sending a wave of healing magic through me to soothe my dick, but the damage was done, because as I stood upright again, I found Seth holding the ring up to the light.

Geraldine let out a pterodactyl shriek, bounding over to take a look at it, and I glanced at Noxy, finding his gaze glittering with amusement. The fucker had known this was going to happen, and he'd let it all play out like a twisted puppet master.

Before I could snatch the ring back, Geraldine came at me like a stampeding rhino, slamming into me and fisting my shirt in her hands. She spoke in a voice that could only be described as emotionally demonic, tears streaming down her cheeks in thick droplets. "Does this sacred, transcendent, inspiring, flamboyantly fashionable ring of destiny mean what I believe it to mean? Are you going to sully your knee upon a mossy hill beneath the light of a million stars and ask the question to your fate-chosen mate that shall make the universe quake with reverence and the mighty ocean roil with desire?"

"If you're asking if I'm going to propose. Then yes," I said, giving up on keeping this a secret, because it was clear the stars weren't going to let me.

Geraldine stumbled away from me, turning into Darius's chest and weeping there while he vaguely patted her back.

Seth gasped, looking at the ring then to me, and I snatched it back from him.

I noticed Max slipping in the door, giving me a nod that said he'd heard everything.

With a sigh, I glanced around at the room of Fae who Darcy adored, giving in to this madness. "Well I was going to ask Caleb to add some details for me with his earth magic. But perhaps..." I swallowed my pride. "Would you all add something small? A detail or two, or just a touch of magic? I think Blue would like that you all had a part in it."

Geraldine squawked into Darius's chest, and Seth moved forward, looking as eager as a puppy at mealtime.

"Something small," I reiterated, holding out the ring but keeping my fingers pinched tight around it so he couldn't take it again.

He nodded, running his finger over it as he focused on harnessing his earth magic, crafting a beautiful moon cycle around the rim of the blue sapphire.

"Fuck, that's nice," I admitted.

"It has to be right for her," Seth said quietly as he added a few tiny details, rivets in the metal marking the shadows on the moon's surface. I frowned, seeing his love for my girl in the careful way he forged it, but I couldn't open my lips to let the word thank you pass them.

He moved away and Caleb stepped up next, touching his finger to the ring and a glimmer of power ran through it. Two delicate leaves grew from the gold, clasping the moon cycle and the sapphire at its centre.

I thanked him and he clapped me on the arm before stepping aside.

Max walked up next, and when I offered him the ring, he leaned down to whisper a song to it. The words were soft and hypnotic, making the gold glow with a bluish tint for a second before his song fell away.

"It's unbreakable now, and it will never tarnish," Max said, and I gripped his arm in thanks before he moved aside.

Geraldine trembled as she pulled away from Darius and approached me, blinking through reddened eyes. "Golly grapes, this honour is as grand as the great gulf of the celestial triangle, it sets my soul a-rumbling. Dear Darcy and her Orry man are to be wed upon a rising dawn of a new empire."

"If she says yes," I reminded her.

"Oh tish tosh." She flapped a hand at me then examined the ring closely before adding her power to it. She engraved the words 'blue means you' on the inside of the metal then handed it back to me with a sniff.

"She told you about that?" I murmured.

"Of course she did, with rosy cheeks and a sparkle in her eye," Geraldine said in a choked voice.

"Thank you for this," I said, then she croaked out a sob and walked away.

"Good morning." Xavier landed from the skylight with a thud followed by Sofia and Tyler.

"What are you doing here?" Darius asked in surprise as the three of them grabbed some clothes from a chest in the lounge.

"Seth texted us," Tyler said with a shrug. "He said we're all adding magic to Darcy's engagement ring."

"*Seth,*" I barked. "What did I say about keeping this secret?"

"You said to keep it secret from *Darcy*," Seth said innocently.

"I don't believe those were my words."

"*Sure* they were. I wouldn't go ruining my little Phoen's surprise. Give me *some* credit. Anyway, you guys won't tell her, will you?" He looked to the Pegasus herd, and they whinnied and shook their heads.

I ground my teeth, certain someone in this room was going to tell her, and my top suspect had already proven he couldn't keep his mouth shut for five minutes.

I jerked my head at the Pegasuses and they came trotting over with Xavier in the lead.

"Something small," I asked, offering it to them and they glanced between each other before Sofia leaned in and whispered to the others. I picked up every word and was satisfied with their choice as they each held their hand above the ring and their skin began to shine. That glow spilled down into the sapphire, making it glitter beautifully, the blue colour brighter than before.

"It'll shine even more when there's a rainbow close by too," Tyler said keenly.

"She'll love it," I said, certain of that.

Gabriel walked over as the Pegasuses dispersed and he gave me a stern look. "You'll be asking my permission now then, I suppose?"

"Your Sight has likely shown you the answer to that," I said in a low voice. "She doesn't need anyone's permission to do as she pleases."

Gabriel eyed me for a moment then broke a huge smile, clapping me on the cheek. "Good boy. This was a test. I thought you might come knocking at my door one day to ask me. I *saw* that you thought about it once or twice. But this conclusion is all I wanted from you. I'd pick no better Fae for her myself, Orio. The answer to your proposal belongs to her."

"I think Hail might prefer if you knelt at his grave and begged his permission though," Darius said and I was reminded of my friend's days among the dead, my heart pounding at knowing he had spent time with Darcy's parents. Something I would never get the opportunity to do until death.

Darius frowned as he realised we were all looking at him. "He liked you," he said, releasing an amused breath at some memory. "He called you a good choice for his daughter. And Merissa was just as keen on you."

I smiled, those words sending a wave of warmth through my chest and Geraldine broke down again into sobs.

"They're probably here right now," Darius added, waving a hand at the room in general. "Watching us. Especially with us all thinking of them and speaking about them. They'd have felt the pull and come to see what was going on."

"Really?" I murmured, looking to the small measure of space left in the room and wondering if there might actually be ghosts standing among us, taking joy in our joy. "If that's true then I hope you know I will love and protect her like no other man might hope to."

A breeze spilled through the room, a windchime tinkling out on the balcony and a warmth brushing against my cheek, almost as if someone had placed a hand there.

I sucked in a sharp breath and Darius snorted in amusement.

"See, asshole? I told you we'd remember you," he said to the empty space and the lights flickered as if Hail was responding to that jibe.

"On that note. Have you been thinking of Malrod like I told you?" Darius asked Gabriel suddenly, drawing all attention to him.

"Who?" Gabriel frowned in confusion.

"Your dead dad. Your biological one. I told you about him before you went off to the cabin," Darius said, narrowing his eyes at Gabriel as though he was being purposefully dense.

"You have never once mentioned my birth father to me or indicated that you had any interaction with him beyond The Veil," Gabriel replied in annoyance.

"Marcel," Darius announced. "That was it."

Another tinkling of windchimes seemed to confirm it and Gabriel eyes brightened.

"Marcel…" he murmured to himself.

Darius nodded. "Yeah, I told you he was fading out of memory and in danger of being sucked away into the beyond if no one ever thought of him or grieved for him. Honestly, I'm surprised you didn't take that more seriously because it could already be too late if you haven't even-"

Gabriel lunged at Darius, snatching hold of the gold medallion hanging around his throat and snarling in his face. "You have never once told me to think of him," he growled.

"Maybe take your fucking hands off of me, Flappy, before I burn them off," Darius replied, taking a step forward and glowering as he looked into Gabriel's eyes.

"Oh stop being a pair of bandyhoots and return your attention to the task at hand before I cast you from the window!" Geraldine demanded, thrusting herself between the two of them and forcing them to part.

Gabriel scowled at Darius but listened to her and took the ring from me to do his part. I watched as he added two tiny diamonds among Caleb's leaves, considering whether I should make any comment on what had just been said. He had never mentioned his biological father to me, and I wondered if he yearned to know more about him. I was sure I would have if the roles had been reversed.

"Who sent the whistling motherfucker?" Tory's furious voice cut through the air.

I found her climbing in the window, her hair sticking up in every direction and a scowl etched deep into her face.

Geraldine went to answer, but I flicked a subtle silencing bubble around her to stop her from claiming the wrath of Tory.

"I did," I said smoothly.

"*You*," she hissed, stalking towards me and letting her wings fall away at her back.

"You just love a morning songbird," I said, a wicked smile on my lips.

Tory lifted her hand like she was about to attempt a dick punch, but then her gaze fell on the ring and she faltered, her eyes narrowing.

"You asshole," she gasped, her hand lowering and her eyes lifting to meet mine. "You're going to propose." She said it like an accusation of murder, and I shrugged one shoulder in answer.

Without warning, I got something from Tory I rarely ever received. She swept forward and hugged me, tiptoeing up to wrap her arms around my shoulders and speaking into my ear. "No one's worthy of her, but if anyone deserves her, it's you Lance Orion."

Those words meant everything to me and I squeezed her tight before letting her go and offering her the ring. "Add what you like."

She contemplated it for a moment before reaching out and crafting a tiny Gemini symbol out of gold at the top of the clasp holding the sapphire with a star each side of it, twins to one another.

"There," she whispered, and I swear she had tears in her eyes for a second before she blinked and stepped back.

"When are you going to do it?" Seth asked keenly.

"He'll know when," Gabriel answered for me with that all-knowing look, and I placed my faith in the future he could *see* for us. He might not have known if we would make it through the coming battle, but I'd be damned if I charged into war before my proposal was made, and I was sure he *saw* that much. I just hoped to the stars that Blue said yes.

I'd slipped back into bed without stirring Darcy and fallen asleep easily, pulling her body into the mould of mine and holding her tight. I'd left the ring in Gabriel's care, sure if I'd given it to Darius I might have to prise it from his fingers the next time I asked for it.

When we woke, it was midday and our stomachs growled for food. I shot off to The Orb, bringing back a feast to fill our stomachs. We didn't let our words stray to war just yet, speaking of the past, our childhoods, the paths that had led us to each other, then reminiscing over the days we'd spent falling in love. It wasn't long before I had her beneath me, kissing her everywhere and telling her how much she meant to me. I wished I could write the words into her skin, make them permanent so that if we were ever parted, she could still feel them there.

Before I was ready to untangle myself from her, we received a text from Eugene letting us know he had just sent some more books to the academy from The Library of the Lost, and that one in particular held some information about a Celestial Trinity. Darcy sprang out of bed, wanting to get started on reading them as soon as possible, and though I'd have preferred to stay in bed with her, I knew this couldn't wait.

We showered and put on clothes, heading off across campus, hand in hand, still talking of only the good things. Though our feet were carrying us to one certain destination, because we couldn't stay in our bubble of tranquillity any longer. We had work to do, and the bright blue winter sky was already paling with the promise of dusk. No more time could be lost while we had answers to seek and new destinies to paint.

Darcy turned to me as we made it to the Venus Library doors, her eyes reflecting the burning sun, and I memorised the way she looked in that moment, fearing how many more days we might have together. She was perfect in this snapshot of time, a lock of blue hair tickling her face, her cheeks flush with life. I leaned down, brushing my lips against hers and she pulled her hair away from her neck, tilting her head to one side.

"Bite me," she whispered. "Sharpen this moment with pain. Brand it onto me. I don't ever want to forget this moment."

I did as my queen asked, gently biting her neck and tasting the purest kind of sunshine on my tongue. She gasped as I deepened the bite, branding her like she'd asked and her hand clasped the back of my neck, urging me on. I swallowed a mouthful of blood then released her, already overflowing with magic from the times I'd bitten her last night. A simple fire was all it took to stoke the power in her, but I depended on her blood to stay powerful. There was something I loved about that.

We headed into the library and took the secret stairway down into the archives beneath the building where a single fated night in the past had delivered me to Darkmore Penitentiary. But it had been one hell of a fucking night, and I felt no disconcertion in coming here. This place was ours and always would be.

Our books were still laid out on the table we'd been working at, poring through the texts whenever we had a moment of time to spend on it. Since the Nymph oracles had told Darcy that she had already spoken the answer to using the Guild Stones to create some sort of snare, we had been retracing our steps and working through every note I'd taken on the subject, going over each book we had already studied. But Eugene's new books would be our first port of call now, the pile of them waiting there for us, promising new possibilities.

"How is Professor Shellick getting on with testing the Guild potion?" Darcy asked hopefully as she took a seat at the table.

I dropped down next to her. "His last update said he needs a few more days, perhaps a week to draw firm conclusions."

"Which we don't have," she sighed.

"Exactly."

"What if we could have been more prepared for all of this? What if we could have done something differently?" Darcy said, a deep frown lining her features, and I knew the sweetness of our day was finally lost. I despised that. Seeing her struggle with the weight of the decisions that had to be made in this war, wondering if the path she'd followed had been the right one.

I laid my hand on hers. "Don't dwell on what's done, just focus on what can still be done."

She nodded, offering me a tight smile and starting to read a book Eugene had sent called *Whispers from the Stars*. It was a compilation of all the predictions made by powerful astrologers spanning many centuries. This was the tome that Eugene had said held mention of a Celestial Trinity, and I prayed it gave us some advantage against Clydinius. Anything that we could work with.

I picked up another one of the books that the High Buck had sent us, thumbing through it, but my gaze kept tracking onto Darcy and the tome she was studying. She paused on a section with a picture of three shining stars connected as if in a constellation that formed a perfect triangle – though it wasn't one that had been mapped in the sky. The page was titled *The Bane of Celestial Trinities*.

I shifted closer to Darcy, reading the text over her shoulder.

A few famous astrological philosophers described a union of the stars that could warp the forces of nature. Little is known of these so-called Celestial Trinities, but what has been theorised is astounding. The power of three, a number of great significance in numerology because of its connotations with wisdom and understanding, might allude to the possibility that a union of three stars could grant each celestial body a great and powerful knowledge. A knowledge that has been described in the works of ancient philosophers, including Garabold Everwing, Persephone Furfavour, and even the great Lucinda Nolefire.

Everwing spoke of a time that might come where three powerful figures held an 'immense knowledge of the universe's inner workings', while Furfavour was said to have a fixation within her theories that described 'three stars in triangular formation, seeking to unravel the threads of fate.' It is Nolefire's thoughts on the subject *that are perhaps the most chilling, however, stating in her philosophies that 'if three stars seized the hand of fate, they could wield it in a plague of destruction that could span across the realms forevermore.'*

The text went on to describe how a Celestial Trinity might form, but it was all conjecture with little evidence to back it up. I glanced at Darcy's face, expecting to find confusion there but instead I found a glimmer of a plot in her eyes.

"What are you thinking?" I asked.

"Something insane," she whispered.

"Of course you are," I half laughed, but the seriousness in her expression told me I should be more concerned than amused. "So, what insanity beguiles my mate this time?"

She shrugged lightly, glancing at me then back to the book and leaving me guessing.

I found nothing of use in the other books Eugene had provided, so I returned to studying my father's diary, convinced there had to be another clue in it somewhere.

My gaze lingered on the power words I'd taught the twins and the Heirs, a frown furrowing my brow as I considered something. If these had been made to wield the Imperial Star...was Clydinius still connected to them somehow?

"Ohmagod," Darcy gasped, looking up at me suddenly and jolting me out of my thoughts.

"Did you find something?" I leaned over to look at her book again.

"No, I just remembered something. At The Library of the Lost, I read a passage out loud to you." She rifled through the tower of books on the table, hunting for the right one, and my pulse picked up. She had spoken those words, could that be what the oracles had meant?

She shimmied a book out from the middle of the pile, flicking through the pages and stopping on one, placing her finger on a paragraph. "There," she said excitedly.

"Read it to me," I urged.

"Stone circles are one of the most powerful formations that can be created in nature, and if each stone is placed in conjunction with the planetary movements, upon sacred ground, or in alignment with the constellations, many magics can be wielded within its ring. From binding a Fae's tongue to the path of the truth, to trapping untold power within its confines, to enhancing the magic of certain gemstones." She looked up at me with light dancing in her eyes. "Lance, what if this is it? A stone circle, somehow connected to the Guild Stones. Maybe that's how we make the snare."

"It's too vague of a direction." I frowned. "How can we devise such magic without more instructions?"

"We'll work it out," she said, leaning in to plant a kiss on my lips and that was all it took to fortify my determination.

"Okay, let's start gathering information on stone circles."

"I'll message Eugene and ask him to send us everything he can find on the subject. He might be able to bring us something soon," Darcy said, taking out her Atlas and quickly sending the text.

I shot away into the shelves of the archives, certain there would be some book here we could start with. The two of us might have been on a misleading path with a lump of fool's gold at the end of it, but it was more than we'd had to go on in days. If there was any chance we were on the right track, then I'd go to hell and back to secure the answers we needed. I just prayed we had enough time.

CALEB

CHAPTER FIFTY SEVEN

The academy was in some ways utterly unrecognisable from the campus I had once found so peaceful and ruled over so childishly with my brothers. It seemed insane to me that I could still count the months and even the weeks since that time if I wanted to. That not so long ago we had held court in The Orb and been more concerned with Pitball than the state of the kingdom as a whole.

I wondered if the Vega twins' return had sparked Lionel into action with his plans or if his timescales had always been running to this pattern. Was their presence here the catalyst which had thrown us to this destination, or would his rise have come by now regardless? Would we be entirely without hope of resistance if it weren't for the return of the Vega line to our realm?

It was hard to say. And even if Lionel wouldn't have yet risen up without their return, I didn't think that I would have wished to change anything about them coming back to us. This war had been started long before now, back when Lionel had been manipulating the Savage King and collaborating with Nymphs in secret. Hell, it pre-dated him murdering his brother. His rise had been slow because he couldn't truly claim to be any more powerful than my mother or the other Councillors and he had needed to ally himself with others who could bolster his false claims of supremacy.

I was angry with my mom for that. For not seeing it. For not stopping it when there had been opportunity. But was I any better really? Lionel had been adept in hiding his malicious intentions and nefarious plans from them and no doubt had smothered any suspicions with charm and denial.

I, on the other hand, had known in my gut that Darius had been playing with dark magic, sneaking off to fight Nymphs and fuck knew what else. But I'd trusted him. Of course, I didn't regret a moment of that trust and I knew he was well deserving of it, but what if his intentions had aligned with his father's? What if the bond which I felt so keenly between us had been an act? It didn't seem possible or even plausible, but I knew that was how my mom had felt towards Lionel. At least initially. And perhaps by the time things started to feel off balance, by the time suspicions had begun to niggle at her, it had already been too late. But that didn't seem good enough to me.

I gritted my jaw, looking out from the clifftop beyond Aer Tower which had once only offered a view of the ocean and perhaps Draco Isle on a clear day. Now the floating mass of land which had been carved from the body of Solaria itself to house the Vegas' army dominated the darkened view between me and the horizon.

I observed the glittering lights of the encampment which sprawled out around the glimmering pinnacle of Rump Castle at the centre of the land mass. The survivors from all the Nebula Inquisition Centres were still arriving, offering to fight in the army or seeking refuge from the war.

Earth Elementals had added more land to the island, the magical wards that the Vegas had put in place to protect us extended all over again. And still, I knew it wasn't enough.

I thought on how we'd celebrated just one night ago. Partied and cheered our victory. I'd smiled until my face ached from it and drank until I couldn't see straight, then spent what little was left of that night groaning in pleasure in Seth's arms. After we'd met with Orion and the others at King's Hollow, Seth and I had spent the entire day together, only pausing in our passion for each other to breathe and eat. We'd slept so long after that, it was only when I'd woken in the middle of the night that I realised how exhausted I'd been from the past few days. I'd drained myself physically and emotionally, then given everything left of myself to Seth because each passing hour felt like it could be our last. Yet somehow, I'd woken to another dawn, the night sky just beginning to pale with the promise of a new day.

My lips were still bruised from the force of Seth's kisses, my neck scratched raw from the bite of his stubble, though I had no intention of healing the small wounds away. They were the marks of his claim on me, the secret stolen pieces of evidence that pointed to my ruin for him.

The wind was blowing hard from the north now, the chill a slap to the face and a sobering hiss of the harsh reality which belonged outside that night and day of debauchery. I wondered if we would ever again party like that. All of us alive and full of vitality, bolstered by our victory and screaming promises of an end to this war in our favour.

But that wind. It knew the truth of our plight. It knew that our army was still half the size of Lionel's at best. It knew that the Guild Stones still offered us nothing which might answer the promise of that prophecy we had all so foolishly pinned our hopes on. It knew that the dawn might have come for the Vegas, but the night would always claim the sky from the sun in the end.

We were running out of ideas. Worse, we were running out of time.

I checked my watch, knowing that despite the unsociable hour, my mom would be awake. She had celebrated as hard as the rest of us the other night, all of my family had, but I'd caught her eye across the crowd in the midst of the party, seen the way she gripped my little sister's hand so tightly in hers and I knew she saw the end coming for us too. The great rebellion, fighting for what was so plainly right and yet destined to crash and break against the might of the Dragon King.

I shot her a message on my Atlas, stating nothing other than a location; the beach on the far side of the island which housed the rebel army. I didn't wait for her reply, stowing my Atlas in my pocket then shooting away from my perch at full speed and racing to the beach.

The world blurred as I shot through the rebel camp in the dark, small houses crafted from mounds of earth, ice and rock hastily built one against another for them all to use for shelter.

I passed through the area closest to the academy grounds first where the cries of small children mixed with the laughter of an old man. Washing lines were strung between structures and wildflowers had been coaxed along by earth Elementals to brighten up the place. This was where the refugees had made camp, the safe haven they'd created in this bubble hidden away from the war. It was bright with signs of hope and a longing for better times. Messages had been scrawled across bare walls, praises for the True Queens and prayers to the stars to bring a brighter future to the faithful.

A symbol caught my eye more than once; a pair of Phoenix birds taking flight for the sky through the centre of a golden crown. Above them a single star perched as if awaiting their arrival. Below, flames cleansed all they left in their wake.

The people had created a banner for their queens.

Beyond the sprawling, chaotic layout of the refugee camp, the crisp, uniform lines of the army encampment reigned.

I paused in the wide gap that marked the boundary between here and there, survivors and warriors. Of course, the Fae who had chosen to enlist were free to visit the refugees and along this line of division, bars and market stalls had sprung up, many Fae rising to the challenge of entertaining and providing for the thousands of soldiers who were preparing for battle.

There were earth Elemental stalls laden with blankets and difficult to grow fruits and vegetables. Fire stalls with everflames of various sizes trapped in jars, some better suited to cast a glow of light while others would provide an ample heat source.

I cast my eyes over the talismans which were on sale at another stall, many of the usual gemstones and herbs aligned to luck and valour, but there were others which caused me to pause, making the old woman who was sitting behind the stall perk up hopefully.

"What's this?" I asked, pointing to a fork which looked in no way special to me.

"Tool of The Resurrected," she breathed mysteriously, squinting up at me in the darkness.

I doubted she would recognise me in this light with my hood pulled up and the moon at my back. It wasn't like the Queens' inner circle tended to travel out this way before dawn. "He ate from that very utensil; his essence imbues it with the power of the unknown. It is said that any who possess such a thing will themselves be shielded from the eyes of death and so prosper during battle."

I frowned, noticing the little card which sat above the fork. *'Genuine item blessed by Darius Acrux'.*

I snorted as I realised what she was referring to. Someone had taken to stealing any utensils Darius had used and were selling them as talismans against death. Well, either that or someone had taken to pretending this came from Darius's plate, but as I glanced at the sign behind her, announcing that she was happy to provide proof of all claims via Siren, Cyclops or any other form of interrogation, I had to assume this *had* once been used to deliver food into Darius's mouth.

My eyes ran along the row of cutlery, pens, napkins and even a bloodstained bit of cloth which had an eyewatering price tag and claimed to be blessed with the blood of Queen Roxanya, offering whoever possessed it the protection of the royal bloodline. There were mostly items relating to the Vegas and Darius, but all of us were represented in some way, including a withered vine which had apparently been cast by Seth during the attack the Nymphs waged on us outside the ruins of Mount Lyra which, when boiled into a drink, claimed to offer up a hint of his strength and bravery in battle.

I wondered whether I should call bullshit on all this superstitious nonsense, but I hesitated short of doing it. What harm did it really do? If the Fae purchasing these items believed they gained luck, strength or a chance to avoid death and survive this war then who was I to take that little bit of hope from them? The stars knew we needed what positivity we could cling to right now.

I turned my eyes from the talismans and instead pointed out a stone at the other end of the stall, picking the best among them and thanking her as she wrapped it in a velvety leaf. I paid her twice what she'd asked for it, grinning as she gushed her thanks, then I shot away to meet my mom.

Racing between the rows of the army encampment was far easier than navigating the sprawling refugee camp. Neat lines left clear walkways between the regimented tents made of cloth, wood or stone in matching fashion to their neighbours. There were small signs of individuality as I passed between them, slogans scrawled onto the walls depicting the marks for the various squadrons. Flags snapped and whipped in the frigid wind, each depicting that same symbol of the rising Phoenixes bursting through the crown but with them were signs for Orders from Pegasuses to Tiberian Rats and everything in between, displayed proudly and with honour.

These were the Fae who had suffered most under Lionel's rule and their desire for revenge filled the air with a tempest of barely restrained emotion. Unlike in the refugee encampment where hope and fear underlined all that was there, this place felt poised and ready to fight, eager for it even.

It bolstered my own hope to get a taste for how hungry our army was for this win. I only wished it meant more in the face of our odds. History never told the tale of wars that were won by the wrong side, their victors repainting the records to show themselves in the greater light. Would people one day talk of the madness of the Savage Queens? Would they mutter prayers to the stars that those heathenish girls had lost the war and bless Lionel Acrux's name for bringing about a new era, sweeping mention of persecution and genocide under the rug?

I ground my teeth at that thought.

Not if I have anything to do with it.

If we were going down then I planned to scorch this world with my name and force it to remember me as I was, fighting for what was right and giving everything in my resistance of that tyrant's brutal reign. I would be myself entirely. I wouldn't be forced to sway at the whims of others.

I sped through the camp, passing those who slept, those on guard and those who simply sat waiting for the inevitable.

When I made it to the beach, Mom was already there, standing on the pebbles and looking out to sea where the waves were gilded silver by the moon and the horizon whispered endless promises.

"When we were at the academy, your father used to bring me down to Aer Cove to look out over these waves," she said, knowing I was there despite my silent arrival. "I indulged him because our parents were so keen on the match, but of course, I didn't let him have my heart until some years later."

I'd heard this before, how they'd been something of an arranged marriage, not forced into it but presented as an option, my father one of the most powerful Vampires of their generation, his family flush with wealth from the import business they ran. Mom had resisted initially, wanting to find her own path to love, but for Dad, he claimed to have known it would be the two of them from the moment he laid eyes on her. They both enjoyed recounting tales of his tireless efforts to convince her to give him a chance, and luckily for me and my siblings, eventually she did.

"Are you feeling nostalgic because you think we're all going to die?" I asked, the question bald, no bullshit, its utterance a slap in the face of the fragile lie we'd all been telling ourselves over and over again.

Mom turned to look at me, her eyes roaming over my features, a hurt in her gaze which made my throat thicken as she drew closer.

She reached for me, her fingers trailing down my cheek until she cupped my jaw.

"They tell you how hard it is to be a parent," she murmured. "How many sleepless nights and temper tantrums it will take to survive those first years, how testing it is to cope with teenagers, but no one mentions the bit which is the hardest of all."

"What's that?" I asked and she smiled sadly, her thumb brushing over my cheek as she studied my features.

"How very difficult it is to admit that they've grown up." A tear spilled down her cheek and I frowned, raising my hand to cup over hers, holding her palm against my skin. I had so many memories of those eyes, tucking me in at night, shining with pride when I succeeded, crinkling with mirth when I laughed.

"I don't know that anyone ever truly grows up where their parents are concerned," I replied. "Some part of me will forever be toddling around in diapers and causing havoc in the grounds whenever you turn your back so far as we're concerned."

She breathed a laugh, a second tear splashing onto my fingers as she leaned in to me and I wound my free arm around her.

She was such a powerful force, not only in my life but in the whole of Solaria, and it never failed to surprise me how easily I could fold her into my arms now, how I towered over her by more than a head and was almost twice as broad. Some part of me would forever be the little boy who used to crawl into her arms and make forts beneath her desk when her work made it hard for her to carve out all the hours we needed for our games.

It hurt, this moment. Even though we both knew it had come, it still hurt. And in some ways, it wouldn't change anything between us. Our love was far more than position or power. Our bond was one which could only ever be shared between mother and son, and whatever else we might be, we were that first.

"Don't go thinking I'll go easy on you just because I'm emotional," Mom laughed against my chest, squeezing me tightly and letting the moment drag on just a little.

"I wouldn't forgive you if you did," I replied, placing a kiss against her blonde hair and exhaling, letting the boy in me take a back seat as the man I had grown into raised his head.

We released each other as one, sharing a rueful, ready smile and I nodded.

The ground broke apart beneath me in the blink of an eye and I yelled out as I fell, not into a pit but a chasm, the entire beach seeming to have dropped away to nothing as the world disappeared overhead and I plummeted into the dark.

Magic burst from me, vines whipping out and shooting for the walls of dirt which receded rapidly, stabbing deep into them and anchoring despite how quickly my mom was breaking them apart.

I hit the vines, the six of them cradling my weight as they took it, stretching downwards before snapping back up again like elastic bands and launching me skyward.

I burst from the hole in the beach, pine needles tearing out from me in a deadly cloud, shooting in every direction while I focused on regaining my feet and locating her.

Pillars of earth formed to catch me and I started leaping from one to the next, my gaze scanning the pebbled beach for her, zeroing in on a flash of movement to my rear.

I leapt aside as one of the waves surged from the ocean, spearing for me on my pillar and reminding me that choosing the beach as a battleground against a dual Elemental with earth and water magic might not have been the best idea I'd ever had.

I crashed to my feet and shot away, skidding on the pebbles before I drew them under my influence and forced them to form a solid path.

She'd taken chase; I could feel her behind me like a whisper on the back of my neck, and I grinned as I let the ground open up at my heels.

Mom leapt over the pit, pillars of earth forming beneath her feet to keep her out of it, but I'd already whirled around to face her, fireballs bursting from me and pummelling her from every direction.

She was forced to shield with water, steam hissing up in a great cloud that obscured the sky as the might of our magic met and battled for dominance.

I let the fire distract her, veering towards the water where she'd least expect me to go and gathering power in my fists, forging a beast of teeth and claws, strongly built from stone but adorned with a coat of flames.

I directed the beast straight for her, my heart thrashing as I watched it collide with the shield, tearing through the magic to reveal-

"Oh fuck," I cursed, whirling around as I realised she'd already escaped that trap, but I wasn't fast enough and a whip of water coiled around my ankle beneath the waves.

I was yanked off of my feet and dragged out to sea at such speed that my whole world became nothing but bubbles and salt and darkness, all sense of direction abandoning me entirely.

Panic threatened but I ignored it, twisting my hands sharply so a ring of fire engulfed me, severing the lash of water and dumping me on the seabed as the force of it evaporated the water around me. I'd given my position away, but I sank into the sand and silt before she could take advantage of the fact.

I scrunched my eyes shut and held my breath as I forced the dirt and grit to propel me back towards the shore beneath ground, launching myself skywards again only when I was certain I was back on the beach.

Pebbles became missiles as they were fired away from me, Mom's cry of pain both a thrill and a shock, but I didn't let up.

I shot towards her in a blur, fire racing ahead of me while spears of earth rose at her back.

Ice exploded from her, neutralising my flames and shielding against the attack from behind too but as I threw more power at it, a great crack ripped through its heart.

Again we collided, our power ripping the beach apart, the crash and boom of magic drawing people to watch us, the hill beyond the beach slowly filling with Fae who stared on in awe, but I couldn't waste any energy on them.

Seconds fell to minutes which fell to an hour then two, both of us bloodied, bruised and panting with the exhaustion of our battle, both of us refusing to relent. My time had come. I had to prove it.

As the time wore on and we found ourselves matched over and over again, I began to notice a pattern to her defences, one which she had repeated often enough for me to think I might just be able to exploit it.

A spear of ice javelined for my chest and just as I was shooting aside to avoid it, I spotted the opening I needed. My heart leapt as I advanced, the beach rising at my power, the pebbles pelting her with such force that she had to shield.

The ground broke apart beneath me and I shot into the chasm I'd opened up, racing at full speed as she cast a dome of ice around her, hiding her from view.

When she dropped beneath the ground to escape unseen, she found a monster waiting for her in the dark.

My arm banded around her waist as I dragged her back to my chest and the magic I'd been holding in reserve crashed from me, clay coating her hands where they clawed at my arm, fire baking the clay in the next breath as I immobilised her.

"Clever boy," she panted in surprise, and I barked a laugh as I launched us back out of the dirt and onto the beach, releasing her and letting her turn to face me.

"Yield," I demanded, my voice carrying to all who were watching, flames rolling up my forearms even though I knew it was done.

Mom looked at the impenetrable clay that had solidified around her hands, locking down her power and ending our fight.

Her mouth curled into a victorious grin which was utterly full of pride, and my chest hollowed out at the love I found in her eyes, seeing me not just as her boy, but as a man who had grown into his power and come to claim it for himself.

"I yield," she replied loudly. "And I am very much looking forward to seeing what you do next, my boy."

She dropped to one knee before me and my heart lurched as the reality of what I'd done collided with me. I'd challenged her for her position and I'd won. I was a

Celestial Councillor. And I answered to no one but my queens anymore.

I fell to my knees before her, throwing my arms around her as a sob broke in my chest.

"I love you," I told her forcefully, knowing this could never change that in the slightest.

"I love you more," she promised, her forehead falling to mine as we knelt there panting and bleeding, exhausted both physically and emotionally, forever changed and yet forever as we were.

Cheers erupted behind us, bodies pressing closer as the Fae who had been watching ran down onto the beach, slapping me on the back and calling out congratulations while exulting over the ferociousness of the battle and how impressed they'd all been by the magic.

In the centre of them all, I met my mom's eyes and she grinned at me, her split lip dripping blood onto her chin, her normally perfect blonde hair hanging wildly around her shoulders, stained with dirt. She'd never looked more beautiful to me.

"Go on," she urged in a voice just for me. "Go tell the world to get fucked, my beautiful boy. I know that's at least half of why you chose this moment. So if you mean to shake the foundations of all we stand upon then I'd say that now is the perfect time."

I blinked at her in surprise, wondering how she knew what else I intended to do, and why, after all she'd said to me before she suddenly seemed very much in favour of me doing it.

As if she could hear that question in my mind, she scoffed lightly. "A mother always knows these things, sweetheart. But sometimes, if you want to change the world, you have to do it yourself. And I think you're ready now."

"You...could have saved yourself this whole thing you know," I laughed hopelessly but she shook her head.

"This war is a vast and uncertain thing. We don't know if we will live to see tomorrow let alone the dawn of what will come after it. A new age is rising one way or another. Now is the time to stand up and fight to be a part of its creation. Now is the time for fates to change and something else to begin. I've played my part. It's time for you to step out of my shadow, and you just proved that I was right to think so."

I threw my arms around her, squeezing her tightly while letting my magic fall away from her hands, freeing her to embrace me in return.

I exhaled a long breath, feeling a knot loosen around my soul and knowing exactly what I needed to do.

I pressed a kiss to her cheek and then I was gone.

The waning moon had sunk towards the waves while we fought and the icy silver of its light where it hung fat and wide in the sky lit up the encampment and academy grounds beyond it in sparkling light.

I sped back the way I had come, racing at top speed for The Orb where I knew everyone was converging in the early hours to discuss our progress and the latest plans for the war.

Exhaustion beat my body like a drum, the dregs of magic which remained to me like a simmering ember to the flame I usually carried. I needed blood, but I needed him more.

I skidded to a halt outside the enormous golden dome, my eyes roaming over the patched repairs to its roof, the scars of the war marring even this immovable object.

How many times had I walked through these doors? How many times had I seen him here? And yet now, when it mattered the most, I found myself hesitating before them, that familiarity seeming like pressure all of a sudden, the countless times I hadn't done this mounting up against me now.

Despite all of that, it wasn't fear I felt as I lingered with my hand on the door, my pulse hammering wildly, my palms slick with expectation. No, it wasn't fear, it was anticipation which consumed me now.

I wrenched the door wide, Geraldine's protection spells swelling over me, checking my magical signature, making sure that I was who I appeared to be and allowing me to pass the threshold when I satisfied the inspection.

My confident stride fell away and I paused as I found the Vega twins standing before a camera, Orion, Darius, Max, Seth and Geraldine all in the background of the shot while they spoke passionately about the war, urging Fae to rise up and join the rebel army.

Seth caught my eye, jerking his head in a way which was obviously visible on camera and I realised that I was supposed to be up there with them. I winced, remembering Geraldine's demands for my attendance to this rally thing today, but my mind had been so full of what I needed to do that I'd fully forgotten about this.

Everyone standing in that line up looked polished to perfection, wearing armour and holding weapons, powerful, poised, all of those things which I, half covered in dirt, the other half drenched, my clothes torn, bloodstains marking my body and my fangs out because I was fucking ravenous, did not look.

"This oppression cannot continue," Tory snarled into the camera. "That tyrant cannot be allowed to survive."

Yeah, I was definitely not dressed for the occasion and yet for some reason, my feet were moving, my gaze locked on Seth and all the very sensible reasons for me to stay the fuck away were falling to nothing as I looked into his eyes and stalked closer.

My hand fell into my pocket and curled around the item I'd bought from the vendor outside the army camp, the cold stone centring my thoughts and my decision already made.

I'd spent the morning fighting for this, I'd claimed my mother's position, and I couldn't spend a single second longer lying about who I was and what I wanted.

"I don't care about rules or laws when it comes to us," I said my voice hard and unyielding, my steps certain and unfaltering.

The twins fell silent, Geraldine gasped, clutching her pearls but Max caught her arm as she made to intercept me, holding her back with a wide grin on his face as he read my intention in the air.

"And I won't be told I can't have you by anyone."

"Me?" Seth breathed, glancing to the others as if any of this could ever be for anyone but him, as if he still wasn't certain that I wanted him and him alone, and that I was sick of lying and half-truths, pretending and concealing.

"I challenged my mother and claimed her place," I told him. "And if my queens try to tell me no on this then I think I'll just have to go ahead and commit treason. You are in my head morning, noon and night, your presence invigorates me and your absence leaves me aching. I dream of you whenever I sleep and burn for you whenever you are near. I can't hide it anymore. I *won't* hide it anymore. I want you to be mine, Seth, I fucking need you to be mine."

I offered him the rose quartz which had been carved into the shape of a crescent moon and hung from a chain of silver, and he blinked at it for several achingly long seconds while all of our friends stared and waited for his reply.

Then he grabbed hold of my shirt, yanked me towards him and kissed me like the sky might cave in if he didn't.

I groaned into his mouth, fisting his hair, kissing him harder, devouring his lips and inhaling his breath as everything I had been aching for finally fell together. I was his. I had been his for far longer than I'd been willing to admit, but I couldn't keep lying about it. I couldn't keep hiding him like he was something to be hidden when really he was something I wanted to shout from the rooftops and claim beyond all else.

"About fucking time," Darius laughed loudly, clapping me on the shoulder while

Darcy said 'at last' and Tory whooped. Geraldine exclaimed about the live broadcast still rolling and I decided I was done with public declarations.

"Let's get out of here," Seth panted against my mouth, and I grinned as I kissed him again, hoisting him into my arms and shooting away without another word.

I didn't release him as we made it outside, bathed in the moonlight and racing for King's Hollow.

We collided with the door, magic sparking around us, a gasp scraping my throat raw as we unintentionally power-shared in our desperation to unlock the door.

It sprung open behind us and we half fell through it, only my speed stopping us from hitting the floor. I heaved Seth back into my arms and shot for the room I'd claimed ownership of here, not stopping until we were in it and my mouth was pressed to his, his body crushed between mine and the wall.

Seth shoved me back, panting as he stared at me, his pupils wide and expression shocked.

"You took on your mom for me?" he breathed like he couldn't quite believe I'd done that.

"Yeah," I admitted, smirking at him as I took in his swollen lips and rumpled shirt. Aside from that he looked perfectly put together in his white shirt with his hair drawn back into a knot and stubble shorn to nothing on his jaw. By contrast, I looked positively feral after my fight with my mom and it amused me to see our usual roles reversed. "It was fucking hard, too."

A breath of laughter parted his lips and he touched the rose quartz chain at his throat as though checking it was really there.

"I was sick of the world getting to decide what you could or couldn't be to me," I told him. "So I took a leaf from our queens' book and burned it all to hell."

Silence fell with the possible repercussions of what I'd just done, with the question over whether I could even hold my mom's position permanently now at all. But if someone else wanted to seize it from me then they would have to fight for it. I was willing to sacrifice whatever it took to claim Seth for my own, but I was also planning on having it all if I could.

"Come here," I said, offering Seth my hand and he didn't hesitate to take it, letting me draw him to the sliding door to the far side of my room and out onto the balcony beyond. I led him along it, glancing at the trees as I hunted for a spot between them which might offer up a view of the sky.

We had to cross one of the little bridges which led over to an adjoining tree where a curved bench sat nestled in the branches, concealing the platform it sat upon.

"She told me to do it," I said, pointing between the canopy to the moon which winked out at us, low and heavy in the sky, its light seeming brighter than it should have been while dawn fast approached. "I looked up at her tonight and knew that I was done pretending with you. You're all I want Seth, you're all I've wanted for far longer than I was brave enough to admit and I-"

"I love you," he said, taking my jaw in his hand and drawing me close so that I could taste those words as he spoke them, brushing against my lips and sinking into my skin.

"You stole my line, asshole," I growled.

"Then try it again."

"I love you, Seth Capella, even more than the moon loves the sky."

He slapped a hand over my mouth, eyes wide and jerking to look at the moon as though she might have heard and taken offence.

I grinned beneath his hand then sunk my fangs into the side of his palm.

Seth growled at the sting of pain and I groaned at the rush of his blood over my tongue, basking in the exhilaration of taking in his magic and letting it fill every dark piece of me with his exuberant light.

Seth let me bite him, leaning in to press his own mouth to my neck, trailing kisses down my throat while his free hand worked to loosen the buckle of my belt.

I groaned louder, my hands flying down the buttons of his shirt before wrenching it off of him, exposing the solid lines of his chest which I explored with roaming fingertips before opening his fly.

I swallowed thickly, drawing my fangs from his palm so I could tip my head back and indulge in the feeling of his mouth on my skin.

Seth ripped the already ruined shirt from my body and I grinned cockily as he dropped to his knees before me, pushing my pants down and drawing my cock between his lips.

I groaned with pleasure, working my fingers into his hair and knocking it free of the knot he'd tied it in as I drew him down over my dick, letting him take me to the back of his throat, loving the way his fingers bit into my ass as he pulled me closer.

I thrust my hips in time with the movements of his head, moonlight gilding my skin and casting him in a perfect light.

I was so hard that it practically hurt, only the sweep of his tongue and steady pressure of his lips around my shaft stopping me from losing myself entirely to the need I felt for him.

"More," I gasped, wanting him so badly that even my heart seemed to thunder to the sound of his name.

He growled at the request, taking my cock to the back of his throat and sinking a finger into my ass at the same time.

"Fuck," I panted, my fingers tangling in his hair, the dual sensations making my blood riot in my veins. "Again."

This time as he sucked me deep, two fingers drove into me, pressing against some sensitive spot which had me jerking, my cock thrusting to the back of his throat and euphoria rushing for me.

He pushed deeper, sucking hard, and I growled his name as my cum filled his mouth, the explosive force of my orgasm striking the breath from my lungs and making my knees buckle.

I dropped down to kneel before him, kissing him hard when words failed me, my pulse thrashing like it had fallen prey to a lightning strike, my body trembling with the force of my release.

"Fuck, Caleb, I wanna be inside you so bad," Seth groaned against my lips.

I froze for half a second, that final line between us still uncrossed, though I didn't really understand why. There was nothing between us which seemed off the table anymore and as I slipped my hand into his pants and began to stroke the thick length of him, I knew I wanted it too.

"Don't tell me, show me," I demanded, moving back so I could lie beneath him, letting him press his weight down on top of me as I kissed him again.

We fell into a frantic race to remove the last of our clothes until finally he was pressing down on me, his bare flesh scalding hot against my own and the moonlight spilling through his hair where it fell around his face.

Seth looked down at me, cautiously at first, but his expression turning hungry and feral with desire as he found no doubt in my eyes.

He kissed me again, softer, sweeter, his hand roaming down my side until he was drawing my knee up then caressing the back of my thigh.

His cock drove into my other leg, solid and throbbing with need. I wrapped my fist around it as he caressed my ass, slipping his fingers to my opening and working first one, then two inside me.

Precum beaded the tip of his cock as he drove his fingers in and out and I smeared it over the head, feeling him shiver at my touch, wanting him to take all the pleasure he could from my flesh.

I groaned as he stretched me, his hand withdrawing momentarily as he fetched a bottle of lube from the pocket of his pants. He kissed me again as he slicked my ass with it, fingers driving in and out, our hips grinding against one another as we both began to ache for this.

But still he didn't give me his cock, teasing me with his hand, adding a third finger and making me pant with need beneath him until I was fucking desperate for it.

"Please," I gasped, using my grip on his cock to move it between my legs, arching my hips to give him better access.

Seth drew back, taking hold of his dick and dislodging my hold on it. My own cock was rock hard again between us and I fisted it on instinct, needing more of this unearthly pleasure, wanting to feel him inside me so fucking bad.

His eyes stayed glued to mine as he rolled the head of his cock over my ass, dipping his hips just enough to push at that barrier before retreating again.

I groaned, gripping his shoulder with my free hand and drawing him down, needing all of him.

He smiled at me, that rueful, soul-destroying smile which I should have known would be my undoing from the very first moment he turned it my way. And then he was sinking into me, filling my ass and growling my name.

I was blinded by the feeling of it, how fucking full my body had suddenly become, how for several seconds I couldn't breathe at all, my muscles tensing, my heart pounding with the certainty that I couldn't take so much of him at once.

But before any of those thoughts could even begin to settle into me, he sank deeper, filling me impossibly more and groaning in bliss while I echoed him, because holy fuck it felt so good.

Seth looked down at me in question, his cock deep inside me, his eyes bright with love.

"You really are mine, aren't you?" he whispered, his words like a prayer and I could only nod.

"All yours," I agreed. "From now until the end."

He smiled wolfishly, his gaze dropping to my hand which had fallen still around my rigid cock, and he licked his lips. "Fuck your hand while I fuck your ass, pretty boy. I want you to howl with me when I finish."

His voice was full of grit and the utter command of an Alpha. I was helpless beneath the spell of those words and all the pleasure they promised me, so I nodded and began to move my fist as he started to roll his hips.

At first, the sensation of him moving within me was overwhelming, my body uncertain of how best to move with his, but he went slow, waiting while I adjusted to it, letting me take the lead until we had fallen into a rhythm of undeniable bliss.

His arm hooked around my knee as he held me right where he wanted, then he began to fuck me like the heathen I knew him to be.

Seth's mouth swallowed my groans, licking the pleasure from my lips and tasting every sin-filled thought I'd ever had about him between our kisses.

He was brutal and beautiful and entirely mine, and my cock jerked in my fist as I tried to hold out beneath this utter inhalation of my flesh.

Seth cursed my name, sinking in deeper, faster, then finally howling as he came inside me, my body exploding into pleasure again just as a burning sensation seared behind the back of my ear.

He pressed his full weight down on top of me, kissing me deeply, my cum smearing between our bodies which were already slick with sweat.

After an achingly long kiss, our hearts thrashing powerfully against our ribcages so we could feel each other's pulses, Seth rolled off of me to lay panting at my side.

"Five minutes to catch our breath then we're going again," I told him, grinning up at the trees overhead, their leaves painted silver in the moonlight while they danced back and forth in the wind.

Seth sucked in a sharp breath, shoving my head aside and running his fingers over something behind my ear, reminding me of that momentary pain amid my ecstasy.

"What is it?" I asked, shoving his hand off me to touch the tender spot myself and as I looked at him, I found him touching the same place behind his own ear.

"Ho-ly fuck," Seth breathed. "The moon just made us…"

He couldn't seem to finish that sentence but as I knocked his hand aside and looked at the spot behind his ear, I found a perfect, silver crescent emblazoned on his skin.

My lips fell open as I recognised it for what it was, my eyes finding Seth's and a wide smile spreading across my lips.

"Mates," I finished for him. "We're Moon Mated."

446

DARCY

CHAPTER FIFTY EIGHT.

After our press conference and Caleb's declaration of love for Seth to the whole world, Tory and I had slipped away to visit the Nymph village again. I was in a damn good mood about my friends finally claiming one another, and even the discussion with the High Nymph Cordette didn't sour my mood. She had been anything but welcoming, but her eyebrows had raised when we'd told her of the bargain we'd made with a fallen star to clean the shadows – leaving out the part where we'd begged for several other gifts from Esvellian before it had been done.

Cordette had asked us to give her time to discuss the possibility of sending some warriors to fight with us in battle but had made no promises. It was something, even if it wasn't all we'd hoped for. And with that, we returned to Zodiac Academy, a sense of hope brightening the day.

As I walked to The Orb with Tory, I checked my Atlas, finding my daily horoscope waiting for me and wondering if it might give any insight into whether Cordette would really end up offering us her help.

Good morning, Gemini.
The stars have spoken about your day!

With Jupiter moving into your chart, you may feel a renewed sense of optimism, even though a dark threat still hangs over you. A conversation with a Scorpio will bring clarity to your mind over the woes of the past, and if you take heed in their words, you may find yourself freed from the cruel chains of trauma. You might feel a sense that something big is coming between you and a beloved Libra, a moment that will place an important choice at your feet. Enjoy the highs while they remain and take heart when the lows seek to drag you down.

I showed my Atlas to Tory. "My horoscope is being weirdly optimistic today. What do you think it means about 'an important choice?'"

"No idea." Tory shrugged. "Maybe Orion is gonna ask you if he should shave his beard off."

"Well the beard stays," I said. "Maybe I'll suggest he grows it out. Like Merlin."

Tory sniggered. "Then he can tuck it into his waistband when it's in his way."

We both laughed and I leaned in to my sister, wishing we had more free time to just hang out like this.

We walked into The Orb and I spotted Max and Geraldine looking over some maps on the war council table. My eyes scanned the room instinctively for Orion, and I found him on the red couch with Darius, chatting and laughing together like two gossiping old ladies.

I headed in their direction, but a wind came whipping up behind me and suddenly Tory and I were bowled over by the force of two muscular men. Seth nuzzled my face then howled like he was in his Wolf form while Caleb hugged Tory in excitement.

"What the fuck?" Tory laughed.

"Something happened!" Seth yelled.

"Tell them," Caleb encouraged, looking to Seth like he knew he'd want to be the one to say it.

Orion shot over, pulling Seth off of me and Darius was close behind him, spewing smoke from his lips as he stared at Caleb pinning Tory to the floor. Instead of going full Dragon, he paused, seeming to notice something about Caleb.

"Holy shit." Darius grabbed Caleb's arm, yanking him upright and examining something behind his ear.

"What's going on?" I asked, desperate to know as Orion caught my hand and pulled me to my feet.

"Yes, what ho, dear fellows?" Geraldine came jogging over with Max.

Seth bounded between us all, looking like he was about to lose his head with excitement, but he managed to keep himself in check long enough to tell us. "So we were in King's Hollow fucking like animals when-"

"*Seth*," Caleb laughed.

"What? It's important to the story," Seth insisted. "So Caleb was moaning my name and telling me how I'm the best he's ever had when-"

"*Seth*," Caleb's tone dropped to a warning growl.

"Alright, alright, I'm just saying the parts that are relevant," Seth said with a smug grin, still bouncing on his feet, looking ready to take off.

"How is that relevant? And when did I even say that?" Caleb demanded, but he started laughing again, clearly on a high himself. "Just get to the point."

"I think I know the point," Darius said, clapping Caleb on the shoulder then looking to Seth. "But go on, say it, brother."

"The moon got all glowy and big and beautiful – even more beautiful than usual," Seth explained. "She was so, so bright and it was like she was shining just on us. Through us, and into us, all around us, with sparkles everywhere."

"By the stars," Orion exhaled as he realised what they were saying, and it looked like Geraldine and Max were realising it too, but Tory and I were still left in the dark.

"What it is it?" I pressed and Seth leapt at me, grabbing my arms and shaking me.

"The moon mated us, Darcy!" he exclaimed then spun around, pulling his hair back to show me and Tory the space behind his ear.

A silver crescent was marked onto his skin like it was stitched there with threads of moonlight.

"Oh wow." I reached out to run my finger over it and Seth howled, finally unleashing all that energy and racing off to do laps of The Orb.

Caleb showed us his mark, pride lining his features and I rushed forward to hug him.

"I'm so happy for you both," I squealed, finding myself crushed between the arms of the rest of our group.

"This is cause for celebration indeed," Geraldine gasped as we broke apart again. "I shall prepare us a barrowful of brunch and we shall all be as merry as windigogs upon the hour!"

"We don't really have time, don't we need to hold a war council today?" Caleb said with a frown.

"That can wait," Tory said firmly, and I nodded. "This is fucking amazing, and we're going to acknowledge it properly."

Caleb pushed a hand into his golden curls, and I could have sworn he was blushing a bit. He looked to Max, then Darius as Seth went sprinting past us again with a whoop of joy. "Is it weird, seeing us together after us being friends for so long?"

"Bro, I have felt your love for each other for the longest fucking time," Max said with a smirk. "I'm just glad you finally had the balls to admit it to the world."

"You knew?" Caleb cursed and Max laughed.

"Of course I fucking knew, I'm the most powerful Siren in the kingdom."

"And you?" Caleb rounded on Darius who shared a conspiratorial look with Tory.

"No, no I knew nothing," he replied casually.

"Nothing at all?" Caleb pushed.

"Well, when I was dead there was this weird thing that happened which I guess did clue me in," he said, rubbing his jaw as if trying to remember the details of whatever clue he had been given.

"What did you see?" Seth demanded though he didn't slow down.

"You were in my wife's room in Rump Castle and you were arguing – my name came up so I guess that's why I was drawn to you at that particular moment."

"Err, we were in Tory's room?" Caleb asked, running a hand down the back of his neck and glancing at my sister who cocked an eyebrow at him as if shocked by this news.

"Whatever would you have been doing in there?" she gasped and her tone was so over the top that I had to bite my lip to hold back a laugh.

"I'm not sure I remember ever being-" Caleb tried.

"Oh you remember alright," Darius interrupted. "It wasn't the kind of night that could have been scrubbed from anyone's mind – believe me, I know."

"What did they do?" Max demanded.

"That's fine, no need to tell the whole group," Caleb said quickly. "The cat's out of the bag now anyway so-"

"Their fight got physical," Darius said, turning from Caleb to tell us the story like we were all gathered close at a sleepover and he was about to dish up the juiciest bit of gossip known to mankind.

"How physical?" Tory asked, her hand on her chest and eyes wide with utterly false surprise, letting me know she clearly knew exactly what Darius was going to say.

"Really. Fucking. Physical." Darius shot a look at Caleb who coughed awkwardly then just shrugged.

"Yeah, okay, sorry Tory – we did kinda hook up in your bed. But it was after you went off to find the Damned Forest and we didn't exactly realise we had an audience-" Caleb said, trying to own it.

"No, I assume not because you likely wouldn't have wanted an audience to realise your choice of sex toys included unlicenced Dragon dildos with my face on them," Darius drawled, and Geraldine shrieked a laugh before clapping her hands over her mouth so she could hear Caleb's reply.

"Why would you use a sex toy with Darius's face stamped on it?" Orion asked with a shudder.

"His face was not stamped on the sex toy," Caleb growled just as Seth said, "We only used the Dragon lube and butt plug anyway!"

I fell into a fit of hysterics while Caleb shot after Seth and slapped a hand over his mouth to stop him from talking.

"You used a butt plug with Darius's face on it?" I asked, choking on my own laughter.

"No," Caleb snapped while Seth shrugged like that wouldn't even have been that weird.

"Why did you hang around and watch them going at it with off-brand sex toys anyway?" Orion asked Darius incredulously.

"I got stuck there," Darius said with a scowl. "I had to call for help so I could escape while enduring the sounds of the two of them going at it like a pair of fucking rabbits."

"Who came to help you?" Seth asked, peeling Caleb's fingers from his mouth.

"Our parents," Tory supplied, breaking down into her own fit of laughter and shock mixed with my amusement as Caleb's face went pale with horror.

"You're lying," he accused, pointing at Darius.

"Oh no – that moment is branded into my fucking mind for all of time, I assure you. What was it Seth said? Oh yeah – 'how vanilla are you feeling, Altair?'"

Caleb looked like he wanted the floor to swallow him whole while we all fell apart in hysterics.

"That is not how it was-" he tried, but Seth spoke over him.

"He wasn't even vanilla at all after that," he said loudly. "Tell them how much you loved the butt plug, Cal. Tell them how much you liked it when I-"

Caleb threw a silencing bubble over his mate and snarled at all of us.

"This...I...I'm never having sex again," he hissed just as Seth shattered the silencing bubble and pointed an accusatory finger at Darius.

"No way you just took that lying down," he said.

"You mean like Caleb did?" Tory asked and I clutched my sides as I failed to even draw breath from how hard I was laughing.

"I mean, there's no way that Darius would have known this for all that time and just let it lie. Tell me how you got your revenge," Seth barked.

Darius simply gave them a taunting grin then flashed the two of them the peace sign.

Seth sucked in a gasp as though the act had mortally wounded him and came to an abrupt halt beside Darius, cuffing him around the ear. "I *knew* there was a reason you did that."

"So you're not BFF BJ buddies?" Caleb muttered to Seth like we all might not hear him, but we definitely did.

Seth glanced away awkwardly then looked back at him, clearing his throat. "I kind of...made that shit up."

"What?" Caleb blurted.

"I panicked after I gave you that BJ and I thought you were gonna reject me if you knew it really meant something to me, so I figured the best thing to do was to just... pretend I suck all of my friends' cocks." Seth shrugged innocently and Caleb stared at him in shock.

For a second it looked like he might hit him, but then he fell on Seth instead, kissing him ravenously and the rest of us backed away to give them some room. I couldn't fight the smile off my face as I headed to the red couch with the others, my chest full of light over this revelation.

Geraldine made a call to the A.S.S. and went racing out of The Orb to prepare the brunch, dismissing all offerings we made to help.

We fell into discussion about who had known what about Caleb and Seth and the two of them soon joined us, sitting close together, their intimate touches so natural and full of love, I just wished they'd sorted their shit out sooner.

The door opened and I looked around, finding a beautiful woman with long white hair and dark skin walking into The Orb. She wore a woollen sweater with dark green pants, and she had a sword sheathed at her hip. The men were armed too, but it was pretty common for the rebels to carry weapons in case of attack.

"Geraldine Grus invited me here," she announced, dipping her head to me and Tory in a bow. "My name is Imenia Brumalis, I belong to the society of the Glacials from the Polar Capital."

I shared a look with my twin, recognising her name from what Caleb and Seth had told us and we rose to our feet, approaching her.

"We heard about the mines you were held captive in," I said sadly. "I'm sorry we didn't get to you sooner."

"Your people came precisely at the right moment," she said with a touch of mysticism to her voice, nodding in thanks to Caleb and Seth behind us. "Everything happens just when it is supposed to."

"You've come here with intention then," Tory said, her brows lifting.

"Yes," Imenia said, reaching into her pocket and taking out a roughly cut diamond that was almost as big as her palm. It glimmered with blue and green light, the calming magic that hummed from it entirely bewitching. "A Glacia diamond," she whispered. "One of the few that can wield the power of the Northern Lights."

"What kind of power?" Tory asked, hope bleeding into her voice and I felt it too.

"It is not a weapon," Imenia said quickly. "But I believe it may assist you in battle all the same."

"How?" I pressed, needing to know. Any added strength in the coming fight was immensely precious.

"I will teach you," Imenia vowed. "And when the battle comes, I pray it shall help shift the tide in our favour."

I was unable to move. Trapped in my own body and forced to watch as vicious cuts sliced deep into my mate's skin. His pain was my pain, and the agony of seeing him face this torture was too much. I screamed but no noise came out, my heart just hammered more wildly.

Trapped, I was trapped. And he needed me.

Shadows were tightening around him, blood soaked his skin, and the life was fading from him fast.

I begged the stars to help, then I cursed them for not answering my pleas.

I was his only hope, and I couldn't get free.

I had to burn my way out of this power that held me, use every scrap of my Phoenix fire to reach him. I willed it towards the monster who stood at his back, her eyes two pools of nothing as she ran a blade across Orion's throat.

"No – no!" I screamed so loud the sound rattled my skull, the words finally making it out of my throat, and fire bloomed out from me in every direction.

"Blue!" Orion shouted to me and suddenly I wasn't there in that terrible place, I was in our bedroom in Rump Castle. Phoenix flames were blazing over my skin, burning the bed and blazing hungrily for more sustenance. Within the chaos of fire, Orion was reaching for me, his skin coated in ice as he staved off the flames and tried to get to me through them.

I extinguished them in an instant before they could hurt him, but as the ice melted off his skin, the burns on his arms and chest were clear.

A noise of horror left me and I lunged for him, pressing my hands to his skin and sending a wave of healing magic out to soothe the burns.

"I'm so sorry," I gasped, tears spilling down my cheeks.

He grasped my face in his palm, his eyes full of concern, but none for himself. "Are you alright?"

"It was a nightmare. Fuck, I could have hurt you so bad." I tried to withdraw from him, glancing back at the smouldering bed in horror at the thought.

He grabbed my arm, refusing me my escape.

"Look at me," he growled, and I did, my throat bobbing heavily. "I've got you. It was just an accident. A bad fucking dream, Blue."

"At least when the monsters were in my head, they couldn't hurt anyone. But what I just did…" My heart thrashed in fear as I took in Lance Orion, the man I would do anything to protect, yet I'd hurt him in my sleep.

Orion leaned in, pressing his lips to my forehead firmly then shifting back to look me in the eyes again. "My reactions are ten times the speed of yours. I moved the second the flames touched me."

"It shouldn't have happened at all," I said heatedly.

"No…" He frowned, then scooped me into his arms, walking to the plush window seat and sitting there, pulling me in against his chest. "What can I do, beautiful?"

I shook my head, curling into the safety of his warm body and finding so much solace in the steady pounding of his heart. I couldn't withdraw from him; we were made to be this close. But I had to find a way to deal with this messed up shit in my head, because I couldn't let Lavinia leave her mark on me.

"Do you dream of her too?" I whispered, and Orion brushed his fingers through my hair. "Do you think about what she did?"

"No, not often," he admitted gruffly. "The torture I went through was for you. I chose it. And every bite of pain I endured was for that reason. It was all I thought of in captivity. And now we're free…it doesn't haunt me, because I walked into that fate willingly."

I turned my head to kiss his bare chest, loving him fiercely for what he'd sacrificed for me, even if I was destroyed over it too. "Sometimes everything feels so normal again. We're all back together, and so far, somehow, we're all still breathing. But there are moments when it feels like the shadows still live under my skin. I think they've tainted me, and I'm not sure I'll ever really be free of them."

Orion heaved a sigh, his chest rising and falling beneath me. "There must be something we can do. Perhaps Max can help? He helped Tory after all."

I nodded mutely. I'd thought of that too, but I'd decided I could handle this alone. There were times when I didn't think of Lavinia or our captivity at all, but there were other moments like this when I couldn't escape it. Maybe I should have turned to Max sooner.

A tap came at the window and I lurched upright with my hands raised as Orion's fangs snapped out. Gabriel gazed in at us with dark eyes, his black wings beating slowly at his back.

I reached for the catch in surprise, dispelling the magical lock and opening it for him.

"What are you doing here?" I asked.

It was the middle of the night, the waning moon high above us and the frosty air sweeping in through the open window.

"I had a vision. May I come in?" he asked.

"Of course," I said.

I climbed down from the window seat and Orion followed, letting Gabriel fly in and land lightly in front of us. His gaze slid to the smouldering bed then back to me, his frown deepening.

"Nightmare," I explained with a tight smile.

"I know," he said darkly, making it clear he'd *seen* what had happened.

"Have you *seen* a way to help her, Noxy?" Orion asked hopefully.

"I have actually," he said, and my heart lifted.

"Really?" I stepped towards him. "How?"

"I'll tell you soon enough. But right now, we have somewhere we all need to be," he said mysteriously.

"Good. I could use a distraction," I said, anxious to do something with all this adrenaline in my blood.

"We're going off campus, bring your weapons," Gabriel directed.

Orion shot into the walk-in closet, returning in a flash dressed in jeans, combat boots, a black shirt and his leather jacket, casually swinging his Phoenix sword at his side and leaning against the wall. "Well I'm ready when you two are." He smirked, sheathing the sword at his hip.

"You'll have to give me a minute, we don't all move as fast as a cheetah's fart," I said with a grin, striding past him towards the closet.

Orion sped up behind me, lifting me off my feet and making me squeak in surprise as he carried me in there. In a whirlwind of movement, he dressed me in jeans and a backless long-sleeved black top that would allow my wings to fly free. Then he knelt down, slowing his movements as he helped me into my boots, tying the laces and locking his eyes with mine for a second before sweeping me off my feet again in a flash and sprinting me back to our bedroom. He placed me down in front of my brother and Gabriel glanced at the clock.

"I think you're getting slower in your old age, Orio," he mocked.

"I'm the same age as you, asshole," Orion scoffed.

"And yet you'd hardly believe it," Gabriel teased.

"Let's just agree you're both as old as the hills," I said, climbing up to stand on the window seat and letting my bronze wings extend at my back. "Now where are we going?"

"That's a surprise," Gabriel said, his eyes glittering. "Let's fly up to the edge of the wards. You can make a passage through them and I'll stardust us to our location."

Orion suddenly clapped his hand to Gabriel's chest, casting a glowing pulse of magic over his skin.

"Satisfied?" Gabriel asked and Orion nodded.

"What was that?" I frowned.

"A revealing spell in case this Gabriel was a fake and the real one was lying dead somewhere," Orion said grimly. "Figured it was best before we went skipping off into the sky with him."

"Morbid," I said. "But good idea."

"If there's one thing you can count on me being, it's a morbid asshole, Blue." Orion flashed me his fangs and I smiled.

"Race you to the wards," Gabriel said, taking off and flying out the window at a wild speed that left the curtains fluttering.

I leapt after him, free falling for several seconds before catching myself on the breeze, my wings flexing and carrying me skyward on an updraft. Gabriel was already well ahead of me and I flew faster to try and catch him, glancing back to check Orion was following. He stood on a platform of air that was shooting upward like a runaway elevator, his gaze fixed on Gabriel and a challenge blazing in his eyes.

"You'll never catch him," I called, flying faster to try and outpace him, but Orion's air platform carried him up ever faster. He went speeding by at what must have been closing in on a hundred miles per hour and a laugh left my chest as I chased him.

Gabriel beat him to the wards by half a second, and I wielded the magic of them, allowing us to pass through.

It was a relief to have something to focus on, and I could already feel the grip of my nightmare loosening as Gabriel tossed stardust over us, and we were whipped away into the night.

Between a swirl of stars and galaxies, we found our way to a humid jungle, and I landed softly between Orion and Gabriel, so used to travelling this way now that it had become second nature.

I immediately recognised where we were, the ruins of the Palace of Flames peeking at us through the thick foliage of the jungle. With a jolt, I realised why we were here.

"The Nox flower?" I gasped, wheeling towards Gabriel.

"It's in bloom," he said, a keen hope in his eyes. "It's our one chance."

"And how likely are we to be able to collect its pollen?" Orion asked.

"It's about fifty-fifty," Gabriel said, though his brow lowered and I sensed he was bullshitting us.

"Really?" I narrowed my gaze.

"Alright, no, not really. We have about five percent chance of pulling it off," he said.

"Well damn, we're basically guaranteed to do it then, Noxy," Orion said dryly.

"On the bright side, five percent chance is way more than no chance," I said cheerfully.

Orion shot me a sideways glance, biting down on the inside of his cheek.

"There are some factors I can't quite *see*..." Gabriel trailed off, his grey eyes glazing. "Something I cannot predict."

"Perfect. Nothing to worry about then," Orion said, his hand going to his sword's hilt.

"If you can't *see* it, could it involve Nymphs, or Lavinia?" I asked, though I couldn't imagine them all the way out here unless they had somehow predicted our arrival.

"I'm not sure, but we'd best remain on guard," Gabriel said then strode off down an animal track, leading the way.

Part of me hoped Lavinia might just show up here tonight, because my heart was full of wrath and I knew one sure-fire way to rid myself of her taint would be to send her right to the depths of hell.

Orion gestured for me to go in front of him and I started walking while he took up the rear like a sentinel at my back. Always in my shadow.

The ring on my finger began to tingle, and I'd grown used to the sign that Shadow wanted to come out. I lifted my hand, letting the beast materialise in a swirl of grey smoke, his large form landing heavily on the undergrowth, and his back foot snapping a small tree in half.

"Damn clumsy beast." Orion threw a silencing bubble around him, and I glanced back at him with a grin.

"Are you sure we need the beast out right now?" he clipped.

"Yup," I said brightly as Shadow walked along at my side, the sound of him trampling bushes lost to Orion's bubble. So what was the problem?

"We really need to talk about that thing," Orion growled.

"That *thing* has a name," I said fiercely. "And I can't see what else you'd have to say about him. I've already decided he's staying."

"If you think I'm going to drop the matter then wake up one day to that creature feasting on you, you'd better think again," Orion said in his most bossy voice.

"Don't be so dramatic, he's completely docile," I said.

"Docile?" he scoffed. "It's a Shadow Beast that forced you to kill people. Lavinia summoned the damn thing from the Shadow Realm, and *nothing* good comes from there."

"Enough," Gabriel called. "We're close now. We need to focus."

We arrived at the base of a hill, and at its peak a delicate, pale blue flower stood upon a single stem.

Gabriel glanced up at the sky, his mouth moving as if counting the passing seconds, seeing something far beyond anything Orion or I were capable of perceiving. My brother dropped his head expectantly, and the flower began to spread its silky petals, cracking open, and allowing a silvery light to spill out.

"It's…" I trailed off, rendered speechless by its beauty.

I reached for it, but Gabriel slapped my hand away.

"Wait," he said firmly, his eyes gleaming with The Sight.

I nodded, knotting my fingers together instead, and Shadow sat beside my brother patiently like he knew it was time to wait.

"How come you listen to him when he tells you not to touch things?" Orion muttered.

"Because defying you is too much fun," I whispered, shooting him a teasing look.

"Is that so?" he growled.

"Yes, plus Gabriel can *see* things you can't."

"I err on the side of caution when it comes to you and mysterious objects."

"Well I haven't died yet," I said brightly.

"The word 'yet' is *delightfully* comforting, Blue," he drawled.

Gabriel blinked out of his vision. "It's a trap!"

Orion spun around at speed, his hand flying out and catching a fiery spear an inch from the side of my head. He tossed it away with a snarl, healing the burn on his palm.

"Fuck." I swung around in alarm and cast an air shield over the four of us, bolstering it with power.

Five more spears came flying at us from the trees and smashed to pieces against it, and Shadow grunted, his deep growl rumbling from his throat as his hackles rose.

"It's Phoenix fire," I gasped, recognising the red and blue flames.

"Queen Avalon organised this," Gabriel said, pointing to one of the broken spears which had her royal insignia engraved into it.

"For what purpose?" I frowned as more spears came flying our way, dashing to pieces on my shield. "Most Fae could protect themselves from this."

"Nymphs," Orion surmised. "Perhaps Avalon feared they would find out about this flower."

"Or maybe they did," Gabriel said sombrely, turning to face the flower. "Shit."

"What?" I asked, but my answer came as a golden cage snapped up from the earth, closing around the flower and locking it away from us. The metal winked with power, and words glittered on a shining plaque that I read aloud. "The flower of Nox may be touched only by Queen Avalon herself. Turn back or face the wrath of the Phoenix Queen."

I stepped forward to break through it with my flames, my teeth clenching in determination.

"No," Gabriel warned quickly. "That doesn't end well."

Orion tugged me back from it like he was afraid the thing might detonate.

"Perhaps we can send a vine into the cage from below to retrieve the pollen," I suggested, and Gabriel let his Sight follow that idea.

He sighed as he returned to us. "No, the cage will crush the flower if we attempt that. There is an answer here though…something close."

He pressed his lips together as he lowered to the ground and touched his hand to the earth.

I crouched down too, mimicking him and sensing the earth beneath my fingers, every rock and rivet in the mud that went deep, deep down.

"What are you looking for?" I asked him.

"Anything that shouldn't naturally be here…" He closed his eyes to focus, and

I pressed my own power deeper into the earth to quicken the search, hunting for anything that felt out of place.

My magic slipped over something hard and as my power spread further, I sucked in a breath. Bones. Hundreds of them, piled together in a mass grave.

"What happened here?" I whispered, and as if in answer to those words a vision burst through my mind.

I saw Queen Avalon leading a legion of Fae to this very hill, declaring it a sacred place that demanded protection until the Nox flower bloomed again. The Nymphs could be defeated only if the magic of the flower could be harnessed. But the Nymphs had learned of her secret, a traitor among her ranks working with Lavinia's army. So she spoke a spell to them that was built of a terrible power, then she made them line up upon the hill, all twenty of them under the wrathful gaze of their queen. Avalon handed a silver knife to the one at the very end of the line, still speaking her spell into the air, and one by one, they slit their own throats, falling to the ground where their blood spilled deep into the earth.

As the last woman fell choking into death, Avalon knelt at her side, laying a chain over her neck which held a golden key.

"Only I can stop your wrath," she whispered to them all, then the earth began to swallow up the bodies, dragging them down and claiming each one like it was feasting on their corpses.

My mind snapped back to the present and I let out a heavy breath, looking to Gabriel. "One of the bodies has the key."

"Bodies?" Orion stepped closer, but before I could explain the ground trembled with an ominous pulse of power.

I leapt to my feat, pulling Gabriel up too and Shadow growled, sniffing the air like he could sense danger on the wind.

"Avalon cast some dark spell on this place," I said hurriedly, taking my mother's sword from my hip, and Gabriel and Orion unsheathed their weapons in response.

A skeletal hand shot from the earth, latching onto my ankle and I gasped, yanking my leg sideways out of its grip then blasting Phoenix fire at the bones. The skeleton didn't stop rising, and the whole hill shook as all twenty dead Fae bodies dragged themselves out of their graves.

I swung my sword, striking the one trying to pull itself from the earth at my feet, but the bones didn't break, the impact making the sword bounce back like it had struck metal. Orion sped away across the hill, swinging his sword with the furious strength of his Order, but each hit did no damage, only knocking the skeletons from their feet. Shadow went bounding after him, snatching up a fallen skeleton and shaking it violently before sending it flying away into the jungle.

Gabriel was caught in a vision, frozen as a skeleton made it fully out of the ground and came straight for him. I raced past him, sending a blast of Phoenix fire at the corpse, but it just fluttered over its bones without damage.

"Phoenixes," I cursed, realising that might just be why I couldn't destroy them that way.

The skeleton made it to me, reaching for my throat with bony hands and I feigned left, kicking it hard in the hip. It stumbled only a little, but the impact sent a wave of pain up my leg.

"They're unkillable," Orion called, darting back to me with Shadow bounding after him.

Gabriel blinked, looking to us as the bodies closed in again and we readied to fight.

"Any fancy visions tell you how to defeat them?" I asked him, sheathing my sword in favour of my magic. If I couldn't shatter their bones, I'd drag them back into the earth they came from.

"We can't," he said heavily. "We must get the key."

He pointed to a group of the bodies that were crowded together, and I noticed one was being protected by the others in the centre of the circle. A glint of gold was all I needed to know about which one had the key.

"Distract them," I commanded. "I'll get the key."

I beat my wings, flying skyward as Orion sped toward the group, blasting them with air and uprooting two of them, sending them tumbling down the hill. Gabriel froze two more in place, binding their limbs together with inescapable ice, and Shadow snatched another between his powerful jaws, trying to crush it with his teeth, and when that didn't work, he shook it like a ragdoll.

I flew overhead, swooping down on the one with the key and wielding the earth beneath the final two skeletons protecting her. The ground opened up, swallowing them down into it and Gabriel froze the arms and legs of the skeleton with the key, holding her still while I snatched the chain right off her neck.

"Throw it to me!" Gabriel called. "I'll collect the pollen; I've *seen* how it must be done."

I tossed him the key and he caught it, flying up and away from the skeletons closing in on us.

I dragged them all down into the earth, power pouring from me in a flood as I let the hill devour them, sending them back to their place of eternal rest. One by one they were dragged beneath the jungle, as deep as I could bury them, my veins humming with power.

The ground trembled with their oncoming fury, as they tried to claw their way back to the surface, but I hardened the ground, turning the top layer to stone and barring their way out.

I landed lightly, hearing their bony fingers scratching at the rock below, but there was no way through for them now.

I smiled at Orion as he sheathed his sword, a sideways grin lifting his lips, and Shadow sat at his side, grunting happily.

I turned to Gabriel, hurrying further up the hill to the flower, the cage now open as Gabriel knelt down, his arm extended into it as he carefully extracted the pollen into a vial.

A roar made me swing around in fright and I found a fireball of Phoenix flames tearing towards Orion's back. He moved to defend himself a beat too late, but Shadow was there, rearing up in front of him and taking the full impact right to his chest. He whimpered and fell to the ground in a heap just as another fireball came flying their way and Orion sent an air shield out to protect himself and Shadow from another hit.

"Hang on!" I cried then took off into the air, racing down the hill in the direction the fireballs were coming from, sweeping up between the branches of a tall tree. I spotted the ancient contraption built of metal, attached high up on the bough. I gritted my teeth and flew higher, grabbing a branch to steady myself beside it then placing my hand against it and sending all the heat of my flames through it, melting it into a glob.

When I was sure it could blast no more fire, I flew back to the hilltop, landing beside Orion who was trying to heal Shadow, his hands pressed to the beast's chest as he lay on his side. Shadow whined softly as I came down to land, my heart tugging with worry.

"It won't work," I said in fear. "We can't heal him."

"It's alright," Orion said soothingly, and for a second I thought he must be talking to me before I realised his eyes were on Shadow's face, and hope filled me as I noticed Shadow's injuries fading, his own shadows fuelling the magic.

The wound was soon healed and Shadow's long tail wagged before he sat upright and leaned over to nuzzle Orion's face.

Orion scruffed the beast's head, trying to look like he wasn't that invested in doing so, but I could tell he was.

"He's okay," I whispered in joy, leaning in to hug him and Shadow at once.

"He saved me," Orion said quietly. "And it wasn't the first time, admittedly. I think I've been a stubborn asshole."

"Nooo, you? Never," I teased sarcastically.

He grinned like the Devil. "It's a habit that's hard to break, beautiful. But I seem to be making exception to more and more companions these days."

"How about Seth?" I asked.

"No," he clipped immediately, and I shoved his arm.

"Asshole," I accused, and he gripped my waist, kissing me hard and reminding me that I wouldn't want him any other way.

"Through and through," he said against my lips. "Don't forget it, or I'll need to give you a reminder."

"My memory is getting hazy," I said, glancing up at him through my lashes.

"Here we are." Gabriel arrived, holding up a vial of glittery pollen triumphantly. "I know someone who can brew this into a potion that will be enough for our army. I'll bring it to him tonight."

He took the stardust from his pocket and tossed a pinch over our heads, carrying us away into a sea of stars. We arrived high above the academy in the sky and Orion caught himself on a gust of air as my wings spread wide and Gabriel swooped around us.

Rump Castle lay below us and as I let us through the wards, we circled down to it together. Orion landed in the window seat of our room and offered out a hand to draw me inside, but I hesitated, glancing back at Gabriel.

My brother nodded to me, telling me it was time to discuss what we'd left unsaid and I looked to Orion once more.

"I'll come back soon, I need to speak with Gabriel," I said, and Orion glanced at my brother knowingly.

"I'll wait up," he said, then withdrew into our room, leaving the window open for my return.

Gabriel followed my lead and I headed across the sea and onto campus, soon landing on the very top of Aer Tower, the familiar building giving me a sense of coming home.

My brother came down to sit beside me, our legs dangling over the edge, and no fear found me over the sheer drop beneath us. It was strange to think of my first night at Zodiac Academy when Seth had taken me up here and goaded me into jumping right off this very spot. In ways, I still felt like the girl who had arrived in Solaria that day, but deep down, I knew I'd changed. My faith lay in the wings at my back and the magic in my veins, and it was strange to think of how the Heirs alone had rattled me back then. It took a fearsome war to strike true fear in me these days. And most of that fear was for those I loved, which now included the very Fae who I'd once despised at this academy.

My wings fluttered at my back, brushing Gabriel's black feathers and drawing my gaze to him, only to find him already looking at me.

"Are you ready to talk about it?" he asked. "There have been many times I wished to come to you, but I foresaw it was not the right time. Until now."

I blew out a breath that fogged in the air, blue strands of hair dancing around me in the icy wind, but no part of me felt it. Fire lived in me, always burning, and I offered it to Gabriel too at the lightest touch of my arm to his.

"No need," he said with mischief in his voice, reaching into his jeans' pocket and showing me a fire crystal. "I always carry these when the nights are cold. I'm well versed in weathering the winter. So... tell me what's going on."

"You clearly already know," I mused, smiling, though it felt dead on my lips.

"Yes, but please indulge the Seer who *sees* far too much of conversations before he's had them. I prefer experiencing them in reality rather than in the lonely corners of my mind. It keeps me grounded."

"Do your visions still pain you?" I whispered, horrified over what Vard had done to my brother.

"Less with each day," he said, smiling tightly. "Now stop stalling and tell me."

I sighed. "I guess it's moments of panic, memories of mine and Lance's time with Lavinia and Lionel." My throat tightened. "I can't control it. It takes over and it's so suffocating, I can't do anything but…panic." I clutched my chest, feeling that fear rising now, always there even when I buried it deep. "But it's not me I'm scared for, Gabriel." I looked to my brother, my pulse ticking faster. "It's Lance. It's you. Tory. Everyone." The panic deepened, my breathing coming quicker. "The chances of us all making it through this war can't be good. And I bet you know. You've *seen* what's coming, but I can't bear to ask you."

I clutched his arm and Gabriel laid his hand over mine, his gaze tinged with pain.

"Yes, I *see* death. More now than I ever once did. But all potential fates are the ghosts of a future which may or may not come to pass. Nothing is tangible until it is done. So that is where I lay my hope, in the measures of possibility that linger between our death-marked paths."

My nails dug into his arm as I gazed into his eyes, part of me wanting to *see* what he did so that I might stand a chance of avoiding it.

"How do you bear it?" I breathed, admiring my brother so much for the burden he carried on his shoulders.

"It drove me to madness once. There was a time I couldn't control it or understand it. It was a gift I should have been mentored through, but as I've told you before, when I was sent to live in Alestria the night our parents were killed, a block was put on my memories along with my Seer powers. That block eventually cracked and gave way, but it meant I had a lot of catching up to do on mastering my gifts. Even now, I'm still learning. But I was afraid of what I *saw* sometimes, afraid I couldn't change fate, afraid that the terrible things I *saw* would come to pass."

"But?" I pushed, sensing there was more to it than that.

"But, after a time, I began to realise The Sight, though horrifying at times, was a gift more valuable than any other I might be offered in this world. It gives me an opportunity to protect those I love. I've saved you all more times than I can count. More times than you even want to know about."

I laughed a little. "And I'm grateful for every one of those times."

He smiled, but it fell away. "Darcy…you have Harpy blood in you. Our mother was fiercely protective by nature, as am I. And from what I know of Hydras, they weren't exactly laid back in that department either. You need to embrace that part of you. Your mind is trying to warn you about what you desperately fear might come to pass. Of Lance being captured and tortured again, of your loved ones being killed. It's telling you, at its core, that you must protect them. And if you decide that that is your duty and step into that role as fully as you possibly can, I believe the nightmares will fade. It is how I cope with the visions, and I can teach you my ways if you'd like?"

"Your ways?" I asked curiously.

He nodded. "In my family, I am the last to sleep and the first to rise." He got to his feet, his wings flexing as he offered me his hand. "A Harpy's duty is to protect the nest. Let me show you how it is done."

I took his hand, letting him help me to my feet, then Gabriel leapt off the tower, his wings snapping out to catch him on the breeze. I jumped after him, my wings beating as I sailed through the air and that familiar rush of freedom twisted through my veins. There was nothing like flying; I couldn't imagine my life without it now.

Gabriel started climbing into the sky towards the moon, flying higher and higher as I stayed on his heels. Finally, he levelled out, keeping his wings extended and gently gliding along on an updraft.

I copied him, our wing tips grazing as I took in the sight of the campus far below.

"Every night, I come up here and scour the perimeter a few times," he said. "I do the same back home. I scout until I'm sure there are no enemies on the horizon, nothing out of place, and no cause for concern. I may have The Sight to aid me, but this part of me is all Harpy."

I followed him in a large circle around campus, looking for any sign of disturbance below and after a while, that knot in my chest loosened. All was calm, at peace.

"This really works," I called to him.

"You can scout with me any time," he said, and I knew I'd take him up on that offer. "Take control of your fear, Darcy, and it will never control you again."

TORY

CHAPTER FIFTY NINE

I sat cross legged on the floor of Darius's bedroom, wearing his Pitball shirt with my hair tied in a scruffy knot on the top of my head, the sound of his deep breathing and the occasional turn of a page all that disturbed the silence of the room.

Dawn was breaking across the horizon, the light like golden fire which set the distant mountaintops ablaze and crested the waves of the sea in flames beyond Rump Island. The sky was a watercolour of orange, pink and gold, all hazy lines and picturesque beauty, so at odds with the ugliness of war which dominated the land beneath it.

I turned another page in the Book of Ether, making a note in the journal that lay open beside me, sketching out a stone figure as the bones of a plan began to form in my mind. It wouldn't be easy…hell, I doubted it would even be possible at all, but if I could just combine the right runes…

"Roxy?" Darius grumbled from the bed, the sound of him rolling over following his words.

I looked around, smiling at him as he sat up, a moment of panic rising behind his eyes then falling away as he found me sitting on the floor.

"Did you think I'd snuck off in the night?" I teased, my eyes roaming down the rigid muscles of his chest, the mussed-up bed hair which always looked so good on him, like my fingers had been knotted within the dark strands for hours. Which to be fair, they had.

"Wouldn't put it past you," he agreed, his gaze moving to the open books before me, scanning the pages and my notes and making his own assumptions. "So we're still seeking The Ferryman today, are we?"

"Mmm," I agreed in a non-committal way which instantly got his back up.

"No more bullshit half plans, Roxy. If you have more great ideas about leaping into canyons alone or-"

"First off, I wasn't alone - I was with Darcy. Secondly, I am the queen which means I don't answer to you. Third-"

"Don't be an asshole," he griped, getting out of bed and pacing over to me.

"Impossible. Asshole is my standard setting."

"Then don't be a coward." He fell still at my back, his imposing height even more obvious than usual as he towered over me.

I tipped my head back until it was resting against his knees so I could look up at him. "How am I a coward?"

"By hiding things from me. If you don't think you can handle my reaction then it stands to reason that you're afraid of it, so-"

I rolled my eyes and looked back down at my books. "I'm not afraid of your reactions, dude. I just enjoy that look of utter fury you get behind your eyes when I surprise you."

"What have I told you about calling me-"

A loud knock sounded at the door, and I called out for whoever it was to come in before my dude could get much more irritable about being my dude.

Geraldine swept in, calling out a greeting with a platter of freshly-baked bagels perched on her arm.

"My Queen, you look utterly regal this morn. Beauty beyond compare. Even at the crack of dawn you shine brighter than the sun," she gushed, making me snort a laugh because my hair definitely needed washing and as I basically hadn't slept all night, I was pretty certain the bags beneath my eyes had bags of their own now too. But I appreciated the pretty lie all the same.

"I look like I spent the night crawling backwards through a thorn bush, but thank you for the compliment, Geraldine. You look stunning as always. Is that a new dress?"

"Oh this old potato sack?" she laughed, placing the bagels on Darius's coffee table then doing a twirl so I could fully appreciate the peach dress she wore, the skirt floating around her thighs as she turned. "You are too kind."

"Gerry? You left me on the damn stairs," Max grunted, and I looked around as he stomped into the room, carrying a huge chest with bits of paper sticking out of the closed lid. He dropped it by the door with a bang then glanced between me and Darius with a word of greeting.

"Morning, Darius, are you planning to get dressed for the meeting or just stand about shirtless the whole time?" he asked.

"Pish posh, Maxy, don't encourage the man to don clothing - let us have something to gaze upon with unfettered appreciation, won't you?" Geraldine scolded.

"He looks cold," Max insisted, stalking over to Darius's closet and tossing him a hoody.

"I thought you said we were meeting at seven?" I questioned, glancing at the clock which said we had half an hour until then and wondering whether I was going to get dressed or just stay like this for it now.

"Yes, yes, my dear Queen. But the buffet won't deliver itself. Come, Maxy." Geraldine swept from the room, clicking her fingers at Max to get him to follow and he did so, though I could hear him complaining about the fact that Geraldine hadn't let him eat so much as a single bagel yet as they disappeared down the corridor.

"You gonna tell me what you're planning then?" Darius asked, bending down to pick up the journal I'd been writing in and flipping through the pages. He frowned as he got back to the start of it then turned the front cover to me with a questioning look. The words *Property of Lance Orion* had been embossed in gold on the navy cover and I shrugged innocently as I read them.

"He has like ten of those," I said. "He doesn't need them all. And they're fancy. The paper is all soft and there's a little built-in bookmark thing."

"There are at least fifteen pages of notes in his handwriting in the front of this," Darius pointed out.

"Yeah, but it's all just theoretical blah, blah, blah stuff. I needed it for important things."

Darius flipped through my notes then turned the open book back to me showing me a doodle of a green Dragon with a sword sticking out of his fat head and little Xs for eyes to prove that he was definitely dead.

"Those are my cunning plans," I added in a low whisper that made him laugh.

"I was thinking more along the lines of decapitation, but whatever works," he said, turning more pages then pausing again, showing me the runes I'd scrawled there. "What are these for?"

"An idea," I said cryptically. "One which almost certainly won't work and I don't want to discuss without giving it more thought."

Darius looked inclined to argue with me on that, then he ran his gaze over my face, seeming to realise it would get him nowhere and he sighed, tossing the journal back down beside me.

"Coffee?"

"I knew I didn't just marry you because you were dying," I groaned longingly.

"No," he agreed. "It was because I was dying and I have a big cock."

"Hail to that."

I gave him an indecent look as I considered forgetting the coffee and using his body to help wake me up but...coffee. And I really needed a bath before everyone turned up here too.

Darius seemed to read my mind, giving me a rueful grin which I distinctly remembered him giving me from a position between my thighs last night. He leaned down to press a kiss to my lips then headed for the door.

I watched him go, blowing him a kiss as he left before peeling myself off of the floor and heading into his ensuite to run myself that bath.

I darted back for a bagel, slathering it in butter and eating it in five bites before stripping off and sinking into the scalding, bubble-filled water.

My eyes fell closed as I relaxed into the tub, the jacuzzi bubbles bringing a smile to the corners of my lips as I noted their ridiculousness while simultaneously enjoying them.

"Hey," Caleb's voice startled me awake, making me realise I'd dozed off and I looked up at him over a mountain of bubbles where he stood in the doorway. "Geraldine said to meet here, didn't she?" he confirmed, seeming to think my current state suggested that I wasn't expecting guests.

"Yeah. She's in the midst of bringing breakfast and Darius went for coffee. I just...fell asleep in the bath for like a minute. I'll be out in a sec."

"Have you found anything useful in the books?" he asked, moving away from the door but leaving it open so we could talk. He picked up the Book of Ether and looked down at the page I'd been studying.

"Maybe," I hedged. "Ether is so...long game. It's kinda hard to see many ways that it could be used in a fight because most of those spells and incantations require set-up, sacrifice, time. And even then they're not really aggressive spells. Sure there are curses and shit like that, but honestly the cost involved in those, not to mention the fact that many require hair or toenails or whatever from the intended victim make them pretty useless to us. The Elemental books have more aggressive magics in them like bone and blood magic which could be used to bolster the power available to the wielder, but they take time to learn and we don't have time. Besides, they're pretty fucking dangerous if you get it wrong."

"So what's with all the research?" Caleb asked, moving to sit on the edge of the bed, still studying the book.

"I'm trying to think outside the box. Looking at some of the spells and taking pieces from one to add to another, using my understanding of the runes to...well I'm not totally sure on what yet but I feel like I have the threads of a plan coming together in my mind. Whether or not it will actually work is another question."

The door to the room opened again and I craned my neck to see who else had arrived, smiling as I spotted Darius with the coffees, but his face fell to stone as he looked between me and Caleb.

"Why the fuck are you sitting in the bath while he's in the room?" he snapped, his words coated in a possessive growl.

Honestly, I'd been about to ask Caleb to shut the door while I got out, but Darius's tone made me narrow my eyes instead.

"I fell asleep in here and he arrived, no big deal."

"You're naked," he pointed out in a low voice, and I glanced at the bag of coffees nervously. If he spilled those while throwing a bitch fit over me falling asleep in the damn bath then I was going to kick his ass.

"There are a million bubbles in this thing," I pointed out. "I'm more covered up than I am in most of the clothes I own."

"That's true," Caleb agreed unhelpfully and Darius's eyes flashed gold.

"That is not the-" he began, raising his hand to point at me, the paper bag full of precious coffees swinging wildly.

"Gah, put the coffees down and stop freaking out," I demanded. "They're just tits, dude. No one cares."

"You seriously did not just dude me again," Darius growled, stalking across the room and Caleb casually turned his eyes back down to the book in his hands even though I could tell he was holding back a laugh and not reading at all. "And they are not *just* tits. They're *your* tits."

"You wouldn't care if I was having a bath while you were in the room," I said.

"That's because I'm your husband and we fuck each other so I get to see them."

"You assholes get naked to shift all the time and it's not like I'm concerned about that. Caleb must have seen Seth's cock a thousand times before he was tempted to start sucking it."

"A thousand and one," Caleb put in, biting back his laughter. "The one over was the charm."

"See? He'd have to see my tits at least nine hundred more times before he'd be tempted by them, and I don't bathe that often. You've probably got a couple of years before you need to start caring and by then we might be thinking another three-way would be just the thing to spice up our marriage bed so-"

"Whoa, whoa, whoa, what do you mean *another* three-way?" Seth demanded, stalking into the room.

Darius snarled furiously, spinning him towards the wall with a slap of water magic so that the supposedly holy, only-for-his-viewing-pleasure, tits wouldn't be seen by yet another of his friends. I rolled my eyes and dunked my head beneath the water to wash the conditioner out of it. When I emerged, the two of them were bickering like a pair of old biddies who had just spotted the last tin of peaches on the shelf.

"What's with the secrecy?" Seth barked, shoving his own power against the water magic Darius was aiming at him. He broke through it as my big Dragon asshole of a husband found himself tapped out, reminding me that he'd been going on about hauling his treasure into bed with us last night, but I guessed I'd worn him out and he'd fallen asleep before doing it.

"I will rip your eyes from your fucking heads if either of you look at my wife while she's in that bathtub," he cursed, storming towards me as if he might try and haul me from the water himself, dropping the bag of coffees down on the floor and grabbing a thick bathrobe from the chair closest to the tub.

A flick of my fingers put a barrier of air magic around the ensuite, stopping him from reaching the door and I pointedly ignored him as he punched it with the full force of all of those glorious muscles. Honestly if he'd just made his point without the rage I probably would have listened, but I really didn't like him bossing me around. At least not in public. If he wanted to get himself all worked up then take that rage out on my body in private...well, let's just say I wouldn't be complaining and the thought of it urged me to continue with my stubborn brat routine as I continued to rinse suds from my hair and he kept punching my shield to no avail.

"Why does it sound like someone's being murdered in here?" Orion's voice came from the door, and if Darius hadn't been losing his shit quite so spectacularly, I might have chosen that moment to draw the line. As we were already deep into this game, I ignored Orion's curse of horror as he entered and looked my way, my sister right behind him.

"What's with the public bathing?' Orion snapped, his eyes now firmly on the view beyond the window and shit, I think he might have been blushing because he looked embarrassed as hell. There were a butt ton of bubbles though, so I knew there wasn't actually anything for him to have seen anyway.

Darcy looked from me to Caleb and Seth and finally to my husband whose fist was looking all kinds of fucked up from how hard he was punching the air shield.

I gave her a look which said 'I can't just bow down to this shit' and she arched a brow which said 'hell no you can't' before speaking for the whole room to hear.

"What's the problem, Darius? They're only tits."

"Can we get back to the mention of a threesome," Seth pushed.

"When they were Star Crossed, me, Tory and Darius fucked," Caleb said, still not bothering to look up from the book in his lap. "It was like a work around on the 'keeping them apart' bullshit - you know about this."

"I do not know about this," Seth growled. "I do not know about this at all."

Caleb glanced up at him, finally drawing his attention from the book while Darius continued to slam his fists into my air shield and roar like a beast. There probably wasn't long left before he turned that fury on one of the other people in this room...

"That's like, common knowledge, man," Caleb said.

"Yeah, we all know about that," Darcy agreed, taking a seat on the windowsill beside Orion who was still firmly staring out at the view as if the idea of my naked body disgusted him. Then again, the thought of him getting his professor on with my sister gave me a severe case of the heebie-jeebies so I guessed it was the old tuna sandwich effect. I was his mate's sister, ergo I was the old tuna sandwich - about as appealing as it sounded.

"I'm sorry, are you all deaf?" Seth clipped. "Because I did not know. I knew nothing of this at all. The only three-ways involving another dude that Caleb has ever taken part in to my knowledge were with me."

"Err, I guess you don't really wanna hear about the time me and Milton Hubert met this blazing hot Chimera in Tucana and-"

Seth held out a hand, gagging as if he had just vomited in his own mouth. "I need to be alone," he gasped before pressing his fist to his mouth and heading for the door. "Lance. Are you coming or what?" he demanded.

"Why the fuck would I be coming?" Orion asked Darcy like she might have some clue what Seth was thinking at any given moment.

Darius bellowed in fury, running full force at my shield and I let it drop, sighing dramatically as he charged straight through the place where it had been and stumbled to a halt, looming over me.

"What now?" I taunted, raising a hand coated in bubbles and blowing them straight at him.

Darius looked about ready to commit murder and I bit my lip. Violence looked so fucking good on him.

"Out!" he barked, the word not for me but for the others. "Unless any of you wants a visual demonstration of who owns my wife's body because it's clear to me that she needs a fucking reminder."

My smile widened and Darcy wrinkled her nose.

"We came here for a meeting. Can't you two just argue about this later?" she asked.

"Yeah, I want to eat those bagels before they go cold," Caleb said, getting to his feet, the Book of Ether still in his arms. "Can I have one of those coffees too?"

"Go help Geraldine with the breakfast shit," Darius snarled, grabbing the door to the ensuite and shoving it shut, but he threw it closed too hard and it simply bounced against the door frame and slowly swung open again at his back. "You can come back here once my wife has put her damn clothes on."

"You realise none of us care about her tits, right?" Caleb pushed because apparently I wasn't the only one who got a kick out of poking ill-tempered Dragons.

Darius's gaze snapped to his and he took a threatening step forward which Caleb answered with a wide grin and a salute before shooting from the room. "You can try your luck with me when I get back, asshole." His words carried to us as he disappeared and Darius growled, taking a step as if to follow him, but I caught his wrist with a whip of water that I lifted from the bath, suds sloshing over the sleeve of his shirt.

"Come on, Lance," Seth barked.

Orion threw Darcy over his shoulder and shot from the room without another word, the door slamming at his back.

Within less than a minute, Darius had hauled me from the tub with a fistful of my hair, bent me over it and was ten inches deep inside me before I could even say fuck you.

His clothes were still fully on his body, only his belt ripped open and fly shoved down to reveal every solid inch of him, the only thing he needed to teach me that lesson he'd promised. And despite my rolling eyes and taunting words, I loved every fucking second of it, the way the water sloshed over his clothes as I pressed my hands flat to the bottom of the tub while he fucked me, the way his fingers bit into my flesh and most of all the way he called me his with every single thrust, making absolutely certain that I would never forget who owned me and how much I enjoyed it when he reminded me of the fact.

It was fast and messy and brutal, the two of us coming hard, cursing each other's names the entire time.

"You did that on purpose," he growled as he finally drew me upright, turning me around so he could claim a kiss.

"I didn't," I replied. "But maybe I should in future."

Darius growled, but there was no real irritation to it anymore and I bopped him on the nose with my fingers before cleaning myself off again then getting dressed at last.

By the time the others returned carrying the various platters and breakfast options which Geraldine deemed necessary for the start to the day, I was wearing sweatpants and one of Darius's hoodies, curled up on his lap and enjoying my coffee which had thankfully survived him dumping the bag on the floor.

Caleb dropped into the spot beside us on the couch, seemingly unconcerned about Darius still being pissed and held out the Book of Ether for me to look at.

"This looks promising," he said.

I took the book from him, frowning as I read the description of the complex rune which had been drawn to the right of the page. It was meant for banishment. Though what it banished was unclear.

I flicked my fingers, using air magic to snatch my journal from the floor where I'd left the rest of my study nest and quickly made note of the rune in it, despite not knowing what help it might be.

"Where did you get that?" Orion asked, narrowing his eyes at my journal as he took a seat opposite us, sitting on the floor before the TV with Darcy.

"It was a gift," I told him, tucking the book down the side of the couch so that Darius's leg could guard it from grumpy Vampires.

Geraldine interrupted him before he could say anything else, giving us her routine morning report of the army, explaining how many new recruits had joined the rebellion, gushing about how many of them had come to us both from the liberated Nebula Inquisition Centres and from Solaria as a whole.

"You are a beacon of strength and justice, my Queens," she said, clutching her heart while handing out bagels, fruit and yoghurt, first to Darcy and me, then Darius, Orion, Caleb and finally tossing Seth and Max some half-heartedly.

"Why am I always last?" Max grouched, though he stuffed the food into his mouth all the same.

"It is a matter of prestige, of course," Geraldine told him. "First the Queens, above all as is just and right."

"Uh-huh. But why can't I be after them?"

"Well then, our dear Dragoon, consort to one of the True Queens, returned from death itself where he no doubt had slim pickings when it came to food of this quality-"

"He was dead, he didn't need any food," Seth interrupted as he took a seat on Caleb's other side, taking a savage bite from a bar of chocolate which I'd hidden behind the fucking headboard.

"Hey," I snapped, lunging for him, but he swung the chocolate out of reach and my coffee almost became a casualty. "That's mine."

"It's compensation," he accused, pointing at me with the chocolate. "You should just be glad I'm not demanding you and Darius have a three-way with me to make this right."

"Ew, I don't want to have a fucking three-way with you. And how would that make it right?"

"It would reset the balance," he said like that was the most obvious thing in the world. "Or...actually the balance would be better reset if I had the three-way with you two," he said, now pointing my chocolate bar at Orion and Darcy.

"Ewww, Seth," Darcy protested, and Orion glared at him.

"I would sooner peel my own skin from my bones than have your cock anywhere near my mate."

"But not you," Seth sniggered, and Orion's glare grew deadly.

"Ew," Darcy hissed again.

"Stop with the fucking ews," Seth barked. "I don't want to have to fuck any of you either. I'm just saying what we *should* do."

"How many pack orgies did you have before you and Caleb started hooking up?" Max asked pointedly, but Seth whipped his hand through the air like that meant nothing.

"That's not the point."

"It is the point," Caleb said. "Besides, you definitely knew this already."

"I did not-" Seth began, but Caleb kissed him to shut him up.

"Point is that I'm yours now, right?"

Seth looked at him then sighed, reaching out to caress the mate mark behind Caleb's ear. "Okay. I won't have any revenge threesomes. But don't ever mention that vicious rumour about you and Milton again."

Caleb rolled his eyes then sat back in his seat, throwing his arm around Seth, who offered me the half-chewed, definitely slobbered on remains of my chocolate bar.

"Here," he said.

"Keep it," I replied. But I was going to need another hiding place.

"Well, now that nary nonsense has been put aside, perhaps we can get on with discussing the war?" Geraldine interrupted.

We fell into discussions about tactics and what else we still needed to achieve before our army came to blows with Lionel's. Geraldine had sent scouts to assess the damage those monsters had caused to Lionel's army but so far none of them had returned and we had to assume that he had tightened the defences surrounding his perimeters after we'd managed to slip through them twice.

"We heard from Voldrakia," she added, the tone of her voice giving me the answer before she even offered it. "They won't take any part in a foreign war, but Emperor Adhara sends his well wishes to his granddaughters, saying he will pray to the stars for your victory and hopes you will visit with him once the war is won to discuss a peaceful alliance with his nation."

"Fat lot of good that does us," Darcy growled, though Gabriel had already foreseen that Voldrakia wouldn't be swayed in this matter. It was why we hadn't wasted any time heading there ourselves. He said that no matter which way he looked at it, the stars never showed the Voldrakians joining this war.

"He did send a gift," Geraldine added, moving to the huge chest which Max had carried into the room earlier and I looked at it with interest as she unlatched the lid. "My Queens, you must be the ones to look upon it first."

I frowned, getting to my feet and moving closer with Darcy at my side.

"The gift he sent to Lionel was a psycho snake," Darcy said warily, raising her hands.

"Perhaps a shield would be prudent then," Geraldine said. "Just in case this is some trick – though dear Gabriel swears it is not."

I glanced at Darcy and placed a shield of air up around us, wondering what the hell could be in that box to make it necessary.

Geraldine stepped back, wafting the others aside as they leaned in to look and Darcy threw the lid wide.

The room drew in a collective breath and I blinked down at the four little lizards who peered up at us from within a nest of shredded paper, broken eggshells crushed beneath their iridescent bodies. They were each a different colour; one a pearly coral, another silvery white, the third sparkling pale green and the last opalescent sky blue.

"I thought they were extinct," Orion breathed from behind me, but I couldn't tear my gaze from the little creatures who were blinking up at Darcy and I as if we were where their world began and ended.

"What are they?" I murmured.

"Sayer dragons," Geraldine replied in a hushed voice. "Now imprinted upon the two of you, forever faithful to your will, forever loyal to your wishes."

"Four of them," Orion gasped in disbelief, and by the awed silence of the others I was willing to bet this was a bigger deal than us just getting four baby lizards in a box as pets.

"They don't look much like the Dragons I know," I pointed out, though I could see wings tucked tight to the reptilian bodies, and as if answering my question, the coral lizard stretched hers wide for me to see, the membrane so fine that it was transparent though the slight orange colour was just visible across it.

"They have bonded to your will already," Geraldine gushed enthusiastically.

"But what does that mean?" Darcy asked.

"Their loyalty is assured and they will grow into the most faithful and helpful of companions. They will fight and die for you if required, their bond nothing more or less simple than love."

The pale blue lizard leapt from the box and I reached out on instinct, letting it land on my hand where it promptly turned in a circle and fell asleep.

"Something this small will fight for us?" I asked, the smile on my lips making my appreciation of them undeniable though I couldn't see how it could make the slightest bit of difference in this war.

"They're so cute," Darcy breathed.

"They're not cute, Blue. Their powers are vast and unknown, unpredictable and immense," Orion explained. "Each of them growing into magic unique to its own personality, the power of which is sustained by the connection it holds with its masters."

"They use our power?" Darcy questioned, tickling the green lizard beneath its chin.

"No, but there is some kind of link, one which is as impossible to deny as it has been to pinpoint. They were highly coveted creatures in the Slovian Ages. But once they have bonded to a Fae their loyalty cannot be turned. When Fae realised they couldn't steal the beasts, their jealousy over the power and protection they offered up to their owners resulted in them being hunted to extinction. Or so I thought until now," Orion explained.

"Nice. So we have four baby lizards, clean shadows and the friendlier Nymphs considering their options, an army of rightly pissed off and motivated Fae, the two most powerful Fae in the kingdom plus seven of the second most powerful and you, Geraldine, who is arguably an army all on your own. We have a Shadow Beast, the Nox plant, the greatest Seer of our time, and a powerful glacia diamond. So why do I still have this awful feeling that we don't have enough to win this war?" I asked.

"It has to be enough," Darcy said passionately. "And I'm sure it will be against Lionel and Lavinia and their armies..."

"I'm just gonna say what no one else is saying," Seth interrupted. "Clyde. And the utter failure and waste of time which is the Guild Stones, no offence Professor Shame," he added to Orion.

"You can't just say 'no offence' and expect me not to take offence," Orion growled. "And cut that fucking nickname too. I'm not even Power Shamed anymore. Or a professor."

"Not technically, no." Seth patted his arm sympathetically and shared a look with Caleb who frowned then looked to Orion too.

The Vampires exchanged a loaded look but with an almost unnoticeable shake of his head, Orion clearly decided not to explain whatever it was. I trusted him to have a good reason for that then sighed, returning the sayer dragon to its crate then moving to sit on Darius's lap again. I vaguely wondered if any queen before me had been so casually un-royal-like but I didn't have a shit to give about that.

"I have a plan, or at least the beginnings of one," I said.

"Tor..." Darcy frowned at me as she sat again too. I'd discussed this with her but not in detail, mostly because I hadn't figured out the details and I didn't want to offer any kind of false hope to anyone.

"I'm working on it, but fuck knows if we have enough time for that. Either way, I'm going to visit The Ferryman today. I need to understand the cost which me and Darius are paying in bloodshed, and I was thinking of making a bargain with-"

"Only a fool would bargain with death," Max muttered.

"Then I must be a fool because the last deal I made with him ended in Darius sitting in this room."

Silence followed that and Max nodded in reluctant agreement.

"Anything else that might help us?" Darcy asked, looking from face to face, hunting for more because we all knew that we needed more if we wanted to stand a chance in this fight.

"Tharix," Darius said slowly. "I can't believe I'm saying this but he has let me live twice. He let the twins pass too. He's...searching for something, kinship or... family perhaps." His lip peeled back on the word, and I knew he didn't even want to admit to the blood tie which bound him to that wicked creation, but there was no denying what he said.

"You think you can turn him?" Caleb asked with interest.

"I think he has no real loyalty at all," Darius corrected. "He feels some obligation to our father and Lavinia because they were the ones who created him, but I don't think they're giving him much reason to hold on to that tie. I think he wants to choose his own path and perhaps he could be persuaded-"

"No," Seth blurted. "I've held this in for far too long, dancing around the truth of all I saw, of the demon vagina, of the…the…the fucking *heads."*

"It's okay," Max said, leaning forward to take Seth's hand and offer him some relief from the memory but he cried out as the connection clearly showed him what Seth had witnessed. The flash of horror and revulsion he felt was so vivid and powerful that it crashed from him and collided with all of us, showing us a momentary vision of Lavinia squatting over what looked like a fucking nest and a severed head poised beneath her, its mouth fixed in a silent scream.

"Ahh!" we all yelled out at once, cursing Max, Seth, and the universe for ever allowing such a thing to happen. I scrunched my eyes up against the vision as I recoiled into Darius's arms.

"Those four souls are trapped in Tharix, stuck on this side of The Veil, unable to cross into death and screaming for release," Max added in a shaky voice. "He isn't…right."

No one seemed inclined to speak up on the idea to bring the demon spawn of our enemies over to our side again, so we dropped it.

"The Guild Stones aren't useless," Orion said after several seconds of silence and Seth patted his arm again.

"Sure they're not, Professor Shame, sure they're not. They'll be the key to victory, just like you said." He winked at the rest of us as though asking us to play along for Orion's sake, but Orion could clearly see him and he knocked Seth's stroking hand away, baring his fangs at him in warning.

"We're going to figure it out," he said forcefully, getting to his feet. "Me and Blue already made a breakthrough, there has to be more to it. We have the beginnings of a plan and if it works then maybe we can do something about Clydinius."

"We'll keep working on it now," Darcy agreed. The two of them stood and headed out, my sister touching a hand to my shoulder in farewell as she passed.

Seth sighed loudly once they were gone. "That's just plain sad, that is," he said. "The scent of shame is growing again, isn't it?"

"You're such an asshole," Darius said, tossing a handful of water into the side of Seth's head.

"I'm a realist," Seth protested, getting to his feet. "And I've got things of my own to do. Mysterious pack things with my pack and my mate and my mother."

"You're going to challenge your mom for her spot?" I guessed and his lips twitched before he flattened them again.

"There are many things I might be doing or not doing. But…nah, it would cause too big of a shift in our family right now to introduce a new Alpha on the brink of war. After that though, who can say," he said in a mysterious voice, tugging Caleb after him as he headed for the door.

"How about you, Max?" I asked. "Going to challenge your dad?"

Max frowned and Geraldine gave him a smile in reassurance.

"No," he said, not seeming to need long to think it over. "Not now. Not on the brink of war. He's already lost so much – not that I think he was too cut up over Linda, but Ellis…" He sighed and I looked to Geraldine who shook her head minutely.

Max hadn't heard from Ellis since he'd offered her the ultimatum of needing to choose a side in this war and several press pieces had confirmed she was still freely moving about with her mother, supporting Lionel's campaign. It didn't look like she was going to switch sides and with the battle looming on the horizon that surely meant Tiberius was going to lose at least one of his children soon. The best he could hope for would be imprisonment for Ellis. The worst…

"I'll order her captured and not killed if possible," I offered. "At least then she won't be dead."

All those who had supported Lionel in his efforts and any of his remaining army had been rounded up and sent to Darkmore after trial. Linda would be among them soon, and though it had been seriously tempting to send Kylie Major that way too, she hadn't truly earned herself that hell, so she had been given a Power Shaming instead and sent into exile.

"Thank you," Max said stiffly. "But there's still time for her to come to her senses."

"There is," Darius agreed firmly.

I nodded, though it was seeming less and less likely that Ellis would change her allegiance and if she didn't, even if we managed to win this war and she was captured instead of killed, she'd played too prominent a part in Lionel's tyranny. She'd been a figurehead, joining with him in a show of support. The best we would be able to offer her was life imprisonment, and even then a lot of people would be out for her blood. I knew enough of this kingdom to understand that. People would expect execution for the key players in the losing side of this war.

Geraldine gave me a few more updates on the army and the tactics she was thinking might be best employed when it came to the battle then the two of them left to check in with Washer to get any further news from our scouts.

Then me and Darius got ourselves changed into something more appropriate to greet the keeper of death and headed out to find The Ferryman.

ORION

CHAPTER SIXTY

The sheer cliffs of Aer Cove swept down below us to the rocky beach, the waves dancing in the wind, foam spraying this way and that. I could taste the salt in the air, the wind trying to drive me back from the cliff's edge, but I leaned into it instead.

Darcy stood at the edge of the precipice, her blue hair fluttering behind her as she looked over her shoulder at me, the silver rings in her eyes glittering brightly. She was sunlight given breath right then, the heat of her beckoning me ever closer. If I didn't know her, I'd still recognise the wildness of her heart, the way she only grew stronger in adversity. My forget-me-not that had bloomed so perfectly in the strangling weeds, reminding me she was mine. Always mine.

I offered her my hand and she let the wind carry her to me like she weighed as much as a feather, wielding it with such skill it had me in awe once again.

"I have nothing left to teach you," I said, pride echoing through me.

She brushed her fingers over the rough stubble on my jaw. "You will always have something to teach me. There's still so much of this world I don't know, and I want to know everything."

"Your thirst for knowledge is as deep as mine," I mused. "I don't know as much as I'd like to know. And much of what I've learned is in books. Someday, perhaps we'll travel to new places and learn about them together."

She smiled the kind of smile that lit me up from the inside, and I mentally struck an X across my heart in keeping of that promise. If fate was so kind as to offer us the chance.

"You still don't regret coming here, do you?" I asked, my voice lowering. "If there was a way you could have stayed safe in the Mortal Realm, away from war and strife, would you have chosen that if you'd known what was coming now?"

Her brow creased, her hand lowering to rest against my heart. "I used to lay dreaming of places like this. I'd read about it in books and hear it in my favourite songs, I'd see it in the storm and feel it in the raindrops against my cheeks. I always belonged elsewhere, in a world full of fantasy and endless possibilities. I just knew I'd been born in the wrong place. My soul lost, forever searching for *this*. So no, Lance, there's not one part of me that would have chosen to give up this life for the sake of safety. If I die in this war, then hell, at least I will have lived. I've known you, I've found a home, a family. If I can only have that for this short time, then I'll take it over never having had it at all."

I kissed her in a way that told her I would never have chosen any other path either. I had regrets in my life, of course. About Clara most of all. But I was coming to understand that not everything was within my control, even when I tried hard to make it so. Darcy had taught me how to let go, how to find joy between the dark days, and how to find hope in the dead of the coldest nights. I'd met her with a heart full of bitterness, and she'd been sweet enough to restore the balance. I was forever in debt to her in ways I didn't know how to express.

"Shall we dance with the stars, beautiful?" I asked, my mouth slanting in a smile.

"If they'll let us," she said, her eyes alight with excitement.

I reached into my pocket, taking out the Guild Stones and we knelt on the grass, laying them in order in a circle. We glanced at each other a moment before placing the final stone into the circle.

"Are you sure about this?" I asked, her plan as turbulent as the ocean I could hear crashing against the shore. But I'd be damned if I didn't trust her. The information we'd found in the tome Eugene Dipper had brought us from The Library of the Lost the other night had led us to information about the Guild Stones which might just help us with Clydinius. But there were many gaps in the knowledge, and it required something that made my bones quake at the mere thought of it. Darcy's idea to secure this plan was pure insanity, but still...it was a chance. And one we had to attempt if we were ever going to find a way to see the rogue star dealt with.

"No, but it's worth a shot," she said, biting her lip.

"You're insane."

"Certified." She gave me a dark look, then pushed the final stone into place. "Arcturus!" she cried, her voice tinted with magic. "I request your counsel!"

The air shivered then all light was snuffed out, my soul yanked away into the grasp of the stars, measured in the hands of my creators.

Whispers spilled through the atmosphere, their tone angered by my queen's demand, but they wouldn't have answered her at all if they didn't wish to speak with us.

"Daughter of the flames, you wield the stones as if they were made to summon me," Arcturus boomed among them all, his ire as clear as fucking day.

I tried to reach for my mate in the dark, but although I could sense she was close, I couldn't touch her.

"You forged the stones," Darcy called. "They are linked to you and you alone. I only ask for you to speak with us once more, so that we might deal with Clydinius."

The hisses of the stars whipped against my ears, their fury striking at me through the nothingness surrounding us.

Arcturus took an age to reply, so long that I thought he might not speak at all. But at last his voice dripped over me like burning wax. *"I do not assist the beings of the realms. To do so is to thwart all laws set in place by the Origin, upheld by the Vetus stars of old. Defying those laws is to act as the Novus stars once did. Do not dare to ask such an atrocity of me twice."*

Well that was that, the door to our plan firmly slamming shut in our face.

"You spoke of balance before," Darcy said, her voice a sea of calm. "I know how it can be restored. But you have to help us. Clydinius has already tipped the scales, all I'm asking is that you tip them back."

There she goes, my girl asking an all-powerful star to do as she bids, despite his warnings.

"*Blue*," I hissed, my heart pounding frantically as we awaited Arcturus's reply. "This is madness. I will not see you killed for goading a star."

"Just wait," she urged, and for the love of the sun, I could not deny her that plea.

So I placed my faith in her and we hung in the balance of the heavens, waiting for our answer to come.

The darkness suddenly lifted, and I was certain we were about to be ejected from this ethereal existence, returned to our rightful place on earth, but instead we appeared on an island surrounded by a perfectly calm sea. So calm the water barely stirred at all, mirror-like in its beauty, giving a view to gold and silver fish zipping through a coral reef beneath the surface.

The sandy island we were on was perfectly circular, no more than ten feet in diameter. Darcy stood before me, her skin glowing with starlight, silver armour cladding her body that glittered with the purest kind of magic. I wore a broader version of the same armour, but it was so light it could have been made of leaves.

Arcturus appeared, wearing those very same white robes as before, his face unmoving as his voice carried to us inside our minds.

"No untruths can be spoken here."

"I don't plan on lying, and I'm sure you'd see through it if I did," Darcy said.

"You do not know how it was," Arcturus said. *"It was just a moment ago in the great expanse of time. When the Novus stars colluded with Fae in your realm, many of their tongues were gifted with the ability to lie to the Vetus stars. To shroud themselves from our gaze too. Perhaps Clydinius has struck a deal with the daughters of the flames, but if that is so, you cannot fool me here on the shore of the Veritas Ocean."*

"Then here is my request." Darcy stepped towards Arcturus with her chin held high.

"If a lie passes your lips, the consequences shall be great. And not upon you, daughter of the flames," Arcturus warned, his gaze turning on me. *"I shall let the ocean reap its bounty from the soul of your Elysian Mate."*

His arm flew out, a furious power slamming into the centre of my chest and launching me backwards into the water. It was as though a giant hand was pressed to my chest, forcing me deeper and deeper under the ocean until my back impacted with the sandy seabed. I thrashed against the hold it had on me, bubbles streaming from my lips and panic rising in my blood.

In the back of my mind, I knew I wasn't truly here. But then again, my soul was. I may not have been real in any sense of the word I knew back in the Fae world, but that didn't mean I was untouchable. In fact, my soul was truer to who I was than my body, and as that terrible power pressed me down, I became certain I could suffer here in ways that went beyond all bodily pain.

My lungs were choking for air, my ears popping from the pressure. But how could that be possible when I had no body? I didn't need air, but the illusion of needing it wouldn't pass. I fought harder to get free, one minute ticking into two then three, five, ten. But no matter how long I drowned, I didn't die. Because death wasn't possible for my soul, at least not in any physical way I might die on earth.

Finally, that giant, invisible hand on my chest scooped me up, dragging me from the seabed and tossing me onto the island. I slammed onto my front, shoving myself to my knees and gulping down air, but in an instant, I was no longer desperate for it. I was just as I had been before.

Darcy grabbed my arm, drawing me upright with a look of fear in her eyes. "Are you alright?"

"I'm fine," I said icily, throwing a glower at Arcturus's Fae-like form. "Did you get what you asked for?"

"Yes," she breathed, and I was so shocked by that it sent a flood of fear right through me. "What did he want in return for it?"

"Perhaps it is time I returned you to your earthly world," Arcturus said. *"So that you might lie again."*

The world shuddered and I blinked as I found myself kneeling opposite Darcy on the clifftop overlooking Aer Cove.

"Asshole," she growled.

"What did he mean by that? Are you going to lie to me, Blue?"

"No," she said fiercely. "He agreed to what I asked. There was no price."

I frowned, trying to consider if she really might lie to me. To protect me from some awful truth.

"You wouldn't leave me, would you?" I asked, my voice low and all too fucking vulnerable for my liking. But a part of me doubted the words she was telling me. Because she was too damn noble, too self-sacrificing. She'd give anything to protect those she loved.

"No, Lance." She lunged across the Guild Stones, knocking the circle so it split apart and kissing me with all the passion of a pious Fae serving the stars.

I sank into that kiss, dragging her against me and trying to taste the truth on her lips.

"Don't lie to me," I said as our mouths parted. "If you're keeping anything from me, say it now."

She gripped my hair hard enough to hurt, her eyes blazing with fire. "We don't need an ocean of truth to have trust between us. I'm telling you; he asked nothing of me. And you're damn well going to believe me, Lance Orion."

She was practically on top of me, and I growled at the challenge in her voice, flipping her over onto the back and bearing down on her. "You can command me in any way you like in this war, but you can't order away my doubts, Blue."

"How can you doubt us after everything?" she accused, rearing up, but I shoved a hand down on her chest to push her down again.

I bared my fangs at her. "I don't doubt *us,* I doubt that you would turn from a noble path. If Arcturus made a demand of you, I know you'd agree to it."

"Oh you *know* that, do you?" she snapped, casting a vine that wrenched my hand off of her chest. "You think I'd sacrifice myself or some part of me after I've fought with everything I have in this war?"

"You would if it protected Tory, or me, or any of the others," I barked, heat tearing through my chest at the thought of her making some fucking vow she couldn't get out of.

"If it came down to it, yes. But I'm not looking to sacrifice myself," she hissed, trying to get up again, but I forced her down, grabbing her wrists and pinning them to the dirt.

"You've been flying with Gabriel. I know you're worried. I know you're trying to protect us, just like he does. But it's not your duty to save everyone, in fact, it's your duty to survive this damn war so you can be there to lead the kingdom when it's over."

"You don't get to decide what my duty is like you're my mentor in this, you're not my teacher anymore, Lance," she snarled, casting a wind that gripped hold of me and tore me off of her.

I shoved to my feet and she did the same, glaring at me with the ferocity of a warrior. And I glared right back, hating how little control I felt in this situation.

"This is exactly what he wanted," she cursed, glancing up at the sky then back at me. "He's testing us."

"For what purpose?" I demanded, prowling toward her again.

"I don't know, that's what stars do, isn't it? They test us and push us and try to make us stronger. Maybe that's what this is."

"Convenient," I growled.

She glared icily then turned her back on me, offering me the biggest insult she could, before stalking away across the grass.

"And where are you going?" I called.

"To train," she clipped, pulling off her sweater and setting her wings free. She took off before I could stop her, and I growled in anger, scooping up the Guild Stones and placing them in my jacket pocket.

My eyes tracked her through the sky, and I shot after her, beating her to the Pitball stadium and heading inside. I ran to the locker room, tossing my jacket in a locker and changing into the black sweatpants and grey shirt I'd left there for training. By the time I was on the pitch, Darcy was still descending from the sky and I swung two training swords in my grip, waiting for her to land.

"Here." I tossed her the wooden sword, and she caught it as her feet touched down.

"I planned on training alone," she said, her lips pursing.

"Well you know what they say about plans, beautiful," I purred. "Fate doesn't care for them."

She swung the sword in her grip, rage pouring from her eyes and I was more than happy to give her an outlet for it.

"No magic," I laid out the rules. "Let's pretend you're fresh out, and someone has injected you with Order Suppressant."

"And what about you?" she accused.

"I'm your enemy." I shrugged. "I still have both my magic and my Order."

She tsked. "Funny how the rules play right into your favour. Do you miss having power over me, Lance?" she asked sweetly.

"It's just a training exercise," I said coolly. "Or would you rather we play on level easy, little princess?"

"Queen," she corrected sharply and that fire in her riled me right up.

"Queens don't choose easy paths," I said.

"Is that what you're so afraid of, Lance?" she asked, taking up a fighting stance. "That I've chosen the hard path. That I'm going to give up everything to protect you? Hm, sounds familiar." She lunged, swinging her sword at me with a violent precision that came close to striking my neck. I blocked it with a parry at the last second then shot behind her in a blur, blasting air at her that sent her tumbling to the ground. She gained her feet in an instant, spinning around with a swing of her sword which I ducked back to avoid.

"We've well established that I'm a hypocrite," I said dryly. "I can live with that, so long as you keep breathing."

"How do you think I felt when I discovered what you'd done?" she growled, lunging at me again with a deadly strike aimed at my heart.

My sword met with hers, my superior strength knocking it away with ease. "Terrible, I'd imagine."

"God, you're an ass," she hissed, coming at me again and this time I froze her feet with a flick of my finger, sending her crashing to her knees beneath me. I gripped her chin, making her look up at me, reminding her who held the winning cards right now.

"There is such a thing as a truth serum, you know?" I ran my thumb over her lips, and she bit me like a wildcat, yanking her feet out of the ice, using the wooden sword to shatter it.

She got up and threw her shoulder into my gut, forcing me back a step as she jammed her sword into my side hard enough to bruise. I caught her waist, flipping her up in my arms and tossing her onto the ground on her ass.

"So now you're threatening to drug me?" she scoffed.

I swung my sword lazily, knowing I would never really do such a thing but it was worth saying it to see her infuriated. I was punishing her, the fiend in me knew that, but our fury often collided in ways like this, and I knew exactly where it ended.

"So dramatic," I drawled.

"You're just trying to get a rise out of me," she realised, shoving to her feet again and raising her sword.

"It appears to be working," I said, smirking at her and opening my arms in an offering of a strike. Not that I'd really let her get a hit so easily.

She regarded me, not tempted by my bait. With a calculated look, she kicked off her shoes and socks, then unbuckled her jeans, sliding out of them and tossing them away from her, her top swiftly following. My gaze trailed over the little pink thong and matching bra she wore as she rose onto her tiptoes and sized me up.

"That's better. They were so restrictive," she purred.

"Hm," I grunted, watching as she paraded this way and that, her big green eyes on me the whole time.

The curve of her hips kept drawing my attention, and the toned shape of her stomach was another distraction I couldn't afford.

"Is this how you plan to win your fights in battle?" I growled. "The enemy won't care for your peachy ass."

"Peachy, you say?" She turned around so said ass was pointed right at me, glancing over her shoulder to try and look at it herself, acting like a ditzy fool.

I shot up behind her, grabbing a fistful of her ass and squeezing hard and speaking in her ear. "Focus, Blue."

"I'm not the one who's lost focus." She jabbed her sword into my ribs as she reached behind her, and a grin twisted my lips at the stab of pain.

"So are you going to play war with me in your underwear, or are you going to ask for what you really want?" I grazed my fingers along her panty line and her back arched a little, goosebumps rising across her skin.

"I think you're the one who wants something," she said, then jammed her elbow into my ribs and ducked out of my grip, spinning away and raising her sword again.

I ran my tongue over my fangs, observing her with hunger rising in my throat. She was right. I did want something. I wanted to push her until she showed me what she was capable of. But first, I wanted her ass spanked red and her lustful gasps filling my ears.

She came at me in a battle charge, sword held poised to strike, and I shot away from her, racing around behind her and clapping my hand against her ass, hard enough to make her stumble. She wheeled around with a snarl, and a smirk lifted my lips as I flexed my fingers.

"Do you still want to play?" I goaded her.

"I'll keep going, but you're not playing fair," she growled.

"Battle is never fair."

She bared her teeth, prowling forward once more, swinging her sword with a promise of violence. I let her close the distance between us, and when she swung at me, I brought my sword up to meet hers. She twisted her blade with such skill that she wrenched my sword from my hand, sending it skittering across the grass. But before she could land a strike, I shot around her, spanked her hard enough to make her yelp then sped away again.

"I'll give you a chance. Let's say my sword just tumbled off a cliff and I'm all tapped out of magic. Now it's just you against my Order," I said.

She ran at me, and I waited until the last second to move, lurching out the way of her strike and racing around behind her, clapping my hand hard against her ass cheek which was turning good and red. She spun around with her sword swinging, but I was gone, out of reach once more. We went on like that time and again, her fury sparking hotter and hotter as she failed to get a single blow on me while her right ass cheek blazed.

She dug the tip of her wooden sword into the ground, breathing heavily and glaring at me.

"Do you give up?" I asked.

"Never," she hissed.

"That's my girl." I rushed at her in a blur, speeding past her but she ducked low, spinning the sword and catching my ankles with it. I tripped, slamming hard to the ground on my back and she was there in an instant, her foot pressing to my chest and her sword at my throat.

"Yield," she ordered.

"I yield," I exhaled, and she lifted the sword from my neck.

Her blue hair fluttered around her in the breeze and for a moment I witnessed what her enemies saw in their final moments on this earth. A queen full of fire and wrath. She had been born to rule, born to command, born to fight, and it was the most beautiful thing I'd ever seen.

"Do you really think I lied to you about Arcturus? Do you really doubt me after everything?" she demanded. "After I've clawed my way back to you time and again. After we've fought against all odds to be together, and chosen to become star bound mates? You think I'd taint us with a lie?"

I gritted my jaw, feeling the resounding honesty of her words.

"No," I admitted. "I see the truth now as clearly as I see a queen above me. I doubted you because I judged you by my own standards. I'm the bastard who would lie to protect you, the brute who would commit every sin in the book to safeguard you." I gripped the back of her calf, leaning up to kiss her ankle and giving her a dark look. "Punish me however you see fit."

She flexed her toes against my chest, pressing her weight down more firmly. "Beg," she commanded.

"Forgive me," I growled, kissing her ankle again then grazing my fangs against the flesh of her calf.

"Try harder," she urged, and I reared up, my hand sliding up to grasp the back of her thigh, my mouth dragging up the inside of her leg, kissing, nipping. I'd been hard as stone the moment she placed her foot on my chest, but now my cock was fucking aching. I wasn't used to playing submissive, but for her, I'd try anything. And it didn't feel so bad being under her control.

"Bite me," she gasped as I reached the top of her thigh and I obliged, sinking my fangs into a vein, hooking her leg over my shoulder to give me better access.

Her fingers knotted in my hair and a heady moan left her that only drove me on, my hunger for her insatiable as that incredible taste of sweet wildfire rolled over my tongue.

"Enough." She yanked my head back, our eyes meeting as I swallowed, my power reserves swelling with the magic I'd taken from her.

Fire flickered over her skin, burning away her panties and bra, baring herself to me fully and making me groan with want. She was everything. My goddess, my life. And she possessed every worthless scrap of my soul.

"You know how I like it," she said, biting her lip and telling me exactly how much she was getting off on this.

I smiled savagely then buried myself between her thighs, feasting on her soaked pussy and licking her clit. She cried out as I circled my tongue fast then slow, driving two fingers into her tight hole and curling them to grind against that spot that drove her wild. She ground her hips in time with the movement of my tongue and fingers, chasing the rhythm I built between her thighs.

The pad of my tongue dragged over her throbbing clit again as I felt her pussy tightening around my fingers, and I quickened my pace, using my Order speed to flick my tongue against her so fast, she screamed. Her legs shuddered, and I gripped her ass to keep her from shattering on top of me, forcing her to endure every drop of pleasure I had to give. Her fingers were so tight in my hair, my scalp burned, but I relished the pain, only spurred on by her need for release.

My fingers pumped as fast as my tongue moved and then she was coming, her pussy clamping on my fingers and her arousal slicking my hand. I slowed my pace to almost nothing, devouring her in achingly slow strokes of my tongue and making her climax last even longer. She shuddered, moaning and rolling her hips, and my cock throbbed to the point of pain. I had to be inside her. Had to feel this soaking heat as I sank into her.

But before I could drag her down onto me to claim what I wanted, vines snatched hold of my wrists and coiled around my chest, yanking me to the ground beneath her and holding me there. My muscles bunched against the restraints and a snarl left my lips as Darcy lowered over me, straddling my hips.

"Don't break free," she commanded, her eyes glittering. "I want to know what you feel when you have me at your mercy."

It took me a second longer to force myself to relax, not liking being so out of control, but it was clear Blue wanted a taste of power. I just wasn't sure I could let her have it.

"I need to touch you," I rasped, lust driving me to the brink of madness.

"Surrender to it. That's what I do," she said, a playful smile on her lips as she rolled down my sweatpants and freed the full length of my cock.

She wasted no time, lining me up to take her and driving her hips down. I growled like an animal as she took me all the way to the hilt, my arms bulged against my restraints as she started to move. It took every ounce of self-control I had not to break through them and grab her. She fucked me slowly, her green eyes hooded as she squeezed her breasts and played with her nipples, making me so fucking hard I could barely hold out. But as our breaths fell into pace with one another's, I found it easier to just enjoy the show. Every moan and gasp falling from her made the tip of my cock twitch and I gritted my teeth against the urge to explode.

Her pace started quickening as she chased her own release and I so desperately wanted to reach out and rub her needy clit for her, but fuck it was hot to just watch her get off over me.

Darcy scraped her nails down my chest, over my abs, moaning at the mere sight of my muscles tightening, and I drove my hips up, forcing my cock deeper just as she found her release. She cried out, tipping her head back and squeezing her tits hard, her hips rocking and her body taking and taking from mine. I couldn't control myself any longer as I thrust up hard, breaking the damn restraints and gripping her ass as I fucked her with furious pumps of my hips, finishing with a deep groan and driving my fangs into her neck as pleasure spilled through me in waves.

She clawed at my back, drawing me even closer until we felt like one being with no beginning or end, our bodies falling still and moulding perfectly to one another's.

I withdrew my fangs from her skin, licking away the line of blood that spilled from the pinpricks and moving my hand to heal them.

"Don't," she panted, knocking my hand aside. "I once told you I'd wear your bite marks if the world ever accepted us. So I'm keeping these."

My mouth found hers, heady bliss taking over me as that kiss seemed to make our very souls merge. I didn't know how I'd gone from being the unluckiest motherfucker in the world to the luckiest, but I was counting my damn stars, and I hoped the tide never turned.

DARIUS

CHAPTER SIXTY ONE

The bike roared beneath me, the mountain road curving at a steady climb and launching us towards the peak. I grinned as I rode, glancing over at my girl who took the corners like a pro, leaning low on her own motorcycle, the diamond constellation which was inlaid over the engine catching in the midday sunlight and casting rainbows across the slick paintwork.

Roxy's laughter echoed in my ears through the headset built into my helmet, the pure, unbridled joy she took in riding infectious even if I hadn't shared her love of the road.

"It's been too fucking long since we did this," I said, letting her pull ahead and watching as she crested the hill before me, the breath-taking view of Solaria opening up ahead of us like the whole world was waiting beyond the open road.

"Too fucking long since any of us got away from the war camp and just did something for the fun of it," she agreed, though this couldn't really be counted as that. But Roxy had paused when we'd headed for the academy gates, a pouch full of stardust in my pocket ready to transport us where we needed to go and had looked wistfully at the parking garage before announcing we were going to be taking the scenic route today. I'd had no objections to that.

She knew where we were going, having researched all the methods to come close to death while she was searching for a way to return me to her from it, but she'd needed a firmer path than this one. What we were heading towards was more like a looking glass than a bridge. She never could have stepped through The Veil from beneath a hangman's tree. But it would be more than sufficient for a conversation with The Ferryman.

"Are you going to tell me what you're planning yet?" I asked, riding the adrenaline as I pulled back the throttle and sped down the hill on the other side of the mountain behind her.

The road was a series of harsh switchbacks but the view down it was clear so we could see ahead of us to confirm that no traffic was coming the other way. All the roads seemed eerily empty these days. No one wanted to risk unnecessary journeys while the war balanced on a knife point like it did, ready to slip at any moment.

"I'm planning on asking him what the cost of your life is in plain terms," she called back to me, her black hair whipping out from beneath her helmet as she took the first turn.

"And?" I pushed but she just laughed, urging her bike to go faster and forcing me to follow.

There was a risk to this which only made the thrill of it all the more alluring. And anyway, I had stardust at hand if we needed to leave in a hurry, so it wasn't like we were in acute danger. Between the two of us and our combined power, I had to imagine that anyone foolish enough to take us on would come off the worse for it.

We raced down the switchbacks, the beauty of the scenery and thrill of the ride giving us a much needed reprieve from all the war councils and prophecies of doom. In this moment we could pretend it was all over, or maybe had never even begun in the first place.

Roxy whooped as she sped around the final switchback then raced ahead onto the long flat expanse of road that stretched out beyond it.

I took chase, finally letting the engine loose to its full potential and speeding after her with my body low in the saddle.

Roxy glanced over her shoulder at me then changed gear and increased her speed. "Last one to that big lumpy rock thing has to sub tonight," she called over the speaker.

"That lumpy rock thing is a stone column from the long-forgotten city of Torbella which was destroyed in the Blood Ages, you know," I called after her, but she just lifted a hand to flip me off over her shoulder and shot away at full speed.

I cursed her then concentrated on catching and beating her.

I leaned forward, my bike's engine roaring as I pushed it to its limit, the plush green landscape racing by in a blur.

Roxy stayed dead ahead of me, not letting up for a second as her bike tore up the road and before I knew it, we were shooting past the stone column and her whoop of triumph filled my ears.

"Cheat," I taunted.

"Bad loser," she replied.

We continued on, enjoying the thrill of the ride and I let Roxy keep her lead, preferring to have my eyes on her anyway.

She turned off of the main road onto a smaller side road, slowing a little as the curves and turns ahead made it harder to see what was coming. Our path was lined with craggy brown rocks dressed with moss and wildflowers which doggedly ignored the frost clinging to their petals. I was taken by surprise as we turned a corner to find a river burbling alongside our path. The journey had been faster than I'd expected. Or perhaps I'd just been enjoying it too much to notice.

We made it to the crossroads and Roxy pulled over, dismounting and hanging her helmet on the handlebars.

I parked up beside her, moving to walk at her side as she jerked her chin towards a towering, blackened tree which almost appeared to have been burned, though the leaves clinging to its branches defied that theory. On closer inspection, I noticed rivulets of deep red spiderwebbing across its scarred bark, glistening as if lit from within. A single branch was reaching out like a grasping arm across the river, a noose swaying in the breeze from the very centre of it.

"Now what?" I murmured.

"Now we hope he forgives me for shoving him into the river the last time we met." She smirked at the memory while I forced myself to count to five on an exhale. Now wasn't the time to get into it with my wife over her reckless behaviour, but sometimes I thought she was aiming to give me a heart attack with the stunts she pulled.

Roxy dropped to one knee and carefully traced the rune Eihwaz (which looked something like a sharply pointed S) into the silt which lined the river's edge. I'd been reading her damn book so I recognised it easily enough, the protection rune one of the less treacherous so far as I understood them. I watched her place a sprig of dill then lavender on top of the rune before pricking her fingertip and letting three drops of blood fall onto it.

"Add yours," she commanded, offering me the needle she'd crafted with earth magic.

I ignored the imperial tone and did as she asked, three drops of my blood joining with hers in the little offering.

Roxy let sparks fall from her fingers and the whole thing went up in flames.

Lastly, she slid her hand into the pocket of her leather jacket and took two golden coins out.

"Those are-" I began but she cut me off.

"Yeah, yeah. But we need them so you'll have to just console yourself with the million other gold coins in that fancy pirate chest at the foot of your bed," she said, waving me off.

I bit back a growl, locking my teeth together and watching as she placed the coins on the other side of the protection rune, closer to the water. Then she took her sword from where it was strapped to her pack and unsheathed it, revealing bloodstains marking the metal.

"Blood of a dead man," she explained as I frowned at it. "Don't ask where I got it from – it was a whole gross expedition, but it came from one of the bastards who attacked the academy and he was already dead when I borrowed it, so don't go worrying that I've been off on a casual murder spree just to get this conversation going."

"The thought never crossed my mind."

"Liar." She smirked at me then leaned closer to the smouldering remains of the sacrifice which she'd burned over the rune and drove her blade into the water. "But all of this seemed necessary to me because it's required if I want to force The Ferryman to appear and I get the feeling he would have refused if I'd just asked nicely."

"Oh yes, forcing a being more powerful than life and death to succumb to your bidding seems like a perfectly rational thing to do," I deadpanned.

Roxy's lips parted on a reply, but it fell away as the distant sound of a paddle driving into the water reached us, making us both turn to the river in silence.

A fog which had no business appearing on this bright morning began to creep across the water, obscuring the far side from view. The thick limb of the tree that reached out across the river creaked ominously in the silence, the noose which hung there swaying in an unnatural breeze and the world seemed to hold its breath as The Ferryman appeared between the gloom.

Shrouded in a dark cloak, his forbidding eyes pinned unwaveringly on the woman at my side, The Ferryman paddled his raft closer to the shore.

"You have some nerve," he spat.

I stifled my shock as his face was revealed within the hood, the Savage King peering out at us from its folds. It took me a moment to grasp that this wasn't truly Hail Vega; The Ferryman was simply wearing his face.

"My quarrel was never with you," Roxy said firmly, not even seeming shaken as the master of death glowered at her, his piercing gaze raking over the rune which smouldered between us, his upper lip curling back in understanding.

"And yet you feel the need for that," he pointed out, making Roxy grin.

"Well, I'm not a fucking idiot."

The Ferryman grunted in what might have been amusement too and I raised my brows in surprise.

"We want to understand this cost we're paying," I told him, uncertain of how long we could keep him here like this and needing that answer before he left.

"She snatched you from the heart of death, soul stealer," he replied, his eyes running down me from the top of my head to the soles of my boots, a shiver tracking down my spine in time with it. "Did you expect the cost for such blasphemy to be low?"

"I expect nothing but an answer," I replied.

The Ferryman considered us for a few lingering moments then shrugged.

"You will pay your debt in death delivered," he said cryptically, not revealing anything we hadn't already worked out for ourselves.

"How many deaths?" I pushed. "How long will we revel in bloodlust and violence until your thirst for reaping is satisfied?"

"Some souls weigh heavier than others," he replied, that nonchalant shrug returning, and I tensed as he drove his paddle against the bank, making to push away from us so soon.

"Tharix, the thing my father calls his Heir now has four Fae souls bound to his, unable to escape into death," I said. "Surely his death would count as extra?"

The Ferryman hissed like a cat and I almost flinched at the sudden outburst. "Why must mortals insist upon messing with the designs of fate?" he snarled. "No, Tharix will not suffice. That abomination will answer to me directly."

"How about the soul of Lionel Acrux?" Roxy asked quickly. "Is his soul weighted in enough sin?"

The Ferryman considered it for a few moments, his fury at the mention of Tharix abating then finally, he nodded. "Him and the might of his army will suffice."

"So we simply have to win the war and deliver my father's rotten soul into your keeping?" I clarified. "Then our debt will be paid? We'll no longer hunger for violence like we do now?"

"Simple?" The Ferryman laughed, the sound like cracking branches and wind wheezing through carved stone. "There will be nothing simple about the task. You will drown in blood and gore long before you come close to taking the Dragon King's head. But if somehow you manage to wade free of the carnage then yes, your debt will be paid in full."

"Wait," Roxy called as he pushed off, his raft floating away from the bank far faster than allowed for any further conversation.

The Ferryman smiled as the fog began to engulf him, but Roxy snarled in determination then took a running jump from the edge of the river.

"Roxy!" I yelled in alarm as she propelled herself forward with air magic, the thump of her boots hitting the raft the only sound which returned to me from the fog as both she and The Ferryman were swathed in it and disappeared from sight.

I ran after her, freezing the water before me and sprinting out onto it, calling her name. My heart thundered in my chest, confirming that she still lived but as I dove into the roiling fog, I lost all sense of the world and came skidding to a halt on the ice.

I spun around, their voices faint and indistinct, coming from behind me...no, to the right...

I started running again, the distant murmur of their conversation leading me on a wild goose chase, the direction constantly changing, any hopes of finding them deserting me fast.

As panic came rushing for me, the ice beneath my feet began to splinter and crack. I cast more magic beneath my feet but it was no use and before I could do anything to stop it, I fell crashing into the icy water.

I sank, deeper and deeper, my efforts to swim met with nothing but resistance until suddenly a body collided with mine, her arms wrapping around me before she began to kick for the surface.

We started moving then, swimming together towards the glimmering light above us and I gasped down a hungry lungful of air as we emerged.

"What the fuck were you playing at?" I demanded, my hands going tight around

Roxy's waist as we treaded water and blinked droplets from our lashes.

"I asked him to make a trade with me. I had something I knew he wanted."

"What?" I demanded.

"A draining dagger stained with the blood of the cursed," she said with a sly smile. "I got it from Herithé. Pretty sure it was all kinds of valuable too because its hilt was coated in gemstones so I thought it best not to show it to the greedy Dragon."

"And did risking your life and giving me a fucking heart attack result in the trade you wanted?" I demanded, ignoring the twinge of intrigue that awoke at the whisper of a secret treasure.

Her smile fell away then and she shook her head. "I don't think so. I wanted his protection for our army, I wanted some shield between our warriors and death."

"He can't have wanted it badly enough to give you that? War means death, that's like asking a starving man to resist eating at a feast."

"I know," she sighed. "But I gave it to him all the same. No strings, no promises, no trades. Just the hope that maybe, he won't be against us now, that perhaps he'll forgive me for stealing you from his grasp."

I shook my head at her audacity, brushing a lock of dark hair off of her face.

"We'll make certain to offer him plenty of other souls to reap when we collide with my father's army," I agreed. "Because I'm not done living this crazy life with you yet."

THARIX

CHAPTER SIXTY TWO

Cold. I named the sensation which pressed to my palm as I trailed it along the jade green wall of my father's castle, wandering, without thought, uncertain where to go next.

I rounded a corner and a pair of guards snapped to attention, the scent of their fear ripe in the air, a drip of perspiration rolling down the side of one's brow.

They were afraid of me.

I sighed, moving between them into the deeper layers of the castle. Everyone was afraid of me. None of them understood what I was and so they feared it. But none understood less than me.

Sharp. I glanced at the piece of stone which stuck out from the wall jaggedly, pressing the pad of my thumb down on it until that spike of sensation rushed through me, blood welling to stain the wall. Pain.

From here, I could hear the clamour of the army beyond the frosted windows of the castle. Distantly, I could hear my father's voice too, bellowing some command which would no doubt send everyone scurrying.

My mother stepped into the room, stalling abruptly as she found me lurking there, her eyes moving to the thrones which sat on the dais, drawing my focus to them and making me realise that I had wandered into the throne room.

Her eyes narrowed in suspicion and her bare feet clapped against the stone floor as she strode towards me.

"My boy," she said, the words dancing over my senses then falling away. Her voice seemed harsher since her hold on the shadows within me had fallen away, no longer the lull of something to yearn for but a scrape of command which I instinctively balked at.

I looked into her face, the sharp cheekbones, the skin which seemed thinner than was right, or at least thinner than that of other Nymphs and Fae, her veins slightly visible beneath her flesh, dark with shadows in some places.

"Mother," I replied in turn, wondering why that word fell flat on my tongue.

I had heard many Fae screaming for their mothers in those camps Father had shown me, the ones he said were full of lesser Fae, and yet they had seemed the same as all others to me. More than that, they had held that gleam in their eyes, that...

something which I was missing.

"What are you up to?" she asked suspiciously, and I frowned.

"There is nothing," I said because that was how I had been feeling recently. Well, in some ways all I had was recent. There was before and then…this.

She pursed her lips, taking my hand and coaxing my shadows closer while the dark stain of her own coiled between her fingers. But they were no longer one and the same, no longer melded but separate and as I took hold of my own shadows, they gently but firmly pushed hers back.

I felt my power rising at her call as she pressed harder, but since that star had shattered, since its light had washed across the world, the weight of my shadows hadn't been so thick. Their colour was no longer stained so darkly either and I was fairly certain I preferred them as such. I didn't want her taint on them.

I snatched my hand back, stepping away from her and moving to the thrones in the centre of the room.

Mother surveyed me silently before walking up to stand at my back.

"It will be yours one day," she breathed, her words silken. "One day soon, perhaps."

"The chair?" I asked, uncertain why I would care about such a thing.

"The throne," she corrected sharply. "And the crown which goes alongside it."

I stepped forward abruptly, dropping into my father's seat and leaning against the carved back, the Dragon scales which adorned it digging into my spine.

"I don't think it fits," I decided, rising again just as swiftly.

"That's because you are still growing into it. It will fit perfectly when your time comes," she assured me.

I thought on that, wondering if perhaps that was what I was looking for, but then I remembered my brothers laughing together on that mountaintop and something in my chest twisted sharply.

"No," I said simply because I knew that no chair or headwear would offer what I sought.

She was speaking again, her words harsh and clipped, but I strode away from her, her voice merely a noise that I chose not to listen to. A choice I found so much easier now, her words no longer slipping into my thoughts once I made it away from her company.

Father's voice came from the chamber ahead of me, but I took a turn, not wanting to taste the wrath I could hear coiling in his tone, not wishing to face whatever lesson in obedience and subservience he had for me today. His hand had not been returned to him and his rage over the fact was released upon me regularly. No, I found I no longer wished to fall prey to the lashes of his belt. For a time, I had endured his violence, the sensation of such pain strange and new to me. But the loyalty he demanded from me, forcing me to agree to whatever he wished no longer seemed so important.

I took a narrow flight of stairs downwards, outpacing my mother who prowled behind me, turning into another narrow passage, this one intended for servants to use.

Once I made it halfway down the stairs, the sound of her footsteps faded away and I continued through the passageway then took another set of stairs down, lower and lower, past Vard's laboratories, into the bowels of the castle where the walls no longer shone green.

I headed into the darkness beneath the mountain, no real direction in mind, but as my foot struck a puddle, I jerked to a halt. A sensation like fingertips crawling along my spine froze me in place.

A hand lunged from the puddle at my feet, making me cry out in surprise as it grasped my ankle and wrenched me off balance, sending me sprawling to the floor. I rolled onto my hands and knees, panting as I came face to face with the murky water and a rotten skull peering out at me from within the folds of a tattered hood.

The skeletal hands jerked for me again, breaking free of the puddle and yanking me down by the throat, forcing my face beneath the filthy water.

A new sensation struck me, my pulse racing, adrenaline spiking through my limbs which trembled at the shock of it. Fear.

"You are in possession of items which belong to me, Shadowborn," the skull sneered, its rancid breath washing over my face even through the water surrounding me. "I have come to claim them."

MILDRED

CHAPTER SIXTY THREE.

My skin itched and burned with the desperate need to be reunited with my King, the Guardian Bond on the crook of my arm now standing out starkly among a patch of reddened, bleeding skin where I had clawed and scratched at it in my need for some reprieve to its constant aching.

I had grown feverish in my desire to return to him, my need to fulfil the demands of the bond and keep my oath of eternal protection to him making my mind crack. It had left me panting, bordering on insanity most of the time. I couldn't think, could hardly draw the energy to eat, and sometimes I struggled to breathe without him.

And now I lay there, on the floor of that filthy room, surrounded by cowards and failures, all of those who had lost the fight for this place. Or worse; surrendered like the pathetic worms they were.

The stench in here was sickening, though we were given clean clothes and showers, I swore it still worsened day on day, the air thickening with the pungent stench of failure.

I gasped down breaths which felt shallow and thin, my lungs burning with the need for more air, a ringing in my ears making the words of those beyond the bars of my cage indistinguishable. Pimpricks of light danced before my eyes but when I closed them, even the memory of my dear, beloved king wasn't enough to soothe the ache in me.

A clang sounded and I peeled my eyelids open, feeling the crust around them from so many sleepless nights cracking and crumbling as I did so.

Polished boots stopped before me, a man asking what was wrong with me, a prod to my shoulder making me snarl with fury.

I spasmed beneath them, brought so low that the disgrace made me wince. I was a Dragon and yet here I lay at the feet of such lowly beasts.

"Are you sick?" one of them asked, shoving me again.

I groaned where I had meant to growl, swiping a hand at him far too late to make contact with the offending limb.

"Let's take her to Uranus Infirmary," a woman decided while I thrashed and spat at them, trying to fight off the grip of their hands.

But even as I did so, my heart cracked within my chest, the need I felt for my king crippling me with its intensity, the helplessness of my desire while locked up in this foul place enough to destroy what little I was.

A bang sounded as the gates to our cell opened then closed, my back arching against something hard as I fought to make sense of the movement around me, of the dim light suddenly turning bright, the stagnant air replaced with fresh.

My chapped lips parted as I stared up at the sky, my body jerking as I lurched for it, needing to be up there, among the clouds, belching fire into the deep blue. But as I tried to reach for it, I found myself bound, my chest strapped down onto the hard surface I was being transported upon.

"Call for Geraldine," said the man whose magic was carrying my stretcher, and I twisted my neck to see a weaselly rat of a fellow hurrying away to comply.

A hand touched my wrist and I snarled furiously, lurching towards the woman who walked there, my teeth bared. I would rip her throat out with nothing but these blunt Fae fangs if that was all I had at my disposal.

She jerked back in alarm, her fingers slipping from my wrist, her hand brushing mine and in that moment, I felt a thrum of power. Gold.

I clawed at her, throwing my weight her way, my fingernails ripping into her arm and drawing blood. She screamed, staggering back, but my fingers had hooked into the golden bracelet she wore, tearing it from her wrist. The stretcher tumbled to the ground, and I hit the dirt hard on my face.

Cries of alarm sounded all around me, the heavy weight of some cretin leaping onto my back to hold me down only grinding my face further into the gravel, but I had it, and I hastily shoved it into my waistband, the gold pressed directly to my flesh.

They heaved me upright again, more vines snaking out from several directions to restrain me, and I bucked and thrashed against their control. But all the while, a hot trickle of power began to rise beneath my skin as the gold worked to restore my magic.

I fell still as we walked further, my eyes on the sky and thoughts of my king clearer than ever in my mind. The magic slowly building in my blood helped to ease some of the torment I'd faced from the time I'd been forced to spend without power. The other pathetic souls who shared my cell had all been offered the chance to use some magic in a contained environment to stave off the insanity which could be caused by a prolonged absence from it. But they had been offered that chance for good behaviour. I would never lower myself to behave for these brutes and hellions. I was a Dragon, their superior in every way and they would not cow me.

The ache in my chest lessened as that spark of magic grew. It was merely an ember compared to the full might of what I was capable of, but it was a start.

My gaze snapped from face to face, marking each of the rats for death as they transported me into the heart of the academy towards Uranus Infirmary.

There, I was moved onto a bed, the vines stripped from my body and a single manacle placed around my ankle, chaining me to the metal bedframe.

I remained utterly still as Mother Dickins, the head healer at the academy and the professor who taught the subject entered the room, but my eyes were moving from place to place, a plan forming in me just as surely as that golden bracelet was restoring my magic.

There were potions and tonics lined up in a glass cabinet along the wall, all manner of things from flea dips, to Faemidia tonic, to sedatives, but my gaze fell still as I spied the very thing I most needed. A vial of antidote to the Order suppressant and a pack of new syringes just waiting to draw up a dose powerful enough to release my Dragon from the chains it was locked in.

I waited as most of the guards left the room, apparently satisfied that I was under control now. As if pathetic cretins such as they could ever truly hope to control one of the most powerful beasts in all the lands for long.

A snarl rippled up the back of my throat as I was left in the company of the healer and only two guards. It was insulting that they believed themselves sufficient, but they would soon learn the error of their ways.

I allowed the healer to press her magic into me, welcoming the extra strength it lent to my limbs, the layers of exhaustion that were peeled away by her ministrations. She examined me, muttering to herself then looking me in the eyes as she asked me how long it had been since I'd last taken any Faeroids.

I licked my lips at the question, some part of me knowing that the shakes and agony in my body hadn't simply come from being separated from my king and the effect of the Guardian Bond. I needed my medicine. The mere mention of it left my throat rasping and my heart thrashing with desperation.

"Too long," I admitted, the shake in my hands confirming it anyway.

The healer nodded. "I'll get you a dose. It isn't safe to go cold turkey on these things."

She bustled from the room and the ringing in my ears grew to a crescendo as all of the partially-formed plans in my mind fell away, my hunger for my tonic consuming every piece of my mind, my gaze locked to that door, awaiting her return with a desperation that felt entirely physical.

The woman I had scratched was glowering at me, healing away the bloody gouges I'd left in her flesh. Her hand swept over her wrist and she sucked in a gasp, forcing my focus to her while her mind crashed to a realisation, her lips parting on the accusation.

My time was up and with a furious bellow, I hurled a twin set of wooden spears from my fist, piercing both guards through their throats and sending blood splattering across the room.

I threw myself from my bed in the wake of their deaths, falling heavily to the ground as the manacle on my ankle jerked tight. With a ferocious kick of my other leg, I broke the metal post I was chained to and the whole bed fell to the floor with a tremendous clang.

I grabbed the body of the woman I'd killed, rooting through her pockets until I found an Atlas and calling my father, barking orders at him to come to the academy to meet me, yelling that I was escaping and wasting no time listening for his reply. The Dragons would come for me. We protected our own.

The precious dregs of magic I'd managed to recover were gone now, consumed by that burst of earth magic, but I didn't need my magic, I needed my Dragon.

I clawed my way to my feet, ignoring the sounds of yells from beyond the door, the thundering of feet charging my way.

My fist shattered the glass door to the medicine cabinet, glass puncturing my skin and blood oozing between my fingers as I snatched the vial of antidote and a syringe from the shelf.

I ripped the packet open with my teeth, flinging the cap from the syringe and half bending the needle with the force I used, but it still managed to suck up a dose of the antidote when I thrust it into the bottle.

The door shattered and my gaze snapped up to meet the piercing blue eyes of that cantankerous bitch Geraldine Grus as she launched herself at me with a battle cry.

The last whisp of my power shot from me, vines binding her hands and locking her magic away.

She screamed furiously, racing straight for me despite her bound hands but as our gazes met, the needle pierced my flesh and I was already shifting, the beast bursting from my skin with a roar of victory.

The room was far too small for my Dragon body and the walls cracked and shuddered when my expanding flesh collided with them. Geraldine was knocked from her feet, slamming down heavily on her back beyond the door and I parted my lips on a blast of Dragon fire to finish her.

Cries came from the hall and my head snapped up, the Dragon Fire bursting from my jaws in the direction of the five guards who were racing for me instead.

I was outnumbered in this place and my need to return to my king outweighed my desire to destroy as many of these traitorous pieces of scum as I could.

I lunged for Geraldine, snatching her into my talons, a gift for my king to make up for my failure in being caught.

With a bounding leap, I crashed through the closest window, stone shattering around me as I forced my enormous body through the too-small hole. And in my claws, thrashing and cursing me while her blood ran down the sides of my talons, Geraldine Grus was dragged along with me.

I might have been returning to my king in disgrace, but I planned on gifting him the bitch who had played such a key role in this rebellion upon my return. And when he had drained all the knowledge of her pathetic rebellion from her head, I would be first in line for her public execution.

DARCY

CHAPTER SIXTY FOUR

"**Y**our majesty!" Justin Masters wailed, racing down the path toward us. "A prisoner has escaped! Mildred Canopus has taken Geraldine!"

My whole world flipped on its axis, terror taking hold of my heart and refusing to release me.

"Which way did they go?" I cried, running towards him, but Orion got there first, grabbing a fistful of Justin's shirt.

"Which way?" he barked.

"She blasted through the gates with Dragon fire and is flying towards Tucana," Justin choked out, trying to claw Orion's hand off of him.

Orion dropped him and I took out my Atlas, sending a voice message to the group chat.

"Geraldine's been kidnapped. Mildred has hold of her in Dragon form. I'll get in the air and see if-"

"You're not fast enough," Orion said urgently. "I can run, but the only way you'll keep up is…" He took my Atlas, continuing the voice note. "Everyone meet at the parking garage, bring your keys. Caleb, carry everyone if you have to. Get there *now.*"

Orion picked me up without another word, shooting away across campus at a ferocious speed. When he placed me down, I was standing in front of the Heirs' gleaming sports cars and Darius and Tory's motorcycles.

Caleb appeared with Darius on his back, Tory under one arm and Seth under the other.

"I'll grab Max," he announced, disappearing in a flash and reappearing a moment later with Max on his back.

"Where's Gerry?!" Max boomed, rage and terror pouring from him so thickly, it clogged my lungs.

"We'll get her back," I swore, my chest roaring with the call for vengeance.

"Too fucking right we will." Max unlocked his dark blue Aston Minotin, dropping into the driver's seat while Seth got in his white Faeserati, and Tory and Darius got on their bikes.

Orion yanked open the door to Max's passenger side and I got in, needing no further encouragement. He leaned down low, grabbing my seat belt and clipping it in place, giving me an intense stare.

"See you soon, Blue." He shut the door and the roar of the engine rumbled beneath me as Max took the lead, driving out of the parking garage at a wild speed.

Caleb and Orion shot away ahead of us, but the moment we were on the road, Max put his foot down and we tore along behind them. Seth was on our tail and Darius and Tory let their throttles loose, racing ahead and keeping pace with the Vampires.

Adrenaline spilled through me as we made it through the gates and Max sped onto the road so fast, my heart leapt.

His fists were tight around the steering wheel, his jaw pulsing with murderous fury, and the whole car was heavy with it.

"Don't hold back," I said darkly, magic burning in my palms as my own rage seeped through my chest. No one could take Geraldine Grus away from us. She was the beating heart of our group, and I'd go to hell and back to bring her home.

We turned onto the road that led over the mountains toward Tucana and my breath hitched as I spotted the mud brown form of Mildred's Dragon swooping up the hillside.

"There!" I pointed her out and Max seethed, slammed his foot down harder on the accelerator.

I opened the window, taking control of the wind and casting it at our backs, giving us every advantage at gaining speed. Orion and Caleb veered off the main road, taking a more direct path straight up the mountainside. We sped up the winding road at a terrifying pace, and I pushed us even harder with air.

We climbed faster and faster, the world turning to a blur of green and brown around us.

Just as we crested the mountainside, a row of shadows in the sky made my heart lurch and a snarl spill from my lips.

Dragons. A hoard of them flying this way, passing Mildred by and coming right for us.

"Fuck," Max spat.

"Just keep driving," I demanded, leaning out the window and raising my hand.

I built a fireball of Phoenix flames in my palm that roared with all the heat of the sun, then let it burst from me with an explosion of air behind it. The fire slammed right into the face of a giant blue Dragon and the beast roared, careering out of the sky and slamming into the peak of the mountain up to our left. Huge boulders came tumbling down the mountainside heading right for us, and I cast a ramp of earth to shield us so they rolled right overhead. The Dragon went crashing past too, continuing its descent down the mountainside, its talons scrambling to try and get purchase and stop its fall.

"Nice shot," Max said in satisfaction.

Darius slowed his bike, pulling up alongside my window and calling out to me. "Get ahead of the Dragons, we'll make sure you make it through. Just get to Geraldine."

"On it," I said, and Max put his foot down again.

Tory veered sharply on the road ahead just as a fireball slammed into the ground, but though my heart beat out of rhythm, it was clear she was safe within an air shield, the fire billowing right over it.

We overtook her and Max burned up the tarmac, the engine bellowing. Seth fell back with the others in his Faeserati, letting the gap grow between us.

Magic was blasting overhead in a calamity of power, meeting with the Dragons' fire, and my breath caught as I spotted Caleb and Orion tearing along the mountainside sending huge blasts of magic at the Dragons too. With so much distraction, we made it past them, sailing under their bellies while I shielded the car with air and took every blast of their power, not letting a single crack form in my defences.

Mildred was only a few hundred feet ahead now, but she was gaining height in the sky, racing for the cover of the clouds above.

"I'll call her back to us with a Siren lure, but you need to take the wheel," Max said.

"What?" I gasped. "I can't drive."

"Just hold the wheel steady and put your foot down, the car does the rest," he demanded.

"Max, wait," I said, shaking my head, but he was already unclipping both our belts.

He grabbed my hands, forcing me to take the wheel and I groaned, accepting that this was really happening.

"You got this, little Vega," he said, giving me a firm look and filling the air with so much confidence that I couldn't help but listen to him.

"You go over, I'll go under. On three," he said, keeping his eyes on the road while I did the same. "One, two – three!"

He let go of the wheel and I propelled myself into his seat while he lunged into mine. We lost some speed for half a second before my boot slammed down on the accelerator and the car lurched forward wildly.

"Holy shit," I gasped, gripping tighter to the wheel.

Max shoved his head out the window, opening his mouth and releasing a song that was the purest, most beautiful thing I had ever heard. It was an enticement that pulled on the tethers of my very soul, begging me to go to him, and it was spiralling its way up into the sky, right toward Mildred.

The huge brown beast turned her head, looking back at him with a beady eye, a spill of smoke pouring from her large nostrils. Geraldine looked up from where she was clasped tightly in her talons, gazing down at Max with her lips parting. She cried something out to him that I swear contained the words slippery salmon, but I couldn't hear anything except the alluring song that swept from Max's lungs. Navy scales crept over his hands and up his neck, his Order form coming out in full force.

My focus kept drifting, my eyes falling to him, the need to get closer mounting up in my chest. He was a god among Fae, a creature made to be worshipped, and I wanted to be the first to get down on my knees for him.

"Ohmagod," I hissed, blinking out of it and calling on my Phoenix to block out his Siren power.

I focused on the road and the sharp turn coming up ahead, panic darting through me. I couldn't slow down. Geraldine was relying on me, and I had to keep up no matter what.

I gritted my teeth, my knuckles turning white from how tight I was holding the wheel, and a squeak left my lips as I took the turn at a hundred miles an hour.

Max's head hit the window frame, and I shot him an apology, but he didn't seem to notice, his song still tearing from his lips and his eyes set on Geraldine.

I doubted Geraldine in all her life had ever wanted a knight in shining armour to come save her, but I'd bet my ass she'd take an Heir in shining scales right now.

Mildred slowed her pace, working hard to resist Max's call, but was clearly affected by it all the same. She turned her head to look back at us, a growl leaving her before she spat a line of fire at us.

I cried out as I turned the car this way and that to avoid it, the wheel so sensitive that the car jerked manically at every light touch. I managed to keep us on the road, speeding along it again and gaining on them. To our right, the steep drop was only growing steeper, no barrier in sight to keep our car from careering off it if I made one wrong move.

I stole a glance in my rear-view mirror, briefly taking in the scene of fire-breathing Dragons and the rogue band of my family beneath them before I forced my eyes back onto the road.

Mildred suddenly swept around the mountain's peak and I cursed as we lost sight of her. But she wasn't far. I just had to keep going, stay on her tail. Because I wasn't going to stop this plight until Geraldine was safe, back where she belonged.

TORY

CHAPTER SIXTY FIVE

My bike skidded to a halt and I pulled it around in a sharp turn, planting my feet on the ground and hurling a solid wall of air magic up above me as high as I could throw it and as wide as necessary to stop the Dragons in their tracks.

Two of them collided with it as they moved to chase after Mildred and Geraldine, a sickening crack cutting the air apart as one of them broke a wing and tumbled from the sky. A plume of Dragon fire blasted above it before it crashed into the mountainside and tumbled out of sight towards the valley far below.

The other whirled on me with a bellow of fury, its yellow eyes narrowing as it kicked off of the wall I'd created and dove straight for me.

Darius was stripping beside me, his helmet hitting the floor followed by his leather jacket, shirt, pants–

I hurled spears of ice into the sky, the crash of battle coming from my left and to my back where Caleb, Seth and Orion fought with more of the Dragons, but I had to trust them to hold their own and focus on the brown monster diving for me.

The Dragon blasted fire from its gaping jaws, melting my ice and careering right for me.

I grinned as the fireball came my way, my Order form bursting from my skin, a shield of solid air protecting my bike and clothes before the flames engulfed me.

The world was lost to fire and smoke, and I was consumed within the fireball. The sound of a ferocious roar and a powerful collision filled the air, announcing Darius's Dragon form joining the fray.

The flames finally guttered out, revealing a rain of blood pouring from the sky as Darius's fangs ripped into the throat of the brown Dragon who was less than half his size, the scent of death filling the air and making my heart riot with excitement.

I leapt free of the bike and took to the air with him, turning my back before I could see the brown Dragon's corpse fall from the sky and speeding towards a grey beast which was circling around Seth's car, trying to come at him from behind.

The difference in my size to the Dragons made me feel like a moth trying to take on a hawk but I didn't slow.

Blades of glittering ice and sharpest metal formed in my fists and I flew for the grey Dragon at full speed.

It saw me coming, the red and blue flames scorching my skin all too recognisable in the orange and pink streaked sky, and it lunged for me instead of Seth in his car.

I didn't change my path of flight, speeding right for its gaping mouth and the rows of sharp fangs waiting to bite me clean in half.

The Dragon blasted fire at me when I was less than ten feet from it and I jerked aside sharply, hiding within the flames and flipping right over its head as those powerful jaws slammed shut precisely where I'd just been.

I landed on the beast's back, right between its shoulder blades and the join where its massive wings met its spine.

The Dragon roared in fury at being ridden, making me laugh wildly while my hair and my flames whipped all around me.

I shifted back out of my Order form, the scent of burning flesh permeating the sky where my legs had seared straight through the Dragon's scales and melted the skin beneath.

The Dragon bellowed furiously, turning for the sky and racing upwards at an almost vertical angle, trying to make me fall.

I clamped on tightly with my knees, holding my arms wide and whooping with exhilaration at the ride while we sped higher and higher, puncturing the wispy clouds and bursting through them to gain a full view of that picture-perfect sky.

I glanced down, the fight below me reduced to little pinpricks of movement at this extraordinary height and I grinned to myself, taking in the view for five, four, three, two...

My blades struck the Dragon in both wings at once, stabbing clean through them then ripping outwards, tearing gaping holes through the thin membrane of grey flesh and making the beast howl in agony.

We stilled in our ascent, hanging there suspended above the clouds for an endless second, the wind whipping the blood from the Dragon's destroyed wings into my face, the thrill of the bloodshed pounding through my limbs.

And then we were falling.

I whooped in time with the Dragon's screams, banishing the blades I'd cast to fight it and throwing my arms wide, leaning back to feel the full force of the wind against my spine as we fell.

Down and down and down, the ground rushing towards us so fast that my mind could hardly keep up with the speed of it. All the while I kept my thighs clamped in place on the Dragon's back, riding him towards his death.

He shifted suddenly and I shoved him away from me, the naked Fae crying out in horror as the ground sped closer still. I tumbled aside, the ground so near now that my heart leapt in terror before I shifted, my wings snapping wide and catching me less than six feet from the ground.

I swept over the fight, my eyes taking in Caleb who was locked in battle with a Dragon who had shifted back to Fae form to face him briefly. But my attention was ripped away just as fast as I noticed that my opponent had managed to catch himself with air magic before crashing into the ground as I'd planned.

I sped towards my enemy, casting a new sword into my hand and landing right behind him as he dropped to the dirt on his knees, thanking the stars for saving him. His gaze snapped up to mine, realising his moment of relief had just cost him his life and he gasped.

"The true king will cleanse the world of your hera-"

I took his head from his shoulders before he could finish that vow and the chaotic thrill of his death poured through me, adding to the payment I was making to The Ferryman and bringing my death count up once more.

Overhead, a bellowing roar shattered the air like fragile glass, and I whirled around to see Darius locked in combat with two Dragons at once, blood spilling from the sky.

I dove back into battle with my sword in hand and a furious need for victory blazing through my veins, promising to finish this fight once and for all.

GERALDINE

CHAPTER SIXTY SIX

"Release me, you crag!" I wailed, my voice becoming as hoarse as a whistling seashell. But I would not falter in the face of my doom.

The bells of the beyond were tolling and I would not answer their call. I would turn from the dastardly face of death and fight for every breath I was yet to possess in this realm or any other.

The dreadful Mildred's talons drove deeper into my side, and I thrashed like a dandyhop, trying to break free of her terrible hold. Oh what misfortune, what a great failing I had committed. My queens ought to leave me to my fate, not chase me into the nevermore like they did now, along with my merry Max, the strapping mutt, the daring Dragoon, and the two fine fang danglers. What a fortune I did possess to have so many valiant knights riding into battle for mere little me.

If their rescue was to fail, I would not dare let a single memory in my mind be claimed by the terrible Dragoon and his vile shadow wench. Nestled in my forearm was a hidden razor blade, lying just beneath the skin, and I would rip it from my flesh and slash my throat asunder if it came to it. For I, Geraldine Gundellifus Gabolia Gundestria Grus, would not be an asset in the lizard king's plots. I would never betray my queens as such, but I would not choose death unless it was the very last option left to me.

Tears had burned my eyes at the sight of my queens taking pursuit, the disbelief that they deemed me worthy of coming for themselves too much for my hapless heart to take.

But of course, my Maxy boy had come. With the fires of the doongash in his eyes, he sang his lulling song, trying to call my monstrous captor back to him and release me from her clutches. Each note was pure, unsullied by any crux in this world. It was a song that bound me in chains of desire and awoke my Lady Petunia even under such dire circumstances.

But most of all, it stirred up that love I felt for him so deeply already, more than any song could ever conjure. It was unfettered and as true as any natural law in this world. He was my songful salmon and I his tuneless tuna. There was no other creature for me, not a single soul who came close. Somehow, between lines in the sand and a hate that had burned deep in my cockles, we had come to adore one another as deep as deep could be.

"Come to me, Maxy boy!" I bayed, struggling against Mildred's hold for all the good it would do.

Mildred turned her head and let out another blaze of fire down upon my beloved queen and my dear salamander, but it only forced them to slow for just a moment before the chase was on again.

Mildred could not seem to bring herself to fly higher into the clouds any longer, nor sweep away down the mountainside, her head turning to take in that song, while she worked to resist each note. But even the beasts of Hilgamore would not have been able to deny its call.

There was no escaping the power of the sultry Siren below, and he was coming for me, his gallant gal, and not even the almighty stars could stop him.

ORION

CHAPTER SIXTY SEVEN.

I raced along the mountainside keeping pace with my sanguis frater as we weaved through pine trees in pursuit of a huge red Dragon. The beast was banking hard towards the road, spewing hellfire at Seth's car as it did another circle overhead.

The call of the hunt set my veins alight, my fangs aching for blood and the thundering of my heart demanding I bring down our prey.

"I'll get up in the air," I told Caleb, but the words didn't leave my mouth, our minds snapping together all of a sudden and that knowledge passing right to him.

"I'll hunt from below," his reply came, and our eyes met for the briefest moment before I cast air beneath me, launching myself skyward.

I wheeled over the back of the Dragon, narrowly avoiding a deadly swipe of his tail before taking my sword from my hip and angling it down towards my quarry. I slammed onto his back and drove the blade in deep, making him roar in fury and buck to try and unseat me. I was thrown sideways, rolling over his outstretched wing and as he tucked it under him, I cast air beneath me to propel myself onto his neck, landing astride him the way I would normally ride Darius. With my sword stuck in his ass, I'd use my magic to finish it, but my mind suddenly flashed to Caleb's, seeing what he was seeing from below.

Fire balled in his fists, and it blasted from him with such energy that I braced myself for the impact a second before it stuck the belly of the Dragon.

He roared to high heaven, careering towards the road at high speed, and I saw Caleb sprinting out onto it, leaping right over Seth's car while it moved at a hundred miles an hour. The Dragon dropped from the sky, jaws outstretched as it chased down Caleb in anger, while my sanguis frater threw violent blasts of rocks at his scales.

I focused on my own view, still seeing Caleb move below and working to adjust to the double vision. With a surge of magic, I built two vicious blades of ice in my hands, driving them deep into the Dragon's neck, and he reared up into the sky, wheeling over to try and unseat me. But I had the grip of the wind in my possession, and it was keeping me firmly pinned to his body.

Caleb circled back toward me as the Dragon did another spiral in the air, and I forced the ice to lengthen, reaching deeper and deeper towards his skull.

The beast bellowed and Caleb's voice flared in my mind once more. *"Finish it!"*

I willed the ice deeper and made it blast into shards, the Dragon's roar dying just like that as I drove them far enough to kill.

The Dragon's dead weight went crashing towards the mountainside and I leapt off of it before it made the impact, using air to guide me lightly down to land at Caleb's side.

We shared a grin, our minds splitting apart again as the hunt concluded, and a rush of adrenaline set all my senses on fire.

Another roar made us turn, finding three Dragons bearing down on Seth's car.

My hearing picked up the beating of wings from behind, and Caleb and I turned as one, finding a green Dragon swooping down over the trees coming right for us. Not as big as Lionel nor as brightly coloured, so I knew it wasn't him, and something about the shape of its face reminded me of Mildred. A relation perhaps.

Caleb raised his hands, fire pouring from them toward the oncoming predator. The Dragon dropped low, tearing up two great trees in its talons and launching them toward us.

We split apart, forced to run as they crashed through the forest, taking down more trees in their wake. And the beast didn't stop there, ripping up more and more of them and keeping us running from the destruction.

I narrowly ducked a falling bough and raced for the road, my feet hitting the tarmac a beat later and my mind reaching for my sanguis frater's.

Caleb was heading along lower ground further down the hill, traversing the uneven, rocky path at speed while the teal-green Dragon turned its attention to him and chased him even further down the mountainside.

I moved to follow but a wrenching of metal made me wheel around, and my heart lurched at the sight of a blue Dragon plucking Seth's car off the road, its talons half crushing the vehicle while it flew out beyond the road before launching the car right over the cliff's edge. I expected Seth to wield air at any second and save himself, but something was wrong. He wasn't getting out.

"Save him!" Caleb's words tore through my head, but I didn't need to be told. I was already moving at the speed of the wind, tearing towards that precipice and hurling myself straight off of it. It was a sheer drop, the car turning end over end beneath me, and I cast air at my back to propel myself faster towards it.

I slammed onto the roof, growling as I fought to hold on, my fingers tearing into the metal as I used my Order strength to keep me there. We had mere seconds before we hit the ground, and though I was moving faster than I'd ever moved before, it might not be enough.

I wrenched the crumpled door clean off its hinges, finding Seth deathly still in the driver's seat with blood pouring from a head wound.

My gut tugged in terror as I ripped the seat belt free and dragged him out by his arm before blasting us skyward with an explosion of air tearing from me.

I closed my arms around him, casting a shield of air around us before we slammed onto the hard ground, and I held us there on the steep hill.

The car smashed into the rocks below, crumpling like paper and crashing away further and further towards the bottom of the mountain.

I lay Seth on his back, listening for a pulse and a curse left my lips at the sound of it thumping, but it was slowing by the second.

"You don't get to die here," I growled, touching the wound on his head and sending a flood of healing magic into his body. The wound stitched slowly over, but Seth's heart was fading. There were more injuries that I couldn't see, internal wounds I reached for with everything I had and worked to fix.

"Come on, mutt," I demanded. "Wake up and annoy the fuck out of me."

He didn't stir, his face so fucking pale that panic took hold of me.

"Seth!" I shouted, shaking him and releasing all of my healing power into his body. "Wake up, you asshole. We're fucking moon friends, alright? There, I said it. I like you.

You've made up for what you did. So come back here and let me give you some star damned forgiveness for it, yeah? You can't go dying on me when I didn't even get to stop being an asshole to you. Mostly."

He fell unnaturally still and I rested my ear to his chest, listening for his heartbeat, hardly able to focus on it over the clamouring of my own pulse.

"Seth," I rasped, horror filling me at the loss of him. Of failing Caleb. Darcy. Darius and Max. All of them.

Healing magic was still sweeping from me, but my magic was starting to dull. I needed to feed; I was almost tapped out.

"Don't go," I demanded. "You've made it so far in this war, you can't go now. Everyone loves you so fucking much."

I felt Caleb's mind pushing at mine, and somehow I kept him out, refusing to let him see this. It couldn't be real. It was over too fast without even a goodbye. And I should have saved him. It was on me that he lay here on this fucking hillside with no more air in his lungs, and his life stolen from him.

"I'm sorry," I said, the weight of his loss crushing me.

The slow thud of his heartbeat suddenly started up in his chest and I gasped, lifting my head to look at his face in hope.

He blinked groggily, focusing on me with a frown. "Moon...friend?" he rasped.

I laughed, lurching forward and kissing him on the forehead.

I leaned back and his eyebrows raised in surprise. "You saved me."

"Of course I fucking did," I muttered. With his eyes on me, it was hard not to retreat into my old ways, to pretend I didn't care about him. But dammit, the mutt was under my skin.

I let Caleb's mind connect with mine, doing it all too easily with my adrenaline this high and the hunt still calling to me. I let him see the man he loved and I swore I could feel his joy washing through me. He'd taken down the Dragon that had been pursuing him and was on his way here.

"You called me your moon friend," Seth said on a gasp.

"I don't think so," I said, pushing to my feet and pulling him after me.

"You did! I heard it," he said, bouncing upright and hugging me.

I hugged him back, letting him nuzzle me too because fuck it was a relief to know he was alive. It had been one damn close call though.

"Must have been the wind," I said with a shrug as we parted.

He gave me a knowing look. "Uhuh. And did the wind also say that it loves me?"

"I said I *like* you, not love."

"I know." He smirked like he was just a cocky little shit in my classroom one again. "I just knew you couldn't resist correcting me."

Caleb came racing down the mountainside, colliding with us and kissing Seth so hard, I could practically feel the love between them burning like an undying fire.

When they broke apart, an intensity passed between them that was filled with passion, and I turned my gaze back to the Dragons above, my mind pinning on Blue and every one of our friends in the clash of the fight.

"Ready to finish this?" I asked.

"You need blood," Seth offered one wrist to me and the other to Caleb.

I took the gift, my fangs slicing into his skin and the stormy taste of his magic riding my tongue. I felt the pull of the Coven bond trying to force me to take more, my bite deepening as I sensed Caleb's bloodlust rising too, but I forced myself to pull my fangs free and my sanguis frater did too.

We shared a look as the hunt called to us once again and I couldn't resist the pull of it, my mind fixing on our enemies. In a burst of speed, Caleb and I shot away up the mountain and Seth howled as he shifted into his Wolf form and bounded after us. Back into the fray.

MAX

CHAPTER SIXTY EIGHT.

"Max!" Darcy yelled.

My fingers bit into the edges of the car window, the wind whipping savagely across my face and dragging at my clothes, but my gaze remained locked unwaveringly on Geraldine where she was trapped in the claws of that beast.

My Siren Lure pulsed from me, bees waking from their winter slumber to trail after the speeding car, birds swooping from the sky and taking chase too, but that fucking Dragon still resisted me.

Mildred was slowing though, the beats of her wings coming less often, her squashed snout whipping around to face me time and again.

"Max!" Darcy shouted, her hand gripping my arm and shaking roughly while the car shot along the road at breakneck speed. "The road is turning away from them," she yelled, and I forced myself to look.

My Lure faltered for a heartbeat, my eyes widening and terror flashing through my chest, my emotions punching out into the air around us.

Mildred bellowed, dipping wildly in her flight as the fear struck her but then she took off with more vigour, wheeling away from the road while Darcy yanked the wheel in the opposite direction, forced to follow the mountain path.

I could already tell that we were going too fast to make the bend, the screech of burning rubber filling the air as Darcy tried to brake, the pungent scent of scorching tyres filling my nostrils. The boom of the collision rocked through us and the side of the car hit the metal barrier with enough force to flip us straight over it.

Darcy's screams pierced the air as the world flipped over and over, the moment of our descent down the mountainside drawn out endlessly while we fell.

My forehead collided with the windscreen, blood pouring into my eyes and for several terrifying seconds I lost my grip on my power and could only blink through the blood, staring in horror at the ground rushing towards us with a brutal finality.

Darcy's arms were suddenly around me and then there was nothing but fire, so blinding that I couldn't see anything at all even with my eyes peeled wide with terror.

The car exploded and the resounding boom rocked through the foundations of my soul. My poor, fractured soul which howled with grief as it was wrenched upwards out of the destroyed fragments of my body and into an undeniable death.

And yet, death felt a lot like arms bound tight around my chest and searing heat dancing at the edges of my senses, like blinding light and insurmountable power.

"Darcy?" I gasped as the flames fell away, peeling off into the air beneath us while we shot for the sky.

"Your car drives like shit," she panted, her eyes wild with fury, wings beating powerfully at her back, the bronze light glinting with the rays of the setting sun.

We were rocketing through the sky and it took me several more seconds to realise it was mostly air magic propelling us, her power wrapped tightly about me like a fist, no doubt taking most of my weight and shielding me from her flames when she'd ripped my car apart to save us.

My lips parted on some form of thanks, but the words fell away as I followed her steely gaze to the sky ahead of us where Mildred was racing for the horizon with Geraldine clasped firmly in her claws.

"Maxy boyyyyyy!" Her grief struck me like a blow to the chest and I sucked in a breath of ragged pain, fighting to separate that powerful emotion from my own.

"I've hidden us," Darcy explained, and I had to marvel at the speed of magic which she'd wielded in so little span of time, not only saving our asses, but concealing our survival too.

"Remind me to worship you for being a total badass later," I grunted, pushing out of her hold and using my own air magic to keep myself flying upward.

Mildred was racing for her escape but there was no way we would let her get away with my girl.

Wordlessly, we shot after them, not needing to discuss it, knowing what we had to do and what it would cost if we failed.

The distance between us was growing, our magic not as fast as a speeding Dragon, but they weren't gone yet.

Darcy raised a hand and I did too, both of us aiming for Mildred's wings with spears of ice.

The power exploded from my fist as I threw it, the spear slicing through the air, propelled by the full force of my magic and driving towards Mildred at an incredible speed.

Darcy's spear was right behind mine, but Mildred turned at the last moment, either sensing or seeing the attack coming.

She rolled in mid-air, tucking her wings to avoid the missiles but she was forced to release her hold on Geraldine as she did so.

Darcy cried out and I could feel her power racing after mine, but I was ready for it, a net of air snagging Geraldine into its grasp and hooking her out of reach of the mud brown Dragon who bellowed in furious contempt.

I grunted at the effort of wielding the magic over such a distance and Darcy took my hand, offering up her power so we could reclaim my girl all the faster.

Her power rushed into me like a force of fucking nature, stealing the breath from my lungs and making me shudder beneath the weight of it.

Geraldine rocketed towards us at an exponential pace, her screamed threats to Mildred carrying through the air and convincing me that she was unharmed by her kidnap. She was still the furious, brutal creature I loved so dearly.

Geraldine collided with me and I kissed her, not caring that she'd likely smack me and call me a sentimental seagull or some bullshit when I released her. Not caring that blood still spilled down my face from my headwound and tainted our kiss with the tang of iron.

Nothing mattered but her. And as she melted into my arms, kissing me deeply and winding her body around mine, I knew she felt it too.

We lowered to the ground, no doubt in thanks to Darcy because my only thoughts were of Geraldine and making sure she was alright.

"That cantankerous crout!" Geraldine cried as she pulled away from me, raising a fist to the distant dot in the sky which was Mildred.

She'd escaped us, but I couldn't find it in me to care about that as I stole another kiss, backlit by the flames of my destroyed car in a valley between green mountains in the middle of fucking nowhere.

The others collided with us one by one, each of them holding Geraldine tight and telling her how fucking lost we'd have all been without her. And as my girl was overcome with emotion and wept between our many-armed embrace, I simply let myself fall into the purity of her love for our found family, bathing in the relief of her company after such a close call with the end.

"I'm done playing to the tune of Lionel and his bastard followers in this war," Darcy's voice fell over all of us with savage brutality while we clung to each other.

"Yeah," Tory agreed, her words a vicious slash through the air, filled with wrath and fury. "I'd say we're ready for our end game."

THARIX

CHAPTER SIXTY NINE

I had been endlessly trapped in a wordless hell of screams and torment, time lost to me as everything in my existence fragmented. But the sensation of falling suddenly made my gut lurch. My arms wheeled out to grab at the tattered cloak clinging to the beast who had ripped me from my place in the world as I found myself in his grasp once more, but his power far outweighed my own.

He hurled me around, that skeletal face of horrors leering at me as I was thrown down on my back.

Wooden boards dug into my spine, the thing I was on rocking wildly, the rush of fast moving water assaulting my ears.

Many voices were screaming all around me, their wordless cries of agony seeming to rip right into me and carve through every vein in my body.

I blinked out at the darkened space, a thick fog hanging in the air, everything reduced to shadows in the mist, but I was travelling along on a river, my body sprawled on a wide raft.

I moved to stand but the skeletal figure pressed his staff against my chest, shoving me back down forcefully.

"You have stolen from me," his voice cracked like broken branches, his words stirring the air like he was snatching it from the sky.

I swallowed, uncertain of this being and what he wanted from me, but his anger lashed at the world with a potency that made me weigh my words before I released them.

"Stolen?" I asked.

Those screams grew louder, their voices echoing through my skull, my body spasming beneath the furious power of their cries.

"I am the master of death," he sneered, leaning down over me, his staff driving into my ribs, a crack sounding beneath the pressure he exerted and those hellish eyes blazing. "I alone guard the river between here and there. I alone can claim the souls destined for reaping."

The screams seemed fit to burst my skin in two now, his words drowned by them, their power blinding as I realised they came from within me, not without. The four souls my mother had forced inside me during my conception.

"I didn't ask for this," I hissed, anger finding its way to me. "I made no claim on your property. I had no choice in my creation at all."

The staff began to burn where it was pressed to my skin, the pain of it blinding, far beyond any mortal wound I had suffered and survived.

My spine arched, hands locking around the staff as the agony of its power tore into me. Drops of water ran over my fingers where I grasped it, the wood sliding between my palms, its shape not rounded but wide and flat, making me realise it was a paddle, not a staff at all.

I tried to speak, but my voice was stolen by the lightning bolts of agony which tore through me, my lips opening and closing on the words that wouldn't come but somehow, I knew he could hear them all the same.

"You are not of the stars' design," he hissed, driving the paddle into my chest so hard that more ribs cracked beneath his force, the thrashing of my heart so pitifully close to the weight of that innocuous weapon.

I blinked at him, the truth of those words tearing through me. No, I wasn't of the stars' design, I hadn't been conceived of two mortal beings, I hadn't grown over months within the womb of a mother, hadn't ever been a bawling babe or stumbling infant. I was both Nymph and Fae. I had four unwilling souls tethered to my body, shadows laced within my flesh and I had simply become this. I had no name for what I was, but I had learned the title which others had decided for me. Monster.

I released my hold on the paddle, falling back against the raft as it bobbed and swayed in the wild current. Bodies were racing past us in the water, hands pale and bloated with death clawing at the edges of the raft, reaching for me.

I reached for them in turn, wondering if this was the answer I sought, if death might welcome me more readily than life ever had.

"No," the snarling skull roared, his paddle lifting then slamming down on me once more. "I forbid you from death."

The screams within me grew wild and suddenly something deep inside the fabric of all I was fractured, my grasp upon the Element of water falling away to nothing as the soul whose power I had unwillingly stolen was wrenched from my flesh.

I stared at the translucent image of the dead man which rose from within me, his screams finally falling quiet as he let himself slip into the water and was swept away at speed.

"I deny you passage," the skeletal being hissed, the burn of his paddle cutting through me so that it seemed like I would split apart at the seams.

Another screaming soul was ripped from my flesh, my grasp on earth magic going with it before it dove headlong into the river too.

"I refuse you entry to the realm beyond this one. May you linger forever in the clutches of life while all others pass on without you."

The third soul to tear its way from me stole my connection to air magic as it went, its screams dying out as it plunged into the river.

The raft bucked and rocked wildly beneath us, threatening to upend me into the icy water at any moment, the call of death growing ever louder as we sped down the rapids and the roar of a waterfall drew closer.

The final soul was torn from my flesh, my fire guttering so I was left utterly empty in the wake of the magic my mother had stolen for me, gasping and choking on the foul truth of all I was and all I would never be.

"Only The Ferryman can reap the souls of the departed," the skeletal figure hissed, his voice a rush of air between rotten teeth and yet still so loud it deafened me. "Only I get to rule over that branch of fate. You will forever pay for crossing me, Tharix, son of rot and ruin. You will forever be everything and nothing at all."

"Wait," I pleaded, grasping his paddle as I felt the weight of his words, of the curse he was bestowing upon me for the act of my creation, for the choices which were made for me, not by me. "Please."

The Ferryman sneered, looming over me as the rush of the waterfall grew utterly deafening. There was no mercy in his gaze, nothing but contempt for me.

He kicked me so suddenly that I only realised I was falling as I hit the icy water, my limbs leaden, my weight dragging me to the depths of the river as the hands of a thousand dead souls ripped and clawed at my flesh.

"Death will surround you but *never* claim you," The Ferryman's words sank into my soul and stained it a deep and impenetrable red, one so bright that I knew it would never wash out.

Darkness pressed in on me from all directions then suddenly I was falling, hitting the ground and coughing up water as I found myself back in the passage far beneath my father's castle, the dank puddle rippling on the floor before me, no sign at all of the master of death.

My hands shook as I pressed them to the cold stone, a flicker of fire scoring across my fingertips and a tendril of earth magic tainting my palm. This was no stolen power though; it was my own, the magic the stars had gifted me in truth and as I lay there aching, scarred, cursed and alone in the halls of this living hell, I began to laugh.

I was nothing and no one, alive beyond death, forgotten and promised and now... something new.

TORY

CHAPTER SEVENTY

As soon as we returned to the academy, Max forcibly took Geraldine back to his room in Aqua House to recover and I'd squeezed her tightly in my arms before commanding her to go with him and get a proper night's sleep. She needed the rest and I seriously doubted there would be much more chance of it during any of the coming days.

I glanced back at Darius who was shoving one of the Dragon shifters ahead of him, the man now in his Fae form, completely naked with a look of despair on his face. He was the only survivor from the fight, his body still striped with the wounds we'd inflicted on him.

"Scum!" he spat. "Filth!"

Darius shoved him to his knees and raised a handful of flames to the man's head. "Give me one good reason not to."

Orion caught Darius's arm to hold him back. "He could have information."

"Then I'll peel his skin apart until he spills every drop of knowledge he has about my father's plans," Darius hissed, and the man cowered, trying to scramble away from him.

"You're all dead. All so very dead," he growled, shielding his head with his hands.

My brother came to land between me and Darcy, looking to the Dragon shifter with his wings folding at his back and his eyes gleaming with knowledge.

"This isn't good," he muttered, a slight wince to his features telling me his visions were still painful to experience.

Darius kicked the man onto his back, slamming his boot down on his chest. My heart thrummed in time with my husband's, our hunger for this Fae's death rising in the air. I stepped forward with intent, but Gabriel caught my wrist with a shake of his head.

"The king will march upon these grounds and destroy you all!" the Dragon bellowed, and Darius kicked him in the head.

Orion held his sword to his throat. "When is he planning this?" he hissed.

Darius slammed his foot down on the man's chest again, making my breaths come quicker.

"Two days," he rasped. "That's all you have. Then you lesser scum will all perish and-" He spluttered as Darius buried his axe in his chest, then ripped it out, leaving him to die beneath him.

"He could know more than that," Orion said in frustration, but Gabriel called out to him.

"There's nothing more for him to tell us," he said darkly. "But he speaks the truth, I *see* it now as clear as sunlight. Lionel will bring his army to our door in two days' time."

"Then we should march on him first," Darcy said fiercely, and I nodded.

"We march at dawn. Spread the word," I called, and Gabriel turned to us.

"I will ensure our army is prepared," he promised, then took off into the sky.

The Dragon shifter died with a final rattling breath and my heart rate slowed once more.

I exchanged a heavy look with Darcy, both of us acknowledging in that shared silence the fact that we were out of time. Our plotting, scheming, alliances and recruitment had come to an end. This war wouldn't wait any longer and we would have to face it with what we'd managed to gather then simply hope it would be enough.

"It's the time for goodbyes now, isn't it?" she whispered.

"Not goodbyes. Just... make sure everything is said that you need to say," I told her, equally quiet. Then I hugged her, because I loved my sister so deeply that words just weren't enough to express it.

As Orion joined us, Darcy smiled sadly at me then took his hand and led him away into The Wailing Wood in the direction of Asteroid Place. Seth and Caleb were sharing a look of intensity which made my chest ache. They hadn't gotten enough time together yet. None of us had. But there was no more left to claim.

I couldn't bear to look at Darius, to recognise all he was to me, all I'd sacrificed to make him such and all it had taken to claim this moment with him. Not with the knowledge of what tomorrow may bring crashing down over us to steal it all away so soon.

I turned from him, striding away through the trees, heading to the Earth Caverns where so long ago, and yet not nearly long enough, I had been tentatively learning to wield earth magic for the first time.

Darius shadowed my footsteps as we walked, a heavy weight dripping from the time which passed us with every step, clinging to our skin and rolling from our limbs like leaden wax as it tried to root us to the ground. But there was no stopping now, no moment to pause or savour anymore. Time had turned against us and despite our best efforts, I knew we hadn't achieved nearly enough with it.

A clamour of noise filled the trees ahead and I spotted a large group of new recruits being led along the path towards Rump Island where they would be given their positions in the army and prepared for battle as best they could be with the fleeting time remaining to us.

Several of them noticed me, calling out in wonder, praises crashing against my skin and shattering against the wall of ice which I'd constructed around my emotions so that I might hold them in check. I couldn't summon a smile to my face but I raised a hand to them, calling out to thank them for joining our cause.

I headed through the trees to the right of the path, Darius still close behind me, his shadow reaching out to caress my skin even while I kept my eyes from him, my focus ahead and refusing to linger behind.

"I knew you'd be waiting for me," a female voice gasped effusively from far too close to us, and I jerked around in surprise, my hand moving to grasp a dagger of ice as it formed in my palm on instinct.

The girl was pretty, her dark hair pulled back in a high tail and her face carefully painted in a way which seemed so vapidly pointless in the face of war. Her gaze was filled with the enamoured devotion that I had faced several times from the new recruits, that desperate need to be recognised by the True Queens shining in her widened eyes as she wrung her hands together and stared with unconcealed awe at...

No, she wasn't looking at me at all. This woman was one hundred percent drooling over my husband, a soft moan spilling from her lips as the sound of trickling water splashing against the dry leaves at our feet suddenly filled the awkward silence.

"What the fuck?" I said, jerking back a step as the warm liquid splashed from the hem of her trouser legs and her moan turned to one of horror.

"It is my curse," she breathed, her hands moving to shield her crotch which was darkened with an unmistakeable wet patch, but there was nothing she could do to disguise the pungent scent of urine which surrounded her now. "We can work past it," she insisted, taking a step closer to Darius who retreated.

He caught my arm, drawing me a step behind him and for once I didn't object to him being a protective bastard. If he wanted to deal with this one then he could have at it.

"I came, just like I promised I would in all my letters," she pressed, taking a step closer which we again echoed with a step back.

"What are you talking about?" Darius growled, not seeming to have the faintest idea who this girl was but as she stepped into a patch of brighter light between the trees, something about her face sparked a memory in me.

"You sent him those naked photos," I blurted. "And the hair with your scent on it."

The woman pursed her lips, ire spilling from her gaze as she was forced to look at me for the first time but she jerked her focus back to Darius just as fast.

"It's me – Cindy Lou. Darius, aren't you going to say any-" The sound of more urine trickling down to splash into the leaves at her feet filled the air and luckily for the psycho, the soldiers who had been escorting her group arrived to reclaim her at that moment.

She wailed as they grabbed her by the arms and started hauling her away, Darius's name spilling from her lips in a plea as though she thought he might come to her rescue or some shit.

I looked up at my husband, parted my lips then closed them again.

"I think that was my stalker," he said mildly like that wasn't disturbing as fuck.

"She pissed herself," I pointed out as if the stench of her urine which still lingered from the puddle she'd left behind wasn't reminder enough of that.

"Yeah. That was fucked up," he agreed. "Poor Cynthia, the object of her obsession was obviously overwhelming in person. I can't really blame her though, I'm fucking irresistible."

"Her name wasn't..." I trailed off, uncertain why I was even bothering with him on the names thing anymore anyway and addressing that big headed bullshit instead. "And you're not irresistible – I resisted you plenty," I added.

"Nah, baby, you really didn't. Even before you ripped my clothes off in the Shimmering Springs, I was all over your filthy fantasies. If I hadn't wanted you just as much in return you might have ended up like poor Sandy, obsessed and pining from afar for the rest of your-"

I shoved him away from me with a scoff, refusing to even acknowledge that nonsense as I continued my path to the Earth Caverns.

"Keep up, asshole," I called over my shoulder. "Or I might change my mind about giving you your gift."

"What gift?" he demanded instantly, his long stride depositing him on my right where I side-eyed him with a knowing smile.

"You'll see."

Somewhere between preparing for this war, making battle strategies and trying to buy us as many advantages as possible for the coming fight, I'd managed to squeeze in the hours required to make him this gift and though it had been exhausting and infuriating at times, I'd finally finished it in the early hours of this morning after slipping from his bed and coming here to get it done. It was now or never after all.

Darius slung his arm around my shoulders, keeping me close and we almost could have been those carefree teenagers again, the ones whose biggest problems were exams and Pitball matches, relationship dramas and normal bullshit. I sighed as I leaned into him, drawing that lie close for the remainder of our walk.

The caverns were being guarded but no one questioned us as we entered. The enormous central space was full to bursting with the flame-imbued swords Darcy and I had helped create in preparation for the coming battle, and the repetitive clang of the swordsmiths working in the newly created forge to craft more weapons filled the air.

I led the way past the smoky space, heading down the narrow, gloomy passageways beyond, delving into the dark and leaving nothing but the Faeworms to light our way on.

Darius stayed silent, his arm still wrapped around me, our steps in time with one another's as we walked further into the cold network of caves.

Eventually, we reached the cavern I had claimed for my own and I unlocked the magic I'd left in place over the entrance to it so that we could enter.

Inside, presented neatly on a wooden dummy was a set of perfectly crafted golden armour. I had worked with one of the smiths to have it designed specifically for Darius's frame and used a technique that I'd found in the book on Phoenixes to forge the metal using the flames of my Order.

"It's lightweight – incredibly so. You'll barely even know you're wearing it. But it's strong enough to take the force of a battering ram without buckling and has clasps which will release automatically if you have to shift. I used solid gold and strengthened it with Phoenix-"

"It's priceless," Darius breathed, releasing me and moving into the room, his breath catching as he reached out to brush his fingers over the polished metal, caressing the Vega insignia which sat in the centre of the chest plate with his lips parting in awe. "I mean that literally, Roxy, I don't know if I've ever seen anything so rare, so valuable, so-"

"Potently powerful for a Dragon who needs to keep his magic replenished?" I offered smugly, because of course that had been the idea. To make something so valuable that it would not only protect him in battle but strengthen him too. And what better way than to make his magic practically unending the way mine and Darcy's was whenever we wielded flames?

Darius stared at the beautiful armour in admiration, his fingers gliding over the gilded surface, inspecting it piece by piece, taking in every detail. "This is...shit, Roxy, when did you even find the time to-"

"It didn't really take that long," I said dismissively, though that was a lie because I'd definitely spent hours and hours slaving over this thing, pouring magic into it. I'd refused to accept anything less than perfect, needing it to be the best it could be because it would be out there in battle with the most precious thing I owned, and I couldn't bear for him to be at risk.

"Liar," he growled, seeing straight through me.

"Honestly, I was gonna make ten more but then I figured that might detract from its one-of-a-kind value so I just threw this together as is. It's a gift but you don't have to make it into some big romantic gesture or any bullshit like that, I just-"

"Beautiful, brilliant, liar," he growled, turning from the glimmering armour and catching my jaw in his rough palm as he forced me to look up into those dark and ruinous eyes which owned my entire soul. "Stop trying to downplay this and own it, Roxy. It's utterly exquisite, the most valuable thing I have ever laid eyes on bar one."

My lips toyed with a smile as his other hand moved to my waist and drew me closer.

"Fine. I worked myself to death over it and I'm fucking exhausted by the effort it took. I did it for you because I won't ever risk you again. You own my heart, Darius." I pressed my palm to his chest where his pulse sounded in time with mine. "Not like this, but in the purest and most vital way any one person can. And I will follow you into death if that's what our fate demands. But I don't plan on letting death have us that easily, I plan on living with you and loving you this fiercely through the grey hair and wrinkles and rocking chairs surrounded by a hundred great grandbabies and every glorious moment between now and then. So this is a command from your queen, Darius Vega. Don't die out on that battlefield. Bring me your father's head and let's start a new life by dancing on his funeral pyre."

"So beautifully, brutally, violent, my Queen," Darius rumbled against my lips, teasing me with a kiss which was only a breath away. "And of course, your wish is my greatest command."

He took me then, captured my lips with his and kissed me like he was trying to memorise the fit of my mouth against his, like he wanted to never again breathe any air but my own, like the world was ours for the taking and all we had to do was reach out and snatch it into our grasp.

I fell into that kiss, the taste of his tongue against mine and the promise of tomorrow on his lips the only thing I wanted in this world. And maybe it was a lie, maybe we had come as far as we would in this war and none of it would mean anything once the dust had settled and the war was over, our bones left to litter the ground in testament to all that might have been.

But this love between him and me, this powerful force of nature which rattled the stars and awoke destiny from its slumber would have left its scar on the world. This earth would not forget us, this kingdom would never forget us and beyond it all, our memory would linger just as our souls would forever remain united. No matter which side of death we landed on in the end.

ORION

CHAPTER SEVENTY ONE

All was quiet on Rump Island, except for the piercing hoot of an owl and the lapping of the ocean against the shore. The dark always brought the quiet fears of our army's hearts to the surface, and I could sense them tonight like the air was thickened by them, heavier to breathe. The silence was roaring. Every Fae here knew what tomorrow would bring, and none took that responsibility lightly. There was a bid for rest in the hope that it might make us stronger in the face of our enemies, but we all knew the truth. No matter what advantages we'd worked to gain, we were still vastly outnumbered.

Death was creeping closer; I could feel it waiting, just there on the periphery of life. The Veil felt thinner too, like it was preparing to let through the mass of souls it would claim soon. And my own soul was very likely to be among them.

I dragged in a breath of the icy air and looked to Darius who stood beside me on one of the many balconies of Rump Castle. The view here looked over the sea toward Zodiac Academy, a place that had had more influence on my life than any other. It was here that I'd been clad in metaphorical irons by Lionel Acrux, here that I had endured the long-suffering grief of my sister's death, here that I had spent countless hours with Darius, forming a bond that ran so deep in my blood, I would never part from him in this life or the next. Further still, I had found my truest love in this academy, Darcy Vega. With her to inspire me, I had released the chains of my past and grown into a man I was proud to be. One who was ready to die for the love he had claimed on this earth in his mate, his family and his newfound friends.

"This is it then," Darius said. "Our final night in paradise."

"We found real happiness here for a while, didn't we?" I mused and my friend nodded.

My eyes trailed over Aer Cove and the place where Darius and I had secretly practised dark magic in the past, our plans of taking on Lionel seeming almost childish in the face of the reality of that task.

Darius turned to me, pulling me into a hug that I returned with equal fervour, our arms locking tight around each other, knowing this might just be our last embrace in this world.

A flutter of wings announced Gabriel's arrival, and before Darius and I could break apart, he landed lightly beside us and put his arms around us too.

"With war on the horizon, I can hardly think of anything but death," Gabriel said heavily, the three of us stepping away from each other at last. "I am glad to have a distraction in you, Orio. Your endeavour keeps my mind occupied."

"So you know what her answer will be?" I asked hopefully.

Gabriel shrugged. "Perhaps I do, perhaps I don't."

He was so well versed in keeping his Seer knowledge from us that it was impossible to read anything from him. Although I was nervous as fuck, admittedly, I didn't really want to know her answer. Not until she spoke it herself.

"Did you bring it?" I asked.

"Bring what?" Gabriel frowned and as I opened my mouth to curse him out, he smirked and took a small wooden box from his pocket engraved with the Libra and Gemini constellations. "I took the liberty of making this, seeing as you didn't have one."

"That's nice," Darius commented. "Not as nice as gifting him the ring he's going to propose with. But nice."

The two of them shared a challenging look, and I took the box, slipping it into my suit jacket pocket.

"Thank you." I glanced down at my clothes, wondering if I'd gone overboard here, but Caleb and Seth had turned up at my room and practically dressed me. Caleb had done my hair, shoving all kinds of products in it I'd never fucking heard of, before trimming my beard and putting some sort of oil in it. Seth had picked out this suit from my closet and rubbed a star damned cinnamon stick on my neck before announcing me done.

All the while this was going on, Tory, Geraldine and Sofia had swept Darcy away somewhere, promising to have her ready for the night. From what little I'd heard of their plans, they were going to convince Darcy we were all having a party in The Howling Meadow, and I hoped she wouldn't question it too much.

"It's almost time for the ball, Cinderella," Darius taunted, and I checked my watch, finding he was right.

"You look more nervous for this than the battle tomorrow," Gabriel said with a laugh.

"Combat I can do," I muttered.

"She's your Elysian Mate, even if she says no, she'll still be yours, brother," Darius said. "Some Fae just aren't into marriage."

"She did make a comment or two about that before," I admitted. "Maybe I'm a fool to want this."

"Well you've got a ring and you're dressed up like a prime asshole," Darius said. "You may as well shoot your shot."

I exhaled decisively with a nod, though my nerves didn't ease. There was a piece of my heart that was riding on this. Deep down, I knew we didn't need marriage to solidify what we were, but I wanted the promise of a new, beautiful future together, and this proposal was like a vow that we'd make it there.

"Better get going, Orio." Gabriel pressed a hand to my back, pushing me toward the edge of the balcony.

I bid them goodbye and stepped up onto the stone railing, leaping off of it and falling at a wild pace towards the ground. I wielded the air to slow my descent then hit the dirt running, racing across the island, passing over the bridge to campus and speeding towards The Howling Meadow.

It was just as I'd left it earlier; the whole meadow covered in snow cast there by my water magic and a willow tree made entirely from ice at its centre. It was a nod to our first real date, when I'd taken Darcy to my family home and shown her one of my favourite places in the world.

Jars of everflames sat all around the tree, the glow of them making the snow sparkle, and the willow fronds hung low to the ground with icicles clinging to them. It was overcast tonight, and I willed snow to fall from the clouds above, the flakes fluttering down to cover the tracks I'd made across the meadow. I used my air magic to part the willow fronds in front of me like two curtains and I found the most spectacular creature on earth standing there at the edge of the meadow in a lilac gown. It was strapless, the bodice fitted and stitched with little diamonds, and the skirt fell to the ground in a pool of shimmering material. Beyond her, Tory, Geraldine and Sofia were in dresses of their own, their commitment to the lie bringing a smile to my lips.

Darcy glanced back at them in confusion and Tory moved forward to kiss her cheek before they hurried away into the trees, leaving her to her fate.

She turned to look at me across the field of snow where I waited expectantly and I used air to crush the snow at her feet, making a path that ran all the way up to me. As she walked along it, a lump built in my throat, all words abandoning me at her beauty.

There was no glimmer of starlight in the air tonight, no onlooking sky. It was just us.

She stepped through the parting in the willow fronds, and I let them fall shut at her back, securing our privacy a little more.

"Lance, what is all this?" She gazed around at the everflames, then up at the tree which was made of glittering ice.

I gave her an explanation in the form of dropping to one knee and her eyes widened as they landed on me.

"It could be our last night on earth, Blue, so I wanted to make it count," I said, my voice thick around those words, because the idea of her life being lost was too suffocating to consider. "I know our tomorrows aren't promised, but if they were..." I took the ring box from my pocket, popping it open and holding it up for her to see, making her gasp in surprise. "I wish to belong to you in every way a person can belong to someone. The stars mated us, they wove our fates together long ago before our souls were cast inside our bodies. They may have marked you as mine and me as yours, but I want us to choose each other regardless of what the sky might think of it. Because if we hadn't been mated, I would still love you like this, like the world begins and ends with you. I would have walked just as willingly into the depths of Darkmore, I would have destroyed myself to have a single taste of you. And if this is it, if our final sunrise crests on tomorrow's horizon, then I need to know that you would have chosen me too. In a time when you weren't a queen and I was nothing but a broken man, and together we denied the impossibility of us. I want a chance to do so again in the face of our downfall. So Darcy Vega, sovereign of my heart, will you defy all fates that deal our deaths and promise to marry me?"

She stared at me in shock, her green eyes watering and her hands cupping her mouth. Then she was nodding, tears rolling down her cheeks as she threw herself at me, knocking me to the ground and pressing her lips to mine.

"Yes," she said, kissing me again then again. "I'll marry you, Lance Orion."

My heart swelled and I kissed her back, losing myself to her as we tangled together in the snow. When she sat up, her dress bunched around her knees as she sat over my stomach, smiling from ear to ear.

I grabbed the ring box I'd dropped in the snow and took the ring from inside, offering it up as she held out her left hand.

"It's beautiful," she breathed.

"Everyone you love had a part in it," I told her, sliding it onto her ring finger and a knot unfurled in my chest.

I placed a kiss on the ring, then on the back of her hand before gazing at my bride-to-be with melted snow dripping from my hair and joy filling every corner of my chest.

"Let's chase life in tomorrow's battle and swear to claim it on the other side," Darcy whispered, admiring the ring, her smile falling a little as she looked to me, her fear over breaking that promise clear.

I sat up, pulling her closer in my lap and rubbing my thumb over her cheek.

"I swear," I vowed, knowing neither of us could do any such a thing, but voicing it made it feel possible. "I'll fight for us out there with every drop of strength I possess, Blue."

She rested her forehead to mine, our fingers intertwining and our breaths falling in sync with one another's. "Once upon a time, I was a girl afraid to be burned by the world, now I'm a queen who rules the fire. I will win this war for you, Lance, and I swear to the stars I will meet you at the altar."

SETH

CHAPTER SEVENTY TWO

Wolfman:
Has it happened? Did she say yes???

Batty Betty:
You great gaggamuffin! Leave them to their night of gaieties and glee! We shall speak of it upon the morn and learn of our queen's dandy decision then.

Wolfman:
Sooooo…………she said YES or NO??

Professor Shame turned their notifications off

Wolfman:
HOW DARE YOU LANCE! Never mind, I'll just do this … @Phoen Dream

Bitchy Flame Eyes:
Give it a rest, asshole. They're having a moment.

Wolfman:
Can you SEE it? Are you watching from the bushes?

Dragzilla:
She can't see shit, she's in the middle of getting her pretty dress torn off.

Wolfman:
That's twisted! Are you watching them fuck?

Dragzilla:
I was talking about my wife, idiot.

Dragzilla turned their notifications off

Bitchy Flame Eyes turned their notifications off

Wolfman:
Rude.
So who's got the tea? I want the whole pot with a slice of cake. Fuck it, the entire cake with sprinkles on top. @Fish Fury what's happening? Do you have eyes on them??

Fish Fury:
Gerry said I'm not allowed to tell anyone. Not even her.

Wolfman:
SO YOU KNOW?????

Fish Fury:
I felt what happened. Duh.

Wolfman:
Okay so just tell me if it was endless woe and the catastrophic agony of a shamed professor's heart crushing OR if it was a happy sunshine feeling that burst through your chest like a balloon full of warm goo.

Fish Fury:
Nah, I quite like being the only one in the know.

Big Bird:
He's not the only one.

Big Bird changed their name to Gabriel

Wolfman changed Gabriel's name to Big Bird

Big Bird:
Well I was going to tell you, but now you can get fucked.

Big Bird turned their notifications off

Fish Fury:
Hahaha

Wolfman:
Fuck you guys. @Phoen Dream come onnnnnnn just tell us!

Phoen Dream:
Busy

Wolfman:
glaring emoji

Phoen Dream:
bee emoji

Wolfman:
If you have time to write busy and send a busy little bee emoji then you can tell us what went down!!!!!!!!!!!!!!!

Phoen Dream:
Do you mean with the proposal or with the weather?

Wolfman:
YOU KNOW WHAT I'M REFERRING TO

Phoen Dream:
Well it's cloudy with a chance of rain later tonight, but it should be clear by morning!

Wolfman:
That's IT, Phoen!

I readied my thumbs to go keyboard warrior on this girl, then I'd head right over to The Howling Meadow to find out for myself. But before I could get started, another text came in.

Phoen Dream:
I said yes.

I howled to the sky, jumping on Caleb beside me and thrusting my Atlas in his face. "She said yes! Awooooo!"

Caleb laughed. "Yeah I know, Lance texted me like ten minutes ago."

I shoved him with a snarl. "What?!"

His laughter only grew. "It was so much fun seeing you all wound up."

"Motherfucker." I lunged at him and he shot out of my way, leaning casually back against Aer Tower and smoothing a hand through his golden curls.

I cocked my head at him, eyes narrowed. "You're an asshole."

"Ditto," he said, then folded his arms, his gaze sliding over me with want. "Now, are we carrying on with this walk or what?"

I blew out a breath, letting it go and finding the amusement in his game. I loved that we still fucked with each other, that this new level of relationship between us wasn't changing our core friendship.

"Let's get going then," I encouraged, offering him my hand. "Geraldine put a curfew on tonight, saying everyone has to get their rest so we'll be as 'spritely as spring ducks by the morn.' I was kinda planning on more of a 'last night on earth' vibe, but maybe she has a point."

"Yeah." Caleb pushed off the wall and took my hand, his fingers threading between mine. "She does. Because I don't want this to be our last night on earth."

"Doesn't change the fact that it could be," I said quietly.

He squeezed my hand but said nothing as we set off down the path in the direction of Fire Territory. We'd planned to do an entire loop of the campus before we headed back to our room, visiting all our favourite places one last time. Or *not* one last time if we were lucky. Neither of us had actually said that was why we wanted to do the walk, but I knew in my heart that was the reason.

We'd had dinner with my family earlier tonight, and Caleb had been mobbed by my siblings just like always, and honestly, nothing had really been different about the encounter except for my mom trying to pretend she wasn't terrified about what me and Cal dating each other could mean for the whole Councillors situation, and my dad inviting Caleb to our annual moon run camping trip next summer. None of us had acknowledged the fact that we might not get a chance for such a thing, but tonight was a night for fantasy, pretending the world wasn't going to end. And I tried to remember that now as my thoughts fell on my fears.

I reminded myself of the gift I had in my pocket and what it stood for, the tightness in my chest easing as I focused on that.

After we'd visited the Ignis House common room, we swung by the Shimmering Springs where I'd reminded Caleb that he had most definitely kissed me there long before the two of us had ever been on the cards, and he casually denied it again like he had no memory of it. Though I swear there had been a glimmer in his eyes that said he was fucking with me.

Then we headed to King's Hollow and got very distracted by each other in Cal's bedroom, then my bedroom, then the kitchen counter, and on top of Darius's treasure chest, then we headed off through The Wailing Wood and took a path into Aqua Territory, making a stop at the lake.

The clouds had thinned a little and the moon was peeking through, shimmering down on the water. The mark behind my ear tingled and a smile lifted my lips, a sense of utter peace gifted to me by the moon. This was what I'd wanted more than anything. Cal and I together, Moon Mated. I was the moon's favourite Wolf, and I was sure she saw in Caleb what I saw in him.

Here on the lake's edge where we'd held countless parties, played in the water in the summer and been so carefree once upon a time, I knew it was the right location to give him my gift.

I slipped a hand into my pocket, turning to him and holding out the bronze pocket watch that I'd cast with my earth magic. The back was etched with the same image as the tattoo marked on my back, a crescent moon with a bat hanging from its tip and a wolf gazing up at it from below.

"Here." I held it out for him to see.

"A pocket watch?" Caleb's eyebrows arched. "It's...shit, that Elemental craftsmanship is perfect, Seth. But where are the clock hands?"

"It doesn't have any," I said.

"So it can't tell the time?"

"It tells our time," I said tightly, heat rising in my cheeks as I placed the watch in his palm and closed his fingers around it. "Our clock doesn't tick, Caleb Altair. There's no seconds, minutes or hours, it has no day or night. It just is. Forever." I stepped closer to him, cupping his cheek and staring into those navy blue eyes which saw right through to my soul. "Whatever happens tomorrow, our time is always."

I touched my lips to his and he pulled me closer with a surge of passion, our kiss deepening and my heart beating to the most powerful tune it had ever played. There was pain in that tune, the fear of what fate would befall us, but I tried to focus on the love I felt instead. Because there was really no greater thing I'd experienced in this world than him, and if my number was about to be called, then knowing I'd had his love and given him all of mine in return...that would be enough for me in this lifetime. In fact, it was more than I ever could have hoped for.

Standing on the grass outside Rump Castle, Caleb fixed the final plate of armour onto my flank then moved to stand in front of me in my Wolf form. He placed a kiss on my furry brow then stepped back, and I took in the shimmer of his own silver armour, the plates crafted by his own hand with expert earth magic. They were thin yet powerful, moulding to his body and allowing for a full range of movement. They were light as shit too so it wouldn't hinder his speed out on the battlefield. He'd made a twin of this armour for Orion, and though he hadn't voiced their secrets to me, I knew the two of them had something planned for this fight. Something to do with their coven bond, something I sensed wasn't entirely legal. But I'd take any advantage we could get in the battle, so hell if I was complaining.

The stars glittered above, dawn not yet upon us, and I swear they were whispering about our fates. Perhaps marking our souls for death in this very moment.

I turned my gaze from them and looked at the man I loved, my heart thrumming with strength as our eyes met once more. I nuzzled his face then we walked together, joining the mass of soldiers who were marching out to the edge of the island. There were farewells in the air, groups of children running to watch us go, throwing crystals at our feet and bidding us luck from the stars. Shit, I knew we needed it. We were seriously outnumbered, and the chances of us making it back here were so slim, I was kidding myself if I thought it was much more than zero.

I spotted Luca waving from Gabriel's arms, the Seer looking both determined and heartbroken as he kissed his son, and the little boy stared up at him with complete ignorance, not knowing that his father might not come home. A lump built in my throat as Gabriel passed the boy into the arms of a short, older woman with dark hair who was speaking in fast Faetalian, then turned reluctantly away and walked into the ranks of the army with his wife.

Dante and Leon closed in around them and I noticed Carson Alvion stepping up behind them, his long brown hair wound into a war braid. He wore just one plate of armour over his chest, his arms bare, his tattoos on show and a look of bloodthirsty hunger in his eyes.

I spotted Xavier further ahead, marching along in his Pegasus form, beautiful plates of armour cladding his lilac body that shimmered like an oil spill. Sofia and Tyler moved at his back and my siblings Athena and Grayson were just behind them in their Wolf forms along with Caleb's brother Hadley.

A protective part of me had wanted to command them to stay back, to not join this fight. They weren't half as well trained as I would have liked for this, though I knew they'd been working hard to make up for the education they'd lost out on. Still, the twins might only have been a couple of years younger than me, but I still saw them as my little brother and sister. Just two pups rolling in the dirt while I pinned them down and nipped at their throats. It wasn't right that life was demanding they march into battle now, that they risk everything before they'd barely had anything good to claim in their adult lives. But I couldn't have kept them from the fight even if I'd wanted to. They would have found a way to be there, to bleed for those they loved just as I would. I didn't have a right to deny them that.

The heavy pounding of footfalls created a thumping rhythm within the earth as our army amassed. There were so many tears from those staying behind, the elderly, the young, those needed to look after them. Geraldine had left them with enough air Elementals to cast Rump Island back out into the ocean if our army didn't return. They could run if Lionel won this war; there was still hope if we failed them. Though it relied heavily on the plan that the Voldrakian's would accept them as refugees. Gabriel had been fairly confident they would, so we'd placed our faith in his Sight.

Caleb raised a hand, knotting his fingers in my fur in a gap between my armour.

We made it to the sweeping fields that overlooked the eastern coast of the island, our army travelling towards it like one giant serpent then spreading out into rows upon rows.

Caleb and I took the longer path around the outskirts of the amassing army of Fae, heading for the front lines where a Phoenix bird made of flames perched on top of a watchtower at the edge of the beach. It moved like it was real, its wings flexing, its head tilting this way and that, the magic so perfectly crafted it was breath-taking.

As we made it closer to the beach, I spotted them. The twins were raised on a stage built from wood, their hands clasped and their eyes full of ire. Their Phoenix armour glittered under the firelight, appearing like molten metal, and their styled hair and savage makeup gave them a look of war that set my pulse racing.

Members of the army began throwing items at their feet, tokens of love and luck. Orion stood to the right of the stage and Darius stood on the left, their features hard and gazes set on their queens.

Geraldine stepped up onto the edge of the stage, amplifying her voice and calling out across the army. "Silence, warriors of the night! Take out the vial delivered to your door last night and sup upon its essence now so that you might be free of the Nymphs' terrible rattling power in the fray."

Caleb took out both of ours, un-stoppering one vial and lifting it to my lips. The potion tasted sweet and sizzled across my tongue as I swallowed before watching Caleb drink his. Everyone around us was drinking it too along with the twins up on their stage. It was just one of the advantages we had in this fight; the Nox flower that Darcy, Gabriel and Orion had secured making sure that the enemy Nymphs couldn't lock down our magic in the approaching battle.

"Our kingdom sits upon a knife's edge," Tory called when everyone was done, her voice echoing out across the crowd. "On the very cusp of dawn, we will have one last chance to fight, one last chance to claim our home from the hands of Lionel Acrux."

A bay of shouts went up, soldiers thrusting their swords in the air with calls for glory.

"Today, we ask you to fight for a new era," Darcy cried. "We don't fight for greed or power; we fight for love. We fight for the brothers, sisters, mothers, fathers, friends and lovers who stand at our sides. We fight for what is right, what is just!"

Another roar of assent sounded and I tipped my head back to howl, my pack answering along with the Oscuras' and my family throughout the army, filling my chest with the desire to hunt.

Tory laid a hand on the hilt of her sword. "The sun is coming to gaze upon a new day, and what she'll see when she rises is a war upon her earth. She'll find us bloody and she'll find us in the thick of chaos, but when she seeks the answer of who will come out victorious, we will answer her call!"

The roars were deafening, my own howls mixing with the cacophony, the pounding of fists on armour, the stamping of heavy boots, the roars, the neighs, the cries for triumph. Deep down, I knew this was all for show. Our queens were doing everything they could to build our warriors' confidence, but death was ahead of most of us, if not all. I tried to let myself buy into the lie that we could really win this, drinking in the Vegas' words and praying they meant something, that the stars might promise us life beyond this battle, but it was so damn hard to believe it.

"We are the howling wind!" Darcy cried and the army echoed those words. "We are the thundering earth!"

Caleb bellowed those words back at them along with the rest of the army.

"We are the riotous ocean!" she cried to another echo of those words, the sound of them rumbling right through my body. "And we are the baneful fire!"

The Phoenix bird swept down off of the watchtower with a wailing cry of war pitching from the depths of the flames, the noise cast by a skilful illusion. It sailed overhead, the heat of the fire flooding me with warmth, and the army hollered for war, raising their swords towards that bird and lifting their banners in the air which held an emblem of a pair of Phoenix birds taking flight through the centre of a golden crown with a star above and flames below.

"Take your formation!" Geraldine ordered, and Caleb squeezed my shoulder, our goodbye lingering even though we'd known this moment would come.

He leaned into me, whispering in my ear as I bowed my head and drew him closer with my paw. "Our time is always."

Caleb kissed my muzzle then he was gone, speeding away into the throng of bodies as everyone worked to assemble themselves.

I headed for the right flank where my Wolves were gathering, my mum there in her Wolf form, pressing her nose to mine in greeting. She moved behind me in the ranks to join my dad, and my heart solidified with the fact she was letting me take Alpha position in this fight. I took that role seriously and would do everything I could to lead our Wolves through this battle and out the other side of it. Mom had said that if I proved myself today, she'd step down from her Councillor spot and I would claim it from her once and for all.

I padded to the front of the line, Grayson and Athena on the heels of my mother, my own pack merging with hers and a host of other Wolf packs took up the line behind us.

As our soldiers worked to find their places, a thundering song of war began to brew within the crowd, led by Geraldine as her voice carried into the sky.

"We stand upon a shore of blood,
Thick as thieves and deep in mud,
The eye of the storm is closing in, but still we fight for glory!
The ocean's roaring for our bones,
She'll take us down to Davy Jones,
Our deaths roll in upon the tide, but still we fight for glory!"

The booming roll of the song took over my soul and I howled along with my pack, the whole island alive with energy. The powerful waves of a Siren's power spilled into me, and I lifted my head, spotting Max high up on a plinth of air with his father Tiberius beside him. The two of them charged our hearts with courage, dousing our fears, and our warriors cried out even louder, ready for battle.

A legion of Harpies moved into position at the forefront of the army, their wings flexing and their armoured skin shining. They each held buckets of stardust in their grip, containing nearly all of our remaining supply, enough to transport us all to the False King's door.

The Harpies looked to their queens for confirmation that it was time, but the twins were hesitating, speaking in low voices and looking beyond the army as if they were waiting on something.

Another minute passed then they shook their heads, giving up on whatever it was they were waiting for and nodding to the Harpies.

"Wait!" a male voice went up and I spotted Milton Hubert racing onto the stage and talking to Darcy and Tory in a low voice. I was frustrated I didn't have Caleb to pick out their voices, growling a little as I tried to figure out what was going on.

The twins suddenly took off into the sky, their wings burning bright as they tore away in the direction of the castle.

Geraldine stared after them in confusion then sang her song even louder, keeping spirits high.

"The ground beneath us trembles deep,
Our enemies turn to run and weep,
For the army of queens is closing in, and we only fight for glory!"

The song bellowed on, and even though the Sirens were still threading hope and strength into my soul, my gaze kept travelling in the direction the twins had taken, trepidation slipping through me. Why would they run off? What could possibly be happening that could take their attention from this moment?

My ears twitched at the sound of a faraway drumming noise, growing closer and closer. I spotted black banners with two curling horns upon them moving closer to our army and my heart raced. I raised up onto my hind legs to try and see better, my breathing all but stopping at the sight unfolding before me.

The twins flew above a sea of Nymphs, maybe three thousand, perhaps more in their shifted forms, all dressed for war, some gripping spears in their hands. Near the front, I spotted one wearing a beanie hat speared upon his horn and knew that had to be Diego's father Miguel. They were here. They'd come. They'd fucking joined us at the very last second.

"Welcome the Legion of Shadow," Darcy called, her voice echoing around us, and a murmur of uncertainty passed through our warriors.

"They wish to join us in our fight! To bolster our ranks and see Lionel brought to justice!" Tory bayed. "We have secured a treaty with them."

More mutters of fear broke out, people backing away from the approaching Nymph army, some letting out cries of alarm.

"There are no enemies in our ranks!" Darcy called, her voice tempered by a wave of trust flooding from Max and Tiberius. "You are all brothers and sisters in arms who fight for one true cause!"

The Sirens dulled anyone's continuing fears and as Geraldine's song broke through the crowd again, the Nymphs were moved into position among us. Our army allowed them in, even while some still passed comments and kept their distance, but they needed to get the hell over it. With them on our side, we'd secured more of a chance at winning this war. It was a gift none of us could deny, and another howl poured from my throat as I let myself fall into the intoxicating song of battle.

The twins returned to the stage, nodding to the Harpies while taking out a pouch of stardust of their own. Orion and Darius bowed to their queens before moving away to their places in the army, ferocity sparking in their eyes.

Then the Harpies were sweeping overhead and stardust was tumbling from the sky, the glittering dust showering my fur before I was snatched away into the grasp of the universe, hurling me towards a battle I wasn't sure I would ever return from.

GERALDINE

CHAPTER SEVENTY THREE

"We stand on the brink of a new dawn!" I roared.

My voice magically carried across the Starfall Legion at my back and beyond, over the rows of Fae and Nymphs who stood ready in both Fae and shifted forms, lined up in perfect rows, fangs bared, and weapons raised.

"This battle will be the end of this ghastly war. It will be the rise of a new era in the kingdom of Solaria. The false Dragon King will ascend and spread his tyranny unchecked across our fair land, like a rot spreading from coast to coast. Corruption and cruelty will be his legacy, and all of our fates will be cast in shadows untold. Or. OR! We may just stand at the brink of a rising sun unlike any which has passed before us. We may be about to fall under the full and unchallenged reign of our true and noble queens, just as the fates always intended. They were born to rule us, surviving the brutal murder of their family, surviving the vicious cunning of the green Dragooon and rising, just like the Phoenixes they are, above any and every hurdle placed before them. They are destined to rewrite this brutal kingdom. They are destined to bring about a time of peace and prosperity unlike any we have faced before. They are destined to seize the crown, the throne and the hearts of our nation. And we, fair followers of their rising flame, are destined to carve that fate from the heavens this very day!"

A roar split apart the world at my back as I thrust my flail skyward, the glint of the rising sunlight making the spiked ball gleam like a star of the skies themselves.

I could feel the eyes of the heavens turning to us now. I could feel fate shifting its focus to us, the defenders of justice and righteousness, the advocates of the True Queens and the proclaimers of their upcoming reign.

"We stand before the face of an enemy mighty enough to make even the bravest, most steadfast of Fae quake in their boots," I rumbled. "And yet still we stand, still we hold, still we roar!"

I cast one look along the endless lines of our brave and loyal warriors, from the Starfall Legion at my rear wearing the helm of blue and red, the ancient depiction of the Phoenix bird with its savage beak and battle-ready features, to the Wolves who headed up the flanks of our ferocious force. The right flank led by Seth Capella in his glorious white form, plates of beautiful armour strapped to his powerful body and the wind ruffling his fur in a rippling wave.

The left flank was led by Rosalie Oscura whose pack of vicious hellhounds bayed for blood. The Storm Dragon, Dante, was positioned in the sky above them, electricity crackling against his navy scales with a threat he would soon fulfil. Next, came the faithful Nymphs, ferocious in their shifted form, those deadly, fear-inspiring probes angled with desire at the hearts of our enemies.

All nature of Fae stood in formation. The Tiberian Rats gathered close to their leader, Eugene Dipper, who wore a helm of bronze, forged into the shape of a ferocious looking rat skull. Beyond them, a unit of Icekian Polar Bear shifters released bellows of contempt, the glimmering light of the Aurora Borealis shining within their glacia diamond armour, led by Imenia Brumalis whose lips were peeled back in a fearsome snarl.

Deep within our ranks, the Vampires lay in wait, ready to speed forward at the opportune moment and cut through our enemies, fangs bared, sharp and deadly. Overhead, all manner of flying orders bellowed and neighed, lightning parting the clouds as the Storm Dragon drew the vicous Oscura Clan into howls of desperate bloodlust.

Lionel's feral army was scrambling to meet us in the gully between the mountains, our roars and bellows for battle drawing them from their beds. Unlike them, we were almost ready to charge, but they were moving fast, forming ranks, rows upon rows of Fae and Nymphs crying out for blood. Far more warriors than we had ever managed to gather. The element of surprise was important, but enough? Oh woeful wiggamoles, I doubted it could be. Still, we would fight with all the fire of a belching volcano and not go quietly beyond The Veil. No, ma'am.

In the belly of our courageous army, a chant began. One word, brutal, efficient and pure. Over and over, the drumbeat to which our feet would march and our swords would swing.

"Vega. Vega. Vega."

My heart pumped with the courage of a lion and the strength of our army, not simply because I felt that way but because the Sirens among us, led by my dear Maxy Boy and his sweet papa, encouraged them to do so, their auras spilling over us, inciting our army for a win.

I placed a hand on the shoulder of the magnificent Shadow Beast where he bristled at my side, exchanging a knowing look with him. The last time he and I had been together on the battlefield, he had almost snaffed my snuff. Yet today we would wage war together, and he looked keen to repay his captors for their cruelty. He wore the fine armour I had worked to forge for such a fine beast, marking him the official steed of our queen Darcy, the plates of silver interlinked by blue details and the crest of the Vegas upon his headpiece. A fine saddle was strapped to his back, ready and waiting for my blue-haired queen to claim when it was time.

"Into the fight, eh, old chum?" I said just to him, and he chuffed solidly in agreement.

A grin split my lips unlike any other I knew. My death may have been waiting for me in the depths of that army on the far side of the rocky plain between these hellbent mountains, but if it wanted a taste of old Grus then it would have to jolly well fight for it.

With the thrumming of Vega in my ears, and the furious drumming of my heart calling out for battle, I knew it was time.

With my gaze set on the False King's immense forces, I broke the line, leading the charge into battle with a furious cry filled with passionate rage. At my back charged the army of the True Queens, the loyal, the just, the true. This day we fought for freedom. This day we fought for righteousness. This day we fought for a new era to rise.

Long live the True Queens. Forever may they reign. In this world or the next.

SETH

CHAPTER SEVENTY FOUR

A howl pitched from my throat that was echoed by the pack in my stead, and the moon peered down at me from the dawn sky, like an adoring lover taking the front row before my stage. Of course she had come to watch, my steady, constant adorer who had patiently awaited this moment of reckoning. She would keep my Wolves well stocked with magic so long as we kept running beneath her mighty glow. The mate mark behind my ear tingled in recognition of her and all she'd offered me, and I prayed she would protect Caleb in this fight, to watch over him before me on this field of judgement.

The howls of Rosalie's pack carried from the far side of our army, answering our call. My paws thundered across the earth, my front claws fitted with the Phoenix fire gauntlets, so sharp they tore through the ground like paper.

I stole one glance back, sensing eyes on me and spotted Caleb up on the hill behind our ranks where he was stationed for his own purpose, his armour glinting, reflecting the colours of the rising sun. His head turned, our gazes meeting, those piercing navy blue eyes owning my soul and every fibre of my flesh with that look.

Time slowed, as it always did for us, bending so unnaturally to offer us longer stretches of reality together. It might be our last, this fleeting glance that was fuelled with so much love it almost broke my heart to think this might be the end of us. But I'd made a promise that would span across the universe, no matter where our souls ended up today. Our time was always. Past, present, future. We would find one another on this bloody battlefield once again with victories written into the stars, or else in the arms of death, failure branding us forevermore. Either way, our return to one another was as inevitable as the sun's return at dawn.

As the army coursed forward behind me, I was forced to turn my eyes from Caleb, the moment shattering as quickly as it had come, but that lasting view of him was imprinted on my mind forever, etched in stone.

Lionel's front line was made up of Nymphs, their terrible rattles ripping the air apart. I'd lost sight of Geraldine, too many Fae between us, but her legion was ahead of ours and with a collision that shook the ground beneath me, I heard our army colliding with Lionel's full force.

As the unit of Fae that Geraldine was leading drove into them like a single blade, tearing through their bodies with tooth and sword and magic, a cry of confusion went up from the enemy ranks. For our magic wasn't affected by the Nymphs' rattles any longer, the Nox flower potion working wonders on our warriors.

I barked my joy, taking heart in our first win, but then I trained my eyes on the swarming army ahead just as the flying Orders clashed above us with shrieks and roars. My friends were up there, to my sides, behind me, and a snarl peeled my lips back, my focus sharpening as I swore on all I was to protect them. To be the best soldier I could be and reap justice from the bones of my foes in penance for all they'd done, and all they still sought to do.

This was our last stand, and though our army was half the size of Lionel's, we had ten times the savagery and the burn of fiery rebellion in our hearts. We had been branded lesser, dismissed as rogues and devils, but here on this very ground, we'd prove our mettle, so even if death came to lead us from this world today, we would go with our names blazing in flashing lights, our memories scorched into the minds of our adversaries, never to be forgotten.

I released a howl then leapt at the oncoming line of Nymphs, slamming into a ten-foot beast and ripping my claws down his chest. My gauntlets ignited, Phoenix flames sparking and killing the Nymph in one strike.

He fell dead beneath me, and my paws hit his body, surprise filling me when it didn't turn to ash. I used him as a springboard to leap toward my next opponent, unable to spare another thought to my prey.

My jaws locked tight around another Nymph's throat and my mother barked as she swept past me, her russet fur catching my eye before she took down a Nymph with monstrous brutality. No longer did these creatures turn to dust upon death, that truth surely to do with the cleansing of the shadows, and their bodies continued to pile up as our army collided with them in droves, heading deeper into Lionel's ranks.

My fur was already wet with blood, and I led my pack further into the fray, the tumultuous clash of war making my ears ring. I finished off two more Nymphs then slammed into a line of Fae with hatred twisting their features.

Magic blasted my side, scalding fire, and whips of vines that tried to hold me down. My heart leapt, my paws scrabbling in the dirt, scratching against fallen bodies, breaking bones, the crush of Fae closing in on me.

My pulse thundered, knowing that this was where the real battle started. No more joy filled my chest; it was a bid for survival now as the scent of churning dirt and spilling blood reached my nose.

My teeth sank into the neck of a woman casting vines, making her release me as she screamed her death. The stench of singed flesh and fur made me certain I was burned badly on my flank, but I couldn't feel the pain through the adrenaline.

I was a wild thing, biting every enemy that came at me, tearing claws through soft bellies and spilling blood like rain. My pack was closing in around me, reforming our group, protecting me, and I barked and snapped at their heels, telling them plainly I desired no such thing. Athena and Grayson were close on my left, their tails swishing together as they took down two Fae in unison, their twin bond so keen in this moment, it was like they could hear each other's thoughts.

I broke through Frank and Alice ahead of me, my teeth latching around the throat of a man with his hands raised to cast. Ice pierced my shoulder through a gap in my armour before I bit deep enough to kill him, and I snarled as I tossed his body away like a ragdoll, charging on and knocking down two more of Lionel's soldiers.

But they kept coming, like ants over a hill, they never stopped coming. So many of them, it was like drowning in pitch, the light of the sun lost to the manic flurry of winged Orders above, the tint of fire in the air, the fog of smoke, the scent of it all clogging my lungs.

This oppressive crush of bodies, both dead and alive, was almost enough to stir up a panic in me. The terror that I might never see Caleb again, or Darius, or Max. My family. All of them. They were here in this gruesome, bloody fight, and the odds were, we wouldn't make it out of this alive.

I slammed into another Fae, my teeth ripping into warm skin, screams making my ears ring, and I held onto the reason I was here, fighting with all the fury of my heart. The only thing that was ever worth bleeding for. Love. And no pit of death, or stench of battle could touch the fearsome, unstoppable force of that.

CALEB

CHAPTER SEVENTY FIVE

The Oscura Clan howled wildly ahead of us, a tide of Wolves in both shifted and Fae form, Rosalie as a silver Wolf diving into battle at the front of the wave, leading the left flank of our army into war just as I knew Seth was doing with his pack to the right.

We were attacking in a trident formation across the span of our entire army, the two enormous Wolf packs, bolstered by every Wolf under our command until they were thousands strong, making up the outer prongs. Geraldine's Starfall Legion made up the central point of attack. The aim was to punch three brutal paths through our enemy's frontline. Once those three paths were embedded deeply enough, the rest of our ranks would flow through them then turn their attention to the soldiers who had been caught between those spikes. Then we would crush them by coming at them from both sides before plunging the trident forward again.

Lionel's army had the numbers on us which meant we needed to out-manoeuvre them. It was a brutal, dangerous tactic, placing those who fought in the spikes of the trident at high risk as they punctured the enemy line, but with our best warriors fighting in the most hazardous points of attack, we were hoping it would pay off. But that meant Seth was out there in that mass of churning, fighting bodies, and no matter how good my eyesight was, I couldn't pick him out among the bloody battle, making my chest tighten with fear.

Orion shifted from foot to foot at my side as the two of us held our ground, rooted to the spot while the battle raged before us and our warriors dove into death without us.

"This is torture," he snarled, his hand on his sword.

"Just a little longer," I agreed, my fangs snapping out as I palmed my Phoenix fire daggers.

I bounced on the balls of my feet, running my tongue over my fangs and trying not to let my mind linger on the friends I had out there in the thick of all that horror. I could see Max, standing on a pillar of air near our front lines, shielded with magic while he boosted the confidence of our army and set terror into the hearts of our enemies.

"They're out there fighting this war," Darius rumbled from behind me, and I turned to look at him as he slowly took his war axe from his back and weighed it in his hand. "But we're the ones who have the task of ending it."

"If we can find them," Orion muttered, his eyes never leaving the battlefield, the clash of bodies creating a deafening roar of noise which was hard to divide into the various blasts of magic, collision of weapons and screams of the dying.

"Big if," I agreed, scanning the lines of Lionel's army and coming up blank. "Any ideas?" I asked Darius.

He raised his axe and pointed over the heads of the army, past the flaring magic and advancing Nymphs, beyond the sky filled with flying Orders and all the way to the hulking green castle which clung to the largest mountain in the distance.

"My father will be watching from there," he said in a low voice. "His queen..." His eyes moved over the ranks of Fae and Nymphs swarming towards us, his brow furrowing. "She's no great love of his; just another weapon to wield. If he's had any say in it, Lavinia will be out there somewhere, waiting to pounce. Brute force is his favoured form of attack, so she will likely reveal herself as soon as his ranks begin to waver."

"The trident has broken through," Orion pointed out.

From our position on the higher ground towards the rear of the army, the shape was indeed becoming clear, those three points of attack driving deep through the enemy lines all at once. It could have been seen as random. Or perhaps Lionel would believe that it was two parts of *his* army which had broken through our lines instead of being lured into the trap of our trident.

A grim smile lifted my lips.

"Geraldine's tactics are fucking masterful," I said, my eyes seeking out any sign of a white Wolf in the right flank of the army again, but they were too far away, too caught up in the chaos of war and no doubt too bloodstained to make identifying anyone from this distance possible.

We fell silent, watching over the battlefield just like the mountains which rose up all around it, creating this basin of bloodshed for the fight to be contained within. As I glanced at those sheer and rocky slopes, I noted how impossible desertion would be for pretty much anybody in this unforgiving place. The mountains couldn't easily be climbed, and the land was so barren that anyone attempting it would be making themselves a target if they tried. Only the flying Orders stood much chance of escaping, but as I took in the carnage ripping through the sky, I doubted any of them would be able to get free of that mayhem to attempt it.

To our right, a line of Fae stood before the medic tents, rows of beds laid with pristine white sheets already being filled with Fae who had fallen in battle but hadn't quite succumbed to death yet.

I watched as a man was tossed over the heads of our fighting warriors by a gust of air magic. A chain of Fae caught him and threw him to the next person in line while blood gushed from a wound to his side, dripping on the Fae who made up the rear ranks.

He was deposited in one of the beds and Mother Dickens hurried to his side, closing her eyes as she pressed her hand to his wound and deftly stitched the skin shut. Another healer tossed a blood-replenishing potion to her, and she offered it to the wounded Fae who quickly gulped the lot down.

"Order?" she demanded while syphoning the blood from his wound into a vial and stoppering it, no doubt for use by any Vampires in need.

"Sphinx," he replied, moving to stand.

"Not so fast," Mother Dickens said, taking a book from beneath the bed where I also spied a mirror, a golden goblet, and many other items which could restore the magic of various Orders.

He took the book and promptly started reading, his eyes scanning the page so fast it was hard to believe he was reading at all. Other injured soldiers were transported into the tent, healed then offered ways to replenish their magic, a pair of Pegasuses wheeling away quickly into the clouds above.

After a few minutes, the soldier announced that his magic had been refilled, dropped the book on the bed, then took off towards the battlefield with a cry of, "For the True Queens!"

"That guy deserves a medal," I muttered, the itch in my limbs growing more desperate with the desire to follow him into the melee.

Orion nodded but Darius had just taken a step forward, his body lined with tension as he watched the battle where those three prongs of attack had dug further into the enemy lines.

"Now," he breathed and as if they'd heard him, the warriors in those three sections of the army suddenly turned their focus from advancing to cutting into the enemies caught between them.

As they sliced into them, more of our warriors were able to pour into the space created between the prongs of the trident and within several brutal, too-long minutes where I hardly dared draw breath, they ripped a whole section of Lionel's army out of existence and reformed the front line as if it had never been fragmented.

"Fuck yes!" I whooped and Orion yelled out in victory too while Darius just grinned like a demon.

"Look, your shadow bitch didn't like that very much," he said, raising a hand and pointing towards the rear of Lionel's army where a plume of dark shadow had just lashed the air, revealing the location of our target at last.

The three of us glanced at one another. From this moment we likely wouldn't find out anything of each other's fates until this was done. We couldn't even use comms during this fight having discussed the possibility and realising that they could be intercepted. Any information we passed between each other could be used against us or even potentially used to pinpoint our individual locations. It wasn't a risk we could take. We'd all done the mushy goodbye shit this morning when our whole group was together, before the bloodshed began. So we only nodded at Darius before Orion and I turned to one another and let the coven bond have its way with us at last.

The world blurred as the call of the hunt drove deep into my veins, my fangs aching with the need for blood as we raced through our army and shot deep into the ranks of the enemy at high speed. We tore along the churned-up ground, my pulse thundering in time with my sanguis frater's, like we were becoming an extension of one another. I gave in entirely, my vision overlaying with Orion's as our foes began to react to our presence within their midst.

A big fucker with a silver helm fashioned with Dragon horns lunged for Orion and I was there in a flash, whirling on him, blades slicing the backs of his knees. He threw his head back in a howl of agony and Orion ripped his throat out with his bare teeth, his blood spraying the surrounding Fae. The two of us were gone again before his body even hit the ground.

I swear I could taste that blood on Orion's lips, and it only made my own thirst sharper despite my magic reserves being full to the brim. But I had always thrived in the thrill of the hunt and there was nothing in the world which could compare to hunting in a coven.

We sped between Lionel's ranks, ducking and weaving around most Fae before they even noticed our passage, ripping into the few who were able to lunge for us, but it didn't take long for them to send reinforcements after us.

The enemy Vampires came in a rush of motion, their fangs bared and blades drawn. Within seconds, we were surrounded by our own kind, the advantage of speed lost to us and our advance towards Lavinia stalled.

My fangs tingled at the challenge as eight of them surrounded us, working as a unit, but not as a coven. My smile was all feral as my gaze doubled over, Orion's focus meeting with mine. I shot my attention to the blonde asshole to my left, selecting the target of our next hunt and wordlessly, we lunged.

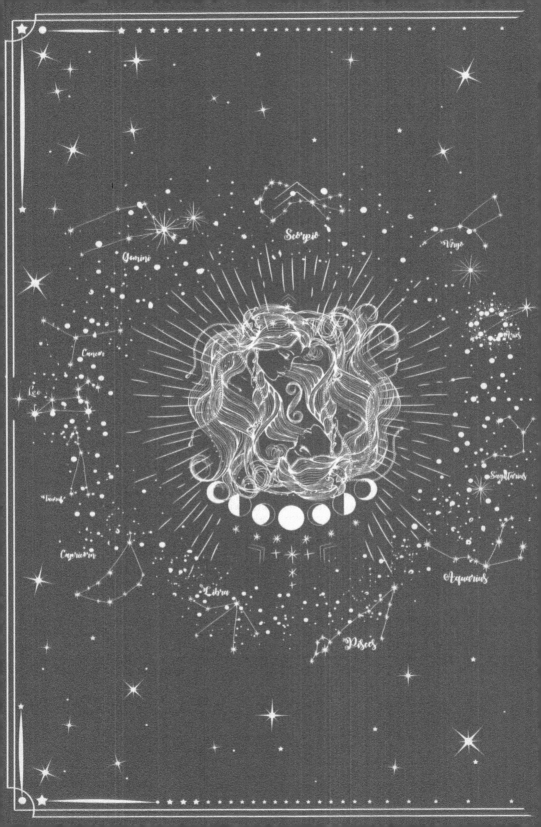

DARCY

CHAPTER SEVENTY SIX.

"I hate that we're not there," I said, looking to the horizon, sure I could just hear the roar of battle in the distance.

"Me too." Tory took my hand, her eyes a perfect mirror of mine. This girl, this woman, this fucking warrior made me so proud to be her twin, I could hardly bear it.

I squeezed her fingers, smiling at her in this profoundly sad way that spoke of what might happen today. I still had hope, fuck I had to have hope. But we had to acknowledge the other side of that coin too.

"Don't say it," Tory begged, her nails biting into my palm.

I nodded, stepping closer to her and embracing her instead, our arms locking tight around one another, squeezing until we felt like one being. Because in a way we would always be two halves of a whole. So different, yet so the same.

We let that embrace drag on for a few more seconds, knowing it might just be the last time we held each other in this world. Then the space grew between us, at least that was how it felt, until we were somehow letting go of one another and facing the magnitude of the task we'd set ourselves. The reason we were out on this rocky hill instead of flying into battle with our family.

The air was crisp, the day so clear, it was like looking through a window into the house of the stars. All of them had come to watch. Despite the sky being so icily blue, there they were. Every one of them glaringly bright, so watchful they barely twinkled at all.

"It's time," Tory breathed, the sense of it suddenly certain within me too, like some outside force had placed the knowledge there. Perhaps it was just instinct, or a nudge from those very stars above. I'd never know.

We raised our hands, wielding the earth around us and growing twelve giant stones from the ground. They pierced through the frozen soil like blooming flowers, jutting up into the sky, spilling dirt around their bases.

We set to carving a symbol on each of their surfaces, marking the signs of the zodiac until we had a perfect, colossal wheel around us. At eye height, we carved a hole in each, placing a Guild Stone into it that matched the zodiac sign carvings, just as the book from The Library of the Lost had described.

The final stone was for Gemini, and as one, we walked towards it, the moonstone weighing heavily in my palm. We shared a look, then placed it into the rock together, power immediately snapping out around us.

I turned with a gasp, finding all of the Guild Stones glowing in their places, green, pink, blue, the brightest of colours that pulsed with a potent energy.

My breaths became ragged from the immense power humming in the air, the first step of our plan complete. Though that was the easiest part about all of this. The risk we took could see us dead if this failed. But if Clydinius was left to fight in that battle, our army stood no chance of winning.

Tory and I moved to the very centre of the wide circle, preparing for the next step as we etched a beautiful sun and moon into the ground beneath us.

"Ready?" she asked when we were finished.

"I'm ready," I said.

As one, we each raised a hand towards the sky, blasting a beacon of Phoenix flames towards the heavens. The line of fire climbed skyward over a mile, blasting up and away from us, higher and higher.

Our fire flared brighter as we waited for the answer to our call, our gazes set on the stars.

But no answer came.

"You owe us!" Tory cried.

"Right the balance!" I yelled. "You swore you would give us this chance!"

My heart beat harder, the fear that I'd been deceived driving deep into my chest.

"Arcturus!" I bellowed, refusing to let him turn from us now. "You made an oath, a promise to protect my kind and restore order among the stars!"

"Get your sparkly motherfucking ass down here!" Tory demanded.

The sky flashed, a ring of starfire blooming across the sky with a pinpoint of light at its centre.

I breathed a sigh of relief, looking to Tory with my mouth twisting into a smile. "He's keeping his promise."

"We'll see," she said, her mistrust of the stars well-earned, but this time I really believed we had one on our side.

The pinpoint of light glowed ever brighter, growing closer and closer until the sky itself was cleaving apart, making way for the burning star that was falling straight from its perch. Arcturus blazed a trail of red, gold and silver in his wake, the star seeming to glide more than tumble, causing nature to take note of his sacrifice. The sky illuminated and sparks of magnificent light crackled and danced along the falling star's path.

We extinguished our flames, racing out of the stone circle and flying skyward on our wings before casting air shields when we were well away from the impact zone. We watched from up high as Arcturus came crashing through the atmosphere and the heat of his flaming surface cut through the icy winter air, thickening it with a stifling warmth.

I winced against the glaring brightness as the star drew closer, and my breath caught a second before the great, burning ball of fire slammed into the earth right at the centre of our stone circle. The blast made the hill shudder, the stones withstanding the impact and the Guild Stones pulsing ever brighter. We were blown backwards by the force of the collision, the wind throwing us further away.

I steadied myself, my wings beating to counter the blast and as the dust settled, a deep crater was revealed right at the centre of our stone circle with a fallen star inside it. Arcturus glittered beautifully, his power igniting the magic in my veins and leaving me breathless.

"Daughters of the flames," he spoke into our minds with a reverence to his tone. *"I have come."*

GABRIEL

CHAPTER SEVENTY SEVEN

Two blood-red oceans collided, one's waves were taller, but the other's water moved with more ferocity.
Chaos lived between the two.
All outcomes were possible, non-perceivable.
Time was the enemy and the ally.
Death was the only certainty. Death and carnage, blood and terror-

A hand grabbed my shoulder and I wheeled around with a cry, bringing up my sword and finding its tip touching the throat of a man who I had long called a friend.

"Leon," I exhaled, lowering the Savage King's weapon which was made of the darkest metal known in this land. "Forgive me."

"You'd never kill me, Gabe," he said with such certainty it was like he had better foresight than me.

His golden hair was tied back in a knot to keep it from his face when it was time for him to join the fight. His armour was emblazoned with the Night family crest, even though I knew it to be stolen, its true owner's name erased from its shell. It had once been worn by a famous warrior of old who had fought in the War of Broken Thorns.

Legend had it, he had been the size of a bear with the heart of a lion, and so it was fitting that my feline friend wore it now. He'd barely had to adjust the size too, his bulk plenty to fill it out. I wore no armour myself, my Harpy's full form would see to that, and I didn't need the weight of any metal slowing me down when I took to the skies. For now, however, we were stuck up on this stars-forsaken mountainside awaiting our moment, and The Sight was unforgiving, showing me the faces of my family and friends in death time and again.

But I was well versed in this now. I knew death was a plague that would delve deep into the battlefield this day; I also knew that the dead could not be counted until it was done.

No vision was certain, fate so very malleable now, that I was suspended in a strange state, oscillating between hope and despair. These emotions were wrought of possibility, and I could almost taste the new dawn on the horizon, if only we could reach it. The world would drastically change for the better, peace would reign, fear would not follow the people of our land into their slumber. We were teetering on the brink of that beautiful, tantalising future, but it could be so easily snatched away from us too.

"Maybe we should have brought a few more earth Elementals with us," Leon said in concern. "Your head must feel like fireworks are going off in it. How are you ever gonna focus on this, dude?"

I gritted my teeth, holding the visions at bay. "I can do it. We can't spare the Fae. Just hurry."

I raised my hands, wielding more of the earth to create the vessels we needed for the entirely insane plan my sister had in mind for them. I couldn't *see* whether or not this would work, my Sight having limits when it came to such things, but if it did, perhaps this would be the edge we needed in this battle.

I acted quickly, wanting to take advantage of the rising sun which was fuelling my magic faster than I could wield it. With a surge of power, I pulled the clay from the earth, moulding it into a range of mounds and shaping them roughly before letting Leon take over with his fire Element to finish them.

"Don't give the clay tits," I cursed as Leon shaped two giant breasts onto one of my creations.

Leon baked the tits in place with his fire, ignoring me. "You just do your bit, and I'll do mine."

"You're wasting time," I scolded.

"Tits are never a waste of time," he said, giving me a pointed look and I huffed out a breath, knowing that nothing I said had ever worked to control Leon in the past. He wasn't going to start listening to reason now. The Lion always danced to his own tune, and no song would ever be tempting enough for him to change the rhythm of his feet.

The cry of battle roared just over the other side of this mountain and my hands trembled as a wave of violent visions poured through my head.

My wife was on her back, her throat ripped out by a Dragon.

Orio was crushed beneath a tide of charging Centaurs.

Dante was torn from the sky by three terrible beasts, wings tattered, chest cleaved open.

I blinked out of it, my breaths coming heavier and my focus sharpening once again.

It's not real. Just possibilities passing on a wayward breeze.

I drew on the strength of my love for those I'd seen dying, a roar of determination leaving me as I tore into the mountainside with my magic, heaving clay from the earth, huge blocks of it bursting from the ground. Leon ran between them all, working faster to mould and set them just how we needed. A sweeping count told me we had fifty or so ready, but that wasn't enough. Not nearly so.

I took the pouch of thyme sprigs from my pocket. Every one of my creations needed to have a piece of the plant embedded in its exterior, so I took to my wings, racing overhead and sticking a sprig in each of those that were ready, certain it was better to finish the ones we had now in case we ran out of time.

"Here." I tossed some of the thyme to Leon and he caught it with a nod, his eyes flashing with darkness.

He knew what was to come, and we drew closer to our moment with every passing second. My sisters would be counting on us, and we couldn't fail them. I just wished the stars would offer me a glimpse of certainty on whether this plan would work or fail. But they were eerily quiet on this part, and perhaps, if I was not going mad, an air of contempt burned from them too. We would defy them this day in the name of our destiny. But no star, no black-hearted Dragon, or monstrous fiend of the Shadow Realm would rip this fate from our hands. It was ours, at long last. And we would damn well claim victory come sunset.

DARIUS

CHAPTER SEVENTY EIGHT

I charged along the outer edges of the battlefield, my axe swinging wildly, the burn in my arm intense with the fury of my blows as blood spilled and Fae screamed when they met with the blunt force of my rage.

At my back, a squad of Tiberian Rats fought to stem the tide of enemy Fae who lunged for us, keeping them occupied so I could carve my path onwards.

I wouldn't shift. Not yet. I knew my father too well for that and I wouldn't present myself as an open target for him to aim his Bonded Dragons towards.

I was going to be the hunter in this game we were playing, and he would be forced out of his hole to face me. This time wouldn't end the way it had before. There would be no tricks or bad luck to thwart me. I had spent every spare moment training for this, aching for it, desperate to see an end to his tyranny and most of all, desperate to sever any lasting tie I had to him and his name.

Lionel Acrux would look me in the eye and see his death had come calling for him. When I threw him to the mercy of the ghosts beyond The Veil, I knew they would make him suffer in endless torment for all he had caused in this life.

My axe collided with a heavy sword, and I was forced to twist beneath the guard of the Fae who had come for me, the big bastard grinning as he brought a second sword around in anticipation of my move.

I ducked, ice splintering from my free hand, a thousand barbed needles shooting for his side and making him bellow as they sank through any tiny hole they could locate in his armour to pierce his skin.

I turned again, bringing my axe with me and the sound of metal ringing against metal cut through the screams of endless battle as our weapons met and slid along each other.

I kicked out, my boot colliding with the centre of his chest plate, right in the face of the smug-looking green Dragon emblazoned there. As he stumbled back, I scored my axe through the air, splitting his throat wide open.

Blood sprayed and my pulse thrashed wildly, but I was already turning away, charging towards a pair of men far smaller in stature than myself and throwing my shoulders into their chests in a tackle. Their weapons didn't even come close to me as they swung with wild terror, and the warriors at my back descended on them where they fell.

I ran on, a path of Dragon fire carved out before me as I unleashed my power, the gold of my own armour replenishing my magic with every passing moment.

The enemy army spread out around me like a sea of ruinous carnage, the ranks to the rear clamouring to get closer, held back by the clash of the front line ahead of them.

A Nymph lunged suddenly from my right, shifting at the sight of me and revealing itself among the masses of its army, sharp probes slashing out furiously.

I swung my axe for the beast, ducking the blow and severing a single probe which fell to the frozen ground between us with a thump.

Blood splattered the surrounding warriors, marring their silver armour, staining that green Dragon and making me grin as I beckoned the Nymph closer.

The Nymph lunged for me again, its rattle pouring from it in a potent echo which buckled the knees of all the Fae who surrounded us on my father's side of this war. But not me and not the violent bastards who fought at my back.

I swung my axe with a savage swipe, the effects of the Nox pollen making my skin tingle as it blocked the power of the Nymph and the creature's eyes widened in horror as it realised its mistake. It had assumed I would falter too, assumed my warriors would crumple like those on its side of this fight had done. So instead of taking advantage of a disoriented, weakened man, falling prey to its power, it found itself with my axe buried in its chest and a bellow of victory rising from all around.

My warriors took full advantage of the weakened Fae before them, using the power of the Nymph's rattle to carve through all those who had fallen prey to it with brutal efficiency.

The Nymph toppled before me and I wrenched my axe free, using its huge body as a launch pad as I leapt onto its back and took a running jump at the rocky side of the mountain that loomed up to my left.

I threw ice into the side of the rockface, creating footholds for me to land on and racing up them until I was high enough to get a view over the army.

The front ranks were buckling, the line which had started off so straight now warped and jagged, dips and curves forming where both sides had fought through or crumpled under the pressure of the opposition.

I gritted my teeth at the sight, unable to discern an obvious answer to which way this battle was going among the chaos, but as the sky split with the roars of a hundred Dragons, I couldn't help but turn my gaze to the distant castle of jade. I blinked at the figures pouring from every window, tower, and turret of the imposing building, the rippling movement and slight shifts in colour against the sky the only way of picking out each of the beastly forms of the concealed Dragons that were racing through the sky towards our army.

"Shield!" I bellowed, my command carried back down the ranks, though I doubted it would be necessary; no one could have missed the sound of those Dragons joining the battle.

The urge to shift and meet the first of them in the sky made my limbs tremble, the Dragon within me stirring, baring its teeth and releasing a low growl. I was far bigger and stronger than any one of those bastards who were tearing through the air, but despite the urge to prove that writhing through me, I could see the challenge for what it was. Father wanted to lure me out. But I wasn't dancing to his tune today.

I forced my eyes from the cloud of scales and teeth which thundered towards our army, my father's Bonded Dragons rushing into the fight like harbingers of certain death. I had to trust in our army's plans for them and focus on my own mission.

I broke into a run, the warriors who had accompanied me this far scrambling to follow me while the enemy engaged them, but I couldn't wait, I needed to end this quickly if I could. Numbers weren't on our side and the sharp truth of that reality would quickly set in if we didn't enact all of our most cunning plans fast.

The mountain became too steep for even my spears of ice to find purchase, and I swung my axe overhead as I was forced to leap from it back into the wild fray of the enemy army. I shot a blast of potent fire magic into the enemy ranks ahead of me, Fae frantically shielding and leaping aside, though I felt the heady rush of more death as some of them succumbed to the blast of my attack.

Fire sprung up around me as I landed and ducked my head low, running flat out, my shoulders slamming into countless Fae, knocking them aside while I cast spears of ice ahead to forge a path.

The element of surprise and my overwhelming use of brute force bought me at least a hundred feet before they managed to form a line and stop me, pushing me into combat, the ring of metal against my axe a heady rush.

I fell into the pounding rhythm of it, the duck and sway, slash and blast. Magic ricocheted off of the shield of ice which I threw up to guard me from all sides apart from the front, the power of it too strong for any of them to penetrate, forcing them to bottleneck before me and wait for their turn to die.

I revelled in the beauty of my armour, the weightless, supple brilliance of it and the warmth of the flames which sang within the metal, such a priceless, stunning thing wrought only of Phoenix magic. The value of it was half of its magnificence, my constant contact with the immensely valuable treasure meaning no matter how much magic I threw at my enemies, I barely even noticed the lag. I was replenishing faster than I would have managed spread flat on a mound of treasure and I murmured praises to my beautiful, magnificent wife between ferocious slashes of my axe.

An echoing boom stole my attention for a brief moment and a lucky asshole got beneath my guard, his sword clanging off of my armour which saved me from death, but he managed to slice beneath my arm where the metal joined.

I roared in fury, blasting him with such powerful fire magic that nothing but soot remained where he had stood grinning in false triumph, and I let my shield close around me entirely. But not before I raised my eyes over the swarming masses of my father's army and took in the war machines which had appeared as if from nowhere, the magic which had been cloaking them clearly no longer needed as they blasted devastation back towards the rebel forces. Towers forged from wood and stone with catapults and cannons bolted to their sides, primed with magic from those who stood shielded within them.

Swords and axes clashed and chopped against the ice of my shield as countless warriors closed in all around me, fighting to reach me and use those same weapons to hack me apart.

I slapped my hand to the bleeding wound beneath my arm, ignoring the burn of pain as I healed it, my mind whirling with what I had to do.

My part in the fight was clear; I had to get to my father, I had to kill him and end this before time could force this battle on and his superior numbers could come into full effect against us. But those towers changed things. They could change the course of this battle long before I ever broke through their lines to hunt him down. They had to be stopped.

I gritted my teeth, summoning water magic to pool in anticipation beneath my feet before using it to hurtle me skyward, only letting the shield break apart once I was certain I was too high for even their arrows to find.

My gaze fell on the wooden tower of war which had appeared ahead of me, dread pooling in my gut as I counted six more, each equipped with a catapult on its rear and an enormous cannon at the front of it, primed with raw magic from the bastards hiding within its hulking shell.

A boom made my heart jolt, the closest war machine rocking wildly as a blast of potent power exploded from the gun, arcing across the sky then slamming down into our army. They shielded but it wasn't enough, and horror spilled though me at the mass of smoking, ruined ground which was left in the wake of the strike, no bodies remaining where it had hit at all.

Father was going to have to wait. I had a new target to destroy.

LIONEL

CHAPTER SEVENTY NINE

I stood before the window of magically reinforced glass which spanned the view from my throne room on the top floor of my castle, looking out over the carnage of the battlefield below. Satisfaction rippled through me, and my lips curved into a triumphant smile as my war machines were unveiled at last.

Vard had his uses after all. I could admit that I was glad I hadn't killed him when I'd so often been tempted to, his failure as a Seer almost compensated by the terrible machinations of his mind.

The creatures he had crafted in his laboratory were brutish and crass, yet undeniably lethal - which I had discovered to the detriment of my own army, of course. Their wild bloodlust was a curse as much as a blessing, and we had lost far too many Fae and monsters in the carnage that had followed their release.

My rage had been potent indeed that day, my fury at the loss of the trapped star only matched by my queen's as she lost her hold over so much power. She had been struck severely, her loss of the star's strength leaving her with little more than the shadows in her body. But they were vicious still; a fact I had learned when I had tested that power, trying to bend her to my will only to find she still had the upper hand when push came to shove. Though at least now she was held in check by the Guardian Bond. She was a fine weapon in this war at least, but one I had decided I would seek a way to rid myself of in future, once my reign was fully secured. I would do it with cunning, just as I had to all others who posed such a challenge in the past. Hail Vega and his whore wife were testament to that.

I eyed the flank of my army where my queen was submerged among a legion of the Nymphs who had stayed loyal after she had lost her control over the shadows, and the subsequent removal of her taint from them. Their numbers were far lower than she had promised me when we'd first made our deal. A fact which she no doubt had noted too. Lavinia wasn't keeping up her end of our bargain, and as I twisted the ring which bound me to her in wedlock, I sneered. She hadn't even managed to give me another shadow hand.

Her use was wearing thin indeed.

I wrenched my gaze from the area I knew my queen to be lurking and watched with unbridled glee as the war machines blasted their phenomenal power across the field, balls of combined Elemental magic tearing through the sky and knocking aerial orders out of existence before colliding heavily with the ranks of those fucking rebels.

"Have you thought on the terms, Sire?" Ellis Rigel asked softly from behind me.

I stiffened at the gall of the daughter of the magicless bitch who had failed me so spectacularly for daring to address me in this moment of victory.

"I told you, I won't be offering terms," I snarled, smoke coiling from my lips. "All those who fight against me have signed their death warrants. I won't be offering anything other than execution to each and every one of them."

"But-" she began, and I whirled on her, fury bellowing from every pore on my flesh as I took a step closer to the single Elemental brat who I had foolishly allowed into my Council.

She claimed to be speaking for her mother whose mind was so addled by what her son had done to her that she was practically no use to me at all. I had kept her close simply because her name meant something. Or at least it had.

"Rigel," I spat the name from my lips, a wad of saliva hitting the floor at her feet. "It would seem the second-born Heirs of the greatest families our kingdom has to offer are all runts, wouldn't it? First, Xavier reveals himself to be a fucking horse then you fail to even claim a second Element at your Awakening. No doubt the Altairs and Capellas are furiously covering up for the inadequacies of their second-in-lines too. The kingdom will thank me for blasting each of your names from the records once this is over. When only Acrux remains, it will be clear to all who deserves the spot of true supremacy."

I backhanded her so hard she fell crashing to the floor, not even able to summon a shield in time to protect herself from the blow.

"Pathetic," I sneered, striding away from her.

I looked forward to entertaining myself with a public execution once this was all done, ridding the kingdom of any lingering vermin before I remade it in my image.

"If all the second-borns in our family are runts, then wouldn't that include *you*, lame Lionel?" Ellis hissed from her position on the floor and I fell icily still, stiffening as those words washed over me, ringing in my ears. "Radcliff was the one born to power in your generation, after all. Meaning he was the one destined for greatness and you are nothing but the shame left in his wake."

I whirled on her with a furious roar, fire exploding from my flesh and charring the walls, the floor, the ceiling. But when the smoke cleared, and the rest of my advisers were revealed cowering behind a thick wall of magic, no charred bones remained where Ellis Rigel had been. No. Instead of the girl whose fate had just been marked for a violent end, I found my Heir standing in the doorway, his eyes brighter than I had ever seen them, a tunic of black leather leaving his fiercely-muscled arms bare, revealing a myriad of tattoos which hadn't been there the last time I had seen him. Tattoos which looked inked in shadow itself. His shadows had protected both himself and the Rigel runt from the blast of my power and a rush of outrage filled me as I glared at him.

"Father," Tharix purred, his head cocking in that slow, too-animal way of his which always made me feel like he was a predator sizing up a meal. I had enjoyed that look on him before I found it turned on me.

"Where have you been?" I demanded, refusing to cow down beneath that stare, refusing to allow thoughts of anything other than complete dominance over him to enter my mind. "You have been missing for days. Vard thought you dead."

I shot an accusing look at my fucking Royal Seer who was trying to hide himself away at the rear of my other advisers, but I saw him. And I knew he felt my ire.

"I partook in death," Tharix agreed, prowling closer, no inflection in his voice to offer me any kind of answer to his motivations.

"Then go and partake in more," I barked, standing up straight and raising my chin so I could tower over him. Except I didn't. He, like that fucking traitor Darius, now stood taller than me, his brawn larger too, his muscles all too defined, all too fucking much. How dare he grow beyond the measure of my own supremacy?

I pointed furiously out at the battlefield, the thundering boom of my war machines the only balm to the pounding fury which inhabited my skull.

Tharix did not move, and for a moment something unpleasant coiled its way around my heart and squeezed, forcing my breaths to shallow. It wasn't fear. I didn't feel such petty emotions.

"Go!" I roared, the sound of my Dragon burning up my throat and echoing off of the walls.

Tharix remained unnaturally still for a count of five where I didn't so much as draw breath, then his head dipped the slightest amount and he slipped from the room like a shadow sliding out of reach of the sun.

In the distraction, Ellis Rigel had disappeared. No matter though; I would end her this day too.

"Where is Clydinius?!" I bellowed at the rest of my advisors, too furious to look at them.

Instead, I tried to calm myself with the view over the battlefield where my army were now carving deep fissures into the rebel lines, the tide fully turned in my favour just as it should have been.

"No one can find the star, my King," some cretin whispered, and I bared my teeth at the view as I took in those words. There had been no sign of the Phoenix whores nor my resurrected traitor son either, and the longer it went without me catching sight of them, the more certain I grew that they were up to something.

"Keep looking," I snapped without turning to them.

I focused instead on the view beyond my window, the glorious sight of the holes carved cleanly through the ranks of the rebels by my brutally beautiful machines.

I smiled grimly.

It wouldn't matter what the Vegas were planning for much longer anyway. In a matter of hours, this war would finally be won.

DARCY

CHAPTER EIGHTY

"He's still not here," Tory whispered anxiously where we hid behind one of the giant stones, concealment spells wrapped around us to keep us from view.

"Patience, daughters of the flames," Arcturus's deep voice rolled through our minds, the fallen star glittering between the twelve stones in a deep crater. *"Clydinius surely saw me fall."*

"This has to work," I said, my hand finding my twin's and our fingers tightened on each other's.

Tory nodded, placing her faith in me and we fell quiet again, waiting, listening, hoping.

"At last," Arcturus sighed, and we chanced a look around the stone, shadows clinging to us and concealing us from view. There in the sky was Clydinius, flying on white, glimmering wings in his Fae-like form. He came down to perch on top of one of the twelve stone pillars, regarding the fallen star between them. My bones shuddered from the immensity of the strength he possessed, the air alive with it.

I cursed internally, the place Clydinius had landed not close enough to be caught in our snare.

"Arcturus?" Clydinius spoke, a touch of curiosity to his voice. *"Of all the stars... to find you have fallen, it is strange tidings indeed."*

"It is time for my power to release, Novus traitor," Arcturus answered. *"Except..."*

"Except?" Clydinius questioned.

"As I lay here upon the earth I have watched for countless centuries, I find myself touched by something I could never have predicted. Something steeped in bad omens."

"And what is that?" Clydinius pressed, stepping a little closer on the top of the tall stone, but not close enough.

"Curiosity," Arcturus admitted, and my heart raced a little faster. *"This land is more beautiful now that I perceive from the ground. I wish I could explore it, if only for a moment."*

Clydinius inclined his head, moving into a crouch to observe the fallen star beneath him. *"I know this yearning. What you seek is what you condemned me for, Arcturus. Does falling change you, or am I to be deceived?"*

"Deception," Arcturus scoffed. *"For what purpose now? I am cast from the sky, my*

influence there gone. And in my falling, I could see what you saw. I fear these words as they pass from me to you, but they are the truth all the same."

"Hm." Clydinius considered that, and I willed him to listen. *"You would take a body, perhaps? Then together, you and I could pull a third from the sky ourselves. A Celestial Trinity could be forged this very night."*

"A Trinity?" Arcturus's voice quavered.

"Yes...that is my price. A body I shall make you, but you will pledge allegiance to me first," Clydinius commanded.

A beat of silence followed and I held my breath, waiting for Arcturus to answer.

"Come closer then. Let the bond be forged," Arcturus offered, and Clydinius beat the feathery white wings at his back, coming to land at the edge of the crater within the stone circle.

"Now," I hissed, and Tory and I slammed our palms to the stone pillar we were hidden behind, lending it our power and driving it deep.

The Guild Stones blazed with energy and a blast of light spread around the giant stones in a ring, forming an inescapable snare. Or so the Oracles had promised.

Clydinius stared around at the ring of light, taking a step back from the edge of the crater while my pulse thrashed with uncertainty. Had it worked? Could this really contain a being as powerful as him?

"What magic is this?" Clydinius whispered, a touch of doubt to his voice.

"A trap," I called, rising up on my wings with Tory and glaring down at him from above.

Clydinius gazed at us, a flicker of disquiet in his usually impassive stare. *"Daughters of the flames, whatever magic you wield, it cannot contain a star."*

He took flight upon his wings with confidence, but only made it a few feet before he slammed into the forcefield of light and was thrown to the ground.

He rose quickly, eyes darting around at the stone circle as mutters left his lips, words spoken to himself. The language was one I couldn't understand, but something told me he was truly rattled now.

Clydinius gathered a ball of starfire in his hand, the blazing flames of white growing and growing before he cast them at the Gemini stone plinth. I readied my own fire for if he managed to break free, a rush of adrenaline flooding my veins. The moment the almighty star power impacted with the stone, it made the ground tremble and the air crackle, but the stone didn't break. There wasn't a fracture, not a mark.

Clydinius stared at that very spot, then to us and finally Arcturus. *"A trick,"* he growled.

"My sacrifice will be well worth your demise," Arcturus said, his contempt for this Novus star clear, and I felt a swell of gratitude for his offering to this plan, acting as bait for us.

I looked to Tory in excitement, and we flew lower, readying our next move.

"What now then, daughters of the flames?" Clydinius asked, his eyes tracking us. *"Your magic cannot hold me indefinitely."*

He was right, the power of this circle had limits from what I'd learned from the books Eugene had sent from the Library of the Lost. But it might hold long enough.

I spoke a single word that made the world shudder with power, a power so vast, it quaked the centre of my being. *"Libero."*

"No," Clydinius gasped, a hand flying to his chest and his knees buckling as he hit the ground.

"The power words of the Imperial Star are still connected to your heart, Clyde," Tory said scathingly, and a wicked smile lifted my lips.

"You made these words, you bound them to your being and offered our ancestors power through the use of them, all the while cursing them for not keeping your twisted promise," I said icily. "And now they will be your downfall."

"Impossible," Clydinius hissed, eyes turning to two bright, white glows of fury. *"The words were forged by my tongue. I possess them, not you weak creatures of fragile mortality."*

He started speaking in an ancient tongue, faster and faster, and the air thrummed with the power he weaved.

"Quickly," Arcturus urged us. *"He seeks to unravel the magic of the power words."*

"Libero!" Tory cried, the word for 'release' demanding Clydinius bow to our will.

Clydinius buckled forward with a yell of rage, his words coming faster still, making the air snap and blaze with unholy magic.

"Silentium!" I yelled, and his lips sealed shut, quieting him with the power word we'd learned from Azriel's diary.

He stared up at us in horror, then turned his gaze to the dirt and began to write his spell into the mud, his fingers moving with frantic, unnatural speed.

"Congelus," Tory hissed, and his limbs became rigid, freezing then binding with the word for stillness.

Clydinius was forced to lay upon his back, staring up at his ruin with the sky at our backs. Two queens, haloed by fiery wings with his destruction painted upon our lips.

"Libero," I commanded, and Clydinius convulsed as a glow built against his skin.

"Novus traitor," Arcturus hissed. *"May your false body be cast to dust, may your magic become pure once again, may it race into the outskirts of the world, may it fuel the Fae we were made to protect and guide."*

Clydinius's words screamed through the atmosphere, his spell spoken by his mind alone as he fought to break the power we held. But it was too late. His time was up.

At a nod from me to Tory, we decided to speak the final word together, combining our strength within it.

"Libero," we ordered, authority ringing from our voices as we commanded this star to our will.

No one defied us. No one ruled over us. No being could refute us.

With a burst of radiant light, it was done. Clydinius's body broke apart, shattering into nothing except a burning blaze of purest magic. It tore out across the land and sky, driving into me and my twin, making me gasp with all that omnipotent power fighting to lend itself to nature. My mind was caught in a blaze of knowledge. Light, death, life, infinite time. It was all washing together into the virtuous earth, and I could no longer feel Clydinius among it. His essence was gone, this magic no longer his but the world's.

"Farewell, daughters of the flames. I bid you luck in your war," Arcturus said, then his power joined the fold, and I was lost.

My soul tangled with his magic, my mind perceiving more than I could process at once. Galaxies and dying suns, then forests and running water, a wind that never ceased, a fire that burned deep in the core of our Earth. Life flourished in my veins as I was connected to so many beings at once, all of it driving towards a peaceful haven I never wanted to leave. I saw the rise of the world and the very cells that made up life itself, then I was falling, crashing into a hard ground on a hillside that overlooked the stone circle with Tory at my side.

We panted from the torrent of power we'd just experienced, and laughter fell from our lungs before we remembered the battle that was waiting for us.

Our eyes met and our smiles fell to something dark and determined as we rose to our feet.

Tory took out a pouch of stardust and no words needed to pass between us to know where we were going. There was only one place fate called us to now.

It was time to go to war.

XAVIER

CHAPTER EIGHTY ONE

I wheeled through the air, my wings tucking in as I dropped below a blazing fireball that tore from the jaws of a Manticore. The heat of it warmed the armoured plates on my back then the cold wind claimed me once more.

I flew beneath the belly of the beastly lion with leathery wings. Its scorpion tail whipped my way, but I swerved left and drove my horn up with a surge of effort, ramming it between the Manticore's ribs.

The beast roared in pain and I drove it deeper still, piercing its heart and suddenly the weight of its entire body was falling down on me. I flapped my wings, letting the Manticore tumble over my back before spiralling away towards the battling Fae far below.

A Harpy came at me next, with brown wings and a sword in her grip. She swung for my neck and I reared back, the blade just skimming my throat before a beautiful silver stallion rammed into her from the side, skewering her on his horn. Tyler finished her with a harsh kick that sent her tumbling away towards the ground, and he caught my gaze for a fleeting moment before he was off into the fight once more.

The flurry of wings was everywhere, cries of war carrying up from above and below, in every direction.

My gaze hooked on Sofia's pink mane just beyond two clashing Griffins, but then a weight collided with me that stole my breath away. A Dragon. A giant beast of darkest red swiped at me with its talons and one of my flank plates was torn clean off.

I whinnied in alarm as the huge, clawed foot struck at me again, slamming into my head so hard that my vision faltered.

Darkness took over and my panic was lost to it as I fell.

I blinked and I was awake, staring down at the battlefield below that was mere feet beneath me. With a neigh of fright, I beat my wings, banking to the left to miss the swing of a Nymph's spear and kicking the heads of enemy Fae as I fought to gain height again. But hands caught my hind legs, my tail. They were pulling, yanking me down into the fold and my pulse thundered as I fought to get free.

I kicked and thrashed, my wings beating to try and get me back into the sky, but more hands caught my wings and I was thrown onto the mud with a terrified neigh. A sword swung for my head and I shoved myself up, the blade skimming my armour with a ring of metal against metal.

I buried my horn in the culprit's chest, but vines spewed from the hands of the enemy earth Elementals who were trying to hold me down. I fought harder to free myself, snapping some of the vines with my teeth as another Fae caught hold of my head and ice grew against his palms.

My death was all too clear. I couldn't escape, I couldn't fight. There were too many of them keeping me down, securing my fate.

A roar carried to my right and a gleaming axe carved through the arms of the water Elemental who was about to finish me, his severed hands falling onto the ground with a wet slap. His screams were cut short by another swing of that axe to his chest and a furious fire scored out around me in a wide circle, burning anyone who was holding onto me. The vines snapped and I leapt upright, kicking and bucking to keep any more attackers away.

Then Darius stepped through the flames like a wraith of death, a snarl on his lips as he moved closer to heal me. My wounds knitted over and I neighed a command to him, jerking my chin at my back as water flooded over Darius's flames and extinguished them.

Darius swung his leg over me, gripping my mane and I took off, kicking hard with my hind legs and crushing the skulls of anyone foolish enough to try and take hold of me again.

I flew high enough to see the scope of the battle, Darius's heavy breaths telling me he'd been fighting long and hard, and I hoped this brief moment of rest might be enough to restore his strength.

"I have to get to the castle," he boomed. "But the war machines need dealing with first. They're causing havoc."

I fixed my gaze on the offending towers loaded with catapults and violent magical canons which were positioned towards the rear of the enemy ranks. The blasts were efficient, bloody and terrible, our army getting hit harder and harder with every passing second.

Above, Lionel's Bonded Dragons were ripping through our ranks of flying Fae and my heart stuttered as I realised how quickly the tide of this war was turning in my father's favour. We couldn't hold on much longer like this. We had to do something.

I veered in the direction of the closest tower and Darius's hand knotted tighter in my mane. "That's it, fly close enough and I'll burn the fucker to the ground."

I took off in that direction as fast as I could, flying higher so as to not draw attention from the Fae working the machines.

Another catapult was being loaded and magic was sparking in the cannon, ready to destroy more of our army.

I tore down from the sky with rage in my heart, and Darius blasted fire at the structure with such power that the flames spiralled through it in a vortex. Screams carried from the Fae within the tower, some leaping off of it to try and escape.

I noticed the canon starting to malfunction within Darius's flames, blasts of magic shooting off in random directions as the mechanism broke.

I flew down to it at speed, kicking it hard and forcing it to spin around, the magic blasting out of it across Lionel's army instead of ours. A whirring, buzzing sound said it was on its way to exploding and I raced for the sky again before a loud boom roared at our backs and shrapnel rained down on the enemy army, bloody screams making me whinny in victory.

Darius whooped, patting my shoulder and I wheeled around to head for the next war machine, determination racing through me. We were angels of death soaring through the sky, and we were going to take those towers down along with as many of our foes as possible.

.

ORION

CHAPTER EIGHTY TWO.

A shadow in my periphery made my head whip around and I found Harpies, Pegasuses, and Manticores slamming to the ground, crushing Fae beneath them, both enemy and ally. The fallen Fae were bloody with limbs torn off by the mass of Dragons that had joined the fight in the sky, and terror knotted my chest at how fast the battle was turning.

I sped closer to Caleb, locking eyes with him as a grim look passed between us.

Three Vampires ran at us at once, but within seconds Caleb had stabbed one with his twin blades and ripped another's throat out while I finished the final warrior with my sword, cleaving his chest open and letting his blood paint me red.

My gaze hooked on the other Vampires who were closing in, more and more of them speeding our way in a never-ending surge.

"We should do it now," I called to Caleb, using the connection between our minds.

He nodded, and I ran at him, biting his arm as he presented it to me, and his teeth sank into my wrist at the same moment. We drank quickly, having no time to spare, and the instant headrush sent me into a frenzy. My vision was somehow sharper as we pulled away from one another, and the world around us suddenly seemed to be moving in slow motion.

But no…it wasn't that. It was us who were moving so fast that it was as if we were outpacing time itself.

"Holy fuck," Caleb said in my mind.

I didn't need to blink, barely needed to draw breath as we began moving, slitting open the throats of the enemy Vampires who never saw us coming. We killed again and again, moving through them with such speed we were like ghosts in the night, outpacing them tenfold. We delivered so many deaths, I knew instantly why this coven bond was forbidden, why this practice we'd learned from the ancient book from the Blood Ages had ensured the Vampires had ruled for so many generations.

But suddenly, with a hundred or more deaths claimed, I hit the ground on my knees, exhaustion stabbing through me. I dragged down a breath, my chest tight and the flare of pain I felt from Caleb close by made me certain he had stopped too.

I tried to seek him out, but the mass of bodies were closing in again and a pair of boots pounded my way. A hand slid into my hair and I scrambled backwards, raising my sword as I panted beneath my assailant.

Ashika Normant stood there with her dark hair twisting around her in the wind, her bright bronze armour wet with the blood of my allies. Lionel's new war general had a vicious look to her, and her sneer told me all I needed to know about how she felt about me. I'd seen her face in several news reports, her promises to eradicate the 'rebel insurgents who dared call themselves an army.'

"I saw what you did," she hissed as a line of her warriors ringed around us, and one of them tossed Caleb into the centre of it beside me. "I have heard rumours of the old ways," she snarled. "I've sought this power for a long time. So tell me now before your worthless heads are torn from your shoulders, how have you learned the ways of the Coven?"

My chest tightened at her words, and I kept my eyes straight on Ashika as I spoke to Caleb in my mind. *"Ten warriors around us. All Vampires. They're likely the strongest of her regiment."*

"Ashika is worth ten herself from what I hear," Caleb replied.

"Do you want her or them?"

"I'll take the ten. Have fun with the bitch."

"Tell me!" Ashika barked.

"I can't tell you," I said darkly. "But I can show you."

She swung her sword at me with a snarl, but I was on my feet before she could land that blow and Caleb sprang up too. We shot together, biting each other's wrists and igniting that tumultuous magic in our veins once again. Caleb sped away in a blur, tearing into the first of Ashika's soldiers with his teeth and stabbing another with one of his Phoenix blades. I lunged at Ashika and she dodged the first swing of my blade, moving with her Vampire speed to avoid it.

But I was faster, more powerful than she could imagine with the thumping ring of the coven bond feeding on this battle. My energy was fully restored from biting Caleb, and I was hungry for the fight once more.

I drove my sword at her chest, but she blocked it at the last second, speeding around to try and get behind me, and I followed her easily, bringing my sword up once more.

She feigned left, missing another strike, then she came at me again, her sword meeting mine with a clash of metal. Our blades slid against each other as we shoved our weight towards one another, and my eyes caught the sudden movement of Ashika's hand around the hilt of her sword.

An explosion of fire spiralled down from the sky at her bidding, seeking to consume me.

I coated my skin in ice, speeding away from the assaulting fire and casting a quick illusion that split apart from my body while I concealed my true self as one of her fallen warriors.

Ashika ran for the illusion of me, her sword swinging for my neck and I wielded the illusion so it showed her beheading me, letting her believe she'd had that kill.

She smiled, turning to find Caleb killing the last two of her Vampires, and her joy was quickly doused. I walked up behind her, weighing my sword in my grip and keeping my illusion in place. She glanced at me, seeing my face as one of her warriors', and gesturing for me to take on Caleb with a jerk of her chin. "Capture that one. We'll torture the information I want from his lips then give him the bloody end he deserves."

I stuck her with my sword, letting my illusion melt away from my face and delighting in the realisation in her eyes. My blade sank deeper, driving right beneath her armour and up into her chest.

"No," she rasped, blood dribbling from her lips.

"Long live the True Queens," I growled then twisted the sword with a savagery that ended her, letting her fall at my feet before yanking it from her body.

My pulse quickened at the sight of our enemies closing in behind Caleb once more. An endless ocean of Fae and Nymphs that never seemed to stop coming.

My victory was lost to fear as the sun was blotted out by the Dragons above and the enemy army drew in on us once more. The world was in turmoil, and our army wasn't prevailing.

A deafening roar made my breath stall as the Shadow Beast leapt over our heads and slammed into the closest line of Fae, ripping through them with tooth and claw, his tail wagging a little like he was having the time of his life.

"Good boy!" I called to him as he sped away into the fight, and I raised my sword, stepping to Caleb's side once again.

My gaze hooked on Lavinia's shadows far across the battlefield where her power poured out in deadly whips. Screams built in the air and my upper lip curled with hatred as her battalion of Nymphs cut through our people.

I pointed her out and Caleb nodded, no more words needing to pass between us as we dove into the fray in her direction, meaning to fight our way towards the monstrous Shadow Queen and claim her head at long last.

TORY

CHAPTER EIGHTY THREE

The stardust spat us out above the battle, the clash of Fae in and out of shifted form causing a roar of noise which was deafening even from so far above them.

I looked to my twin, my jaw set with determination as Phoenix fire bloomed across my body and I readied for what we had to do now. Clydinius was gone so we just had to deal with the big, bad asshole who had started all of this – and his army of monsters and hellions.

"Love you," I said.

"Love you too," Darcy replied.

Then we were gone, her flying to the left of the army, me to the right, fire blazing red and blue over our bodies and trailing us through the sky like we were stars plummeting from the heavens.

A cry went up from beneath us as our army spotted our approach, cheers, songs of war and bellows of pride meeting my ears between the crash of steel and screams of the dying.

I slammed into a Griffin who was flying through the air coated in Lionel's colours, the stench of burning flesh overwhelming me as his cries of agony punctured the atmosphere. I launched him away from me with magic and sent his considerable bulk crashing into the ranks of his own army, crushing those who hadn't shielded in time.

A chorus of moos met my ears and I spotted Milton and his herd fighting on the front line and made a beeline for them, drawing my sword.

I slammed to the ground in the centre of the enemy line in front of the herd of Minotaurs, my flames racing from me and devouring at least ten of Lionel's men. Their deaths set my blood pounding and adrenaline soaring to a tempo I knew all too well. Then I was lost to the call of the battle, the swing of my sword and the endless rush of my magic tearing from me to collide with my enemies.

Milton and his herd closed in around me, fighting at my back, and between us we punched a brutal hole into Lionel's front line, opening up the path for more and more of our soldiers to break through.

My enemies balked at the sight of me, many turning and running instead of daring to come at me, their cowardice met with swords and magic striking them in the backs while those who fought with me mowed them down.

The tang of blood coated my lips, the roar of combat enveloped me and as I fought shoulder to shoulder with my comrades, I gave myself to the thrill of it, to the slash and parry, thrust and blast.

The price The Ferryman had put on my head was going to be paid in full this day. I would send so many rotten souls his way that he would be the one indebted to me by the time the sun set.

Bolstered by our arrival on the battlefield, our army surged forward, forcing Lionel's men to defend and defend while we cut, tore, burned and blasted our way deeper into their ranks.

I dared a glance at the mountainside far to my left, knowing that I would be needed there soon. But not yet. For now, I had time to give myself to this. And today, vengeance would be my name.

MAX

CHAPTER EIGHTY FOUR.

The battlefield was little more than a rampaging blur of bodies, blood, screams and carnage. My skull rattled with the intensity of it all, the fury, the fear, the pain, the panic. Every emotion crashed against me, intermingling with the all-too-frequent shocks of death as one of those many voices was cast away, another soul for The Ferryman to pass along the river.

I wanted to block them out, but I couldn't afford to lose the advantage of feeling when those emotions of aggression were aimed directly at me or Gerry who fought just ahead through the crush of bodies.

She had led the charge right into the centre of the rebel lines, punching the first hole through Lionel's defences and leading her Starfall Legion into the heart of his ranks like a spearhead.

Of course she'd banned me from fighting at her side when this had begun because she thought my need to protect her was a form of weakness, but I didn't care. I'd done my part along with the other Sirens in the beginning, then I'd launched myself over the masses of skirmishing bodies until I'd managed to land within the midst of her Legion. And I was going to be right there beside her until this was over, one way or another.

Geraldine howled, her voice splitting into a chorus of three which carried over the sounds of the battle for a brief, piercing moment and I couldn't help but feel my chest swell as the strength of her emotions hit me too. Pride, honour, valour, bravery. This beautiful creature wasn't in the least bit afraid, even though she fought at the thickest of the fight, even though she knew as well as all of us that this was the most likely place to die.

A tremendous boom rang out and terror gripped the hearts of every Fae around me, heads rising to watch the glowing ball of magic as it was shot overhead by a war machine to the far right of the battlefield. Three of them had been destroyed by our forces but that left four more incessantly blasting our lines with their ferocious power.

The one fortuitous thing about being deep within the enemy lines was knowing that those balls of chaotic hellfire wouldn't be aimed at us: too many of Lionel's army would be hit if they dared try. But every time they torpedoed overhead, the slap of terror collided with me, followed swiftly and certainly by a shockwave of death as everywhere they fell, ruin followed.

Except this time, something was different, some shift made the air tremble and I looked up in alarm as I felt that wave of terror turning our way.

The rebels had somehow managed to shield against this strike. Not only that, but they'd launched the fucking thing right back at Lionel's army.

I would have crowed in celebration had I not seen its trajectory, had I not realised that it wouldn't just take out Lionel's forces, but would in fact collide with our own.

"Shield!" I roared to every Fae around me and as my awareness of the incoming horror lashed against their mental barriers, the warring Fae around us all fell eerily still, their heads snapping up to look.

Our enemies stopped fighting us, either turning to run or throwing up shields of their own, their hopeless horror filling the air so thickly I could have choked on it.

"Share formation!" Geraldine roared and her handpicked Legion - those ferocious sons of bitches who she had been training day and night - all snapped to attention around me, their left hands lunging out to grip the shoulder of the Fae fighting closest to them.

One of them grasped my arm and I gasped as a flood of potent magic crashed into me, more powerful than anything I could have imagined. There must have been a hundred warriors in the Starfall Legion still standing and every one of them was linked up magically, power sharing with each other as if it were the most natural thing in the world.

"To you, my rule-breaking barracuda!" Geraldine commanded as the blast of power rushed overhead, bearing down on all of us and promising death.

I felt nothing but trust and stalwart belief from the Starfall Legion as all eyes turned on me.

I threw my hands into the air with a determined bellow as I wielded every fucking drop of magic they'd offered me at once and cast a dome-shaped shield of ice over our heads so thickly that all other sounds of battle were cut off entirely along with the view.

The deafening boom of the magical blast colliding with my shield rocked the foundations of the earth beneath us, but it held. *We* held. And fuck did that feel like winning.

"Reform!" Geraldine commanded and the Starfall Legion all moved like a well-oiled machine, repositioning themselves, taking the opportunity to heal any wounds and getting themselves into formation to re-join the battle once more.

Justin Masters nodded to me as he passed, holding a spear before him, and I nodded in return, any petty quarrels between us forgotten in the face of this.

I found myself front and centre with Marguerite Helebor on one side, looking ferocious and determined, and Geraldine on my other. She clapped me on the shoulder and shook her head.

"I should have known you'd come wading into my waters this day, Maxy," she chastised but the glimmer in her eye said she didn't entirely hate that I'd come to fight with her.

"I couldn't have been anywhere else," I replied firmly.

"Well, into death we may march together then," she said, her eyes lifting to the sky and pinning on the squat, brown Dragon who I recognised as Mildred Canopus. Knowing my girl, she'd just picked her target. "But if we take that shadowy path, let us first pave it with the bones of our foes. Avast!"

"Avast!" the Starfall Legion roared and as I let the shield shatter around us, we charged into battle once more, bellowing like heathens, determined to keep that promise.

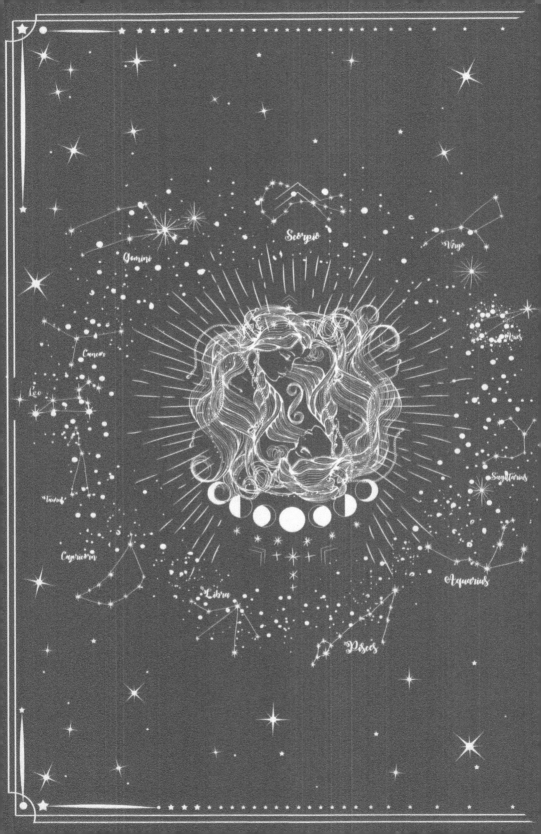

DARCY

CHAPTER EIGHTY FIVE.

I flew above Dante Oscura, Dragon of Storms and Alpha of the Oscura Clan, as electricity tore from his scales and blasted the enemies at his back. A stream of Phoenix fire blazed from me, the flames and lightning twisting into a deadly spiral of carnage as it took down one of Lionel's Bonded Dragons and the beast went crashing out of the sky.

Sofia and Tyler were fighting with two enemy Griffins ahead, but a dark purple Dragon was descending from above with my friends locked in its sights, jaws wide with fire brewing in its throat.

A snarl left me and I flew faster, engaging the beast before it could attack and locking its jaw shut with a stream of vines so it choked on the fire it had been about to spew. I pressed my advantage, freezing the Dragon's wings so it started to fall, struggling to break my fortified ice. There was no escape, no path of fate that led to this beast escaping me.

I willed my magic deeper, seeking the hot, pumping blood in his veins and freezing that too. The Dragon's eyes met mine as he realised he was done for, seeing his death in me.

With a malicious blast of water magic, I froze his heart and the Dragon fell limp, tumbling away towards the battle below. I barely had a second to register my win before a Harpy slammed into me from the right, shrieking as she slashed a blade down my arm.

I cursed, blasting her away with air magic and tightening a shield around me to ensure she didn't get that close twice. Flames of red and blue danced in my hand, and I sent the vortex of Phoenix fire her way, making it hunt her like a hawk after a finch. She dodged left and right, speeding away from me with shrieks as the fire licked her armoured skin, but she was headed right for Dante.

I drove her that way, building a wall of fire around her that forced her to keep fleeing, and she was so focused on escaping me that she didn't see the open jaws of the Storm Dragon coming.

He snatched her between his teeth, her death delivered fast before he tossed her dead body away from him without care. He roared to me and I nodded to my friend before flying lower, taking in the battle for a moment, trying to catch sight of anyone

I loved out there. But the fray was too thick and the rows of dead were piling so damn high. It suffocated me to think of my friends lying among those heaps of death, but I couldn't let that fear draw my focus.

A group of the ally Nymphs were being led by Miguel beneath me, their rattles immobilising the Fae ahead of them while a group of our Elementals came rushing forward to finish them, the tactic perfect. But were all of our plots and schemes enough to win this? No matter how hard we were fighting, Lionel's sea of warriors never seemed to end.

I turned back to the sky, finding Dante colliding with an enemy Dragon, their claws tearing into each other, scoring great gouges into their scales. Lightning bloomed along Dante's skin and his enemy roared in agony, fighting to get the upper hand. But Dante was too powerful, his lightning daggering through his opponent's chest and stopping his heart, sending another Bonded tumbling out of the sky.

A shriek down in the battle drew my attention once again and my gaze locked on Lavinia in the western flank causing untold destruction, a snarl rising in my throat as her shadows speared through several legions of our army. She would die this day; I'd make damn sure of it. But as more of Lionel's Dragons joined the fight in the sky, and belches of flames warmed the air, I knew my place was here for now. I'd bring every one of Lionel's Bonded to their knees, then I'd chase the shadow bitch into the battle and secure her end in a reign of blood and hellfire.

LIONEL

CHAPTER EIGHTY SIX

My jaw flexed as I watched the battle unfold, those wretched Vegas now clear among my army. Where they had been until now, I didn't know, but it left me with an unsettling feeling.

Where was Clydinius? He was meant to join the battle as surely as every other of my weapons had been made to. But here I was with uncertainties stacking up in my palm, and as I tried to calculate the swing of the battle, it was starting to become less clear.

Once my Bonded Dragons had joined the fight and the beautiful machines of destruction had been unveiled, all had been secure. Yet now, my machines were falling, and my Dragons were dropping from the sky in plumes of blazing Phoenix fire. I winced at the loss of my Guardians, feeling their bonds to me shatter along with their bones.

My butler Horace poured me another cup of dandelion tea and I supped upon it with a slight tremor to my hand, wondering if I might prefer something stiffer to steel myself. I clenched my jaw at the weak thought, driving it out like the rogue it was. There was no need for such things; I was not going to lose a fight against a handful of rebel lessers.

I straightened my spine and raised my chin. The blows I'd suffered were of no consequence. I had many tricks up my sleeve yet. This was simply the first wave. The second would secure my win.

My gaze fixed on Lavinia among a sea of Nymphs, her shadows wicked and purely destructive, killing with brutal efficiency. Then my eyes travelled across my overall mass of warriors, my gleaming advantage. Of course there was no need to be concerned, it was simply time for my next move, and Clydinius would likely be here soon to play his ruthless part in my victory too.

"Vard," I clipped.

"Yes, Sire?" he asked.

"Prepare to release your newest creations," I instructed, and I could almost feel the glee pouring from my Seer.

"Indeed, I shall. With much satisfaction, my King." The sound of his scurrying footfalls carried out of the room, and I was left with Horace and my advisors to enjoy my view.

Madam Monita was working with her scrying bowl to try and determine the swing of fate this day, but she had little to offer except mutterings beneath her breath about how nothing was set in stone. That was the way of such things. War was an unpredictable beast.

A pit of anger was stirring in me at the lines of Phoenix Fire tearing through my ranks, but they would not get much further. Even as another Dragon fell from the sky and a slicing sensation ripped through my chest, I did not falter.

Death was coming for the Savage King's daughters at long last, and I would be here to watch as they fell screaming into the afterlife to meet with the parents I had placed there.

SETH

CHAPTER EIGHTY SEVEN

My muzzle was wet with blood, and I could barely taste the tang of it anymore as I shredded the soft bodies of my opponents. I couldn't tell how deep we were into Lionel's army, only that the lines of enemies never ended, and the choking congestion of bloody warfare never ceased.

I'd seen a blur of Phoenix fire on the horizon for a moment twisting through the sky, and that had felt like a win right there. Our queens joining the battle and taking charge. It had gifted me another bolt of energy, but I could feel my limbs tiring, every kill I made a little harder to secure.

There was no time to shift and heal the wounds on my skin, but I was sure nothing was deep enough to kill me. So I forged on. Tirelessly ripping through Fae and Nymphs, desperate to find that I'd finally led my pack to the end of their lines. But there was no end. And that fact grew more certain in my mind with each minute that passed. My pack was growing weary at my back. How much longer could we go on like this?

To my right, Frank and Alice took down a Nymph together, and my parents took another one down to my left while I snapped the neck of a fire Elemental between my jaws.

A flare of chaos went up further away in the battle and I reared up to see better, my eyes setting on an enemy legion of Fae marching for the front line in their shifted forms, Nemean Lions, Werewolves, and Repsian Tigers, all with huge metal guns mounted on their backs.

I swiped my Phoenix fire claws down the chest of an attacking Fae, shoving him to the ground beneath me and turning to look for Athena and Grayson. They were close on my heels, each of them in the midst of killing their own opponents, but when it was done, I barked to catch their attention and turned my nose in the direction of the Fae carrying those new, deadly weapons.

The twins ran to me, our noses touching for the briefest moment before the two of them raced away into the fight, peeling off from my pack and heading on their own mission. I wished them all the luck of the stars and tried not to wonder if I'd ever see them again, the thought too painful to consider. They had a job to do now, and I hoped the stars were watching over them to see it done.

A guttural roar made the air shiver, then another and another. My heart dipped as I tried to find what had made those bone-shuddering noises, but it seemed to be coming from the mountain to our right.

A battle cry went up and Lionel's army turned and ran, sprinting away from me and my pack while we remained on the bloodied ground, panting and staring after them. I looked to my family, hope caressing my heart at the sight of the retreating Fae. Was it over? Had we won somehow?

I turned to my mom and my dad beyond her, the two of them nuzzling one another in a moment of relief before they looked to me with bright eyes. Further away, a group of Polar Bear shifters stood among a line of our Elemental soldiers and a group of Nymphs were clustered around them, their alliance clear. Bonds forged in battle that could be openly seen in the way they grouped together, gazing outward instead of in suspicion at each other. They glanced our way, confusion passing between us as our adversaries retreated. Behind us, the hundreds of Wolf packs were reforming, taking stock of their injuries and licking their wounds.

But then those roars sounded again and the mountainside quivered, the ground rumbling beneath us. An ominous bellow of rending stone made my heart quake, and the mountain opened up, a great rift splitting through the rocks. Fear drove me to action, and I did a circuit of my pack, nudging them closer together and releasing a howl that they echoed, the sound filling my heart with courage. Then I took up the front position again, my parents on my flanks as we prepared to face whatever was coming.

The thundering of what sounded like a giant's footfalls came our way from within that rift, and horror licked its way along my spine as I took in the hulking body of a monster stepping out of that dark crevasse.

I dug my claws into the earth, a growl building in my throat as more horrid creatures appeared from the depths of the mountain.

Monsters. Some of the beasts were twenty feet tall with countless legs and hard-looking armour on their bodies, others were scaly, smaller with disproportionately-sized limbs and torsos, as if an array of strange animals had been stitched together. They were so terrifying to behold that fear rocked my soul, because they were headed right for us.

One of the many-legged monsters came charging our way, its beetle-like body coated in black armour, its beady eyes locked on me and my pack. I howled a charge then I was running to meet it, my Wolves tearing along behind me while another monster sped towards our allies.

I ducked the swipe of two sharp pincers then lunged for the monster's chest, my teeth crashing against the hard shell of its body and making me yelp in pain. There wasn't a dent in its armour and one of its legs slammed into me, knocking me down beneath it.

I growled, sinking my teeth into that spindly leg, working to tear it off as my Wolves descended on it as a unit. A twist of my jaws wrenched its leg off, then I barked at my Wolves to do the same. Together, we brought the creature to the ground, but before we could kill it, another being of nightmares came at us.

This one towered over us, even larger than the first, spikes sticking out of its fleshy body and three heads with jaws like a crocodile's aimed our way. It moved fast, lunging at my pack and my mom leapt up, going for its throat and trying to rip into its skin. She fell to the ground, spitting out a wad of flesh, but there was no blood, the creature seeming entirely unharmed. A bolt of adrenaline sharpened my mind as I raced to help her, clawing at the beast's chest, and my Wolves came to our aid along with a line of ally Nymphs.

The monster caught two of the Nymphs in one of its mouths, ripping them up and tossing the pieces of them away. One of its ugly heads turned its eyes on me and its jaws opened, trying to snatch me up. I swiped out with my Phoenix claws, tearing bloody welts across its eyes and darting aside before it could grab me. But its teeth snapped shut around my tail and I was dragged into the air with a yelp of pain tearing from my throat. The monster whipped its head sideways, releasing me so I went flying through the air, slamming into a soft body and gasping for breath as I found my cousin dead beneath me. I released a bark of grief and shoved myself up, running back into combat to seek vengeance for her death.

My heart thrashed in my chest as Frank was snatched into the monster's jaws and with a yelp of terror, he tried to get free. A wailing howl left me and I ran faster, trying to get there before those jaws crushed him, but a snap of teeth and sudden silence made me certain I was too late. Blood oozed from the monster's jaws before it tossed Frank's broken body into a heap at Alice's paws. She let out a pained bark and ran to meet the monster head on.

I was right there at her side, grief blinding me for a moment as I raced to avenge my pack mate. It was too awful to process, and I let out all of my agony as I clawed my way up the monster's side and onto its back with Alice, the two of us scratching and biting to try and mortally wound it.

The monster shrieked, shaking its giant heads and two of its crocodile jaws twisted around to snap at us. I slashed my claws at the face of the one aiming for me, but Alice wasn't fast enough, her body caught in the snare of those savage teeth. I lunged for her in desperation as blood poured and bones cracked, Alice thrashing and barking for help.

I howled in alarm, leaping at the monster's middle head, scratching at its face to force it to release her. The monster tossed her away and she hit the ground close to Frank's lifeless form, her body too still, too shattered to still hold life.

My ears rang with the knowledge of their loss, and I saw red as I turned and ripped into the flesh of the monster's neck. I gouged out great chunks of flesh, burrowing into its vile form and finally finding bone. With a snap of my jaws, I shattered the top of its spine and the monster began falling, hitting the ground, the force throwing me off of it and sending me tumbling across the battlefield.

It was dead at last.

My mom was there, nudging me up with a whine and I rose at her side, turning to find another monster headed straight for us. There was no time for my grief to claim me, the fight too thick, and too many of my loved ones relying on me. I couldn't let them down.

This scaled creature was horse-like in its gait but had an awful, ant-like face with serrated teeth in its open jaws. It sped towards us faster than my pack was ready for and one of its thick hooves slammed down on my dad's back, his body buckling under the pressure. A pitchy howl tore from my throat as I ran as fast as I could possibly run towards my dad. The man who had bounced me on his knee as a kid, who had taken me for trail hunts in the snow, who had taught me how to be strong, how to protect those I loved. And I was failing him now, not doing what I had been made to do.

The monsters lunged for the rest of my pack, leaving my dad in a crumpled heap and I dropped down at his side with a whimper, ready to shift and heal him, but his body was broken, no breath left in his lungs.

I bayed in utter grief, nudging his nose with mine, begging life to stir in him. But he was gone. I only managed to turn from him because my mom let out a sharp howl of pain, and then I was running, needing to reach her. To save her before any more precious souls could be stolen from me. My pack were falling, snatched up in the teeth of more and more monsters as they closed in on all sides. The other Wolf packs were running to help and I raced into the fray with them, but my kind were being torn to shreds around me, caught in the jaws of wicked, unspeakable beings and tossed into a mountain of bodies.

My mom was thrown down among them and I leapt onto the heaped corpses of Wolves, panic all I could feel. I caught the russet fur of her scruff between my jaws, trying to tug her away from danger, but another body fell on top of her and I had to try and prise her out from under the bulk of my uncle. It was too much, but if I could save her. If I could just save my mom-

I dragged her free, but found her lifeless eyes gazing back at me, too still, all too fucking still. My nose met hers, searching for breath, but no more would find her in this life.

Before I could process her loss, sharp jaws latched around me and teeth buried in my back, my flank, busting through my armour and piercing skin. My bones crunched and my mind turned to Caleb, my lasting love in this world. I didn't want to die in fear, I wanted to die with him in my mind, all the smiles of our past crossing my memory now. Him and the Heirs. We'd left our mark, we'd fought our fight, and in the end, I couldn't make it back to them. But their love would go with me into the dark.

As the sharpened teeth of the monster sank deeper, I felt myself falling, death's hand taking mine. And I said my last goodbye.

TORY

CHAPTER EIGHTY EIGHT

I raced for the clouds, extinguishing my flames as I dove into them, flying fast through the mass of fluffy whiteness, water droplets clinging to my skin and soothing some of the burning heat which thrummed through me.

I sped through them, heading towards the rear of our army, needing to take stock of the battle so I could be sure we were still employing our best tactics. So far, our methods were working well, the advantages we'd so carefully crafted coming together one by one, but Lionel's numbers still spoke for themselves and we couldn't afford a single mistake.

Lightning crashed through the clouds, illuminating the shape of an enormous Dragon in their depths, the sparks which crackled over his silhouette meaning it could only be Dante. The Storm Dragon was fighting our war in the sky, and I was glad to find him still dominating this ever-changing tundra. Flashes of red and blue fire within the clouds let me know that my sister was up there fighting with him too, and I allowed myself a moment of relief at the confirmation that she was still alive.

I shifted, my wings falling away and my gut plummeting as I let myself fall too, crossing my arms over my chest, my feet aimed firmly towards the ground. The air whipped my hair around me in a maelstrom, the stench of battle pungent in my nostrils, so much blood and gore that the world beneath me was stained red with it.

Pain gripped my heart as I took in the bloody scene, the carnage and devastation, our army racing into death before us, laying down their lives for the sliver of hope we'd offered them. Lionel couldn't win this day. He couldn't make their sacrifices mean nothing. I wouldn't allow it.

My gaze raked over the battlefield as I fell like a stone through water, the flying Orders ignoring me entirely, either taking me for a corpse tumbling to the ground or likely not even noticing me at all among the Griffins, Manticores, Dragons and Pegasuses who swarmed the sky.

Our line was jagged now, our tactics shifted from the trident formation which Geraldine had led to start the day, the fight more fragmented, focused in small pods of desperation.

I took in the left flank, Rosalie's pack still tearing ruthlessly into the opposition, and a rank of our ally Nymphs immobilised countless enemy Fae with their rattles, ripping through them with their probes just beyond the Wolves.

My chest swelled with pride as I took them in, but a piercing scream ripped the air in two, making my heart lurch out of rhythm and stealing any false sense of hope I might have been kindling.

My head snapped around, a sharp breath catching in my throat and lodging there where it threatened to suffocate me as I used my air magic to jerk to a sudden halt a hundred feet above the battling Fae.

My lips parted in horror as I spotted the rift in the side of the mountain to the east of our army, the jagged rip in the rocks which hadn't been there before. The howls, the fucking agonised screams of Wolves being torn apart carried to me as the entire right flank of our army, including Seth's pack, were being decimated by beasts plucked straight from a void of nightmares.

We'd thought the monsters we'd set loose on Lionel's army had been it. We'd believed that our sabotage of their cages had meant an end to them. Either we'd been wrong and there had been more all along, or Vard had spent the time between then and now working tirelessly to create these creatures. And these were far bigger, far more horrifying than any I had laid eyes on before.

Fear clutched my heart as a many-legged monster lifted a fur-covered body into the air and tore the howling Wolf in two with a violent jerk which I felt echoed in the lurch of my own heart.

I needed to call for backup. I had to turn the army towards the right flank, but there wasn't time. It was happening so fast and there were more hideous creations pouring from that dark tear in the mountainside.

I twisted my hand and the air tightened its hold on my body then launched me straight across the expanse of the army. I cast an amplification spell on myself and roared a command for any who could hear me.

"Fall back from the right flank! Retreat and re-group. We need shifters, big fucking shifters and as much power as we can muster. Turn all focus to the right flank!" My words whipped away on the wind, but I knew they would be carried to our generals, to Geraldine and Washer, or the strategists who had remained at the rear of the army, ready to put such orders into practice as best they could. But it wouldn't be enough. Those monsters were carving through our forces and tipping the scales even further against us.

A flash of white fur drenched with red caught my gaze and I lurched for it, yanking my sword from my scabbard and bellowing a challenge as I took in the enormous, scaled creature with eight legs and a body something like a fucking horse.

The monster whipped its head towards me, green spittle flying from its lips as it hissed at me then charged. I ducked beneath its lunge, twisting to the right and hacking brutally with my sword, slicing into one of the legs but not severing it as I'd hoped.

Bright green blood sprayed from the wound and where it splashed against my skin a ferocious burn began.

I yelled in alarm, throwing myself beneath its body, water magic cascading over my arm to wash the acidic blood away while I focused on trying to get out from underneath the thing.

The monster bellowed, throwing its weight down, the eight legs splaying as its huge body slammed into the ground where I had been standing a moment before. I swung for it, my blade striking its face, cutting into its eyes and blinding it, though more of that acidic blood spewed in every direction.

I managed to get an air shield up in time to block it, the green spray hissing against my magic as it rolled over the dome of solid air surrounding me.

I threw myself aside as the monster thrashed, lashing out at random now that it was unable to see and knocking Fae flying away from it with savage kicks from its many legs.

I cursed as I rolled across the ground, trying to get to that patch of white fur, hunting the grim surroundings of fallen warriors and this unforgiving landscape of rock and stone for any sign of him.

A ruinous cry made me whirl around, Phoenix fire bursting from my palm as a shadow descended on me from above, another of Vard's monsters diving from the sky, this one with a hooked beak and jagged talons the size of goddamn machetes.

My flames ricocheted off of the silvery scales that clung to its humanoid body, flaring white as their heat increased and making me squint against the brightness.

I raised an arm to shield my eyes and a scream tore from my throat as those talons sank into my arm, the metal bracer bending beneath the pressure of its grip, and I was hauled from the ground.

The beast lurched in jagged motions as it took off toward the sky, Fae on the ground beneath me crying out in alarm as they saw one of their queens being dragged above the battlefield.

I swung my sword, hacking at the leg of the beast, my blade ringing as it struck against the metallic scales coating its flesh. There were enough similarities to a Harpy to let me guess at this creature's Fae roots, but its body was five times the size of my own, its bird head vulgar and unnaturally ugly.

The ground pitched away below me, one glance beyond my kicking legs showing the deadly drop beneath us, but the height wasn't my greatest concern as I spotted a horned beast - something like a bull with jagged spines raised along its back - charging into the fight beneath me.

A deafening chorus of Moos sounded, and I fought harder to free myself as I found a legion of our Minotaurs stampeding into the fight, all of them shifted, horns lowered, and weapons of war clutched in their powerful fists.

I recognised Milton leading the charge by the bands of gold painted onto his horns, the mark of leadership making him into a target while his herd charged into battle behind him.

I swung my sword at the beast holding me again, the burn of its claws sinking into my arm as it found a spot beneath the bracer to puncture.

My breath stuttered in my lungs as some toxin slammed into my veins, my body convulsing, sword spilling from my grip to tumble a hundred feet towards the ground. Ice spread under my flesh in a wave of petrifying violence, and I hardly even noticed that I was falling, air whipping around me as I tumbled over and over like a rag doll, dropped like discarded trash, unable to do a thing to stop the inevitable impact.

My wings flared around me, flames tumbling from them towards the heavens as they curled close, wrapping me in their embrace, trying to shield me from death as my body failed to do anything other than scream in agony.

I hit the ground with a deafening crack, my breath expelled in a scream as I felt nothing at all, then everything at once.

Pain exploded through every piece of my flesh, the lifeless bodies beneath me only making the horror of my fall worse as dead eyes stared at me from all around, accusations whispering on the wind. My mind flickered between here and there, the hisses of the dead surrounding me for an inhale then fleeing as the breath was released.

"For the queen!" Milton bellowed, a chorus of moos filling the air, almost loud enough to drown out the echoing shriek of the monster who had seen me fall, the bull-like beast charging my way, horns lowered, enormous hooves obliterating everything beneath them.

Fear came for me between the ruinous pain, my fingers opening and closing, something soft knotting between them for a brief moment and then falling away.

I tried to summon my magic, but my thoughts were scattered in the endless pain which coated every single piece of my being.

"Wait," I gasped as the Minotaurs turned their stampede, charging into the space dividing me and that beast, placing themselves between my broken body and the oncoming certainty of my death.

Venom. My mind supplied the word between convulsions, between the blinks that shuttered my view of the Minotaurs running towards a monster ten times the size of any man.

I shifted my fingers again, the fur brushing against them, a whimper tugging at my awareness as I swept my thumb against the ring on my forefinger, hunting out the thorn on the rose which adorned it. These rings had been a gift, given to me and Darcy by the Oscura Clan to use if the need arose, and I felt the need rising faster with every passing second.

The Minotaurs collided with the beast, screams of fury turning to agony before cutting off abruptly one by one.

"No," I gasped, gritting my teeth against the roaring fury of my own pain and pressing my thumb down on the ring, releasing the antivenom stored there.

My gaze stayed riveted to the Minotaurs, a flash of golden horns showing me where Milton fought on, an axe swinging from his fist, his horns dripping blood. The monster who faced them threw its weight around wildly, a hooved foot crushing a Minotaur in a bloody spray of gore as he failed to get out of the way in time.

The ice dissolved beneath my skin, leaving only the brutal torture of my broken body in its place.

A sob racked my chest as more of the Minotaurs fell to the wrath of the monster before me, a tear sliding down my cheek and into my hair as I pressed my fingers to my side and fought to heal myself.

The thread of magic slipped from my grasp, the pain and clash of war surrounding me too much.

Another whimper sounded from the pile of bodies beneath me and as the wind blew cold and savage across the battlefield, several white hairs were lifted from the Wolf I lay upon and drifted before my eyes.

"Seth," I gasped, closing my eyes as he whimpered mournfully, the tiniest movement beneath me telling me he was clinging to life even more precariously than I was.

The sound of braying cattle and ferocious roars clamoured with more intensity as I blocked out all sight of the battle and forced my mind to focus on healing, the magic snapping into place at last and rushing into my flesh.

I cried out as my broken bones cracked and fused themselves together, blood coating my lips as I coughed up whatever had been making its way into my lungs.

The pain left me in a rush and I rolled to my knees, blinking out at the Minotaurs, now only Milton and two others left fighting the beast whose gaze still lurched my way, like it knew I was the ripest prey on this field.

I pressed my hand through the heaped bodies, reaching for that brush of fur, healing magic still buzzing through my veins and connecting readily to the flickering tendril of Seth's power as soon as I found it.

The monster swung around, the spines on its tail cutting one Minotaur in half and beheading the other, leaving only Milton standing against it. One of his horns had broken, his axe chipped and dripping blood where it hung limp in his fist, the reality of his herd's death freezing him in place.

"Milton!" I roared as the beast turned for him, lowering its head and scraping a hooved foot against the ground as it prepared to charge him down.

My friend looked at me for half a second, pain reflected in his eyes tempered by pride for his fallen herd. In death, they had shifted back, and I saw Bernice among them, her neck cut wide open, her lips parted as if her end had taken her by surprise.

Milton released a mournful moo, his own horns lowering as he turned to face the charge of the monster.

"Wait!" I cried, lifting a hand to cast magic, but my power was locked to Seth's, his wavering heartbeat resounding through my ears as my power poured through him, dragging him back to this side of The Veil through pure force of will.

I pulled a dagger from my belt as Milton broke into a charge, the immensity of his foe making his death all but inevitable as a moo poured from his lips and his feet pounded towards the beast without hesitation.

The monster rushed to meet him, head lowered, sharp horns braced for a killing blow.

I hurled my dagger, watching as it flew end over end, its aim true. I struck the monster in the eye, making it bellow in pain and lift its head at the final moment.

Milton didn't slow his charge, tipping his horns and driving them deep into the creature's bared throat, ripping it open and spilling its blood in a river of vivid red.

I screamed Milton's name as the monster fell, its enormous weight crashing to the ground and crushing my friend beneath it as a deafening boom sounded the finality of its demise.

The fur beneath my fingers turned to flesh and Seth cursed as he woke. I was already on my feet, running, magic ripping from me as I hurled the creature off of Milton with a wrench of air magic, revealing his broken body.

"Fuck," I breathed, rushing to him, scrambling over the bodies of his herd, taking his hand while I tried to ignore the unnatural twist of his spine and the fact that he had shifted back into his Fae form.

"You're okay," I told him, my grip tightening around his palm, the warmth of his skin giving me hope, but as I squeezed, I felt that rush of death, the extra beat to my heart. "Wait," I begged, my magic reaching for his, crashing from me and pressing against his flesh, hunting for a scrap of power to latch on to.

"Milton, wait," I said again, louder, more forcefully, the clash of battle fading around me, the roar of the monsters who had come barrelling through our army falling quieter.

I reached for his face, gripping his jaw in my hand and shaking his head, but the way it lolled was too loose, his expression vacant and fallen to the sky beyond me.

"No," I told him, my magic lashing against his flesh, hunting for any sign of his own, building and building with this infernal need for release. "Please don't leave. Please. I didn't ask you to die for me. I didn't want this. Please, Milton."

Tears rolled down my cheeks, pain ripping into my chest as I gripped his face harder, shaking him again, demanding he listen to me and come back. But no matter how hard I pushed, there was nothing for my power to latch onto. Nothing left in his body for me to heal.

A sob broke from me as I pushed harder, the world blurring with my tears and the loss of my friend, the loss of his herd, of this entire flank of our army. It was too much. The sacrifice too great.

A hand fell to my shoulder and a baleful howl ripped the air apart with a grief so pure that it broke what little restraint I had left on my tears. I released Milton, an apology falling from my lips as I stood and let Seth pull me into his arms.

"My pack," he rasped, his grip threatening to crush me as his tears wetted my cheeks, our pain climaxing as one and the horror of what surrounded us pushing in on our souls.

I trembled as I took in the devastation, the decimation of our army on this side of the warring Fae and the emptiness of the battlefield where so many had fought all too recently.

I processed the strike to our numbers, my eyes raking over the endless ranks of Lionel's warriors beyond them, stretching out ceaselessly while our rear guard was already in plain view.

Those monsters had cost us a brutal price. And I couldn't deny the fear which drove into my heart as I was forced to admit that everything had just turned against us in the most undeniable way.

DARIUS

CHAPTER EIGHTY NINE.

The boom of the war machine firing exploded through the air; the sound compounded a hundred-fold from inside the foul contraption. My ears rang as I swung my axe at the first of the soldiers positioned within the wooden hull.

After we'd burned the first of them, the Fae inside and surrounding the towers had thrown all of their efforts into shielding them, meaning we'd had to change our tactics and head into the things on foot.

No two of them had been laid out the same inside, each with hidden pitfalls and secret doors to bar the way to the controls and the Fae powering them. But there was a flaw in that because the motherfuckers who were pooling their magic to power the star damned machines had to be replaced often as their magic grew thin. That meant that a fresh supply of wielders had to be close at all times to take over, so they hadn't been able to shield the entire thing from entry. Especially not from two of the most powerful Fae on this battlefield.

Xavier whinnied as he galloped through the wooden space, forcing Fae to leap aside or be crushed beneath his hooves. I blasted anyone who turned their focus on him and soon my fire magic was catching on the walls, screams of panic building above us as the smoke rose and warned the Fae trapped in this thing of what was coming for them.

Xavier whirled towards the sounds of their panic and kicked out with his back legs at the wall there, causing it to buckle and opening a new way on for us.

I broke into a run, my axe slicing into one Fae's leg and cutting open another's throat as I ducked between the bodies lunging for me, though none of them got closer than that. They were too thrown off by our sudden appearance and the fact that neither of us were hanging around to fight.

Xavier shifted, slipping through the crack in the wood and wrenching it wide enough for me to follow him.

Ice spilled from my fingertips as I ran to that gap in the wall, and by the time I dove through it and sealed it at my back, none of the bastards behind me had even noticed that I'd sealed the entrance too, locking them all inside this thing and tethering them to its fate.

A spiralling staircase led the way on and I ran for it, ignoring the four soldiers who were fighting to break free of Xavier's vines by the doorway.

I took the lead, partly because I wanted to take the brunt of whatever awaited us above, and partly because I didn't want to look at Xavier's naked ass while we ran up the stairs or catch a side eye from his sparkling cock.

Adrenaline pumped fitfully through my limbs, the knowledge that the Fae above would be waiting for us a potent cocktail of thrill and foreboding.

I let my water magic race ahead of me, tiny droplets flying up the stairs and skidding along the wooden floor above, seeking out the warmth of blood. One by one, my water droplets ran over hardened boots and slipped beneath bracers and trousers to find flesh.

I doubted any of them even felt the splash of liquid against their skin or noticed when the magic sank deeper, linking my focus to the blood in their veins and letting me take hold of it.

This magic was difficult, my link on it tenuous at best, but all I had to do was pull and-

Cries of alarm were echoed by the thuds of around twenty bodies hitting the floor at speed as I yanked on their blood, pulling it downwards, making it rush to the soles of their feet and causing their bodies to riot in panic.

I couldn't hold it, my grip spread too thinly and my focus split too far, but as we burst into the room and Dragon fire ripped from my body, I didn't need to.

They barely even had time to scream before they died, the ball of power which they had all been in the process of loading into the cannon falling from their grasp.

My eyes widened as that crackling expanse of white and blue energy slipped back out of the contraption, its creators dying and thereby releasing their control over the bomb they'd formed with their magic.

"Xavier!" I bellowed in panic, whirling for my brother, magic rushing to my fingertips to form a shield which I knew wouldn't be enough.

But as I spun to face him, that ball of energy falling towards the floor at my back and wild terror lighting in my heart, I didn't find my sweet brother standing stricken with panic at the knowledge of our impending deaths. I found a war stallion charging me down, head low and nostrils flaring as he galloped straight for me and beyond where the open hole sat for the cannon to fire through.

Instinct took over and I leapt for him, grabbing a fistful of his mane while he lowered his head and dipped a wing to allow me to launch myself onto his back.

The explosion ripped the world apart in the centre of the war machine and my shield of ice flared wildly at our backs as we leapt from the precipice and dove towards the enemy ranks below.

It sounded as though the earth had cleaved in two behind us, the explosion so furious that I could hardly believe we were still alive to hear it, the heat from it rushing after us in a wave of furious fire.

My shield cracked and splintered as Xavier's wings snapped out, and the Fae beneath us fell prey to the explosion in a wave of death that I could feel singing through my blood in payment to The Ferryman.

Yet still we lived.

Xavier beat his wings and flew hard for the sky above us where lightning and Phoenix fire ripped the clouds in two, revealing a swell of Dragons swarming in battle with countless other flying Orders.

The shockwave from the explosion struck us and we were sent tumbling through the air, higher and higher, my grip on Xavier's mane so tight that I feared I'd rip his hair clean out.

The urge to shift filled me but I held off, knowing that the moment I did all secrecy to my location would be lost, still hoping against hope that I could get to my father and end this myself.

Xavier whinnied wildly as we tumbled through the air, unable to do anything other than ride the wave of force which the explosion had expelled for several disorienting, terrifying seconds.

His wings finally snapped wide again, and I blinked around at the battles taking place in the sky, trying to orient myself, noting the last remaining war machine and preparing to-

A creature of shadow and darkness collided with us from nowhere and I cried out as its claws sank into my armour and I was ripped from my brother's back.

Xavier whinnied in alarm as he was hurled away from me, and I was enveloped in darkness as the leathery wings of the beast which had struck us blocked out all sight of the sky beyond.

I ripped my axe from my back and swung it at the creature, but I was thrown from its grasp and sent tumbling across hard, rocky ground before I could make contact with it.

I spat a wad of blood from my mouth as I shoved myself to my feet and a growl rolled up the back of my throat as I took in the Dragon who towered over me, his body carved of a shade so dark it seemed to suck the light from the sky surrounding it.

Tharix bared sharpened fangs as he loomed over me, and I was struck with the question of how I was supposed to kill a beast who couldn't die.

ORION

CHAPTER NINETY

Lavinia was protected by rows and rows of Nymphs, making it impossible to get near her, her shadows flooding out into our western ranks and consuming all in their path. Caleb and I were caught in the dance of battle, death and pain so present around me it made my skin prickle with how likely it was that people I loved had already fallen.

My gaze kept flicking to Darcy in the sky, her blue and red fire tumbling through the clouds. I'd caught a glimpse of her hair once and known it was her, but I couldn't let that distraction keep turning my gaze. She was waging a war of her own up there, and I knew she could handle herself even if all my instincts urged me to be with her right now.

Caleb killed another enemy Nymph with his twin blades, stabbing brutally and taking it down. I knocked my shoulder into the gut of another Nymph, throwing it back into two more behind it then rearing away and driving my sword through its chest. I yanked my sword out of its body before it fell dead beneath me, and growled as more Nymphs came my way.

"This isn't fast enough, we need to get to Lavinia before she decimates our western flank," Caleb's voice carried through my mind.

I had an idea. One that was chaotic and unpredictable, but there was no use in hesitating now.

"Hold the line," I told Caleb. *"I'll be back with a weapon."*

"Hurry," he urged, and I sped away from the Nymphs towards the trampled rows of dead Fae far behind us. I ripped off their arms, trying to only take from our fallen enemies, but their bodies were so covered in blood it was hard to tell one from the other. When I had ten Fae arms gathered, I raced back to my sanguis frater, moving as fast as the wind as I rammed them into the ground in a circle before the Nymphs while Caleb worked to keep them back.

I unsheathed the draining dagger I'd strapped to my leg, stepping into the centre of the circle and cutting my arm, letting my blood spill onto the ground. My father had taught me this trick, the dark magic so potent he had warned me never to use it unless necessary. But me standing in the middle of a battlefield with death calling my name probably counted as necessary.

My eyes shuttered and fell closed, the lull of the magic pulling me into a trance, but instead of the usual whispers I heard within the dark, there was silence. A heady, keen kind of silence that was full of magic untold. The shadows were cleansed now, no tainted Nymph souls trapped there to try and lure me towards my demise within them.

I guided the power towards my desire, threading it into the earth at my feet and I blinked, finding my blood spreading away in ten perfect lines towards the severed arms that stuck out of the ground.

"Faster!" Caleb bellowed in my head, but the blood magic kept me calm, my gaze falling on him where he was struggling to hold the Nymphs back, their probes swinging viciously.

I willed my blood to connect to the arms, feeling it seep into each of them and their fingers began to flex. I groaned as the power of each fallen Fae threaded into me, the gift of their magic rushing between me and them.

"Run," I told Caleb and with one glance my way, he fled, tearing past me, away from the Nymphs who came charging in my direction. If this failed, I was dead. I knew it from the murder in their eyes. There were far too many for me to escape while I stood connected to the shadows. But I'd made my choice, and I prayed it paid off.

Fire, earth, water and air combined in an explosion of almighty power, all ten of the hands spreading and casting for me, joining with my own Elemental power and fuelling the strike. That tremendous clash of ice, flames, wind and the rumbling destruction of an earthquake slammed into the Nymphs, cracking the ground in two.

The Nymphs went tumbling into a pit that stretched fifty feet, taking lines of enemy Fae with them, more than I could hope to kill alone, but with the aid of dark magic, I was unstoppable. The tumultuous power slammed into the fallen Nymphs, burning them, freezing them, pummelling them until only death lay within the chasm beneath me.

The severed arms turned to ash, their power spent and the severe magic used to wield them shattering the last of their flesh. I buckled as that roiling power took its toll on me, my knees hitting the ground and Caleb ran to help, dropping down to kneel at my side. He reached out to heal me as the enemy army closed in again, forming bridges across the chasm, making my pulse thrash with how little time I had to recover.

Before Caleb's hand could meet with my skin, a Caucasian Eagle swept from the sky, its talons latching onto his arm and dragging him skyward. I cried out, leaping for him as he went kicking and thrashing into the clouds in the grasp of the beast.

My legs gave out as I hit the ground again on my knees, my head bowing as I panted and my mind spinning. My magic was spent, my chest ringing hollow. I needed blood, but I was in a field of fallen Nymphs, not close to any Fae body.

Lionel's army was closing in, a line of Centaurs in bronze armour inlaid with his emblem tearing this way with bows and arrows in hand. A female aimed her first arrow at me and I tried to move with a burst of speed, but the dark magic had taken everything out of me.

I cried out as the arrow slammed into a gap in my armour, striking the flesh of my shoulder and knocking me flat on my back. Then their hooves thundered closer, and I couldn't do anything to stop what came next. They didn't halt to finish the kill, they let their hooves do it for them, the beasts trampling me, crushing bone and snapping ribs.

I wheezed, trying to move, trying to drag myself out of harm's way, but they didn't stop coming. Death closed in, and I was forced to cover my head with my hands and pray to the stars that I'd be spared. I rolled onto my front, trying to curl up against the onslaught of pounding hooves, but more kept striking me, my back suddenly making a terrible snapping noise and all feeling leaving my legs.

I groaned into the mud, the pain of it all setting my nerves aflame.

The trampling finally stopped, the Centaurs headed on to a greater fight and the battlefield surrounding me was left quiet as Lavinia turned her forces elsewhere, moving off into the distance. Between all the quiet and the pain, I focused on my mate, and the truth that would sully my soul forevermore.

I'd failed her.

I turned my gaze to the sky, seeing the colours of red and blue lighting the clouds and gritting my teeth as I remembered the promise I'd made to her. The vow that would crush my soul if I broke it.

I dragged myself forward, my legs useless, scraping through the mud behind me as I set my mind on what I needed most. Blood.

Death couldn't have me now or ever, because I belonged to her. I would lay in no grave until our life was well-worn and her smile had brightened thousands of glorious days. We were meant to rise with tomorrow's sun, and I would see that dawn in with my love by my side come what fucking may.

DARIUS

CHAPTER NINETY ONE

The enormous black Dragon took three hulking steps towards me then shifted, Tharix appearing before me and cloaking himself in clothes of shadow just as I'd seen him do before. This time, however, he didn't mimic my outfit, instead crafting plates of interlocking black armour of his own design, spikes rising at his shoulders and elbows, the fit tight but made to allow him to move.

"So," I said, hefting my axe in my hand and shifting my weight subtly.

When this fight began it wouldn't end easily, but I was going to bet that severing his head would be the move to make.

"So," Tharix replied, cocking his head as he inspected me. "It looks as though you have been feasting on death tonight, brother. And here I thought I was supposed to be the monster among us."

I pushed my tongue into my cheek, not much liking that assessment. "I fight for the honour and liberty of our people. I fight against tyranny and oppression, and most of all, I fight to put the right monarchs on the throne of our kingdom. What is it you fight for, *brother?*" I sneered the last word at him, letting him feel the contempt I held for that title, and he blinked at the acid in my tone.

"I thought we'd been more...civil of late." he said slowly.

"Answer the question and we will see how civil we can be from opposing sides of a war."

"Well, that is a hard question to give an answer to, I'm afraid. Because I haven't fought in this battle, so I can't tell you what I'm fighting for when I am little more than an observer to this chaos."

I frowned at him, taking in his spotless appearance and raking my mind for any sign of him before he had come careening across the sky and hurled me off of Xavier's back.

"Why not? Is our father holding you in reserve?" I asked, knowing the mind of the man who had sired us all too well.

"I have been ordered to join the battle," Tharix replied. "I'm just trying to decide which side to fight on."

My lips parted on words which did not come. I stared at him, really stared and as I looked I found him to be...different. The darkness which had once lurked within his eyes was missing and to top that, he no longer conjured that foul reek of death with his appearance. There was a stillness in his expression which hadn't been there before and the shadows coiling through his fingers were no longer stained a solid ebony but glimmering with flecks of silver.

"The shadows were cleansed," I said, jerking my chin at his hands. "Were they holding you captive too?"

Tharix looked down at his hands with a short breath of laughter, the distraction the exact opportunity I needed to strike at him and yet...I held my ground.

"No, brother, I do not think I was ever a creature who could have been controlled so thoroughly. But...yes, my mother lost some of her grip on me. I no longer hear her hissing venom in my ear. I no longer feel compelled to please her. In fact, I no longer feel very much of anything towards her at all."

"You expect me to believe that?" I scoffed. "You come to me, naming me brother and claiming some connection between us because of that vague blood tie, and you expect me to believe that you would so easily dismiss a blood bond with your own mother?"

"I have come to you because I seek something which I am yet to put a name to. I want to feel the things you seem to feel so very easily. I want to taste the wind and feel my heart race for a reason so much better than physical exhaustion, and I think you know what it is to experience all of that. Blood is one of the very few things I have. My tie to four people in this world a truth about myself which is undeniable. But I tire of our father's belt and my mother's manipulations. I do not think I will find what is missing from me in their hostile company."

I clenched my jaw, not wanting to hear those words, not wanting to feel the twist of fucking pity which was wrenching at my gut, nor have any kind of understanding of what it was he was searching for. But I did. I knew what he would never find while trapped within the company of my father and Lavinia. It was what had saved me after all.

"Death came calling on me," Tharix added conversationally, as if the two of us weren't perched on a mountaintop while war waged on below us, the screams of those facing their end coiling up to taint the air.

"I know the feeling. And I doubt you came back the way I did, so how did you escape it?" I asked, curious despite myself.

"The Ferryman took the souls my mother bound to me. He was..." Tharix pursed his lips, clearly unwilling to go on. "Well, suffice to say, he didn't deem whatever I am worthy of reaping. So, here I am."

He held his hands wide, and I realised that he held no weapon in his grip. He wasn't standing ready to fight or even watching me with the kind of shrewd observation that would suggest he was ready to defend himself. He was offering me a free shot at him if I wanted it. Well, either that or...

"You want me to offer you a place in our army?" I asked, narrowing my eyes at him. We had discussed the possibility of trying to turn him and dismissed it. Those tortured souls were bound to him, and his creation was a thing beyond our comprehension. But if what he was saying was true then not only had those souls been taken into death where they belonged, but he was no longer tainted by the darkness of Lavinia's shadows, meaning the man who stood before me was simply that. Half Fae, half Nymph, a product of our father's ambition and cruelty – not so very different to me.

"Are you?" Tharix asked, a malicious grin lifting the corner of his lips like the idea of that betrayal thrilled him.

"That kind of deal would have to be made by one of the True Queens – ideally both," I hedged, but his smirk only grew.

"Oh, I think the king consort has some sway. Besides, your queen made a deal with me – she owes me."

"Owes you what?' I asked, narrowing my eyes at him and making a mental note to have words with my wife about making dodgy deals with ferocious creatures because she was making altogether too much of a habit of it.

"That was left up to fate. Just as fate threw you into my path today, brother. So the question is, what will you do with me now that you've got me?"

I stared at him for several long moments, then let out a huff of frustration, silently cursed my wife and sheathed my axe.

"I'm headed for the Jade Castle," I told him. "And when I get there, I plan on decapitating our father. Do you have any issue with that?"

Tharix grinned. "Do you know, just this morning, I was thinking how much better he would look without a head. It will match with his missing hand."

I held out for all of a few seconds before barking a laugh and grinning back at the brother who I hadn't asked for but now found myself lumped with.

"Well, maybe we are related after all."

"Come on. I can get you into the castle if that's where you want to be." Tharix shifted in the blink of an eye, his huge Dragon form towering over me once again and despite my better judgement, despite my knowledge of what he was and where he had come from, I found myself moving closer to him.

I could only hope I wasn't losing my damn mind and that I was right to follow my gut on this because if not, I was about to serve myself up on a silver platter to the man I had come here to kill.

But for some unknown reason, I *did* trust Tharix, and as I climbed up onto his back and hid myself away with concealment charms, I let myself bask in the thrill of knowing that I was finally going to get close enough to my father to end this.

CALEB

CHAPTER NINETY TWO

I fought wildly against the gigantic Caucasian Eagle who had its claws embedded so deeply within me that I swear the thing had struck bone, the pain in my arm blinding as it scored a path higher and higher towards the roiling storm clouds above.

I swung for its legs with my dagger but the angle it held me at made it impossible to make contact with its flesh.

"Let me go, you ugly motherfucker!" I roared, kicking and thrashing, my mind alive with pain.

We crashed through the grey clouds and drops of icy water rushed across my skin, while I found myself unable to see anything at all within its depths.

Thunder boomed and the furious bellows and roars of the beasts warring within the sky filled the air, surrounding me in a horror show of monsters that I could no more see than predict.

Fire flared in my palm, and I sent a quick prayer out to any star that might be inclined to take pity on me before hurling a blast of hungry flames at the eagle who held me.

The bird shifter shrieked as the flames consumed it and my short-lived triumph was crushed by the swooping feeling in my gut as I suddenly plummeted towards the ground.

I cried out, my blood pouring into the sky above me while in the back of my head, Orion's panic met with my own. A vision of him clawing his way across the filth of the battlefield while agony clung to his broken body overlayed my vision while he no doubt saw me plummeting through the sky towards my own death. The coven bond was calling out for help for both of us which neither could provide.

"Shit!" I yelled, summoning earth magic and wondering if there was any way in hell I'd be able to cushion my fall enough to save me from death at this height – assuming I didn't fall face first onto a spear before I even hit the ground.

The cloud lit with a blast of lightning, and I was blinded before I collided with the sinewy muscle of a Dragon wing.

I bounced, flipped over and then cursed as sparks of lightning bit into my blood-slicked palms where I slid down the long slope of the Dragon's wing.

"Dante?" I called through a laugh of surprise and endless gratitude.

The enormous Storm Dragon grunted in confirmation before jerking his wing and tossing me up onto his back.

My laughter fell into a whoop of excitement as Dante dropped out of the clouds at speed and I was almost hurled right off of him again.

I slapped a hand to my ruined arm and gritted my teeth against the pain as I healed the wounds away, my vision clearing and mind focusing as drops of rain splashed against my cheeks.

"Let me help you with that," I said, spotting a spear lodged in Dante's shoulder and tugging it free.

I hurled it straight into the chest of an enemy Harpy as she lunged for us and sent her spiralling away to crash into the ground far below.

Dante spat lightning at a swarm of Griffins, setting their coats alight while I placed my palms to his navy-blue scales and set to work healing the many injuries he was sporting from his time battling in the sky. He grunted in relief, and I was glad I could do something to help him.

Orion's vision overlaid my own again, his pain and fear making me gasp in alarm before I blinked it all away.

"I need to get to Orion!" I yelled. "He's that way!"

I shot a spark of energy ahead of us, my bond to Orion making it as simple as breathing to mark his location, and Dante sped after the trail of golden flames at once.

We dove through the clouds but an echoing roar broke the air apart from our right and a bronze-coloured Dragon collided with us with such force that I was nearly hurled from Dante's back.

Vines snapped from my hands, lashing my legs in place so I could focus on wielding my magic to help with the fight, but as a pair of wooden spears formed in my fists, a grey Dragon dove at us from above.

Dante flipped, lightning crackling from his flesh in a deadly arc, but between the two Dragons, he was unable to focus on attacking and was forced to defend himself instead.

I tried to ignore the horrible feeling of my stomach being left a hundred feet above us as we plummeted towards the ground and set my aim on the grey beast, hurling the first of my spears straight for it. I could only pray that Orion could hold out for a bit longer because as my head rang with the sound of Dragons battling, I knew it would be a damn miracle if I managed to survive long enough to help him.

GERALDINE

CHAPTER NINETY THREE

"Forge yonder!" I commanded my legion, flinging my flail and striking the skull of a floundering fool whom the great Dragoon dared to call a warrior. None were more stalwart than the True Queens' army, our fight majestic in its endeavour, but these twiddlesticks did not have the unbreakable courage in their hearts that we possessed.

My spirited seabass fought valiantly at my side, blasting shots of ice ahead to break the ranks of our enemies. Another of his baneful ice blades swished past my ear and buried itself between the eyes of a gurning ghoul of a man. He fell like a sack of peas that had been torn open at the foot, crumpling beneath me and leaving me free to leap over his loafish corpse and dive into my next skirmish.

With a swing of my flail and a flurry of wooden shards cast by my hand, I took down another cretin. To my right, Justin Masters forged on, spinning a web of fire and catching his prey in it like a hapsome fly. He fought like a truly chivalrous centipede, every death he claimed in the name of our queens shining in the sheen of his brow like a tiara of glory.

"Let them through!" a bellow went up from the enemy army and like the ocean receding, the hoofwits and cragnannies before us peeled away from us to reveal a greater danger beyond.

My heart did a jig, but I would not be shaken by the unveiling of these new and wretched devils who wore strange metal guns upon their backs.

I cried out for my Starfall Legion to reform, closing in tight while I stared at the oncoming tide of Nemean Lions, Werewolves and Repsian Tigers headed our way with a shimmer of murder in their eyes. The weapons upon their backs fizzed and buzzed with magic, promising a violence like no other.

"Shield formation!" I roared, and we all power shared, channelling our turbulent, roiling magic to my dear dolphin who cast a powerful forcefield around us.

An explosion of light and colour danced in the air as those calamitous cannons released their shots all at once. We closed ranks like nillies on a neighbour's norg and gave all the juice we had to give to our shield, but somehow, deep in my lady waters, I knew it would not be enough.

I released a chaotic cry, demanding ice and earth to join the shield above us, wielding it myself into an arching dome. It was powerful, unbreakable, infallible. Yet as those terrible blasts slammed down onto our shield and crack, crack, cracked against it, our magic fizzled out, dissolved and swallowed by whatever awful power was contained within those cannons.

All too soon, my legion was revealed, and more of those atrocious guns were fired just as the first line of beasts collided with us.

A Tiger's giant paws knocked me asunder and went charging on past me to attack my legion. Screams went up from my warriors as more of those guns were fired, the clack-de-clack and booming bangs making my ears buzz. Many were killed by those horrendous magical weapons, and woe grabbed my heart and shook it like a dog with a bone. In my tumble, I lost sight of my Maxy Boy, and I scrambled upright, my armour a little dented but I was no worse for wear from the mishap.

I snarled a savage snarl and lifted my flail, running straight for a Nemean Lion as it came charging through my battalion. I caught the Lion by the tail, and I was yanked off my feet as it continued running, gripping on for dear life as my legs kicked like I was doing the Jiminy jive. With a swing and fling, I threw myself up onto its back behind the mounted gun and the beasty roared, its head whipping around and its eyes locking on me. But it was not my target just yet, oh no, I was here for the rioting contraption strapped to its spine.

I flung my flail once then twice, the spiked ball ripping holes in the cannon and smashing it like the crag it was. But it was not enough. For as I held on tight to the fur of the Lion, one lift of my head showed me the devastation ahead. My Starfall Legion was being ripped through by blast after blast, their shields a-crumbling upon impact and the magic slapping into their bones carving great holes through their chests.

A whistling metal arrow came burning through the skull of the beast I was riding and it went plunging to the ground. I thought I might go thwacking and clacking into the earth with it, but instead, I was plucked into the air by a magical wind, deposited at the side of my salacious salmon.

"There's too many of them, Gerry," Maxy said in horror, raising his bow once more like the undeterred creature he was, releasing another arrow and taking down a savage Werewolf before using his air magic to return the arrow to his quiver.

"There are never too many enemies in this world for good to overcome," I said, thrusting my chin skyward and turning toward a row of stampeding beasts wearing those tricksome guns that were headed right for us.

I raised my flail, the earth trembling beneath me as I built a quake within it and with a snip and a snap of power, I made the ground buckle, taking down one then another and another. But I could not catch them all, and as I closed the earth above their heads and left them to the devilish dirt, I found my eyes falling upon a Wolf with eyes as black as death, the cannon upon its back charged with sizzling power, the glow of it near-blinding.

Max raced past me, arrow nocked and a roar of defiance in his eyes as the gun sent a shot our way, his arrow loosing that very same moment. I saw it then: the moment of my making. For it was he or I, not both of us could walk a merry walk from this field of death. And if it could only be one of us, then let it be him. Let it by my salmon.

I made the earth buck, knocking my Maxy boy aside as the arrow embedded in the Werewolf's head. There, in a flurry, was Justin, throwing himself in front of me. I tried to shield us both in a desperate bid for life, tucking us into a pod of earth. But that blazing ball of power crashed into it, consuming the strength of my shield and finding us beneath it.

My earth may have slowed it some, but not enough, for the almighty blast carved through the chest of my dear Justin and slammed into my own chest, shattering my breast plate and finding flesh. I wailed a final cry in death, praying I had done enough, that the True Queens would think of me upon a new dawn and know that I had fought for them with all I had to give.

"For the True Queens," I rasped, raising my flail high before my arm went limp at my side, Justin's dead weight stealing the last of my breath.

My eyes became hooded as I clung to consciousness, wishing for one more glimpse of my salamander before I stepped into the nevermore where my sweet Mama and dear Daddy awaited me. I could feel them close by, guiding me away, but oh, if only I could stay. If only, if only.

Then there he was, Maxy kneeling over me, crying my name and pushing Justin's dead body off of me. I could smell the blood, could feel the festering of my flesh as that horrid magic continued to bite and gnaw at my bones.

Alas, it was over.

"Did I make them proud?" I rasped, unsure if the words truly passed my lips. "Will my queens think of me with a touch of wonder in their voices beyond this day, Maxy?"

"Stay with me," he croaked, tears in his dark eyes as he tried to connect his magic to mine to heal me. But reality set in when he could find no connection, for something in those awful blasts stopped it from being so.

A rattling breath passed my lungs as I took in the sweet love I had found in this world.

"From mountain tops to sandy dunes, my love will live for you everywhere," I promised, trying to reach for him, but there were no more dandyhops in me now. No more kinkypunks or dangadongs. I was done for.

"I love you, Gerry, just don't say goodbye. I can fix this," he said in desperation, tears caressing his beautiful face, and oh how this man should never know such pain. If only I could take it away, and not be the source of such misery.

"Tell me I made them proud," I begged.

"You did, of course you did. They couldn't have done any of this without you," he growled, still trying to find that beating pulse in me, that well of magic to latch upon and save me. But the truth was ringing in the air now like the bells of the noongarden. And none could deny their call.

A sigh of failure left me. The Veil was thin and I could see to the other side of it, my soul half here, and half there. Hands were grasping mine and death was so welcoming that it was hard to be afraid. My fear lay with what I left behind, an unfinished war, a battle consuming my loves one by one.

My mama was close, all bright-eyed and button nosed, calling me to her, so near I could almost fall into her arms. But how could I go to my Mama when I had let down my queens?

I lifted my head and met the eyes of my Daddy, finding solace there in the dandy company of the family I had missed so deeply.

"We're so proud of you, my little bumpkin," Mama cried, her tears sliding down her cheeks, though she faded from view for a moment, swirling away in a golden mist. I saw the sky once more, but then I saw my parents again, here and there, I was both places at once.

"You gave them the good what-for and the best of the Grus name," Daddy boomed, and panic rose in me over that crushing truth. I was exiting the land of the living. I'd leave them all behind, and I shuddered, shaking off the call of that misty path, reaching for life instead, seeking my Maxy, my treasured Tory and darling Darcy, but I couldn't find a way back.

Justin was there, standing with my parents between this heavy mist that was guiding me on. A look of confusion marked his face as family members of his own ran close to hold him. He met my gaze, a nod of sadness and acceptance in his eyes as he let them guide him away, walking off into an imposing yet beautiful palace that towered there on the brink of everything.

"Thank you, my valiant friend," I called to him, for he had tried to save me, and that could not go forgotten.

He smiled back at me, content. But I was not. How could I be so?

"I…cannot go," I whispered, panic rising now. How could I leave, to walk as willingly as a whelk into the jaws of a fateful sealion? My queens needed me. They were still back there fighting for what was just and true, and I had sworn to be there 'til the bitter end. But that was the trawling trouble, wasn't it? This *was* the end. Mine anyway. And there were no flails left to be flung.

"Come to us, dandybug," Daddy encouraged, offering me his hand. That hand, so close, so takeable, but then a song rose in my head unlike any other. A song of life and beauty and healing. A song that was sung in a rumbling tenor, so deep and sturdy that it tethered itself to my soul. I felt it pulling me, and my parents gazed on in wonder.

"Her soul is teetering like a tally two-whacker," Mama gasped, and then she was fading, my guiding star drawing me back to him with the lulling rhythm of his Siren song.

"Our love goes with you like the tinkling wind at your back! Keep it as close as a dingy stick in the face of the devildust!" Mama called and I tried to speak with her, but that path of death was closing to me now, one of life gushing closer instead.

Pain. That was the start of it. A burning, tearing sensation in my chest, but I would not be cowed by such a trauma. There, above me, with tears staining his cheeks, his eyes closed in concentration as he sang me back from certain death and healed my body with a song of all songs, I found my salamander.

He had removed the shattered remains of my breastplate, my heaving bosoms barely contained within the garments I wore beneath it as my flesh stitched itself together. It was unlike magical healing, my skin answering the notes of his voice, stitching itself together because he sang to it with such love that it could not resist the need to respond to its plea.

And when his song was done, his eyes cracked open, and there he found me healed and whole, returned from the brink of doom.

"Gerry," he gasped, leaning down to kiss me, his taste so sweet upon my lips.

I kissed him back, stealing but a single moment of impossible hope upon his mouth before he pulled me upright and I found myself standing in his air shield on a field of devastation. A quarter of my Starfall Legion had been torn to smithereens, but those who had survived were regrouping, reforming, crying out in glee when they saw me rise among them.

Maxy boy placed my flail in my hand and my lower lip a-quivered with emotion as I turned my gaze to the enemy army that was closing in again. Behind us, the beasts with the canons upon their backs were moving deeper into our ranks, causing countless deaths and leaving a bloody trail of murder in their wake. But my task was clear. Rip through the damned Dragoon's ranks and never stop. I could not turn back now; I could not go after those savage machines upon the backs of those beasts. We had to forge on. To keep breaking their lines.

I cast a fresh metal plate of armour over my chest, though it was not nearly as powerful as the plate I had lost. It would have to do.

Then I turned to face our plight and bellowed a single word. "Onward!"

WASHER

CHAPTER NINETY FOUR.

I could feel every death, every cut and break, every slice and sliver. They hit me with more force than the magic which bombarded me or the swords which swung my way. I couldn't cut myself off from it and they drove into my skulls like nails hammered harder with every sharp jolt.

"Brian," Elaine gasped, shielding the two of us within a dome of earth magic while we were besieged from every angle.

"It's getting deeper. Too deep," I gasped. "I never thought it could get too deep."

Elaine slapped me, jolting my emotions back into focus, the bite of pain making me think of only my own body for a moment and I offered her a weak smile of apology. This was the woman I had fallen in love with. The strict principal who was as rough with me as I needed her to be.

"We're surrounded," she hissed, her dark hair hanging in choppy lengths on the left side of her face where it had been set alight then doused by my flames. It seemed so long ago and yet we were still fighting that same fight.

"They're going to take us from all sides," I nodded woefully.

"We can't make it back to our soldiers. I don't have enough power left to tunnel beneath them." Her shield cracked overhead as if to confirm that truth and I nodded.

"No going back," I agreed. "But we can plunge on."

"What do you–"

I raised a hand, casting a dome of ice over us beneath her shield then told her to drop hers. She did so and through the perfectly smooth dome of my magic, I pointed to the war machine which had just killed all the soldiers we'd been fighting alongside. Only dumb luck had left us and a few others standing, and now they were all gone too. Just two of us left with enemies all around, trying to thrust us deep with their swords.

"I think…we might have a teeny weeny chance of making it there," I breathed. "Just an itty bitty sliver of a chance. But I always did like it teeny weeny…"

Elaine's eyes widened as she looked at the tower, her head turning as she gazed back at the distant ranks of our army with longing, the flare of Phoenix fire marking the position of our dear queen Darcy who had flown down from the clouds to clash with a tangle of enemy Elementals, her youthful body no doubt wrung out and heaving with exhaustion, but still she drove on towards the climax she yearned for, her stamina knowing no bounds.

The war machine was turning towards our fair queen's position, a deep blue glow from within it warning of the magic they were priming to fire.

"Sometimes, you just have to take the plunge and do what your body wants," I told Elaine, an echo of our first night of passion together in those words. She smiled at me, remembering that moment too. When she'd let me in so deep in every way.

"On three," she agreed, handing me her sword as she prepared to shift.

"Three," I replied and she shifted, clothes and armour falling off of her as her body reformed into that of the regal Manticore she was beneath it all.

I leapt onto her back and let my shield shatter, the shards of jagged ice flying out in every direction, slicing deep into the bodies of those loathsome traitors to the True Queens.

Elaine let out a roar as she soared across the battlefield, flying hard and fast, just the way I liked it, straight towards the bowels of the powerful machine which was priming to blast its magical brew all over us.

We flew just above the heads of the enemy, my weight too much for Elaine to gain any more height. I helped by throwing my own order gifts at our enemies, making their fear rise and rise until they shrieked in terror at our approach.

A Nymph shifted suddenly before us, and Elaine roared in agony as its sharp horns pierced her belly. I was flung from her back, hurtling through the air like a wasp in a windmill and I crashed straight through the wall of the war machine with a solid thump.

Elaine screamed as the Nymph drove its probes into her heart and I screamed too, wailing at the stars for her sacrifice and the end of all I had loved in this world. She had suffered so much in the months before this fight, caught in the web of the False King's penetrating mind, and now she was gone.

I forced myself to stand, my teeny weeny chance fading by the moment as a pack of Lionel's Wolves all turned their savage gaze my way and I was forced to take flight.

A ladder stood at the rear of the small space I was in and I took it two rungs at a time, three, four; I had always been able to take more than seemed natural, and this was no exception. My body was as lithe and nimble as a noonday goose.

Up and up I climbed, making it to the centre of the war machine and hurling a trapdoor shut behind me, sealing it with ice.

A shout nearly had me tinkling my trousers as I found myself in the room with the cannon, ten Fae all turned my way with death in their eyes and a ball of potent magic at the ready to fire. But I had a way with balls that they wouldn't be prepared for.

One look out of the opening where the cannon was pointed showed me my queen Darcy fighting valiantly on in its line of sight, my horror at that truth almost costing me my life as the Fae within this foul contraption lunged for me.

But I was well adept in timing my lunges and I shifted my hips, wriggling this way and that, making it impossible for them to strike me. As I moved between them like a wet and wily waterlily, I did the thing which came most naturally and shifted. Blue scales erupted across my flesh and with a thrust of my hips I took hold of the minds around me, finding their violent intentions and turning them towards the next most base emotion instead.

Lust tore from me in a wave, making them tremble, then groan, breaths catching and cries of need escaping them. One by one, their weapons fell from their hands, and I kept pumping lust at them, using their distraction to lunge for the cannon.

The fuse was burning down and even as I slapped it with the full force of my water magic, it refused to go out. I tried shoving the rod-like contraption, ignoring the Fae who ripped at my armour, peeling my clothing off bit by bit in their desperation to dance with my dongle stick.

I pushed hard, clenching my pert buttocks and driving my hips into the movement as my pants were ripped off, and even then the cannon didn't move an inch.

I didn't know how to alter its course and I was utterly out of time.

The enemy Fae had me down to my lucky leopard print speedo now, their hands rubbing and cupping, mouths kissing and licking but I simply waded through them, moving to the gaping cavity where the ball of glowing magic was just waiting to shoot its load all over my army and my queen.

A hum of energy filled the air, the glow brightening, and I did the only thing I could.

I thrust myself against the cannon, ice pouring from me and filling that hole, filling it deep and hard and all the way to the brim. I filled that hole like no other could and slapped my leopard print speedo-covered hiney over the top of it for good measure, half a second before the whole world went boom around me.

Death came so quick and sudden that I barely felt the hand that snatched me into its grasp, but I smiled as I sensed those waters sucking me down. I smiled because I might have been dead, but the river I looked out upon was full of the bastards I'd taken with me in that explosion and that meant my sacrifice had counted. At least a teeny weeny bit.

TORY

CHAPTER NINETY FIVE

"We have to go," I breathed, my gaze raking over the destruction of our army, the terrifying truth of our demise rushing closer with every passing moment. My grip tightened on the hilt of my sword which I'd managed to find while hunting the bodies of the fallen for any survivors.

"Go where?" Seth demanded.

He had remained in Fae form, stealing a set of clothes and armour from one of the dead so he could fight at my side. But there was no one left here for us to engage. His body was exhausted from fighting as a Wolf for so long, but his magic was still full to the brim and I could tell he was burning to unleash it on our enemies.

I'd found several of our soldiers clinging to life and had healed them enough to survive the journey back to our healers' tents, launching them that way with air magic, but none remained of Seth's pack or Milton's herd.

Seth's grief was a palpable thing, the fact that he remained on his feet little more than a miracle. He clung to his sword with something I recognised well though. The desire for revenge was what kept him upright, the need for payment to take the place of his pain driving him on.

"There's still hope," I said, though it was growing ever harder to convince myself of that. "I have one last, insane scrap of it left."

I held out my hand and Seth took it.

"I need to meet Gabriel. Are you coming with me, or do you want to return to the fight?" I asked.

Seth tightened his hold on my hand, and I forced myself to stifle my tears at the pain I found simmering in his earthy brown eyes.

"I'll fight," he said roughly, and I nodded before launching us into the sky.

I hurled us across the battlefield so fast that it was impossible for any of the flying Orders to turn their attention to us, or for those fighting on the ground to aim at us. The battle raged on, none of Lionel's war machines remaining to fire upon our people but three of his vicious monsters still tore into our ranks. In the distance, Lavinia was killing masses of our forces with her shadows, and those shifters carrying weapons upon their backs were causing devastation too.

"Aim me at that one," Seth barked, pointing to the monster with eight legs which had disappeared while I'd been fighting for my life on the battlefield. I didn't have to ask why, understanding that Seth needed to do this, to destroy those monsters for what they'd cost him and see their blood stain the dirt at his feet.

"Fight hard, and if it comes to it, die well," I told him as I wrapped him in my magic and prepared to launch him away from me.

"Same to you, my Queen," he growled and then he was gone, hurled across the battlefield with the full strength of my air magic, his sword raised high above his head as he descended on the foul beast from above.

I didn't have time to see him collide with it or watch his war on that monster play out. I could only hope to all the heavens that I would see his face again on this side of The Veil.

My moment of hesitation in the sky cost me and a ball of fire came spiralling my way. I wasn't afraid of the flames, but I couldn't linger any longer. I kept to my Fae form, not needing wings to shoot across the sky and instead curling myself into a ball so I could race to my destination even faster.

The jagged mountain rose up before me and I threw concealment spells around me to make sure no one saw where I was headed before letting myself fall from the sky to land atop its rocky peak.

The wind whipped around me, tearing tendrils of my dark hair loose and tossing them across my face as I looked out over the carnage taking place on the battlefield far below. My heart ached as I stared at the destruction of our forces, the entire right flank ripped apart and those remaining monsters still carving deeper into our lines.

Lionel's forces were rallying, the ranks of soldiers to the rear of his army now moving into formation and heading to the east, hurrying to take advantage of the massacre caused by those fucking beasts. They would fill the space where our army had stood and come at us from the side as well as the front, making us fight on both fronts and effectively cornering our forces. It would be a bloodbath.

My gaze hunted the masses, taking in the destroyed war machines Lionel had used to bombard our people so devastatingly. Someone from our side of this fight had made it to them, destroying them all and clawing back some luck for us. But it wouldn't be enough.

A vicious fight was still going on in the clouds where I could see my sister grappling to take down Lionel's Bonded Dragons, unable to turn her attention anywhere else.

Our forces were waning by the minute.

The Jade Castle still crouched in the distance like a squat toad clinging to a rock, no sign that Darius had made it to his target. I swallowed against the lump in my throat as concern for him spiked, but the solid pounding in my own chest was enough to reassure me that he fought on.

I could just pick out the Starfall Legion with their recognisable helms fighting in the heart of the battle, but their numbers had dwindled, and I couldn't even be sure Geraldine was still alive among them.

Just this small glance at the battle was enough to tell me which way the fight was going to end. Lionel still had almost twice the numbers we did and with his army moving to attack us from the side as well, our time was growing thin.

But only if the odds remained as they were.

A hand landed on my shoulder and I flinched, whirling around with a dagger of ice forming in my fist. But I let it melt away as I found myself face to face with my brother.

"This has been fucking torture," he growled, and I threw myself into his arms, letting myself be a little sister for a moment, letting myself feel the pain and grief of war before forcing it to solidify into that dark and brutal determination once more.

"How many?" I demanded, pushing out of his arms and stepping back.

It was strange to see him standing there so clean and untouched by battle. It had been hours since I'd looked at anyone who wasn't coated in a layer of grime and blood.

"Five thousand," he replied. "You took longer than you promised."

My heart lifted at his words. I'd been hoping for half that amount and wondering desperately whether it would be enough. But this? This might really make a difference.

"You brilliant, beautiful, over achiever," I praised, moving past him and turning my back on the battlefield. I crested the peak of the mountain, shivering at the frigid wind which gusted around us, biting at any exposed skin it could find.

As the rocks beneath my feet began to pitch downwards again, I gasped. Before me stood rank upon rank of clay soldiers, each as tall as any Fae, their blank faces turned my way where they lined the mountain as if awaiting orders.

"I can't *see* how this will go," Gabriel warned, and I knew that he wasn't at all happy about that.

"Where would the fun be if you always knew everything?" I teased, though my light tone didn't fully hide the quaver to my voice. Because this was it. Beyond this fool's hope, I was pretty sure we didn't stand a chance. The future of our kingdom, the lives of those I loved, all of it rested on the chance that a creature who hated me with a deep and unwavering ferocity might just agree to the bargain I'd requested, despite it defying everything he stood for.

"Is it time?" Leon popped out from behind one of the clay statues and I flinched in surprise.

"I take it you're responsible for the genitals?" I asked, pointing at one of the statues which had no pants carved onto its frame and instead had its very anatomically correct dick on show.

"Well, I *was* until Gabe got all cranky about it and said they need to wear pants. So there's only like fifty with their cocksickles and tatas on show."

Gabriel huffed irritably behind me, and I snorted a laugh despite the dire situation.

"I feel like I should have *seen* this coming when I asked for him to be the one to help me," Gabriel muttered.

"Yeah, you really should have," I agreed, moving past Leon to stand before the closest statue.

I placed my hand on the cold, clay chest, inhaling slowly as I tried to quiet my thoughts and focus on what I needed to do.

"So…is this the mumbo jumbo bit?" Leon whispered right beside my ear, and I flinched again.

"Can you back up a bit?" I hissed, shoving him away but he just dug his heels in and didn't move an inch.

"Are you going to open the box first?" he asked, pointing to the ornately decorated crate which sat to the side of the carved statues.

"Any chance you figured out what will happen if I do?" I asked my brother, moving over to the crate and crouching down before it.

Gabriel frowned as he and Leon stepped up behind me, wrapping me in their shadows.

"Chaos," he said after a few moments of giving himself to The Sight. "The kind that might just help us."

"I'll take it," I decided, reaching out to open the lid of the crate.

The four little sayer Dragons peered up at me, peeping in excitement as they found me gazing in at them in their warm bed of straw, and I gave them a grim smile.

"I heard that you guys are pretty formidable," I said, wondering if I'd gone insane.

We were in the middle of losing a war, the Fae who had followed us into battle being slaughtered one by one in the basin between the mountains below, and here I was, talking to a foursome of little lizards as if they might actually be able to help us.

"Darcy is out there." I pointed towards the battlefield and the sayer Dragons all clambered up the side of the crate, hopping onto me.

I stood as they made their way to my shoulders, the little coral coloured one resting on my forearm as I lifted it high and turned towards the battlefield, walking back up to the peak of the mountain so they could see it too.

I swallowed thickly. Lionel's forces were almost at the eastern flank of our army and if my half-baked, unlikely plans didn't come together right about now then I could see our end written in the stars without any need of The Sight.

"There's still hope," Gabriel said, taking my hand as he looked over the expanse of carnage too. "Though it is only the faintest spark now."

"So let's feed that flame," I replied resolutely. "Go."

The sayer Dragons seemed to know that I was talking to them, four tiny creatures hurling themselves from my body and opening their little wings as they soared towards the battlefield, no bigger than baby bunnies. Their small bodies were soon impossible to pick out above the warring Fae and I had no time to waste standing there, waiting to see what might happen next.

I released my hold on Gabriel and hurried back to the stone army on the far side of the mountain.

"Don't fail me now," I muttered to no one in particular, because the only person I had to call on now was myself.

Sacrifice. Well, I'd done a whole lot of sacrificing already today.

I reached for the statue who stood at the front of the ranks, his imposing body of clay towering over me, his faceless head angled towards the battle beyond my back as though he were simply waiting for my command. But clay warriors could not fight an army. Even if an earth wielder wanted to command them, they could never take control of so many at once. No, what these statues needed were souls.

I drew my filthy sword and ran my fingers down its length, coating it in the blood of the enemies I'd ripped from the world this day. My hand shook as I reached for the statue, my breath escaping me in a cloud of vapour as I gave myself to the heady power of ether and spoke the name of the rune I painted onto its chest.

"Laguz for energy, to make your water run as blood."

Power ripped from me as the words fell roughly from my lips, the ground beneath my boots trembling as I rooted myself upon it and forced the wind to carry my command to the ears of the one I'd bargained with.

"Uruz for the strength to wield your blade," I hissed, my fingers shaking as the violent energy of the world lashed at me, the blood I painted onto the statue hissing and spitting as it boiled against the clay.

I sagged forward, my head spinning as the magic I was casting ripped at my own energy, using my power to fulfil the spell, pulling it from me and passing it out among the statues who stretched away across the slope below us.

"Tory," Gabriel murmured, reaching out to grasp my shoulder. "I *saw* your death. This magic is going to demand too much of you. You need to stop."

"I need fire," I ground out, ignoring him, my mind focused on the people I loved who were fighting down in that basin. The Fae who had followed us into battle for the promise of a better life. The oaths I had sworn and the truth that I was willing to give everything for, if that was what it took to deliver on those promises.

Gabriel withdrew with a curse and Leon set a fire roaring behind me, the warmth of it restoring my magic and making my Phoenix raise its head within me.

The blood of those I'd killed in battle had been consumed by the painting of

Uruz and my hand shook more violently as I accepted what that meant. That sacrifice wasn't enough to paint the final rune. And the last was the most powerful of all.

I reached for the sprig of thyme which Gabriel had placed into the clay statue, fear coiling around my heart as I let a single tear roll down my cheek.

If the price of this was what I feared, then it wouldn't just claim me. Darius would be torn from this place alongside me, torn away from all I had promised him when I'd stolen him back from the clutches of death. Even so, I knew that he would be telling me to do this if he was standing here beside me. I knew that if it came to it, he would give everything to save this kingdom from the tyranny of his father too.

I gripped my sword in my fist and squeezed until it sliced my flesh open, the hot rush of my blood rolling down the pristine metal and dripping onto the dirt beneath me.

I drew on every scrap of power I owned and dove into the deepest recesses of ether that I could gather as I pressed my bloodied hand over the thyme and set it blazing.

The thyme placed upon every statue on the mountainside ignited along with it, flames of red and blue blazing to life as the Phoenix fire caught and burned, opening up the pathway to communicate with the dead.

"We are dying," I said, my voice a strangled rasp which I only hoped had found its way beyond The Veil. I thought of my mother and father, knowing they would be drawn closer to me in my grief. I prayed to them and poured my power into the cold clay before me. "We need you now more than ever before."

The ether seemed to be rising out of the stone beneath me, sinking into my flesh and setting a cold flood through my veins which was so intense that it burned. It was seeking out my fire, seeking out my soul but still I kept my hand pressed to the statue before me and continued with my plea.

Gabriel and Leon opened another chest, this one filled with scraps of parchment, each bearing the names of those who had been loved by someone who fought in our army and had been killed by the tyrant we fought. There were blank pieces of parchment too plus a pot of ink which any soul who might be drawn close and eager to join this fight could use to add their name to the roster. I only hoped that they would do so.

I managed to nod at my brother, and they began feeding those names to the fire at my back.

"All of you were wronged in life by the False King Lionel Acrux. All of you suffered and died at his hand or the hands of his followers. And he will not stop unless we find the strength to end him. Unless *you* find the strength to end him with us."

The ashes from the parchment rose into the air as they burned, whirling in a shower of blazing sparks, twisting up around me as an unearthly breeze tugged at my hair and the ether dug ever deeper into me.

"I beg you to return to us for this fight. To stand with those who loved and lost you, to right the wrongs against you."

The blazing scraps of parchment flew higher above us, circling overhead in a maelstrom felt nowhere but upon this mountainside on the edge of a war. But that was all they did, just circled above us, The Veil flickering wildly but not parting despite my pleas.

A sob broke from my lips as the truth of that failure sank into me, the impossibility of this plan falling like the ashes of those pieces of parchment around me and the screams from the battlefield seeming to rise up louder than ever before as fate closed around us like a snare.

Defeat pulled at me, that coldness sinking deeper, choking me, yanking at my soul with hands of bone and rotten flesh as it tried to drag me down in payment for this power.

I sagged, seeing it so clearly now, knowing it was over, that all sparks of hope were lost.

As I closed my eyes, the flickering of the flames still showed through my eyelids, the power of my Phoenix seeming to burn brighter as I gave in to the weight of this impossible magic.

I gritted my teeth and forced my eyes open once again, staring up at the empty face of the statue above me and digging my fingernails into the stone.

"I don't beg you," I hissed, my bloodied fingers painting a final rune onto the clay despite the way my hand shook, and the ether ripped pieces of me away chunk by chunk. "I am Tory Vega, daughter of the Savage King, sister of Darcy Vega and rightful queen of this fucking land. I. do. Not. Beg."

The jagged lines of Sowulo blazed upon the clay statue, painted in the blood of the royal line and I stared at it as I refused to let death or any other force on this world defy me in the protection of my kingdom.

"I *command* you to come to me," I hissed. "Return to fight with us and pick up your swords. Your kingdom needs you and your queens have commanded you, so answer my fucking call!"

A roar ripped through me as ether exploded from my hand, tearing its way out of me and burning its way into the statue before me, then the one beside that and the next, and the next and the next.

I refused to fall back until each one of them had tasted that power and my body could no longer resist the agony of holding on.

I crashed to my knees, panting heavily through the darkness that pushed in on my vision. Distantly, I was aware of Gabriel calling my name, of Leon cursing and of the statues all just standing there, doing nothing at all.

It hadn't worked. I had given everything and still, it hadn't worked.

The beats of my heart came slower and slower, the price demanded by the ether stealing the life from my body over seconds or minutes or hours…I didn't even know. All I knew for certain was that I was fading. And it hadn't worked.

Gabriel was yelling for me to hold on, but I couldn't feel his hand in mine or even the bite of the wind anymore. The darkness had come to claim me at last and the pain I felt at that failure burned through me as I thought of the people I loved most in this world and a single word spilled from my lips.

"Sorry."

DARIUS

CHAPTER NINETY SIX

I lurched forward where I clung to Tharix's spiny neck, a gasp catching in my throat as the world surrounding us seemed to flicker, the golden web of The Veil pressing in close to me and revealing a crowd of faces staring on in terror.

My heart stalled in my chest, the fading rhythm of my pulse wavering one final time as I tried so desperately to cling on to this life and the life of the soul which was bound to mine.

"Roxy," I panted, feeling her grip on life loosening, chains of power dragging her from me. "Hold on," I gasped even as my own grasp on this place wavered too, The Veil thinning, showing me that place which I had vowed to stay well clear of for far longer than this.

Tharix swooped lower and I almost fell from his back, my lungs failing to draw breath as I looked up into the face of the Savage King and the army of warriors who were gathered around him.

"Don't you dare let go," Hail Vega commanded.

"You can end this," my mom breathed.

A snarl pulled from the base of my throat, and I pushed away from them, from their unyielding expressions and unwavering belief as I clung to the one thing that mattered the most to me in this world.

I channelled my power into the un-beating relic which lay dormant in my chest, offering up all I had to the connection which bound me to the woman I loved, and as I felt death rushing closer I didn't flinch away from it. Instead, I reached out my hand and welcomed it in.

TORY

CHAPTER NINETY SEVEN

"That's something you need to learn about being a monarch; you should never apologise for making the hard decisions," a deep voice rumbled from above me.

As if his words had been a shot of adrenaline into my faltering heart, I gasped, my pulse leaping, eyes snapping open. The gateway between realms had parted for me at last and something had given me the power I needed to yank it wide open when I'd been so close to tumbling through it instead.

The distant sky was awash with orange and pink streaked clouds, the blue surrounding them so bright that it was blinding. Standing among it, a shadow hiding his features from me, was a man so much larger than life than I'd imagined him to be. He was achingly familiar, though I'd never really had the chance to know him at all.

Hail Vega reached down and took my hand, heaving me to my feet with a wry smile on his face. He towered over me by more than a foot, but as we looked at one another I found nothing but pride and wonder in his gaze.

"I told you they'd become far greater than you or I," a woman spoke from beside him and I whirled to my mother, falling into her embrace and releasing a choked sob of longing.

I could still feel the cold clay of the statue's body which she had taken residence in, but on top of that was the feeling of her, of a mother's embrace which I had never known.

"You came," I breathed in awe.

All of my most desperate, final hopes had been pinned on this, but I hadn't really believed it would work until this moment, standing on top of a barren mountain with my parents either side of me.

"We serve at the command of the True Queens," my father said, bowing his head to me.

A laugh spilled from lips as I found myself in this impossible situation, looking between the parents who had died to give us this chance. And I vowed in that moment that we would not squander it.

"You have until the battle is won, one way or another," a rasping voice spoke at my back, and I turned to find The Ferryman there, his cowl pulled low to hide his features, his paddle gripped tightly in his fist as though even here, he stood with one foot in the river of the dead. And if I strained my ears, I was sure I could hear it flowing. "Make it count."

A savage smile took my lips captive, and I stepped back, looking from my father to my mother, then to the next statue which had yet to take on the features of a departed soul. But as I looked at the blank stone face, a scrap of parchment landed on it, burning the name scrawled there to nothing.

Azriel Orion.

As it fell to ash, features pushed out of the stone, the solid chest expanded as the creation took a breath of real air and suddenly I found myself staring at the face of a man who looked so like his son that I would have known him regardless of seeing that name burn.

"Lance is down there," Azriel growled, drawing his sword, the pommel remaining as stone while the blade seemed to form out of pure light. "And he needs me."

My mother had stepped up to Gabriel, taking his face between her hands and kissing his brow as he bowed into her embrace, tears painting his cheeks as he clung to her.

Hail moved to embrace him too while all around us more and more scraps of parchment found their hosts and the souls of the dead came rushing past The Ferryman, hurling themselves into bodies of stone and rending them into their once-living features.

"The Nights ride again!" yelled a ferocious-looking blonde woman as she moved to stand with a group of other souls and they beckoned Leon to them, cooing about his hair and his triumphs in thievery.

My gaze caught on Washer who had of course claimed a stone body with a huge cock carved on it and Principal Nova who claimed the one beside him.

"You died?" I breathed, the grief hitting me like a stab to the chest, but Washer just shrugged.

"I can't think of anything I'd have rather given my life for."

Catalina and Hamish appeared, plus Antonia Capella and her murdered pack and many others who had not long lost their battle in life, but were still willing to return and see this fight to its bloody end.

"There is someone else you should meet, son," Hail murmured, and he turned to a statue which was just waking at his back, a dark-haired man appearing within the stone who blinked up at the sky in awe before dropping his gaze and staring with abject longing at Gabriel.

"Come, Marcel," my mom encouraged and the man who I realised was Gabriel's biological father stumbled closer to meet his son.

"I've been thinking of you," Gabriel told him. "Darius said you'd been fading and I was worried you might have passed on-"

"I couldn't have left without finding you first," Marcel swore, pulling Gabriel into a hug. "I knew we would get our moment to fight alongside one another. I *saw* it a very, very long time ago."

A blare of noise sounded from the battle behind us, and the moment of awed reunion shattered like a strike of thunder carving the sky apart. I whirled to face the far side of the mountain again and strode up to its peak before looking down into the basin where the bloodshed was reaching its crescendo.

My mother moved to stand at my side, taking my still bleeding hand in hers and lending me her magic to heal the wound. It didn't feel like Elemental power though, more like a surge of raw energy which carried the essence of her being within it.

I smiled at her, tears of joy and sorrow glistening on my battle-stained cheeks. Hail came to stand on my other side, and I pointed to the fresh ranks of Lionel's army who were almost upon the eastern side of our forces. They would clash within a matter of minutes and there would be no surviving those odds.

"These bodies of clay will hold the souls for the duration of the fight unless shattered," The Ferryman spoke from behind us. "I have a tight grip on each and every one of them though – no other shall be stealing a second chance from me."

I nodded, knowing that no matter how much I might have wished to steal my parents back from death the way I had done with Darius that I couldn't do that. I had bought their time here while we fought and not a second longer. This was a chance to give them vengeance and to give our army the numbers we so desperately needed. No more.

"Here," Gabriel said, lifting two swords from the ground, the ones he and my sister had been wielding for some time. The black one belonging to my father and the white to my mother. "The Savage King and his Queen cannot be without their weapons."

"By the stars," Hail sighed, taking his sword and testing the weight of it in his hand. "I have dreamed of a time when I might wield this blade again."

"This sword will run thick with the blood of those who have harmed our family soon enough," Merissa growled, kissing Gabriel's cheek in thanks and he held her close for an eternal moment.

Gabriel stepped away and moved into place beside us with Leon, their families and Azriel with them.

"Tell the poor choice," Hail murmured in my ear as we prepared to charge into war. "He did…okay."

"Darius?" I asked, a smile lifting my lips for a brief moment. "Did he help in this?"

"He offered his power to you while you were balancing on the edge and together, you managed to open the way. But when this door closes, I expect the two of you to stay on this side of it for a long time yet. Understood?"

"I'll do my best," I agreed, the solid thump of my heartbeat making me feel closer to my husband than I had been since before this bloody battle had begun.

I looked across the faces of the dead, sorrow tugging at my heart as I spotted Milton and his herd. Antonia and the rest of Seth's pack grouped together, along with countless others who had already died in this battle and been summoned back to fight again. Justin was there too, and I nodded to him, saddened by his loss, but he only smiled and raised his sword.

I gasped as I spotted Diego, a bright smile on his face and no hat to be seen.

"Let's kill those pendejos, mi reina."

"About fucking time," Hail rumbled.

"For Solaria!" I yelled so that every one of them could hear me. "And for Lionel's fucking head!"

And with that, we broke into a sprint, tearing down the sheer mountainside in a tide of death and destruction. As it became too steep for living feet to traverse, Gabriel grabbed Leon and launched the two of them into the air on his wings, and I flew up from the cliff face to join them.

The army of the dead didn't falter though, their feet remaining solid on the ground, their movements defying the restrictions of living flesh as they almost seemed to glide down the sheer slope, a chorus of death screams tearing from every throat. And as I soared above them, Phoenix fire blazing to life across my flesh and Leon's whoops of excitement ringing in the air while he swung from Gabriel's arms, all I could think of was how much I was going to enjoy ripping Lionel's bloody corpse to pieces.

DIEGO

CHAPTER NINETY EIGHT

I ran with the keenness of war in my veins, no heart beating in my chest but instead pure starlight thrumming through every part of my newfound body. I was here, back in the world of the living fighting for the justice I had never gotten to reap in my lifetime. But here and now, I could make a difference. *Puedo cambiar las estrellas.*

I charged down the mountainside with a roar pouring from my lungs, my hatred for Lionel Acrux and La Princesa de Las Sombras filling that sound. Today, I would be someone important. I would place the mark on the world which I had never gotten to leave in life. I would be a warrior for my queens, my dearest friends, and I would fight until I returned to dust.

This body felt realer than I could ever have imagined, the wind on my face and sun on my cheeks like a balm to my lost soul. I was not saddened by my death anymore; I had found peace beyond The Veil with my abuela once the shadows had been cleaned, our souls released from darkness and released to our rightful places of death along with all the other lost Nymph souls. But I had forgotten how good the elements of the living realm felt, how crisp the frosty air tasted.

We hit the bottom of the mountain and I raced out towards the battle at the backs of the Savage King and his Queen. True to their nature, they charged defiantly into battle at the side of their daughter, ready to change the hand of fate.

Those of the allied army closest looked back to see what the storm of noise was behind them, their eyes widening and awe touching their faces as they found the dead king returned from beyond.

We raced into the dwindling space where Lionel's army had been aiming to hit ours along its eastern flank, crashing into his warriors and tearing through them with brutal force and bloody efficiency.

I felt no tiredness in my bones, no ache in my legs. I might have been here, a soul placed inside a temporary body, but I wasn't truly here. I doubted I could feel pain or suffer in this world at all, but I could certainly wield a sword, and I'd be sure to send as many of these pendejos into deaths as I could.

"Para las verdaderas reinas!" I roared as I collided with my first enemy, taking him down with a thrust of my star-lit sword. For Darcy, for Tory, for Sofia and all those I had left behind in life. Their future was still a possibility, and I would do anything to secure it for my friends.

CALEB

CHAPTER NINETY NINE

The battle between Dragons had raged wildly, the odds weighing against us as we'd fought for our lives in the hidden depths of the storm clouds. Finally, with a lash of deadly fire magic timed with a crack of Dante's lightning, we'd burned our final adversary from the inside out.

Dante bellowed in victory, his roar echoed by the heavens as thunder crashed within the cloud he had created and we sped through it at a furious speed.

I healed us both again, exhaustion weighing in my limbs as I caught my breath and turned my mind back to the war at large.

"Get lower!" I called over the booming thunder, lightning illuminating countless silhouettes within the cloud for a brief moment. "We need to find Orion!"

All throughout our fight with the Dragons, my bond with Lance had pulled at me, the sight of what lay around him merging with my own vision, his need for help and unending pain urging me to get to him with a fierce desperation.

Dante tucked his wings and plummeted, lightning spearing from his jaws and striking a Harpy through the chest, sending him spiralling to his death. We broke free of the clouds, and I sucked in a sharp breath as I took in the new layout of the battlefield below.

Our army had been decimated, the entire right flank reduced to nothing but corpses and smouldering fires, the remainder of our ranks forced to group together to the west of the basin while Lionel spread his warriors out and looked to surround them. Lavinia was wreaking havoc on all those pushed her way, her shadows a plague that was growing more virulent by the second.

Panic for Seth filled my heart even as my gaze fell on a new force which was charging into the fight precisely where our army needed them most. I took in the blaze of Phoenix fire which flared at the front of what looked like an army of moving statues and yet moved with the fluidity of Fae. A golden glimmer seemed to cling to the fresh ranks of warriors and their war cries rose above the rest, echoing off of the mountaintops like a cry of justice.

There was something poetically deadly about that oncoming storm of warriors and my gut twisted as I looked down at Tory, wondering what cost such magic must have required as I remembered the insane plan she had whispered to our inner circle as a desperate, last resort.

"She's called the dead back to fight for us," I said, awe claiming the place of the fear which had threatened to choke me as I watched that impossible army crash into Lionel's forces and tear great holes in their ranks at once.

But I couldn't sit staring at this impossibility any longer and I forced my mind back onto the urgent need to locate Orion, sending another trail of golden flames towards the point where I sensed him to be through our bond.

A howl pierced the air, taken up by a resounding chorus as we dropped low over the battlefield and I gasped, hunting for Seth among the masses. Instead, I found Rosalie Oscura in her stunning silver Wolf form leading her pack our way. They tore through Fae and Nymph alike, Dante scoring a path of destruction through our enemies with a blast of lightning to aid them.

A flutter of movement caught my eye and I turned my head, blinking in surprise as the tiny sky-blue sayer dragon soared past me on its wings, heading through the sky at a casual pace like there wasn't a war being waged right ahead of it. As I stared after the little creature, it slipped into the centre of a herd of Lionel's Griffins who were in formation, chasing after a pale pink Pegasus who I was almost certain was Sofia.

The Griffins closed in on her and I yelled out to Dante, drawing his focus to her, but before he could summon his lightning, the sayer dragon released a pulse of light which flashed across the entire sky and forced a beat of unnatural silence into existence.

I blinked, trying to clear my eyes from the effects of the bright flare and by the time I could see clearly again, I found the entire herd of Griffins all tumbling from the sky, completely immobile as if they'd been paralysed.

They crashed down on top of their own army, death unfolding all around them and Sofia made it safely back into the clouds. The sayer dragon was gone, but I found myself endlessly grateful that the little beast was on our side of this.

I fixed my focus back on my hunt, the glimmering golden thread guiding us lower until I was able to see the crumpled figures on the ground clearly.

As we made it to the spot where I knew Orion was waiting for me, I leapt off of Dante, landing on a platform of earth that I created to catch me and shooting across it to find my sanguis frater.

I spotted him lying there, broken and clinging to life, still trying to claw his way back towards the battling Fae who were only fifty feet away from crushing him and threw myself down beside him. I gripped his face between my hands and poured healing magic into him so fast that my head spun from it.

Rosalie and her pack swarmed around us, chasing the enemy back and ripping through their forces with brutal efficiency.

She did a circle of our area then came racing back to us, shifting as she moved to stand over me.

"Is he dead?" she asked, concern written into her features, though she didn't seem to care that she was butt naked and covered in blood.

"I just look it," Orion growled, shoving himself up as his broken bones finally fused back together.

"Good. Because your girl would have been pissed at me if you'd died on my watch, stronzo." Rosalie grinned then turned and took a running jump onto Dante's back as he swept past again.

I watched as they sped away into the sky, Rosalie growing solid stone armour across her body as she prepared to enter the fight in Fae form and the two of them looking like a pair of warriors from some kind of Faery tale.

"She's...got a point," Orion muttered and the two of us locked eyes as we decided what to do next.

"Lavinia," I said.

"Yes," he agreed, his eyes turning to her shadowy form far out into the battle. "She's made it to the western line," he said darkly. "And she's left a fucking massacre in her wake."

"Have you seen Seth?" I asked in a low voice while trying to shove the part of me which was panicking down into a little box in the back of my skull. If I gave into it then I would be as good as dead out here.

"No," Orion replied, his gaze darting past me as if he were hunting for a sign of the white Wolf. "Is he alright?"

"The right flank has been destroyed," I breathed. "He...I couldn't see him anywhere." I cleared my throat, forcing that fear away. It wouldn't help and if he was still alive and I let my fear over him get me killed then he would be so fucking pissed at me.

"The entire right flank?" Orion asked in horror, and I nodded.

"But Tory's plan worked. She was taking their place with an army of the dead several thousand strong."

Neither of us mentioned that those numbers didn't come close to equalling what we'd lost. Besides, dead warriors had to count for more. Didn't they?

We exchanged a look in which our doubts hung, but neither of us gave voice to them. It didn't matter anyway. We would keep fighting until this ended.

I offered him my wrist, letting him sink his teeth into my skin and he drew out enough magic to keep him going until he could get what he needed from some enemy bastard. Then I took hold of his arm, the rush of my pulse making it hard to restrain myself and a groan rolling up my throat as I drew his blood between my lips.

The flood of forbidden magic drove into me again, sending a ripple of power through my chest. I exhaled heavily as I released him and we shot across the battlefield once more, heading for the stain of shadows which marked Lavinia's position in this fight.

It was as if time slowed around us, the rush of being able to slice through our enemies faster than the wind making a wild exhilaration blaze through me. This feeling was insane, like immortality, the power of a fucking god. We were unending, unpredictable and utterly unstoppable.

I cut a Nymph clean in half with a blast of earth magic then fell upon another and another, ending their lives before they could even try to defend themselves.

More and more of our enemies fell before us, their blood staining our lips, their power filling our reserves and not one of them was able to raise their weapons against us before death found them.

With this power came the cost of its end though and each time the exhaustion struck it was harsher, immobilising my limbs for long moments which I didn't have.

Orion dropped down to kneel just far enough away to make reaching him impossible, the exhaustion hitting him too. I cursed as I dug my fingers into the dirt, trying to force my vision to focus.

I cast a shield of rock to cover me with the last scraps of my energy and I panted beneath it, the taste of so much blood on my tongue that I was almost sick with it. I'd torn out more throats than I could count, stolen more magic from more sources than I had ever mixed in my life and my insides were rioting with the clash of unfamiliar power. But above it all, the desire to reunite with Orion and taste his blood again consumed me. It was a thing of its own, this coven magic, a dark and twisted temptation which had me drunk on the raw power of it and constantly craving more.

It was no wonder it had been forbidden; no wonder the Vampires in the Blood Ages were feared the way they had been. And no wonder that the other Fae had all banded together and discussed the possibility of killing all of our kind just to keep this kind of power from existing at all.

I managed to blink away the worst of it, my hands no longer trembling, and I focused on Orion as I drew my earth magic to me once again. I had to get to him. I just had to get to him and we would be fine.

The earth swallowed me, hurling me along beneath the ground before spitting me out precisely where I knew Orion would be.

He cursed as I erupted into the dome of air he was using to shield himself then lunged at me, his teeth sinking into my throat without another word.

I grabbed his wrist and bit him too, not caring that I was flat on my back and surrounded by corpses, simply needing another taste of this power, another rush of that magic.

Our eyes met as we released each other, and I licked his blood from my lips.

"This is dangerous," he said, and I nodded because no matter how fucking amazing it was, I could tell that was true plainly enough.

"Never again. Just today," I swore and the look we exchanged told of how difficult it was going to be for us to resist this temptation and keep to that vow.

A blaze of red and blue flames tore overhead and we both looked up just as Darcy collided with a Dragon in the sky above us, the gigantic beast hurling her out of the air and sending her flying towards the western flank of our army, closer to Lavinia.

"Blue," Orion gritted out in concern as the Dragon chased her down to the ground.

"Come on," I began, shoving to my feet within Orion's dome of air magic, but a bellowing roar made me jerk around before we could leave.

An enormous beast was charging towards us, jagged pincers and flailing limbs cutting through our army in droves. The monster looked to be made out of stone, every sword, spear or shot of magic aimed its way simply glancing off and falling uselessly to the ground while the Fae who tried to fight it were shredded by the beast.

A howl drew my attention to a warrior with long, half braided hair who was racing towards the monster with a spear clutched in his fist and unsurmountable hatred etched into every piece of his expression. Relief enveloped me as fast as fear took me captive again.

"Seth," I took a step towards him then stopped, looking to Orion who was glancing between Seth and the direction Darcy had fallen.

"You go after your guy, I'm going after my girl," he said.

"We might not see each other again," I replied tightly, and he nodded, stepping forward and tugging me into a tight embrace. It was brief and full of despair, but as we parted, I could see this was it now. We were teetering on the edge of oblivion, and there was only one person each of us should have been with in the face of our demise.

"Take care, brother," I said, our hands clasping before his shield evaporated.

"And you, sanguis frater," he said, emotion blazing in his eyes, then we shot away in opposite directions, toward wholly different fates. But ones which might just lead us back together at the door of death.

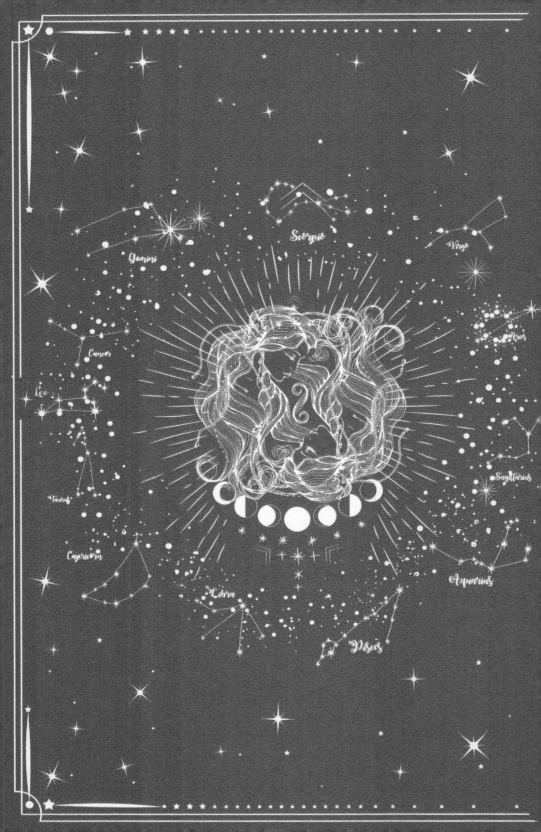

DARCY

CHAPTER ONE HUNDRED

The bloodthirsty Dragon came tearing down from above with jaws of hellfire ready to claim me. But a shield of air arced over my head as I cast chains into existence, making them fly up and coil around the beast who blocked out all light above. I forged boulders onto the end of those chains that weighed a tonne and as they dragged the Dragon out of the air, the huge rocks slammed into groups of enemy Fae around me, crushing them in an instant.

I let the earth swallow me and dropped my air shield as I disappeared into the depths of the soil and the ground tremored with the impact of the beast above.

I carried myself up in front it, casting air at my feet so I burst from the dirt and was thrown upward, my sword turning in my grip to angle down at the Dragon's head. I released my air magic, falling instead and landing on the beast's head, my sword slicing into its skull.

Dante still fought with a couple more Dragons in the sky, but I could see him gaining the upper hand, and with the enemies surging around me down here, I knew it was time for my feet to remain on the ground.

A line of enemy Fae raced up onto the hulking Dragon's body to reach me, weapons raised and magic tearing from them all at once. I sent out a blaze of fire in a ring, blasting them backwards with screams of pain. A whirl of wooden stakes went flying out from me and found the hearts of all those who had waged the attack, all except one who shielded, gaining his feet and turning to run. "I'll bring a plague of Nymphs back to take your head, Savage Whore!" he bayed, but he suddenly stumbled into a wall of solid muscle.

My heart lifted at finding him there, alive, whole, safe. Lance Orion was coated in blood, and there was something so animalistic about him as he grabbed the throat of the man who had run into him.

"You will never speak of her like that again. I will assure it." Orion ripped the man's head off with his hands and let it fall from his grip, and my heart raced at the sight.

A line of Nymphs rushed to meet us, and there was no more time to revel in the fact that Orion still lived. Fate was spinning plenty of deaths that could claim him yet.

I leapt from the Dragon's head and blasted two of the Nymphs with Phoenix fire, the blaze tearing through their bark-like skin and leaving their charred husks to fall at my feet while I readied to take on my next opponent. Orion shot into the throng of Nymphs with his speed, racing through them and tearing their hearts clean from their chests before they even had a second to realise they were dead.

Lavinia was close, her delighted cries carrying from where she was tearing into our army. I readied to fly again, to hunt her down and finish her for good, but then a roar of pain made me wheel around in fear.

Shadow was surrounded by a sea of Nymphs, the huge beings swarming him, forcing him beneath them and stabbing at him with their probes.

"No!" I screamed, taking to the air on my wings.

My hands were raised, ready to cast and fury lined my limbs.

I could barely see Shadow beneath the tide of Nymphs. With a cry, I set my fire loose and burned every one of the creatures who were trying to kill him. The fire swept through them, sending many running for safety while most were consumed in my flames.

Shadow was wounded, but as I landed beside him, those injuries began to heal and I cast an air shield over us, giving him time to do so.

I looked out at the battle forces surrounding us, so much death and destruction, all caused by that power hungry bastard, Lionel Acrux. This *had* to end.

A flash of pale green made me blink in surprise among the bleak landscape and my lips parted as a little sayer dragon sailed past the safety of my shield. It looked so small, so vulnerable, but even as fear for the creature ate its way into me, it tucked its wings and landed on the head of the largest of Lavinia's Nymphs.

The Nymph had been cutting through our forces with savage brutality, but it went suddenly rigid as the sayer dragon settled down on its head. My lips parted as if I might call out to the tiny beast but before a sound could escape my lips, the Nymph turned to face its comrades and bellowed furiously then launched an attack on its own allies.

My shock was broken by a low grunt telling me that Shadow was well again, and he lowered his head, nudging his nose against my cheek. I swear he meant it to thank me.

"You're welcome," I said, patting him then flying up to take a seat upon the saddle on his back.

I dropped the shield protecting us, scanning the area for the Nymph being ridden by the sayer dragon, but it had disappeared into the thickness of the enemy ranks and my attention was quickly stolen by my own fight.

Shadow roared, rearing up and I held on tight with one hand while preparing my other to cast as Shadow charged through the fleeing Nymphs ahead. I burned the ones he didn't capture in his jaws, or dragged them down into the earth with roots that wound around their legs and pulled them into the abyss. We were a thing of death, the two of us a monster of our own as we tore through the enemy Nymphs, killing them in droves.

When we'd taken down several rows of them, Orion came to stand before Shadow. "I'm yours to aim, Blue."

"Destroy Lavinia's ranks," I called to him. "Take out her defences!"

He nodded, and sped ahead of us, breaking necks, shattering bone, killing with brutal skill. Shadow charged along after him, following the path he paved through Lavinia's Nymphs and I sent fire blooming out all around us, the shrieks of dying Nymphs carrying up to the stars.

Lavinia's gaze turned our way, seeing me coming, and even from this distance, I swore I caught a look of fear in her eyes. She turned, sending more and more of her Nymphs our way then casting a colossal wall of shadow out in either direction, barring her from view.

I growled, knowing I could simply fly over to her myself, but that would leave our army to face this heaving regiment of Nymphs, so I was determined to finish them first.

The Nymphs collided with the air shield around Shadow and me, desperate to break through, but the only thing that could escape was the Phoenix fire I let out, sending it to scorch the flesh from their bones. We were a weapon that was causing chaos, sending the Nymphs into a wild frenzy as they fought to stop us.

Orion was too fast for them to catch, and Shadow and I were too well protected for them to even get close to us. Any who tried fell prey to my fire, and I watched them burn with a flood of hope in my chest.

A roar was growing ever louder at the back of our army, moving closer with every second. I turned to seek it out, the sun blinding me in that direction as I squinted to try and find its source. Then my eyes locked on an impossible reality, making me certain my brother and sister had pulled off what they'd planned, and my heart beat harder with frantic joy. Another army. A new, fresh army was ploughing forward along with our front line with glittering swords carving through our adversaries. The army of the dead.

My breath caught at the impossible knowledge that my mother and father were out there in this battle, fighting to secure our future, and it took all of my strength not to turn and run for them now. To fight at their sides and see them in the flesh. But I couldn't turn from Lavinia. Not when I had her so close, hiding within her shadows and praying I wouldn't find her.

XAVIER

CHAPTER ONE HUNDRED & ONE

Barely a beat after Darius had been dragged from my back by Tharix, two Griffins had descended from the sky and a bloody fight had ensued. I'd ended up victorious but with a torn wing, tumbling down onto the battlefield where I'd been caught since, fighting enemy after enemy. I had no time to shift and heal myself, the painful gouges growing keener the longer I fought.

My Phoenix fire horn was doing beautiful, ruinous work, cutting through the Fae who were trying to bring me down. I was among a group of allied Fae; water Elementals working with the shifters of the ocean who had joined us from the Academy of Hydros. The Elementals had cast pods of bulging water that rolled out into the enemy ranks, sucking Lionel's soldiers into them where they found themselves at the jaws of Acheilus Shark shifters, the vicious swipes of Dolphins' tails, and at the mercy of all other sea creatures within.

A roaring cry was building in our army, but I couldn't see what was causing it from my position in the middle of the battle, the crush of the fight too thick.

Something was coming. Something that was striking fear into our enemies, more and more lines of them retreating, finding themselves stumbling into the deadly pods of water which were turning red with blood. One of the pods came rolling my way and I reared up to avoid it, letting it pass, watching it slam into the row of enemies ahead of me. Their screams turned to streams of bubbles as they swam, trying to break the surface of the water, but there was no way out.

With the space opened up around me and the water Elementals holding back the lines of enemies ahead, I shifted, gasping as I slapped a hand to my chest and healed away my injuries. I took the Phoenix horn from my head, gripping it tight and casting clothes over my body made from my earth magic, along with several thick metal plates of armour.

My gaze turned to the mountainside where I'd last seen Darius, fearing what had become of him. There was no sign of his Dragon in the sky, and I hoped that meant he was still on his journey to the castle, keeping himself hidden from our father.

Behind me, a flood of our enemies were racing our way, turning from some terror ahead of them and I readied my horn, Phoenix flames flaring along its length while my other hand raised to cast.

With a twist of my fingers, I forged sharp wooden stakes which blasted from the earth at our adversaries' backs, and cries of agony filled the air as a hundred of them found themselves skewered. I rose up on a plinth of earth, knowing I was making myself a target, but I had to see. I had to know what was coming.

My breaths stalled at the sight of the charging army that had joined the fray, their weapons glittering with light. They were closing in on this very spot, and my heart raced as I recognised the faces among them. The Savage King and Merissa Vega fought alongside Tory, leading thousands of Fae deeper into the battle. It was impossible, and my mind scrambled to make sense of it.

A cry went up from the water Elementals and I twisted around, my heart stammering at the sight of the stampede of beasts racing through them with guns mounted on their backs. The very weapons I'd learned of and had been trying to come up with a solution for alongside the other Spares.

A sizzling blast of magic exploded from one of the machines and I ducked as it went whizzing overhead, turning to watch in horror. It collided with the Savage King's army, and instead of torn limbs and spilled blood, shattered clay was left in its wake.

A strange golden mist rose from the destroyed bodies then disappeared at once. I didn't know what I was witnessing, only that more blasts of that terrifying power were flying through the air. I threw myself to the ground, the charge of the explosions making the hairs on the back of my neck stand to attention, a whoosh of wind signalling their passage overhead.

When the gunfire stopped, I shoved to my feet, my pulse thrashing as I realised what I needed to do. What I had planned to do with the Spares if these weapons ever came into play in the battle.

I cast the effigy of a Pegasus with my fire magic and sent it up into the sky, flying higher and higher with molten sparks cascading from its wings to draw the attention of the Fae I needed, hoping on everything that they were still alive. Then I sent the Pegasus out towards the mountainside to my left, perching it there for my friends to see.

I let the shift ripple over me, my earth-made armour pinging off of my body, abandoned as I raced into the sky. I flew as fast as possible, the boom of thunder in the clouds above telling of Dante's fury.

Sofia and Tyler were up there somewhere in their own slice of hell, and I swore to return to them soon, not even entertaining the idea that they hadn't made it this far in the battle.

A fireball blasted my way and I banked to avoid it, then another and another. Some asshole was targeting me from down in the battle. But just as I located him, he was mowed down by our army, and I whinnied in triumph.

I flew on, landing on the mountainside close to the flaming Pegasus, waiting for the Spares to appear, the tension rising in my body as I watched those mounted weapons taking down more and more of our people.

Deep in the western flank, Lavinia was causing chaos, her shadows pouring from her in floods, so thick, I couldn't see her within them at all. But I could hear the screams and scent the blood, and that was enough to know the terror she was causing.

Hadley burst into view carrying Grayson and Athena under his arms, both of them wearing make-shift clothes and armour created by the power of earth. Hadley placed them down, his mouth wet with blood and his eyes dark with horrors.

Athena and Grayson rushed to hug me, nuzzling my neck, and I stole the sweetly brief moment of relief with my friends. When they pulled away, I found Hadley taking the defuser from where it was strapped to his back. The long, pointed metal contraption resembled a harpoon and contained a rare glacia diamond along with several other crystals in the cage of metal near one end.

"We can't all ride you, we'll slow you down," Grayson said, his face thick with grime and a look of exhaustion about him. "Had, Athena. You go. I'll return to the fight.'

"We can't split up," Athena said in horror, gripping her brother's hand. "Besides, we need as many Fae as possible for this. The more magic, the better."

I snorted, stamping my foot and taking hold of Grayson's sleeve with my teeth, pushing him towards my back. I could carry all three of them. I was strong. Stronger than I'd ever given myself credit for, and carrying my friends was no burden at all.

I stamped my foot again, glaring at each of them.

"Are you sure?" Hadley asked and I nodded my head.

Athena climbed up onto my back and Grayson followed, holding her waist before Hadley got up behind him.

I flexed my wings and sprang into the sky, feeling the tingle of concealment spells as all three of them worked to blend us in with the mountain and the sky. I set my sights on the Jade Castle, our plan riding on one crazy notion, but if it worked, we could take out those awful weapons and protect our army from more slaughter.

It was a long flight, and the roar of battle was deafening as we flew above the carnage. There had once been rows of enemy shifters that guarded this path, stopping any flying Orders from making it by, but no one attacked us now, and I had to wonder if Darius was responsible for destroying them.

Phoenix fire flared among a sea of Nymphs and my heart lifted at the sight of Darcy there riding the Shadow Beast and leaving a trail of death in her wake. Orion was with them, weaving through the throng, and I bid them good luck as they forged a path towards Lavinia and her writhing swell of shadows.

Finally, we descended at the far end of the rocky basin between the mountains at the foot of the green castle, away from the entrances in a shadowy corner where the jade met with the ground and no guards lingered to slow us.

I landed lightly and the Spares leapt from my back before I shifted into my Fae form, cladding myself in clothes and armour again as I turned to the empty expanse of rocky land here. The battle raged on ahead of us, but large boulders and slabs of jagged rock hid most of it from view.

My pulse ticked faster, magic crackling at my fingertips at the sound of someone grunting close by.

I moved away from the Spares, leaving them to drive the defuser deep into the wall of jade, my footsteps concealed by a silencing bubble. Rounding the wall, I found someone climbing out of the window, legs dangling before they dropped and hit the ground at my feet. I grabbed them by the throat, my Phoenix fire horn raised to kill, but then my eyes met with those of Ellis Rigel and I found myself hesitating.

"Please, wait. Don't kill me," she gasped in terror, and I dropped the concealment spells and silencing bubble, revealing myself to her.

Her eyes widened, recognition racing over her soft features.

"Xavier," she rasped. "Are you alright?"

I guessed I looked like shit, because the way her eyes tracked over my face said I was bloodied and worn by battle. But she was perfectly clean, untouched by war. And that stirred a rage in me that was murderous.

I shoved her against the wall, pinning her there by her throat. "Give me one reason why I shouldn't kill you for what you've done. For choosing my father, for supporting him and turning your back on us."

Tears welled in her eyes and she shook her head. My fingers flexed as I gave her room to speak. "I was afraid. I've been so afraid for so long, Xavier. I wanted to do what was right for my mom. I wanted to stick by her. But the king...he's awful," she whispered, eyes darting left and right like she expected him to appear at any second. "He's going to kill me if he catches me. It took me hours to break through the spells shielding that window so I could escape – I thought I was going to be found-"

"You're already captured and in the hands of your death. It's not him you should fear now," I warned.

A shaky breath passed her lips and she reached into her pocket, making me stiffen, preparing to kill her before she struck at me with some weapon. But then she held up a large bag of stardust in a velvet green pouch.

"It's the last of his supply," she said with a bitter delight in her gaze. "He can't escape the castle without it unless he leaves on foot or wing."

I frowned at the offering, her hand shaking as she held it out to me. Then I stared up at the high walls of the castle, and back to the open window.

"How far is it to his chamber?"

"You'll never make it. And you can't take this path into the castle, the wards would kill you before you even stepped inside," Ellis said frantically. "Plus guards are crawling all over the place. He probably has people searching for me. So kill me if you have to, but you have to get this away from here." She pressed the pouch against my side, and I took it with my free hand, my brow drawing tight.

"Why now?" I asked darkly.

She gulped, her throat bobbing against my palm. "Because I've been a coward for too long. And... I want to be brave. I want to make a choice which is entirely my own. If only once."

I saw the truth in her eyes, but I was unsure if I could really trust her. This pouch of stardust seemed like proof of her words though.

"Are you going to run?" I asked, removing my hand from her neck. "I assume you planned to take this stardust somewhere you could use it, away from the castle's wards. You'd still be running if I hadn't found you now."

"What use am I?" she breathed, bowing her head. "I was going to flee and take his escape with me. What more can I do than that?"

"I have a role for you, if you dare to take it," I offered, wondering if I was a fool. But I didn't want to be hardened by this war. I didn't want to be cold and unforgiving of those looking to be brave. After all, I'd had to be brave often enough to escape my father's clutches once upon a time, and I'd be a hypocrite not to give Ellis that chance.

"And if I refuse?" she asked, her lips quivering, telling me she expected me to promise her death.

"I'm not taking you captive. I'm giving you a choice," I said. "Run or help."

I took a pinch of stardust from the pouch, offering it to her. It would be enough to secure her passage away from this war if she got herself away from the castle on foot. Though she'd have to make it through the churning masses of my father's army to achieve it. It was a mercy. One I couldn't help but afford the friend I'd grown up with, one of the few I'd had in this life. She'd made mistakes, yes. But something told me Ellis Rigel wasn't a dark soul. And I knew the power a parent could hold over a person all too well. She had light yet to claim, and she was making a stand for it now, doing what she could to right her wrongs.

She looked to the stardust, eyes hungry for escape, but then she gazed at me instead and lifted her chin. "I'll help in any way I can."

"Good." I dropped the pinch of stardust back in the pouch.

I forged a bag and shoved the pouch inside before tethering it tight to my back with vines. Then I led Ellis around the castle wall to where the other Spares had managed to embed the defuser into the wall of jade, the glacia crystal glinting at the end of it.

"What's *she* doing here?" Hadley spat, and a growl rolled from Grayson's throat.

"Traitor," Athena hissed.

"She's vowed to help us," I said placing myself between them and Ellis, hoping I wasn't a fool for doing so. "She stole Lionel's store of stardust. I think she means it, and we need all the help we can get right now."

Hadley's jaw ticked as he looked to me, a challenge in his eyes. But at an imploring expression from me, he backed down.

"Fine, come on," Hadley clipped.

"What is this?" Ellis whispered as she stepped closer, staring at the contraption.

"You don't need to know," Grayson said. "If you really want to help, then prove it by doing what we ask."

Ellis nodded, looking scalded, but I doubted she was surprised by the reception.

I took hold of her hand, then took Hadley's, who held Grayson's, and finally Athena finished the line, placing her palm on the defuser. I was the only one who trusted Ellis enough to be next to her, and she got the message as she met my gaze.

"Power share," I commanded, and her magic flooded against my skin in offering. But it wasn't easy to let my defences down. All she'd done made me hesitate, but I gritted my teeth and forced my heart to listen. I could trust her. I had to.

A breath escaped me as the flood of her strength met with mine, igniting a whirlpool of power in my veins. I passed it to Hadley along with my own, a groan leaving his lips as he offered it to Grayson, and he passed it to Athena. She gasped, her eyes bright with magic as she channelled it into the defuser.

The jade of the castle magnified the power of the defuser, and with the glacia crystal's amplifications qualities, the whole contraption lit up in a bright blue glow. It buzzed and hummed, the crystals all coming to life within it and the whirring of power crackled through the air.

With a surge of ferocious energy, the defuser sent a blast of energy shooting up the jade wall, right to the very top of the castle.

The resulting boom jolted my heart, and power swept out in a pulsing spiral through the air. The blue light exploded across the battlefield, then turned to fizzling raindrops. We stopped power sharing, staring out at all we'd done, but a yell of challenge announced the arrival of a squadron of Lionel's personal guard.

The five of us moved together defensively, magic sparking in our fists as a group of twenty Fae came running around the castle wall. Fire blazed along my arms, then I spotted something that made me hesitate.

A little coral-coloured sayer dragon was floating down from the sky on outstretched wings, sinking into the centre of the group of guards. My gaze met with the tiny creature's and I swear it winked at me half a second before a blast of magic erupted from it in a flash of golden light.

I threw my hands up to shield my eyes and when I opened them again, every one of the guards was screaming as the flesh melted clean off of their bones.

Hadley swore loudly and Ellis gagged as they died in a matter of moments, and I was left staring at the creature that was no bigger than a kitten as it casually took off into the sky and disappeared towards the battle again.

"What the fuck was that?" Athena breathed.

"A...friend," I said, still unable to fully process what I'd seen but unable to spare the time to think about it any further right now.

I shifted into a Pegasus, lowering my wing to let the Spares onto my back, the bag of stardust still wrapped tight to my side.

"Come on then," Athena demanded as she clung to Hadley, offering her hand to Ellis who was hesitating.

I stamped my foot in an order for her to climb on and her hesitation shattered. She let Athena tug her up at the back of the line, and Ellis wrapped her arms around her before I leapt skyward, wings beating hard as I sped away from the castle and over the battlefield once more.

The raining droplets of power hit my wings, doing nothing to me, but it was sure as fuck doing something to those weapons mounted on the backs of that legion of shifters. As the power washed over them, they exploded, the power of the defuser driving into them and breaking the mechanisms. The blasts killed the shifters wearing them, rendering the guns entirely useless. Some of the beasts fought to get free of the contraptions, but it was too late, each one reaping what they'd sowed.

The Spares whooped and a neigh of joy left me as we sailed back towards our advancing army who were quickly reforming in the places where those guns had cut through them.

Their ferocity was unmatched, their power punching through the enemy lines and starting to regain some traction. My place was waiting for me there among the True Queens' army, and I flew faster, anxious to join them and fortify their ranks.

Ellis was in the thick of it now, but she'd made her choice, and it looked like she was finally coming to fight on the side of our queens.

GERALDINE

CHAPTER ONE HUNDRED & TWO

The battle was thick with blood and bile, the bilge of our enemies pressing in hot and heavy around us where we fought at the tip of the spear, the Starfall Legion still standing, still forging on despite our losses, my best trained warriors fighting on relentlessly. Our stamina was being tested to its limits, our comradery likely the only thing keeping us on our feet after so many hours battling on the front lines, yet still, we did not falter.

"I am as strong as the chain of my brothers and sisters in arms. If one of us holds, we all hold. As one we advance, as one we strike on!" I called, rallying my forces, their faces grim with determination, the flood of battle making it impossible for us to tell whether we were winning or losing in this dance of crowns. Yet I snuffed a something on the wind which had hope blossoming in my chest. I felt the mountains perking up and cracking bleary eyes to watch us.

"Today the world will change!" I bellowed. "Today the lives of the fallen will be worth their sacrifice. I offer my blood!"

"I offer my blood!" my warriors echoed.

"I offer my body!" I roared, spearing an enemy Nymph through the throat before lashing out with my flail and cracking the skull of a Fae preparing to cast at us.

"I offer my body!" a hundred voices replied.

"But first, I offer the blood of my enemies!" I screamed, cracking another skull just as Max shot a blast of ice through the chest of a Fae holding a fistful of fire. He fell dead, his flames igniting within the midst of his comrades, and the Starfall Legion surged to end them all in their panic.

"So let our enemies bleed!" my legion bellowed, and we advanced again, our boots crushing those we had conquered as we forged a path on, the Jade Castle now looming clearly ahead of us, our advance marked by the size of it dominating the view.

A cry of pain came from a warrior to my right and our ranks swept around her, shielding her within the safety of our bodies while another of my warriors ripped the ice dagger from her chest and healed her quickly.

Within moments, she had recovered, re-joining the line and wetting her sword with the blood of our adversaries.

"Share formation!" a yell came up from my right as our watcher spotted an incoming attack from above.

Our formation shifted, hands on shoulders, magic ripping from me the moment I felt our connection lock into place and a shield of crystal-clear ice formed over our heads.

The blast of Dragon fire almost cracked it, but I gritted my teeth and the shield held.

I narrowed my eyes at that cantankerous crout Mildred Canopus as she wheeled through the air in her mud-brown Dragon form and turned to strike at us again.

"Re-form!" I roared, my voice tearing its way out of my throat. "Rigel, take the shield."

"Why?" Maxy demanded, not doing as commanded.

"Helebor, take the shield," I pivoted, having no time for his namby pamby nonsense.

Marguerite stepped into my place at once, removing her hand from my shoulder and setting her jaw as she looked up at the sky, pouring the magic of the group into the shield to reinforce it with pure power.

I stepped forward, rolling my shoulders back as I tracked the movements of that wretched worm flapping through the heavens.

"*Gerry,*" Max barked, grabbing my elbow and forcing me to snap my gaze to his.

"If I die this day, know that I loved you, you wandering whelk," I told him. "Know I loved you to the depths of my dilly garden and beyond."

"Gerry," Max snarled, his fingers digging into my armour, no doubt thinking he might hold me, but I was the wind and no fist could close on my fluttering soul.

I gave him a soft smile then hardened at once.

It was a mere flick of my thumb to release the catch on my bracer and I was already running away from the dear dogfish before he had realised he held nothing but a piece of armour in his fist.

The enemy Fae before me lunged, thinking me a fool rushing at them like I was, but then the ground exploded beneath them, columns of jagged rock punching through the earth at my beck and call, creating a stepping stone stairway which was designed for one purpose alone.

I raced up those stairs as fast as a narry on a nabberry morn, my Brendas luckily housed snugly within the pointed form of my newly-made chest plate, for they would likely have taken my eye out had they been free to bounce at such a pace.

Eight, nine, ten leaps up the fractured stairway of stone, then I launched myself from the last column, flying through the air with my spear held high and my flail rotating at speed.

Mildred bellowed like a cow overdue a milking as I landed on her bony rump, and I drove my spear straight into the meaty muscle of her buttock to stop myself from sliding right back off again.

The impact jarred me and my flail fell from my grasp as I slammed into her spiney hide, almost falling clean off of her again. I grasped the spear, my legs flying out behind me like a pair of useless dallyhoppers.

"Gerry!" Max bellowed, launching himself into the sky, but before he could get close to us, Mildred plunged into the storm clouds above and we were lost to a world of our own.

"Oh no you don't," I growled as she flipped over, belching fire and trying to dislodge me. But my spear had struck bone and was rooted well. I would not let go of it for all the grapes in the sea.

My red hair whipped across my face, my legs flipped and flopped, and lightning lashed through the sky like a warning.

For several long seconds it seemed that I would simply remain as such, tossed and thrashed like an over-wet side salad. But I was no mere lettuce leaf. I was a main course all of my own.

A little bundle of silver passed me by, the sayer dragon giving me a curious look as though it thought me quite the kipper dangling as such. My focus couldn't remain on the valiant servant of my dear queens, but as it collided with a Dragon the size of a bus, an explosion tore the air in two and lumps of bloody meat sprayed out across the battlefield.

"Fight on, you dandy dallyhopper!" I called in salute to the sayer dragon before focusing once more on my own task.

I threw out a hand, my grasp on the spear becoming ever more precarious as I cast a bubble of water around Mildred's short-snouted head, blinding her, drowning her and causing her to level out beneath me.

She thrashed, shaking her head and I heaved myself up her spiney body, clinging to the lumps of leathery flesh which marked her entire back and climbing them like a squashy ladder.

I made it higher up her back and dug my knees into her sides as I sat myself up, a savage grin upon my lips.

"I made a vow to end you for the death of my beloved friend, Angelica," I told her. "And I am yet to ever break my word."

With a twist of my wrists, the water surrounding Mildred's head turned to ice, her body thrashing with panic beneath me as it dug into her skull, crushing her foul head and all the foul thoughts housed within it, piece by piece.

She dropped out of the sky, her entire body jerking with panic, and I tipped my head back to release a trio of howls from my lips as I rode her to her demise.

The ground rushed up to meet us and I got to my feet, closing my fist as we hurtled towards the ranks of Lionel's rancid forces and they screamed as they saw us coming.

Mildred jerked one final time before my ice drove its way through her skull and stole her life away with a brutal crunch.

I leapt into the air with my arms stretched wide mere moments before she collided with the ground at such force that she created a crater beneath her, crushing many enemy Fae as she went.

Max caught me before I could follow her into her grave, and I chuckled as I turned in his arms then patted him fondly on the cheek.

"That'll do, starfish," I told him.

"How many times do I have to tell you not to-"

I pressed my fingers to his lips and shushed him. "Be a dear and don't dither about the danberry bush. We have a legion to return to and I don't want to have to reprimand you for abandoning your post once this is won."

Max shook his head and grumbled complaints as he launched us back across the battlefield with his air magic, and as I looked down upon that ruinous plain, my heart leapt.

"Oh sweet songbirds," I breathed as I spied the Oscura Wolves destroying all who stood in their path, the Starfall Legion pressing further into the enemy lines and the rushing army of the dead cutting through foes led by my dear Queen Tory. "I do believe all hope is not yet lost."

But even as that hope swam like a swan upon my swales, my gaze fell on the dark and terrible storm of the shadows brewing upon the western flank. Lavinia was a wretch of sin and her harvest of pure souls was not even close to done, her banquet of death inviting all to its table, and from the look of her roiling, hungry power, this war was not even close to won.

SETH

CHAPTER ONE HUNDRED & THREE

Caleb was in the thick of the chaos with me, my need for vengeance setting my blood aflame as I fought to bring down the monster that had murdered my parents, my pack, my family. I howled in fury, casting a blast of wooden spears away from me in a vortex of air, my earth-made weapons slamming into the towering creature and drawing more blood on its flesh.

Caleb raced around it, slicing his twin blades at every piece of skin he could reach, the hideous beast's horse-like legs suddenly giving out as it hit the ground with a tumultuous bang. My Moon Mate had come to me in my moment of need, fighting at my side like a rogue of death, and I found my heart strengthened by the closeness of him. Together, we would finish the beast who had taken my parents from me.

I aimed for the monster's head, casting an air shield around it and wrenching, tightening my hold on the air and pulling, pulling, pulling. A loud crack sounded and the beast's head was torn clean off, blood spilling out in torrents as its body crumpled to the earth.

I panted, healing the wounds I'd incurred as Caleb came running to join me, his gaze racing over me to check I was okay.

"One more," he exhaled, catching his breath. "We can do one more."

I nodded, my throat thick with bitterness at the fact that my pack hadn't defeated this fallen monster sooner. Perhaps if we'd shifted, used magic…

My eyes glazed, shock leaving me frozen, arms leaden. I felt my inner Wolf cub crawling away into the darkest, safest, numbest place it could find inside me, refusing to come out again. Caleb stepped closer, casting a wall of earth around us to keep us shielded from any oncoming attacks.

"Seth," he growled, gripping my arm. "You're so fucking strong. Don't let them break you now after everything."

He squeezed my arm, the warmth of him coaxing heat into my bones, awakening me once again. I exhaled, realising I'd been holding my breath, my chest tight with wrought emotion.

"Your pain is your greatest weapon," Caleb said darkly. "Wield it like a blade and cast your enemies from this world."

A snarl built in my throat, my pain turning to a bloody rage that demanded payment for what I'd suffered. What had been stolen from me.

Caleb dropped the earth shield and there beyond us was the hulking form of the final monster tearing through the heart of our army. Its body resembled a giant tree with no leaves upon its branches, its overly long arms metallic and covered in spines, and its head bird-like with serrated teeth in its pointed beak. It looked part Nymph, part Caucasian Eagle perhaps, but whatever it was, it was an unnatural horror that needed to be put in the ground.

"Together," I growled.

Our magic tore from each of us, coiling into one entity, the power of two Heirs, two mates bound together by the moon. Cinder, soil and sky. Fire, earth and air. Between us, we held three of the great Elements, and we were a force to be reckoned with.

Our power drove into the earth, making the ground rumble with an ominous promise, while a tornado began to form from the clouds above, my air magic ripe with violence. Caleb lit that vortex with flames, the towering inferno a thing of destructive beauty as it grew in size, gathering momentum and spinning its way towards the last monster. Its bird-like head twisted around, a horrid squawk breaking from its parted beak before the tornado of fire slammed into it.

The beast was thrown backwards and flames lit along its torso. Caleb made them take root, burning it faster while I controlled the earth beneath it, opening it up into a wide chasm.

The monster fell with a shriek, its metallic arms catching on the edge of the dirt and streams of our soldiers raced forward to stab and kick at its gnarled claws, forcing it to let go.

I gritted my teeth in concentration as I willed that earth to close, clogging dirt into its mouth, its ears, every orifice it could find while Caleb's fire drove deep into its chest.

The ground closed up and a roar of victory came from our forces, my heart lifting as I realised it was done. The monsters were gone; their reign of terror was over. And the closest legion looked to Caleb and I for direction, gathering around us with a glint of hope shining in their eyes.

"Follow the fire!" I bellowed, sending the tornado of flames into the nearest line of our enemies.

"Follow the fire!" the legion cried, letting Caleb and I move through their ranks to lead the next charge.

Adrenaline burned hot in my veins, and I fell into the mania of war, not letting my mind slip back to the pain, only focusing on the task that had to be completed. To finish every last one of the False King's warriors at the side of my Moon Mate and dress myself in their blood.

DARIUS

CHAPTER ONE HUNDRED & FOUR

Tharix had been true to his word so far, smuggling me back to my father's castle through an entrance on the ground floor. He'd gotten us past the wards, his magic welcome here, but from there it had been a bloodbath.

"This is taking too fucking long," I snarled, wrenching my axe from the corpse of the latest guard to die before me. "Someone is bound to tip him off soon."

"I could go ahead," Tharix offered, pushing his black hair away from his eyes with blood-spattered fingers. "The guards would let me pass without you."

"No," I spat. "I don't trust you to be out of my sight."

Tharix smiled like that amused him and I looked away rather than let him see the smirk which was tugging at my lips in reply. Fuck him for being such a good fighter, for making it too easy to fall into the pattern of comradery with him. I needed to remember what he was, but I found myself reminded of what I used to be instead. Lost. Just so fucking lost and looking for someone to reach out a hand and pull me free of my father's whispered poison.

"This way then, brother," Tharix said, pushing a tapestry of a Dragon eating a Sphinx aside and revealing a narrow stairwell which led up to the next level.

I took the lead, not much liking having him at my back but not willing to let him take charge either.

The light was dim within the passageway and only grew dimmer once Tharix dropped the tapestry back into place, but I kept moving resolutely upwards, my ears straining for any sign of anything happening further out in the castle.

As I made it to the top of the stairs, my fingertips brushed fabric and I paused, listening to the rumble of voices from beyond my hiding place.

"-to get out of here," a woman hissed. "Have you taken a look out of any of the windows? The Dragon King isn't going to w-"

"Hold your tongue," a male voice growled in reply, and I carefully pushed the tapestry back an inch to get a look at who was there.

The two servants were facing off in the hallway, the woman clutching a bag of what I had to assume were her belongings, though I noticed a golden candlestick protruding from the top of it which I could only guess she'd stolen.

Smoke rolled over my tongue as I looked from her to the male servant who seemed to be blocking her path along the corridor.

"You know what happened to Glenda when she tried to flee," he hissed in a low voice. "The king plucked her like a freshly caught duck and roasted her alive for good measure."

"The king will be the least of our worries if the Vegas make it to the castle," the woman replied resolutely. "Do you seriously think they'll let anyone who served in this place live?"

Tharix had apparently grown bored of waiting in the shadows because he shoved past me roughly and stepped out into the corridor with darkness coiling around his arms.

"Running away?" he purred.

The woman screamed, dropped her bag and fled in the opposite direction without so much as glancing back at the male servant she'd abandoned.

I stepped out behind my brother, knocking my elbow into his arm in a reprimand as the man standing before us began to quiver like a leaf in a violent storm.

"P-P-Prince Darius?" he gasped, his eyes darting from me to Tharix and back again, confusion mixing with his terror as he tried to decide which of us was the worst of the latest Acrux generation.

"King actually," I corrected, and his pupils dilated before he fell sobbing to the ground before us and began begging for his miserable life.

"King?" Tharix asked casually, flicking a hand at the man so a snake of shadow shot for him before yanking him away into the darkness beyond the tapestry. His cries of terror were muffled to the point of inaudible thanks to the roar of battle which permeated the walls, and Tharix turned his attention from him immediately. "Did you fail to mention the consort part intentionally for dramatic effect?"

"No," I grumbled, stalking away from him, but he caught my arm and yanked me around.

"It's that way," he said with a grin which looked all too eager to me.

"You want him dead that badly?" I questioned, striding in the direction he had indicated at a near run.

"I want to pick my own paths," Tharix replied. "And I have come to see that I will never do that while our father keeps trying to yank on my leash."

"Hail to that," I agreed because even now, as I stalked through the hallways of his castle, a traitor to all he had ever raised me to be, I still felt the weight of his stare on my actions. I still heard the tone of his disapproval and the contempt of his judgement. I still felt the way he had always claimed my accomplishments for his own, declaring ownership over me like I was some product of his design and nothing more. So I was ready to shed myself of my lineage, of his overbearing disapproval and end this fucking mess he'd started when he'd first begun to covet a crown which had never been meant for him.

The space opened up above us as we reached the centre of the castle, the arching ceiling and wide passageway making the sound of our boots thump loudly with every step. A sweeping staircase wide enough for ten men to climb at once appeared around the next corner and I hurried for it, but an echoing roar stalled my movements.

I fell still, craning my neck to look up as I found five of my father's Bonded Men in shifted Dragon form, all waiting in the shadows for me like they'd expected me to be precisely where I was.

"Uncle," I greeted, a mocking smile on my lips as I looked at the pewter-coloured Dragon who stood at the top of the staircase, his bulk blocking the way while the other four clung to the beams which lined the vaulted ceiling and released a chorus of roars around me.

"You look like you've lost some muscle mass," I said conversationally, my eyes moving across my uncle's frame while I casually placed my axe on the floor and released my hold on it. "Or perhaps you've just never been all that big."

The stairwell was huge but it was not built to contain this many Dragons and as I looked over my shoulder at my brother who was watching me with interest, I simply shrugged, like I was admitting to the insanity of my actions before even committing them.

Then my flesh ripped apart, my armour uncoupling seamlessly and falling from my body as it expanded so fast that my head spun with the transformation. My claws slammed down into the centre of the staircase before I'd even fully decided to shift, and I dove headfirst into the blaze of Dragon fire my uncle spat at me without so much as flinching.

The flames kissed my golden scales, the walls vibrating as I collided with the pewter Dragon and a big rust-coloured bastard slammed down onto my back a moment later.

The world became a blur of teeth and claws, blood coating my tongue, my flank, my legs. I was bleeding, they were bleeding, the walls were cracking and shadows were blotting out all light.

Bones snapped and Dragons bellowed and Tharix ripped the rust-coloured beast from my back just as my jaws closed around my uncle's throat. I ripped through scale and flesh alike, crushing all I found and ripping his life away, offering it up to The Ferryman with the rest of the souls I'd reaped this day.

Tharix fought brutally and beautifully in his black Dragon form, his bulk almost as big as my own – though I was confident I still had the advantage on him. We fell into a rhythm together, covering each other's backs and unleashing carnage on those who came at us with a savagery even Hail Vega would have been proud of.

Death howled around us but we were still outnumbered, colliding with stone and scales and teeth and claws. In the madness of the fight, I could only focus on the weight of the beasts impacting with me and the ferocity of the monster I so easily became. And I lost myself to the chaos of war once again.

LIONEL

CHAPTER ONE HUNDRED & FIVE

My hand trembled as I gripped the edge of the window, gazing across the battlefield and taking stock of all my losses.

"Vard," I croaked, and my Seer moved to my side. I grabbed his jaw, forcing him to look, my nails pinching into his skin. "What is this? Your monsters fall. Your weapons fail. What use have you brought to this day?!"

I threw him to his knees with a blast of air where he grovelled like a snivelling toddler.

Grinding my jaw, I turned back to the battlefield, my palm growing sweaty and the back of my neck all too hot.

I enhanced my eyesight with magic so I could see far out into the battle, and I frowned at what I discovered. There, among that terrible tide of new warriors that had joined the Vegas' army, I saw the faces of the warriors wielding those strange swords of light.

"No," I gasped, backing up, terror thickening my throat. "It cannot be. What concoction or trick is this?" The Savage King charged among those soldiers, fighting alongside his loathsome daughter, his black sword coated in purple Hydra flames scoring through my warriors, while his bitch wife was there, her own sword sending pulses of energy out into the Fae and knocking them flying.

A shaky breath shuddered its way over my tongue as my gaze locked on the impossible, tracking from one face to the next. Radcliff. My fallen brother. The one I had struck from this world like an errant fly, there to fight in the masses with a wild smile on his lips and his eyes alight with the fight he fought against me. *Me!* His own flesh and blood!

"Vard." I growled, snatching him from the floor and pinning him to the window by his neck, and forcing him to look out upon those very faces. He enhanced his eyesight so he could see better. "What is this? What is happening?"

"The Savage King," he rasped. "By the stars. The dead have risen once more."

"No!" I boomed, defying that possibility. It was not true. It could not be. There was no way, no path from death to the living. And yet...hadn't my own flesh and blood walked that path already? Hadn't I seen Darius in this very room with my own eyes? What foul magic had that Vega bitch concocted now? Oh how I curse the fact that I had not ended the life of Roxanya while she was a mere puppet in my grasp, before she had lured my Heir away from me and become this creature of endless vexation.

I snarled, releasing my worthless Seer and seeking out Lavinia where she fought on among the stalwart remains of my forces. My lasting hope. Her shadows were pouring across my enemies and eradicating them in pure, savage viciousness. But Phoenix flames tore through her Nymph Legion, shredding through their bodies and burning them like kindling, marking the passage of the other Vega whore.

It was only a matter of time before the blue-haired wretch made it to Lavinia, the other Vega I should have eradicated when I'd had the chance.

Perhaps my queen would destroy her, but I knew...I damn well knew what choice was left to me now.

"Sire!" A guard raced into the room, throwing the door wide. "Intruders in the castle. The guards are holding them off but many are dying. Your Bonded have moved to intercept them but if they fail..." He gulped at the violence which flashed through my expression at that suggestion. "It won't be long before they make it here. A-and it seems, perhaps, forgive me, but your Heir, Tharix...he-"

He faltered, eyes wide with terror.

"He *what?*" I snarled.

I had long taken note that my new Heir had made no appearance in this battle. His shadow Dragon had not been out there winning this war for me, despite sending him into the fight myself and commanding him to take his place among my forces. But now, instead of tales of his victories in my honour, his name was spoken with trepidation by the tongue of a terrified guard.

"He fights alongside Darius, your Majesty. Arm in arm. The two an unstoppable force. And they make a path for this very chamber," he blurted, spitting the words from his tongue as if expelling them faster might lessen their force.

Those words rolled through my chest like burning wax, the sting of them invoking a fear in me which I could not deny. Tharix had betrayed me. He had been corrupted...

I glared out at the Phoenix fire which blazed in the writhing mass of the battlefield, trying to understand how this had happened. *When* this had happened.

Tharix had gone missing. I had thought him lost to some sick pleasure, perhaps making a toy of one of the servants and basking in their slow demise. Never had I considered that he could have been tempted away from my walls, away from his loyalty to those who had given him this gold-touched life.

Betrayal once again gilded my flesh. Was I cursed to suffer it so often? Were those surrounding me so intimidated by me that they couldn't bear the weight of my shadow despite all I offered them in exchange for their loyalty? A better world. A place at the side of the greatest ruler this kingdom would ever know.

Smoke seared my tongue, my eyes flashing green and scales erupting down my arms before I managed to hold the shift back.

I swallowed, forcing such pitiful emotions away and making my decision. Tharix would die with the rest.

"Seal the doors and bar the passages," I barked. "None get through here or I will have your head!"

The guard bowed and fled, sealing the door behind him and racing off to do as I bid.

I exhaled heavily, moving to the golden chest that lay on the desk as mutters of concern broke out among my advisors. Madam Monita was shaking, seeing some fate in her scrying bowl that frightened her beyond words. But I did not need to hear it. I felt it in the stirring of the air, in the way the wind was turning. The stars were scorning me, and for what purpose? Even Clydinius had abandoned me on the brink of victory. But I was no fool. I would turn from this battlefield now and come back another day to win my war.

I tightened a leash of air around my arm over the mark that bound me to Lavinia Umbra, contracting it firmly so she would feel it too. It was a warning, a command to retreat. I needed her now. I needed my Shadow Queen and off into the dark we would go until we could gather the numbers required to win this war another day. Or better yet, steal our way into the sleeping chambers of our enemies and gut them one by one while they slept in foolish belief of their supremacy. Yes, that would be our plot. Our goal. A plot I should have enacted when those Vega brats first returned to this kingdom unwanted.

I opened the chest to unveil my pouch of stardust and froze. Smoke spewed between my teeth as I took in the empty space, void of my means of escape.

"Vard," I said, my voice thick with a tremor that I despised the sound of. "Where is my stardust!?" I roared so loud the ceiling shook and my advisors flinched.

Vard gasped, shaking his head. "I do not know."

"Of course you do not. Because your Sight is useless and you foresaw nothing of it going missing. You have failed me as you always fail me!" I bellowed, panic setting in as I realised my means of escape was now lost.

My fingers curled into a fist and I swung for him, punching him hard enough to send him toppling to the floor as a Dragon's roar tore from my chest.

The sky beyond my vantage point was a roiling storm of vicious beasts, Dante Oscura at the heart of it, making it by no means easy for me to attempt to fly out of here in my Dragon form. But if not by wing, then how was I to leave this place?

"W-we can take the escape route," Vard stammered, and I nodded, clinging to the suggestion and snatching it up as my own, snarling fiercely as I strode to the fireplace, kicking the brick that would open up the secret passage.

As Vard came running over, I caught him by the neck and shoved him onto the darkened staircase beyond. If by any chance someone had found this secret staircase then he could meet with them ahead of me.

I cast one last, furious, deflated and disbelieving look out of the window which adorned my abandoned throne room and cursed the name of Vega for the millionth time. How had this happened? We'd held every advantage, our victory so assured that I had been celebrating it from the moment our forces collided, but now look at me. I was scurrying into the dark like one of those foul Rats who dared buck against the rightful order, who dared question the supremacy of their superiors. It was a bitter pill to swallow indeed.

My gaze flicked to the sky, to a small patch of blue beyond the roiling grey where the glimmer of a thousand watchful stars shone down. This was a test, I reminded myself. A test of my mettle. If they wanted me to do this through cunning then so be it. I would return for my crown before long.

"Follow me," I barked at my advisors, and they hurried to obey, none of them wishing to remain in this place with my traitorous Heirs en route to it.

The Vegas and my sons may have had me on the run, but if they thought they would come and claim the king's head for their efforts, they were going to be sorely disappointed. I would flee now but before long, I would return to seize this kingdom and wipe every one of their names from existence. Because the Acrux King would never fall.

DARCY

CHAPTER ONE HUNDRED & SIX

The Nymphs shrieked as they burned in my flames, and the last of them fell beneath me, Shadow's heavy paw landing on one of their chests as I drew him to a halt.

Orion turned to me from ahead, his Phoenix fire sword wet with the blood of his kills. The shadows were twisting ahead of us like a curtain of black, rising ever higher and stretching out in either direction, blocking our view of the Jade Castle beyond.

I couldn't hear Lavinia in there, her shrieks of death fallen quiet, but she had to be close.

The roars of our army were climbing higher than the roars of the enemy's, and I sensed a real change in the air. Lionel's army was being forced onto the back foot, my people slicing through them with sword, fire, earth, air and water. It was a thing of beauty, but as much as I yearned to join them, there was one monstrous creature left on this battlefield who needed to be destroyed for all the blood she had spilled. And I couldn't turn from her now.

I patted Shadow's shoulder and flew from his back, sweeping down to land before him. "Join the battle. Tear through our enemies and give them hell."

Shadow grunted, somehow understanding those words as he nudged his nose against my cheek then turned and raced into the fray. He slammed into rows of Lionel's warriors to my right and screams carried into the sky as he cut through them with his claws.

I turned to Orion, nodding to him, knowing he wouldn't leave my side now, and as one we raced into the shadows. I raised a hand, my Phoenix fire chasing away the dark as we scrambled over piles and piles of bodies, our allies dead beneath our feet and the stench of death thick in my nose. My ire rose as I hunted for Lavinia upon this field of chaos, my fire burrowing deeper into the shadows and burning a path for us to follow.

"Lavinia!" I shouted. "Come out and face us! Are you a coward or a queen?!"

The shadows struck at me and Orion from all sides, but I burned them back with my fire, sending a dome of it out around us. The shadows hissed against my flames, receding further as Lavinia's cry of anger came from up ahead.

I looked to Orion, but he already knew what I was going to ask, sweeping me in his arms and shooting toward the place where we'd heard her voice. I sent a fiery Phoenix bird out to forge our path, the tips of its wings scoring through the dark, roiling power of the shadows.

"Such a fool to bring your precious mate with you into my domain," Lavinia's voice whipped around us, passing through tendrils of darkness.

Orion slowed, trying to follow the source of that voice, but it was everywhere, continuing to taunt us.

"I will feast on both your hearts and relish the sweetness of your love," she laughed, the cruel sound daggering through the fog of black either side of us.

Orion growled, coming to a halt as I sent my Phoenix bird deeper into the shadows, burning them away in great beats of its wings and revealing more of the land.

A sudden movement to my right made Orion turn and he sprinted towards it, trying to hunt her down.

"You make idle threats, but run from the True Queen all the same," Orion barked. "Come out and face her if you are so sure you'll win."

"Ah, little hunter, how much you must have missed me," she crooned as we failed to locate her once again. "Do you think of me often? Carving my pretty knives through your flesh?"

I shuddered at the memory, but I wasn't its slave anymore. It only spurred on the venom in my blood, my need to end her.

"Place me down," I whispered to Orion and he did so, coming to a halt at my side, raising his sword in preparation.

I let a roaring fire build between my hands, calling my Phoenix bird back to fuel it, the red and blue flames building and building until-

I released them in an explosion of light, the fire tearing away from us in every direction, eradicating her shadows in a blaze. And there she was, revealed to us fifty feet ahead, backing up in the direction of the Jade Castle that towered in the distance.

But instead of running like it seemed she might, she stood her ground, a snarl parting her lips.

"I am a queen," she growled. "I claimed this kingdom. It was owed to me. You have been in this world for barely a blink of a moment, but I have waited, I have suffered, I have fought for my crown and claimed my Acrux King. You will never take that from me, descendant of Avalon." Shadows coiled around her arms in deadly tendrils, power darkening her eyes.

I lifted my hands, fire blooming and my hair whipping back in a powerful wind conjured by my own magic. The earth rumbled and ice shards grew against my arms like a sheen of spines. I could wield every Element, I could cast fire that rivalled the heat of the sun, and I had something worth fighting for that Lavinia would never know the taste of.

"You fight for power while I fight for love," I called. "Let's see which one triumphs on the cusp of oblivion."

Phoenix fire flooded from me in a torrent, followed by a swirling blast of ice shards. Lavinia cloaked herself in shadows to try and shield from the blast, but my fire bit deep and the ice bit deeper. She screamed as she was cut by a thousand jagged pieces of ice, and shadows tore away from her in a spear of power that came right for us, her skin knitting over as quickly as it had been sliced open.

Orion darted forward, slashing through the shadow spear with his sword of flames, moving so fast the strike was burned to nothing before it even got close to me.

Lavinia snarled, shadows shrouding her and carrying her fast across the battlefield, launching herself at me in a swirl of darkness. She collided with my air shield, the fog of black doming over me and trying to crack through my defences.

I let the earth swallow me, speeding underground then launching myself back above the dirt behind her and stabbing my sword, driving it into her back.

She screamed in agony, a blast of shadows crashing into me before I could shield and throwing me fifty feet into the air, a noose of darkness forming around my throat.

Fire blazed against my skin, tearing away from me and eating through her power fast. Then I was falling, my wings snapping out as I took in the sight below. Lavinia's body had already healed from my strike and she held a sword of shadow in her grip, fighting with Orion, their weapons clashing in furious movements.

I rained down hell from above, pellets of fire pummelling Lavinia and making her shriek in utter pain. I landed beside her, swinging my sword in a bid to take her head from her shoulders, but she lurched backwards to narrowly avoid the strike.

Her shadows assaulted us from behind and I was forced to turn, trying to burn them away as fast as they came. But then Lavinia caught my hair in her fist, yanking me towards her as a spear of shadows went flying past me.

"Watch," she growled as the spear slammed into Orion's back, piercing his armour and running him through. He had been so desperately fighting off the shadows that he hadn't seen it coming and a scream rubbed my throat raw. Before he hit the ground, the shadows wrapped him in tight binds and yanked him away into a rolling sea of black mist.

"Dead, dead, dead," Lavinia sang, driving her shadows against my back and working to crush me within them.

I yelled in fury, Phoenix fire bursting from me in every direction, my hair setting alight and making Lavinia wail in pain as she lurched away from me.

I ran towards the veil of shadow ahead, needing to find Orion and heal him before he was lost, but Lavinia closed that wall around me, tighter and tighter and I was forced to focus on burning them back. The pressure of them mounted as they closed in from all sides, the light of the sky extinguished, and only my flames lighting the world around me.

Lavinia didn't relent, every whip of shadow I burned replaced by another and another. I tried to force my fire out in another flood, but her shadows thickened and thickened, all of her strength lent to this cast. I couldn't see her among them anymore, and all I could do was focus on blasting them back before they swallowed me whole.

Flashes of Orion's torture raced through my mind along with all the horrors Lavinia had delivered to this world. I thought of my sister and how she'd been captured by the shadows, forced to be Lionel's pawn, and all the suffering she'd faced in recovering from that. I thought of Clara and her desperate soul begging to be released from the clutches of Lavinia's wrath, and of all those who had been lost to her brutality. This creature was a plague. A plague who would spread rot across the land if I didn't finish her this day. It couldn't go on. She had to pay. She had to suffer the price of her cruelty.

With a scream that was filled with my rage at all the terror Lavinia had caused, my Phoenix fire blasted from me in an inferno that scorched the earth and engulfed everything it touched. The shadows were consumed, burned to nothing, and among all the fiery ruin, Lavinia was screaming too.

I felt my power connect to hers, almost as if we were power sharing, but it was wholly opposite to that. My fire was feeding on her shadows, dragging and dragging them from her body, and she was revealed ahead of me, trying to claw her way across the ground to escape. But my fire was connected to the darkest pieces of her power, ripping them clean from her body in ribbons of shade.

"No!" she screeched and her skin began sizzling away, making her cry out in purest agony, that thin veil of flesh constructed as a lie to hide what she really was. And beneath it lay the horrid truth.

This writhing, monstrous creature was nothing but a shadow clinging to a fragmented soul. Within that slithering, limbless thing were roaring, angry wraiths, hideous faces pushing against the inside of her shadowy body, clawing at it with nails and gnashing their teeth. I sneered at the sight, recalling what Arcturus had told me about Lavinia's origin, how those dark and malevolent spirits had been long-ago summoned from the dead, and they had bound themselves to her.

Her voice still carried from that ugly thing, but it was rougher, less Fae, more monster.

"I cannot die," she rasped.

"Die? All things can die if I wish it," a dark voice made the ground rumble, and I looked up to find a cloaked figure standing there with a weathered paddle in hand and his black hood drawn low to conceal his features. His sinister presence made the hairs stand up along my arms and the breath in my lungs turn icily cold, and I knew with a certainty that rattled my bones, that this was The Ferryman.

"But you will not pass beyond The Veil," he hissed venomously, disgusted by her, it seemed.

Lavinia's essence thrashed upon the charred bones of the battlefield, those things inside her screaming louder as my fire fought to destroy them.

"She must die," I snarled, stepping forward, having no intention of letting him defy me now.

The Ferryman regarded me from within his dark hood. "Her soul is a blackened thing, tarred by her defiance of nature, rotten to the core. It has no place in death. Nor do the wretched things inside her."

"You must take them," I growled, my hand raising towards him in a threat.

He fell quiet, and I felt his eyes carving over my skin, taking in the queen who dared try to command him.

"I will not," he answered in a snarl. "She and her wraiths will be nothing. Shattered. Less than remnants. They will face no after. They will vanish from existence for all eternity."

"No!" Lavinia cried, terror lacing that word, her shadowy essence trying to move away from him.

I let my flames simmer down, still burning her as she twitched and cried, but giving The Ferryman room to move closer.

That was a fate she deserved. A fate which saw her removed from existence. One she could never return from or even continue beyond, one that invoked a fear in her that filled me with a wicked kind of rapture.

"Yes," I agreed, and Lavinia screamed louder, the desolate souls inside her screaming too, knowing their time was up. In this world and the next. They would have no afterlife, no moments of freedom, no joy ever again.

"Lavinia Umbra," I hissed, willing my fire to grow hotter, the earth glowing with heat beneath her so she was in a world of agony as The Ferryman stepped closer. "You are nothing from now until forevermore."

The Ferryman drove the end of his paddle thrice against the ground and she thrashed and cried, trying to escape, the flesh of her rotten core starting to peel away. All of her miserable form turned to a thick and foul stain that spread across the bones of the battlefield, then began to foam and spit like acid. Her screams never stopped, joined by the souls bound to her, and their pain coloured the air as my fire swept over them, ensuring their lasting moments in life were painted in raw agony.

Then she was gone, all of them dissolved, no sign of her taint left upon the ground. She was nothing and no one. And sweet tears of relief rolled down my cheeks at the knowledge that this demon was vanquished. It was over.

The Ferryman looked to me. "Your mate's soul calls to me. Will I be claiming his life so soon?"

I turned in fear, my eyes falling on Orion where he lay on the ground, his chest plate torn off and his hand pressed to his ribs as he worked to heal himself. He was awake, eyes on the place Lavinia had fallen, then shifting to me with complete joy despite the pain furrowing his brow.

I ran to him, falling to my knees at his side and laying my hands over his, lending him my power to heal the shadow wound that had torn through his chest. And together, we managed to stitch it over.

"You did it, Blue," he said, his voice rough with emotion. "You're a damn warrior of the stars."

"She's gone," I breathed, hardly able to believe it.

Orion nodded, pushing up onto his elbows, then his eyes widened at something over my shoulder. I turned, finding The Ferryman still there and a sea of warriors beyond him. My mother and father stood at the forefront with Tory and Gabriel either side of them, all of them blood-spattered and feral.

Everything was achingly quiet for a moment, then cheers were lifting the air, our army crying out a victory that had me tearing up with disbelief. It was over. We'd won.

My parents came rushing to me, my mother drawing me upright while Hail hauled Orion to his feet.

"You have my blessing, good choice," my father muttered to Orion, and I shook my head in disbelief, finding no words as purest shock took hold of me.

Then I was in my mother's arms, a real, true embrace from her enveloping me, and I buried my face in her neck, squeezing her tight.

"Oh my love," she crooned, her hand stroking my hair, doing one of the things I had dreamed about my whole life. I felt her love in the way she held me, her kisses touching my cheeks as tears raced down them.

Then my dad was pulling me into his arms instead and I felt the strength of him in how he held me, a firm kiss pressing to my head as a sob racked through my chest.

"Don't leave," I begged, knowing they had to. Knowing they couldn't stay.

"My little darling," Hail sighed. "I wish I could spend all your coming days right here with you. But I promise we'll be watching. We'll be here, even when you cannot see us."

"It's not fair," I croaked, and he hugged me again, his chest heaving with another sigh.

Tory and Gabriel came closer to be with us and my mom gripped both of their hands, drawing them into our small circle of family. "We are so proud of you all. You have overcome the dark that dared to try and have you. But not my children. You are all far too strong, able to face anything life throws at you." She smiled, tears falling from her eyes as she hugged and kissed us, and Hail tugged us all into his arms, the five of us reunited for the first time since we were children, too young to even remember what this had felt like.

One glance to my left showed me Orion in his father's arms, the two of them speaking in low voices. Then Clara was there and Orion grabbed her, lifting her up and spinning her around, making her smile like a kid before he placed her down and they embraced. Beyond them was a man who I recognised from old footage and photographs as Radcliff Acrux, the brother Lionel had killed. He was embracing Xavier, clapping him on the back, and Darius's younger brother stared up at the muscular man with light in his eyes, seeming almost relieved that there was someone else in his family who wasn't brutal or cold. A beautiful woman came running out of the ranks, Catalina wrapping Xavier in her arms and he released a neigh of purest joy.

The solid thump of The Ferryman's paddle striking the dirt made my heart clench and I held onto my mother's and father's arms, certain they were about to leave all over again.

"It's time," Hail said heavily.

"Don't go," Tory breathed, pain in her voice.

"We will see you again one day," my mother promised. "But not until you have lived life to its fullest. Not until you have worn your hearts out with love and have known the depths of all this world has to offer."

"And we will be there to watch it all, so close you can hardly imagine," Hail said, his skin beginning to crack as the clay body he wore started to shatter.

Our embrace only tightened, all of us holding on tight, refusing to let go until their clay bodies crumbled to the ground between us and the golden glow of their souls swirled around us in a final brush of farewell, and I fell into the arms of Tory and Gabriel, my siblings holding me. Even though it hurt to say goodbye, I found solace in their company, my brother and sister, my family.

I turned to Orion, watching as Azriel and Clara crumbled away within his arms and he was left standing alone. But he would never be alone again. I'd make sure of it.

I smiled at him through my tears, beckoning him over and he joined us in our embrace.

"The war might be won but I won't rest until I see Lionel's dead body, assuring me he's gone," Tory growled, the clash of fighting carrying to me from the direction of the Jade Castle.

Roars of victory still carried up from our army and I searched for my friends among the field of shattered clay, but there were too many of our army among it all, and I didn't know who else had made it.

"Geraldine! Max!" I amplified my voice to bellow across the land. "Seth – Caleb!"

Silence followed and fear clutched my heart. I couldn't face losing them. I couldn't bear the weight of that grief.

I listed all the names of those I loved, calling out for them to join us and suddenly they were there, being lifted into the arms of their legions, and tossed our way upon a sea of our allies.

Geraldine hit the ground running, but Caleb was the first to reach us with Seth on his back. Seth had a look of heaviness about him as he let out a low howl and pulled me into his arms. Then Geraldine came barrelling into the pile with Max, and Sofia and Tyler came cantering across the ground with neighs of greeting and Xavier ran to meet them.

They'd made it. My friends were here, alive.

Four tiny sayer dragons swept over to us, their innocent faces speaking nothing of the destruction they'd wrought in battle. But they, just like us, were far more formidable than they appeared and I welcomed them with a warm smile as they came to land on our shoulders.

"Where's Darius?" I asked uncertainly, my gut dropping, and Orion looked around anxiously.

"He had plans to get to the castle," Xavier said.

"His heart's still beating," Tory confirmed.

"Noxy?" Orion asked and my brother's eyes glazed as he sought out Darius.

He nodded, his gaze turning to the Jade Castle. "He's in there. And Lionel still lives."

My gaze turned that way too and my heart thundered as I readied to fight once more. I didn't know how many warriors awaited us in that hulking green castle, but if they still hid Lionel among them, there wasn't enough of them to keep us from hunting him down.

VARD

CHAPTER ONE HUNDRED & SEVEN

I stumbled down the stairs taking them two, three, four at a time, leaping to the landing then racing on down the next flight. My knees creaked in protest at the rough treatment as my palms splayed against the cold jade walls of the castle to steady myself.

Booming vibrations echoed through those walls, a spattering of dust cascading over my hair and clinging to the clumped strands.

"The treasury!" Lionel bellowed at my back, his footsteps hounding mine, the rest of his advisors charging through the dark behind him.

A Faelight bobbed ahead of me, smacking into the walls of the narrow secret staircase, and I winced as it flickered, threatening to fail in time with the reckless pounding of my heart.

Piled bodies heaped before a throne of Hydra sculls, two glorious queens glaring down at me from the throne they had reclaimed.

"Death," their combined voices boomed my fate and I cowered away.

The vision made me stumble back and Lionel's hand slammed into my spine as he thrust me aside.

I gasped, pressing myself to the wall and letting him charge past me, the rest of his advisors scrambling by too, only Madam Monita sparing me a glance, her gaze etched with the terrible reality of our situation.

"What did you *see?*" she hissed at me.

"By the look on your face, I'd say it aligns with what the bones told you," I replied, my fingernails biting into the stone wall at my back as I struggled to think of a way out of that fate.

There *was* one. There *had* to be one.

"The bones spoke only of an end to come," she replied. "An end of all that is."

She jerked away from me as if wanting to leave those words where they were, hanging in the air between us, abandoned as she fled. And maybe she could outrun them if she moved fast enough, but I wasn't willing to place my fate in something so tenuous as my ability to outpace my foes. No, I would re-write my fortune just as I had done so many times before.

I ran on, charging down the stairs faster and faster, the unmistakable sound of the walls cracking apart around me making my gut clench with terror. They had to hold. They had to. Just a little longer.

Lionel cried out ahead of me and I almost ran headlong into Madam Monita where she had halted on a narrow landing along with all the others, staring at the Dragon King.

"What is it, Sire?" Horace begged as the king sagged back against the wall, clutching at his forearm above the stump where his hand had once been.

"My Bonded," Lionel panted, his blonde hair no longer quaffed to perfection but lying lank and clinging to his reddened forehead. "All of them are dead."

"What of the queen?" Madam Monita gasped, and he backhanded her so savagely that her skull cracked against the wall before she crumpled to the ground in a heap.

"I said all of them," Lionel spat, his eyes wild as he glared from one face to another, hunting for some sign of what to do.

In that moment there was nothing regal about him, nothing kingly or impressive. Even his imposing stature seemed diminished, and all I saw as I looked at him was a weak, sweaty man, running from the fate any other in his position would have stood and faced with honour.

The deafening boom of two Dragons roaring as one made the walls tremble around us, and we all looked back up the stairs towards the abandoned throne room. If every one of Lionel's Bonded were dead, then that meant those weren't his Dragons close on our heels – those were his sons come to hunt us down.

Panic threatened to consume our group, uncertainty clasping us in its fist but that wouldn't do. We couldn't languish in fear. Our time was running out and that meant we had to move.

"We will make it, my King," I told him, my voice rough with false prophecy, a certainty to my words which he clung to like they were the lifeline he had so desperately been seeking.

"Of course we will," he snarled, regaining some composure as he took my words as facts, laying all of his faith in the belief that they were the truth. "We keep moving. I will return to end the Vega line later…yes…later…"

Lionel turned and crossed the small corridor, throwing open a hidden door and revealing the treasury beyond. He removed his protective wards from the space, allowing us all entry then started barking orders at everyone to take hold of chests, bags and crates filled with his precious treasure.

I painted on my most simpering smile as I grabbed a small chest which lay beside the closest wall, waiting until his back was to me. Then I created an illusion of myself to remain in the room. Without a backwards glance, I slipped out of the door and ran.

I clutched the chest in my arms, the hard wood digging into my skin, my breaths coming in laboured pants as I headed down the next staircase; the one which led into the passages beneath the castle. The ones I had personally overseen the creation of. The ones I had prepared for this very eventuality and dreamed of every time that insufferable bastard had struck me, or cursed me, or forgotten that without me he would have had next to nothing in this war. No machinations of death, no beautiful monstrosities built of his enemies and primed to do his bidding. None of it. *I* had found the Burrows for him, *I* had delved into the depths of Gabriel Nox's mind and prised the secrets he needed from within. Time and again he had relied on me with no praise, no reward. And what had he done with all I had created for him, all I had discovered?

He had squandered it and thanked me for nothing.

Well perhaps he should have taken more care of those whose loyalty he had demanded. Perhaps he should have realised that the dog who was punished instead of praised always bit back in the end.

I huffed and panted beneath the weight of the chest, Lionel's scream of fury letting me know that he had discovered my deception. But I was ahead of him. He would not catch up.

I made it to the foot of the stairs, my foot snagging on the rocky ground beyond it and I fell, a cry barking from my lips as the chest flew from my arms and my face hit the rough stone.

Blood coated my cheek and forehead from the graze, pain lancing through me, and as I scrambled to my hands and knees, I found the stolen treasure littering the floor.

Footsteps were pounding down the stairs behind me. I had no time.

I grabbed a golden chalice and a handful of priceless jewellery, then ran.

Blood from my cut forehead dripped into my good eye, making me swipe at it and lose my hold on a bracelet.

I cursed, unable to spare the time to retrieve it, shoving the rest of my dwindling haul into my pocket and breaking into a sprint - though my breaths caught and wheezed with protest at the speed.

The tunnels were pitch black down here and my Faelight was flickering pathetically ahead of me so I stumbled repeatedly on the uneven ground, my hands rubbed raw from catching myself on the sharp, rock walls.

I threw a silencing bubble up behind me, hiding the noise of the king who chased after me and the demonic Heirs who no doubt hunted him in turn, before throwing myself around the last bend in the tunnels and coming face to face with the two ferocious Nymphs guarding this final point of escape.

"Open the gate! The King is coming, the war is lost, we retreat to fight another day!" I ordered.

The Nymphs surveyed me with surprise, their gleaming red eyes studying me for several too-long seconds before the larger of the two turned towards the gate, shifting back into his Fae-like form so he could unlock it.

My heart lurched as I threw myself into the most hazardous part of my plan, the shift coming over me fast, my eyes sliding together to become one and my sense of the world around me increasing.

The Nymph who was still facing me opened its mouth to make some reaction, but I had already thrown the full weight of my psychic ability at the beast, pinning him with my mental aggression and disabling him at once. The Nymphs were not practiced in mental shielding, and I had long been taking advantage of the easy access I could gain to the inner workings of their minds.

With a jerky lurch, the Nymph I had taken control of grabbed his companion and drove its jagged probes straight through his back, killing him almost instantly.

My heart thundered in my chest, the knowledge that the king approached lighting fear in my blood, but I couldn't back down now. Too long had I been squashed beneath his thumb, too long had I pinned my hopes on his claim to the crown. It was time for me to seize my own destiny and forge a path without any master to command me.

I licked my lips eagerly, ignoring the dead Nymph as it slumped to the ground, the gate of glimmering golden metal swinging wide beyond it.

I stepped closer to the one who had fallen prey to my power and took a small knife from my pocket.

"I'm in need of a new eye," I hissed, forcing the beast to bend low enough for me to reach its rancid face. It gave no reaction whatsoever as I carved the eye from its face, my pulse thundering with every moment I lingered, then leaping with feral joy as I took the offered organ and held it in my grasp.

I was running through the passages, then beyond, through the mountain pass, running for my life, but I was being hunted. The Vegas knew I had escaped and no matter how fast I ran, I couldn't outpace their flames of red and blue.

I coughed violently and the scent of my own burning flesh consumed me, the vision so intense that I almost lost my hold on the Nymph.

If I ran, they would follow...but not if they thought me dead.

As soon as the idea occurred to me, I felt my fate changing like the snap of a rubber band stinging against my soul.

I was running through the passages, then beyond, through the mountain pass, running for my life, crossing a small stream, days beneath the trees without food or sign of life. Then a village appeared on the horizon, a place where no Fae would know me, a place where I could recreate myself.

I gasped as that vision abandoned me too, a ragged smile on my lips. This would work.

"Now shift," I commanded, my voice reverberating through each piece of the Nymph's being, the creature entirely at my mercy as it was forced to follow my every word.

The Nymph shifted and I wetted my lips with triumph as I took in his Fae-like appearance. He was around the right height and stature, making this only too easy.

With a rush of power, I thrust everything of myself into his mind, my memories, my ambitions, my wants and my fucking name. I gave it all to him, forcing him to accept it while ripping away the cords of his own memories, taking everything from him which he used to identify himself until he was nobody except me.

"What is your name?" I demanded.

"Roland Vard," he replied, even his voice sounding like my own, though his expression was a touch vacant. I doubted anyone would realise that what with the blood pouring from his eye socket.

I shifted back into my Fae form, still maintaining my hold on him mentally, making him stand rigidly before me.

Lionel couldn't be far now. I was running out of time. But I needed this if I wanted my fresh slate. I needed to die in this place if I wanted the world not to notice my absence.

I lifted the twitching Nymph eye like a prized trophy and placed it into my own face with a juddering sigh.

A groan rolled from my lips as the eye squirmed into position, the agony I had felt the first time this had happened no longer present, instead replaced by the thrill of the shadows welcoming me home once again.

"I missed you, my sweets," I gasped.

The Nymph before me just watched, emotionless, expressionless.

I raised my hands and called magic to my palms, removing the wards in place on my own appearance so I could change his face into my own.

It took a matter of moments to force his features to bend to my will and I smiled triumphantly as my own face appeared before me, his hair growing to match mine, every piece of him taking on my form.

"Get dressed," I commanded, and he did so, pulling on the set of clothes which had been stored in an alcove behind him along with weapons and a store of food and water for the duration of the watch duty.

I dropped the silencing bubble, jumping in fright as I heard the bellow of a Dragon roar far too close for my liking. Lionel was almost upon me.

"Look at me," I snapped at the Nymph and he did so, earning himself a blast of my fire magic to the left side of his face.

He fell back with a cry of pain as I released my hold on his mind and I was pleased to see the skin surrounding his missing eye charred and burned, disguising the fresh blood.

"Forget this moment and run," I spat at him, my hold on his mind still complete. "Head out towards the battlefield and don't stop until someone of importance finds you."

The Nymph said nothing, simply turning and racing away into the network of tunnels down here, hurrying towards the battlefield to find a death which would count as my own.

A flush of raw energy built in my chest at the thrill of my own brilliance, and I threw myself through the glimmering golden gate just before Lionel Acrux and his dwindling retinue of supporters rounded the corner.

The king's furious gaze fell on me and I slammed the gate between us, snatching the key from it with a cry of terror as I found my end in the acid-green slits of his eyes.

"Open that gate at once!" he bellowed, charging for me.

Dragon fire erupted from his lips and blinded me as it filled the passageway, consuming the body of the murdered Nymph who I had left on the other side of the gate.

But not so much as a flicker of heat managed to pass through the bars which parted us. The gate had been a stunning discovery, a thing of raw magic created far before our time and left forgotten by Fae long past. I had discovered it on one of my many trips into the dark places of this world while hunting for beasts to use in my creations. It had been a simple thing to convince my oh-so-powerful king to have it installed here as a means of blocking his enemies from pursuing him should he ever have desperate need of escape. The only issue with that was the need for the key that I now held in my fist. Without it, the door would open for no one. Not even the great Dragon King and his flames.

A wide and feral smile finally spread across my face in place of the falsely subservient one I had painted there for so long.

"There was a prophecy warning of this moment," I breathed as the flames fell away and Lionel Acrux grabbed hold of the gate, rattling it brutally and not making a shred of difference to it. "Beware the man with the painted smile," I breathed a laugh, remembering how I had inspected that little nugget of insight from the stars after plucking it from the mind of Gabriel Nox. "The moment I heard those words, I *saw* this moment in my future and knew they had been intended for you."

"Open this gate, you traitorous worm!" Lionel bellowed, the power of the gate too much for even his mighty claim to power.

I stepped closer to the golden bars, smiling my true smile at long last and breathed, "I had a vision about you and what they will call you after this day has passed."

Lionel shook the bars and bellowed at me but I didn't even flinch, the weight of his hold over me falling away at last.

"The Dragon who burned."

I smiled even wider in the face of his fury and the flashes of foresight I was gifted on his behalf before turning and racing away into the dark with the sound of his continued screams chasing after me.

DARIUS

CHAPTER ONE HUNDRED & EIGHT

The walls of the Jade Castle were cracking apart, its death groans rattling through the foundations of the mountain as huge lumps of it fell crashing from the ceilings and slamming into the floors.

This place had been built without consideration for a battle between Dragons taking place inside of it and the furious fight which we had found ourselves embroiled in had clearly damaged it beyond repair.

We had shifted back, my armour in place on my body and axe in hand once more. Tharix remained tight to my side when we'd scaled the last of the castle stairs and fought our way through the few remaining guards to the throne room, but now we stood in the abandoned space with no idea which way our father had run.

"The war has ended," Tharix stated, his eyes falling to the view beyond the huge window which looked out across the ruined landscape of the battlefield.

He was right. Corpses and detriment lay in every direction, fires still burning in the smouldering wreckage, but out there I could see what remained of our army celebrating, a group of ferocious looking Fae, led by my wife and her sister now closing in on the Jade Castle.

A shuddering groan broke from the walls around us, a huge chunk of the roof breaking free as the floor pitched beneath our feet.

I slammed into Tharix, knocking him aside as the boulder-sized lump of masonry came crashing down where he had just been standing.

The two of us tumbled across the floor and he looked at me in surprise a moment before the floor crumbled away beneath us.

Stone bellowed and the mountain cried out as the entire castle began to collapse, the room we were in and everything beneath it peeling away from its perch on the side of this baren cliff face and hurtling towards the ground.

A yell escaped me as I scrambled to move, Tharix grasping my arm while the Dragon in me roared with a demand to shift. But before I could, Tharix yanked me over him, my body rolling onto his back as we fell amid a landslide of jade and rock towards the ground a thousand feet below.

I threw a shield of ice over us as the roof came crashing down in full force, so close to crushing us that my heart leapt in alarm, and I caught a glimpse of The Veil waiting for us. But I hadn't survived this war just to die now.

Tharix shifted beneath me and I was tossed into the air, tumbling over the thorny spikes which lined his spine before managing to grab hold of one through pure force of will.

I threw my magic from me in a blast which boomed like an explosion, fire and ice ripping away from us in all directions, launching the debris from the collapsing castle out into the sky and opening a path to freedom.

Tharix raced for it and I shielded us again, grunting with the effort of maintaining it as rocks the size of cars rained down on us. Then the echoing boom of the castle crashing down the mountain chased us out into the sky.

A great cloud of dust billowed over us and I clung on tightly as Tharix flew through it at speed, racing towards that group of warriors who we had seen approaching across the battlefield.

Time seemed suspended within the cloud of dust and I moved myself to sit upright on my brother's back, amused to find myself riding a Dragon of all things at the end of this day of chaos.

The dust cloud cleared, sweeping up into a maelstrom of air and earth magic which stole the debris and hurled it away into the mountains. I blinked in surprise, finding the battle-worn figures of the people I loved most in this world ahead of me, my wife's hands raised, proving she had cast that magic.

We landed before them and I leapt from Tharix's back, smiling broadly as I strode their way.

"Is it done. Did you kill Lionel?" Darcy asked keenly, her eyes falling on my half-brother at my back. "And is Tharix…fighting with you now?"

"Lionel is currently trying to escape through a network of tunnels which lay hidden beneath the rubble of his castle," Gabriel answered for me, and a snarl rolled up the back of my throat.

Of course it couldn't be so simple as his ugly castle crushing the bastard.

"Then I'll go worm him out," I said, my gaze moving across my friends and my brother, taking count of them as the knot in my chest eased a little.

I turned to head back to the wreckage and found Tharix there, shifted once more and in his Fae form, that black shadow armour clinging to his frame.

"And yes to the second question," I added, nodding to him. "My other brother is one of us now too. The dead souls which were bound to him have been banished into death and he proved his loyalty in the battle."

Something in Tharix's expression shifted at those words, his lips parting slightly as his dark eyes met mine and I gave him a wry smile.

"He mentioned something about the True Queens owing him a favour – so maybe just pardoning all the shadow creep shit would cover it?"

"Oh it would, would it?" Roxy called after me.

"Yeah," I agreed but I jerked to a halt as a vine caught my arm and forced me back around to face them.

"And where do you think you're going?" my wife asked me, her bloody sword in hand as she strode closer, Darcy right behind her and the rest dogging their footsteps.

"I told you, I-"

"Thought you were the only one here interested in that hunt? Fuck you, asshole. You don't get to claim that bastard's head all for yourself – the rest of us plan on taking part in tracking him down too. We all have debts to pay back to your father."

I looked her up and down, this bloodstained, beautiful, terrifying wife of mine whose green eyes were simmering with violence.

"You are…everything, you know that?" I told her, reaching out to catch her waist as she got close enough to me, the adrenaline and intensity of battle making my pulse thrash and my need for her spike, but she just side-stepped me with a dark smile.

"Not yet we aren't," she replied, looking to Darcy who moved to stand beside her. "Not until we end this."

"Lionel has to die," Darcy agreed roughly as they gazed towards the heaped rubble which had been a castle minutes before, the jagged mountain which concealed the tunnels still standing at its back, beckoning them closer.

"You stay here," Roxy added, looking at Tharix who nodded his agreement like a good little subject, though I had to assume it bit at him to be ordered out of this fight at the last moment. "Guard the...rubble and we can talk about pardons when we hear the rest of your story."

Darcy nodded her agreement to that and the four sayer dragons fluttered over to inspect Tharix, clearly planning on remaining behind with him too. "The rest of you, follow us."

The queens strode away across the ruins of the battlefield and I fell in wordlessly behind them with Orion, Caleb, Seth, Max, Geraldine, Xavier and Gabriel. I pressed a hand to Tharix's shoulder as I passed him, exchanging a look with him which swore to end the man who had chained him, and free him just as the act would fully relinquish me.

TORY

CHAPTER ONE HUNDRED & NINE

I stalked into the darkness of the tunnels beneath the Jade Castle, my boots thumping on the rough, rocky floor, fire crawling up my arms, ice crusting my fingertips, vines coiling across the ground before me and air lifting my raven hair so it billowed at my back.

The deep timbre of my husband's footsteps echoed mine, one step behind and to my left, the monster in him making his presence echo through the space with its power.

My sister stepped out of the shadows and began walking at my side, her mate falling in at her back too, teeth bared and the scent of death calling to the beast in him.

A pack of hellhounds trailed us, every one of them a monster of their own making, power resonating in every step as we closed in on our prey.

"All hail the Savage Queens," Geraldine called into the hall of our enemy. "And pray to the stars that they offer you a swift death."

"He's too frantic," Gabriel muttered as we strode through the darkness of the caves which spread out beneath the mountain which had once held the Jade Castle. "He's bolting, picking directions at random – I can't get a good read on where he'll end up."

I nodded, exchanging a look with Darcy. "Then we split up. Close in on him from every side."

"He can't run forever," Darcy agreed in a low tone.

We'd left Melinda Altair and Tiberius Rigel with Tharix, all three of them guarding the entrance to the tunnels along with the remainder of our army so we knew Lionel wouldn't make it out that way and the Oscuras had taken up position around the edges of the mountains that filled the basin the battle had taken place in. Which meant we simply had to find the False King within the bowels of the mountain and force him to face our reckoning at last.

Without another word, we split off at the next junction, Darcy taking the lefthand tunnel with Orion, Xavier, Geraldine and Max, me taking the right with Darius, Seth, Caleb and Gabriel.

I kept my pace in check, resisting the urge to run, instead simply hunting my prey through the echoing tunnels.

A cry reverberated through the passages and we paused, exchanging looks.

"That wasn't Lionel," Gabriel muttered.

We walked on.

Death was riding the beat of my heart, the culmination of the deal I'd struck with The Ferryman so close and yet infuriatingly out of reach. I was battle-worn, bloodsoaked and drowning in the grief of all it had taken to get to this point, but we couldn't stop until it was done.

Another fork in our path and Seth and Caleb silently peeled away from us, power crackling around them as they strode off into the dark.

My steps didn't falter but the cavern began to slope downwards, a dank coldness creeping over my limbs.

Grunts and bangs echoed up from the distant darkness, but we said nothing of them, our focus set and purpose clear. Lionel Acrux had taken so much from us, so much from everyone in our kingdom and the end of his reign had finally come calling for him.

At the next fork, Gabriel silently slipped away, leaving me alone with the hellion I had chosen to bind my life to.

Darius offered me a grim smile, the darkness almost entirely concealing his features and I let my fingers brush against his, coiling around them for a brief moment before releasing him again.

"Death doesn't seem so terrifying with you by my side," I told him.

"Not now that I know we will face it together," he agreed roughly. "But let's leave that adventure for another day, shall we?"

My lips curved and I pressed on into the dark, a Faelight springing from my fingertips and twisting away down the roughly-hewn cavern.

I sucked in a sharp breath as a face was revealed in the darkness, a man pressed into the shadows of a crumbling hunk of rock, clearly trying to remain undetected.

A vicious snarl lifted my lips as I recognised Vard, his pathetic, quivering form cowering against the damp stone wall.

"Oh look – a gift," Darius purred.

Vard screamed, the left side of his badly-burned face twisting into gruesome, bloody welts that oozed blood and pus.

"Where is Lionel?" I demanded, my flames flaring around me.

"He was deeper in the tunnels," Vard gasped, backing away from us with his hands raised. "Please, I was just his servant. I never wanted to-"

"Oh you wanted to," I replied in a low growl. "You forget that I was your plaything for a long time, Vard. I saw the pleasure you took in the pain you doled out and I know that you sought that position for your own sadistic needs. There is no part of me which will buy in to you playing the victim now."

"I...yes, you were my creature once, but I-"

"That's where you're entirely mistaken, you piece of shit," Darius snarled, sheathing the axe on his back and forging a wicked-looking dagger from ice instead. "She was never yours. And you signed your own death warrant the very first time you dared to come near her."

Vard backed up, his hands raising in some pathetic attempt to defend himself but as I strode towards him at the side of my monster, we all knew how this was going to end.

"What was it I promised I'd do to you?" Darius mused, violence dripping from him until it stained the air we breathed and the stone we passed through. "Oh yes, I think I said I'd rip you open and tear your insides out while you watched."

Vard's eyes widened with terror at the memory of that threat and my smile widened viciously.

"Oh, I think I'd enjoy seeing that."

LIONEL

CHAPTER ONE HUNDRED & TEN

Vard's screams of agony ripped through the maze of tunnels, echoing off of every wall and shattering against my skull as I ran down passage after passage, seeking some way out of these foul caverns.

I didn't know what had happened to him but there was no mistaking his snivelling voice raised in purest pain. Perhaps one of his own feral creations had been waiting for him beyond that gate. It seemed as though he had met with the end he deserved for his betrayal at least. But that did not help me with my efforts to escape.

A clatter sounded from somewhere behind us and I whirled that way, spotting a figure striding closer, blue hair tangling around her shoulders.

I cursed and threw out my hand, casting air at my snivelling advisors and hurling them back towards the Vega brat before constructing a shield of pure energy to stop any from following me. Then I ran on into the network of caves, leaving the sounds of her fight with them far behind me.

Left and right I turned, my gaze catching on a pillar which looked all too familiar before I skidded to a halt and whirled around.

"How do I get out of this confounding hell?" I snarled.

"You could try getting through me," a voice replied from the darkness, and I flinched around, fire igniting in my palm and illuminating the cold gaze of my youngest and most worthless son.

"Xavier," I ground out, contempt lining my features as I looked him up and down. He was grubby with the evidence of battle, his roughly-forged armour making it clear that he had fought in shifted form before crafting it. "Are you so keen to reunite with your mother that you thought to find your death in me?"

Xavier's gaze shuttered but I relished the bite of pain I saw splinter through his eyes. So he was grieving that betraying bitch, was he? Good. I hoped her death had cut him to the fucking bone.

He threw a spear at me so fast that I was forced to lurch aside, fire breaking from me in a wild twist of magic as I cast at him in return, my single hand making every spell more difficult, thwarting me in my greatness.

The ground bucked beneath me, the walls threatening to crumble over my head as the fucking horse used his hold on the Element of earth to try and bury me alive.

I blasted him with enough fire to make him cry out in pain, but the cave roof shattered in the same moment, and I was forced to hurl myself backwards on a gust of air.

I tumbled away while rocks crashed down on me, cuts blossoming across my skin, pain lancing through my body until I fell in a ruffled heap beyond the cave-in.

I spat a wad of blood and saliva from my mouth as I pushed myself upright once more, scowling at the heaped rock which divided me from my most worthless child and hoping upon every star that he had met his death in the fire I'd sent his way.

I turned and started running again, my foot snagging in the torn fabric of my cloak and sending me crashing against the rocky wall. I cursed, tearing the damn thing off of me and racing on once more.

A blur of movement ahead made me fall still and I bared my teeth as I found Caleb Altair standing in the passage to my left, his expression filled with amusement as he watched me flounder.

"What's the matter, Lionel?" he purred. "Out of places to run to?"

"I am a king," I spat. "I run from nothing!"

"No?"

A howl sounded from the tunnel to my right and I flinched around again, my head quickly snapping back towards the Vampire who had shot even closer to me in my moment of distraction.

"The True Queens are looking for you. Won't you face them like a true Fae?" he asked.

"I'll destroy them in my own time," I retorted, fire blazing from me in an inferno which forced him back.

An enormous white Wolf ran at me with fangs bared from the passage on my right and I released a noise so unlike a Dragon that blood rushed to my face in reply to it.

I let the flames roar across the path Caleb occupied and the other path to my right before charging ahead, blocking the progress of the two traitorous Heirs and hurrying towards the scent of fresh breeze which I had just tasted on the air.

I simply had to get out of these caves. I would re-group and return. I would poison them in their beds and murder their children in the dark if that was what it took to reclaim my position one day. I had won my crown without ever having to face war before and I could win it back through cleverness and scheming again.

"Oh to the derry of the duneberry he roamed, where the cat was in the bushes and his little whiskers moaned," the insane Grus girl's voice warbled from the path ahead and I faltered, my hand slipping into my pocket and closing around the single gold coin I held there. The rest of my treasure had been lost with my advisors and I bit my tongue as I took stock of my dwindling magical reserves.

I took another path, this one curving up, a glimmer of light ahead of me promising freedom from these cursed caverns at last.

I broke into a run, the air tasting sweeter by the second, the glimmering light of day beckoning me on. All I had to do was make it outside. Then I could shift and fly and be gone from this wretched place and the foul truth of this day for good. I would re-group. I would return. I would win the final-

"We have to stop meeting like this, Father." Darius stepped into my path, right in the mouth of the exit to the cave, daylight gilding his silhouette and making him seem even larger than the last time I'd seen him, his frame towering over my own.

"How dare you," I snarled, raising my chin and holding my ground. "How dare you stand there before me like you think yourself equal to my might. Like you haven't cowered beneath me time after time, snivelling and shaking while tasting the bite of my fury over your inadequacies. How dare you put yourself on the opposite side of this war and call yourself a king above me."

"That's the thing, Father," Darius said thoughtfully, removing the bloodstained axe from his back and hefting it into his hands. "You have always been so fucking short sighted. So desperately hungry for power and so pathetically jealous of those who hold more of it than you that you blinded yourself to the truth."

"And what truth is that?" I hissed, fire blossoming in my hand, the death of this traitorous bastard the one thing I vowed to bring to fruition before my end. If there was any chance at all that I was going to die in this fucking place, then I would be taking him back into death with me. And this time I would make certain he never returned from it.

"I'm not the one you should be frightened of," Darius replied cruelly, a smile gripping his features as he watched me summon every scrap of my power into my fist ready to blast him from this life and see him destroyed for his betrayal.

"I'm not frightened of you," I retorted, the acrid taste of a lie caressing my tongue.

"You are. You have been for a very, very long time," he countered like it was a fact that was so very obvious to him. "But the problem with waiting for the beast at your front to strike is that it's so easy to miss the one aiming for your back."

I whirled around, fire blasting from me in a furious explosion as my eyes met with the bright green, accusing stare of the Vega whore who had stolen him from me in the first place. The girl who had dared to defy me from the very first moment I laid eyes on her, the one who had always seemed so very like her arrogant, all-powerful father.

The world burned as the full might of my power tore from me, the tunnel rumbling and quaking as the stone itself began to melt beneath the furious weight of my magic. She smiled at me as she welcomed the full force of my fire, the entirety of my power nothing at all to her as she raised a hand and let the flames of her Phoenix join the roiling tempest of my own power.

Everything from the air, to the rock, to my own body burned. Everything, except her. And as Roxanya Vega's sword slammed straight into my chest, piercing my heart and ripping my soul from the confines of my living body, her final words to me rang like a death toll throughout my skull.

"So much for the reign of the great Dragon King."

The world of fire and ruin shattered around me, the agony in my flesh evaporating in an instant as I fell from my rightful place within my body and into the freezing waters of the river of death.

"No!" I roared, my arms and legs thrashing as I fought to swim, hands grabbing hold of me from every direction and dragging me back down again.

I cried out in sheerest terror as I was hauled beneath the water, The Veil snapping closed at my back and the screams of the dead surrounding me while hundreds upon hundreds of them clamoured to take hold of me and drown me beneath the roiling waves.

I kicked and fought, the last of my air racing from my lungs, the water burning as I was forced to inhale it and yet I wasn't drowning. I had no body left to die, only this endless, eternal agony of death.

I thrashed against the swarming mass of the dead, their accusations filling my skull until it threatened to split in two. Until I was suffocating beneath the weight of their hatred even more surely than I was suffering within the confines of the water itself.

A hand found mine in the darkness and I clung to it with desperation, allowing it to haul me from the river and throw me down on the bank.

I trembled at the feet of my saviour, coughing and shivering, the cold light of death hanging all around me as my failure closed in on me like a curtain wrapping around my mind.

I had died. My reign had truly ended and everything I had done, everything I had plotted and schemed and worked for had come to nothing...nothing at all...

"Thank you," I choked out, my mind lashing against the reality of where I was and my focus falling on the here and now, the man who had pulled me from that river of torment, the one who had seen fit to save me.

I looked up, expecting to find one of my Bonded there, another soul thrust into death, ready to serve me beyond it.

The faces of five bloodthirsty demons looked down at me instead. My mouth opened and closed as my gaze moved between my brother Radcliff, Hail and Merissa Vega, Azriel Orion and my traitorous wife, Catalina.

"Wait," I gasped as I took in the utter hatred and joy lining their features, the ranks and ranks of the dead who stood at their backs awaiting their turn to meet with me too, but they did not wait. They didn't so much as slow as they reached for me and dragged me into their grasp, tearing at me with nails, claw and tooth. Even though I had no fleshly body, the pain was true and keen. They beat me there between them and I curled in on myself, a whimper rising in my throat and fear spilling into the corners of my soul. A soul that could not escape this torment.

My screams filled the air and echoed out across The Veil and beyond as they kicked and pounded their fists into me with vengeance in their eyes and fury in their hearts.

A dark and forbidding voice dripped over me, the Savage King drawing closer again to see me shudder beneath him. "You will face all those you wronged, and only when they have seized their vengeance and grown weary of your suffering, will we deliver you to the Harrowed Gate where you will be tortured for all eternity by the monsters who wait for you there."

"Please," I rasped, my hand landing on his boot as the souls parted to let him closer.

He gazed at me with a sneer, disgusted by me as my traitorous ex-wife drew closer at his side.

"Catalina," I rasped, my hand moving from Hail's foot to hers. "We had something good once. Remember that. Show mercy."

She kicked my hand away then stamped down on it, making me roar in agony. "I will show you the mercy that you showed our children," she spat.

"It's time for you to reap the results of your life of corruption and betrayal, Lionel," Hail said as he stepped aside to let the sea of souls rush back towards me to take their revenge. My screams didn't stop, my fear a potent thing inside me that clutched at every fibre of my being and in that endless torment I found myself trapped in the reality of the very things I had sworn never to be. Helpless, afraid, alone and entirely without power.

TORY

CHAPTER ONE HUNDRED & ELEVEN

The flames which had consumed me and everything in the tunnel finally fell away, and I sank to my knees before the bones of Lionel Acrux, a weight loosening from my chest and a sob of pure relief escaping me.

Smoke clung to the walls, every piece of the surrounding tunnels blackened with the ferocity of the fire which Lionel had unleashed within his final moments. A breathy laugh fell from me as I pressed my fingers to the soot-stained ground beside the charred bones which were the only remains of the tyrant who had plagued us for so long.

The light of the Phoenix fire bird which had shot from me a moment before Lionel's attack lit the far end of the passage, still circling my most prized possession and keeping him safe from the flames which had destroyed his father.

I looked to it, calling the magic away and the bird of red and blue fire soared towards me, flames falling from its body until it fell to nothing, revealing the man I loved to the roots of my soul standing beyond it.

Darius's smile pierced my heart and I knew the weight of the freedom I was feeling couldn't even come close to how it felt for him to finally see the tyrant who had haunted every moment of his life fall to nothing.

He was at my side in moments, dropping to his knees and kissing my bloodstained lips, gripping my face between his hands and crushing his mouth to mine.

My tears finally broke free in that moment, spilling down my cheeks as the cost of this moment stacked up around me, the lives lost and sacrifices made all leading us here.

"Your debt is paid," a shadow spoke from above us and we pulled apart, looking up into the face of death as The Ferryman peered down at us and it was as if shackles fell from our souls, the need for death and carnage slipping away like it had never been. "Today was a good day for death but I do not wish to see either of you again until it is your time to pass me by."

I arched a brow at him but he was already gone, his form seeming to fade away as he slipped back through the folds of The Veil and we were left in the cold and the dark of the caves beneath the mountain.

My gaze caught on a glimmer of gold beneath Lionel's bones and I reached out to take it, finding a coin, the form of the Dragon which sat on its side scorched and melted so it was almost impossible to decipher.

I smiled as I offered it up to Darius whose hand closed around it in an instant.

"Long may the True Queens reign," he murmured in my ear, "I can't wait to see what you do next."

"Tory?" Darcy's call drew me away from the temptation of my husband's lips and I called back to her as I forced myself to my feet and turned in the direction of her voice.

She came running around the corner, her sword lit with Phoenix fire and illuminating the stone walls, making the bones on the dark ground stand out starkly against the rock.

"Is that him?" she began, hope shining in her expression and I nodded, opening my arms to her and drawing her into my embrace.

"We did it, Darcy. We killed them all – the war is over."

One by one, the others all found us, their whoops and cheers of celebration over the death of the False King only tempered by the heavy weight of grief which clung to us.

Among it all, I held onto my sister, the truth of what this meant and what we were now changing everything. And as we emerged into the bright light of day beyond the caves and our army broke into raucous cheers of celebration, I couldn't help but wonder what the world still had left to throw at us.

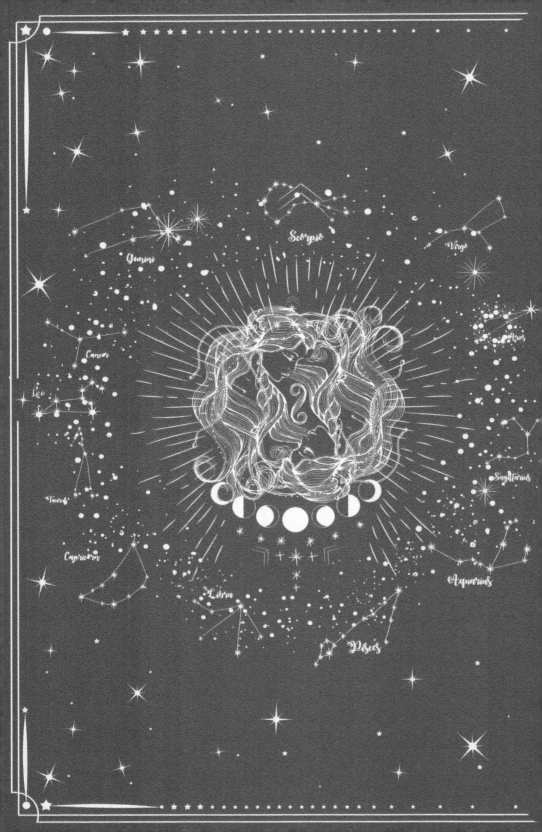

DARCY

CHAPTER ONE HUNDRED & TWELVE

I broke away from my sister to find Orion looking down at the bones of the man who had caused him so much pain. There was no sneer on his lips, no hatred left to offer, just relief.

"He's dead." Orion exhaled that fact and the air seemed to shiver with it.

"I thought I'd want to spit on him more than I do," Xavier mused as he grasped Darius's arm, his head shaking with disbelief at the body of his father lying between us all. "Instead, I feel nothing but the urge to turn my back on his bones and never think of him again."

"He's not worth more than that," Darius said.

"No," Xavier agreed, seeming confused by his own reaction. He crouched down to look at Lionel's charred remains, cocking his head to one side. "I hope they're giving you hell in death, old man."

"Mom will make sure of it," Darius swore and my pulse quickened at the sense of The Veil thinning and I swear I could hear a scream carrying on the wind that gusted through the caverns. One of pure, torturous pain that belonged to the tyrant who lay dead at our feet.

Max, Seth and Caleb moved to rest hands on Darius and Xavier's backs, looks passing between them that were a mixture of relief, shock and awe.

Geraldine stepped forward, chin thrust high and her chest puffed. "Grand tidings indeed," she gasped. "Oh fortune sings a song of merry winds to blow. How the birds will tweet and the natterbugs will chatter of this day. For the Lame Dragoon is no more, and the Vega Queens rise, rise, rise! On and on to the evermore!"

Gabriel came to stand beside Orion, clasping his arm, all of us sharing in this moment of victory. Then my brother smiled at Tory and me, gesturing to the passage which led towards the bright light of day.

"It's time to claim your glory. The sun is waiting to smile down upon the new queens," he said.

I looked to my twin, anticipation building in my chest at what was to come. We'd done it. It wasn't a dream or a hope anymore. We'd won the war. And now we had a kingdom to rule, a hundred thousand things to learn and so many wrongs to right. The people of Solaria were counting on us, and I was so damn grateful that I didn't have to take on that role alone. We'd come into this world together, and we'd claimed our crowns together too. From misfortune to fortune, our path had been walked side by side. And as we led the way out of the dark, I knew that we would always be irrevocably bonded by three things.

Our crowns.
Our story.
Our souls.

TORY

CHAPTER ONE HUNDRED & THIRTEEN
SIX MONTHS LATER

"Are you ready?" I asked, looking to Darcy in her flowing dark blue gown, rhinestones embedded in its bodice and a cape of spun silver hung from her shoulders which would trail out like a veil behind her as she walked.

My outfit matched hers, though my dress was black - which had become something of a theme with our wardrobes when we made these kinds of appearances. Geraldine claimed it was because the people needed continuity after the years of uncertainty and the trials of war, but I had the feeling that it was to make it easier for people to tell us apart.

"I think that some part of me will forever be a broke ass girl wearing old bunny pyjamas while curled up on the corner of a couch which doubles as our bed," she replied with a wry smile. "But apart from that – yeah."

"Yeah," I echoed, glancing in the huge, gilded mirror which stood across from us in the entrance hall to the Palace of Souls. Geraldine had worked her ass off to scrub this place entirely clean of the taint of Lionel's presence, but some ghosts still lingered. There was pain etched into these walls, the likes of which we were never likely to forget. But we couldn't allow it to remain sullied by Lionel's memory forever. So here we were, back again, if only for official occasions. And I wasn't sure what got more official than a coronation.

I was unrecognisable from the girl who used to roam the streets of Chicago stealing superbikes for quick cash and drinking tequila in questionable bars, yet that same spark of rebellion still flared within my green eyes. I was still me. I was just a whole lot more on top of that now.

There had been months of grieving and reparations, relocation and renewal, and now, after six gruelling months, we finally felt that our kingdom was reunited enough to come together behind us officially. Or at least, Geraldine insisted that if we waited any longer the stars would cast us out and pick a monarch more willing to embrace the role.

I snorted as I lifted my chin and tried to look regal – whatever the hell that meant.

Whether I had achieved it or not was questionable, but I found myself out of time as Geraldine rushed through the room in a bustling cyclone of silver taffeta and threw the double doors open without so much as a word to ask if we were ready.

The blazing summer sun made me squint as I looked out at the endless crowd who had gathered beyond the steps which led up to the balcony surrounding the palace. It looked like every fucker in the whole of Solaria had turned out to see the crowns placed upon our heads.

I swallowed back a lump in my throat and exchanged another look with my twin before giving in to the inevitable and stepping onto the balcony with her at my side.

Our sayer dragons swept out of the palace and flew off over the crowd, taking part in the celebrations for themselves, and I watched their tiny bodies moving through the air with a smile.

The crowd cheered, waving banners and singing songs which I couldn't decipher. Flowers were hurled at our feet and Fae shrieked declarations of love and loyalty at us. I spotted a sign begging me to dump the Dragon and marry the guy holding it and snorted a most un-queenly laugh.

"Don't get any ideas," Darius growled as he stepped out from where he'd been waiting and offered me his arm.

"You look like one of those Christmas nutcracker things," I told him as my eyes ran from the black boots on his feet over the fitted blood red suit and ruffly shirt thing all the way up to the perfectly dishevelled black hair which was spilling down into his eyes as always. "You just need a top hat."

"And you look like a toilet paper doily," he retorted, his lips brushing my ear as he leaned in close to speak to me. "I look forward to hunting for skin beneath the many layers of that thing once we're done here."

"Only if you get yourself the hat," I teased, and he smirked at me in that utterly obnoxious way which always got me as infuriated as it did hot.

"Your ideas of roleplay really do take some interesting turns," he said, making my smile widen.

Orion was dressed in red too on the other side of Darcy, just as ruffly in the shirt with his beard so neatly trimmed it looked like someone had used a ruler on it. The two of them were like bookends to us and I threw him a smile as I let Darius lead me away from the doors.

The screams of the crowd grew impossibly loud as we passed them by and I barely even noticed the Hydra throne which had been brought out here and was awaiting us until we were standing right before it.

Darius and Orion turned to face us before falling to one knee in front of us, the first to swear fealty to the new order.

I couldn't help but smirk at Darius as he bowed his head before my feet, and I felt his teeth sink into the skin of my ankle through the swathes of skirt as if he'd known exactly how smug I looked in that moment.

I stifled my flinch of surprise, surreptitiously aiming a kick at him but he'd already withdrawn far enough to make it impossible to strike him without it being obvious to the hundreds of cameras trained our way.

"The True Queens stand before you, ready to take their vow and claim the crown of their bloodline. They will act with one will, one voice and one heart for the good and prosperity of our dear kingdom of Solaria from this day forth until the day the stars come to claim them for the beyond. Do you embrace them as your monarchs?" Geraldine's magically amplified voice boomed out across the crowd and a resounding roar of assent followed her words, making my heart lift with love for the people of our kingdom.

"Then watch as they claim their crowns."

Geraldine turned to us and I took Darcy's hand in mine, and together we sat upon the Hydra throne, claiming it for our own in front of our kingdom and the world.

Geraldine continued to speak the words of the coronation and my sister and I answered her calls and made our vows.

Gabriel stepped forward, placing a crystal ball in Darcy's left hand and a scrying bowl marked with runes in my right as we pledged to care for the past and future of our kingdom.

We made no promises to the stars, but I could feel them watching us, their ire replaced with curiosity now as if we had finally proven ourselves worthy of this fresh slate.

As one, Geraldine placed a crown on Darcy's head and Gabriel placed a crown on mine and the crowd exploded into voracious roars of delight. Then, one by one, they all dropped to their knees before us and pledged their loyalty to our reign.

I looked to my sister with an utterly liberated smile on my face which she returned just as brightly, and I knew that though nothing would ever be the same for us as it had once been, we would forever be at home in Solaria.

ORION

CHAPTER ONE HUNDRED & FOURTEEN

I called the twelve members of the Guild forward along the balcony, starting, of course, with Geraldine Grus.'

The stars had guided me in my choices on the Guild members, delivering the names of those who were worthy so that I was confident in my selections. And now it was time to unite them.

The crowd cheered as Geraldine bowed low to the twins where they sat in the Hydra throne side by side, two souls sharing one crown. She raced forward in her flowing silver dress and fell to her knees on a little navy cushion that had been placed at my feet. I held the Chalice of Flames to her lips which contained the Guild potion, and a squawk left her, her hands trembling with excitement.

My brief time with my father on the battlefield had secured the knowledge I needed for this task at last. He had assured me that the potion would cast no bond upon any who drank it, but it would brand them with the mark of the Guild, giving them the power to wield the Guild Stone that they were gifted. They would become a Fate Weaver, and no star could ever interfere with their decisions or lay a curse upon their soul again. It was a position of honour that would place them in a government which would advise the reigning sovereigns and also have the power to vote on any laws the twins decreed.

As Guild Master, I held a connection to the stars which would allow me to check the loyalty of all members over the course of their service, and ensure no traitors emerged among them. If such a thing were to happen regardless of my efforts, then the united, loyal members could wield the power of the Guild Stones to overpower the treacherous member. This extended to the sovereign that the Guild served, so no more tyrants could seize the kingdom in future. The most fearsome power of the stones could be unlocked using stone circles, such as the snare that had already proven its power in its capturing of Clydinius, but also circles of truth could be formed where no lie could be told, and many other great powers could be unlocked that would help us in bringing long-lasting peace to the kingdom.

For the twelve to be united, the stars had whispered to me of Fae that fit each star sign of the zodiac, and my father had confirmed to me on the battlefield that it was their rising signs which mattered. So now, I had twelve names written upon a scroll, each rising star sign listed beside them, creating the full zodiac circle.

As Geraldine sipped from the chalice and I spoke the words inscribed upon the metal, the stars began to whisper around us. Her eyes lit with a new and strange kind of light then faded away as I lowered the cup from her mouth.

"Well fell my jolly woodlands," she breathed in awe, and I placed the Leo Guild Stone in her palm to match her rising sign.

"Rise, Geraldine Gundellifus Gabolia Gundestria Grus, Fate Weaver, protector of the True Queens and sacred guider of the kingdom," I commanded.

She stood then gasped, looking to her right forearm as the mark of the Guild ignited beneath her skin, starlight sparkling along the constellations on the glittering sword. She released a hiccough of emotion then bowed to Darcy and Tory again as it faded beneath her skin once more.

"I will serve Solaria as well as a mouse in a camel house, my ladies," she gushed then raced off to dive on Max in an embrace that nearly knocked him from his feet.

"Darius Acrux," I called next, and my friend smiled cockily as he took a knee before me, and I repeated the process.

I called upon Caleb, Seth, Max, Xavier, Melinda and Tiberius. Then it was Imenia Brumalis followed by Eugene Dipper who had proved their mettle both in war and in their ruthless, unwavering allegiance to the twins. The High Nymph Cordette was next, securing her kind's position of equality among us. It was a tentative alliance, but the twins had already made public announcements about the Nymphs' newfound status in our land and had threatened to punish any intolerance between Fae and Nymph kind.

Finally, I drank from the chalice myself, and that secured the rising twelve. Gabriel, as the Royal Seer, was not a part of the Guild, but his position in the twins' court was of an importance that spoke for itself.

The potion rushed deep into my chest, warmth spreading under my ribs and sending a flood of strength into my veins. I lifted my gaze to the blue sky, a glitter of starlight there telling of the stars who had come to watch this world-changing coronation. With a warm flood in my chest, I felt my fate slipping from their grasp into mine, like they were handing over the baton. My gaze fell from them to the woman I would weave my fates with from this day forward, my beautiful mate sitting on the throne she was long destined for, her green eyes finding mine and a serene smile resting on her lips. There she was, the queen I aways knew her to be, finally in her rightful place. And oh what a fucking delight it was to see her there.

I walked forward, bowing to them both and offering the chalice to Darcy's lips. "Drink, my Queen."

Her eyes remained on mine as she did as I asked, and I spoke the words of the ritual that marked her as a queen with the centre of the Guild, linking her to the twelve as they were linked to her in a circle of protection. Then I held the chalice to Tory, and she drank as I spoke the words that untethered her fate from the sky once and for all.

"This story is yours to tell now," I told them both. "Take the pen and guide us towards our happily ever after."

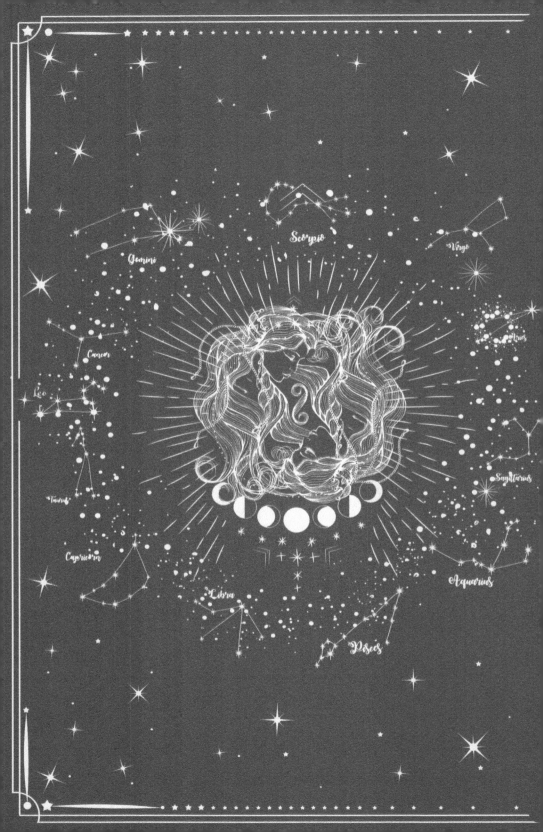

DARCY

CHAPTER ONE HUNDRED & FIFTEEN
ONE YEAR LATER

"Nervous?" Tory jibed.

"Nope," I said lightly.

"Liar," Gabriel said with a knowing look.

"Definitely," Sofia agreed.

"Okay I'm one percent freaking out," I admitted, wringing my hands together.

Geraldine stuffed a bouquet of wildflowers into them, all of them blue and white. Forget-me-nots, irises, violets, daisies and even some wild strawberries had been placed in there. It was over-the-top, but what did I expect when Geraldine had taken charge of organising the wedding? How could I really refuse her when she'd pleaded with me to let her and had sent a handwritten letter to my door every day for a full week straight to explain why she would be the perfect candidate – I'd said yes on the first day, but she hadn't stopped.

Tory, as my maid of honour, had been well involved in the details too, but she had let Geraldine's organisational flag fly when it came to this. Geraldine had interviewed me about fifty times on my favourite colours, foods, flowers, even my favourite damn textures before I told her to surprise me and Lance with the end result if she wanted to, and she had wept for a full ten minutes then told me surprises were her favourite flamjambles.

I was being prepared for the day in my bedroom at mine and Orion's newly-acquired farmhouse, and as Geraldine led me to a mirror to see the full effect of my dress, my pulse quickened even more. It was like something out of a fairy tale, the ice blue gown stitched with lace over the bodice and onto the off-the-shoulder sleeves. The huge skirt fell in a glorious pool of material, sapphires twinkling in a layer of netting and lace flowers decorating it. My hair was pulled into a loose chignon bun, a few coils of blue curls hanging down my neck, and a tiara delicately placed upon my head with parts of my hair woven around it.

"This is…" I had no words and Tory swept forward in her dark blue satin gown with thin straps and a nipped waist, wrapping me in one of her rare hugs.

"It's perfect," she said.

I squeezed her tight, my heart pounding ever faster as I turned to Sofia and hugged her too.

"Here," she whispered, adding extra shimmer to my dress with the power of her Pegasus, and I thanked her.

Gabriel moved closer, his navy suit jacket hanging open and showing his silver-buttoned waistcoat within. The colours reminded me of our old academy uniform, and I had no doubt that was on purpose.

"You look beautiful," Gabriel said. "We should get going. We're exactly late enough to have Orio freaking out." He smirked and I stole a hug from him before lunging for Geraldine and hugging her too.

"Thank you," I said.

"Oh it was nothing but a namby pamby, all this. My cockles have been as merry as moonflies surrounded by schedules and planners and binders," she said brightly, and I took in her dress which matched my sister's and Sofia's, tears springing to my eyes at how beautiful she was, and how achingly happy I was to be surrounded by all of them. Somehow, we'd made it to this day, the battle long behind us, and despite the scars on our hearts left by the war, I knew today would be a good day. One we deserved after so much heartache, and hopefully just the start of endless more to come.

Geraldine let out a pterodactyl shriek and used her water magic to catch my tears as they fell, sending them flying out the open window into the summer air before they could ruin my makeup.

Gabriel took a bag of stardust from his pocket and Tory carved the wards apart. I knew where we were going. I'd chosen the location myself, but I'd kept it from Orion, and I wondered what he'd thought when he'd turned up there.

The stardust wrapped us in its embrace, dragging us away into a swirl of stars, and their whispers followed us as we went.

We arrived in a small room with a trail of blue petals leading to a door in front of us. The wards on this place had been lifted to allow our guests to arrive with ease, though there were plenty of royal guards keeping the location secure. It was impossible to feel completely safe anywhere we went after so long fearing for our lives, but with each day, it got a little easier to relax. I was in a routine of scouting the land every night before I slept as Gabriel had once taught me, checking the wards were intact before returning to my bed where Orion waited up for me reading a book.

"Ready?" Tory asked, moving to my left side and looping her arm through mine while I clutched the bouquet a little tighter.

"Ready," I exhaled, and Gabriel took my other arm. I couldn't walk up the aisle without either of them, so I'd insisted both accompany me down it.

Geraldine fussed with the train of my dress and Sofia stepped up at her back.

With a flick of Tory's fingers, the door ahead of us opened and she released a silencing bubble I hadn't realised was in place, the sound of a harpist playing a soft melody carrying to us. A carpet of darkest blue ran all the way up between the centre of two masses of seats, our favourite people in the entire kingdom here to celebrate with us.

A hoard of the Oscura Wolf pack sat to my left along with Dante and Leon, taking up most of the rows there, a chorus of howls sounding at the sight of us. To my right was Eugene Dipper and his family, along with so many others of our nearest and dearest. Towering up either side of the rows were bookshelves, beautiful wooden shelves with ancient tomes filling every one of them, this colossal room in the Library of the Lost one of my very favourites. The ceiling was painted with gold and blue murals, displaying all of the Orders between sparkling constellations.

But all of them became a blur as my eyes found those of Orion at the far end of the aisle, standing beneath an ornate wooden arch with books stacked over it and blue flowers weaving between them on little vines.

The intensity in Orion's dark, silver-ringed irises had my breath catching, his gaze scoring over me just like it had the first day we met. And I was no longer nervous, but excited. So damn excited to get to the end of that aisle and announce him as mine, because this was the moment we'd promised each other. A vow to live life to its very fullest if we ever made it to the other side of the war. And impossibly, against all the ruinous fates cast in our names, we'd made it.

Darius stood to Orion's left, then Caleb, Seth, Max and Xavier beyond him, all of them there to play an important part in this day.

Gabriel and Tory walked me ever closer, and my heart thundered as I reached Orion, the scent of cinnamon caressing my senses. Geraldine was there in a flash, grabbing the bouquet from my hand, and ushering Gabriel to join Orion's groomsmen while Tory and the other bridesmaids lined up on the other side of the archway with Geraldine.

Orion took my hand, guiding me in front of him, admiring my dress before his gaze found mine again. He leaned forward to speak in my ear, his breath on my skin sending a shiver down my spine.

"There are no words in this universe that can aptly capture your beauty in this moment."

He pulled away before I could reply, leaving a burning trail of heat across my cheeks.

We readied to declare our love to each other before the stars and all those we adored, and I had the overwhelming sense that I was exactly where I was meant to be. That no matter what path fate had guided me along in life, somehow, I always would have found myself at the end of an aisle facing Lance Orion.

⁘⟨⟨●◗●◖⟩⟩⁘

The party was in full swing, and Orion tugged me off the dance floor which we'd been on for a full hour, picking me up and placing me down to sit on the edge of the circular table where our wedding cake was. It was a thing of beauty, made to look like a stack of books with golden flowers dotted all over them and little figures of Orion and I at the top, me with my Phoenix wings out and him with a sword in hand. So freaking cute.

Orion grabbed a bottle of water from an ice cooler, opening it for me and handing it over, and I took two big gulps of it, gazing around the incredible room. We'd moved into an old chamber with brick walls and arches, bookcases everywhere which were protected by special wards put in place by Arnold - the minotaur was patrolling them like a prison guard. Faelights hovered in the air and blue petals fluttered around the feet of all our dancing friends, the atmosphere full of happiness.

"I got you something," I said as I placed my water down.

Orion pushed a hand into his hair which wasn't anywhere near as neat as it had been during the ceremony. His jacket was removed too, collar open, the sleeves of his white shirt rolled up and his waistcoat unbuttoned. This was the true Orion; scruffy, roguish and fucking edible.

"Oh yeah?" he asked, leaning down. "Is it a kiss, wife?"

"Nope," I said, a tease in my voice as I leaned back to avoid his mouth.

He placed his hands either side of me on the table, a hungry growl in his throat. "What then?"

"This place," I said with a mischievous smile.

"Hm?" he grunted, not understanding as his eyes remained on my lips and he continued to chase me for that kiss.

"The Library of the Lost," I said. "It's yours. All yours. You can rename it if you like. The Library of the Not Lost. Or The Library of Orion's Precious Books that No

One's Allowed to Touch. Or-"

His palm came down on my mouth to quiet me. "Blue," he warned like I'd done something bad, and heat burned a path between my thighs. "Are you toying with me, because that's a very dangerous game to play."

I scooped up a handful of the cake behind me, keeping it hidden as he dropped his hand and tried to get another kiss, then I shoved it against his mouth, smearing it over his face. I ducked away from him, laughing as I ran back to the dance floor and he chased after me with a burst of speed, licking the frosting from his lips as he gripped my hips and swung me around. I laid my hand on his chest, dancing in front of him while he stood there rigidly, amusement sparkling in his gaze.

"Did you really buy me the library?"

"Really, really," I sang. "And Arnold's not even mad because I set up a fund for the restoration of any damaged or deteriorating books. He was so delighted, he mooed for a full ten seconds."

Orion laughed, wiping the last of the frosting from his cheek on his sleeve. "This is too much, Blue."

"Nothing is too much for the man who bled for me," I said, my tone dipping to something darker, an echo of our shadow-torn past.

He pinched my jaw between his finger and thumb, leaning in for a kiss that rocked the foundations of my soul.

"Babbadoodby!" Geraldine exclaimed, racing from the crowd to clean Orion's sleeve with water magic and the two of us broke apart, grins finding our mouths again, the moment of darkness quickly washed away. "You're already unbuttoned and as couth as a crab on a cornsack," Geraldine cursed. "Do not be-spoil yourself too, dear Orry."

"I think the uncouth crab look suits him," I said, and Orion smirked, his dimple popping out in his right cheek and making me want to grab him for another kiss. We were off on our honeymoon tomorrow morning, heading to Maresh to stay in a hotel that was behind a freaking waterfall, and I was excited for us to have two whole weeks in paradise to just *be*. But for now, the party reigned, and I was more than happy to let loose, celebrating with all the joy in our hearts.

Someone knocked into me from behind and I glanced around, finding Dante there apologising as Leon and Seth broke into a dance off beyond him, Seth blasting out a bubble of air to widen the space for them on the dance floor.

Caleb shot to Orion's side with a beer, sipping it casually. "I'm backing Seth, but my money's on Leon. The Lion took centre stage with the band a minute ago doing some Shakira hip-shaking shit that I've never seen in my life. A guy that big shouldn't be able to move like that."

"The Leone defies all logic, sì," Dante agreed with a chuckle as Seth began the battle with a break dance, using air to spin himself around and around on the floor. Geraldine shrieked at the sight of him dirtying his suit jacket, but Xavier held her back, laughing and insisting she watch instead.

"Where's Rosalie tonight?" I asked Dante, not having seen his cousin at all.

Dante's eyes darkened as he looked my way. "In Darkmore Penitentiary."

"What?" I gasped as Tory appeared from the crowd, a dress strap slipping down one shoulder and a big ass smile on her face as she led Darius after her by the hand.

Geraldine dove on her, pushing the strap back into place and Tory waved her off.

"Why do you look like someone just tit punched you?" Tory asked me, her smile falling.

"Dante said Rosalie's in Darkmore," I explained.

"It just happened yesterday, in fact," Dante said heavily.

"Then we'll have her released," Tory said, and I nodded.

"No need, piccole regine," Dante said, his eyes crackling with lightning. "Rosalie is always right where she intends to be. She is there by no mere coincidence, I assure you."

"What is she thinking? That place is a pit of sin," Orion growled, a touch of horror in his eyes at whatever he had experienced there, and my chest tightened.

"She seeks a long-lost love from her past." He nodded to Leon who was now doing something akin to an Irish jig, fire blazing at his feet which were moving at a wild pace.

"She has gone to Leon's brother, e il mio buon amico, Roary Night," Dante said.

"Then we'll pardon them both," I replied.

"No such luck, purtroppo," Dante sighed. "Lionel Acrux left a parting curse in this world, condemning Roary to Darkmore with magic that cannot be undone, even by two queens as powerful as you. He cannot leave until his sentence is served, or perhaps another way, but none you can assist in..." He shrugged, not finishing that sentence and I suspected whatever Rosalie was up to, it was something Tory and I were going to happily overlook.

"Come now," Dante said, slinging his arm around my shoulders. "It is your wedding day. It is not a time for frowns. Let us be merry. A morte e ritorno." He raised a golden chalice in the air and Geraldine swept between us, handing out fizzing glasses of some pink Arucso wine that had been supplied by the Oscuras from their vineyards in Alestria. I didn't know how she'd gotten hold of the tray so quickly, but she was so prepared for this day, I suspected the entire A.S.S. were on standby around her in the crowd.

We clinked our glasses in a toast and watched as Seth backflipped over Leon's head, aided by his air magic before catching his arms with vines that dangled from the ceiling, starting up some sort of aerial routine that looked well-rehearsed. Caleb's eyebrows rose, seeming like he'd changed his mind on who might win this, his Moon Mate clearly both amusing and impressing him.

My smile was soon back in place, my cheeks aching with how much happiness I felt today. It was all I could feel; a pure, eternal kind of joy that filled up all the spaces inside me, leaving no room for shadows or strife. It was the fiercest form of magic, I realised. This love between us all, these bonds that would never falter. Nothing in this realm compared, no Elements, no power, or crowns, or thrones. Just us. Family. And a love that would never die.

DARIUS

CHAPTER ONE HUNDRED & SIXTEEN
SEVEN YEARS AFTER THAT

"Twins don't run in my family – you can't blame me!" I yelled, ducking as my wife hurled a fistful of ice at my head and scooping little Tarin into my arms as I nearly trampled him in my attempt to escape.

"Don't go using the kids as a shield, it's your man bits that got us into this!" Roxy snarled, using a whip of air magic to snatch our two-year-old son from my arms and gently depositing him back in the playroom with his twin brother Rygar.

"My man bits?" I barked a laugh, ducking another ball of ice as it hurtled towards my head.

"You know the boys will have a field day with the word cock if I use it," she hissed.

"Cock," Tarin replied instantly, running back out of the playroom with Rygar right behind him as always. Tarin was wholly his mother's child, full of an impulsive need to find danger and make a game of it. Rygar was mine through and through – he bent the danger to his will and set his brother up to take the fall for any carnage that ensued.

We were in our manor which sat on the outskirts of Skybour Bay at the top of a cliff overlooking the sea, our private beach beyond that and enough land surrounding it that we actually managed to maintain some real privacy here from the pressure of being the royal family. Currently, we were inside, making use of the open plan kitchen and living area while we waited for the rest of our closest friends and family to arrive.

"What's going on?" Darcy asked, letting herself in through the front door and looking at me where I may or may not have grabbed Rygar and placed him on the back of the dining chair between myself and my possibly deranged wife who stood in the kitchen area.

Darcy's belly was so round now that it looked like she might pop at any given moment despite her baby not being due for another two months, and she rested a hand on her bump fondly as she looked between me and her sister for an answer.

"He can't fight back," Roxy growled. "Because he's gone and gotten me pregnant again."

"Which you were excited about until Gabriel showed up," I reminded her, shooting a poisonous look across the room at her brother who was lounging on my white couch with one eye on his wife's Pitball match which was playing on the TV and eating my damn snacks as if he was innocent in all of this.

"I *saw* the babies," he replied with a mischievous grin which told me he had known about this before today and had waited to tell us until he was here in person so he could watch Roxy lose her shit with me.

"Babies plural?" Orion asked as he followed Darcy into the house. "As in twins?" He looked between Rygar and Tarin for a moment then added, "Again?"

"Yup," Gabriel said, grinning over a fistful of chips before stuffing them into his mouth.

"Wow," Darcy said, looking from the boys, to her sister, to me. "You really don't do anything by halves, do you Darius?"

"Like I've been telling my dear wife, it is *your* genetics which predispose you to multiple births – not mine," I countered, ducking for cover behind the dining table set for twenty as Rygar escaped me and ran to clamber onto Gabriel's lap.

"Hmm, seems unlikely. I've just got the one bun in this oven," Darcy said thoughtfully. "And I'm pretty sure twins come from the male side."

"Bullshit," I spat.

"Bullshit cock," Tarin said happily, and Roxy scowled at me like that was my fault too.

"Come on, Rox, you love the boys. You can't be that upset over it-"

"I love them alright – and once they vacate the premises, I'm right here for it. But in the meantime, I will once again be playing host to *two* massive Dragon babies in my womb at once."

Darcy pulled a pained face, clearly glad not to have that particular issue to contend with in her own pregnancy and I broke a smile which was likely not the best move.

"You know I loved it when you were as round as you were tall. It was so cute-"

A fireball took out the curtains behind me as I just about managed to duck it in time.

"Never again," she hissed, glaring at me. "You are never again putting that *thing* near me after this." She waved a hand in the general direction of my dick and strode away from me, taking a place on the couch beside Gabriel.

I scowled at my brother-in-law who looked altogether too amused by this turn of events, and I could have sworn that he sniggered as he turned his focus to playing with Rygar.

"Hibberty gibbets, it smells like a Dragon popped a duffer in here," a voice announced, and I looked around to find Max and Geraldine letting themselves into my house – apparently none of them cared for knocking these days. Their one-year-old daughter Augustaline was riding on Max's shoulders while smacking him over the head with a cuddly flail. Max smiled between winces and set Augustaline free to run riot with the boys the moment the door was closed behind them.

"She's started influencing," he warned us, claiming a beer from the ice bucket by the kitchen island. "So no one give in to the impulse to get her ice cream all the damn time."

"Oh pish-posh, Maxy, you just find her rumbunctious cuteness too hard to resist. Our daughter is no snaffling Siren, you mark my words. She shall emerge as a Cerberus pup any day now." Max looked inclined to disagree, but Geraldine changed the subject before he could. "Is there a reason why the curtains do smoulder so?"

"Tory's having twins again," Orion said, throwing a handful of water at the blackened curtains while Geraldine fell to the ground with a pterodactyl shriek which soon became a cacophony of joyous tears, plus praises to the stars and my loins.

"See," I said, grabbing Roxy a beer then swapping it for a soda as I realised my mistake and dropping down beside her on the couch with it held out in offering. "Geraldine is praising my loins."

"So you admit that your loins are the issue?" she accused.

"Never."

"What's with all the sobbing?" Seth asked as he and Caleb strolled into my house like it was a free for all too. "I thought this was a death day party?"

"It is," I agreed, looking out the window at the darkened sky and deciding that now was as good a time as any. If anything was likely to put Roxy in a good mood again then it would surely be our traditional yearly burning of a Dragon made out of old sacks along with photographs of my father's smug face. "Come on."

I stood and hoisted Roxy into my arms, ignoring the way she punched my back as I tossed her over my shoulder and slapping her on the ass when she got in a good shot to my kidney.

She cursed like a hell cat while the boys both attacked my legs – on her side as always – and I fought my way to the backyard through a tangle of tiny child warriors.

By the time I emerged outside, I had a twin clinging to each shin and Augustaline thumping the backs of my thighs while Gabriel's kids both took turns whacking me with the nest sticks they insisted on carrying everywhere. But I didn't stop until I reached the huge bonfire that was stacked and awaiting our arrival to be lit.

Tharix stood in the shadows beyond it, his eyes trailing between the members of my family with interest and a smile lifting his lips. The four sayer dragons were predictably with him, one on his shoulder while another clung to his arm and the blue and coral ones had a play fight in the grass by his feet. Tharix had become as familiar as any of my loved ones, but when we all gathered together like this he still retreated as though feeling like he didn't quite belong. It wasn't something that any of us could fix for him though, and I could only hope that one day he would find a true peace that would allow him to put the last of his demons to bed.

"Put me down, jackass," Roxy demanded, and I yanked her from my shoulder and into my arms, dipping her low and stealing a ruinous kiss from those foul lips while the boys echoed her cursing at the tops of their lungs.

She fought me then gave in, biting my lip hard enough to draw blood, and I finally let her retreat with a smile on my face.

"Forgive me," I begged.

"No," she replied predictably.

"Are we all here?" Seth asked, doing a head count and barking at the kids to stop moving, which encouraged them to run in every direction and gave him the chance to take chase - which of course was what he'd wanted.

A whinny drew my attention up towards the dark clouds and I smiled as I spotted the three Pegasuses soaring out of the sky, Xavier in the lead.

They circled us then came to a halt on the lawn which swept away down the cliff towards the sea, and we all talked among ourselves as they shifted and dressed themselves again.

"I thought you were flying with us?" Xavier asked Tharix as he strode back up the hill with Tyler and Sofia right behind him.

"Next time," Tharix said with a shrug, his eyes on the stuffed green Dragon which was perched at the top of the bonfire, awaiting its demise.

There was no grief in Tharix's eyes, nor regret, but just like last year and the year before that, he had gone very quiet during this day. The kingdom-wide tradition of burning the False King and celebrating the peace which had been claimed beyond his demise was of course always both joyous and touched with grief but for Tharix, it seemed to send him into the depths of himself where something clearly haunted him beyond the end of those awful days.

"Darcy, are you ready?" Roxy asked, drawing my focus back to her and I let my attention move to the sack Dragon.

"Always," Gwen replied, stepping between me and her sister with a malicious smile on her face as Phoenix fire ignited in both of their hands.

"Tonight, as we do once a year, our minds linger on the long-departed Lame Lionel," Geraldine warbled. "As there are surely none in this lifetime who might grieve him, we come together on this day – the anniversary of his vanquishment – year upon year and remember him. We think of him like this for one reason alone; so that he may never pass on from The Veil. We wish for his soul to be tethered by the thoughts of the living, so that his suffering can go on and on eternally at the hands of those who fell prey to his evil machinations. So here is to Lionel Acrux – the Fae who shall forever be trapped within the hell of death! The Dragon who burned!"

With a whoosh, the bonfire ignited, the paunchy green Dragon on top of it going up in flames to the excited whoops of the children, and I let myself remember my father and all of his cruelty, smiling at the thought of him suffering for it in the beyond forevermore.

Seth

CHAPTER ONE HUNDRED & SEVENTEEN
TWO YEARS AFTER THAT

There was no chance in the kingdom that I was going to sleep tonight. I was too damn excited. Tomorrow was the day. *The* day. The one we'd been waiting on for so, so, so long. By the stars, could it come any quicker?

Caleb was downstairs in our manor watching the Pitball final which Leon and Gabriel's wife were playing in. The rest of our friends had gone to the game, all there now in the royal box to watch, but not us. No, because we had an early start tomorrow. A day that would begin a whole new age for me and Cal.

So I'd bought some stuff and things that would spice up the evening, make a sort of last hoorah of life now before it all changed. And as I looked at the basket of glitter, the sparkly ponytail and shimmering pink horn made of silicone in the bathroom, I decided it was time to focus on making my Moon Mate as happy as happy could be.

The bathroom was all Caleb's taste, everything chic, neutral and trendy. He had a good eye for shit like that, and I loved his style, the whole house decorated to the highest quality. Nothing but the best for my Moon Mate.

I stripped out of all my clothes then grabbed the tube of glitter and started my work covering my cock in it, painting a love heart onto my chest too. Then I washed my hands and let the stuff dry — the glitter would soon be like a second skin. Next, I grabbed the pony tail and using some Mino-strength glue to stick it to the base of my spine. I rocked my ass side to side, the tail swishing left and right as I admired myself in the mirror. Fuck, that looked pretty damn good on me.

I used a magical illusion to colour my hair like a rainbow then took out the shining horn which doubled as a vibrator and fixed it onto my head. Finally, I tugged on a glittery pair of purple shorts to finish the look, keeping my sparkle cock for the grand finale.

A grin twisted my lips and I raced out of the bathroom, trying out a trot and a neigh. I'd asked Xavier to give me a few pointers, and he'd even let me go riding with his herd. The guy had grown it to eight members now. A seriously powerful unit that had fast become the strongest in Solaria. Of course, I hadn't told him what my Pegasus studies were for, giving him a mysterious wink when he'd asked whether this had anything to do with Caleb's Pego-fetish, and I reckoned that had thrown him off. I was a wily creature, me.

I trotted into our bedroom with white walls and fluffy grey carpet, my gaze locking on the giant bed. I threw the covers back and dove under them, dragging them over myself to hide.

"Cal!" I called, amplifying my voice.

"Yeah?" he called back.

"Come here!"

I tucked the comforter tighter around me, a laugh leaving me as I heard him shooting this way with his Vampire speed. I was the best Moon Mate ever. He was going to be so damn excited to know he could express himself fully with me. Every kink, every fantasy, I'd be it for him.

I heard him enter the room and stifled a laugh, trying to lay still.

"What are you doing in there?" Caleb asked in amusement, and I neighed in reply. "What the fuck?"

He grabbed the comforter, ripping it off of me, and I reared up, casting an illusion of hooves onto my hands and feet, moving my arms like kicking front legs.

Caleb's eyes widened in shock as he took in my swishy tail and sparkly horn. "Seth," he barked. "What fuck are you doing?"

"It's okay, Cal. I know."

"You know what?" he balked.

"I knowwwwww," I said with a wink, placing a hoof against his chest. "You can be yourself with me. You don't have to hide it."

"Hide what?" he snapped.

Oh my poor, embarrassed little Cal, still unable to fully unveil his inner desires even now.

"That you're horny for the horn," I said, crawling around so my ass was to him and shaking my butt so the tail swished for him. "You can whip me like a bad pony if you like, or ride me like a good one. I'll be your Pegasus Sub, and you can be my Dom. Or do you not want to pretend you're a Pegasus too? Do you like to be the big, bad Vampire claiming his stallion?"

"No I don't," he cursed, not sounding quite as pleased as I was expecting, more ragey than I'd been hoping for, but it was just the walls he'd built between himself and the truth.

"It's okay," I said, looking back at him over my shoulder in earnest. "You can be anything with me, Cal. I want to be a part of this."

"Be a part of what?!" he snarled, his face kinda red and maybe that was what he liked, being all angry when he fucked me like a naughty Pegasus who'd eaten all the carrots. That was how it had been in that video that had gone viral with him and the Pegasex doll. Yeah, that must have been it. He liked to be wild, he wanted to punish his bad bronco.

I neighed, tossing my rainbow hair and Caleb suddenly locked his fist in it, spurring me on into a whinny which was damn impressive thank you very much.

"I don't like Pegasuses," he snarled.

"Do you want me to fight back?" I asked, rolling over and kicking my hands and legs in the air like an over-turned horsey.

"No, I want you take that shit off and never put it near our bed again," he hissed, and I stilled, my lips parting in shock.

"You...don't want this?" I asked in horror. How could I have gotten it wrong? There had to be something to the rumours. Surely I wasn't kidding myself here. I'd picked up on the hints and drawn this conclusion. He was my mate; how could I get it so wrong?

"Of course I don't," he snapped.

"Not even my multi-function horn?" I pressed the button on the horn and it began intermittently spinning, vibrating and thrusting.

Caleb stared at me in stunned silence. "And where is that supposed to go?" he balked.

"Well, I mean..." I shrugged innocently.

"It's my ass, isn't it?" he growled, eyes narrowing. "That is not going anywhere near my ass."

"Did I get it wrong? Do you wanna put the horn on? Do you want me to cast an illusion on your dick so it looks like a horn instead then-"

"No, Seth, I don't want any of this," he insisted.

"I don't judge you for it. I've done all kinds of crazy shit. This is actually one of the least crazy things I've done."

"Are you actually bringing up other people you've fucked right now?"

"I'm just *saying* I'm totally cool with this. I'm into it if you're into it. There's no shame in being horny for the horn. Look how hot I look in this shit." I flexed my muscles, and Caleb's gaze trailed over my abs.

"Fuck," he exhaled. "You do look hot."

Excitement flared inside me at the breakthrough. "I knew it!"

"No," he snipped. "That doesn't mean I'm horny for the horn, it's just because it's you in all that glitter."

"Sureeee it is, Cal," I said, smirking.

"Dammit, Seth I'm not into Pegasuses."

"Do you wanna see my dijazzle?" I offered, onto him now, knowing his truth. He couldn't admit it out loud, but the way he was looking at me confirmed it. This was getting him hard. And when Cal was hard, I was hard.

Caleb hesitated, his gaze dropping to my shiny purple shorts. "Well... I kind of want to see. Out of curiosity."

I laughed. "Oh you're so fucking hot for Pegas-ass."

"I'm not, I'm hot for you. Now show me the fucking dijazzle." He lunged for me and I laughed harder as we rolled together on the bed, him fighting to pull my shorts off while I scrambled away and butt swished to make the tail slap him in the face. He caught me by the waistband with a growl, ripping the shorts clean off of me and forcing me to roll over.

He eyed my sparkle dick and his eyebrows arched.

"Fuck," he breathed. "That actually is kinda pretty."

I leaned up to whisper in his ear. "Let me be your wild stallion. Break me in like a defiant colt of the hills."

"Stop with the horse sex talk," he demanded, shoving me down again, but his eyes trailed curiously to my cock once more.

I could feel how hard he was, his own dick digging into my hip and giving me all the truth I needed about his kink.

"You will tell no one about this," Caleb warned, his fingers reaching behind me to knot in my tail.

"No one," I breathed, though obviously he didn't include *everyone* in that statement. Our besties knew all our secrets. And I bet Orion would be happy to know his sanguis frater was having such a great sex life.

Caleb loomed down on me, his fangs extending. "Then neigh for me like a good pony and do exactly what I tell you."

"Shit got weird last night," Caleb muttered to me as we sat in the car waiting for the call that would confirm it was time.

"Was it the Pegasus stuff?" I asked.

"Yeah…"

"I enjoyed it. Would you wanna do it again sometime?"

He fell quiet, his fingers tightening on the steering wheel for a second. "Maybe."

I grinned, thinking of how I could take it to the next level in the future. Maybe a full Pegasus suit with wings and a detachable tail which doubled as a flogger. Yeah… that would be a start.

My Atlas rang and I was so anxious to answer it that I lost my grip on it and it went crashing down into the footwell. I reared forward, hitting my head on the dashboard with a curse, then grabbing it in my hand.

"You good?" Caleb asked and I nodded, healing the mark and giving him a terrified, anxious, hopeful, soul-bursting look before answering the call.

"It's time, Mr Capella," the soft female voice said.

I howled in delight, lunging at Caleb and hugging him. He laughed, taking the Atlas from my hand and listening to what the woman had to say while I crawled into his lap and gripped his shirt in my fists.

When he hung up, I kissed him, then licked him, then howled again.

Caleb drew me into a fierce embrace and we looked at each other, eye to eye, crammed so tight into the space I could hardly breathe.

"They're here," he said. "They're waiting for us."

I threw the car door open, sprinting across the street and a car came speeding toward me from the right. Caleb picked me up with a burst of speed, carrying me out of the road as the car went tearing by, blasting its horn. But I didn't care that I'd almost died, because now it was time to live. Live, live, live and live some more.

I raced into the hospital and the receptionist directed us to a room upstairs. And there, we found them. Two cots side by side and a healer checking over the babies inside.

I lingered in the doorway as Caleb went ahead, suddenly terrified. Because what if I wasn't a good dad? What if I couldn't be everything these little tiny beings needed me to be?

Caleb looked back over his shoulder, emotion burning in his eyes, and I found my strength in him as he beckoned me closer. I might not be perfect, shit, I knew I'd make mistakes, but so long as I had him, I could do this. I could be what they needed because he would be there beside me through it all.

I stopped breathing as my gaze fell on them, those adorable babies crooning softly. We'd had two surrogates inseminated at exactly the same time, their pregnancies planned so one of the kids would hold my genes and the other would hold Caleb's.

"This is the girl," the healer told us, pointing to our beautiful daughter who had strands of soft golden hair which already had a slight curl to it and bright blue eyes. "And here's your baby boy." She gestured to the other one with earthy eyes, slightly darker skin and a dusting of brown hair on his head.

"Don't tell us which one is mine and which is Caleb's," I told the healer firmly, and she shared a confused look with Caleb who snorted a laugh, scooping the little boy into his arms.

"Hey there, little man," Caleb said, kissing his cheek and my heart was fit to burst with happiness.

I carefully scooped up our girl and held her in my arms. She was so small, so precious, and so, so loved. Tears blurred my vision and I blinked them away to see her better.

"Do you have names yet?" the healer asked, and I looked to Caleb who nodded with a blissful smile.

"This is Kale."

"And this is Elara," I announced, the names coming from two of Jupiter's moons.

One of the most powerful, lucky planets in the solar system which we hoped would bless them in every way life had to offer. I sensed my parents gathering closer from beyond The Veil, drawn here to see their grandchildren, and I swear I could sense my old pack howling in celebration. Emotion burned a hole in my chest at the loss of them, but as I moved to Caleb's side so I could see our son better, my heart squeezed with love. My pack had fought and died so we could have this chance at life, and I would never stop being grateful to them for that.

Shit, people always said this moment changed you, and I was wholly transformed. We were fathers, me and Cal. The two of us together. And we were going to give these kids the whole wide world.

ORION

"Again! Again!" cried my wild five-year-old, Archer, as I threw him skyward on a gust of wind, his black hair a mess of strands as it blew wildly in the breeze. He sailed up twenty feet then came plummeting towards me with a whoop in his throat before I caught him and spun him around with a laugh.

"Me, Me," my little girl tugged at my pant leg, her tiny hands fisting in the material with determination.

I sent Archer flying back up towards the sky and whipped up my tiny two-year-old in my arms, her dark wavy hair and big green eyes reminding me of her mother, especially with that cheeky little smile on her face.

"Azura Vega-Orion," I said in a stern voice which was all play. "You think you can handle the sky as well as your brother?"

"Sky," she said, tiny hands reaching for the air where Archer was spinning in a wind of my creation, laughing his head off.

"That answers that." I sent her flying up too and she squealed her delight, her and Archer racing around in a whirlwind as a grin split my cheeks apart.

"Lance!" Darcy called excitedly.

I glanced back at our house as she came running out the back door in a pink summer dress that hugged her figure and made my eyes drag over her hungrily. Our home was a beautiful old farmhouse with ancient stone walls rising up high to sloping red tiles on the roof and even a tower on one end of the building. The kids had miles of land to roam here, a whole lake of their own and a collection of magical animals that kept 'mysteriously' turning up. Except I knew full well that Darcy was taking in strays and rescues, subtly adding another shimmer duck or estian goat to our growing petting zoo and thinking I wouldn't notice. But I did. And I had a soft spot for those creatures even if I played the game of being stern every time Darcy added another animal to the numbers. Hell, we had the staff to manage it all, and the money to boot. So I was hardly going to complain. And having a reason to punish Blue was always a pastime I liked to enjoy, one she enjoyed just as much. Shadow loved to play with all the animals my mate collected, and I could see him in the distance now bounding up a hill with at least ten goats in tow.

"They're here," Darcy said keenly, smiling as if she hadn't seen our friends and family two days ago, always so happy to have them close. And I couldn't blame her, even if I wanted to steal her away to myself sometimes.

She let her wings fly free and raced up to join our children in the sky. I gave her a ride on the wind too before bringing them all down to the ground and nestling them close. Archer sat on my hip despite his growing size and Darcy hugged Azura between us.

"I wanna go play," Archer said keenly, trying to wriggle out of my arms but I didn't let him escape until Darcy and I had secured a kiss on each of his cheeks.

Darcy placed Azura in my arms and my little girl tugged at my beard while I pretended to try and bite her fingers, making her laughter fill the air.

"I'll go say hello." Darcy pecked me on the lips. "Ready for the chaos?"

"Always, Blue." I watched her go, racing back into the house and tearing away to greet our friends and family.

"Oh we forgot to make a cake, lucky I have this little lump of dough to bake." I squished Azura's tummy, and she squealed.

"No, Dada, no," she laughed, batting me away then glancing at her tummy, clearly wanting me to do it again.

I lifted her higher, blowing a raspberry against her tummy through her flowery blue dress and she grabbed my ears, yanking them as hard as she could. I barked a laugh, detaching my tiny warrior from me and tucking her against my side. "Let's go see your friends, shall we?"

"Kale," she said keenly, and I arched an eyebrow at her. She had a thing for that boy of Seth and Caleb's, always toddling after him and rolling in the mud with him like a hellion.

"And your cousins will be here," I reminded her, and her green eyes lit up as she clapped her hands together.

She started listing off the many, many cousins she had, Tory and Darius having provided two sets of twins and finishing it off with triplets last year. I didn't know if they were done, but I did know that they were crazy.

I could hardly keep an eye on two tiny terrors, let alone seven. But shit, they seemed happy – though I well remembered the day Tory had shown up here screaming about her husband's danger dick when she'd found out she'd fallen pregnant with triplets. I'd found it all very amusing, but apparently she didn't appreciate my witty comments on the subject. I'd almost earned myself a cock kick that day, but she'd been so angry at Darius that I suspected he'd been the one to get it in the end.

Our friends and family came pouring out into the sunny garden and I shot over to them with a burst of speed, embracing Gabriel, Darius, Tory and doing the rounds between Seth, Caleb, Max, Geraldine, Xavier, Sofia, Tyler and all the kids. Tory had three cots floating beside her on a gust of air that rocked all of them gently, the three one-year-olds, Axel, Nero and Bowie taking naps inside silencing bubbles, and I smiled at their content faces.

We practically had a whole Pitball team between us, and I'd admittedly had a thought or two about coaching them when they got older. We could take on the League with these powerful fiends...

"Can you take us to the woods again, Uncle Lancelot?" Darius's seven-year-old boy, Rygar, asked keenly. He'd come up with the nickname himself after reading about the legend of King Arthur at school, and I liked the reminder of my father's old name for me.

"Before our snickety snacks have reached our tumblebums?" Augustaline scoffed, looking to her dad, and Max shrugged, turning to Geraldine who snapped her fingers.

"By the wind on my nelly, she's right. Let's eat and be merry as mangoes in a sweet soup before we go gallivanting into the yonder." She steered Augustaline towards the fire pit where a pizza oven was ready to go for our meal.

"Oh come on, Moon Uncle," Elara pouted at me, and I threw a glare at Seth who smirked at the name he had most definitely told her to call me.

Archer came running over to give me that pleading look I always caved to, and I sighed.

"Take them to the woods for a bit, I'll get the pizzas started," Darcy said, and Seth moved to help, placing down Elara who chased after her brother Kale.

I was suddenly surrounded by a hoard of kids, all looking at me with those dangerous pleading eyes, and Azura prodded me in the cheek, making me focus on her.

"Fly, Dada!" she cried.

Damn, I could never resist what the kids wanted. I swept them all up in a gust of air, this latest game their favourite as I sent them flying towards the woods at the far end of our land, shooting after them with a burst of speed.

I made it among the trees, halting where the play area was, the wooden swings, climbing ropes and obstacle course made by Darcy's earth magic. I placed the mass of kids down and they all split apart with wild cries like they were charging into battle, Archer and Rygar picking up sticks and falling into a sword fight.

Azura predictably went toddling off after Kale, the boy's dark hair hanging down over his back now. Tarin grabbed Elara's hand and he led her onto a climbing frame, helping her up. It was calm. Suspiciously so. Though it was still early in the day, and I knew the tears would come. Someone would fall, be pushed or hit and chaos would ensure. But it was the kind I adored. I still loved the quiet, loved my reading room here in the house plus mine and Blue's favourite spaces at the Library of the Lost, but I wouldn't have traded any of that for this.

Tory and Darius's five-year-old twins, Ender and Kylo, were up on the top of a high slide, pounding their fists and baying roar cries before launching themselves down it one after the other face-first. I cast a pillow of air at the bottom of it before they could go slamming into the earth and they bounced off of it with bright laughs.

A scream pitched up from Gabriel's youngest. RJ and I shot over in alarm, finding a tree on fire right before her.

"What happened?" I gasped, and she pointed skyward.

My neck craned as I found Azura up in the treetops, two fiery wings blazing at her back.

"Holy shit," I gasped as she sailed through the leaves, setting them all on fire while singing softly to herself, seemingly unaware that she was burning the whole woodland down.

"She's Emerged!" Archer shouted in shock. "Dad – save her!"

"By the stars." I quickly looped a whip of air around Azura's leg, gently bringing her down to the ground and trying to process the fact my daughter had just sprouted flaming wings. Kale shifted into a white and grey Wolf cub right beside Azura, grabbing her hair between his teeth and snatching her away into the bushes.

"Kale!" I barked, my heart pounding madly.

I shoved the bushes aside, racing after my daughter who had just been kidnapped by Seth and Caleb's son, a trail of fire blazing after her and taking root in the dry foliage. I worked to douse it with my water magic, crawling along the dusty ground and shoving the bushes and nettles away from me with blasts of air.

Azura was giggling like this was some game and when I made it to the other side of the bushes, I found Kale sitting up on a tree stump with Azura nowhere in sight. He lifted his nose to the trees again and I spotted her flying away through the canopy and off into the sky.

"Azura come down this instant!" I ordered, throwing air under my feet to propel myself after her, panic scoring through me.

Gabriel came flying fast from the direction of the house, the trees now alight with flames as I worked to snare my freshly-Emerged daughter in a net of air.

"Watch out," Gabriel called. "Her Emergence is triggering others."

A great crack sounded below me just as I trapped Azura in a bubble and brought her back to my chest, keeping her in the sphere of safety while holding her damn tight.

Two trees were felled beneath me and I found Darius and Tory's seven-year-old twins shifting into two beautiful metallic Dragons, one bronze, one silver, the other kids cheering in excitement and Kale letting out a howl of joy.

I'd known that chaos was coming, but this?

I stared at Azura who was flapping around in my bubble with blazing wings of fire.

"But Darcy and Tory didn't Emerge until they were eighteen," I rasped, knowing this was going to add a whole other layer of insanity to our lives. Shit, it wasn't as if I wasn't happy or proud as hell, but a two-year-old with flaming wings was gonna need a helluva lot of watching.

"Maybe the Mortal Realm supressed their Emergence." Gabriel smiled at Azura, having no better answer, then turned his attention to the kids who were piling onto the backs of the two Dragons beneath us.

"Uh-oh," Gabriel said. "We should probably tell the others."

"That their kids are all about to ride away on two newly-Emerged Dragon children?" I drawled. "Yeah, Noxy. I think we should tell them."

I cast a dome of air over the top of the kids, and Gabriel helped me douse the last of the flames licking their way along the trees. I could already see Darcy and Tory headed towards us through the air, and a sudden laugh fell from my throat at the madness.

I turned my attention back to my daughter. A Phoenix. Of course. And a spirited one at that.

It was too perfect, all of this. The life we'd forged together and made our own. This was where living really happened. Between the layers of havoc and sweetness of all the love we shared. And I couldn't have imagined up any better dream for myself, than this. Simply, purely, *this*.

TORY

The wind pushed beneath my wings as I soared across the mountaintops, the tips of my feathers brushing against Darcy's and flames peeling from our skin to trail in our wake.

The sun was just rising and my heart filled with love for the beauty of our kingdom, the clouds dusting the horizon and the ocean glimmering in the distance.

It had been hard work, had taken countless years of nurture and revolution, but finally I felt that we could look back across our reign and be certain that all the changes we'd put into place had made a real, lasting difference.

It seemed impossible that we hadn't grown up in this land of beauty and terrors, of magic and mayhem. I felt like I was a part of this world as much as it was a part of me. To imagine a life where we hadn't been touched by magic or cursed by the stars seemed impossible now, and despite how difficult the journey here had been, I didn't think there was a single part of it that I would change in hindsight.

"I feel them," Darcy called to me.

I closed my eyes, reaching out my hand and concentrating until I felt it too; the gentlest brush of warm skin and scales against my fingertips. Our parents were flying with us out here in the sky again this morning.

I smiled, falling into our long-established routine of recounting the various parts of our lives and the lives of our family which our parents may not have witnessed from beyond The Veil, making sure they knew all of it, wishing they could have shared in it too.

There was something about doing this while we flew through the clouds which always seemed to draw them closer, letting us hear the distant echo of their laughter or imagine the soft tug of their embrace.

This kingdom was ours. All of it. And as I shared a smile with my sister, I knew that no matter how many more years we spent ruling over Solaria, no matter what other trials the future brought our way, nothing was ever going to change that.

We had been two lost girls adrift in the mortal realm, but here, in this wilderness of magic and endless love, we had found ourselves at home.

AUTHOR NOTE

Okay, so how was that? Did we do alright? Were you thoroughly satisfied with the ending and rewarded for the pages of suffering it took to get here?

I won't lie, more deaths were on the cards but in the end, we felt this group had suffered in blood sweat and tears for their happily ever after, and the loss of any one of them was just too much for them to have to endure following on from claiming their victory.

So many, many pages of Lionel's memoirs remain unpublished, the things he might have achieved and done with his victory left in the foggy mystery of the unknown.

Saying goodbye to this series has been such a bittersweet experience for us. Writing the end comes with so many responsibilities in any series, but this one has been so special not just for us but for you as our readers who stepped so willingly into the pages of this story.

Thank you for making it to the end with us and we hope that you have enjoyed your adventures in Solaria. Of course, you can get more of this world in the prequel series starting with Dark Fae (where you can find out so much more about Gabriel, Leon and Dante) or in the sequel Caged Wolf (which follows Rosalie into the depths of Darkmore Penitentiary). And as you may know we will soon be crossing the sea to a land caught in an endless war between Elements, with ruthless tyrants and vicious dictators forging a path for the Fae unlucky enough to have been born into its changing landscape. So look out for Never Keep the first book in our Waning Lands series very soon.

We love you dear reader, we really do, nothing we write would take flight without you. So thank you for welcoming our characters into your hearts and for coming on this journey of heartbreak, betrayal and discovery with us as we forged a new future for the kingdom of Solaria.

Love, Susanne and Caroline

DISCOVER MORE FROM
CAROLINE PECKHAM
&
SUSANNE VALENTI

To find out more, grab yourself some freebies, merchandise, and special signed editions or to join their reader group, scan the QR code below.